D0101356

CHRONICLES OF THE CANONGATE

WALTER SCOTT was born in Edinburgh in 1771, educated at the High School and University there, and admitted to the Scottish Bar in 1792. From 1799 until his death he was Sheriff-Depute of Selkirkshire, and from 1806 to 1830 he held a well-paid office as a principal clerk to the Court of Session in Edinburgh, the supreme Scottish civil court. From 1805, too, Scott was secretly an investor in, and increasingly controller of, the printing and publishing businesses of his associates, the Ballantyne brothers.

Despite crippling polio in infancy, conflict with his Calvinist lawyer father in adolescence, rejection by the woman he loved in his twenties, and financial ruin in his fifties, Scott displayed an amazingly productive energy and his personal warmth was attested by almost everybody who met him. His first literary efforts, in the late 1790s, were translations of romantic and historical German poems and plays. In 1805 Scott's first considerable original work, *The Lay of the Last Minstrel*, began a series of narrative poems that popularised key incidents and settings of early Scottish history, and brought him fame and fortune.

In 1813 Scott, having declined the poet-laureateship and recommended Southey instead, moved towards fiction and devised a new form that was to dominate the early-nineteenth-century novel. *Waverley* (1814) and its successors draw on the social and cultural contrasts and the religious and political conflicts of recent Scottish history to illustrate the nature and cost of political and cultural change and the relationship between the historical process and the individual. *Waverley* was published anonymously and, although many people guessed, Scott did not acknowledge authorship of the Waverley Novels until 1827. Many of the novels from *Ivanhoe* (1819) on extended their range to the England and Europe of the Middle Ages and Renaissance. Across the English-speaking world, and by means of innumerable translations throughout Europe, the Waverley Novels changed for ever the way people constructed their personal and national identities.

Scott was created a baronet in 1820. During the financial crisis of 1825–6 Scott, his printer Ballantyne, and his publishers Constable and their London partner became insolvent. Scott chose not to be declared bankrupt, determining instead to work to generate funds to pay his creditors. Despite his failing health he continued to write new novels, to revise and annotate the earlier ones for a new edition, and to write a nine-volume *Life of Napoleon* and a history of Scotland under the title *Tales of a Grandfather*. His private thoughts during and after his financial crash are set down in a revealing and moving *Journal*. Scott died in September 1832; his creditors were finally paid in full in 1833 from the proceeds of his writing.

CLAIRE LAMONT is Professor of English Romantic Literature at the University of Newcastle upon Tyne, specialising in the study of English and Scottish poets and novelists of the late eighteenth and early nineteenth centuries. She has published editions of *Waverley* (1981) and *The Heart of Midlothian* (1982), and is Advisory Editor for the Waverley Novels in Penguin and Textual Adviser for the new Penguin edition of the novels of Jane Austen.

DAVID HEWITT, born in 1942, was brought up in the Borders, and studied English at the University of Edinburgh. Since 1994 he has been Professor in Scottish Literature at the University of Aberdeen. He has published widely on Scottish and Romantic literature, and is editor-in-chief of the Edinburgh Edition of the Waverley Novels. He is editor of Scott's *The Antiquary* and co-editor of *Redgauntlet* for Penguin Classics.

WALTER SCOTT

CHRONICLES OF THE CANONGATE

Edited with an introduction by
CLAIRE LAMONT

PENGUIN BOOKS

PENGUIN BOOKS

Published by the Penguin Group
Penguin Books Ltd, 80 Strand, London WC2R ORL, England
Penguin Putnam Inc., 375 Hudson Street, New York, New York 10014, USA
Penguin Books Australia Ltd, 250 Camberwell Road, Camberwell, Victoria 3124, Australia
Penguin Books Canada Ltd, 10 Alcorn Avenue, Toronto, Ontario, Canada M4V 3B2
Penguin Books India (P) Ltd, 11, Community Centre, Panchsheel Park, New Delhi – 110 017, India
Penguin Books (NZ) Ltd, Cnr Rosedale and Airborne Roads, Albany, Auckland, New Zealand
Penguin Books (South Africa) (Pty) Ltd, 24 Sturdee Avenue, Rosebank 2196, South Africa

Penguin Books Ltd, Registered Offices: 80 Strand, London WC2R ORL, England

www.penguin.com

First published 1827
Published in the Edinburgh Edition of the Waverley Novels by
the Edinburgh University Press 2000
Published with revised critical apparatus in Penguin Classics 2003

5

Text, historical notes, explanatory notes and glossary © The University
Court of the University of Edinburgh, 2000
Editor-in-chief's Preface and Chronology © David Hewitt, 1998
Introduction and Note on the Text © Claire Lamont, 2003
All rights reserved

The moral right of the author has been asserted

Printed in England by Antony Rowe Ltd, Chippenham, Wiltshire

Except in the United States of America, this book is sold subject
to the condition that it shall not, by way of trade or otherwise, be lent,
re-sold, hired out, or otherwise circulated without the publisher's
prior consent in any form of binding or cover other than that in
which it is published and without a similar condition including this
condition being imposed on the subsequent purchaser

ISBN 978-0-14-043989-2

Learning Resources
Centre

12962511

CONTENTS

ACKNOWLEDGEMENTS

The editors of a critical edition incur many debts, and the indebtedness of the editors of the Edinburgh Edition of the Waverley Novels and of its paperback progeny in the Penguin Scott is particularly heavy. The universities which employ the editors (in this case Newcastle University) have, in practice, provided the most substantial assistance; but in addition the Universities of Edinburgh and of Aberdeen and the Humanities Research Board of the British Academy have been particularly generous in their support of the costs of editorial preparation.

The Edinburgh Edition of the Waverley Novels has been most fortunate in having as its principal financial sponsor the Bank of Scotland, which has continued its long and fruitful involvement with the affairs of Walter Scott. In addition the P. F. Charitable Trust and the Robertson Trust have given generous grants.

The manuscript of *Chronicles of the Canongate* and most of the letters and papers relating to the publication of the work are in the National Library of Scotland in Edinburgh. Without the preparedness of the National Library to make these manuscripts readily accessible, and to provide support beyond the ordinary, this edition would not have been feasible.

The editors have had, perforce, to seek specialist advice on many matters, and they are most grateful to their consultants: the late Alan Bruford, Professor John Cairns, Professor Thomas Craik, Caroline Jackson-Houlston, Professor David Nordloh, Roy Pinkerton, and Professor David Stevenson. They owe much to their research fellows, Mairi Robinson, Dr Alison Lumsden, and Gerard Carruthers. They have continuously sought advice from the members of the Scott Advisory Board, and are particularly grateful for the support of the late Sir Kenneth Alexander, Professor David Daiches, Professor Douglas S. Mack, Professor Jane Millgate, and Dr Archie Turnbull.

The editor of *Chronicles of the Canongate* is grateful to the Bodleian Library, Oxford (in particular the Indian Institute Library); the Carlisle Public Library; the Cumbria Record Office; the Edinburgh Room of Edinburgh Public Library; the Newcastle Central Public Library; the Public Record Office, Kew; and the Robinson Library, University of Newcastle. In addition she would like to thank the following for specific information or assistance: Dr Cedric Barfoot, Professor G. W. S.

Barrow, Dr D. H. Caldwell, Professor Ian Campbell, Rev. Dr Ian
Clark, Irene Dunn, Matthew Elliot, Dr Andrew Fairbairn, Professor
Ina Ferris, Dr John Goodridge, Dr Judith Hawley, Martin Holt, Dr
Gillian Hughes, Dr A. B. Hunt, Richard D. Jackson, E. J. Lamont,
Dr Sara Lodge, T. R. A. Mason, Dr Donald Meek, Professor Chris
Perriam, Professor Jonathan Powell, Dr John Riddy, Dr W. G. Roberts,
the late William Ruddick, Dr Sheena Sutherland, the late Margaret
Tait, Professor Mark Weinstein, Dr Diana Whaley, and Dr Michael
Winship. Alexander Murray has been not only a source of information
on all matters historical and Cumbrian but a never-flagging source of
strength.

To all of these the editors express their thanks, and acknowledge
that the production of the Edinburgh Edition of the Waverley Novels
and the Penguin Scott has involved a collective effort to which all
those mentioned by name, and very many others, have contributed
generously and with enthusiasm.

David Hewitt
Editor-in-chief and General editor of this title

Claire Lamont
Advisory editor, the Penguin Scott

J. H. Alexander,
P. D. Garside,
G. A. M. Wood
General editors

The novels of Walter Scott published in Penguin are based on the volumes of the Edinburgh Edition of the Waverley Novels (EEWN). This series, which started publication in 1993 and which when complete will run to thirty volumes, is published in hardback by Edinburgh University Press. The Penguin edition of *Chronicles of the Canongate* reproduces the text of the novel, Historical Notes, Explanatory Notes, and Glossary unaltered from the EEWN volume. It does not reproduce the substantial amount of textual information in the Edinburgh Edition but instead provides, in the following paragraphs, a summary of general issues common to all Scott's novels and, in the Note on the Text, a succinct statement of the textual history of *Chronicles of the Canongate*. A new critical introduction has been written specifically for the paperback, as well as a Chronology of Scott's life and a list of recommended further reading.

The most important aspect of the EEWN is that the text of the novels is based on the first editions, corrected so as to present what may be termed an 'ideal first edition'. Normally Scott's novels gestated over a long period: for instance, the historical works on which he drew for *The Tale of Old Mortality* (1816) had all been read by 1800. By contrast the process of committing a novel to paper, and of converting the manuscript into print, was in most cases extremely rapid. Scott wrote on only one side of his paper, and he used the blank back of the preceding leaf for additions and corrections, made both as he wrote and as he read over what he had written the previous day. Scott's novels were published anonymously---hence the title 'the Waverley Novels', named after the first of them—which meant that only a few people could be allowed to see his handwritten manuscript. Before delivery to the printing-house, therefore, the manuscript was copied and it was the copy that went to the compositor. The person who oversaw the printing of Scott's novels was his friend and business partner James Ballantyne, with whom he jointly owned the printing firm of James Ballantyne & Co. from 1805 (except for the period 1816–22 when Scott was sole partner) until they both became insolvent in 1826.

The compositors in the printing-house set the novels as copy arrived, and while doing so they inserted the great majority of the punctuation marks, normalised and regularised the spelling without standardising it, and corrected many small errors. It was in the printing-house that the presentation of the texts of the novels was changed from the conventions appropriate to manuscript to those of a printed novel of the early nineteenth century. Proofs were corrected in-house, and then a new set of proofs was given to Ballantyne, who annotated them prior to sending them to the author. Scott did not read his proofs against his manuscript or against the printer's copy; he read for sense and, making full use of the prerogatives of ownership, he took the opportunity of revising, amplifying, and even introducing new ideas. Thus for Scott reading proofs was a creative rather than just a corrective engagement with his texts. The proofs went back to Ballantyne, who oversaw the copying of Scott's new material on to a clean set of proofs and its incorporation into the printed text. Only occasionally did Scott see revised proofs. Two points in particular might be noted about the above procedures. First, Scott delivered his manuscript in batches as he wrote it, and the result was that the first part of a novel was set in type, and proofs corrected, before the end was written. And secondly, in the business of turning a rapidly written text from manuscript to print Scott was indebted to a series of people, copyist, printer, proof-reader, whom Scott editors have come to refer to as 'the inter-mediaries'.

The business of producing a Waverley novel was so pressurised that mistakes were inevitable. The manuscript was sometimes misread or misunderstood (Scott's handwriting is neat but his letters poorly differentiated); punctuation was often inserted in a mechanical way and the implication of Scott's light manuscript punctuation lost; period words were sometimes not recognised and more obvious, modern terms were substituted for them. The EEWN has examined every aspect of the first-edition texts in the light of the manuscript and the full textual history of the novel. This has enabled the editors to correct the text where Scott's intentions were clearly not fulfilled in the first edition. The EEWN corrects errors, but it does so conservatively bearing in mind that the production of the printed text was a collective effort to which Scott had given his sanction.

Most of the Waverley Novels went through many editions in Scott's lifetime; Scott was not normally involved in the later editions although very occasionally he did see proofs. But in 1827, after his insolvency the previous year, it was decided to issue the first full collected edition of the Waverley Novels, and much of Scott's time in the last years of his life was committed to writing introductions and notes, and to reviewing his text for what he called his 'Magnum Opus' ('Great Work'), or Magnum for short. Scott had acknowledged his authorship of the novels in 1827, and this enabled him to describe the origins of

INTRODUCTION

Walter Scott's *Chronicles of the Canongate*, first published in 1827, contains two of his best-known tales, 'The Highland Widow' and 'The Two Drovers', and a third, 'The Surgeon's Daughter', which is less well known but is remarkable for being one of the earliest pieces of English historical fiction set in India. *Chronicles* was started in May 1826 at the lowest point in Scott's fortunes. He had come to fame as a poet in 1805 with his verse romance *The Lay of the Last Minstrel*; in 1814 he published a novel, *Waverley*, which was the first of a prolific series which became known as the Waverley Novels, and made their author rich. In 1826, however, in the course of a national financial crisis, Scott became insolvent and on 24 February undertook to write to pay off the debts for which he was responsible.[1] On 15 May his wife died. He started to write what became *Chronicles of the Canongate* on 27 May, and an elegiac note is detectable in the passage where he first put pen to paper, at the beginning of Chapter 6 on page 55 of this edition.

Although Scott wrote other tales, *Chronicles of the Canongate* was the only collection published in his lifetime. It has suffered from a lack of profile because in the collected editions of Scott's novels, which dominated the market after his death in 1832, the tales were separated to make weight in volumes containing the shorter novels. The present edition reinstates the collection as it was originally published: as three tales preceded by an autobiographical Introduction, and a narrative by the fictitious narrator and compiler, Chrystal Croftangry. The name of the collection is taken from the Canongate in Edinburgh, where its narrator, Croftangry, had retired. Its significance is that this was an area which had come down in the world, being inhabited by 'greyheaded eld' (124) now that people of fashion had moved to Edinburgh's famous New Town. Apart from the linking idea of the Canongate, Scott did not impose a plan on the collection. As he wrote in his journal, 'I intend the work as an *olla podrida* into which any species of narrative or discussion may be thrown.'[2]

The Penguin edition aims to enable the reader either to read the collection straight through as Scott originally published it or to take one tale at a time. For this reason this Introduction and the Explanatory Notes are divided into sections. A Historical Note before the Explanatory Notes gives an account of the sources and setting for each tale.

Note: the sections devoted to the three tales each reveal the conclusion to the tale.

INTRODUCTION

The Introduction with which the text starts is not an introduction to the contents of *Chronicles of the Canongate*, but an explanation of some circumstances relating to the work's publication. Scott's novels, starting with *Waverley* in 1814, had been published anonymously, and the anonymity had been maintained in his later novels despite the intelligent guesses of reviewers and readers which had more or less exploded any claim to it. Scott's financial crash in 1826, however, had obliged him to acknowledge his authorship of the Waverley Novels at least to the lawyers dealing with its aftermath; and in February 1827 an unexpected opportunity was afforded him of acknowledging his authorship to a public gathering in Edinburgh. After that it remained to admit to his faithful readers that he was 'the sole and unaided author of these Novels of Waverley' (4), which he does in this Introduction signed Walter Scott, the first occasion upon which he attached his name to a work of prose fiction.

The discarding of his anonymity also allowed Scott to acknowledge in print the help he had had down the years from friends and strangers who had supplied him with material. The result is that the Introduction is interesting for what it says about Scott's anonymity and its consequences. For the modern reader wishing to read the tales of *Chronicles of the Canongate* it may be left till last; but it is worth recalling that the Introduction—an apparently frank avowal by an author who had meant so much to them—was what the first readers of *Chronicles* particularly relished.

CHRYSTAL CROFTANGRY'S NARRATIVE

This section introduces two narrators: Chrystal Croftangry, the compiler of the whole work, and Mrs Martha Bethune Baliol, the source for 'The Highland Widow'. Croftangry, a first-person narrator, is a man in his sixties who had squandered his inheritance through youthful folly, then recouped his fortunes by years abroad, and is now occupying his retirement by writing. He looks back with remorse and disillusion. His return home has not led to the reinstatement which is usually the reward of younger heroes in Scott's fiction. He had gone back to his family home in Upper Clydesdale to find the house replaced with a modern building, itself empty. The old family retainer, Christie Steele, had been sour and did not remember him with any warmth. And not only him: she would not allow any comforting comparison between his family and that of his successor, Mr Treddles. The purchaser of

Croftangry's estate of Glentanner had founded a mill on the property; but his son had overreached himself financially and it was again for sale. For Scott, whose name is associated with respect for the old ways and the negotiation between old and new, there is pessimism in the description of Glentanner, which thrives under neither. There is little politics in this presentation: the Croftangrys were not Jacobites to the new man's Whiggery. Instead Chrystal had been a 'paughty, petted, ignorant, dissipated, broken-down Scotch laird' (28), and Mr Treddles's son was a *nouveau riche* with fashionable tastes. Both families had lost the estate through the extravagance of their heirs; but the businessman had at least brought employment to the poor during his prosperity.

The only person to welcome Croftangry back was a poor Highland landlady, Janet MacEvoy, with whom he had lodged many years before when he had taken sanctuary for debt in Holyrood. She is from a dispeopled Highland glen—a victim of what we have come to call 'the Highland clearances'. Croftangry humours Janet's Highland love of genealogy by acquiescing in the (false) derivation of his name from 'Croft-an-ri', Gaelic for 'the King his Croft' (23). For the reader, a significant element in that name is *angry*. The narrator is angry—at modern developments like mail coaches, and at his own powerlessness to command respect. He turns his back on Glentanner, and settles into the favour of two old women in the Canongate: Janet MacEvoy and Mrs Martha Bethune Baliol.

Mrs Bethune Baliol is an old lady with a long memory. Described in her richly furnished house, entertaining guests according to the conventions of an earlier age, she represents cultivated, cosmopolitan Edinburgh, with its links to the Continent. One thing only betrays unease in her negotiation with the modern world. She 'did not like to be much pressed on the subject of the Stuarts . . . the rather that her father had espoused their cause' (65). Her family had been Jacobite,[3] but she has reconciled herself to 'the present dynasty'. She has witnessed many changes in society, and undertakes to supply Croftangry with material for his work. Although Scott had not announced a theme for his work, Croftangry does: 'The work of the whole publication is, to throw some light on the manners of Scotland as they were, and to contrast them, occasionally, with such as now are fashionable in the same country' (53). Both Mrs Bethune Baliol and Chrystal Croftangry are the last of their families, and what they give to the future is the memory of the past. As Croftangry embarks on his description of Mrs Bethune Baliol's house he laments that it has been pulled down (56)—making it one with the cottages in Janet's glen and the old house of Glentanner. Only writing survives in *Chronicles*—signified by the formidable family history left by Croftangry's great-grandfather in Chapter 2; houses and families do not.

It was recognised from the first that Scott had put a lot of himself into the character of Chrystal Croftangry.[4] Early readers were thirsty for details about Scott, and, like the printer James Ballantyne, did not care much for the lower-class and unromantic heroes of the tales that followed.[5] This led to a tradition of criticism which found the Croftangry narrative the most pleasing part of the work. John Buchan, for instance, remarked that 'It is the narrator of the tale, and the narrator's friends, that give the book its virtue.'[6] For other readers the Croftangry narrative has been found too long, delaying the reader's approach to the tales themselves. Edgar Johnson remarks that the characters introduced in it 'float as mere sketches having no purpose beyond themselves'.[7] More recently Chrystal Croftangry has been interesting to those studying the enabling personas chosen by fiction writers. Scott in the Waverley Novels has a rich list of these—Jedidiah Cleishbotham, Peter Pattieson, Laurence Templeton—and there is no doubt that Croftangry is better realised and less of a caricature than his predecessors.[8]

Chrystal Croftangry has a different relation to each of the three tales in *Chronicles of the Canongate*. 'The Two Drovers' is based on an experience in his own early manhood (142) and is narrated by him. The story which is the base of 'The Surgeon's Daughter' was told to Croftangry by Katie Fairscribe, the daughter of his lawyer, with supplementary material from her father. From that oral source the tale is narrated by Croftangry. The case of 'The Highland Widow' is less clear. Croftangry's source is Mrs Bethune Baliol, who undertook to give him material for his collection only after her death. Accordingly, what he receives is in writing, prompting the question, what alteration, if any, is Croftangry supposed to have made to Mrs Bethune Baliol's material? 'The Highland Widow' fills Chapters 7–11 of *Chronicles*. Chapter 7, describing Mrs Bethune Baliol's tour and her meeting with 'the Woman of the Tree', is plainly written by the traveller herself. The narrator of Chapters 8–11, which tell the story of Elspat and her son, is reticent and makes few self-references: although the 'I' at 81.33 appears to be Mrs Bethune Baliol, the 'I' at 120.28 and the 'we' at 121.7 are clearly Croftangry, leaving it to be supposed that Croftangry is contributing to a text written by Mrs Bethune Baliol.[9]

Chrystal Croftangry is not only involved in the tales' origins: he also arranges to measure their reception by, in Volume 1, reading what he has written to Janet MacEvoy and, in Volume 2, seeking the verdict of the Fairscribes. Janet 'wept most bitterly' over 'The Highland Widow' (68), and some acknowledgement that the Croftangry narrative is too self-indulgent in places appears in the fact that Janet MacEvoy does not enjoy it (55). She does not comprehend the passage towards the end of Chapter 5 in which Croftangry rehearses his plan for his literary undertaking in a somewhat jocose manner. He knows he ought to rewrite it, but refuses to do so with an assertion of wilfulness: ' "Know that I alone am king of me" ' (55).[10] Perhaps that ungratifying bloody-mindedness, an aspect of character rarely seen in his work, reflects the mental state with which Scott struggled to confront his financial and personal disasters of 1826.

THE HIGHLAND WIDOW

Robert Louis Stevenson wrote in a letter of 1890, 'I say, have you ever read "the Highland Widow"? I never had till yesterday. I am half inclined, bar a trip or two, to think it Scott's masterpiece . . ."[11]

'The Highland Widow' is a tragic tale of human will—the will of a mother defending the values of an older generation against her son's striving towards a new life. It is set in the Highlands of Scotland some years after the defeat of the Jacobite rising of 1745–6,[12] and the individuals in the tale represent more than themselves in that their tragedy is produced by the circumstances of that time and place. As Chrystal Croftangry remarked in prompting Mrs Bethune Baliol's memory:

> "You have witnessed the complete change of that primeval country, and have seen a race not far removed from the earliest period of society, melted down into the great mass of civilization; and that could not happen without incidents striking in themselves, and curious as chapters in the history of the human race."
> (65)

Elspat MacTavish's husband had been a Highland warrior and freebooter, a Jacobite who had been killed in a skirmish with Hanoverian soldiers shortly after the decisive defeat of the Jacobites at Culloden in 1746. Elspat was left alone with her infant son, Hamish, and nursed the sole ambition of bringing him up to follow the career of his father. But, as the years passed, MacTavish Mohr's way of life became an anachronism in a society organised under the rule of law rather than by the claims of tradition and personal strength.

The tale starts when Hamish is a young man, and ready to take charge of his life. He frets under the domination of his strong-willed mother and, after a quarrel, signs up with a recruiting officer for a newly formed Highland regiment destined to fight in America. Elspat is appalled, because the regiment is a creation of the Hanoverian government and its recruiting officer is a Campbell (a clan traditionally

Whig and anti-Jacobite). In return for her son's service she receives money and the promise of protection—a deal which the old widow finds both dishonourable and only partly comprehensible. To Hamish it is his only hope of freeing them both from poverty and isolation. The way of life of a freebooter is no longer honourable, or even possible, in post-Culloden Scotland, and enlisting in the army promises Hamish scope for the martial qualities he inherits, in keeping with the new political reality. As a soldier he is allowed to wear tartan, which is both a link with his father and, less visibly, an example of the government's manipulation of his culture for its own ends.[13] The appearance of the ghost of his father, beckoning him away from his mother's cottage, implies that his father would have agreed with his taking this step; only his mother does not.

The theme of the tale is desertion—military desertion in the sense of failing to return to barracks when ordered to, and the larger sense of desertion of one's family's values. Hamish's dilemma is that he can avoid one of these sorts of desertion only by committing the other. He is caught between opposing forces, each using its own weapons. His mother's are manipulative language and the weapons of the weak, namely guile, avoidance, and flight. She uses traditional Highland skill to produce a drugged drink so that Hamish sleeps through the moment of decision until, in Elspat's view, the decision has been made for him. The Hanoverian army uses weapons of strength: command, inflexibility, and violence. Its attitude to Hamish's predicament is confrontational: the punishment for desertion is flogging. Punishments often distinguish cultures—what is accepted in one culture is regarded with revulsion in another. In the tale, Highland culture regards punishment of the body as dishonourable, and would even find capital punishment preferable, death in action being the expectation of a warlike culture. An aspect of colonial relationships is the imposing of alien punishments on a people who do not deny the need for punishments, but do not accept sorts which are offensive to them. In Scott's first novel, *Waverley*, his Highland chieftain Fergus Mac-Ivor, facing the brutal penalty for high treason (hanging and disembowelling), points out to the hero that it was '"one of the blessings . . . with which your free country has accommodated poor old Scotland"',[14] and the theme occurs again with variations in the later tales of *Chronicles*. In 'The Highland Widow' the case against Highland culture, which builds up relentlessly, is suddenly reversed by the fact that the reader is likely to share the Highland view of corporal punishment (as did liberal opinion in Scott's day).

A contributory factor to Hamish's tragedy is that he has no advisers. It is an indication of the mother and son's cultural isolation that they have no friends in the neighbourhood—Elspat despises any others whom she mentions, and they fear her. There is only one representative of a community in the tale, the minister of the church at Dalmally, Mr McIntyre. He is well-intentioned, but sadly inadequate to the task. When Hamish meets him after waking from his drugged sleep, all the minister can do is reprove him for not being in church on Sunday. After the death of Cameron, the officer who came to arrest Hamish, he intervenes to help, comforts the young man in his last hours, and conveys the news of his execution to his mother. Elspat, a Catholic, addresses him with contempt. Her religion is presented as one of spiritual barter and subjection, implying that the passions of the old Scotland can be curbed only by the dogmatism of the old religion (118–19).[15] The new Scotland has a more moderate religion, and a minister more celebrated for showing tourists the beauty of Loch Awe than for grappling with a recalcitrant parishioner like Elspat MacTavish. Mr McIntyre's disabling modernity emerges again at the end of the tale. The last paragraph speculates on the cause of Elspat's death: some people thought she had been carried away by an evil spirit, others that she had disappeared into the gulf of the Corrie Dhu, either by accident or suicide.

> The clergyman entertained an opinion of his own. He thought, that impatient of the watch which was placed over her, this unhappy woman's instinct had taught her, as it directs various domestic animals, to withdraw herself from the sight of her own race, that the death-struggle might take place in some secret den, where, in all probability, her mortal remains would never meet the eyes of mortals. (122)

This is the view of a man educated in the scientific outlook of the Scottish Enlightenment. It does not appear to trouble him that he has attributed the death of an unhappy old woman to the instinct of a domestic animal.[16] He rejects a supernatural explanation of her death—he is modern in that—but, in replacing superstition with rationality, human values have gone too.

'The Highland Widow' is a pessimistic tale. In Scott loyalty is usually a positive value, even loyalty to a doubtful cause. In this tale Elspat's loyalty is stubborn and destructive, and Hamish's loyalty is not recognised by the army from which he refuses to flee. In Scott's Jacobite novels, in particular *Waverley* and *Redgauntlet* (1824), the young heroes are able to make the transition from an older to the modern world, with the losses involved being acknowledged in the unhappy fate of other characters. 'The Highland Widow', being a tale, has no subplot, and lower-class characters who would be on the margins of a novel are here at the centre, with devastating result. Lilian Dickins pointed out the paradox that Scott's fiction respects the old, but endorses to the hilt the right of the young to rebel.[17] Youthful rebellion would hardly surprise us, were it not for the nature of that rebellion in Scott's Jacobite fiction. The young rebel *against* rebellion. In *Redgauntlet* Darsie rebels against his uncle's plans for his life, and in so doing he rebels into the mainstream. Hamish's tragedy is particularly painful because what he was trying to do was join the society of which the narrator, and many readers, are members. He fails, and he and his mother, able neither to find a foothold in the new world nor to retain one in the old, can only die in grief and anonymity.

The tale is mediated by the framing narrative of Mrs Bethune Baliol's tour. It is a feature of the post-Culloden world that the Highlands are being opened up to visitors. This is an example of what is a commonplace today: the remains of earlier societies after defeat being presented for tourists, and landscapes previously regarded as dangerous and unproductive being offered as examples of the sublime and the beautiful. At the beginning of the journey the postilion, Donald MacLeish, is described as willing to 'point out ... the principal clan-battles, and recount the most remarkable legends' (69). This is Scottish history rendered into a narrative for travellers, and does not promise that the traveller will be confronted with the raw actuality, which is what happens. Donald tries to deflect Mrs Bethune Baliol's interest in the old woman; but her curiosity draws Elspat's history reluctantly from him. What can Mrs Bethune Baliol do? She offers sympathy and money, both of which are ignored. The other thing she can do is remember the story, which she gives to Chrystal Croftangry. Mrs Bethune Baliol is a decent representative of the new Scotland. The reader has been told in Croftangry's narrative that her family had been Jacobite, but that she had unobtrusively come to terms with the post-Culloden changes. She is a woman who has negotiated with change, and when she met Elspat she confronted one who could not. The inadequacy of Mrs Bethune Baliol's actions probably also implicates the reader; griefs so intense render ordinary modern people helpless, and memory is the only recompense they can offer.

THE TWO DROVERS

'The Two Drovers', which had a cool reception from his printer James Ballantyne,[18] is now regarded as one of the most perfectly executed of Scott's works. It invites comparison with 'The Highland Widow', since it too is a tragedy resulting from confrontation between a Scottish Highlander and the culture of southern Britain in the post-Culloden world.[19] It differs, however, in its pace —being faster and more economical in narration—and in the tenor of the plot that drives it. An important part of the plot of 'The Highland Widow' is a trick which goes wrong: the drugged drink designed to resolve the characters' problem in fact makes it worse. The trick is almost folkloric, the resource of the poor and quick-witted. 'The Two Drovers', on the other hand, is more akin to those classical tragedies where the plot unfolds in response to a prophecy. As the Highland drover, Robin Oig, prepares to set forth with his drove he is stopped by his aunt—another powerful old Highland woman—who, having the gift of second sight,[20] has seen English blood on his dirk: '"Blood, blood—Saxon blood again. Robin Oig McCombich, go not this day to England!"' (128). To avert the prophecy, Robin hands over the dirk to a Lowland drover, Hugh Morrison, for safe keeping. But in tragedy it is in the nature of a prophecy to *come true* no matter what the protagonist may do in relation to it. (The *locus classicus* in ancient Greek drama is the story of Oedipus; in the English tradition it is *Macbeth*.) When Robin, having parted with his dirk, gets into a quarrel he has to go in search of Hugh Morrison to retrieve it. The time that takes is used by the judge at the end of the tale to declare him guilty of murder rather than manslaughter. The theme of an inexorable prophecy, against which the actions of men are vain, has resonated in European literature from the earliest times and drives Scott's plot.

Robin Oig is unlike Elspat MacTavish in that he is a Highlander who has taken a step into the world of the late eighteenth century. He is distinguished as a drover, and by driving Highland cattle to English markets he contributes to the opening of the Highlands to commerce with the rest of the kingdom. In the course of his trade he has made a friend of an Englishman, Harry Wakefield. Robin accommodates himself to his situation when he is in the Lowlands and England. For instance, he keeps his counsel about his birth, in which he takes pride. His grandfather had been a friend of the celebrated outlaw Rob Roy. Robin's surname McCombich, '*son of my friend*' (126), had been given to his father by Roy Roy, disguising the real name, MacGregor—the name of a clan proscribed for its lawless conduct.[21] This is an ominous ancestry, and its distinction is not likely to be recognised outside Robin's 'own lonely glen' (126). Robin, however, has made that transition into a more modern Scotland which is symbolised by replacing cattle-rieving with cattle-droving. Exactly how modern he is in outlook is raised by his aunt's prophecy. Does Robin hand over his dirk because he believes the prophecy? Or to placate his aunt and stop her hindering his journey?

The friendship between the Highlander and the Englishman is spoiled by an accident, caused by a difference between a landowner and his bailiff over the letting of a field of which the drovers could have no knowledge. Robin is the beneficiary of the mistake, and although he offers to help his friend, who is the loser, he is rebuffed. In the inn that evening Harry Wakefield suggests that they '"take a tussle for love on the sod"' (135).[22] This suggestion precipitates the disaster that follows. Wakefield wants a pugilistic meeting, an encounter with fists. This is repugnant to the Highlander, who finds such physical body-contact demeaning. If an encounter were to take place at all, Robin would countenance only a duel with swords, the weapons of a gentleman. This attitude inflames the crowd gathered in the inn, who had already taken sides with their countryman and revealed their prejudice against the Scot. It is made plain, with considerable complacency on the English side, that boxing is regarded in England as a 'natural' way of solving disputes, using nature's weapons (145). But it will do so only if both participants agree on its symbolic function. The Highlander, from what was until recently a warrior culture, does not understand it.

There is a serious question why any such tussle should take place at all. Robin has not intentionally wronged Harry Wakefield. If Harry thinks he has, as Robin sensibly points out, they should take the matter to a court. '"If you think I have done you wrong, I'll go before your shudge, though I neither know his law nor his language"' (136). This course is rejected; but Harry is now being taunted with cowardice by the bailiff, and something is needed to set the situation to rights. As Robert Gordon has remarked, Harry wants the tussle 'for the purpose of relieving his feelings and clearing the air'.[23] It is for just such a nebulous purpose that the tussle for love exists. It is an archaic ritual, displacing a grievance of the mind on to an encounter of physical skill. It is not rational, but it would work if both sides believed it. It could be useful to a society to have a method of getting over grievances which are below the concerns of a court of law. For the Highlander the sticking point about Harry's proposal is the use of the fists, in which he has never been trained. We note that the use of either fists or swords would be a shared encounter. When the quarrel becomes serious it is one-sided: Harry knocks Robin over as he tries to leave the inn, and Robin takes revenge for the insult with his dirk, a notoriously one-sided weapon. As the judge points out later, revenge is another archaic ritual.

The trial takes place in Carlisle, symbolically the town in the west nearest the Anglo-Scottish border. Critical opinion has divided on the issue of the judge's speech which dominates the end of the tale. For some it has been seen as offering a 'true' verdict on the story of Robin Oig, directing our thoughts in a way that Scott might have endorsed. For others—probably the majority of modern readers—the judge is simply another character in Croftangry's tale, albeit one with the role of commentator. In this he is similar to the minister, Mr McIntyre, in 'The Highland Widow'. The minister and the judge are both educated men, of basic good will; but they cannot see their own limitations.

The judge refuses to allow the prosecution's case that the 'laws of the ring' (143) enshrine natural and universal values. He points out that they are culture-specific, adding astutely that their applicability even within England is limited by social class. He acknowledges the composure of Robin while being mocked in the inn, and the provocative behaviour of the English bystanders. He ensures that the jury are aware of recent Highland history, and edifies them with the comparison, common in Scottish Enlightenment thought, between Highlanders and the American Indians. He is in many ways a good judge; but at a certain point his understanding fails. He finds Robin guilty of murder rather than manslaughter because of the two hours it took him to retrieve his dirk from Hugh Morrison—two hours after which he appeared like a 'wraith' (139), bent only on his revenge. For the judge, his passions would have cooled in those two hours, making his stabbing of Harry Wakefield an act of murder. But the whole business of how one gets over a slight has been one of the themes of the tale. The narrator regards placability as a peculiarly English quality. Even so, Harry Wakefield needed a fist fight to return him to his usual frame of mind after an unintended slight. What would be needed for a person sprung from a revenge culture to get over a physical affront? The judge, who was sound about the cultural specificity of boxing, fails to acknowledge the cultural determinants involved in acting placably after an insult. For that failure he can be blamed. But there is more—a cultural gap too great for the ready attribution of blame. The judge does not know what the reader knows: that the question whether two hours is long enough for Robin's passion to have subsided is unanswerable, because as he left the inn he remembered his aunt's prophecy. 'The recollection of the fatal prophecy confirmed the deadly intention which instantly sprang up in his mind' (138). The prophecy which he had attempted to avert he now determined to fulfil.

Compared with the previous tale, 'The Two Drovers' is a tragedy in the classical sense—its hero has stature and awareness of what he has done. Hamish MacTavish is a young man destroyed by forces too big for him, and Elspat's inscrutability in her grief prevents us knowing to what extent she recognises herself to be the cause of her distress. Hamish's poignant last message to his mother places him back in the world of his boyhood: '"Tell her Hamish Bean is more glad to die than ever he was to rest after the longest day's hunting"' (115–16). Robin Oig by contrast is an adult. He had left Scotland to trade in the

English market and pay fair price. The verdict is his: ' "I give a life for the life I took . . . and what can I do more?" ' (146).

THE SURGEON'S DAUGHTER

'The Surgeon's Daughter' differs from the tales that precede it in *Chronicles* by being set partly in India, but shares with them the theme of people leaving Scotland to take up the opportunities offered them elsewhere in the late eighteenth century. It has never been highly esteemed among Scott's works. The traditional view is succinctly stated by George Gordon: ' "The Surgeon's Daughter", which begins well enough in a Scottish village, is smothered in melodrama and curry-powder.'[24] While it is not possible entirely to refute that criticism, contemporary interest in the literature of imperialism, and in the presentation of 'the Orient' in the light of Edward Said's *Orientalism*,[25] help us to recognise in it aspects which were previously overlooked.

The story which forms the plot of 'The Surgeon's Daughter' is told to Chrystal Croftangry, the narrator, by Katie Fairscribe, and concerns a young woman who was a relation of the Fairscribes.[26] Mr Fairscribe, a Presbyterian Lowland lawyer, has not entirely approved of the two previous tales in *Chronicles of the Canongate*, with their imaginative sympathy for Highlanders, and it is he who suggests to Croftangry that he set his tale among the British in India:

> "If you want rogues, as they are so much in fashion with you, you have that gallant caste of adventurers, who laid down their consciences at the Cape of Good Hope as they went out to India, and forgot to take them up again when they returned. Then, for great exploits, you have in the old history of India, before Europeans were numerous there, the most wonderful deeds, done by the least possible means, that perhaps the annals of the world can afford." (155)

This passage promises both rogues and 'wonderful deeds', and stresses, as the tale does throughout, that the incidents described are set not in Croftangry's present (1826–27), but fifty years earlier. The Indian part of 'The Surgeon's Daughter' is set in the 1770s, in Madras and Mysore.

The tale starts, however, in Scotland, in the little town of Middlemas, where three young people live in the house of the local doctor, Gideon Grey. One is his daughter, Menie, and the other two are his apprentices, Adam Hartley and Richard Middlemas. Both young men love Menie; she prefers Richard and is secretly engaged to him. Richard is the illegitimate son of a Jacobite father and a Jewish mother, whose family had abandoned him at birth except for the payment of a modest maintenance to Gideon Grey. The child's fantasies about his origin had been encouraged by his nurse, who had led him to believe that his family would one day reclaim him and establish him in rank and money. Disappointed in this hope as a young man, and restless at the limited prospects offered him as a doctor in Scotland, he transfers his fantasies to India: ' "Oh, Delhi! oh, Golconda! . . . India, where gold is won by steel; where a brave man cannot pitch his desire of fame and wealth so high, but that he may realize it, if he have fortune to his friend!" ' (198). Through the offices of a disreputable recruiting agent of the East India Company army, Richard sets out for India. Independently the disappointed lover, Adam Hartley, also goes to India, as a doctor. In due course Menie, now fatherless, accepts Richard's invitation to join him.

The tale is set just after the first phase of British territorial expansion in India, which had seen Bengal come under British rule following Robert Clive's victory at Plassey in 1757. In south India, however, the East India Company's activities had met with resistance from the ruler of Mysore, Haidar Ali (or Hyder Ali as Scott spells him). From their fort in Madras the British had fought a war with Haider Ali in 1767–69, and the three young people in the tale arrive in Madras during the years of uneasy truce that followed it.[27]

The sense of entrepreneurial energy present in the activities of the East India Company in India is reflected in the behaviour of individual characters in the tale, in particular Richard Middlemas. Such energy flouts morality and destabilises character. In their self-seeking, Richard Middlemas and the Begum Montreville, his associate in India, cross boundaries of political allegiance, religion, race, and gender. Richard has no loyalty except to himself, and only slight regret at what he inflicts on Menie. The Begum is a Scots adventuress, condemned as an 'unsexed woman, who can no longer be termed a European' (259). She deploys the visible attributes of femininity: she dresses with regal flamboyance, and Richard's relationship with her is expressed in terms of sordid gallantry. It is her idea, however, to offer Menie to Hyder Ali's son, Tippoo (or Tipu), as a contribution to his *zenana*, or harem, in the hope of securing Richard's appointment as governor of Bangalore—justifying her soubriquet 'Mother Montreville' (251), which implies a procuress. By contrast Menie Grey has no shifting elements in her personality. Described contemptuously by the Begum as ' "this northern icicle" ' (262), she is treated as something to trade, some 'fair-skinned speculation of old Montreville's' (251). In Bangalore her presence is revealed only by a scream from within 'a close litter' (280–82), a muffled and inarticulate protest. The advantage which the villains seek by their intrigue is the opportunity to betray Bangalore to the British. This, were it to succeed, would be conquest by betrayal, not by fighting of the sort worthy to be recorded in 'the annals of the world' (155).

What saves Menie and unravels the plot is Adam Hartley's success in enlisting the help of Hyder Ali. To achieve it he journeys up the mountain pass to Mysore, a journey like Edward Waverley's to the Highlands in Chapter 16 of *Waverley* in that it takes him to a different society. In one sense Mysore is presented in 'The Surgeon's Daughter' in terms of the clichés of the Western view of the Orient: Hyder Ali, its Muslim ruler, is a despot; his son Tippoo is lustful; its court ceremonies are luxurious. It is a Muslim sense of justice, however, which rescues Menie from the machinations of renegade Christians. Adam is an example of a different sort of Briton in India, of which there were some in the eighteenth century: he cures the sick, learns the local languages, and has studied enough of the Muslim religion to sustain an exchange with Hyder Ali. His meeting with the Fakir— Hyder Ali in disguise—has this in common with Jeanie Deans's meeting with Queen Caroline in Chapter 37 of *The Heart of Mid-Lothian*: he and Jeanie have only speech to persuade rulers to save a young woman who is far below their usual notice, and both succeed by offering the rulers a religious view of their power, as the source of justice and mercy.

The outcome is the action of a just despot. Hyder Ali reproves his son and enacts justice on the traitor by having him trampled to death under the foot of an elephant. As the tales in *Chronicles of the Canongate* demonstrate, methods of punishment are conditioned by culture, and shock those from outside. Richard has, however, crossed the boundary into the service of Mysore, and dies according to the conventions of the culture he was attempting to betray. Hyder Ali's action is sudden and drastic—an example of what Bruce Beiderwell describes as 'swift, and certain acts of righteousness'[28]—and contrasts with the modern use of a court of law exemplified in 'The Two Drovers'.

There is no difficulty in discovering rogues in 'The Surgeon's Daughter', but what about the 'wonderful deeds' that Fairscribe promised? The tale expresses the astonishment of the ordinary Briton that an empire so recently founded should have grown so that by the 1820s almost all of the Indian peninsula was ruled by Britain either directly or indirectly.[29] This is a matter of 'wonder' in the tale, and the narrator gives us the names of military leaders—Clive, Caillaud, Lawrence, Smith—and commends the 'hardy and persevering policy' (219) of the directors of the East India Company (as opposed to their unscrupulous and incompetent representatives in Madras). The text seems to want to establish a difference between the behaviour of rogues like Richard Middlemas and the activities of those who had created this empire. Yet that distinction is hard to sustain, and not only because there are no characters to speak for the empire in the tale. There are several passages which express anxiety about the imperial venture in India. Talking of the speed of the foundation of the empire in India, the narrator explains that it 'rose like an exhalation, and now astonishes Europe, as well as Asia, with its formidable extent, and stupendous strength' (201)—a compliment undercut by the fact that 'rose like an exhalation' comes from Milton's description of Hell in *Paradise Lost*.[30] Any suggestion that a European might be in India innocently, as perhaps Adam Hartley is, is undermined by a remark of his colleague, Mr Esdale: '"we are all upon the adventure in India, more or less"' (253). A similar ambivalence is present in a passage towards the end of the tale. Hyder Ali declares to an envoy from the British, '"You have brought to me . . . words of peace, while your masters meditated a treacherous war . . . Hitherto I have been in the Carnatic as a mild prince—in future I will be a destroying tempest!"' The narrator continues, 'It is well known how dreadfully the Nawaub kept this promise, and how he and his son afterwards sunk before the discipline and bravery of the Europeans' (284–5). This acknowledges both the discreditable actions of the British—punished by Haider Ali's descent on Madras in 1780—and the dynamic of their ultimate triumph, outside the tale—the death of Tipu and the defeat of Mysore in 1799.

In the fate of the characters there is no such ambivalence. Even for the survivors there is no happy ending. The source story as Scott (rather than Croftangry) received it allowed Menie to marry her rescuer.[31] 'The Surgeon's Daughter' is less romantic: Menie's 'feelings were too much and too painfully agitated, her health too much shattered' (285) for her to think of marriage; and before she had recovered Adam had died of disease. Menie returns home to her native village and devotes the rest of her life to charitable works. Even that is not held up to unmixed admiration, since Mr Fairscribe recalls, '"There was something very gentle, but rather tiresome, about poor cousin Menie"' (156).

The framework surrounding the three tales in *Chronicles of the Canongate* offers the response of folk in the Canongate to each tale. 'The Surgeon's Daughter' ends with the tale's being read by Croftangry to Katie Fairscribe's literary circle, allowing us to see the impact of this tale of the British in India on a group of women at home. Two things gain their attention. One is reference to the luxury goods from India that have now become consumer desirables in Britain: 'mention of shawls, diamonds, turbans, and cummmberbands, had their usual effect in awakening the imaginations of the fair auditors' (287). The other is the description of the death of Richard Middlemas. It excited 'that expression of painful interest, which is produced by drawing in the breath through compressed lips; nay, one Miss of fourteen actually screamed' (287). In 'The Surgeon's Daughter, the masculine story of the British in India yields only death and defeat; and when recounted in Britain is feminised into a matter of shawls and exotic horrors.

CONCLUSION

The three tales in *Chronicles of the Canongate* differ in length and setting. They are, however, linked thematically. They all take place in the second half of the eighteenth century, and all are tales of people leaving Scotland to seek their fortune elsewhere. In 'The Two Drovers' Robin Oig is involved in the relatively uncomplicated export of cattle from the Highlands to English markets. In the other two tales the exports are young people for whom Scotland offers no opportunity. In 'The Highland Widow' Hamish MacTavish enlists with a Highland regiment to be sent to protect the American colonies against the French. In 'The Surgeon's Daughter' Richard Middlemas enlists with the East India Company forces and goes to Madras. Through the stories of individuals, the tales in *Chronicles* tell a wider history of Scotland's relationship with the outside world. Each tale is, however, tragic in its conclusion, preventing any sense of triumph at Scotland's growing internationalism. In each case the Scottish protagonist falls foul of the law and suffers under an alien judicial system. There the similarities end: the tales do not work to the same pattern. While both Hamish MacTavish and Robin Oig suffer as a result of misunderstanding between their Highland background and British culture and law, Richard Middlemas is a British imperialist whose abandonment of principles shared ideally by both the British and Hyder Ali is punished by the Indian culture he opposes. In none of the tales is there a male survivor. Both 'The Highland Widow' and 'The Surgeon's Daughter' have a female survivor, who is the link between the tragic events of the past and their narration.

As has been suggested, there are in these tales many instances of the crossing of borders, some of them geographical, others cultural. These include boundaries between Highland and Lowland, Scottish and English, British and Indian, Jewish and Christian, Christian and Muslim, male and female, white and black. This raises the question: *ought* these boundaries to be crossed? Zahra A. Hussein Ali has argued persuasively that 'The Two Drovers' endorses the cultural assimilation of Highlanders into Britain through the successful prosecution of cross-border trade,[32] lamenting only the tragic outcome in Robin Oig's case. A similar claim could be made for the British bias of 'The

Highland Widow'. 'The Surgeon's Daughter', which presents so many different boundaries, seems to present those of gender and race as not to be crossed, but the others as open to debate.

The second half of the eighteenth century saw Scotland reap at last the social and economic benefits of the parliamentary union with England of 1707. The history of the country in the period can be told in terms of triumph: its universities and cities were renowned for the intellectual and cultural advances commonly referred to as the Scottish Enlightenment (and Croftangry's narrative gives glimpses of Enlightment Edinburgh); Scottish inventiveness contributed to the Industrial Revolution; and Scots abroad contributed to international trade and the founding of the British Empire. *Chronicles of the Canongate*, the work of the country's most celebrated poet and novelist, writing towards the end of his life when he was stricken with grief and personal disaster, shows the other side of such wide-ranging achievement. Three starkly tragic tales show the personal toll exacted on ordinary Scots who stepped out of the settled cultures in which they had grown up. They reveal the difficulties of social transition. That is to look back. To look forward, the two Highland tales in particular are prophetic of the experience of other small societies in their relation to imperial power. The submersion of one culture under the privileged position of another, supported by force and assumptions of rightness, may have been the history of the recent past for the Scottish Highlands, but it has turned out to be the future for many other parts of the world as empire and globalisation have expanded.

The tales in *Chronicles of the Canongate* stand at the beginning of a literary tradition in that they tell that story 'from below'. None of their main characters is a leader, able to speak for British military policy, the judicial system, or the British presence in India. They are not all good people, but all are attempting to carve out a life for themselves on the interface between an indigenous culture and the modernity that opposes and undermines it.

NOTES

1 National Library of Scotland, MS 112, p. 41. For a fuller account of Scott's circumstances as he started to write *Chronicles of the Canongate* see the beginning of the 'Essay on the Text' in *Chronicles of the Canongate*, ed. Claire Lamont, Edinburgh Edition of the Waverley Novels 20 (Edinburgh, 2000), 289–93.

2 *The Journal of Sir Walter Scott*, ed. W. E. K. Anderson (Oxford, 1972), 151, entry for 28 May 1826. *Olla podrida*, literally 'rotting pot', is a Spanish term for a stew or hash made from leftovers.

3 A supporter of the claim of the Stewart dynasty to the throne of Britain. Since 1714 Britain had been ruled by the Hanoverian kings (George I to

IV), and the Jacobites had been defeated at the Battle of Culloden in 1746. See the Historical Note to 'The Highland Widow', 319–20. In British politics Jacobites were usually Tories; the opposing party was the Whigs, who had the support of the Hanoverian monarchs and were in power for much of the eighteenth century.

4 Specific examples are indicated in the Explanatory Notes.

5 As he worked on 'The Highland Widow' Scott noted, 'I may be mistaken but I do think the Tale of Elspat McTavish in my bettermost manner but J. B. roars for chivalry' (*Journal*, 168–69, entry for 8 July 1826).

6 John Buchan, *Sir Walter Scott* (London, 1932), 314.

7 Edgar Johnson, *Sir Walter Scott: The Great Unknown* (London, 1970), 1069.

8 He has been celebrated by Frank Jordan in 'Chrystal Croftangry, Scott's Last and Best Mask', *Scottish Literary Journal*, 7 (1980), 185–92.

9 Since there was a gap in the writing of 'The Highland Widow' of almost a year at 102.20 (see A Note on the Text, xliii), it is possible that in a text where the narrator is not intrusive Scott had forgotten which of his fictitious narrators was responsible for the last part of the tale.

10 From John Dryden, *Almanzor and Almahide, or, the Conquest of Grenada* (1672), Part I, 1.1.206.

11 Letter to Edward L. Burlingame, ?7 October 1890, in *The Letters of Robert Louis Stevenson*, ed. Bradford A. Booth and Ernest Mehew, 8 vols (New Haven and London, 1994–95), 7.12.

12 For the historical setting of the tale see the Historical Note on pp. 320–21.

13 The wearing of Highland dress had been banned after the defeat of the Jacobite rising of 1745–46, but an exception was made in the case of Highland regiments. The ban was lifted in 1782.

14 *Waverley*, ed. Claire Lamont (Oxford, 1981), 326.

15 This contrasts with the Catholicism of Janet MacEvoy, which is presented positively in terms of chapel-going, prayer for her benefactor, and giving to the poor (47).

16 Graham Tulloch gives an interesting reading of 'The Highland Widow' in terms of its use of images of wild and domesticated animals in his 'Imagery in "The Highland Widow"', *Studies in Scottish Literature*, 21 (1986), 147–57.

17 Lilian Dickins, 'Scott's Masterpiece', *The Englishwoman*, 19 (July 1913), 62–71.

18 On the day he finished writing the tale, 15 July 1827, Scott noted in his journal, 'J. B. will I fear think it low; and if he thinks so others will' (*Journal*, 328). His fears were justified: 'James Ballantyne dislikes my drovers. But it shall stand. I must have my own way sometimes' (*Journal*, 331, entry for 22 July 1827).

19 For an account of the Highlands in the eighteenth century see the Historical Note to 'The Highland Widow', 319–20.

20 The ability to see things distant in time or place, attributed particularly to Scottish Highlanders.

21 The first Act proscribing the MacGregors, making anyone using the name an outlaw, was passed in 1603; it was renewed on occasions subsequently until 1775, when all Acts against the clan were repealed.

22 That is, a fight on the ground which is engaged in for pleasure rather than competitively.

23 Robert C. Gordon, *Under Which King? A Study of the Scottish Waverley Novels* (Edinburgh and London, 1969), 168.

24 George Gordon, '*The Chronicles of the Canongate*', in Thomas Seccombe and others, *Scott Centenary Articles* (London, 1932), 174–84 (180).

25 Edward W. Said, *Orientalism* (New York, 1978); some idea of the debate provoked by the book can be found in *Orientalism: A Reader*, ed. A. L. Macfie (Edinburgh, 2000).

26 For Scott's sources for the tale see the Historical Note, 355–58.

27 For the historical setting of the tale see the Historical Note, 358–60.

28 Bruce Beiderwell, *Power and Punishment in Scott's Novels* (Athens, GA, 1992), 82.

29 British rule in India was exerted through the East India Company until 1858, when the Company was wound up and the Crown took over its functions.

30 *Paradise Lost*, I.711.

31 See Historical Note, 356–57.

32 Zahra A. Hussein Ali, 'Adjusting the Borders of Self: Sir Walter Scott's *The Two Drovers*', *Papers on Language and Literature*, 37 (2001), 65–84.

1771	*15 August.* Born in College Wynd, Edinburgh. His father, Walter (1729–99), son of a sheep-farmer at Sandyknowe, near Smailholm Tower, Roxburghshire, was a lawyer. His mother, Anne Rutherford (1732–1819), was daughter of Dr John Rutherford, Professor of Medicine at the University of Edinburgh. His parents married in April 1758; Walter was their ninth child. The siblings who survived were Robert (1767–87), John (1769–1816), Anne (1772–1801), Thomas (1774–1823), and Daniel (?1776–1806).
1772–73	*Winter.* Contracted what is now termed poliomyelitis, and became permanently lame in his right leg. His grandfather Rutherford advised that he be sent to Sandyknowe to benefit from country air, and, apart from a period of 'about a year' in 1775 spent in Bath, a spell in 1776 with his family in their new home on the west side of George Square, Edinburgh, and a time in 1777 at Prestonpans, near Edinburgh, he lived there until 1778. From his grandmother and his aunt Janet he heard many ballads and stories of the Border past, and these narratives were crucial to his intellectual and imaginative development.
1779–83	Attended the High School of Edinburgh; he was particularly influenced by the Rector, Dr Alexander Adam, and his teaching of literature in Latin. After the High School, he spent 'half a year' with his aunt Janet in Kelso, where he attended the grammar school, and read for the first time Thomas Percy's *Reliques of Ancient English Poetry.*
1783–86	Attended classes at Edinburgh University, including Humanity (Latin), Greek, Logic and Metaphysics, and Moral Philosophy.
1786	Studies terminated by serious illness; convalescence in Kelso. Apprenticed as a lawyer to his father.
1787	Met Robert Burns at the house of the historian and philosopher, Adam Ferguson.
1789	Decided to prepare for the Bar.
1789–92	Attended classes at Edinburgh University, including History, Moral Philosophy, Scots Law, and Civil Law.
1792	*11 July.* Admitted to the Faculty of Advocates.

Autumn. First visit to Liddesdale, in the extreme south of Scotland, with Robert Shortreed, in search of ballads and ballad-singers. Seven such 'raids' followed over seven years. Shortreed later commented: 'He was makin' himsell a' the time'. His tours took him into many parts of Scotland and the north of England: e.g. in 1793 to Perthshire and the Trossachs; in 1796 to the north-east of Scotland; and in 1797 to Cumberland and the Lake District.

1794   In April involved in a brawl with some political radicals and bound to keep the peace. In September attended the trials of the radicals Watt and Downie, and in November Watt's execution.

*c.*1794–96   In love with Williamina Belsches, culminating in April 1796 with an invitation to her home, Fettercairn House, Kincardineshire.

1796   Anonymous publication of *The Chase and William and Helen*, Scott's translations of two of Bürger's poems.
October. Announcement of the engagement of Williamina Belsches to William Forbes.

1797   Volunteered for the new volunteer cavalry regiment, the Royal Edinburgh Light Dragoons, and appointed quarter-master.
September. Met Charlotte Carpenter (1770–1826), at Gilsland, Cumberland, and within three weeks proposed marriage. Charlotte's parents were Jean François Charpentier and Margaret Charlotte Volère (d. 1788), of Lyons. Some time after the break-up of the marriage around 1780, her mother brought Charlotte and her brother Charles (1772–1818) to England; Charlotte and Charles later became the wards of the 2nd Marquess of Downshire, and changed their name to Carpenter.
24 December. Married Charlotte in Carlisle, and set up house at 50 George Street, Edinburgh.

1798   Met Matthew Gregory ('Monk') Lewis, and agreed to contribute to *Tales of Wonder* (published 1801).
Rented cottage in Lasswade near Edinburgh for the summer, and made many political and literary contacts, including Lady Louisa Stuart, who proved to be one of the most acute and trusted of his friends and critics.
Moved to 19 Castle Street, Edinburgh.
October. Birth and death of first son.

1799   Publication of *Goetz of Berlichingen*, Scott's translation of Goethe's tragedy.

April. Death of Scott's father.

Met John Leyden and the publisher Archibald Constable, and had his first discussion with the printer James Ballantyne about undertaking book-printing: Ballantyne brought out Scott's anthology *An Apology for Tales of Terror* in 1800.

October. Birth of daughter, Charlotte Sophia Scott.

December. Appointed Sheriff-Depute of Selkirkshire.

1801   *October.* Birth of son, Walter Scott.

Moved to 39 Castle Street, Edinburgh.

1802   Publication of *Minstrelsy of the Scottish Border*, Vols 1 and 2. The *Minstrelsy* was the first publication in a lifetime of scholarly editing, and it shows both the strengths and weaknesses of Scott as editor. He found new texts (of the 72 ballads he published, 38 had not appeared in print before), and his literary, historical, and anthropological essays and notes are always illuminating; but, following the editorial practice of the time, he had no settled methods or principles for choosing or establishing a text.

Met James Hogg.

1803   *February.* Birth of daughter, Anne Scott.

Second edition of *Minstrelsy of the Scottish Border*, Vols 1 and 2, and first edition of Vol. 3.

Began to contribute reviews to the *Edinburgh Review*. Scott was an acute reviewer, in the expansive manner characteristic of heavyweight reviews in the early nineteenth century, and was particularly perceptive about such contemporaries as Jane Austen, Byron, and Mary Shelley.

September. Visit from William and Dorothy Wordsworth.

1804   Took the lease of Ashestiel near Selkirk as his country house in place of the cottage in Lasswade.

Publication of Scott's edition of the medieval metrical romance, *Sir Tristrem*.

1805   Publication of *The Lay of the Last Minstrel*, the first of a series of verse romances which established his fame as a poet.

Entered into partnership with James Ballantyne in the printing business of James Ballantyne & Co. Until the financial crash in 1826, the partnership was not just a financial arrangement, but a unique collaboration: Ballantyne managed the business, but also acted as Scott's editor; Scott seems to have been responsible for much of the financial planning, and it was a standard part of his contracts with publishers that his works should be printed by James Ballantyne & Co.

December. Birth of son, Charles Scott.

1806   Hurried to London to secure his appointment as one of the Principal Clerks to the Court of Session, a position which had been under negotiation for much of the previous year but which was imperilled by the advent of a new government after the death of William Pitt on 23 January. The appointment was announced on 8 March. Scott took the place of an elderly Clerk, but, as there was no retirement and pension scheme, allowed his predecessor to keep the salary of £800 per annum for life. While in London Scott was 'taken up' by high society.

1807   Brother Tom bankrupt. It also emerged that Tom, a lawyer who had inherited his father's practice, and who had been retained as agent for the Duddingston estate of the Marquess of Abercorn, had misappropriated some of his client's money. Scott felt financially and morally endangered by his brother's breach of trust, and extended efforts were required over several years to protect his own financial credit and provide for his brother and his family.

1808   Publication of poem *Marmion* (the rights of which the publisher Archibald Constable had bought for £1050 in 1807).

Appointed secretary to the Parliamentary Commission to Inquire into the Administration of Justice in Scotland. The Commission ended its work in 1810.

Publication of *The Works of John Dryden . . . with Notes . . . and a Life of the Author*, 18 vols.

Cancelled his subscription to the *Edinburgh Review* because of its 'defeatist' view of the war in Spain, and began (with others) planning the *Quarterly Review* and the *Edinburgh Annual Register*, both launched in 1810. The political disagreement developed into a quarrel with Archibald Constable & Co., and Scott and the Ballantyne brothers, James and John, set up and became the partners in a rival publishing business, John Ballantyne & Co. Scott entrusted his own works to the new business and whenever possible directed other writers and new ventures to it, but Constable withdrew printing work from James Ballantyne & Co., and the printing firm stopped making significant profits.

1809   Publication of *A Collection of Scarce and Valuable Tracts*

(Somers' Tracts), Vols 1–3; completed in 13 vols 1812.

1810   Publication of *The Lady of the Lake*, his most commercially successful poem.

1811   Scott's predecessor as Clerk of Session agreed to apply for a pension, and from 1812 Scott was paid a salary of £1300 per annum.

Publication of poem *The Vision of Don Roderick*.

Purchase of Cartley Hole, the nucleus of the Abbotsford Estate, between Galashiels and Melrose.

1812   Byron began correspondence with Scott.

Removal from Ashestiel to Abbotsford, and plans for rebuilding the small farmhouse there.

1813   Publication of poems *Rokeby* and *The Bridal of Triermain*. First financial crisis. It became apparent in 1812 that the publishing firm of John Ballantyne & Co. was making losses on every publication except Scott's poetry, and that the *Edinburgh Annual Register* was losing £1000 per issue. The firm was undercapitalised, and depended overmuch on bank credit. The national financial crisis of 1812–14 led to reduced orders for books from retailers, late payments, and the bankruptcy of many companies whose debts to John Ballantyne & Co. were either not paid or paid in part. John Ballantyne & Co. found itself unable to pay its own bills and repay the banks on time, and *Rokeby*, greatly profitable though it was, failed to generate enough ready money to meet obligations. Protracted negotiations with Constable over much of 1813 led to the purchase of Ballantyne stock, on the condition that John Ballantyne & Co. ceased to be an active publisher, to the sale of a share in *Rokeby*, and later to the advance sale to Constable of rights for the publication of the long poem *The Lord of the Isles*. Scott had to ask the Duke of Buccleuch to guarantee a bank loan of £4000, and many friends gave small loans. All the personal loans were repaid in 1814, and the publishing business was eventually wound up profitably in 1817, largely through Scott's efforts. As part of the reconciliation Constable commissioned essays on Chivalry and the Drama for the Supplement to the *Encyclopaedia Britannica* (published 1818 and 1819 respectively). Offered and declined the Poet Laureateship.

1814   Publication of his first novel, *Waverley*. The novel was probably begun in 1808 (the date '1st November, 1805' in the first chapter is part of the fiction), continued in

1810, and completed 1813–14; it was first advertised in 1810, and again in January 1814. The early parts (up to the beginning of Chapter 5, and Chapters 5–7) were probably written in parallel with Scott's autobiography (first published at the beginning of Lockhart's *Life of Scott* in 1837).

Publication of *The Works of Jonathan Swift . . . with Notes and a Life of the Author*, 19 vols.

Toured the northern and western isles of Scotland with the Lighthouse Commissioners. His diary of the voyage is published in Lockhart's *Life of Scott* (1837).

1815	Publication of poem *The Lord of the Isles* and *Guy Mannering*, his second novel.

First visit to the Continent, including Waterloo and Paris, where he was lionised.

1816	Publication of *Paul's Letters to his Kinsfolk*, *The Antiquary*, and *Tales of my Landlord* (*The Black Dwarf* and *The Tale of Old Mortality*).
1817	Publication of *Harold the Dauntless* (Scott's last long poem) and *Rob Roy* (1818 on title page).
1817–19	First phase of the building of Abbotsford.
1818	Publication of *Tales of my Landlord*, second series (*The Heart of Mid-Lothian*).

Offered and accepted a baronetcy (announced March 1820).

1819	Seriously ill, probably from gallstones. From 1817 Scott had been suffering stomach cramps, but in the spring and early summer of 1819 he was thought to be dying. Nonetheless he continued to work, dictating to an amanuensis when he was too ill to write. He completed *The Bride of Lammermoor* in April (the greater part of the manuscript is in his own hand) but the latter part of the novel and most of *A Legend of the Wars of Montrose* must have been dictated. The two tales constitute *Tales of my Landlord*, third series, and were published in June 1819.

Purchase by Constable of the copyrights of the 'Scotch novels' and publication of the first collection of Scott's fiction as *Novels and Tales of the Author of Waverley*, 16 vols. All the novels eventually appeared in collected editions in three formats: 8vo, 12mo, and 18mo. Publication of three articles in the *Edinburgh Weekly Journal*, later issued as a pamphlet entitled *The Visionary*, which was in essence political propaganda for the constitutional status quo in the period after Peterloo, when there was a real possibility of a radical rising in the west of Scotland. *December*. Death of Scott's mother.

Publication of *Ivanhoe* (1820 on title-page).

1820   Publication of *The Monastery* and *The Abbot*.

Marriage of daughter Sophia to John Gibson Lockhart.

Elected president of the Royal Society of Edinburgh.

1821   Publication of *Kenilworth* and *The Pirate* (1822 on title-page).

1821–24   Publication of *Ballantyne's Novelist's Library*, for which Scott wrote the lives of the novelists.

1822   Publication of *The Fortunes of Nigel* and *Peveril of the Peak* (1823 on title-page).

Visit of King George IV to Edinburgh.

1822–25   Demolition of the original house and second phase of the building of Abbotsford.

1823   Bannatyne Club founded and Scott made first president.

Publication of *Quentin Durward* and *St Ronan's Well* (1824 on title-page).

1824   Publication of *Redgauntlet*.

1825   Marriage of son Walter to Jane Jobson.

Publication of *Tales of the Crusaders* (*The Betrothed* and *The Talisman*).

Began his journal.

1826   *January*. Scott insolvent. There was a severe economic recession in the winter of 1825–26 and many companies and individuals became bankrupt. Scott's principal publishers, Archibald Constable & Co., and the printers James Ballantyne & Co., in which he was co-partner, had always been undercapitalised, and relied on bank borrowings for working capital. In paying for goods and services, including such things as paper, printing, and publication rights, all parties used promissory bills, a system in which the drawer promised to pay stated sums on stated dates, and which the acceptor 'discounted' at the banks, i.e. got the money in advance of the date less the amount the banks charged in interest for what was in fact a loan. Both Constable's and Ballantyne's hoped that the money coming in from the sale of books when they were published would be sufficient to pay off the money due to the banks, but in practice both firms too often borrowed more money to pay off debts when they were due, and acted as guarantors for each other's loans. In December 1825 it was realised that they were unable to get further credit from the banks; and in January the bankruptcy of the London publishers of Scott's works, Hurst, Robinson & Co., precipitated the collapse of Constable's, then Ballantyne's, and the ruin of all the partners. Scott, the only one of those involved with a capacity to generate a large income, signed a trust deed undertaking to repay his own private debts (£35,000), all the debts of the printing business for which he and James Ballantyne were jointly liable (£41,000), the debts of Archibald Constable & Co. for which he was legally liable (£40,000), and a mortgage on Abbotsford (£10,000), amounting in all to over £126,000. Such were the profits from works like *Woodstock*, *The Life of Napoleon Buonaparte*, and above all the Magnum Opus, the collected edition of the Waverley Novels with introductions and notes specially written by Scott, and issued in monthly parts from 1829–33, that by Scott's death in 1832 more than £53,000 had been repaid, and the remaining debts were paid in 1833.

Publication of three letters in the *Edinburgh Weekly Journal*, later issued as *The Letters of Malachi Malagrowther*, in which Scott attacked a government proposal to restrict the rights of the Scottish banks to issue their own banknotes; Scott was so effective that the government withdrew its proposal.

Sale of 39 Castle Street, Edinburgh, on behalf of creditors.

15 May. Death of wife, Charlotte Scott.

Publication of *Woodstock*.

Autumn. Visit to Paris.

1827	Public acknowledgement of the authorship of the Waverley Novels.
	Publication of *The Life of Napoleon Buonaparte*, 9 vols, *Chronicles of the Canongate* (Chrystal Croftangry's Narrative, 'The Highland Widow', 'The Two Drovers', and 'The Surgeon's Daughter'), and *Tales of a Grandfather* (Scotland to 1603).
1828	Publication of *Chronicles of the Canongate*, second series (*The Fair Maid of Perth*), and *Tales of a Grandfather*, second series (Scotland 1603–1707).
1829	Publication of *Anne of Geierstein*, *History of Scotland*, Vol. 1, and *Tales of a Grandfather*, third series (Scotland 1707–45). The first volume of the Magnum Opus, completed in 48 vols in 1833, appeared on 1 June.

1830   *February.* First stroke.
       November. Retired as Clerk to the Court of Session with pension of £864 per annum. Second stroke.
       Publication of *Letters on Demonology and Witchcraft*, *Tales of a Grandfather* (France), and *History of Scotland*, Vol. 2.

1831   *April.* Third stroke.
       Publication of *Tales of my Landlord*, fourth series (*Count Robert of Paris* and *Castle Dangerous*).
       October. Departure on HMS *Barham* to the Mediterranean, Malta and Naples.

1832   Overland journey home, via Rome, Florence, Venice, Verona, the Brenner Pass, Augsburg, Mainz, and down the Rhine, but had his fourth stroke at Nijmegen. Travelling by sea to London and then Edinburgh, he reached Abbotsford on 11 July.
       21 September. Death at Abbotsford.

FURTHER READING

THE WORKS OF SCOTT

The Journal of Sir Walter Scott, ed. W. E. K. Anderson (Oxford, 1972).

The Letters of Sir Walter Scott, ed. H. J. C. Grierson and others, 12 vols (London, 1932–37). The index to this edition is by James C. Corson, *Notes and Index to Sir Herbert Grierson's Edition of the Letters of Sir Walter Scott* (Oxford, 1979).

'Memoirs', in *Scott on Himself: A Selection of the Autobiographical Writings of Sir Walter Scott*, ed. David Hewitt (Edinburgh, 1981).

The Poetical Works of Sir Walter Scott, ed. J. Logie Robertson (Oxford, 1904; frequently reprinted).

The Poetical Works of Sir Walter Scott, Bart. [ed. J. G. Lockhart], 12 vols (Edinburgh, 1833–34).

The Prose Works of Sir Walter Scott, Bart., 28 vols (Edinburgh, 1834–36).

Waverley Novels, 48 vols (Edinburgh, 1829–33), known as the 'Magnum Opus'.

The Waverley Novels were among the most frequently reprinted works of the nineteenth century, and all editions after Scott's death were based upon the edition of 1829–33. Of these, the best are the Centenary Edition, 25 vols (London, 1871), the Dryburgh Edition, 25 vols (London, 1892–94), and the Border Edition, ed. Andrew Lang, 24 vols (London, 1892–94). The first critical edition is the Edinburgh Edition of the Waverley Novels (1993–   ), on which the volumes of the new Penguin Scott are based.

The complete listing of the works of Scott is in:

William B. Todd and Ann Bowden, *Sir Walter Scott: A Bibliographical History 1796–1832* (New Castle, DE, 1998).

There are two simpler listings:

J. G. Lockhart, 'Chronological List of the Publications of Sir Walter Scott', in *Memoirs of the Life of Sir Walter Scott, Bart.*, 7 vols (Edinburgh, 1837–38; many times republished), 7, 433–39.

J. H. Alexander, 'Sir Walter Scott', in *The Cambridge Bibliography of English Literature, Volume 4: 1800–1900*, 3rd edn, ed. Joanne Shattock (Cambridge, 1999), 992–1063.

BIOGRAPHY

There are very many biographies of Scott. The most important still is by J. G. Lockhart, for, although it is unreliable in some of its detail, it is the work of someone who knew Scott and his circle intimately. The most comprehensive of the modern works is by Edgar Johnson; it is generally reliable. John Buchan's one-volume life is the most sympathetic of all the studies of Scott, while John Sutherland takes a harsher view of the way in which Scott used those in his circle for his own advantage.

James Hogg, *Anecdotes of Scott*, ed. Jill Rubinstein (Edinburgh, 1999).

J. G. Lockhart, *Memoirs of the Life of Sir Walter Scott, Bart.*, 7 vols (Edinburgh, 1837–38; many times republished).

John Buchan, *Sir Walter Scott* (London, 1932).

Sir Herbert Grierson, *Sir Walter Scott, Bart.: A New Life supplementary to, and corrective of, Lockhart's Biography* (London, 1938).

Arthur Melville Clark, *Sir Walter Scott: The Formative Years* (Edinburgh, 1969).

Edgar Johnson, *Sir Walter Scott: The Great Unknown*, 2 vols (London, 1970).

John Sutherland, *The Life of Walter Scott* (Oxford, 1995).

CRITICISM

Complete listings of critical works on Scott are to be found in:

James C. Corson, *A Bibliography of Sir Walter Scott: A Classified and Annotated List of Books and Articles relating to his Life and Works 1797–1940* (Edinburgh, 1943).

Jill Rubenstein, *Sir Walter Scott: A Reference Guide* (Boston, MA, 1978) [covers the period 1932–77].

Jill Rubenstein, *Sir Walter Scott: An Annotated Bibliography of Scholarship and Criticism 1975–1990* (Aberdeen, 1994).

THE FOLLOWING ARE USEFUL FOR THE STUDY OF CHRONICLES OF THE CANONGATE:

General

George Douglas, 'Scott's Short Stories', *Sir Walter Scott Quarterly*, 1 (1927), 6–13.

David Cecil, Introduction to *Short Stories by Sir Walter Scott* (London, 1934), vii–xx.

J. T. Christie, 'Scott's *Chronicles of the Canongate*', *Essays and Studies for the English Association*, n.s. 20 (1967), 64–75.

A. O. J. Cockshut, *The Achievement of Walter Scott* (London, 1969), 54–62.

Teut Andreas Riese, 'Sir Walter Scott as a Master of the Short Tale', in *Festschrift Prof. Dr. Herbert Koziol zum Siebzigsten Geburtstag*, ed. Gero Bauer and others (Vienna, 1973), 255–65.

Susan Manning, 'Scott and Hawthorne: The Making of a National Literary Tradition', in *Scott and His Influence*, ed. J. H. Alexander and David Hewitt (Aberdeen, 1983), 421–31.

Christopher Harvie, 'Scott and the Image of Scotland', in *Sir Walter Scott: The Long-Forgotten Melody*, ed. Alan Bold (London, 1983), 17–42 (33–42).

Graham Tulloch, Preface to Sir Walter Scott, *'The Two Drovers' and Other Stories* (Oxford, 1987), xxi–xxx.

Introduction and Chrystal Croftangry's Narrative

Frank Jordan, 'Chrystal Croftangry, Scott's Last and Best Mask', *Scottish Literary Journal*, 7 (1980), 185–92.

Frank Jordan, 'Scott, Chatterton, Byron, and the Wearing of Masks', in *Scott and his Influence*, ed. J. H. Alexander and David Hewitt (Aberdeen, 1983), 279–89.

Claire Lamont, 'Walter Scott: Anonymity and the Unmasking of Harlequin', in *Authorship, Commerce and the Public: Scenes of Writing, 1750–1850*, ed. E. J. Clery, Carolyn Franklin and Peter Garside (Basingstoke, 2002), 54–66.

'The Highland Widow'

Lilian Dickins, 'Scott's Masterpiece', *The Englishwoman*, 19 (July 1913), 62–71.

Seamus Cooney, 'Scott and Progress: The Tragedy of "The Highland Widow"', *Studies in Short Fiction*, 11 (1974), 11–16.

Graham Tulloch, 'Imagery in "The Highland Widow"', *Studies in Scottish Literature*, 21 (1986), 147–57.

Claire Lamont, 'Jacobite Songs as Intertexts in *Waverley* and "The Highland Widow"', in *Scott in Carnival*, ed. J. H. Alexander and David Hewitt (Aberdeen, 1993), 110–21.

'The Two Drovers'

Kenneth Robb, 'Scott's "The Two Drovers": The Judge's Charge', *Studies in Scottish Literature*, 7 (1970), 255–64.

Coleman O. Parsons, Foreword to *'The Two Drovers': A Short Story* (Westwood, NJ, 1971), i–x.

Seamus Cooney, 'Scott and Cultural Relativism: "The Two Drovers"', *Studies in Short Fiction*, 15 (1978), 1–9.

Walter Allen, *The Short Story in English* (Oxford, 1981), 9–10.

W. J. Overton, 'Scott, the Short Story and History: "The Two Drovers"', *Studies in Scottish Literature*, 21 (1986), 210–25.

Christopher Johnson, 'Anti-Pugilism: Violence and Justice in Scott's "The Two Drovers"', *Scottish Literary Journal*, 22 (1995), 46–60.

Zahra A. Hussein Ali, 'Adjusting the Borders of Self: Sir Walter Scott's *The Two Drovers*', *Papers on Language and Literature*, 37 (2001), 65–84.

'The Surgeon's Daughter'

P. R. Krishnaswami, 'Sir Walter Scott's Indian Novel: "The Surgeon's Daughter"', *Calcutta Review*, n.s. 7 (1919), 431–52.

Edgar Rosenberg, *From Shylock to Svengali: Jewish Stereotypes in English Fiction* (Stanford, CA, 1960), 103–15. On the character of Zilia and the 'half-Jewishness' of her son, Richard Middlemas.

Linda Gertner Zatlin, *The Nineteenth Century Anglo-Jewish Novel* (Boston, 1981), 28–30, 70–72. On the character of Zilia.

Margaret Tait, 'Illustrated Editions of *The Surgeon's Daughter*', *Scott Newsletter*, 13 (1988), 8–11.

J. M. Rignall, 'Walter Scott, J. G. Farrell, and Fictions of Empire', *Essays in Criticism*, 41 (1991), 11–27.

Marilyn Butler, 'Orientalism', in *The Romantic Period*, ed. David B. Pirie (London, 1994), 395–447. On the treatment of the East in English literature c. 1780–1820.

Tara Ghoshal Wallace, 'The Elephant's Foot and the British Mouth: Walter Scott on Imperial Rhetoric', *European Romantic Review*, 13 (2002), 311–24.

Claire Lamont, 'Scott and Eighteenth-century Imperialism: India and the Scottish Highlands', in *Configuring Romanticism*, ed. Theo D'haen, Peter Liebregts and Wim Tigges (Amsterdam, 2003), 35–49.

A NOTE ON THE TEXT

The text of *Chronicles of the Canongate* in this edition is based on the first edition, published in two volumes in Edinburgh in 1827. *Chronicles of the Canongate* was the first work of fiction undertaken by Scott after his financial crisis in 1826, and its writing took longer than was characteristic of him.[1] The first mention of it is on 12 May 1826, when the publisher Robert Cadell recorded in his diary a meeting with the printer James Ballantyne, who 'stated the wish of a certain person to try to raise £500 by writing a small Eastern Tale'.[2] Scott started to write on 27 May 1826, and the work was published on 30 October 1827 in an edition of 8,750 copies. The chief reason for the delay was that at the outset *Chronicles* was not the most important task he had in hand: he was writing a *Life of Napoleon Buonaparte*, whose proceeds were to help repay the debt of over £126,000 which had been incurred on the collapse of the printing house of James Ballantyne & Co., of which Scott was a partner. *Chronicles* was always intended as an incidental work, although it did ultimately make its contribution to the repayment of the debt.

Chronicles of the Canongate was written in two bursts of creativity. The first was between 27 May and 9 July 1826, when Scott wrote Chrystal Croftangry's Narrative and 'The Highland Widow' up to 102.20. The second was between 20 June and 1 October 1827, when he finished 'The Highland Widow' and wrote 'The Two Drovers', 'The Surgeon's Daughter', and the Introduction. The gap in the writing was caused by the rush to finish the *Life of Napoleon*, which was published in nine volumes in June 1827.

The manuscript of *Chronicles* survives in 134 leaves, covering about two-thirds of the work, and is in the National Library of Scotland (MS 23048). The manuscript survives for Chrystal Croftangry's Narrative and 'The Highland Widow' in Volume 1, but is missing for the Introduction, the Croftangry linking passage after 'The Highland Widow', and the whole of 'The Two Drovers'. In Volume 2 the manuscript survives for a substantial part of 'The Surgeon's Daughter', but is missing for the introductory passage by Croftangry and the beginning and end of the tale.

Scott did not start writing *Chronicles* either with his 'small Eastern Tale' or at what is now the beginning. He started with the description of Mrs Martha Bethune Baliol in Chapter 6 (55.28). He broke off before completing his description (at 65.28) and wrote the Croftangry chapters which were to precede it. He then completed his description of Mrs Bethune Baliol and started on 'The Highland Widow', but his first period of composition ended before he had finished it. 'The Two Drovers' was not part of the original plan for the work: the decision to add it was taken in late June, and it was finished on 15 July 1827. The rest of that summer he was writing 'The Surgeon's Daughter' and, having got his story to India, in September he was grateful to a neighbour, Colonel James Ferguson, for some sketches of India on which he drew for descriptive passages towards the end of the tale.[3]

Although a second edition of *Chronicles* was advertised in 1828, no evidence of a second typesetting has been found, and the next appearance of the work was in the collected edition of the Waverley Novels which appeared towards the end of Scott's life and is known as the 'Magnum' edition (48 vols, Edinburgh, 1829–33). This edition started the tradition of splitting up the work: in the Magnum the first volume of *Chronicles* appears in Vol. 41, and the second in Vol. 48. Scott added an appendix to the Introduction in Vol. 1, and made a few corrections and notes. An aim of the current edition is to restore the identity of the work by reuniting its different elements.

The procedures by which a work of fiction by Scott was turned from manuscript copy into a printed book are described by David Hewitt in 'The Waverley Novels in Penguin' on pp. viii–ix of this volume. They worked satisfactorily on the whole for *Chronicles of the Canongate*, but inevitably some errors and misjudgements survived into the first edition. The present edition aims to provide a first-edition text, corrected to bring it as close as possible to what would have been an ideal state of the text in 1827.[4] The source of the majority of the corrections is the manuscript. Comparison between the manuscript and the first edition shows instances where the manuscript had been read wrongly, and instances where it had been misunderstood and hence punctuated wrongly (the compositor was responsible for inserting most of the punctuation). An example of misreading is the first edition's 'perfumed their voluptuous Eastern domes', which in the present text is emended to the manuscript reading 'performed their voluptuous Eastern dances' (203.10). More difficult to handle are places where the manuscript text has been altered, presumably in proof (the proofs do not survive). Some of these additions are clearly by Scott and show him continuing the process of composition at proof stage. In a few cases, however, Scott's alterations in proof caused difficulty in the text, and some emendation has been made to the text to remove it. The chief example in *Chronicles* is in Chapter 6 of Chrystal Croftangry's Narrative, which was divided into two at proof stage, with

Scott writing more than a paragraph of new material for the opening of the new chapter. As this material overlaps and conflicts with
what has already been said (about Mrs Bethune Baliol's promise of
material for Croftangry's work), the present text has removed the new
chapter division and restored the reading of the manuscript.[5] This
has the consequence of renumbering the subsequent chapters in
Volume 1.

There were also some proof alterations in 'The Surgeon's Daughter'
which in adding clarity to one passage brought confusion to another,
for instance in the passage concerning Richard Middlemas's meeting
with his mother, and it has sometimes been possible to remove the
confusion by returning to the manuscript. However, 'The Surgeon's
Daughter' contains other errors in the text which it is better to recognise
than to attempt to remove. A serious interference with the plot, should
the reader notice it, is that Middlemas leaves the miniature of Menie
Grey with Adam Hartley before he goes to India (223.22–24; 262.8,
13). A similar oversight leads the narrator to forget that Witherington
is a Catholic (164.8; 240.16–17).

No attempt has been made to render the first edition's spellings
consistent where the variants were acceptable in the period. An exception to this rule is made in the case of names of people and places,
which have been rendered consistently throughout. In choosing which
spelling to adopt, particular attention has been paid to the predominant
manuscript spellings and to the level of consistency achieved in the
first edition. It is the custom of the first edition to italicise words which
are not in English, and some consistency in this was achieved in Volume
1, in which the languages involved are French, Latin and Gaelic. In
Volume 2, however, there are many words of Anglo-India origin, some
of them derived from Colonel Ferguson's sketches. The compositors
were inconsistent in italicising these, and this inconsistency has been
allowed to remain. Most of these Anglo-Indian words are in spellings
acceptable at the time, but two words—'motakul' and 'naggra'—were
clearly wrong in the first edition and have been emended (see the
Explanatory Notes to 'molakat' at 278.27 and to 'nagara' at 279.2).

NOTES

1 For a full account of the writing, publication, and textual history of the
  work see the 'Essay on the Text' in *Chronicles of the Canongate*, ed. Claire
  Lamont, the Edinburgh Edition of the Waverley Novels 20 (Edinburgh:
  Edinburgh University Press, 2000), 289–356.
2 National Library of Scotland MS 21016, f. 22r.
3 For an account of Colonel James Ferguson's sketches see the Historical
  Note to 'The Surgeon's Daughter' (364–66).

CHRONICLES

OF

THE CANONGATE;

BY

THE AUTHOR OF "WAVERLEY," &c.

SIC ITUR AD ASTRA.
Motto of the Canongate Arms.

IN TWO VOLUMES.

VOL. I.

EDINBURGH:

PRINTED FOR CADELL AND CO., EDINBURGH;

AND SIMPKIN AND MARSHALL, LONDON.

1827.

INTRODUCTION

ALL WHO ARE acquainted with the early history of the Italian stage
are aware, that Arlechino is not, in his original conception, a mere
worker of marvels with his wooden sword, a jumper into and out
of windows, as upon our theatre, but, as his party-coloured jacket
implies, a buffoon or clown, whose mouth, far from being eternally
closed as amongst us, is filled, like that of Touchstone, with quips, and
cranks, and witty devices, very often delivered extempore. It is not
easy to guess how he became possessed of his black vizard, which was
anciently made in the resemblance of the face of a cat; but it seems
that the mask was essential to the performance of the character, as will
appear from the following theatrical anecdote:—

An actor on the Italian stage permitted at the Foire de St Germain,
in Paris, was renowned for the wild, venturous, and extravagant wit,
the brilliant sallies and fortunate repartees, with which he prodigally
seasoned the character of the party-coloured jester. Some critics,
whose good will towards a favourite actor was stronger than their
judgement, took occasion to remonstrate with the successful performer on the subject of the grotesque vizard. They went wilily to their
purpose, observing that his classical and attic wit, his delicate vein of
humour, his happy turn for dialogue, were rendered burlesque and
ludicrous by this unmeaning and bizarre disguise, and that those
attributes would become far more impressive, if aided by the spirit of
his eye and the expression of his natural features. The actor's vanity
was easily so far engaged as to induce him to make the experiment. He
played Harlequin barefaced, but was considered on all hands as having made a total failure. He had lost the audacity which a sense of
incognito bestowed, and with it all the reckless play of raillery
which gave vivacity to his original acting. He cursed his advisers, and
resumed his grotesque vizard; but, it is said, without ever being able to
regain the careless and successful levity which the consciousness of
the disguise had formerly bestowed.

Perhaps the Author of Waverley is now about to incur a risk of the
same kind, and endanger his popularity by having laid aside his incognito. It is certainly not a voluntary experiment, like that of Harlequin;
for it was my original intention never to have avowed these works
during my lifetime, and the original manuscripts were carefully preserved, (though by the care of others rather than mine,) with the
purpose of supplying the necessary evidence of the truth when the

period of announcing it should arrive. But the affairs of my publishers having unfortunately passed into a management different from their own, I had no right any longer to rely upon secrecy in that quarter; and thus my mask, like my Aunt Dinah's in Tristram Shandy, having begun to wax a little threadbare about the chin, it became time to lay it aside with a good grace, unless I desired it should fall in pieces from my face.

Yet I had not the slightest intention of choosing the time and place in which the disclosure was finally made; nor was there any concert betwixt my learned and respected friend Lord MEADOWBANK and myself upon that occasion. It was, as the reader is probably aware, upon the 23d February last, at a public meeting, called for establishing a professional Theatrical Fund in Edinburgh, that the communication took place. Just before we sate down to table, Lord MEADOWBANK asked me, whether I was still anxious to preserve my incognito on the subject of what was called the Waverley Novels? I did not immediately see the purpose of his Lordship's question, although I certainly might have been led to infer it, and replied, that the secret had now become known to so many people that I was indifferent on the subject. Lord MEADOWBANK was thus induced, while doing me the great honour of proposing my health to the meeting, to say something on the subject of these Novels, so strongly connecting them with me as the author, that, by remaining silent, I must have stood convicted, either of the actual paternity, or of the still greater crime of being supposed willing to receive indirectly praise to which I had no just title. I thus found myself suddenly and unexpectedly placed in the confessional, and had only time to recollect that I had been guided thither by a most friendly hand, and could not, perhaps, find a better public opportunity to lay down a disguise, which began to resemble that of a detected masquer-ader.

I had therefore the task of avowing myself, to the numerous and respectable company assembled, as the sole and unaided author of these Novels of Waverley, the paternity of which was likely at one time to have formed a controversy of some celebrity. I now think it further necessary to say, that while I take on myself all the merits and demerits attending these compositions, I am bound to acknowledge with gratit-ude, hints of subjects and legends which I have received from various quarters, and have occasionally used as a foundation of my fictitious compositions, or woven up with them in the shape of episodes. I am bound, in particular, to acknowledge the unremitting kindness of Mr Joseph Train, supervisor of excise at Dumfries, to whose unwearied industry I have been indebted for many curious traditions, and points of antiquarian interest. It was Mr Train who recalled to my recollection the history of Old Mortality, although I myself had a personal interview with that celebrated wanderer so far back as about 1792, when I found him on his usual task. He was then engaged in repairing the gravestones of the Covenanters who had died while imprisoned in the Castle of Dunnottar, to which many of them were committed prisoners at the period of Argyle's rising; their place of confinement is still called the Whigs' Vault. Mr Train, however, procured for me far more extensive information concerning this singular person, whose name was Patterson, than I had been able to acquire during my short conversation with him. He was (as I may have somewhere already stated,) a native of the parish of Closeburn, in Dumfries-shire, and it is believed that domestic affliction, as well as devotional feeling, induced him to commence the wandering mode of life, which he pursued for a very long period. It is more than twenty years since Robert Patterson's death, which took place on the high road near Lockerby, where he was found exhausted and expiring. The white pony, the companion of his pilgrimage, was standing by the side of its dying master; the whole furnishing a scene not unfitted for the pencil. These particulars I had from Mr Train.

Another debt, which I pay most willingly, is that which I owe to an unknown correspondent (a lady), who favoured me with the history of the upright and high principled female, whom, in the Heart of Mid-Lothian, I have termed Jeanie Deans. The circumstance of her refusing to save her sister's life by an act of perjury, and undertaking a pilgrimage to London to obtain her pardon, are both represented as true by my fair and obliging correspondent; and they led me to consider the possibility of rendering a fictitious personage interesting by mere dignity of mind and rectitude of principle, assisted by unpretending good sense and temper, without any of the beauty, grace, talent, accomplishment, and wit, to which a heroine of romance is supposed to have a prescriptive right. If the portrait was received with interest by the public, I am conscious how much it was owing to the truth and force of the original sketch, which I regret that I am unable to present to the public, as it was written with much feeling and spirit.

Old and odd books, and a considerable collection of family legends, formed another quarry, so ample, that it was much more likely that the strength of the labourer should be exhausted, than that materials should fail. I may mention, for example's sake, that the terrible catastrophe of the Bride of Lammermoor actually occurred in a Scottish family of rank. The female relative, by whom the melancholy tale was communicated to me many years since, was a near connexion of the family in which the event happened, and always told it with an appearance of melancholy mystery, which enhanced the interest. She had known, in her youth, the brother who rode before the unhappy victim to the fatal altar, who, though then a mere boy, and occupied almost entirely with the gallantry of his own appearance in the bridal procession, could not but remark that the hand of his sister was moist, and cold as that of a statue. It is unnecessary further to withdraw the veil from this scene of family distress, nor, although it occurred more than a hundred years since, might it be altogether agreeable to the representatives of the families concerned in the narrative. It may be proper to say, that the events are imitated; but I had neither the means nor intention of copying the manners, or tracing the characters, of the persons concerned in the real story.

Indeed, I may here state generally, that although I have deemed historical personages free subjects of delineation, I have never on any occasion violated the respect due to private life. It was indeed impossible that traits proper to persons, both living and dead, with whom I have had intercourse in society, should not have risen to my pen in such works as Waverley, and those which followed it. But I have always studied to generalize the portraits, so that they should still seem, on the whole, the productions of fancy, though possessing some resemblance to real individuals. Yet I must own my attempts have not in this last particular been uniformly successful. There are men whose characters are so peculiarly marked, that the delineation of some leading and principal feature, inevitably places the whole person before you in his individuality. Thus, the character of Jonathan Oldbuck, in the Antiquary, was partly founded on that of an old friend of my youth, to whom I am indebted for introducing me to Shakspeare, and other invaluable favours; but I thought I had so completely disguised the likeness, that it could not be recognised by any one now alive. I was mistaken, however, and indeed had endangered what I desired should be considered as a secret; for I afterwards learned that a highly respectable gentleman, one of the few surviving friends of my father, and an acute critic, had said, upon the appearance of the work, that he was now convinced who was the author of it, as he recognised, in the Antiquary, traces of the character of a very intimate friend of my father's family.

I may here also notice, that the sort of exchange of gallantry, which is represented as taking place betwixt the Baron of Bradwardine and Colonel Talbot, is a literal fact. The real circumstances of the anecdote, alike honourable to Whig and Tory, are these:—

Alexander Stewart of Invernahyle,—a name which I cannot write without the warmest recollections of gratitude to the friend of my childhood, who first introduced me to the Highlands, their traditions, and their manners,—had been engaged actively in the troubles of

1745. As he charged at the battle of Preston with his clan, the Stewarts of Appine, he saw an officer of the opposite army standing alone by a battery of four cannon, of which he discharged three on the advancing Highlanders, and then drew his sword. Invernahyle rushed on him, and required him to surrender. "Never to rebels!" was the undaunted reply, accompanied with a longe, which the Highlander received on his target; but instead of using his sword in cutting down his now defenceless antagonist, he employed it in parrying the blow of a Lochaber axe, aimed at the officer by the Miller, one of his own followers, a grim-looking old Highlander, whom I remember to have seen. Thus overpowered, Lieutenant Colonel Allan Whitefoord, a gentleman of rank and consequence, as well as a brave officer, gave up his sword, and with it his purse and watch, which Invernahyle accepted, to save them from his followers. After the affair was over, Mr Stewart sought out his prisoner, and they were introduced to each other by the celebrated John Roy Stewart, who acquainted Colonel Whitefoord with the quality of his captor, and made him aware of the necessity of receiving back his property, which he was inclined to leave in the hands into which it had fallen. So great became the confidence established betwixt them, that Invernahyle obtained from the Chevalier his freedom upon parole; and soon afterwards, having been sent back to the Highlands to raise men, he visited Colonel Whitefoord at his own house, and spent two happy days with him and his Whig friends, without thinking, on either side, of the civil war which was then raging.

When the battle of Culloden put an end to the hopes of Charles Edward, Invernahyle, wounded and unable to move, was borne from the field by the faithful zeal of his retainers. But as he had been a distinguished Jacobite, his family and property were exposed to the system of vindictive destruction, too generally carried into execution through the country of the insurgents. It was now Colonel Whitefoord's turn to exert himself, and he wearied all the authorities, civil and military, with his solicitations for pardon to the saver of his life, or at least for a protection for his wife and family. His applications were for a long time unsuccessful: "I was found with the mark of the Beast upon me in every list," was Invernahyle's expression. At length Colonel Whitefoord applied to the Duke of Cumberland, and urged his suit with every argument which he could think of. Being still repulsed, he took his commission from his bosom, and, having said something of his own and his family's services to the House of Hanover, begged to resign his situation in their service, since he could not be permitted to show his gratitude to the person to whom he owed his life. The Duke, struck with his earnestness, desired him to take up his commission, and granted the protection required for the family of Invernahyle.

The Chieftain himself lay concealed in a cave near his own house, before which a small body of regular soldiers was encamped. He could hear their muster-roll called every morning, and their drums beat to quarters at night, and not a change of the sentinels escaped him. As it was suspected that he was lurking somewhere on the property, his family were closely watched, and compelled to use the utmost precaution in supplying him with food. One of his daughters, a child of eight or ten years old, was employed as the agent least likely to be suspected. She was an instance among others, that a time of danger and difficulty creates a premature sharpness of intellect. She made herself acquainted among the soldiers, till she became so familiar to them, that her motions escaped their notice; and her practice was, to stroll away into the neighbourhood of the cave, and leave what slender supply of food she carried for that purpose under some remarkable stone, or the root of some tree, where her father might find it as he crept by night from his lurking-place. Times became milder, and my excellent friend was relieved from proscription by the Act of Indemnity. Such is the interesting story which I have rather injured than improved, by the manner in which it is told in Waverley.

This incident, with several other circumstances illustrating the Tales in question, was communicated by me to my late lamented friend, William Erskine, (a Scottish Judge, by the title of Lord Kinedder,) who afterwards reviewed with far too much partiality the Tales of my Landlord, for the Quarterly Review of January 1817. In the same article, are contained other illustrations of the Novels, with which I supplied my accomplished friend, who took the trouble to write the review. The reader who is desirous of such information, will find the original of Meg Merrilees, and I believe of one or two other personages of the same cast of character, in the article referred to.

I may also mention, that the tragic and savage circumstances which are represented as preceding the birth of Allan MacAulay, in the Legend of Montrose, really happened in the family of Stewart of Ardvoirlich. The wager about the candlesticks, whose place was supplied by Highland torch-bearers, was laid and won by one of the MacDonalds of Keppoch.

There can be but little amusement in winnowing out the few grains of truth which are contained in this mass of empty fiction. I may, however, before dismissing the subject, allude to the various localities which have been affixed to some of the scenery introduced into these Novels, by which, for example, Wolf's-Hope is identified with Fast-Castle in Berwickshire,—Tillietudlem with Draphane in Clydesdale, —and the valley in the Monastery, called Glendearg, with the dale of the Allan, above Lord Somerville's villa, near Melrose. I can only say, that, in these and other instances, I had no purpose of describing any particular local spot; and the resemblance must therefore be of that general kind which necessarily exists betwixt scenes of the same character. The iron-bound coast of Scotland affords upon its headlands and promontories fifty such castles as Wolf's-Hope; every county has a valley more or less resembling Glendearg; and if castles like Tillie-tudlem, or mansions like the Baron of Bradwardine's, are now less frequently to be met with, it is owing to the rage of indiscriminate destruction, which has removed or ruined so many monuments of antiquity, when they were not protected by their inaccessible situation.

The scraps of poetry which have been in most cases tacked to the beginning of chapters in these Novels, are sometimes quoted either from reading or from memory, but, in the general case, are pure invention. I found it too troublesome to turn to the collection of the British Poets to discover apposite mottos, and, in the situation of the theatrical mechanist, who, when the white paper which represented his shower of snow was exhausted, continued the storm by snowing brown, I drew on my memory as long as I could, and, when that failed, eked it out with invention. I believe that, in some cases, where actual names are affixed to the supposed quotations, it would be to little purpose to seek them in the works of the authors referred to.

And now the reader may expect me, while in the confessional, to explain the motives why I have so long persisted in disclaiming the works of which I am now writing. To this it would be difficult to give any other reply, save that of Corporal Nym—It was the humour or caprice of the time. I hope it will not be construed into ingratitude to the public, to whose indulgence I have owed much more than to any merit of my own, if I confess that I am, and have been, more indifferent to success, or to failure, as an author, than may be the case with others, who feel more strongly the passion for literary fame, probably because they are justly conscious of a better title to it. It was not until I had attained the age of thirty years that I made any serious attempt at distinguishing myself as an author; and at that period, men's hopes, desires, and wishes, have usually acquired something of a decisive character, and are not eagerly and easily diverted into a new channel. When I made the discovery,—for to me it was one,—that by amusing myself with composition, which I felt a delightful occupation, I could also give pleasure to others, and became aware that literary pursuits were likely to engage in future a considerable portion of my time, I felt some alarm that I might acquire those habits of jealousy and fretfulness which have lessened, and even degraded, the character of the children of imagination, and rendered them, by petty squabbles and mutual irritability, the laughing-stock of the people of the world. I resolved, therefore, in this respect to guard my breast (perhaps an unfriendly critic may add, my brow,) with triple brass, and as much as possible to avoid resting my thoughts and wishes upon literary success, lest I should endanger my own peace of mind and tranquillity by literary failure. It would argue either stupid apathy, or ridiculous affectation, to say that I have been insensible to the public applause, when I have been honoured with its testimonies; and still more highly do I prize the invaluable friendships which some temporary popularity has enabled me to form among those most distinguished by talents and genius, and which I venture to hope now rest upon a basis more firm than the circumstances which gave rise to them. Yet feeling all these advantages as a man ought to do, and must do, I may say, with truth and confidence, that I have tasted of the intoxicating cup with moderation, and that I have never, either in conversation or correspondence, encouraged discussions respecting my own literary pursuits. On the contrary, I have usually found such topics, even when introduced from motives most flattering to myself, rather embarrassing and disagreeable.

I have now frankly told my motives for concealment, so far as I am conscious of having any, and the public will forgive the egotism of the detail, as what is necessarily connected with it. The author, so long and loudly called for, has appeared on the stage, and made his obeisance to the audience. Thus far his conduct is a mark of respect. To linger in their presence would be intrusion.

I have only to repeat, that I avow myself in print, as formerly in words, the sole and unassisted author of all the Novels published as the composition of the "Author of Waverley." I do this without shame, for I am unconscious that there is anything in their composition which deserves reproach, either on the score of religion or morality; and without any feeling of exultation, because, whatever may have been their temporary success, I am well aware how much their reputation depends upon the caprice of fashion; and I have already mentioned the precarious tenure by which it is held, as a reason for displaying no great avidity in grasping at the possession.

I ought to mention, before concluding, that twenty persons at least were, either from intimacy or from the confidence which circumstances rendered necessary, participant of this secret; and as there was no instance, to my knowledge, of any one of the number breaking the confidence required from them, I am the more obliged to them, because the slight and trivial character of the mystery was not qualified to inspire much respect in those intrusted with it.

As for the work which follows, it was meditated, and in part printed, long before the avowal of the novels took place, and originally commenced with a declaration that it was neither to have introduction nor preface of any kind. This long proem, prefixed to a work intended not to have any, may, however, serve to show how human purposes, in the most trifling as well as the most important affairs, are liable to be controlled by the course of events. Thus, we begin to cross a strong river with our eyes and our resolution fixed on the point of the opposite shore, on which we purpose to land; but, gradually giving way to the torrent, are glad, by the aid perhaps of branch or bush, to extricate ourselves at some distant and perhaps dangerous landing-place, much farther down the stream than that on which we had fixed our intentions.

Hoping that the Courteous Reader will afford to a known and familiar acquaintance some portion of the favour which he extended to a disguised candidate for his applause, I beg leave to subscribe myself his obliged humble servant,

WALTER SCOTT.

ABBOTSFORD, *October* 1, 1827.

CHRONICLES
OF THE CANONGATE

VOLUME I

Chapter One

Sic itur ad astra.

"THIS IS THE PATH to heaven." Such is the ancient motto attached
to the armorial bearings of the Canongate, and which is inscribed,
with greater or less propriety, upon all the public buildings, from the
church to the pillory, in the ancient quarter of Edinburgh, which
bears, or rather once bore, the same relation to the Good Town that
Westminster does to London, being still possessed of the palace of the
sovereign, as it formerly was dignified by the residence of the principal
nobility and gentry. I may, therefore, with some propriety, put the
same motto at the head of the literary undertaking by which I hope to
illustrate the hitherto undistinguished name of Chrystal Croftangry.

The public may desire to know something of an author who pitches
at such height his ambitious expectations. The gentle reader, therefore—for I have some touch of Captain Bobadil's humour, and could
to no other extend myself so far—the *gentle* reader, then, will be
pleased to understand, that I am a Scottish gentleman of the old
school, with a fortune, temper, and person, rather the worse for wear.
I have known the world for these forty years, having written myself
man nearly since that period—and I do not think it is much mended.
But this is an opinion which I keep to myself when I am among
younger folks, for I recollect, in my youth, quizzing the Sexagenarians
who carried back their ideas of a perfect state of society to the days of
laced coats and triple ruffles, and some of them to the blood and blows
of the Forty-five. Therefore I am cautious of exercising the right of

censorship, which is supposed to be acquired by men arrived at, or approaching, the mysterious period of life, when the numbers of seven and nine multiplied into each other, form what sages have termed the Grand Climacteric.

Of the earlier part of my life it is only necessary to say, that I swept the boards of the Parliament-House with the skirts of my gown for the usual number of years during which young Lairds were in my time expected to keep term—got no fees—laughed, and made others laugh —drank claret at Bayle's, Fortune's, and Walker's—and eat oysters in the Covenant Close.

Becoming my own master, I flung my gown at the bar-keeper, and commenced gay man on my own account. In Edinburgh, I ran into all the expensive society which the place then afforded. When I went to my house in the shire of Lanark, I emulated to the utmost the expenses of men of large fortune, and had my hunters, my first-rate pointers, my game-cocks, and feeders. I can more easily forgive myself for these follies, than for others of a still more blameable kind, so indifferently cloaked over that my poor mother thought herself obliged to leave my habitation, and betake herself to a small inconvenient jointure-house, which she occupied till her death. I think, however, I was not exclusively to blame in this separation, and I believe my mother afterwards condemned herself for being too hasty. Thank God, the adversity which destroyed the means of continuing my dissipation, restored me to the affections of my surviving parent.

My course of life could not last—I ran too fast to run long. And when I would have checked my career, I was perhaps too near the brink of the precipice. Some mishaps I prepared by my own folly, others came upon me unawares. I put my estate out to nurse to a fat man of business, who smothered the babe he should have brought back to me in health and strength, and, in a dispute with this honest gentleman, I found, like a skilful general, that my position would be most judiciously assumed by taking it up near the Abbey of Holyrood. It was then I first became acquainted with the quarter, which my little work will, I hope, render immortal, and grew familiar with those magnificent wilds, through which the Kings of Scotland once chased the dark-brown deer, but which were chiefly recommended to me in those days, by their being inaccessible to those metaphysical persons, whom the law of the neighbouring country terms John Doe and Richard Roe.

Dire was the strife betwixt my quondam doer and myself; during which my motions were circumscribed, like those of some conjured demon, within a circle, which, "beginning at the northern gate of the King's Park, thence running northways, is bounded on the left by the

King's garden-wall, and the gutter, or kennel, in a line wherewith it crosses the High Street to the Water-gate, and passing through the same, is bounded by the walls of the Tennis-court and Physic-garden, &c., follows the wall of the Church-yard, joins the north-west wall of St Anne's Yards, and going east to the Clackmill-house, turns southward to the turnstile in the King's Park-wall, and includes the whole King's Park within the Sanctuary."

These limits, which I abridge from the accurate Maitland, once marked the Girth, or Sanctuary, belonging to the Abbey of Holyrood, and which, being still an appendage to the royal palace, has retained the privilege of an asylum for civil debt. One would think the space sufficiently extensive for a man to stretch his limbs in, as, besides a reasonable proportion of level ground, (considering that the scene lies in Scotland,) it includes within its precincts the mountain of Arthur's Seat, and the rocks and pasture land called Salisbury Crags. And yet it is inexpressible how, after a certain time had elapsed, I used to long for the Sunday, which permitted me to extend my walk without limitation. During the other six days of the week I felt a sickness of heart, which, but for the speedy approach of the hebdomadal day of liberty, I could hardly have endured. I experienced the impatience of a mastiff, who tugs in vain to extend the limits which his chain permits.

Day after day I have walked by the side of the kennel which divides the Sanctuary from the unprivileged part of the Canongate; and though the month was July, and the scene was the old town of Edinburgh, I preferred it to the fresh air and verdant turf which I might have enjoyed in the King's Park, or to the cool and solemn gloom of the portico which surrounds the palace. To an indifferent person either side of the gutter would have seemed much the same—the houses equally mean, the children as ragged and dirty, the carmen as brutal, the whole forming the same picture of low life in a deserted and impoverished quarter of a large city. But to me the gutter, or kennel, was what the brook Kidron was to Shimei. Death was denounced against him should he cross it, doubtless because it was known to his wisdom who pronounced the doom, that from that time the devoted man's desire to transgress the precept would become irresistible, and he would be sure to draw down on his head the penalty which he had already justly incurred by cursing the anointed of God. For my part, all Elysium seemed opening on the other side of the kennel, and I envied the little blackguards, who, stopping the current with their little dam-dikes of mud, had a right, during the operation, to stand on either side of the nasty puddle which best pleased them. I was so childish as even to make an occasional excursion across, were it only for a few yards, and felt the triumph of a school-boy, who, trespassing upon an orchard, hurries back again with a fluttering sensation of joy and terror, betwixt the pleasure of having executed his purpose, and the fear of being taken or discovered.

I have sometimes asked myself, what I should have done in case of actual imprisonment, since I could not bear without impatience a restriction which is comparatively a mere trifle; but I really could never answer the question to my own satisfaction. I have all my life hated those treacherous expedients called *mezzo-termini*, and it is possible with this disposition I might have endured more patiently an absolute privation of liberty, than the more modified restrictions to which my residence in the Sanctuary at this period subjected me. If, however, the feelings I then experienced were to increase in intensity according to the difference between a jail and my actual condition, I must have hanged myself, or pined to death; there could have been no other alternative.

Amongst many companions who forgot and neglected me of course, when my difficulties seemed to be inextricable, I had one true friend; and that friend was a barrister, who knew the laws of his country well, and, tracing them up to the spirit of equity and justice in which they originate, had repeatedly prevented, by his benevolent and manly exertions, the triumph of selfish cunning over simplicity and folly. He undertook my cause, with the assistance of a solicitor of a character similar to his own. My quondam doer had intrenched himself chin-deep among legal trenches, hornworks, and covered ways; but my two protectors shelled him out of his defences, and I was at length a free man, at liberty to go or stay wheresoever my mind listed.

I left my lodging as hastily as if it had been a pest-house; I did not even stop to receive some change that was due to me on settling with my landlady, and I saw the poor woman stand at her door looking after my precipitate flight, and shaking her head as she wrapped the silver which she was counting for me in a separate piece of paper, apart from the store in her own moleskin purse. An honest Highlandwoman was Janet MacEvoy, and deserved a greater remuneration, had I possessed the power of bestowing it. But my eagerness of delight was too extreme to pause for explanation with Janet. On I pushed through the groups of children, of whose sports I had been so often a lazing, lounging spectator. I sprung over the gutter as if it had been the fatal Styx, and I a ghost, which, eluding Pluto's authority, was making its escape from Limbo Lake. My friend had difficulty to restrain me from running like a madman up the street; and in spite of his kindness and hospitality, which soothed me for a day or two, I was not quite happy until I found myself aboard of a Leith smack, and, standing down the Firth with a fair wind, might snap my fingers at the retreating outline of Arthur's Seat, to the vicinity of which I had been so long confined.

It is not my purpose to trace my future progress through life. I had extricated myself, or rather had been freed by my friends, from the brambles and thickets of the law, but, as befell the sheep in the fable, a great part of my fleece was left behind me. Something remained, however; I was in the season for exertion, and, as my good mother used to say, there was always life for living folk. Stern necessity gave my manhood that prudence which my youth was a stranger to. I faced dangers, I endured fatigue, I sought foreign climates, and proved that I belonged to the nation which is proverbially patient of labour and prodigal of life. Independence, like liberty to Virgil's shepherd, came late, but came at last, with no great affluence in its train, but bringing enough to support a decent appearance for the rest of my life, and to induce cousins to be civil, and gossips to say, "I wonder who old Croft will make his heir? He must have picked up something, and I should not be surprised if it prove more than folks think of."

My first impulse when I returned home was to rush to the house of my benefactor, the only man who had in my distress interested himself in my behalf. He was a snuff-taker, and it had been the pride of my heart to save the *ipsa corpora* of the first score of guineas I could hoard, and to have them converted into as tasteful a snuff-box as Rundell and Bridge could devise. This I had thrust for security into the breast of my waistcoat, while, impatient to transfer it to the person for whom it was destined, I hastened to his house in —— Square. When the front of the house became visible, a feeling of alarm checked me. I had been long absent from Scotland, my friend was some years older than I—he might have been called to the congregation of the just. I paused, and gazed on the house, as if from the outward appearance I had hoped to form some conjectures concerning the state of the family within. I know not how it was, but the lower windows being all close and no one stirring, my sinister forebodings were rather strengthened. I regretted now that I had not made inquiry before I left the inn where I alighted from the mail-coach. But it was too late; so I hurried on, eager to know the best or the worst which I could learn.

The brass-plate bearing my friend's name and designation was still on the door, and when the door was opened, the old domestic appeared a good deal older I thought than he ought naturally to have looked, considering the period of my absence. "Is Mr —— at home?" said I, pressing forwards.

"Yes, sir," said John, placing himself in opposition to my entrance, "he is at home, but"——

"But he is not in," said I. "I remember your phrase of old, John. Come, I'll step into his room, and leave a line for him."

John was obviously embarrassed by my familiarity. I was some one, he saw, whom he ought to recollect—at the same time it was evident he remembered nothing about me.

"Ay, sir, my master is in, and in his own room, but"——

I would not hear him out, but passed before him towards the well-known apartment. A young lady came out of the room a little disturbed, as it seemed, and said, "John, what is the matter?"

"A gentleman, Miss Nelly, that insists on seeing my master."

"A very old and deeply indebted friend," said I, "that ventures to press myself on my much-respected benefactor on my return from abroad."

"Alas, sir," replied she, "my uncle would be happy to see you, but"——

At this moment, something was heard within the apartment like the falling of a plate, or glass, and immediately after my friend's voice called angrily and eagerly on his niece. She entered the room hastily, and so did I. But it was to see a spectacle, compared with which that of my benefactor stretched on his bier would have been a happy one.

The easy-chair filled with cushions, the extended limbs swathed in flannel, the wide wrapping-gown and night-cap, showed illness; but the dead eye, once so replete with living fire, the blabber lip, whose dilation and compression used to give such character to his animated countenance, the stammering tongue, that once poured forth such floods of masculine eloquence, and had often swayed the opinion of the sages whom he addressed,—all these sad symptoms evinced that my friend was in the melancholy condition of those in whom the principle of animal life has unfortunately survived that of mental intelligence. He gazed a moment at me, but then seemed insensible of my presence, and went on—he, once the most courteous and well-bred—to babble unintelligible but violent reproaches against his niece and servant, because he himself had dropped a tea-cup in attempting to place it on a table at his elbow. His eyes caught a momentary fire from his irritation; but he struggled in vain for words to express himself adequately, as, looking from his servant to his niece, and thence to the table, he laboured to explain that they had placed it (though it touched his chair) at too great a distance from him.

The young person, who had naturally a resigned Madonna-like expression of countenance, listened to his impatient chiding with the most humble submission, checked the servant, whose less delicate feelings would have entered on his justification, and gradually, by the sweet and soft tone of her voice, soothed to rest the spirit of causeless irritation.

She then cast a look towards me, which expressed, "You see all that remains of him whom you call friend." It seemed also to say, "Your longer presence here can only be distressing to us all."

"Forgive me, young lady," I said, as well as tears would permit;—"I am a person deeply obliged to your uncle. My name is Croftangry."

"Lord! and that I should not hae minded ye, Maister Croftangry," said the servant. "Ay, I mind my master had mickle fash about your job. I hae kenned him order in fresh candles as midnight chappit, and till't again. Indeed, ye had aye his gude word, Mr Croftangry, for a' that folk said about you."

"Hold your tongue, John," said the lady, somewhat angrily; and then continued, addressing herself to me, "I am sure, sir, you must be sorry to see my uncle in this state. I know you are his friend. I have heard him mention your name, and wonder he never heard from you." —A new cut this, and it went to my heart. "But" she continued, "I really do not know if it is right.—If my uncle should know you, which I scarce think possible, he would be much affected, and the doctor says that any agitation——But here comes Dr —— to give his own opinion."

Dr —— entered. I had left him a middle-aged man; he was now an elderly one; but still the same benevolent Samaritan, who went about doing good, and thought the blessings of the poor as good a recompence of his professional skill as the gold of the rich.

He looked at me with surprise, but the young lady said a word of introduction, and I, who was known to the doctor formerly, hastened to complete it. He recollected me perfectly, and intimated that he was well acquainted with the reasons I had for being deeply interested in the fate of his patient. He gave me a very melancholy account of my poor friend, drawing me for that purpose a little apart from the lady. "The light of life," he said, "was trembling in the socket; he scarcely expected it would ever leap up even into a momentary flash, but more was impossible." He then stepped towards his patient, and put some questions, to which the poor invalid, though he seemed to recognize the friendly and familiar voice, answered only in a faltering and uncertain manner.

The young lady, in her turn, had drawn back when the doctor approached his patient. "You see how it is with him," said the doctor, addressing me; "I have heard our poor friend, in one of the most eloquent of his pleadings, give a description of this very disease, which he compared to the tortures inflicted by Mezentius, when he chained the dead to the living. The soul, he said, is imprisoned in its dungeon of flesh, and though retaining its natural and inalienable properties, can no more exert them than the captive inclosed within a prison-house can act as a free agent. Alas! to see *him*, who could so well describe what this malady was in others, a prey himself to its infirmities! I will never forget the solemn tone of expression with which he summed up the incapacities of the paralytic,—the deafened ear, the dimmed eye, the crippled limbs,—in the noble words of Juvenal—

> ——omni
> Membrorum damno major, dementia, quæ nec
> Nomina servorum, nec vultum agnoscit amici."

As the physician repeated these lines, a flash of intelligence seemed to revive in the invalid's eye—sunk again—again struggled, and he spoke more intelligibly than before, and in the tone of one eager to say something which he felt would escape him unless said instantly. "A question of death-bed, doctor—a reduction *ex capite lecti*—Withering against Wilibus—about the *morbus sonticus*. I pleaded the cause for the pursuer—I, and—and—Why, I shall forget my own name—I, and— he that was the wittiest and the best-humoured man living——"

The description enabled the doctor to fill up the blank, and the patient joyfully repeated the name suggested. "Ay, ay," he said, "just he—Harry—poor Harry"—— The light in his eye died away, and he sunk back in his easy-chair.

"You have now seen more of our poor friend, Mr Croftangry," said the physician, "than I dared venture to promise you; and now I must take my professional authority on me, and ask you to retire. Miss—— will, I am sure, let you know if a moment should by any chance occur when her uncle can see you."

What could I do? I gave my card to the young lady, and, taking my offering from my bosom—"If my poor friend," I said, with accents as broken almost as his own, "should ask where this came from—name me and say from the most obliged and most grateful man alive. Say, the gold of which it is composed was saved by grains at a time, and was hoarded with as much avarice as ever was a miser's:—to bring it here I have come a thousand miles, and now, alas, I find him thus!"

I laid the box on the table, and was retiring with a lingering step. The eye of the invalid was caught by it, as that of a child by a glittering toy, and with infantine impatience he faltered out inquiries at his niece. With gentle mildness she repeated again and again who I was, and why I came, &c. I was about to turn, and hasten from a scene so painful, when the physician laid his hand on my sleeve—"Stop!" he said, "there is a change."

There was indeed, and a marked one. A faint glow spread over the pallid features—they seemed to gain the look of intelligence which belongs to vitality. His eye once more kindled—his lip coloured—and drawing himself up out of the listless posture he had hitherto maintained, he rose without assistance. The doctor and the servant ran to give him their support. He waved them aside, and they were contented to place themselves in such a position behind as might ensure against accident, should his newly-acquired strength decay as suddenly as it had revived.

"My dear Croftangry," he said, in the tone of kindness of other days, "I am glad to see you returned—You find me but poorly—but my little niece here and Dr ———— are very kind—God bless you, my dear friend! we will not meet again till we meet in a better world."

I pressed his extended hand to my lips—I pressed it to my bosom—I would fain have flung myself on my knees; but the doctor, leaving the patient to the young lady and the servant, who wheeled forward his chair, and were replacing him in it, hurried me out of the room. "My dear sir," said he, "you ought to be satisfied; you have seen our poor invalid more like his former self than he has been for months, or than he may be perhaps again until all is over. The whole Faculty could not have assured such an interval—I must see whether anything can be derived from it to improve the general health—Pray, begone." The last argument hurried me from the spot, agitated by a crowd of feelings, all of them painful.

When I had overcome the shock of this great disappointment, I renewed gradually my acquaintance with one or two old companions, who, though of infinitely less interest to my feelings than my unfortunate friend, served to relieve the pressure of actual solitude, and who were not perhaps the less open to my advances, that I was a bachelor somewhat stricken in years, newly arrived from foreign parts, and certainly independent, if not wealthy.

I was considered as a tolerable subject of speculation by some, and I could not be burdensome to any: I was therefore, according to the ordinary rule of Edinburgh hospitality, a welcome guest in several respectable families. But I found no one who could replace the loss I had sustained in my best friend and benefactor. I wanted something more than mere companionship would give me, and where was I to look for it?—Among the scattered remnants of those that had been my gay friends of yore?—alas!

> Many a lad I loved was dead,
> And many a lass grown old.

Besides, all community of ties between us had ceased to exist, and such of my former friends as were still in the world, held their life in a different tenor from what I did.

Some had turned misers, and were as eager in saving sixpence as ever they had been in spending a guinea. Some had turned agriculturists—their talk was of oxen, and they were only fit company for graziers. Some stuck to cards, and though no longer gamesters, rather played small game than sat out. This I particularly despised. The strong impulse of gambling, alas! I had felt in my time—it is as intense as it is criminal; but it produces excitation and interest, and I can conceive how it should become a passion with strong and powerful minds. But to dribble away life in exchanging bits of painted pasteboard round a green table, for the piddling concern of a few shillings, can only be excusable in folly or superannuation. It is like riding on a rocking-horse, where your utmost exertion never carries you a foot forward; it is a kind of mental treadmill, where you are perpetually climbing, but can never rise an inch. From these hints, my readers will perceive I am incapacitated for one of the pleasures of old age, which, though not mentioned by Cicero, is not the least frequent resource in the present day—the club-room, and the snug hand at whisk.

To return to my old companions: Some frequented public assemblies, like the ghost of Beau Nash, or any other beau of half a century back, thrust aside by tittering youth, and pitied by those of their own age. In fine, some went into devotion, as the French term it, and others, I fear, went to the devil. A few found resources in science and letters; one or two turned philosophers in a small way, peeped into microscopes, and became familiar with the fashionable experiments of the day. Some took to reading, and I was one of them.

Some grains of repulsion towards the society around me—some painful recollections of early faults and follies—some touch of displeasure with living mankind, inclined me rather to a study of antiquities, and particularly those of my own country. The reader, if I can prevail on myself to continue the present work, will probably be able to judge, in the course of it, whether I have made any useful progress in the study of the olden times.

I owed this turn of study, in part, to the conversation of my kind man of business, Mr Fairscribe, whom I mentioned as having seconded the efforts of my invaluable friend, in bringing the cause on which my liberty and the remnant of my property depended, to a favourable decision. He gave me a most kind reception on my return. He was too much engaged in his profession for me to intrude on him often, and perhaps his mind was too much trammelled with its details to permit his being willingly withdrawn from them. In short, he was not a person of my poor friend ———'s expanded spirit, and rather a lawyer of the ordinary class of formalists, but a most able and excellent man. When my estate was sold, he had retained some of the older title-deeds, arguing, from his own feelings, that they would be of more consequence to the heir of the old family than to the new purchaser. And when I returned to Edinburgh, and found him still in the exercise of the profession to which he was an honour, he sent to my lodgings the old family-bible, which lay always on my father's table, two or three other mouldy volumes, and a couple of sheep-skin bags, full of parchments and papers, whose appearance was by no means inviting.

The next time I shared Mr Fairscribe's hospitable dinner, I failed not to return him due thanks for his kindness, which acknowledgment, indeed, I proportioned rather to the idea which I knew he entertained of the value of such things, than to the interest with which I myself regarded them. But the conversation turning on my family, who were old proprietors in the Upper Ward of Clydesdale, gradually excited some interest in my mind; and when I retired to my solitary parlour, the first thing I did was to look for a pedigree, or sort of history of the family, or House of Croftangry, once of that Ilk, latterly of Glentanner. The discoveries which I made shall enrich the next chapter.

Chapter Two

What's property, dear Swift? I see it alter
From you to me, from me to Peter Walter.
POPE

"CROFTANGRY Croftandrew—Croftanridge—Croftandgrey—for sa mony wise hath the name been spellit—is weel known to be ane house of grit antiquity; and it is said, that King Milcolumb, or Malcolm, being the first of our Scottish princes quha removit across the Firth of Forth, did reside and occupy ane palace at Edinburgh, and had there ane valziant man, who did him man-service, by keeping the croft, or corn-land, which was tilled for the convenience of the Kingis household, and was thence callit Croft-an-ri, that is to say, the King his Croft; quhilk place, though now coverit with biggings, is to this day callit Croftangry, and lyeth near to the ryal palace. And whereas that some of those who bear this auld and honourable name may take scorn that it ariseth from the tilling of the ground, quhilk men account a slavish occupation, yet we ought to honour the pleugh and spade, seeing we all derive our being from our father Adam, whose lot it became to cultivate the earth, in respect of his fall and transgression.

"Also we have witness, as weel in holy writt as in profane history, of the honour in quhilk husbandrie was held of old, and how prophets have been taken from the pleugh, and great captains raised up to defend their ain countries, sic as Cincinnatus, and the like, who fought not the common enemy with the less valiancy that their arms had been exercized in halding the stilts of the pleugh, and their bellicous skill in driving of yauds and owsen.

"Likewise there are sindry honorable families, quhilk are now of our native Scottish nobility, and have clombe higher up the brae of preferment than what this house of Croftangry hath done, quhilk shame not to carry in their warlike shields and insignia of dignity, the tools and implements the quhilk their first forefathers exercised in labouring, or, as the poet Virgilius calleth it eloquently, in subduing the soil. And no doubt this ancient house of Croftangry, quhile it continued to be called of that Ilk, produced many worshipful and famous patriots, of quhom I now prætermit the names; it being my purpose, if God shall spare me life for sic ane pious *officium*, or duty, to resume this first part of my narrative touching the House of Croftangry, when I can set down at length the evidents, and historical witness anent the facts which I shall allege, seeing that words, when they are unsupported by proofs, are like seed sown on the naked rocks, or an house biggit on the flitting and faithless sands."

Here I stopped to draw breath; for the style of my great-grandsire, the inditer of this goodly matter, was rather lengthy, as our American friends say. Indeed, I reserve the rest of the piece until I can obtain admission to the Bannatyne Club, when I propose to throw off an edition, limited according to the rules of that erudite Society, with a fac-simile of the manuscript, emblazonry of the family arms, surrounded by their quartering, and a handsome disclamation of family pride, with *Haec nos novimus esse nihil*, or *Vix ea nostra voco*.

In the meantime, to speak truth, I cannot but suspect, that though my worthy ancestor puffed vigorously to swell up the dignity of his family, we had never, in fact, risen above the rank of middling proprietors. The estate of Glentanner came to us by the intermarriage of my ancestor with Tib Sommeril, called by the southron Somerville, a daughter of that noble house, but I fear on what my great-grandsire calls "the wrong side of the blanket." Her husband, Gilbert, was killed fighting, as the *Inquisitio post mortem* has it, "*sub vexillo regis, apud prœlium juxta Branxton, l.e. Floddenfield.*"

We had our share in other national misfortunes—were forfeited, like Sir John Colville of the Dale, for following our betters to the field of Langside; and in the contentious times of the last Stuarts, we were severely fined for harbouring and resetting intercommuned ministers; and narrowly escaped giving a martyr to the Calendar of the Covenant, in the person of the father of our family historian. He "took the sheaf from the mare," however, as the MS. expresses it, and agreed to accept of the terms of pardon offered by government, and sign the bond, in evidence he would give no farther ground of offence. My great-grandsire glosses over his father's backsliding as smoothly as he can, and comforts himself with ascribing his want of resolution to his unwillingness to wreck the ancient name and family, and to permit his lands and lineage to fall under a doom of forfeiture.

"And indeed," said the venerable compiler, "as, praised be God, we seldom meet in Scotland with these belly-gods and voluptuaries, who are unnatural enough to devour their patrimony bequeathed to them by their forbears in chambering and wantonness, so that they come, with the prodigal son, to the husks and the swine-trough; and as I have the less to dreid the existence of such unnatural Neroes in mine own family to devour the substance of their own house like brute beasts out of mere gluttonie and Epicurishnesse, so I need only warn mine descendants against over hastily meddling with the mutations in State and in Religion, which have been near-hand to the bringing this poor house of Croftangry to perdition, as we have shown more than once. And albeit I would not that my successors sat still altogether when called on by their duty to Kirk and King; yet I would have them wait till stronger and walthier men nor themselves were up, so that either they may have the better chance of getting through the day; or, failing of that, the conquering party having some fatter quarry to live upon, may, like gorged hawks, spare the smaller game."

There was something in this conclusion which at first reading piqued me extremely, and I was so unnatural as to curse the whole concern, as poor, bald, pitiful trash, in which a silly old man was saying a great deal about nothing at all. Nay, my first impression was to thrust it into the fire, the rather that it reminded me, in no very flattering manner, of the loss of the family property, to which the compiler of the history was so much attached, in the very manner which he most severely reprobated. It even seemed to my aggrieved feelings, that his unprescient gaze on futurity, in which he could not anticipate the folly of one of his descendants, who would throw away the whole inheritance in a few years of idle expense and folly, was meant as a personal incivility to myself, though written fifty or sixty years before I was born.

A little reflection made me ashamed of this feeling of impatience, and as I looked at the even, concise, yet tremulous hand in which the manuscript was written, I could not help thinking, according to an opinion I have heard seriously maintained, that something of a man's character might be conjectured from his handwriting. That neat, but crowded and constrained small hand, argued a man of a good conscience, well regulated passions, and, to use his own phrase, an upright walk in life. But it also indicated narrowness of spirit, inveterate prejudice, and hinted at some degree of intolerance, which, though not natural to the disposition, had arisen out of a limited education. The passages from Scripture and the classics, rather profusely than happily introduced, and written in a half-text character to mark their importance, illustrate that peculiar sort of pedantry which always considers the argument as gained, if secured by a quotation. Then the flourished capital letters, which ornament the commencement of each paragraph, and the name of his family and of his ancestors, whenever these occurred in the page, do they not express forcibly the pride and sense of importance with which the author undertook and accomplished his task? I persuaded myself, the whole was so complete a portrait of the man, that it would not have been a more undutiful act to have defaced his picture, or even to have disturbed his bones in his coffin, than to destroy his manuscript. I thought, for a moment, of presenting it to Mr Fairscribe; but that confounded passage about the prodigal and swine-trough—I settled at last it was as well to lock it up in my own bureau, with the intention to look at it no more.

But I do not know how it was, that the subject began to sit nearer my heart than I was aware of, and I found myself repeatedly engaged in reading descriptions of farms which were no longer mine, and boundaries which marked the property of others. A love of the *natale solum*, if Swift be right in translating these words, "family estate," began to awake in my bosom. The recollections of my own youth added little to it, save what was connected with field sports. A career of pleasure is unfavourable for acquiring a taste for natural beauty, and still more so for forming associations of a sentimental kind connecting us with the inanimate objects around us.

I had thought little about my estate, while I possessed and was wasting it, unless as affording the rude materials out of which a certain inferior race of creatures, called tenants, were bound to produce (in a greater quantity than they actually did) a certain return called rent, which was destined to supply my expenses. This was my general view of the matter. Of particular places, I recollected that Garval-hill was a famous piece of rough upland pasture, for rearing young colts, and teaching them to throw their feet,—that Minion-burn had the finest yellow trout in the country,—that Seggy-cleuch was unequalled for woodcocks,—that Ben-gibbert moor afforded excellent moorfowl-shooting, and that the clear bubbling fountain called the Harper's Well, was the best recipe in the world on the morning after a *Hard-go* with my neighbour fox-hunters. Still these ideas recalled, by degrees, pictures, of which I had since learned to appreciate the merit—scenes of silent loneliness, where extensive moors, undulating into wild hills, were only disturbed by the whistle of the plover, or the crow of the heath-cock; wild ravines creeping up into mountains, filled with natural wood, and which, when traced downwards along the path formed by shepherds and nutters, were found gradually to enlarge and deepen, as each formed a channel to its own brook, sometimes bordered by steep banks of earth, often with the more romantic boundary of naked rocks or cliffs, crested with oak, mountain-ash, and hazel,—all gratifying the eye the more that the scenery was, from the bare nature of the country around, totally unexpected.

I had recollections, too, of fair and fertile holms, or level plains, extending between the wooded banks and the bold stream of the Clyde, which, coloured like pure amber, or rather having the hue of the pebbles called cairn-gorum, rushes over sheets of rock and beds of gravel, inspiring a species of awe from the few and faithless fords which it presents, and the frequency of fatal accidents, now diminished by the number of new bridges. These alluvial holms were frequently bordered by triple and quadruple rows of immensely large trees, which gracefully marked their boundary, and dipped their long arms into the foaming stream of the river.—Other places I remembered, which had been described by the old huntsman as the lodge of tremendous wild-cats, or the spot where tradition stated the mighty stag to have been brought to bay, or where heroes, whose might was now as much forgotten, were said to have been slain by surprise, or in battle.

It is not to be supposed that these finished landscapes became visible before the eyes of my imagination, as the scenery of the stage is disclosed by the rising of the curtain. I have said, that I had looked upon the country around me, during the hurried and dissipated period of my life, with the eyes indeed of my body, but without those of my understanding. It was piece by piece, as a child picks out its lesson, that I began to recollect the beauties of nature which had once surrounded me in the home of my forefathers. A natural taste for them must have lurked at the bottom of my heart, which awakened when I was in foreign countries, and becoming by degrees a favourite passion, gradually turned its eyes inward, and ransacked the neglected stores which my memory had involuntarily recorded, and when excited, exerted herself to collect and to complete.

I began now to regret more bitterly than ever the having fooled away my family property, the care and improvement of which I saw might have afforded an agreeable employment for my leisure, which only went to brood on past misfortunes, and increase useless repining. "Had but a single farm been reserved, however small," said I one day to Mr Fairscribe, "I should have had a place I could call my home, and something that I could call business."

"It might have been managed," answered Fairscribe; "and for my part, I inclined to keep the mansion-house, mains, and some of the old family acres together; but both Mr —— and you were of opinion that the money would be more useful."

"True, true, my good friend," said I, "I was a fool then, and did not think I could incline to be Glentanner with L.200 or L.300 a-year, instead of Glentanner with as many thousands. I was then a paughty, petted, ignorant, dissipated, broken-down Scotch laird; and thinking my imaginary consequence altogether ruined, I cared not how soon, or how absolutely, I was rid of everything that recalled it to my own memory, or that of others."

"And now it is like you have changed your mind." said Fairscribe. "Well, fortune is apt to circumduce the term upon us; but I think she may allow you to revise your condescendence."

"How do you mean, my good friend?"

"Nay," said Fairscribe, "there's ill luck in averring till you're sure of your facts. I will look back on a file of newspapers, and to-morrow you shall hear from me—Come, help yourself—I have seen you fill your glass higher."

"And shall again," said I, pouring out what remained of our bottle of claret; "the wine is capital, and so shall the toast be—To your fireside, my good friend. And now we will go beg a Scots song without foreign graces, from my little siren Miss Katie."

The next day accordingly I received a parcel from Mr Fairscribe with a newspaper enclosed, among the advertisements of which, one was marked with a cross as requiring my attention. I read to my surprise—

"DESIRABLE ESTATE FOR SALE.

"By order of the Lords of Council and Session, will be exposed to sale in the New Sessions House of Edinburgh, upon Wednesday the 25th November 18—, All and Whole the Lands and Barony of Glentanner, now called Castle-Treddles, lying in the Upper Ward of Clydesdale, and shire of Lanark, with the teinds, parsonage and vicarage, fishings in the Clyde, woods, mosses, moors, and pasturages," &c. &c. &c.

The advertisement went on to set forth the advantages of the soil, situation, natural beauties and capabilities of improvement, not forgetting its being a freehold estate, with the particular polypus capacity of being sliced up into two, three, or, with a little assistance, four freehold qualifications, and a hint that the county was like to be eagerly contested between two great families. The upset price at which "the said Lands and Barony and others" were to be exposed, was thirty years' purchase of the proven rental, which was about a third more than the property had fetched at the last sale. This, which was mentioned, I suppose to show the improvable character of the land, would have given another some pain; but let me speak truth of myself in good as in evil—it pained not me. I was only angry that Fairscribe, who knew something generally of the extent of my funds, should have tantalized me by sending me information that my family property was in the market, since he must have known the price was far out of my reach.

But a letter, dropped from the parcel on the floor, attracted my eye, and explained the riddle. A client of Mr Fairscribe's, a monied man, thought of buying Glentanner, merely as an investment—it was even unlikely he would ever see it; and so the price of the whole being some thousand pounds beyond what cash he had on hand, this accommodating Dives would gladly take a partner in the sale for any detached farm, and would make no objection to its including the most desirable part of the estate in point of beauty, providing that the price was made adequate. Mr Fairscribe would take care I was not imposed on in the matter, and said in his card, he believed, if I really wished to make such a purchase, I had better go out and look at the premises, advising me, at the same time, to keep a strict incognito; an advice somewhat superfluous, since I am naturally of a retired and reserved disposition.

Chapter Three

Then sing of stage-coaches,
And fear no reproaches
      For riding in one;
But daily be jogging,
Whilst, whistling and flogging,
Whilst, whistling and flogging,
      The coachman drives on.
                    FARQUHAR

DISGUISED in a grey surtout which had seen service, a white castor on my head, and a stout Indian cane in my hand, the next week saw me on the top of a mail-coach driving to the westward.

I like mail-coaches, and I hate them. I like them for my convenience, but I detest them for setting the whole world a-gadding, instead of sitting quietly still minding their own business, and preserving the stamp of originality of character which nature or education may have impressed on them. Off they go, jingling against each other in the rattling vehicle till they have no more variety of stamp on them than so many smooth shillings—the same even in Welsh wigs and great coats, each without more individuality than belongs to a party of the company, as the waiter calls them, of the North coach.

Worthy Mr Piper, best of contractors who ever furnished four frampal jades "for public use," I bless you when I set out on a journey myself; the neat coaches under your contract render the intercourse, from Johnie Groat's house to Ladykirk and Cornhill Bridge, safe, pleasant, and cheap. But, Mr Piper, you, who are a shrewd arithmetician, did it ever occur to you to calculate how many fools' heads, which might have produced an idea or two in the year, if suffered to remain quiet, get effectually addled by jolting to and fro in these flying chariots of yours; how many decent countrymen turn conceited bumpkins after a show dinner, which they could not have attended save for your means. How many decent country parsons return critics and spouters, by way of importing the newest taste from Edinburgh? and how will your conscience answer one day for carrying so many bonny lasses to barter modesty for conceit and levity at the metropolitan Vanity Fair?

Consider, too, the low rate to which you reduce human intellect. I do not believe your habitual customers have their ideas more enlarged than one of your coach-horses. They *knows the road*, like the English postilion, and they know nothing beside. They date, like the carriers at Gadshill, from the death of John Ostler; the succession of guards forms a dynasty in their eyes; coachmen are their ministers of state, and an upset is to them a greater incident than a change of administration. Their only point of interest on the road is to save the time, and see whether the coach keeps the hour. This is surely a miserable degradation of human intellect. Take my advice, my good sir, and disinterestedly contrive that once or twice a quarter, your most dexterous whip shall overturn a coachful of these superfluous travellers, *in terrorem* to those who, as Horace says, "delight in the dust raised by your chariots."

Your current and customary mail-coach passenger, too, gets abominably selfish, schemes successfully for the best seat, the freshest egg, the right cut of the sirloin. Your mode of travelling is death to all the courtesies and kindnesses of life, and goes a great way to demoralize the character, and cause it to retrograde to barbarism. You allow us excellent dinners, but only twenty minutes to eat them; and what is the consequence? Bashful beauty sits on the one side of us, timid childhood on the other; respectable, yet somewhat feeble age is placed on our front; and all require those acts of politeness which ought to put all degrees upon a level at the convivial board. But have we time—we the strong and active of the party—to perform the duties of the table to the more retired and bashful, to whom these little attentions are due? The lady should be pressed to her chicken—the old man helped to his favourite and tender slice—the child to his tart. But not a fraction of a minute have we to bestow on any other person than ourselves; and the *prut-prut-tut-tut* of the guard's discordant note, summons us to the coach, the weaker party having gone without their dinner, and the able-bodied and active threatened with indigestion from having swallowed victuals like a Lei'stershire clown bolting bacon.

On the memorable occasion I am speaking of I lost my breakfast, sheerly from obeying the commands of a respectable-looking old lady, who once required me to ring the bell, and another time to help the tea-kettle. I have some reason to think she was literally an *Old Stager*, who laughed in her sleeve at my complaisance; so that I have sworn in my secret soul revenge upon her sex, and all such errant damsels of whatever age and degree, whom I may encounter in my travels. I mean all this without the least ill-will to my friend the contractor, who, I think, has approached as near as any one is like to do towards accomplishing the modest wish of the Amatus and Amata of the Peri Bathous,

> Ye gods, annihilate but time and space,
> And make two lovers happy.

I intend to give Mr P. his full revenge when I come to discuss the more recent enormity of steam-boats. Meanwhile, I shall only say of both these modes of conveyance, that

> There is no living with them or without them.

I am perhaps more critical on the —— mail-coach on this particular occasion, that I did not meet all the respect from the worshipful company in His Majesty's carriage that I think I was entitled to. I must say it for myself, that I bear, in my own opinion at least, not a vulgar point about me. My face has seen service, but there is still a good set of teeth, an aquiline nose, and a quick grey eye, set a little too deep under the eye-brow; and a cue of the kind once called military, may serve to show that my civil occupations have been sometimes mixed with those of war. Nevertheless, two idle young fellows in the vehicle, or rather on the top of it, were so much amused with the deliberation which I used in ascending to the same place of eminence, that I thought I should have been obliged to pull them up a little. And I was in no good-humour, at an unsuppressed laugh following my descent, when set down at the angle, where a cross road, striking off from the main one, led me towards Glentanner, from which I was still nearly five miles distant.

It was an old-fashioned road, which, preferring ascent to sloughs, was led in a straight line over height and hollow, through moor and dale. Every object around me, as I passed them in succession, reminded me of old days, and at the same time formed the strongest contrast with them possible. Unattended, on foot, with a small bundle in my hand, deemed scarce sufficient good company for the two shabby genteels with whom I had been lately perched on the top of a mail-coach, I did not seem to be the same person with the young prodigal, who lived abreast with the noblest and gayest in the land, and who, thirty years before, would, in the same country, have been on the back of a horse that had been victor for a plate, or smoking along in his travelling chaise-and-four. My sentiments were not less changed than my condition. I could quite well remember, that my ruling sensation in the days of heady youth, was a mere school-boy's eagerness to get farthest forward in the race in which I had engaged; to drink as many bottles as ———; to be thought as good a judge of a horse as ———; to have the knowing cut of———'s jacket. These were thy gods, O Israel!

Now I was a mere looker-on; seldom an unmoved, and sometimes an angry spectator, but still a spectator only, of the pursuits of mankind. I felt how little my opinion was valued by those engaged in the busy turmoil, yet I exercised it with the profusion of an old lawyer retired from his profession, who thrusts himself into his neighbour's affairs, and gives advice where it is not wanted, merely under pretence of loving the crack of the whip.

I came amid these reflections to the brow of a hill, from which I expected to see Glentanner; a modest-looking yet comfortable house, its walls covered with the most productive fruit-trees in that part of the country, and screened from the most stormy quarters of the horizon by a deep and ancient wood, which overhung the neighbouring hill. The house was gone; a great part of the wood was felled; and instead of the gentlemanlike mansion, shrouded and embosomed among its old hereditary trees, stood Castle-Treddles, a huge lumping four-square pile of freestone, as bare as my nail, except for a paltry edging of decayed and lingering exotics, with an impoverished lawn stretched before it, which, instead of boasting deep green tapestry, enamelled with daisies, and with crowsfoot and cowslips, showed an extent of nakedness, raked, indeed, and levelled, but where the sown grasses had failed with drought, and the earth, retaining its natural complexion, seemed nearly as brown and bare as when it was newly dug up.

The house was a large fabric, which pretended to its name of Castle only from the front windows being finished in acute Gothic arches (being, by the way, the very reverse of the castellated style), and each angle graced with a turret about the size of a pepper-box. In every other respect it resembled a large town-house, which, like a fat burgess, had taken a walk to the country on a holiday, and climbed to the top of an eminence to look around it. The bright red colour of the freestone, the size of the building, the formality of its shape, and awkwardness of its position, harmonized as ill with the sweeping Clyde in front, and the babbling brook which danced down on the right, as would the fat civic form, with bushy wig, gold-headed cane, maroon-coloured coat, and mottled silk stockings, with the wild and magnificent scenery of Corehouse Linn.

I went up to the house. It was in that state of desertion which is perhaps the most unpleasant to look on, for the place was going to decay, without having been inhabited. There were about the mansion, though deserted, none of the slow mouldering touches of time, which communicate to buildings, as to the human frame, a sort of reverence, while depriving them of beauty and of strength. The disconcerted schemes of the Laird of Castle-Treddles, had resembled fruit that becomes decayed without ever having ripened. Some windows broken, others patched, others blocked up with deals, gave a disconsolate air to all around, and seemed to say, "There Vanity had purposed to fix her seat, but was anticipated by Poverty."

To the inside, after many a vain summons, I was at length admitted by an old labourer. The house contained every contrivance for luxury and accommodation;—the kitchens were a model, and there were hot closets on the office stair-case, that the dishes might not cool, as our Scotch phrase goes, between the kitchen and the hall. But instead of the genial smell of good cheer, these temples of Comus emitted the damp odour of sepulchral vaults, and the large cabinets of cast-iron looked like the cages of some feudal Bastille. The eating-room and drawing-room, with an interior boudoir, were magnificent apartments, the ceilings fretted and adorned with stucco-work, which already was broken in many places, and looked in others damp and mouldering; the wood pannelling was shrunk and warped, and cracked; the doors, which had not been hung for more than two years, were, nevertheless, already swinging loose from their hinges. Desolation, in short, was where enjoyment had never been; and the want of all the usual means to preserve, was fast performing the work of decay.

The story was a common one, and told in a few words. Mr Treddles, senior, who bought the estate, was a cautious money-making person; his son, still embarked in commercial speculations, desired at the same time to enjoy his opulence and to increase it. He incurred great expenses, amongst which this edifice was to be numbered. To support these he speculated boldly, and unfortunately; and thus the whole history is told, which may serve for more places than Glentanner.

Strange and various feelings ran through my bosom, as I loitered in these deserted apartments, scarce hearing what my guide said to me about the size and destination of each room. The first sentiment, I am ashamed to say, was one of gratified spite. My patrician pride was pleased, that the mechanic, who had not thought the house of the Croftangrys sufficiently good for him, had now experienced a fall in his turn. My next thought was as mean, though not so malicious. "I have had the better of this fellow," thought I; "if I lost the estate, I at least spent the price; and Mr Treddles has lost his among paltry commercial engagements."

"Wretch!" said the secret voice within, "darest thou exult in thy shame? Recollect how thy youth and fortune were wasted in those years, and triumph not in the enjoyments of an existence which levelled thee with the beasts that perish. Bethink thee, how this poor man's vanity gave at least bread to the labourer, peasant, and citizen; and his profuse expenditure, like water spilled on the ground, refreshed the lowly herbs and plants where it fell. But thou! whom hast thou enriched, during thy career of extravagance, save those brokers of the devil, vintners, panders, gamblers, and horse-jockeys?" The anguish produced by this self-reproof was so strong, that I put my hand suddenly to my forehead, and was obliged to allege a sudden megrim to my attendant, in apology for the action, and a slight groan with which it was accompanied.

I then made an effort to turn my thoughts into a more philosophical current, and muttered half aloud, as a charm to lull my more painful thoughts to rest—

> *Nunc ager Umbreni sub nomine, nuper Ofelli*
> *Dictus, erit nulli proprius; sed cedet in usum*
> *Nunc mihi, nunc alii. Quocirca vivite fortes,*
> *Fortiaque adversis opponite pectora rebus.* *

In my anxiety to fix the philosophical precept in my mind, I recited the last line aloud, which, joined to my previous agitation, I afterwards found became the cause of a report, that a mad schoolmaster had come from Edinburgh, with the idea in his head of buying Castle-Treddles.

As I saw my companion was desirous of getting rid of me, I asked

---

* HORACE, Sat. II. Lib. 2. The meaning will be best conveyed to the English reader in Pope's imitation:—

> What's property, dear Swift? you see it alter
> From you to me, from me to Peter Walter;
> Or in a mortgage prove a lawyer's share;
> Or in a jointure vanish from the heir. . . .
> Shades, that to Bacon could retreat afford,
> Become the portion of a booby lord;
> And Helmsley, once proud Buckingham's delight,
> Slides to a scrivener and a city knight.
> Let lands and houses have what lords they will,
> Let us be fix'd, and our own masters still.

where I was to find the person in whose hands were left the map of the estate, and other particulars concerned with the sale. The agent who had this in possession, I was told, lived at the town of ————; which I was informed, and indeed knew well, was distant five miles and a bittock, which may pass in a country where they are less lavish of their land, for two or three more. Being somewhat afraid of the fatigue of walking so far, I inquired if a horse, or any sort of carriage, was to be had, and was answered in the negative.

"But," said my cicerone, "you may halt a blink till next morning at the Treddles Arms, a very decent house, scarce a mile off."

"A new house, I suppose?" replied I.

"Na—it's a new public, but it's an auld house: it was aye the Leddy's jointure-house in the Croftangry-folk's time. But Mr Treddles has fitted it up for the convenience of the country. Poor man, he was a public-spirited man when he had the means."

"Duntarkin a public house!" I exclaimed.

"Ay?" said the man, surprised at my naming the place by its former title, "ye'll hae been in this country before, I'm thinking?"

"Long since," I replied—"And there is good accommodation at the what-d'ye-call-'um Arms, and a civil landlord?" This I said by way of saying something, for the fellow stared very hard at me.

"Very decent accommodation. Ye'll no be for fashing wi' wine, I'm thinking, and there's walth o' porter, ale, and a drap gude whisky—(in an under tone) Fairntosh, if you can get on the lee-side of the gude-wife—for there's nae gudeman—They ca' her Christie Steele."

I almost started at the sound. Christie Steele! Christie Steele was my mother's body servant, her very right hand, and, between our-selves, something like a viceroy over her. I recollected her perfectly; and though she had, in former times, been no favourite of mine, her name now sounded in my ear like that of a friend, and was the first word I had heard somewhat in unison with the associations around me. I sallied from Castle-Treddles, determined to make the best of my way to Duntarkin, and my cicerone hung by me for a little way, giving loose to his love of talking; an opportunity of which, situated as he was, the seneschal of a deserted castle, was not like to occur frequently.

"Some folks think Mr Treddles might as weel have put my wife as Christie Steele into the Treddles Arms, for Christie had been aye in service, and never in the public line, and so it's like she is ganging back in the world, as I hear—now, my wife had keepit a victualling office."

"That would have been an advantage, certainly."

"But I am no sure that I wad ha' looten Eppie take it, if they had put it in her offer."

"That's a different consideration."

"Ony way, I wadna ha' liked to have offended Mr Treddles; he was a wee toustie when you rubbed him again the hair—but a kind, weel-meaning man."

I wanted to get rid of this species of chat, and finding myself near the entrance of a footpath which made a short cut to Duntarkin, I put half-a-crown into my guide's hand, bade him good-evening, and plunged into the woods.

"Hout, sir—fie, no, sir—no from the like of you—Stay, sir, ye winna find the way that gate—Odd's mercy, he maun ken the gate as weel as I do mysell—Weel, I wad like to ken wha the chield is."

Such were the last sounds of my guide's drowsy, uninteresting tone of voice; and glad to be rid of him, I strode out stoutly, despite large stones, briers, and *bad steps*, which abounded in the road I had chosen. In the interim, I tried as much as I could, with verses from Horace and Prior, and all who have lauded the mixture of literary with rural life, to call back the visions of last night and this morning, imagining myself settled in some detached farm of the estate of Glentanner,

> Which sloping hills around enclose—
> Where many a birch and brown oak grows;

when I should have a cottage with a small library, a small cellar, a spare bed for a friend, and live more happy and more honoured than when I had the whole barony. But the sight of Castle-Treddles had disturbed all my own castles in the air. The realities of the matter, like a stone plashed into a limpid fountain, had destroyed the reflection of the objects around, which, till this act of violence, lay slumbering on the crystal surface; and I tried in vain to re-establish the picture which had been so rudely broken. Well, then—I would try it another way; I would try to get Christie Steele out of her *public*, since she was not thriving in it, and she who had been my mother's governante should be mine. I knew all her faults, and I told her history over to myself.

She was a grand-daughter, I believe, at least some relative, of the famous Covenanter of the name, whom Dean Swift's friend, Captain Crichton, shot on his own staircase in the times of the persecution, and had perhaps derived from her native stock much both of its good and evil properties. No one could say of her that she was the life and spirit of the family, though, in my mother's time, she directed all family affairs; her look was austere and gloomy, and when she was not displeased with you, you could only find it out by her silence. If there was cause for complaint, real or imaginary, Christie was loud enough. She loved my mother with the devoted attachment of a younger sister, but she was as jealous of her favour to any one else as if she had been the aged husband of a coquettish wife, and as severe in her reprehensions as an abbess over her nuns. The command which she exercised over her, was that, I fear, of a strong and determined over a feeble and more nervous disposition; and though it was used with rigour, yet, to the best of Christie Steele's belief, she was urging her mistress to the best and most becoming course, and would have died sooner than have recommended any other. The attachment of this woman was limited to the family of Croftangry, for she had few relations; and a dissolute cousin, whom late in life she had taken as a husband, had long left her a widow.

To me she had ever a strong dislike. Even from my early childhood, she was jealous, strange as it may seem, of my interest in my mother's affections; she saw my foibles and vices with abhorrence, and without a grain of allowance; nor did she pardon the weakness of maternal affection, even when, by the death of two brothers, I came to be the only child of a widowed parent. At the time my disorderly conduct induced my mother to leave Glentanner, and retreat to her jointure-house, I always blamed Christie Steele for having inflamed her resentment, and prevented her from listening to my vows of amendment, which at times were real and serious, and might, perhaps, have accelerated that change of disposition which has since, I trust, taken place. But Christie regarded me as altogether a doomed and predestinated child of perdition, who was sure to hold my course, and drag downwards whosoever might attempt to afford me support.

Still, though I knew such had been Christie's prejudices against me in elder days, yet I thought enough of time had since passed away to destroy all of them. I knew, that when, through the disorder of my affairs, my mother underwent some temporary inconvenience about money matters, Christie, as a thing of course, stood in the gap, and having sold a small inheritance which had descended to her, brought the purchase-money to her mistress, with a sense of devotion as deep as that which inspired the Christians of the first age, when they sold all they had, and followed the apostles of the church. I therefore thought that we might, in old Scottish phrase, "let byganes be byganes," and begin upon a new account. Yet I resolved, like a skilful general, to reconnoitre a little before laying down any precise scheme of proceeding, and in the interim I determined to preserve my incognito.

Chapter Four

Alas, how changed from what it once had been!
'Twas now degraded to a common inn.
                                        GAY

HALF AN HOUR'S brisk walking, or thereabouts, placed me in front
of Duntarkin, which had also, I found, undergone considerable
alterations, though it had not been altogether demolished like the
principal mansion. An inn-yard extended before the door of the
decent little jointure-house, even amidst the remnants of the holly
hedges which had screened the lady's garden. Then a broad, raw-
looking, new-made road intruded itself up the little glen, instead of
the old horseway, so seldom used that it was almost entirely covered
with grass. It is a great enormity of which gentlemen trustees on the
highways are sometimes guilty, in adopting the breadth necessary for
an avenue to the metropolis, where all that is required is an access to
some sequestered and unpopulous district. I do not say anything of
the expense; that the trustees and their constituents may settle as they
please. But the destruction of sylvan beauty is great, when the breadth
of the road is more than proportioned to the vale through which it
runs, and lowers of course the consequence of any objects of wood or
water, or broken and varied ground, which might otherwise attract
notice, and give pleasure. A bubbling runnel by the side of one of
these modern Appian or Flaminian highways, is but like a kennel,—
the little hill is diminished to a hillock,—the romantic hillock to a
mole-hill "almost too small" for sight.

Such an enormity, however, had destroyed the quiet loneliness of
Duntarkin, and intruded its breadth of dust and gravel, and its associations of po–chays and mail-coaches, upon one of the most sequestered spots in the Upper Ward of Clydesdale. The house was old and
dilapidated, and looked sorry for itself, as if sensible of a derogation.
But the sign was strong and new, and brightly painted, displaying a
heraldic shield, three shuttles in a field diapré, a web partly unfolded
for crest, and two stout giants for supporters, each one holding a
weaver's beam proper. To have displayed this monstrous emblem on
the front of the house might have hazarded bringing down the wall,
but for certain would have blocked one or two windows. It was therefore established independent of the mansion, being displayed in an
iron framework, and suspended upon two posts, with as much wood
and iron about it as would have builded a brig; and there it hung,
creaking, groaning, and screaming in every blast of wind, and fright-

ening to five miles' distance, for aught I know, the nests of thrushes and linnets, the ancient denizens of the little glen.

When I entered the place, I was received by Christie Steele herself, who seemed uncertain whether to drop me in the kitchen, or usher me into a separate apartment. As I called for tea, with something rather more substantial than bread and butter, and spoke of supping and sleeping, Christie at last inducted me into the room where she herself had been sitting, probably the only one which had a fire, though the month was October. This answered my plan; and, as she was about to remove her spinning-wheel, I begged she would have the goodness to remain and make my tea, adding, that I liked the sound of the wheel, and desired not to disturb her housewife-thrift in the least.

"I dinna ken, sir,"—she replied in a dry *revêche* tone, which carried me back twenty years, "I am nane of thae heartsome landleddies that can tell country cracks, and make themsells agreeable; and I was ganging to pit on a fire for you in the red room; but if it is your will to stay here, he that pays the lawing maun choose the lodging."

I endeavoured to engage her in conversation; but though she answered with a kind of stiff civility, I could get her into no freedom of discourse, and she began to look at her wheel and at the door more than once, as if she meditated a retreat. I was obliged, therefore, to proceed to some special questions that might have interest for a person, whose ideas were probably of a very bounded description.

I looked round the apartment, being the same in which I had last seen my poor mother. The author of the family history, formerly mentioned, had taken great credit to himself for the improvements he had made in this same jointure-house of Duntarkin, and how, upon his marriage, when his mother took possession of the same as her jointure-house, "to his great charges and expenses he caused box the walls of the great parlour, (in which I was now sitting,) empannel the same, and plaster the roof, finishing the same with ane concave chimney, and decoring the same with pictures, and a barometer and thermometer." And in particular, which his good mother used to say she prized above all the rest, he had caused his own portraiture to be limned over the mantel-piece by a skilful hand. And, in good faith, there he remained still, having much the visage which I was disposed to ascribe to him on the evidence of his hand-writing,—grim and austere, yet not without a cast of shrewdness and determination; in armour, though he never wore it, I fancy; one hand on an open book, and one resting on the hilt of his sword, though I dare say his head never ached with reading, nor his limbs with fencing.

"That picture is painted on the wood, madam," said I.

"Ay, sir, or it's like it would not have been left there;—they took a' they could."

"Mr Treddles's creditors, you mean?" said I.

"Na," replied she, drily, "the creditors of another family, that sweepit cleaner than his, poor man, because I fancy there was less to gather."

"An older family, perhaps, and probably more remembered and regretted than later possessors?"

Christie here settled herself in her seat, and pulled her wheel towards her. I had given her something interesting for her thoughts to dwell upon, and her wheel was a mechanical accompaniment on such occasions, the revolutions of which assisted her in the explication of her ideas.

"Mair regretted—mair missed?—I liked ane of the auld family very weel, but I winna say that for them a'. How should they be mair missed than the Treddleses? The cotton mill was such a thing for the country! The mair bairns a cottar body had the better; they would make their awn keep frae the time they were five years auld. And a widow wi' three or four weans was a wealthy woman in the time of the Treddleses."

"But the health of these poor children, my good friend—their education and religious instruction——"

"For health," said Christie, looking gloomily at me, "ye maun ken little of the warld, sir, if ye dinna ken that the health of the puir man's body, as weel as his youth and his strength, are all at the command of the rich man's purse. There never was a trade so unhealthy yet, but men would fight to get wark at it for twa pennies a-day aboon the common wage. But the bairns were reasonably weel cared for in the way of air and exercise, and a very responsible youth heard them their carritch, and gied them lessons in Reediemadeasy.* Now, what did they ever get before? Maybe on a winter day they wad be called out to beat the wood for cocks or siclike, and then the starving weans would maybe get a bite of broken bread, and maybe no, just as the butler was in humour—that was a' they got."

"They were not, then, a very kind family to the poor, these old possessors?" said I, somewhat bitterly; for I had expected to hear my ancestors' praises recorded, though I certainly despaired of being regaled with my own.

"They werena ill to them, sir, and that is aye something. They were just decent bien bodies;—ony poor creature that had face to beg got an awmous and welcome; they that were shame-faced gaed by, and twice as welcome. But they keeped an honest walk before God and

* "Reading Made Easy," usually so pronounced in Scotland.

man, the Croftangrys, and, as I said before, if they did little good, they did as little harm. They lifted their rents and spent them, called in their kains and eat them; gaed to the kirk of a Sunday, bowed civilly if folk took aff their bannets as they gaed by, and looked as black as sin at them that keeped them on."

"These are their arms that you have on the sign?"

"What! on the painted board that is skirling and groaning at the door?—Na, these are Mr Treddles's arms—though they look as like legs as arms—ill pleased I was at the fule thing, that cost as muckle as would hae repaired the house from the wa' stane to the rigging-tree. But if I am to bide here, I'll hae a decent board wi' a punch bowl on it."

"Is there a doubt of your staying here, Mrs Steele?"

"Dinna Mistress me," said the cross old woman, whose fingers were now plying their thrift in a manner which indicated nervous irritation—"there was nae luck in the land since Luckie turned Mistress, and Mistress my Leddy. And as for staying here, if it concerns you to ken, I may stay if I can pay a hundred pund sterling for the lease, and I may flit if I canna; and so gude e'en to you, Christie,"—and round went the wheel with much activity.

"And you like the trade of keeping a public house?"

"I can scarce say that," she replied. "But worthy Mr Prendergast is clear of its lawfulness, and I hae gotten used to it, and made a decent living, though I never made out a fause reckoning, or give ony ane the means to disorder reason in my house."

"Indeed," said I, "in that case, there is no wonder you have not made up the hundred pounds to purchase the lease."

"How do you ken," said she sharply, "that I might not have had a hundred punds of my ain fee? If I have it not, I am sure it is my ain faut; and I winna ca' it faut neither, for it gaed to her wha was weel entitled to a' my service." Again she pulled stoutly at the flax, and the wheel went smartly round.

"This old gentleman," said I, fixing my eye on the painted pannel, "seems to have had *his* arms painted as well as Mr Treddles—that is, if that in the corner be a scutcheon."

"Ay, ay—cushion, just sae, they maun a' hae their cushions; there's sma' gentrice without that; and so the arms, as they ca' them, of the house of Glentanner, may be seen on an auld stane in the west end of the house. But to do them justice, they didna propale sae mickle about them as puir Mr Treddles did;—it's like they were better used to them."

"Very likely.—Are there any of the old family left, goodwife?"

"No," she replied; then added, after a moment's hesitation—"not that I know of,"—and the wheel, which had intermitted a little, began again to revolve.

"Gone abroad, perhaps?" I suggested.

She now looked up, and faced me—"No, sir. There were three sons of the last laird of Glentanner, as he was then called; John and William were hopeful young gentlemen, but they died early—one of a decline, brought on by the mizzles, the other lost his life in a fever. It would hae been lucky for mony ane that Chrystal had gane the same gate."

"Oh—he must have been the young spend-thrift that sold the property? Well, but you should not have such an ill-will against him: remember necessity has no law; and then, goodwife, he was not more culpable than Mr Treddles, whom you are so sorry for."

"I wish I could think sae, sir, for his mother's sake; but Mr Treddles was in trade, and though he had no preceese right to dae, yet there was some warrant for a man being expensive that imagined he was making a mint of money. But this unhappy lad devoured his patrimony, when he kenned that he was living like a ratten in a Dunlap cheese, and diminishing his means at a' hands—I canna bide to think on't." With this she broke out into a snatch of a ballad; but little of mirth was there either in the tone or the expression—

> "For he did spend, and make an end
> Of gear that his forefathers wan:
> Of land and ware he made him bare,
> So speak nae mair of the auld gudeman."

"Come, dame," said I, "it is a long lane that has no turning. I will not keep from you that I have heard something of this poor fellow, Chrystal Croftangry. He has sown his wild oats, as they say, and has settled into a steady respectable man."

"And wha tell'd ye that tidings?" said she, looking sharply at me.

"Not perhaps the best judge in the world of his character, for it was himself, dame."

"And if he tell'd you truth, it was a virtue he did not aye use to practise," said Christie.

"The devil!" said I, considerably nettled; "all the world held him a man of honour."

"Ou, ay! he would hae shot onybody wi' his pistols and his guns, that had evened him to be a liar. But if he promised to pay an honest tradesman the next term-day, did he keep his word then? And if he promised a poor silly lass to make gude her shame, did he speak truth then? And what is that, but being a liar, and a black-hearted deceitful liar to boot?"

My indignation was rising, but I strove to suppress it; indeed, I should only have afforded my tormentor a triumph by an angry reply. I partly suspected she began to recognise me; yet she testified so little emotion, that I could not think my suspicion well founded. I went on, therefore, to say, in a tone as indifferent as I could command, "Well, goodwife, I see you will believe no good of this Chrystal of yours, till he comes back and buys a good farm on the estate, and makes you his housekeeper."

The old woman dropped her thread, folded her hands, as she looked up to heaven with a face of apprehension. "The Lord," she exclaimed, "forbid! the Lord in his mercy forbid! Oh, sir! if you really know this unlucky man, persuade him to settle where folk ken the good that you say he has come to, and dinna ken the evil of his former days. He used to be proud enough—O dinna let him come here, even for his own sake.—He used ance to have some pride."

Here she once more drew the wheel close to her, and began to pull at the flax with both hands—"Dinna let him come here, to be looked down upon by ony that may be left of his auld reiving companions, and to have the decent folk that he looked ower his nose at lang syne look ower their noses at him, baith at kirk and mercat. Dinna let him come to his ain country to be made a tale about when ony neibour points him out to another, and tells what he is, and what he was, and how he wrecked a dainty estate, and brought harlots to the door-cheek of his father's house, till he made it nae residence for his mother; and how it had been foretauld to him by a servant of his ain house, that he was a ne'er-do-weel, and a child of perdition, and how her words were made good, and"——

"Stop there, goodwife, if you please," said I: "you have said as much as I can well remember, and more than it may be safe to repeat. I can use a great deal of freedom with the gentleman we speak of; but I think were any other person to carry him half of your message, I would scarce insure his personal safety. And now, as I see the night is settled to be a fine one, I will walk on to L——, where I must catch a coach to-morrow, as it passes to Edinburgh."

So saying, I paid my moderate reckoning, and took my leave, without being able to discover whether the prejudiced and hard-hearted old woman did, or did not, suspect the identity of her guest, with the Chrystal Croftangry against whom she harboured so much dislike.

The night was fine and frosty, though, when I pretended to see what its character was, it might have been raining like the deluge. I only made the excuse to escape from old Christie Steele. The horses which run in the Corso at Rome without any riders, in order to stimulate their exertions, carry each his own spurs, namely, small balls of steel, with sharp projecting spikes, which are attached to loose

straps of leather, and, flying about in the violence of the agitation, keep
the horse to his speed by pricking him as they strike against his flanks.
The old woman's reproaches had the same effect on me, and urged
me to a rapid pace, as if it had been possible to escape from my own
recollections. In the best days of my life, when I won one or two hard
walking matches, I doubt if I ever walked so fast as I did betwixt the
Treddles Arms and the borough town for which I was bound. Though
the night was cold, I was warm enough by the time I got to my inn; and
it required a refreshing draught of porter, with half an hour's repose,
ere I could determine to give no farther thought to Christie and her
opinions, than those of any other vulgar prejudiced old woman. I
resolved at last to treat the thing *en bagatelle*, and, calling for writing
materials, I folded up a cheque for L.100, with these lines on the
envelope:

> Chrystal, the ne'er-do-weel,
> Child destined to the Deil,
> Sends this to Christie Steele.

And I was so much pleased with this new mode of viewing the subject,
that I regretted the lateness of the hour prevented my finding a person
to carry the letter express to its destination.

> But with the morning cool reflection came.

I considered that the money, and probably more, was actually due
by me on my mother's account to Christie, who had lent it in a moment
of great necessity, and that the returning it in a light or ludicrous
manner was not unlikely to prevent so touchy and punctilious a person
from accepting a debt which was most justly her due, and which it
became me particularly to see satisfied. Sacrificing then my triad with
little regret, (for it looked better by candle-light, and through the
medium of a pot of porter, than it did by daylight, and with bohea for a
menstruum,) I determined to employ Mr Fairscribe's mediation in
buying up the lease of the little inn, and conferring it upon Christie in
the way which should make it most acceptable to her feelings. It is only
necessary to add, that my plan succeeded, and that Widow Steele even
yet keeps the Treddles Arms. Do not say, therefore, that I have been
disingenuous with you, reader; since, if I have not told all the ill of
myself I might have done, I have indicated to you a person able and
willing to supply the blank, by relating all my delinquencies, as well as
my misfortunes.

In the meantime, I totally abandoned the idea of redeeming
any part of my paternal property, and resolved to take Christie
Steele's advice, as Young Norval does Glenalvon's——"although
it sounded harshly."

Chapter Five

——If you will know my house,
'Tis at the tuft of olives here hard-by.
                              As You Like It

BY A REVOLUTION of humour which I am unable to account for, I
changed my mind entirely on my plans of life, in consequence of the
disappointment, the history of which fills the last chapter. I began to
discover that the country would not at all suit me; for I had relinquished field-sports, and felt no inclination whatsoever to farming,
the ordinary vocation of a country gentleman; besides that, I had no
talents for assisting either candidate in case of an expected election,
and saw no amusement in the duties of a road trustee, a commissioner
of supply, or even the magisterial functions of the bench. I had begun
to take some taste for reading; and a domiciliation in the country must
remove me from the use of books, excepting the small subscription
library, in which the very book which you want is uniformly sure to be
engaged.

I resolved, therefore, to make the Scottish metropolis my regular
resting-place, reserving to myself to take occasionally those excur-
sions, which, spite of all I have said against mail-coaches, Mr Piper
has rendered so easy. Friend of our life and of our leisure, he secures
by dispatch against loss of time, and by the best of coaches, cattle, and
steadiest drivers, against hazard of limb, and wafts us, as well as our
letters, from Edinburgh to Cape Wrath in the penning of a paragraph.

When my mind was quite made up to make Auld Reekie my headquarters, reserving the privilege of *exploring* in all directions, I began to
explore in good earnest for the purpose of discovering a suitable
habitation. "An' whare trew ye I gaed?" as Sir Pertinax says. Not to
George's Square—nor to Charlotte Square—nor to the old New
Town—nor to the new New Town—nor to the Calton Hill. I went to
the Canongate—and to the very portion of the Canongate in which I
had formerly been immured, like the errant knight, prisoner in some
enchanted castle, where spells have made the ambient air impervious
to the unhappy captive, although the organs of sight encountered no
obstacle to his free passage.

Why I should have thought of pitching my tent here I cannot tell.
Perhaps it was to enjoy the pleasures of freedom, where I had so long
endured the bitterness of restraint; on the principle of the officer,
who, after he had retired from the army, ordered his servant to continue to call him at the hour of parade, simply that he might have the

pleasure of saying—"Damn the parade," and turning to the other side to renew his slumbers. Or perhaps I expected to find in the vicinity some little old-fashioned house, having somewhat of the *rus in urbe*, which I was ambitious of enjoying. Enough, I went, as aforesaid, to the Canongate.

I stood by the kennel, of which I have formerly spoken, and, my mind being at ease, my bodily organs were more delicate. I was more sensible than heretofore, that, like the trade of Pompey in Measure for Measure—it did in some sort——pah—an ounce of civet, good apothecary!—Turning from thence, my steps naturally directed themselves to my own humble apartment, where my little Highland landlady, as dapper and tight as ever, (for old women wear a hundred times better than the hard-wrought seniors of the masculine sex,) stood at the door, *teedling* to herself a Highland song as she shook a table napkin over the fore-stair, and proceeded to fold it up neatly for future service.

"How do you, Janet?"

"Thank ye, good sir," answered my old friend, without looking at me; "but ye might as weel say Mrs MacEvoy, for she is na a'body's Shanet—umph."

"You must be *my* Janet, though, for all that—have you forgot me?—Do you not remember Chrystal Croftangry?"

The light, kind-hearted creature threw her napkin into the open door, skipped down the stair like a fairy, three steps at once, seized me by the hands,—both hands,—jumped up, and actually kissed me. I was a little ashamed; but what swain, of somewhere inclining to sixty, could resist the advances of a fair contemporary? So we allowed the full degree of kindness to the meeting,—*honi soit qui mal y pense*,—and then Janet entered instantly upon business. "An' ye'll gae in and see your auld lodgings, nae doubt, and Shanet will pay ye the fifteen shillings of change that ye ran away without, and without bidding Shanet good day. But never mind," (nodding good-humouredly,) "Shanet saw you were carried just for the time."

By this time we were in my old quarters, and Janet, with her bottle of cordial in one hand and the glass in the other, had forced on me a dram of usquebaugh, distilled with saffron and other herbs, after some old, personal Highland receipt. Then was unfolded, out of many a little scrap of paper, the reserved sum of fifteen shillings, which Janet had treasured for twenty years and upwards.

"Here they are," she said, in honest triumph, "just the same I was holding out to ye when ye ran as if ye had been fey. Shanet has had siller, and Shanet has wanted siller, mony a time since that—and the gauger has come, and the factor has come, and butcher and baker—

Cot bless us—just like to tear puir auld Shanet to pieces; but she took good care of Mr Croftangry's fifteen shillings."

"But what if I had never come back, Janet?"

"Och, if Shanet had heard you were dead, she would hae gien it to the poor of the chapel, to pray for Mr Croftangry," said Janet, crossing herself, for she was a Catholic;—"you maybe do not think it would do you cood, but the blessings of the poor can never do no harm."

I agreed heartily in Janet's conclusion; and, as to have desired her to consider the hoard as her own property, would have been an indelicate return to her for the uprightness of her conduct, I requested her to dispose of it as she had proposed to do in the event of my death, that is, if she knew any poor people of merit to whom it might be useful.

"Ower mony of them," raising the corner of her checked apron to her eyes, "e'en ower mony of them, Mr Croftangry.—Och, ay— There is the puir Highland creatures frae Glenshee, that came down for the haarst, and are lying wi' the fever—five shillings to them, and half-a-crown to Bessie MacEvoy, whose coodman, puir creature, died of the frost, being a shairman, for a' the whisky he could drink to keep it out o' his stamach—and——"

But she suddenly interrupted the bead-roll of her proposed charities, and assuming a very sage look, and primming up her little chattering mouth, she went on in a different tone—"But, och, Mr Croftangry—Bethink ye whether ye will not need a' this siller yoursell, and maybe look back and think lang for ha'en kiven it away, whilk is a creat sin to forthink a wark o' charity, and also is unlucky, and moreover is not the thought of a shentleman's son like yoursell, dear. And I say this, that ye may think a bit, for your mother's son kens that ye are no so careful as you should be of the gear, and I hae tauld ye of it before, jewel."

I assured her I could easily spare the money, without risk of future repentance; and she went on to infer, that, in such a case, "Mr Croftangry had grown a rich man in foreign parts, and was free of his troubles with messengers and sheriff-officers, and siclike scum of the earth, and Shanet MacEvoy's mother's daughter would be a blithe woman to hear it. Put if Maister Croftangry was in trouble, there was his room, and his ped, and Shanet to wait on him, and tak payment when it was quite convenient."

I explained to Janet my situation, in which she expressed unqualified delight. I then proceeded to inquire into her own circumstances, and, though she spoke cheerfully and contentedly, I could see they were precarious. I had paid more than was due; other lodgers fell into an opposite error, and forgot to pay Janet at all. Then, Janet being ignorant of all indirect modes of screwing money out of her lodgers, others in the same line of life, who were sharper than the poor simple Highland woman, were enabled to let their apartments cheaper in appearance, though the inmates usually found them twice as dear in the long-run.

As I had already destined my old landlady to be my housekeeper and governante, knowing her honesty, good-nature, and, although a Scotchwoman, her cleanliness and excellent temper, (saving the short and hasty expression of anger which Highlanders call a *fuff*,) I now proposed the plan to her in such a way as was like to make it most acceptable. Very acceptable the proposal was, as I could plainly see. Janet, however, took a day to consider upon it; and her reflections against our next meeting had suggested only one objection, which was singular enough.

"My honour," so she now termed me, "would pe for biding in some fine streets apout the town; now Shanet wad ill like to live in a place where polish, and sheriffs, and bailiffs, and sic thieves and trash of the world, could tak puir shentleman by the troat, just because they wanted a whin dollars in the sporran. She had lived in the bonny glen of Tomanthoulich—Cot, an ony of the vermint had come there, her father would hae wared a shot on them, and he could hit a buck within as mony measured yards as e'er a man of his clan. And the place here was sae quiet frae them—they durst na put their nose ower the gutter. Shanet owed nobody a bodle, put she couldna bide to see honest folk and pretty shentlemen pu'd away to prison whether they would or no; and then if Shanet was to lay the tangs ower ane of the ragamuffins' heads, it would be, maybe, that the law would gie it a hard name."

One thing I have learned in life,—never to speak sense when nonsense will answer the purpose as well. I should have had great difficulty to convince this practical and disinterested admirer and vindicator of liberty, that arrests seldom or never were to be seen in the streets of Edinburgh, and to satisfy her of their justice and necessity, would have been as difficult as to convert her to the Protestant faith. I therefore assured her my intention, if I could get a suitable habitation, was to remain in the quarter where she at present dwelt. Janet gave three skips on the floor, and uttered as many short shrill yells of joy; yet doubt almost instantly returned, and she insisted on knowing what possible reason I could have for making my residence where few lived, save those whose misfortunes drove them thither. It occurred to me to answer her by recounting the legend of the rise of my family, and of our deriving our name from a particular place near Holyrood Palace. This, which would have appeared to most people a very absurd reason for choosing a residence, was entirely satisfactory to Janet MacEvoy.

"Och, nae doubt! if it was the land of his fathers, there was nae mair to be said. Put it was queer that his family estate should just lie at the town tail, and covered with houses where the King's cows, Cot bless them hide and horn, used to craze upon. It was strange changes."— She mused a little, and then added, "Put it is something, Maister' Croftangry, when the changes is frae the field to the habited place, and not from the place of habitation to the desert; for Shanet, her nainsell, kent a glen where there were men as weel as there may be in Croftangry, and if there werena altogether sae mony of them, they were as good men in their tartan as the others in their broad-cloth. And there were houses too, and if they were not bigged with stane and lime, and lofted like the houses at Croftangry, yet they served the purpose of them that lived there; and mony a braw bonnet, and mony a silk snood, and comely white curch, would come out to carry to kirk or chapel on the Lord's day, and little bairns toddling after; and now, —Och, Och, Ohellany, Ohonari! the glen is desolate, and the braw snoods and bonnets are gane, and the Saxon's house stands tall and lonely, like the single bare-breasted rock that the falcon builds on— the falcon that drives the heath-bird frae the glen."

Janet, like many Highlanders, was of imagination all compact; and, when melancholy themes came upon her, expressed herself almost poetically, owing to the genius of the Celtic language in which she thought, and in which, doubtless, she would have spoken, had I understood the Gaelic. In two minutes the shade of gloom and regret had passed from her good-humoured features, and she was again the little busy, prating, important old woman, undisputed owner of one flat of a small tenement in the Abbey-yard, and about to be promoted to be housekeeper to an elderly bachelor gentleman, Chrystal Croft-angry, Esq.

It was not long before Janet's local researches found out exactly the sort of place I wanted, and there we settled. Janet was afraid I would not be satisfied, because it is not exactly part of Croftangry; but I stopped her doubts, by assuring her it had been part and pendicle thereof in my forefathers' time, which passed very well.

I do not intend to possess any one with an exact knowledge of my lodging; though, as Bobadil says, "I care not who knows it, since the cabin is convenient." But I may state in general, that it is a house *within itself*, or according to a newer phraseology in advertisements, *self-contained*, has a garden of near half an acre, and a patch of ground with trees in front. It boasts five rooms and servants' apartments— looks in front upon the palace, and behind upon the hill and crags of the King's Park. Fortunately the place had a name, which, with a little improvement, served to countenance the legend which I had imposed on Janet, and would not perhaps have been sorry if I had been able to impose on myself. It was called Littlecroft; we have dubbed it Little Croftangry, and the men of letters belonging to the Post Office have sanctioned the change, and deliver letters so addressed.

My establishment consists of Janet, an under maid-servant, and a Highland wench for Janet to exercise her Gaelic upon, with a handy lad who can lay the cloth, and take care besides of a pony, on which I find my way to the Portobello sands, especially when the cavalry have a drill; for, like an old fool as I am, I have not altogether become indifferent to the tramp of horses and the flash of weapons, of which, though no professional soldier, it has been my fate to see something in my youth. For wet mornings, I have my book—is it fine, I visit or I wander on the Crags as the humour dictates. My dinner is indeed solitary, yet not quite so neither; for though Andrew waits, Janet, or, —as she is to all the world but her master, and certain old Highland gossips,—Mrs MacEvoy, attends, bustles up and down to see everything is in first-rate order, and to tell me, Cot pless us, the wonderful news of the Palace for the day. When the cloth is removed, and I light my cigar, and begin to husband a pint of port, or a glass of old whisky and water, it is the rule of the house that Janet takes a chair at some distance, and nods or works her stocking, as she may be disposed; ready to speak, if I am in the talking humour, and sitting quiet as a mouse if I am rather inclined to study a book or the newspaper. At six precisely she makes my tea, and leaves me to drink it; and then occurs an interval of time which most old bachelors find heavy on their hands. The theatre is a good occasional resource, but it is distant, and so are one or two public societies to which I belong; besides, these are all incompatible with the elbow-chair feeling, which desires some employment that will divert the mind without fatiguing the body.

Under the influence of these impressions, I have sometimes thought of literary undertakings. I must have been the Bonassus himself to have mistaken myself for a genius, yet I have leisure and reflections like my neighbours. I am a borderer also between two generations, and can point out more perhaps than others of those fading traces of antiquity which are daily vanishing; and I know many a modern instance and many an old tradition, and therefore I ask—

> What ails me, I may not, as well as they,
> Rake up some thread-bare tales, that mouldering lay
> In chimney corners, wont by Christmas fires
> To read and rock to sleep our ancient sires?
> No man his threshold better knows, than I
> Brute's first arrival and first victory,
> Saint George's sorrel and his cross of blood,
> Arthur's round board and Caledonian wood.

No shop is so easily set up as an antiquary's. Like those of the lowest order of pawnbrokers, a commodity of rusty iron, a bag or two of hob-nails, a few odd shoebuckles, cashiered kail-pots, and fire-irons declared incapable of service, are quite sufficient to set him up. If he add a sheaf or two of penny ballads and broadsides, he is a great man—an extensive trader. And then—like the pawnbrokers afore-said, if he understands a little legerdemain, he may, by dint of a little picking and stealing, make the inside of his shop a great deal richer than the out, and be able to show you things which cause those who do not understand the antiquarian trick of clean conveyance, to wonder how the devil he came by them.

It may be said, that antiquarian articles interest but few customers, and we may bawl ourselves as rusty as the wares we deal in without any one asking the price of our merchandize. But I do not rest my hopes upon this department of my labours only. I propose also to have a corresponding shop for Sentiment, and Dialogues, and Disquisition, which may captivate the fancy of those who have no relish, as the established phrase goes, for pure antiquity;—a sort of green-grocer's stall erected in front of my ironmongery wares, garlanding the rusty memorial of ancient time with cresses, cabbages, leeks, and water purpy.

As I have some idea that I am writing too well to be understood, I humble myself to ordinary language, and avow, with becoming mod-esty, that I do think myself capable of sustaining a publication of a miscellaneous nature, as like to the Spectator, or the Guardian, the Mirror, or the Lounger, as my poor abilities may be able to accom-plish. Not that I had any purpose of imitating Johnson, whose general learning and power of expression I do not deny, but many of whose Ramblers are little better than a sort of pageant, where trite and obvious maxims are made to swagger in lofty and mystic language, and get some credit only because they are not easily understood. There are some of the Great Moralist's papers which I cannot peruse without thinking on a second-rate masquerade, where the best-known and least-esteemed characters in town march as heroes, and sultans, and so forth, and by dint of tawdry dresses, get some consideration until they are found out.—It is not, however, prudent to commence with throwing stones, just when I am striking out windows of my own.

I think even the local situation of Little Croftangry may be con-sidered as favourable to my undertaking. A nobler contrast there can hardly exist than that of the huge city, dark with the smoke of ages, and groaning with the various sounds of active industry or idle revel, and the lofty and craggy hill, silent and solitary as the grave—one exhibit-ing the full tide of existence, pressing and precipitating itself forward with the force of an inundation—the other resembling some time-worn anchorite, whose life passed as silent and uninvolved as the slender rill which escapes unheard, and scarce seen, from the fountain of his patron-saint. The city resembles the busy temple, where the modern Comus and Mammon hold their court, and thousands sacrifice ease, independence, and virtue itself, at their shrine; the misty and lonely mountain seems as a throne to the majestic but terrible Genius of feudal times, when he dispensed coronets and domains to those who had heads to devise, and arms to execute, bold enterprises.

I have, as it were, the two extremities of the moral world at my threshold. From the front door, a few minutes' walk brings me into the heart of a wealthy and populous city; as many paces from my opposite entrance, places me in a solitude as complete as Zimmerman could have desired. Surely with such aids to my imagination, I may write better than if I were in a lodging in the New Town, or a garret in the old. As the Spaniard says, "*Veamos—Caracco!*"

I have not chosen to publish periodically, my reason for which is twofold. In the first place, I don't like to be hurried, and have had enough of duns in an early part of my life, to make me reluctant to hear of, or see one, even in the less awful shape of a printer's devil. But, secondly, a periodical paper is not easily extended in circulation beyond the quarter in which it is published. This work, if published in fugitive numbers, would scarce, without a high pressure on the part of the booksellers, be raised above the Netherbow, and never could be expected to ascend to the level of Prince's Street. Now I am ambitious that my compositions, though having their origin in this Valley of Holyrood, should not only be extended into those exalted regions I have mentioned, but also that they should cross the Forth, astonish the Long Town of Kirkaldy, enchant the skippers and coalliers of the East of Fife, venture even into the classic arcades of St Andrews, and travel as much farther to the north as the breath of applause will carry their sails. As for a southward direction, it is not to be hoped for in my fondest dreams. I am informed that Scotch literature, like Scotch whisky, will be presently laid under a prohibitory duty.—But enough of this. If any reader is dull enough not to comprehend the advantages which, in point of circulation, a compact book has over a collection of fugitive numbers, let him try the range of a gun loaded with hail-shot, against that of the same piece charged with an equal weight of lead consolidated in a single bullet.

Besides, it was of less consequence that I should publish periodically, since I did not mean to solicit or accept of the contributions of friends, or the criticisms of those who may be less kindly disposed.

Notwithstanding the excellent examples which might be quoted, I will establish no begging-box, either under the name of a lion's-head or an ass's. What is good or ill shall be mine own, or the contribution of friends to whom I may have private access. Many of my voluntary assistants might be cleverer than myself, and then I would have a brilliant article appear among my chiller effusions, like a patch of lace on a Scotch cloak of Galashiels grey. Some might be worse, and then I must reject them, to the injury of the feelings of the writer, or else insert them, to make my own darkness yet more opaque and palpable. "Let every herring," says our old-fashioned proverb, "hang by his own head."

One person, however, I may distinguish, as she is now no more, who, living to the utmost term of human life, honoured me with a great share of her friendship, as indeed we were blood-relatives in the Scottish sense—Heaven knows how many degrees removed—and friends in the sense of Old England. I mean the late excellent and regretted Mrs Bethune Baliol. But as I design this admirable picture of the olden time for a principal character in my work, I will only say here, that she knew and approved of my present purpose; and though she declined to contribute to it while she lived, from a sense of dignified retirement, which she thought became her age, sex, and condition in life, she left me some materials for carrying on my proposed work, which I coveted when I heard her detail them in conversation, and which now, when I have their substance in her own handwriting, I account far more valuable than anything I have myself to offer. I hope the mentioning her name in conjunction with my own, will give no offence to any of her numerous friends, as it was her own express pleasure that I should employ the manuscripts, which she did me the honour to bequeath me, in the manner in which I have now used them. It must be added, however, that in most cases I have disguised names, and in some have added shading and colouring to bring out the narrative.

Many of my materials, besides these, are derived from friends, living or dead. In some cases they may be inaccurate, and in such I shall be happy to receive, from sufficient authority, the correction of the errors which must creep into traditional documents. The object of the whole publication is, to throw some light on the manners of Scotland as they were, and to contrast them, occasionally, with such as now are fashionable in the same country. For my own serious opinion—it is in favour of the present age in many respects, but not in so far as it affords means for exercising the imagination, or exciting the interest which attaches to other times. I am glad to be a writer or a reader in 1826, but I would be most interested in reading or relating what

happened from half a century to a century before. We have the best of
it. Scenes in which our ancestors thought deeply, acted fiercely, and
died desperately, are to us tales to divert the tedium of a winter's
evening, when we are engaged to no party, or beguile a summer's
morning, when it is too scorching to ride or walk.

Yet I do not mean that my essays and narratives should be limited to
Scotland. I pledge myself to no particular line of subjects; but, on the
contrary, say with Burns,

> Perhaps it may turn out a sang,
> Perhaps turn out a sermon.

I have only to add, by way of postscript to these preliminary chapters,
that I have had recourse to Molière's receipt, and read my manuscript
over to my old woman, Janet MacEvoy.

The dignity of being consulted delighted Janet; and Wilkie, or
Allan, would have made a capital sketch of her, as she sate upright
in her chair, instead of her ordinary lounging posture, knitting her
stocking systematically, as if she meant every twist of her thread,
and inclination of the wires, to bear burden to the cadence of my
voice. I am afraid, too, that I myself felt more delight than I ought
to have done in my own composition, and read a little more orator-
ically than I would have ventured to do before an auditor, of whose
applause I was not so secure. And the result did not entirely encourage my plan of censorship. Janet did indeed seriously incline to the
account of my previous life, and bestowed some Highland maledictions more emphatic than courteous on Christie Steele for her
reception of a "shentlemans in distress," and of her own mistress's
house too. I omitted, for certain reasons, or greatly abridged, what
related to herself. But when I came to treat of my general views
of publication, I saw poor Janet was entirely thrown out, though,
like a jaded hunter, panting, puffing, and short of wind, she endeavoured at least to keep up with the chase. Or rather her perplexity
made her look all the while like a deaf person ashamed of his infirm-
ity, who does not understand a word you are saying, yet desires you
to believe that he does understand you, and who is extremely jealous
that you suspect his incapacity. When she saw that some remark
was necessary, she resembled exactly in her criticism the devotee
who pitched on the "sweet word Mesopotamia," as the most edifying
note which she could bring away from a sermon. She indeed hastened to bestow general praise on what she said was all "fery fine."
But she chiefly dwelt on what I had said about Mr Timmerman,
as she was pleased to call the German philosopher who wrote upon
Solitude, and supposed he must be of the same descent with the
Highland clan of McIntyre, which signifies Son of the Carpenter.

"And a fery honourable name too—Shanet's own mither was a McIntyre."

In short, it was plain the latter part of my introduction was altogether lost on poor Janet; and so, to have acted up to Molière's system, I should have cancelled the whole, and written it anew. But I do not know how it is; I retained, I suppose, some tolerable opinion of my own composition, though Janet did not comprehend it, and felt loath to retrench those delilahs of the imagination, as Dryden called them, the tropes and figures of which are caviar to the multitude. Besides, I hate the re-writing, as much as Falstaff did the paying back—it is a double labour. So I determined with myself to consult Janet, in future, only on such things as were within the limits of her comprehension, and hazard my arguments and my rhetoric on the public without her imprimatur. I am pretty sure she will "applaud it done." And in such narratives as come within her range of thought and feeling, I will, as I at first intended, take the benefit of her unsophisticated judgment, and attend to it deferentially—that is, when it happens not to be in peculiar opposition to my own; for, after all, I say with Almanzor—

> Know that I alone am king of me.

The reader has now my who and my whereabout, the purpose of the work, and the circumstances under which it is undertaken. He has also a specimen of the author's talents, and may judge for himself, and proceed, or send back the volume to the bookseller, as his own taste shall determine.

Chapter Six

> The moon, were she earthly, no nobler.
> *Coriolanus*

WHEN WE SET OUT on the jolly voyage of life, what a brave fleet there is around us, as stretching our fresh canvass to the breeze, all "ship-shape and Bristol fashion," pennants flying, music playing, cheering each other as we pass, we are rather amused than alarmed when some awkward comrade goes right ashore for want of pilotage! —Alas! when the voyage is well spent, and we look around us, toil-worn mariners, how few of our ancient consorts still remain in sight, and they, how torn and wasted, and, like ourselves, struggling to keep as long as possible off the fatal shore, against which we are all finally drifting!

I felt this very trite yet melancholy truth in all its force the other day, when a packet with a black seal arrived, containing a letter addressed to me by my late excellent friend Mrs Martha Bethune Baliol, and marked with the fatal indorsation, "To be delivered according to address, after I shall be no more." A letter from her executors accompanied the packet, mentioning that they had found in her will a bequest to me of a painting of some value, which she stated would just fit the space above my cupboard, and fifty guineas to buy a ring. And thus I separated, with all the kindness which we had maintained for many years, from a friend, who, though old enough to have been the companion of my mother, was yet, in gaiety of spirits, and admirable sweetness of temper, capable of being agreeable, and even fascinating society, for those who write themselves in the vaward of youth; an advantage which I have lost for these five-and-thirty years. The contents of the packet I had no difficulty in guessing, and have partly hinted at them in the last chapter. But to instruct the reader in the particulars, and at the same time to indulge myself with recalling the virtues and agreeable qualities of my late friend, I will give a short sketch of her manners and habits.

Mrs Martha Bethune Baliol was a person of quality and fortune, as these are estimated in Scotland. Her family was ancient, and her connexions honourable. She was not fond of specially indicating her exact age, but her juvenile recollections stretched backward till before the eventful year 1745; and she remembered the Highland clans being in possession of the Scottish capital, though probably only as an indistinct vision. Her fortune, independent by her father's bequest, was rendered opulent by the death of more than one brave brother, who fell successively in the service of the country; so that the family estates became vested in the only surviving child of the ancient house of Bethune Baliol. My intimacy was formed with the excellent lady after this event, and when she was already something advanced in age.

She inhabited, when in Edinburgh, where she regularly spent the winter season, one of those old hotels, which, till of late, were to be found in the neighbourhood of the Canongate, and of the Palace of Holyrood-house, and which, separated from the street, now dirty and vulgar, by paved courts, and gardens of some extent, made amends for an indifferent access, by showing something of aristocratic state and seclusion, when you were once admitted within their precincts. They have pulled her house down; for, indeed, betwixt building and burning, every ancient monument of the Scottish capital is now like to be utterly demolished. I pause on the recollections of the place, however; and since nature has denied a pencil when she placed a pen in my hand, I will endeavour to make words answer the purpose of delineation.

Baliol's Lodging, so was the mansion named, reared its high stack of chimneys, among which were seen a turret or two, and one of those small projecting platforms called balconies, above the mean and modern buildings which line the south side of the Canongate, towards the lower end of that street, and not distant from the palace. A *porte cochère*, having a wicket for foot passengers, was, upon due occasion, unfolded by a lame old man, tall, grave, and thin, who tenanted a hovel beside the gate, and acted as porter. To this office he had been promoted partly by my friend's charitable feelings for an old soldier, and partly by an idea, that his head, which was a very fine one, bore some resemblance to that of Garrick in the character of Lusignan. He was a man saturnine, silent, and slow in his proceedings, and would never open the *porte cochère* to a hackney coach; indicating the wicket with his finger, as the proper passage for all who came in that obscure vehicle, which was not permitted to degrade with its ticketed presence the dignity of Baliol's Lodging. I do not think this peculiarity would have met with his lady's approbation, any more than the occasional partiality of Lusignan, or, as mortals called him, Archie MacReady, to a dram. But Mrs Martha Bethune Baliol, conscious that, in case of conviction, she could never have prevailed upon herself to dethrone the King of Palestine from the stone bench on which he sat for hours, knitting his stocking, refused, by accrediting the intelligence, even to put him upon his trial; well judging, that he would observe more wholesome caution if he conceived his character unsuspected, than if he were detected, and suffered to pass unpunished. For after all, she said, it would be cruel to dismiss an old Highland soldier, for a peccadillo so appropriate to his country and profession.

The stately gate for carriages, or the humble accommodation for foot-passengers, admitted into a narrow and short passage, running between two rows of lime-trees, whose green foliage, during the spring, contrasted strangely with the swart complexion of the two walls by the side of which they grew. This access led to the front of the house, which was formed by two gable ends, notched, and having their windows adorned with heavy architectural ornaments. They joined each other at right angles; and a half circular tower, which contained the entrance and the staircase, occupied the point of junction, and rounded off the acute angle. The other two sides of the little court, in which there was just sufficient room to turn a carriage, were occupied, one by some low buildings answering the purpose of offices; the other, by a parapet surmounted by a highly-ornamented iron railing, twined round with honey-suckle and other parasitical shrubs, which permitted the eye to peep into a pretty suburban garden, extending down to the road called the South Back of the Canongate, and boasting a number of old trees, many flowers, and even some fruit. We must not forget to state, that the extreme cleanliness of the entrance and court-yard was such as intimated that mop and pail had done the utmost in that favoured spot, to atone for the general dirt and dinginess of the quarter where the premises were situated.

Over the doorway were the arms of Bethune and Baliol, with various other devices carved in stone. The door itself was studded with iron nails, and formed of black oak; an iron rasp,* as it was called, was placed on it, instead of a knocker, for the purpose of summoning the attendants. He who usually appeared at the summons was a smart lad, in a handsome livery, the son of Mrs Martha's gardener at Mount Baliol. Now and then a servant girl, nicely but plainly dressed, and fully accoutred with stockings and shoes, would perform this duty; and twice or thrice I remember being admitted by Beauffet himself, whose exterior looked as much like that of a clergyman of rank as the butler of a gentleman's family. He had been valet-de-chambre to the last Sir Richard Bethune Baliol, and was a person highly trusted by the present lady. A full stand, as it is called in Scotland, of garments of a dark colour, gold buckles in his shoes, and at the knees of his breeches, with his hair regularly dressed and powdered, announced him to be a domestic of trust and importance. His mistress used to say of him,

> He's sad and civil,
> And suits well for a servant with my fortunes.

As no one can escape scandal, some said that Beauffet made a rather better thing of the place than the modesty of his old-fashioned wages would, unassisted, have made it amount to. But the man was always very civil to me. He had been long in the family; had enjoyed legacies, and laid by a something of his own, upon which he now enjoys ease with dignity, in as far as his newly-married wife, Tibbie Shortacres, will permit him.

The Lodging—Dearest reader, if you are tired, pray pass over the next four or five pages—was not by any means so large as its external appearance led people to conjecture. The interior accommodation was much cut up with cross walls and long passages, and that neglect of economizing space which characterizes old Scottish architecture. But there was far more room than my old friend required, even when she had, as was often the case, four or five young cousins under her protection; and I believe much of the house was shut up. Mrs Bethune Baliol never, in my presence, showed herself so much offended, as once with a meddling person who advised her to have the windows of these supernumerary apartments built up, to save the tax. She said in ire, that, while she lived, the light of God should visit the house of her fathers; and while she had a penny, king and country should have their

* See CHAMBERS's Traditions of Edinburgh.

due. Indeed, she was punctiliously loyal, even in that most staggering test of loyalty, the payment of imposts. Mr Beauffet told me he was ordered to offer a glass of wine to the person who collected the income tax, and that the poor man was so overcome by a reception so unwontedly generous, that he had wellnigh fainted on the spot.

You entered by a matted anteroom into the eating parlour, filled with old-fashioned furniture, and hung with family portraits, which, excepting one of Sir Bernard Bethune, in James the Sixth's time, said to be by Jameson, were exceedingly frightful. A saloon, as it was called, a long narrow chamber, led out of the dining-parlour, and served for a drawing-room. It was a pleasant apartment, looking out upon the south flank of Holyrood-house, the gigantic slope of Arthur's Seat, and the girdle of lofty rocks, called Salisbury Crags, objects so rudely wild, that the mind can hardly conceive them to exist in the vicinage of a populous metropolis. The paintings in the saloon came from abroad, and had some of them much merit. To see the best of them, however, you must be admitted into the very pene-tralia of the temple, and allowed to draw the tapestry at the upper end of the saloon, and enter Mrs Martha's own special dressing-room. This was a charming apartment, of which it would be difficult to describe the form, it had so many recesses which were filled up with shelves of ebony, and cabinets of japan and *or moulu;* some for holding books, of which Mrs Martha had an admirable collection, some for a display of ornamental china, others for shells and similar curiosities. In a little niche, half screened by a curtain of crimson silk, was disposed a suit of tilting armour of bright steel, inlaid with silver, which had been worn on some memorable occasion by Sir Bernard Bethune, already mentioned; while over the canopy of the niche, hung the broad-sword with which her father had attempted to change the fortunes of Britain in 1715, and the spontoon which her elder brother bore when he was leading on a company of the Black Watch at Fontenoy.

There were some Italian and Flemish pictures of admitted authen-ticity, a few genuine bronzes and other objects of curiosity, which her brothers or herself had picked up while abroad. In short, it was a place where the idle were tempted to become studious, the studious to grow idle—where the grave might find matter to make them gay, and the gay subjects for gravity.

That it might maintain some title to its name, I must not forget to say, that the lady's dressing-room exhibited a superb mirror, framed in silver filigree work; a beautiful toilette, the cover of which was of Flanders lace; and a set of boxes corresponding in materials and work to the frame of the mirror.

This dressing apparatus, however, was mere matter of parade: Mrs Martha Bethune Baliol always went through the actual duties of the toilette in an inner apartment, which corresponded with her sleeping-room by a small detached stair-case. There were, I believe, more than one of those *turnpike stairs*, as they were called, about the house, by which the public rooms, all of which entered through each other, were accommodated with separate and independent modes of access.

In the little boudoir we have described, Mrs Martha Bethune Baliol had her choicest meetings. She kept early hours; and if you went in the morning, you must not reckon that space of day as extending beyond three o'clock, or four at the utmost. These vigilant habits were attended with some restraint on her visitors, but they were indemnified by always finding the best society, and the best information, which was to be had for the day in the Scottish capital. Without at all affecting the blue stocking, she liked books—they amused her and if the authors were persons of character, she thought she owed them a debt of civility, which she loved to discharge by personal kindness. When she gave dinner to a small party, which she did now and then, she had the good-nature to look for, and the good luck to discover, what sort of people suited each other best, and chose her company as Duke Theseus did his hounds,

> ——matched in mouth like bells,
> Each under each,

so that every guest could take his part in the cry; instead of one mighty Tom of a fellow, like Dr Johnson, silencing all besides by the tremendous depth of his diapason. On such occasions she afforded *chère exquise;* and every now and then there was some dish of French, or even Scottish derivation, which, as well as the numerous assortment of *vins extraordinaires* produced by Mr Beauffet, gave a sort of antique and foreign air to the entertainment, which rendered it more interesting.

It was a great thing to be invited to such parties, and not less so to be invited to the early *conversazione*, which, in spite of fashion, by dint of the best coffee, the finest tea, and *chasse café* that would have called the dead to life, she contrived now and then to assemble in her saloon already mentioned, at the unnatural hour of eight in the evening. On such occasions, the cheerful old lady seemed to enjoy herself so much in the happiness of her guests, that they exerted themselves in turn to prolong her amusement and their own; and a certain charm was excited around, seldom to be met with in parties of pleasure, and which was founded on the general desire of every one present to contribute something to the common amusement.

But although it was a great privilege to be admitted to wait on my excellent friend in the morning, or to be invited to her dinner or her evening parties, I prized still higher the right which I had acquired, by old acquaintance, of visiting Baliol's Lodging, upon the chance of finding its venerable inhabitant preparing for tea, just about six o'clock in the evening. It was only to two or three old friends that she permitted this freedom, nor was this sort of chance-party ever allowed to extend itself beyond five in number. The answer to those who came later, announced that the company was full for the evening; which had the double effect, of making those who waited on Mrs Bethune Baliol in this unceremonious manner punctual in observing her hour, and of adding the zest of a little difficulty to the enjoyment of the party.

It more frequently happened that only one or two persons partook of this refreshment on the same evening, when in the former case and supposing the individual a gentleman, Mrs Martha, though she did not hesitate to admit him to her boudoir, after the privilege of the French and the old Scottish school, took care, as she used to say, to preserve all possible propriety, by commanding the attendance of her principal female attendant, Mrs Alice Lambskin, who might, from the gravity and dignity of her appearance, have sufficed to matronize a whole boarding-school, instead of one maiden lady of eighty and upwards. As the weather permitted, Mrs Alice sate duly remote from the company in a fauteuil behind the projecting chimney-piece, or in the embrasure of a window, and prosecuted in Carthusian silence, with indefatigable zeal, a piece of embroidery, which seemed no bad emblem of eternity.

But I have neglected all this while to introduce my friend herself to the reader, at least so far as words can convey the peculiarities by which her appearance and conversation were distinguished.

A little woman, with ordinary features and an ordinary form, and hair which in youth had no decided colour, we may believe Mrs Martha, when she said herself she was never remarkable for personal charms; a modest admission, which was readily confirmed by certain old ladies, her contemporaries, who, whatever may have been the youthful advantages which they more than hinted had been formerly their own share, were now, in personal appearance, as well as in everything else, far inferior to my accomplished friend. Mrs Martha's features had been of a kind which might be said to wear well; their irregularity was now of little consequence, animated as they were by the vivacity of her conversation; her teeth were excellent, and her eyes, although inclining to grey, were lively, laughing, and undimmed by time. A slight shade of complexion, more brilliant than her years promised, subjected my friend amongst strangers to the suspicion of having stretched her foreign habits as far as the prudent touch of the rouge. But it was a calumny; for when telling or listening to an interesting and affecting story, I have seen her colour come and go as if it played on the cheek of eighteen.

Her hair, whatever its former deficiencies, was now the most beautiful white that time could bleach, and was disposed with some degree of pretension, though in the simplest manner possible, so as to appear neatly smoothed under a cap of Flanders lace, of an old-fashioned, but, as I thought, a very handsome form, which undoubtedly has a name, and I would endeavour to recur to it, if I thought it would make my description a bit more intelligible. I think I have heard her say these favourite caps had been her mother's, and had come in fashion with a peculiar kind of wig used by the gentlemen about the time of the battle of Ramillies. The rest of her dress was always rather costly and distinguished, especially in the evening. A silk or satin gown of some colour becoming her age, and of a form, which, though complying to a certain degree with the present fashion, had always a reference to some more distant period, was garnished with triple ruffles; her shoes had diamond buckles, and were raised a little at heel, an advantage which, possessed in her youth, she alleged her size would not permit her to forego in her old age. She always wore rings, bracelets, and other ornaments of value, either for the materials or the workmanship; nay, perhaps she was a little profuse in this species of display. But she wore them as subordinate matters, to which the habits of moving constantly in high life had rendered her indifferent. She wore them because her rank required it, and thought no more of them as articles of finery, than a gentleman dressed for dinner thinks on his clean linen and well-brushed coat, the consciousness of which embarrasses the rustic beau of a Sunday.

Now and then, however, if a gem or ornament chanced to be noticed for its beauty or singularity, the observation usually led the way to an entertaining account of the manner in which it had been acquired, or the person from whom it had descended to its present possessor. On such and similar occasions my old friend spoke willingly, which is not uncommon, but she also, which is more rare, spoke remarkably well, and had in her little narratives concerning foreign parts, or former days, which formed an interesting part of her conversation, the singular art of dismissing all the usual protracted tautology respecting time, place, and circumstance, which is apt to settle like a mist upon the cold and languid tales of age, and at the same time of bringing forward, dwelling upon, and illustrating, those incidents and characters which give point and interest to the story.

She had, as we have hinted, travelled a good deal in foreign countries; for a brother, to whom she was much attached, had been sent upon various missions of national importance to the continent, and she had more than once embraced the opportunity of accompanying him. This furnished a great addition to the information which she could supply, especially during the last war, when the continent was for so many years hermetically sealed against the English nation. But, besides, Mrs Bethune Baliol visited distant countries, not as is the modern fashion, when the English travel in caravans together, and see in France and Italy little besides the same society which they might have enjoyed at home. On the contrary, she mingled when abroad with the natives of those countries she visited, and enjoyed at once the advantage of their society, and the pleasure of comparing it with that of Britain.

In the course of her becoming habituated with foreign manners, Mrs Bethune Baliol had, perhaps, acquired some slight tincture of them herself. Yet I was always persuaded, that the peculiar vivacity of look and manner—the pointed and appropriate action with which she accompanied what she said—the use of the gold and gemmed *taba-tière*, or rather I should say *bonbonnière*, (for she took no snuff, and the little box contained only a few pieces of candied angelica, or some such lady-like sweetmeat,) were of real old-fashioned Scottish growth, and such as might have graced the tea-table of Susannah, Countess of Eglinton, the patroness of Allan Ramsay, and of the Hon. Mrs Colonel Ogilvy, who was another mirror by whom the maidens of Auld Reekie were required to dress themselves. Although well acquainted with the customs of other countries, her manners had been chiefly formed in her own, at a time when great folks lived within little space, and when the distinguished names of the highest society gave to Edinburgh the *éclat*, which we now endeavour to derive from the unbounded expense and extended circle of our pleasures.

I was more confirmed in this opinion, by the peculiarity of the dialect which Mrs Baliol used. It was Scottish, decidedly Scottish, often containing phrases and words little used in the present day. But then her tone and mode of pronunciation were as different from the usual accent of the ordinary Scotch *patois*, as the accent of St James's is from that of Billingsgate. The vowels were not pronounced much broader than in the Italian language, and there was none of the disagreeable drawl which is so offensive to southern ears. In short, it seemed to be the Scottish as spoken by the ancient court of Scotland, to which no idea of vulgarity could be attached; and the lively manner and gestures with which it was accompanied, were so completely in accord with the sound of the voice and the manner of talking, that I cannot assign them a different origin. In long derivation, perhaps the manners of the Scottish court might have been originally formed on that of France, to which it had certainly some affinity; but I will live and die in the belief, that those of Mrs Baliol, as pleasing as they were peculiar, came to her by direct descent from the high dames who anciently adorned with their presence the royal halls of Holyrood.

This was a subject on which my mind was so much made up, that when I heard her carry her descriptions of manners far back beyond her own time, and describe how Fletcher of Salton spoke, how Graham of Claverhouse danced, what were the jewels worn by the famous Duchess of Lauderdale, and how she came by them, I could not help telling her I thought her some fairy, who cheated us by retaining the appearance of a mortal of our own day, when, in fact, she had witnessed the revolutions of centuries. She was very much diverted when I required her to take some solemn oath that she had not danced at the balls given by Mary of Este, when her unhappy husband occupied Holyrood in a species of honourable banishment;—or asked, whether she did not recollect Charles the Second, when he came to Scotland in 1650, and did not possess some slight recollections of the bold usurper, who had driven him beyond the Forth.

"*Beau cousin*," she said, laughing, "none of these do I remember personally; but you must know that there has been wonderfully little change in my natural temper from youth to age. From which it follows, cousin, that being even now something too young in spirit for the years which Time has marked me in his calendar, I was, when a girl, a little too old for those of my own standing, and as much inclined at that period to keep the society of elder persons, as I am now disposed to admit the company of gay young fellows of fifty or sixty like yourself, rather than collect about me all the octogenarians. Now, although I do not actually come from Elfland, and therefore cannot boast any personal knowledge of the great personages you inquire about, yet I have seen and heard those who knew them well, and who have given me as distinct an account of them as I could give you myself of the Empress Queen, or Frederick of Prussia—And I will frankly add," said she, laughing and offering her *bonbonnière*, "that I *have* heard so much of the years which immediately succeeded the Revolution, that I sometimes am apt to confuse the vivid descriptions fixed on my memory by the frequent and animated recitation of others, for things which I myself have actually witnessed. I caught myself but yesterday describing to Lord M—— the riding of the last Scottish Parliament, with as much minuteness as if I had seen it, as my mother did, from the balcony in front of Lord Moray's Lodging in the Canongate."

"I am sure you must have given Lord M—— a high treat."

"I treated him to a hearty laugh, I believe," she replied; "but it is you, you vile seducer of youth, who lead me into such follies. But I will be on my guard against my own weakness. I do not well know if the Wandering Jew is supposed to have a wife, but I should be sorry a decent middle-aged Scottish gentlewoman should be confused with such a supernatural person."

"For all that, I must torture you a little more, *ma belle cousine*, with my interrogatories; for how shall I ever turn author unless on the strength of the information which you have so often promised me upon the ancient state of manners?"

"Stay, I cannot allow you to give your points of inquiry a name so very venerable, if I am expected to answer them—ancient is a term for antediluvians. You may catechise me about the battle of Flodden, or ask particulars about Bruce and Wallace, under pretext of curiosity after ancient manners; and that last subject would wake my Baliol blood, you know."

"Well, but, Mrs Baliol, suppose we settle our æra—You do not call the accession of James the Sixth to the kingdom of Britain very ancient?"

"Umph!—no, cousin, I think I could tell you more of that than folks now-a-days remember,—for instance, that as James was trooping towards England, bag and baggage, his journey was stopped near Cockenzie by meeting the funeral of the Earl of Winton, the old and faithful servant and follower of his ill-fated mother, poor Mary! It was an ill omen for the *infare*, and so was seen of it, cousin."

I did not choose to prosecute this subject, well knowing Mrs Bethune Baliol did not like to be much pressed on the subject of the Stuarts, whose misfortunes she pitied, the rather that her father had espoused their cause. And yet her attachment to the present dynasty being very sincere, and even ardent, more especially as her family had served his late Majesty both in peace and war, she experienced a little embarrassment in reconciling her opinions respecting the exiled family, with those she entertained for the present. In fact, like many an old Jacobite, she was contented to be somewhat inconsistent on the subject, comforting herself, that *now* everything stood as it ought to do, and that there was no use in looking back narrowly on the right or wrong of the matter half a century ago.

"The Highlands," I suggested, "should furnish you with ample subjects of recollection. You have witnessed the complete change of that primeval country, and have seen a race not far removed from the earliest period of society, melted down into the great mass of civilization; and that could not happen without incidents striking in themselves, and curious as chapters in the history of the human race."

"It is very true," said Mrs Baliol; "one would think it should have struck the observers greatly, and yet it scarcely did so. For me, I was no Highlander myself, and the Highland chiefs of old, of whom I certainly knew several, had little in their manners to distinguish them from the Lowland gentry, when they mixed in society in Edinburgh, and assumed the Lowland dress. Their peculiar character was for the clansmen at home; and you must not imagine that they swaggered about in plaids and broadswords at the Cross, or came to the Assembly-Rooms in bonnets and kilts."

"I remember," said I, "that Swift, in his Journal, tells Stella he had dined in the house of a Scotch nobleman, with two Highland chiefs, whom he had found as well-bred men as he had ever met with."

"Very likely," said my friend. "The extremes of society approach much more closely to each other than perhaps the Dean of Saint Patrick's expected. The savage is always to a certain degree polite. Besides, going always armed, and having a very punctilious idea of their own gentility and consequence, they usually behaved to each other and to the Lowlanders, with a good deal of formal politeness, which sometimes even procured them the character of insincerity."

"Falsehood belongs to an early period of society, as well as the deferential forms which we style politeness," I replied. "A child does not see the least moral beauty in truth, until he has been flogged half-a-dozen times. It is so easy, and apparently so natural, to deny what you cannot be easily convicted of, that a savage as well as a child lies to excuse himself, almost as instinctively as he raises his hand to protect his head. The old saying, 'confess and be hanged,' carries much argument in it. I observed a remark the other day in old Birrel. He mentions that MacGregor of Glenstrae and some of his people had surrendered themselves to one of the Earls of Argyle, upon the express condition that they should be conveyed safe into England. The Maccallan Mhor of the day kept the word of promise, but it was only to the ear. He indeed sent his captives to Berwick, where they had an airing on the other side of the Tweed but it was under the custody of a strong guard, by whom they were brought back to Edinburgh, and delivered to the executioner. This, Birrel calls keeping a Highlandman's promise."

"Well," replied Mrs Baliol, "I might add, that many of the Highland chiefs whom I knew in former days had been brought up in France, which might improve their politeness, though perhaps it did not amend their insincerity. But considering, that, belonging to the depressed and defeated faction in the state, they were compelled sometimes to use dissimulation, you must set their uniform fidelity to their friends against their occasional falsehood to their enemies, and then you will not judge poor John Highlandman too severely. They were in a state of society where bright lights are strongly contrasted with deep shadows."

"It is to that point I would bring you, *ma belle cousine*,—and therefore they are most proper subjects for composition."

"And you want to turn composer, my good friend, and set my old tales to some popular tune? But there have been too many composers, if that be the word, in the field before. The Highlands *were* indeed a rich mine; but they have, I think, been fairly wrought out, as a good tune is grinded into vulgarity when it descends to the hurdy-gurdy and the barrel-organ."

"If it be a real good tune," I replied, "it will recover its better qualities when it gets into the hands of better artists."

"Umph!" said Mrs Baliol, tapping her box, "we are happy in our own good opinion this evening, Mr Croftangry. And so you think you can restore the gloss to the tartan, which it has lost by being dragged through so many fingers?"

"With your assistance to procure materials, my dear lady, much, I think, may be done."

"Well—I must do my best, I suppose; though all I know about the Gael is but of little consequence—Indeed, I gathered it chiefly from Donald MacLeish."

"And who might Donald MacLeish be?"

"Neither bard nor seannachie, I assure you, nor monk nor hermit, the approved authorities for old traditions. Donald was as good a postilion as ever drove a chaise and pair between Glencroe and Inverary. I assure you, when I give you my Highland anecdotes, you will hear much of Donald MacLeish. He was Alice Lambskin's beau and mine through a long Highland tour."

"But when am I to see these anecdotes?—you answer me as Harley did poor Prior—

> Let that be done which Mat doth say.
> 'Yea,' quoth the Earl, 'but not to-day.'"

"Well, *mon beau cousin*, if you begin to remind me of my cruelty, I must remind you it has struck nine on the Abbey clock, and it is time you were going home to Little Croftangry. For my promise, be assured, I will one day keep it to the utmost extent. It shall not be a Highlandman's promise, as your old citizen calls it."

I by this time suspected the purpose of my friend's procrastination; and it saddened my heart to reflect that I was not to get the information which I desired, excepting in the shape of a legacy. I found accordingly, in the packet transmitted to me after the excellent lady's death, several anecdotes respecting the Highlands, from which I have selected that which follows, chiefly on account of its possessing great power over the feelings of my critical housekeeper, Janet MacEvoy, who wept most bitterly when I read it over to her.

It is, however, but a very simple tale, and may have no interest for persons beyond Janet's rank of life or character or understanding.

Chapter Seven

The Highland Widow

It moaned as near as near could be,
But what it is she cannot tell;
On the other side it seemed to be,
Of the huge broad-breasted old oak tree.
COLERIDGE

MRS BETHUNE BALIOL'S memorandum begins thus:—

It is five and thirty, or perhaps nearer forty years ago, since, to relieve the dejection of spirits occasioned by a great family loss sustained two or three months before, I undertook what was called the short Highland tour. This had become in some degree fashionable; but though the military roads were excellent, yet the accommodation was so indifferent that it was reckoned a little adventure to accomplish it. Besides, the Highlands, though now as peaceable as any part of King George's dominions, was a sound which still carried terror, while so many survived who had witnessed the insurrection of 1745; and a vague idea of fear was impressed on many, as they looked from the towers of Stirling northward to the huge chain of mountains, which rises like a dusky rampart to conceal in its recesses a people, whose dress, manners, and language, differed still very much from those of their Lowland countrymen. For my part, I come of a race not greatly subject to apprehensions arising from imagination only. I had some Highland relatives, knew several of their families of distinction; and, excepting the company of my bower-maiden Mistress Alice Lambskin, I went on my journey fearless, though without an escort.

But then I had a guide and cicerone, almost equal to Greatheart in the Pilgrim's Progress, in no less a person than Donald MacLeish, the postilion whom I hired at Stirling, with a pair of able-bodied horses, as steady as Donald himself, to drag my carriage, my duenna, and myself, wheresoever it was my pleasure to go.

Donald MacLeish was one of a race of post-boys, whom, I suppose, mail-coaches and steam-boats have put out of fashion. They were to be found chiefly at Perth, Stirling, or Glasgow, where they and their horses were usually hired by travellers, or tourists, to accomplish such journeys of business or pleasure as they might have to perform in the land of the Gael. This class of persons approached to the character of what is called abroad a *conducteur;* or might be compared to the sailing-master on board a British ship of war, who follows out after his own manner the course which the captain commands him to observe. You explained to your postilion the length of your tour, and the objects you were desirous it should embrace; and you found him perfectly competent to fix the places of rest or refreshment, with due attention that those should be chosen with reference to your convenience, and to any points of interest which you might desire to visit.

The qualifications of such a person were necessarily much superior to those of the "first ready," who gallops thrice a-day over the same ten miles. Donald MacLeish, besides being quite alert at repairing all ordinary accidents to his horses and carriage, and in making shift to support them, where forage was scarce, with such substitutes as bannocks and cakes, where the raw oats were not to be had, was likewise a man of intellectual resources. He had acquired a general knowledge of the traditional stories of the country which he had traversed so often; and, if encouraged, (for Donald was a man of the most decorous reserve,) he would willingly point out to you the site of the principal clan-battles, and recount the most remarkable legends by which the road, and the objects which occurred in travelling it, had been distinguished. There was some originality in the man's habits of thinking and expressing himself, his turn for legendary lore strangely contrasting with a portion of the knowing shrewdness belonging to his actual occupation, which made his conversation amuse the way well enough.

Add to this, Donald knew all his peculiar duties in the country which he traversed so frequently. He could tell, to a day, when they would "be killing" lamb at Tyndrum or Glenuilt; so that the stranger would have some chance of being fed like a Christian; and knew to a mile the last village where it was possible to procure a wheaten loaf, for the comfort of those who were little familiar with the Land of Cakes. He was acquainted with the road every mile, and could tell to an inch which side of a Highland bridge was passable, which decidedly dangerous.* In short, Donald MacLeish was not only our faithful attendant and steady servant, but our humble and obliging friend; and though I have known the half-classical cicerone of Italy, the talkative French valet-de-place, and even the muleteer of Spain, who piques himself on being a maize-eater, and whose honour is not to be

---

* This is, or was at least, a necessary accomplishment. In one of the most beautiful districts of the Highlands was, not many years since, a bridge bearing this startling caution, "Keep to the right side, the left being dangerous."

questioned without danger, I do not think I have ever had so sensible and intelligent a guide.

Our motions were of course under Donald's direction; and it frequently happened, when the weather was serene, that we preferred halting to rest his horses even where there was no established stage, and taking our refreshment under a crag, from which leaped a waterfall, or beside the verge of a fountain, enamelled with verdant turf and wild flowers. Donald had an eye for such spots, and though he had, I dare say, never read Gil Blas or Don Quixote, yet he chose such halting-places as Le Sage or Cervantes would have described. Very often, as he observed the pleasure I took in conversing with the country people, he would manage to fix our place of rest near a cottage where there was some old Gael, whose broadsword had blazed at Falkirk or Preston, and who seemed the frail yet faithful record of times which had passed away. Or he would contrive to quarter us, as far as a cup of tea went, upon the hospitality of some parish minister of worth and intelligence, or some country family of the better class, who mingled with the wild simplicity of their original manners, and their ready and hospitable welcome, a sort of courtesy belonging to a people, the lowest of whom are accustomed to consider themselves as being, according to the Spanish phrase, "as good gentlemen as the king, only not quite so rich."

To all such persons Donald MacLeish was well known, and his introduction passed as current as if we had brought letters from the High Chief of the country.

Sometimes it happened that the Highland hospitality, which welcomed us with all variety of mountain fare, preparations of milk and eggs, and girdle-cakes of various kinds, as well as more substantial dainties, according to the inhabitant's means of regaling the passenger, descended rather too exuberantly on Donald MacLeish in the shape of mountain dew. Poor Donald! he was on such occasions like Gideon's fleece, moist with the noble element, which, of course, fell not on us. But it was his only fault, and when pressed to drink *doch-an-dorroch* to my ladyship's good health, "it would have been ill taken to have refused the pledge, nor was he willing to do such discourtesy." It was, I repeat, his only fault, nor had we any great right to complain; for if it rendered him a little more talkative, it augmented his ordinary share of punctilious civility, and he only drove slower, and talked longer and more pompously than when he had not come by a drop of usquebaugh. It was, we remarked, only on such occasions that Donald talked with an air of importance of the family of MacLeish; and we had no title to be scrupulous in censuring a foible, the consequences of which were confined within such innocent limits.

We became so much accustomed to Donald's mode of managing us, that we observed with some interest the art which he used to produce a little agreeable surprise, by concealing from us the spot where he proposed our halt to be made, when it was of an unusual and interesting character. This was so much his wont, that when he made apologies at setting off, for being obliged to stop in some strange solitary place, till the horses should eat the corn which he brought on with them for that purpose, our imagination used to be on the stretch to guess what romantic retreat he had secretly fixed upon for our noontide baiting-place.

We had spent the greater part of the morning at the delightful village of Dalmally, and had gone upon the lake under the guidance of the excellent clergyman who was then incumbent at Glenorquhy, and had heard an hundred legends of the stern chiefs of Lochawe, Duncan with the thrum bonnet, and the other lords of the now mouldering towers of Kilchurn. Thus it was later than usual when we set out on our journey, after a hint or two from Donald concerning the length of the way to the next stage, as there was no good halting place between Dalmally and Oban.

Having bid adieu to our venerable and kind cicerone, we proceeded on our tour, winding round the tremendous mountain called Cruachan Ben, which stoops down in all its majesty of rocks and wilderness on the lake, leaving only a pass, in which, notwithstanding its extreme strength, the warlike clan of MacDougal of Lorn were almost destroyed by the sagacious Robert Bruce. That King, the Wellington of his day, had accomplished, by a forced march, the unexpected manœuvre of forcing a body of troops round the other side of the mountain, and thus placed them in the flank and in the rear of the men of Lorn, whom at the same time he attacked in front. The great number of cairns yet visible, as you descend the pass, on the westward side, shows the extent of the vengeance which Bruce exhausted on his inveterate and personal enemies. I am, you know, the sister of soldiers, and it has since struck me forcibly that the manœuvre which Donald described, resembled those of Wellington or of Bonaparte. He was a great man Robert Bruce, even a Baliol must admit that; although it begins now to be allowed that his title to the crown was scarce so good as that of the unfortunate family with whom he contended—But let that pass.—The slaughter had been the greater, as the deep and rapid river Awe is disgorged from the lake, just in the rear of the fugitives, and encircles the base of the tremendous mountain; so that the retreat of the unfortunate fugitives was intercepted on all sides by the inaccessible character of the country, which had seemed to promise them defence and protection.

Musing, like the Irish lady in the song, "upon things which are long enough a-gone," we felt no impatience at the slow, and almost creeping pace, with which our conductor proceeded along General Wade's military road, which never or rarely condescends to turn aside from the steepest ascent, but proceeds right up and down hill, with the indifference to height and hollow, steep or level, indicated by the old Roman engineers. Still, however, the substantial excellence of these great works—for such are the military highways in the Highlands—deserved the compliment of the poet, who, whether he came from our sister kingdom, and spoke in his own dialect, or whether he supposed those whom he addressed might have some national pretension to the second sight, produced the celebrated couplet—

> Had you but seen these roads *before* they were made,
> You would hold up your hands, and bless General Wade.

Nothing indeed can be more wonderful than to see these wildernesses penetrated and pervious in every quarter by broad accesses of the best possible construction, and so superior to what the country could have demanded for many centuries for any pacific purpose of commercial intercourse. Thus the traces of war are sometimes happily accommodated to the purposes of peace. The victories of Bonaparte have been without results; but his road over the Simplon will long be the communication betwixt peaceful countries, who will apply to the ends of commerce and friendly intercourse that gigantic work, which was formed for the ambitious purpose of warlike invasion.

While we were thus stealing along, we gradually turned round the shoulder of Ben Cruachan, and descending the course of the foaming and rapid Awe, left behind us the expanse of the majestic lake which gives birth to that impetuous river. The rocks and precipices which stooped down perpendicularly on our path on the right hand, exhibited a few remains of the wood which once clothed them, but which had, in latter times, been felled to supply, Donald MacLeish informed us, the iron-founderies at Bunawe. This made us fix our eyes with interest on one large oak, which grew on the left hand towards the river. It seemed a tree of extraordinary magnitude and picturesque beauty, and stood just where there appeared to be a few roods of open ground lying among huge stones, which had rolled down from the mountain. To add to the romance of the situation, the spot of clear ground extended round the foot of a proud-browed rock, from the summit of which leaped a mountain stream in a fall of sixty feet, in which it was dissolved into foam and dew. At the bottom of the fall the rivulet with difficulty collected, like a routed general, its dispersed forces, and, as if tamed by its descent, found a noiseless passage through the heath to join the Awe.

I was much struck with the tree and waterfall, and wished myself nearer them; not that I thought of sketch-book or portfolio,—for, in my younger days, Misses were not accustomed to black-lead pencils, unless they could use them to some good purpose,—but merely to indulge myself with a closer view. Donald immediately opened the chaise door, but observed it was rough walking down the brae, and that I would see the tree better by keeping the road for a hundred yards farther, when it passed closer to the spot, for which he seemed, however, to have no predilection. "He knew," he said, "a far bigger tree than that nearer Bunawe, and it was a place where there was flat ground for the carriage to stand, which it could jimply do on these braes—But just as my leddyship liked."

My ladyship did choose rather to look at the fine tree before me, than to pass it by in hopes of a finer; so we walked beside the carriage till we should come to a point, from which, Donald assured us, we might, without scrambling, go as near the tree as we chose, "though he wadna advise us to go nearer than the road."

There was something grave and mysterious in Donald's sun-browned countenance when he gave us this intimation, and his manner was so different from his usual frankness, that my female curiosity was set in motion. We walked on the whilst, and I found the tree, of which we had now lost sight by the intervention of some rising ground, was really more distant than I had at first supposed. "I could have sworn now," said I to my cicerone, "that yon tree and waterfall was the very place where you intended to make a stop to-day."

"The Lord forbid!" said Donald, hastily.

"And for what, Donald? why should you be willing to pass so pleasant a spot?"

"It's ower near Dalmally, my leddy, to corn the beasts—it would bring their dinner ower near their breakfast, the poor things:—an', besides, the place is not canny."

"Oh! then the mystery is out. There is a bogle or a brownie, a witch or a gyre-carlin, a bodach or a fairy, in the case?"

"The ne'er a bit, my leddy—ye are clean aff the road, as I may say. But if your leddyship will just hae patience, and wait till we are by the bit and out of the glen, I'll tell ye all about it. There is no much luck in speaking of such things in the place they chanced in."

I was obliged to suspend my curiosity, observing, that if I persisted in twisting the discourse one way while Donald was twining it another, I should only make his objection, like a hempen cord, just so much the tougher. At length the promised turn of the road brought us within fifty paces of the tree which I desired to admire, and I now saw, to my surprise, that there was a human habitation among the cliffs which surrounded it. It was a hut of the least dimensions, and most miserable description, that I ever saw even in the Highlands. The walls of sod, or *divot*, as the Scots call it, were not four feet high—the roof was of turf, repaired with reeds and sedges—the chimney was composed of clay, bound round by straw ropes—and the whole walls, roof and chimney, were alike covered with the vegetation of house-leek, rye-grass, and moss, common to decayed cottages formed of such materials. There was not the slightest vestige of a kale-yard, the usual accompaniment of the very worst huts; and of living things we saw nothing, save a kid which was browsing on the roof of the hut, and a goat, its mother, at some distance, feeding betwixt the oak and the river Awe.

"What man," I could not help exclaiming, "can have committed sin deep enough to deserve such a miserable dwelling!"

"Sin enough," said Donald MacLeish, with a half-suppressed groan; "and God he knoweth, misery enough too;—and it is no man's dwelling neither, but a woman's."

"A woman's!" I repeated, "and in so lonely a place—What sort of woman can she be?"

"Come this way, my leddy, and you may judge that for yourself," said Donald. And by advancing a few steps, and making a sharp turn to the left, we gained a sight of the side of the great broad-breasted oak, in the direction opposed to that in which we had hitherto seen it.

"If she keeps her old wont, she will be there at this hour of the day," said Donald; but immediately became silent, and pointed with his finger, as one afraid of being overheard. I looked, and beheld, not without some sense of awe, a female form seated by the stem of the oak, with her head drooping, her hands clasped, and a dark-coloured mantle drawn over her head, exactly as Judah is represented in the Syrian medals as seated under her palm-tree. I was infected with the fear and reverence which my guide seemed to entertain towards this solitary being, nor did I think of advancing towards her to obtain a nearer view until I had cast an inquiring look on Donald; to which he replied in a half whisper—"She has been a fearfu' bad woman, my leddy."

"Mad woman, said you," replied I, hearing him imperfectly; "then she is perhaps dangerous?"

"No—she is not mad," replied Donald; "for then it may be she would be happier than she is; though when she thinks on what she has done, and caused to be done, rather than yield up a hair-breadth of her ain wicked will, it is not likely she can be very well settled. But she neither is mad nor mischievous; and yet, my leddy, I think you had best not go nearer to her." And then, in a few hurried words, he made me acquainted with the story which I am now to tell more in detail. I heard the narrative with a mixture of horror and sympathy, which at once impelled me to approach the sufferer, and speak to her the words of comfort, or rather of pity, and at the same time made me afraid to do so.

This indeed was the feeling with which she was regarded by the Highlanders in the neighbourhood, who looked upon Elspat Mac-Tavish, or the Woman of the Tree, as they called her, as the Greeks considered those who were pursued by the Furies, and endured the mental torment consequent on great criminal actions. They regarded such unhappy beings as Orestes and Œdipus, as being less the voluntary perpetrators of their crimes, than as the passive instruments by which the terrible decrees of Destiny had been accomplished; and the fear with which they beheld them was not unmingled with veneration.

I also learned farther from Donald MacLeish, that there was some apprehension of ill luck attending those who had the boldness to approach too near, or disturb the awful solitude of a being so unutterably miserable; that it was supposed that whosoever approached her must experience in some respect the contagion of her wretchedness.

It was therefore with some reluctance that Donald saw me prepare to obtain a nearer view of the sufferer, and that he himself followed to assist me in the descent down a very rough path. I believe his regard for me conquered some ominous feelings in his own breast, which connected his duty on this occasion with the presage of lame horses, lost linch-pins, overturns, and other perilous chances of the postilion's life.

I am not sure if my own courage would have carried me so close to Elspat, had not he followed. There was in her countenance the stern abstraction of hopeless and overpowering sorrow, mixed with the contending feelings of remorse, and of the pride which struggled to conceal it. She guessed, perhaps, that it was curiosity, arising out of her uncommon story, which induced me to intrude on her solitude—and she could not be pleased that a fate like hers had been the theme of a traveller's amusement. Yet the look with which she regarded me was one of scorn instead of embarrassment. The opinion of the world and all its children could not add or take an iota from her load of misery; and, save for the half smile that seemed to intimate the contempt of a being rapt by the very intensity of her affliction above the sphere of ordinary humanity, she seemed as indifferent to my gaze, as if she had been a dead corpse or a marble statue.

Elspat was above the middle stature; her hair, now grizzled, was still profuse, and had been of the most decided black. So were her eyes, in which, contradicting the stern and rigid features of her countenance, there shone the wild and troubled light that indicates an unsettled mind. Her hair was wrapt round a silver bodkin with some attention to neatness, and her dark mantle was disposed around her with a degree of taste, though the materials were of the most ordinary sort.

After gazing on this victim of guilt and calamity till I was ashamed to remain silent, though uncertain how I ought to address her, I began to express my surprise at her choosing such a desert and deplorable dwelling. She cut short these expressions of sympathy, by answering in a stern voice, without the least change of countenance or posture— "Daughter of the stranger, he has told you my story." I was silenced at once, and felt how little all earthly accommodation must seem to the mind which had such subjects as hers for rumination. Without again attempting to open conversation, I took a piece of gold from my purse, (for Donald had intimated she lived on alms,) expecting she would at least stretch her hand to receive it. But she neither accepted nor rejected the gift—she did not even seem to notice it, though twenty times as valuable, probably, as was usually offered. I was obliged to place it on her knee, saying involuntarily, as I did so, "May God pardon you, and relieve you!" I shall never forget the look which she cast up to Heaven, nor the tone in which she exclaimed, in the very words of my old friend, John Home—

> "My beautiful—my brave!"

It was the language of nature, and arose from the heart of the deprived mother, as it did from that gifted imaginative poet, while furnishing with appropriate expressions the ideal grief of Lady Randolph.

Chapter Eight

> O, I'm come to the Low Country,
>   Och, och, ohonochie,
> Without a penny in my pouch
>   To buy a meal for me.
> I was the proudest of my clan,
>   Long, long may I repine;
> And Donald was the bravest man,
>   And Donald he was mine.
>   *Old Song*

ELSPAT HAD ENJOYED happy days, though her age had sunk into hopeless and inconsolable sorrow and distress. She was once the beautiful and happy wife of Hamish MacTavish, for whom his strength and feats of prowess had gained him the title of MacTavish Mhor. His life was turbulent and dangerous, his habits being of the old Highland stamp, which esteemed it shame to want anything that could be had for the taking. Those in the Lowland line who lay near him, and desired to enjoy their lives and property in quiet, were contented to pay him a small composition, in name of protection-money, and comforted themselves with the old proverb, that it was better to "fleech the deil than fight him." Others, who accounted such composition dishonourable, were often surprised by MacTavish Mhor, and his associates and followers, who usually inflicted an adequate penalty, either in person or property, or both. The creagh is yet remembered, in which he swept one hundred and fifty cows from Monteith in one drove; and how he placed the laird of Ballybught naked in a slough, for having threatened to send for a party of the Highland Watch to protect his property.

Whatever were occasionally the triumphs of this daring cateran, they were often exchanged for reverses; and his narrow escapes, rapid flights, and the ingenious stratagems with which he extricated himself from imminent danger, were no less remembered and admired than the exploits in which he had been successful. In weal or woe, through every species of fatigue, difficulty, and danger, Elspat was his faithful companion. She enjoyed with him the fits of occasional prosperity; and when adversity pressed them hard, her strength of mind, readiness of wit, and courageous endurance of danger and toil, were said often to have stimulated the exertions of her husband.

Their morality was of the old Highland cast, faithful friends and fierce enemies: the Lowland herds and harvests they accounted their own, whenever they had the means of driving off the one, or of seizing upon the other; nor did the least scruple on the right of property interfere on such occasions. Hamish Mhor argued like the old Cretan warrior:

> My sword, my spear, my shaggy shield,
>   They make me lord of all below;
> For he that fears the lance to wield,
>   Before my shaggy shield must bow,—
> His lands, his living, must resign,
> And all that cowards have is mine.

But those days of perilous, though frequently successful depreda-tion, began to be abridged after the failure of the expedition of Prince Charles Edward. MacTavish Mhor had not sate still on that occasion, and he was outlawed, both as a traitor to the state, and as a robber and cateran. Garrisons were now settled in many places where a red coat had never before been seen, and the Saxon war-drum resounded among the most hidden recesses of the Highland mountains. The fate of MacTavish became every day more inevitable; and it was the more difficult for him to make his usual exertions for defence or escape, that

Elspat, amid his evil days, had increased his family with an infant child, which was a considerable encumbrance upon the necessary rapidity of their motions.

At length the fatal day arrived. In a strong pass on the skirts of Ben Cruachan, the celebrated MacTavish Mhor was surprised by a detachment of the Sidier Roy. His wife assisted him heroically, charging his piece from time to time; and as they were in possession of a post which was nearly unassailable, he might have perhaps escaped if his ammunition had lasted. But at length his balls were expended, although it was not until he had fired off most of the silver buttons from his waistcoat, that the soldiers, no longer deterred by fear of the unerring marksman, who had slain three, and wounded more of their number, approached his stronghold, and, unable to take him alive, slew him, after a most desperate resistance.

All this Elspat witnessed and survived, for she had, in the child which relied on her for support, a motive for strength and exertion. In what manner she maintained herself it is not easy to say. Her only ostensible means of support were a flock of three or four goats, which she fed wherever she pleased on the mountain pastures, no one challenging the intrusion. In the general distress of the country, her ancient acquaintances had little to bestow; but what they could part with from their own necessities, they willingly devoted to the relief of others. From Lowlanders she sometimes demanded tribute, rather than requested alms. She had not forgotten she was the widow of MacTavish Mhor, or that the child who trotted by her knee might, such were her imaginations, emulate one day the fame of his father, and command the same influence which he had once exerted without control. She associated so little with others, went so seldom and so unwillingly from the wildest recesses of the mountains, where she usually dwelt with her goats, that she was quite unconscious of the great change which had taken place in the country around her, the substitution of civil order for military violence, and the strength gained by the law and its adherents over those who were called in Gaelic song, "the stormy sons of the sword." Her own diminished consequence and straitened circumstances she indeed felt, but for this the death of MacTavish Mhor was, in her apprehension, a sufficing reason; and she doubted not that she should rise to her former state of importance, when Hamish Bean (or Fair-haired James) should be able to wield the arms of his father. If, then, Elspat was repelled rudely when she demanded anything necessary for her wants, or the accommodation of her little flock, by a churlish farmer, her threats of vengeance, obscurely expressed, yet terrible in their tenor, used frequently to extort, through fear of her maledictions, the relief which was denied to her necessities; and the trembling goodwife, who gave meal or money to the widow of MacTavish Mhor, wished in her heart that the stern old carline had been burned on the day her husband had his due.

Years thus ran on, and Hamish Bean grew up, not indeed to be of his father's size or strength, but to become an active, high-spirited, fair-haired youth, with a ruddy cheek, an eye like an eagle, and all the agility, if not all the strength, of his formidable father, upon whose history and achievements his mother dwelt, in order to form her son's mind to a similar course of adventures. But the young see the present state of this changeful world more keenly than the old. Much attached to his mother, and disposed to do all in his power for her support, Hamish yet perceived, when he mixed with the world, that the trade of the cateran was now alike dangerous and discreditable, and that if he were to emulate his father's prowess, it must be in some other line of warfare, more consonant to the opinions of the present day.

As the faculties of mind and body began to expand, he became more sensible of the precarious nature of his situation, of the erroneous views of his mother, and her ignorance respecting the changes of the society with which she mingled so little. In visiting friends and neighbours, he became aware of the extremely reduced scale to which his parent was limited, and learned that she possessed little or nothing more than the extreme necessaries of life, and that these were sometimes on the point of failing. At times his success in fishing and the chase was able to add something to her subsistence; but he saw no regular means of contributing to her support, unless by stooping to servile labour, which, if he himself could have endured it, would, he knew, have been like a death's-wound to the pride of his mother.

Elspat, meanwhile, saw with surprise, that Hamish Bean, although now tall and fit for the field, showed no disposition to enter on his father's scene of action. There was something of the mother at her heart, which prevented her from urging him in plain terms to take the field as a cateran, for the fear occurred of the perils into which the trade must conduct him; and when she would have spoken to him on the subject, it seemed to her heated imagination as if the ghost of her husband arose between them in his bloody tartans, and laying his finger on his lips, appeared to prohibit the topic. Yet she wondered at what seemed his want of spirit, sighed as she saw him from day to day lounging about in the long-skirted Lowland coat, which the legislature had imposed upon the Gael instead of their own romantic garb, and thought how much more he would have resembled her husband, had he been clad in the belted plaid and short hose, with his polished arms gleaming at his side.

Besides these subjects for anxiety, Elspat had others arising from the engrossing impetuosity of her temper. Her love of MacTavish Mhor had been qualified by respect and sometimes even by fear; for the cateran was not the species of man who submits to female government; but over his son she had exerted, at first during childhood, and afterwards in early youth, an imperious authority, which gave her maternal love a character of jealousy. She could not bear, when Hamish, with advancing life, made repeated steps towards independence, absented himself from her cottage at such season, and for such length of time as he chose, and seemed to consider, although maintaining towards her every possible degree of respect and kindness, that the control and responsibility of his actions rested on himself alone. This would have been of little consequence, could she have concealed her feelings within her own bosom; but the ardour and impatience of her passions made her frequently show her son that she conceived herself neglected and ill used. When he was absent for any length of time from her cottage, without giving intimation of his purpose, her resentment on his return used to be so unreasonable, that it naturally suggested to a young man fond of independence, and desirous to amend his situation in the world, to leave her, even for the very purpose of enabling him to provide for the parent whose egotistical demands on his filial attention, tended to confine him to a desert, in which both were starving in hopeless and helpless indigence.

Upon one occasion, the son having been guilty of some independent excursion, by which the mother felt herself affronted and disobliged, she had been more than usually violent on his return, and awakened in Hamish a sense of displeasure, which clouded his brow and cheek. At length, as she persevered in her unreasonable resentment, his patience became exhausted, and taking his gun from the chimney corner, and muttering to himself the reply which his respect for his mother prevented him from speaking aloud, he was about to leave the hut which he had but barely entered.

"Hamish," said his mother, "are you again about to leave me?" But Hamish only replied by looking at, and rubbing the lock of his gun.

"Ay, rub the lock of your gun," said his parent, bitterly; "I am glad you have courage enough to fire it, though it be but at a roe-deer." Hamish started at this undeserved taunt, and cast a look of anger at her in reply. She saw that she had found the means of giving him pain.

"Yes," she said, "look fierce as you will at an old woman, and your mother; it would be long ere you bent your brow on the angry countenance of a bearded man."

"Be silent, mother, or speak of what you understand," said Hamish, much irritated, "and that is of the distaff and the spindle."

"And was it of spindle and distaff that I was thinking when I bore you away on my back, through the fire of six of the Saxon soldiers, and you a wailing child? I tell you, Hamish, I know a hundred-fold more of swords and guns than ever you will; and you will never learn so much of noble war by yourself, as you have seen when you were wrapped up in my plaid."

"You are determined at least to allow me no peace at home, mother; but this shall have an end," said Hamish, as, resuming his purpose of leaving the hut, he rose and went towards the door.

"Stay, I command you," said his mother; "stay! or may the gun you carry be the means of your ruin—may the road you are going be the track of your funeral!"

"What makes you use such words, mother?" said the young man, turning a little back—"they are not good, and good cannot come of them. Farewell, just now we are too angry to speak together—farewell, it will be long ere you see me again." And he departed, his mother, in the first burst of her impatience, showering after him her maledictions, and in the next invoking them on her own head, so that they might spare her son's. She passed that day and the next in all the vehemence of impotent and yet unrestrained passion, now entreating Heaven, and such powers as were familiar to her by rude tradition, to restore her dear son, "the calf of her heart;" now in impatient resentment, meditating with what bitter terms she should rebuke his filial disobedience upon his return, and now studying the most tender language to attach him to the cottage, which, when her boy was present, she would not, in the rapture of her affection, have exchanged for the apartments of Taymouth Castle.

Two days passed, during which, neglecting even the slender means of supporting nature which her situation afforded, nothing but the strength of a frame accustomed to hardships and privations of every kind, could have kept her in existence, notwithstanding the anguish of her mind prevented her being sensible of her personal weakness. Her dwelling, at this unhappy period, was the same cottage near which I had found her, but then more habitable by the exertions of Hamish, by whom it had been in a great measure built and repaired.

It was on the third day after her son had disappeared, as she sat at the door rocking herself, after the fashion of her countrywomen when in distress, or in pain, that the then unwonted circumstance occurred of a passenger being seen on the road above the cottage. She cast but one glance at him—he was on horseback, so that it could not be Hamish, and Elspat cared not enough for any other being on earth, to make her turn her eyes towards him a second time. The stranger, however, paused opposite to her cottage, and dismounting from his pony, led it down the steep and broken path which conducted to her door.

"God bless you, Elspat MacTavish!"—She looked at the man as he addressed her in her native language, with the displeased air of one whose reverie is interrupted; but the traveller went on to say, "I bring you tidings of your son Hamish." At once, from being the most uninteresting being, in respect to Elspat, who could exist, the face of the stranger became awful in her eyes, as that of a messenger descended from Heaven, expressly to pronounce upon her death or life. She started from her seat, and with hands convulsively clasped together, and held up to Heaven, eyes fixed on the stranger's countenance, and person stooping forward to him, she looked those inquiries, which her faltering tongue could not articulate. "Your son sends you his dutiful remembrance and this," said the messenger, putting into Elspat's hand a small purse containing four or five dollars.

"He is gone, he is gone!" exclaimed Elspat; "he has sold himself to be the servant of the Saxons, and I shall never more behold him. Tell me, Miles MacPhadraick, for now I know you, is it the price of the son's blood that you have put into the mother's hand?"

"Now, God forbid!" answered MacPhadraick, who was a tacksman, and had possession of a considerable track of ground under his Chief, a proprietor who lived about twenty miles off—"God forbid I should do wrong, or say wrong, to you, or to the son of MacTavish Mhor! I swear to you by the hand of my Chief, that your son is well, and will soon see you; and the rest he will tell you himself." So saying, MacPhadraick hastened back up the pathway, gained the road, mounted his pony, and rode upon his way.

Chapter Nine

ELSPAT MACTAVISH remained gazing on the money, as if the impress of the coin could have conveyed information how it was procured.

"I love not this MacPhadraick," she said to herself; "it was his race of whom the Bard hath spoken, saying, 'fear them not when their words are loud as the winter's wind, but fear them when they fall on your ear like the sound of the thrush's song.' And yet this riddle can be read but one way: My son hath taken the sword, to win that with strength like a man, which churls would keep him from with the words that frighten children." This idea, when once it occurred to her, seemed the more reasonable, that MacPhadraick, as she well knew, himself a cautious man, had so far encouraged her husband's dangerous trade, as occasionally to buy cattle of MacTavish, although he must have well known how they were come by, taking care, however, that the transaction was so made, as to be accompanied with great profit and absolute safety. Who so likely as MacPhadraick to indicate to a young cateran the glen in which he could commence his perilous trade with most prospect of success, who so likely to convert his booty into money? The feelings which another might have experienced on believing that an only son had rushed forwards on the same path in which his father had perished, were scarce known to the Highland mother of that day. She thought of the death of MacTavish Mhor as that of a hero who had fallen in his proper trade of war, and who had not fallen unavenged. It was a tame and dishonoured life which she dreaded for her son, the subjection to strangers, and death-sleep of the soul which is brought on by what she regarded as slavery.

The moral principle which so naturally and so justly occurs to the mind of those who have been educated under a settled government of laws that protect the property of the weak against the incursions of the strong, was to poor Elspat a book sealed and a fountain closed. She had been taught to consider those whom they called Saxons, as a race with whom the Gael were constantly at war, and she regarded every settlement of theirs within reach of Highland incursion, as affording a legitimate object of attack and plunder. Her feelings on this point had been strengthened and confirmed, not only by the desire of revenge for the death of her husband, but by the sense of general indignation entertained, not unjustly, through the Highlands of Scotland, on account of the barbarous and violent conduct of the victors after the battle of Culloden. Other Highland clans, too, she regarded as the fair objects of plunder when that was possible, upon the score of ancient enmities and deadly feuds.

The prudence that might have weighed the slender means which the times afforded for resisting the efforts of a combined government, which had, in its less compact and established authority, been unable to put down the ravages of such lawless caterans as MacTavish Mhor, was unknown to a solitary woman, whose ideas still dwelt upon her own early times. She imagined that her son had only to proclaim himself his father's successor in adventure and enterprise, and that a force of men as gallant as those who had followed his father's banner, would crowd around to support it when again displayed. To her, Hamish was the eagle who had only to soar aloft and resume his native place in the skies, without her being able to comprehend how many additional eyes would have watched his flight, how many additional bullets would have been directed at his bosom. To be brief, Elspat was one who viewed the present state of society with the same feelings with which she regarded the times that had passed away. She had been indigent, neglected, oppressed, since the days that her husband had been feared and powerful, and she thought that the days of her ascendance would return when her son had determined to play the part of his father. If she permitted her eyes to glance farther on futurity, it was but to anticipate that she must be for many a day cold in the grave, with the coronach of her tribe cried duly over her, before her fair-haired Hamish could, according to her calculation, die with his hand on the basket-hilt of the red claymore. His father's hair was grey, ere, after a hundred dangers, he had fallen with his arms in his hand—That she should have seen and survived the sight, was a natural consequence of the manners of that age. And better it was— such was her proud thought—that she had seen him so die, than to have witnessed his departure from life in a smoky hovel—on a bed of rotten straw, like an over-worn hound, or a bullock which died of disease. But the hour of her young, her brave Hamish, was yet far distant. He must succeed—he must conquer, like his fathers. And when he fell at length,—for she anticipated for him no bloodless death,—Elspat would ere then have lain long in the grave, and could neither see his death-struggle, nor mourn over his grave sod.

With such wild notions working in her brain, the spirit of Elspat rose to its usual pitch, or rather to one which ascended higher. In the emphatic language of Scripture, which in that idiom does not greatly differ from her own, she arose, she washed and changed her apparel, and ate bread, and was refreshed.

She longed eagerly for the return of her son, but she now longed not with the bitter anxiety of doubt and apprehension. She said to herself, that much must be done ere he could in these times arise to be an eminent and dreaded leader. Yet when she saw him again, she almost expected him at the head of a daring band, with pipes playing, and banners flying, the noble tartans fluttering free in the wind, in despite of the laws which had suppressed, under severe penalties, the use of the national garb, and all the appurtenances of Highland chivalry. For all this, her eager imagination was content only to allow the interval of some days.

From the moment this opinion had taken deep and serious possession of her mind, her thoughts were bent upon receiving her son at the head of his adherents in the manner in which she used to adorn her hut for the return of his father.

The substantial means of subsistence she had not the power of providing, nor did she consider that of importance. The successful caterans would bring with them herds and flocks. But the interior of the hut was arranged for their reception—the usquebaugh was

brewed or distilled in a larger quantity than it could have been supposed one lone woman could have made ready. Her hut was put into
such order as might, in some degree, give it the appearance of a day of
rejoicing. It was swept and decorated with boughs of various kinds,
like the house of a Jewess, upon what is termed the Feast of the
Tabernacles. The produce of the milk of her little flock was prepared
in as great variety of forms as her skill admitted, to entertain her son
and the associates whom she expected to receive along with him.

But the principal decoration, which she sought with the greatest
toil, was the cloud-berry, a scarlet fruit, which is only found on very
high hills, and there only in small quantities. Her husband, or perhaps
one of his forefathers, had chosen this as the emblem of his family,
because it seemed at once to imply by its scarcity the smallness of their
clan, and by the places in which it was found, the ambitious height of
their pretensions.

For the time that these simple preparations of welcome endured,
Elspat was in a state of troubled happiness. In fact, her only anxiety
was that she might not be able to complete all that she could
do to welcome Hamish and the friends who she supposed must have
attached themselves to his band, before they arrived, and found her
unprovided for their reception.

But when such efforts as she could make had been accomplished,
she once more had nothing left to engage her save the trifling care of
her goats; and when these had been attended to, she had only to
review her little preparations, renew such as were of a transitory
nature, replace decayed branches and fading boughs, and then to sit
down at her cottage door and watch the road, as it ascended on the one
side from the banks of the Awe, and on the other wound round the
heights of the mountain, with such a degree of accommodation to hill
and level as the plan of the military engineer permitted. While so
occupied, her imagination, anticipating the future from recollections
of the past, formed out of the morning mist or the evening cloud the
wild forms of an advancing band, of what were then called "Sidier
Dhu,"—dark soldiers dressed in their native tartan, and so named to
distinguish them from the scarlet ranks of the British army. In this
occupation she spent many hours of each morning and evening.

Chapter Ten

Though justice ever should prevail,
The tear my Kitty sheds is due;
For seldom shall she hear a tale
So sad so tender and so true.
                              SHENSTONE

IT WAS IN VAIN that Elspat's eyes surveyed the distant path, by the earliest light of the dawn and the latest glimmer of the twilight. No rising dust awakened the expectation of nodding plumes or flashing arms—the solitary traveller trudged listlessly along in his brown lowland great-coat, his tartans dyed black or purple, to comply with or evade the law which prohibited their being worn in their variegated hues. The spirit of the Gael, sunk and broken by the severe though perhaps necessary laws, that proscribed the dress and arms which he considered as his birthright, was intimated by his drooping head and dejected appearance. Not in such depressed wanderers did Elspat recognise the light and free step of her son, now, as she concluded, regenerated and free from every sign of Saxon thraldom. Night by night, as darkness came, she removed from her unclosed door to throw herself on her restless pallet, not to sleep, but to watch. The brave and the terrible, she said, walk by night—their steps are heard in darkness, when all is silent save the whirlwind and the cataract—the timid deer comes only forth when the sun is upon the mountain's peak; but the bold wolf walks in the red light of the harvest-moon. She reasoned in vain—her son's expected summons did not call her from the lowly couch, where she lay dreaming of his approach. Hamish came not.

"Hope deferred," saith the royal sage, "maketh the heart sick;" and strong as was Elspat's constitution, she began to experience that it was unequal to the toils to which her anxious and immoderate affection subjected her, when early one morning the appearance of a traveller on the lonely mountain-road, revived hopes which had begun to sink into listless despair. There was no sign of Saxon subjugation about the stranger. At a distance she could see the flutter of the belted-plaid, that drooped in graceful folds behind him, and the plume that, placed in the bonnet, showed rank and gentle birth. He carried a gun over his shoulder, the claymore was swinging by his side, with its usual appendages, the dirk, the pistol, and the *sporran mollach*.* Ere yet her eye had scanned all these particulars, the light step of the traveller was hastened, his arm was waved in token of recognition—a

* The goat-skin pouch worn by the Highlanders round their waist.

moment more, and Elspat held in her arms her darling son, dressed in the garb of his ancestors, and looking, in her maternal eyes, the fairest among ten thousand.

The first outpouring of affection it would be impossible to describe. Blessings implored mingled with the most endearing epithets which her energetic language affords, in striving to express the wild rapture of Elspat's joy. Her board was heaped hastily with all she had to offer; and the mother watched the young soldier, as he partook of the refreshment, with feelings how similar to, yet how different from, those with which she had seen him draw his first sustenance from her bosom!

When the tumult of joy was appeased, Elspat became anxious to know her son's adventures since they parted, and could not help greatly censuring his rashness for traversing the hills in the Highland dress in the broad sun-shine, when the penalty was so heavy, and so many red soldiers were abroad in the country.

"Fear not for me, mother," said Hamish, in a tone designed to relieve her anxiety, and yet somewhat embarrassed; "I may wear the *breacan** at the gate of Fort-Augustus, if I like it."

"Oh, be not too daring, my beloved Hamish, though it be the fault which best becomes thy father's son—yet be not too daring! Alas, they fight not now as in former days, with fair weapons, and on equal terms, but take odds of numbers and of arms, so that the feeble and the strong are alike levelled by the shot of a boy. And do not think me unworthy to be called your father's widow, and your mother, because I speak thus; for God knoweth, that, man to man, I would peril thee against the best in Breadalbane, and broad Lorn besides."

"I assure you, my dearest mother," replied Hamish, "that I am in no danger. But have you seen MacPhadraick, mother, and what has he said to you on my account?"

"Silver he left me in plenty, Hamish; but the best of his comfort was, that you were well, and would see me soon. But beware of MacPhadraick, my son; for when he called himself the friend of your father, he better loved the most worthless stirk in his herd, than he did the life-blood of MacTavish Mhor. Use his services, therefore, and pay him for them—for it is thus we should deal with the unworthy; but take my counsel, and trust him not."

Hamish could not suppress a sigh, which seemed to Elspat to intimate that the caution came too late. "What have you done with him?" she continued, eager and alarmed. "I had money of him, and he gives not that without value—he is none of those who exchange barley for chaff. Oh, if you repent you of your bargain, and if it be one which

* That which is variegated, *i. e.* the tartan.

you may break off without disgrace to your truth or your manhood, take back his silver, and trust not to his fair words."

"It may not be, mother," said Hamish; "I do not repent my engagement, unless that it must make me leave you soon."

"Leave me! how leave me? Silly boy, think you I know not what duty belongs to the wife or mother of a daring man! Thou art but a boy yet; and when thy father had been the dread of the country for twenty years, he did not despise my company and assistance, but often said my help was worth that of two strong gillies."

"It is not on that score, mother; but since I must leave the country"——

"Leave the country!" replied his mother, interrupting him; "and think you that I am like a bush, that is rooted to the soil where it grows, and must die if carried elsewhere? I have breathed other winds than these of Ben Cruachan——I have followed your father to the wilds of Ross, and the impenetrable deserts of Y Mac Y Mhor——Tush, man, my limbs, old as they are, will bear me as far as your young feet can trace the way."

"Alas, mother," said the young man, with a faltering accent, "but to cross the sea——"

"The sea? who am I that I should fear the sea? Have I never been in a birling in my life—never known the Sound of Mull, the Isles of Treshornish, and the rough rocks of Harris?"

"Alas, mother, I go far, far from all of these—I am enlisted in one of the new regiments, and we go against the French in America."

"Enlisted!" echoed the astonished mother—"against *my* will—without *my* consent—You could not—you would not,"—then rising up, and assuming a posture of almost imperial command, "Hamish, you DARED not!"

"Despair, mother, dares everything," answered Hamish, in a tone of melancholy resolution. "What should I do here, where I can scarce get bread for myself and you, and when the times are growing daily worse? Would you but sit down and listen, I would convince you I have acted for the best."

With a bitter smile Elspat sate down, and the same severe ironical expression was on her features, as, with her lips firmly closed, she listened to his vindication.

Hamish went on, without being disconcerted by her expected displeasure. "When I left you, dearest mother, it was to go to MacPhadraick's house, for although I know he is crafty and worldly, after the fashion of the Sassenach, yet he is wise, and I thought how he would teach me, as it would cost him nothing, in which way I could best mend our estate in the world."

"Our estate in the world!" said Elspat, losing patience at the word; "and went you to a base fellow with a soul no better than that of a cowherd, to ask counsel about your conduct? Your father asked none, save at his courage and his sword."

"Dearest mother," answered Hamish, "how shall I convince you that you live in this land of our fathers, as if our fathers were yet living? You walk as it were in a dream, surrounded by the phantoms of those who have been long with the dead. When my father lived and fought, the great respected the Man of the strong right hand, and the rich feared him. He had protection from MacAllan Mhor, and from Caberfae, and tribute from meaner men. That is ended, and his son would only earn a disgraceful and unpitied death, by the practices which gave his father credit and power among those who wear the breacan. The land is conquered—its lights are quenched,—Glengary, Lochiel, Perth, Lord Lewis, all the high chiefs are dead or in exile—We may mourn for it, but we cannot help it. Bonnet, broadsword, and sporran—power, strength, and wealth, were all lost on Drummossie-muir."

"It is false!" said Elspat, fiercely; "you, and such like dastardly spirits, are quelled by your own faint hearts, not by the strength of the enemy. You are like the fearful waterfowl, to whom the least cloud in the sky seems the shadow of the eagle."

"Mother," said Hamish, proudly, "lay not faint heart to my charge. I go where men are wanted who have strong arms and bold hearts too. I leave a desert, for a land where I may gather fame."

"And you leave your mother to perish in want, age, and solitude," said Elspat, essaying successively every means of moving a resolution, which she began to see was more deeply rooted than she had at first thought.

"Not so, mother," he answered; "I leave you to comfort and certainty, which you have yet never known. Barcaldine's son is made a leader, and with him I have enrolled myself; MacPhadraick acts for him, and raises men, and finds his own in it."

"That is the truest word of the tale, were all the rest as false as hell," said the old woman, bitterly.

"But we are to find our good in it also," continued Hamish; "for Barcaldine is to give you a shieling in his wood of Letter-findreight, with grass for your goats, and a cow, when you please to have one, upon the common; and my own pay, dearest mother, though I am far away, will do more than provide you with meal, and with all else you can want. Do not fear for me. I enter a private gentleman; but I will return, if hard fighting and regular duty can deserve it, an officer, and with half a dollar a-day."

"Poor child!—" replied Elspat, in a tone of pity mingled with contempt, "and you trust MacPhadraick?"

"I might, mother—" said Hamish, the dark red colour of his race crossing his fair forehead and cheeks, "for MacPhadraick knows the blood which flows in my veins, and is aware, that should he break trust with you, he might count the days which could bring Hamish back to Breadalbane, and number those of his life within three suns more. I would kill him on his own hearth, did he break his word with me—I would, by the great Being who made us both!"

The look and attitude of the young soldier for a moment overawed Elspat; she was unused to see him express a deep and bitter mood, which reminded her so strongly of his father. But she resumed her remonstrances in the same taunting manner in which she had commenced them.

"Poor boy!" she said; "and you think that at the distance of half the world your threats will be heard or thought of! But, go—go—place your neck under Him of Hanover's yoke, against whom every true Gael fought to the death—Go, disown the royal Stuart, for whom your father, and his fathers, and your mother's fathers, have crimsoned many a field with their blood.—Go, put your head under the belt of one of the race of Dermid, whose children murdered—Yes," she added, with a wild shriek, "murdered your mother's fathers in their peaceful dwellings at Glencoe!—Yes," she again exclaimed, with a wilder and shriller scream, "I was then unborn, but my mother has told me—and I attended to the voice of *my* mother—well I remember her words!—They came in peace, and were received in friendship, and blood and fire arose, and screams and murder!"

"Mother," answered Hamish, mournfully, but with a decided tone, "all that I have thought over—There is not a drop of the blood of Glencoe on the noble hand of Barcaldine—with the unhappy house of Glenlyon the curse remains, and on them God hath avenged it."

"You speak like the Saxon priest already," replied his mother; "were you not better to stay, and ask a kirk from MacAllan Mhor, that you may preach forgiveness to the race of Dermid?"

"Yesterday was yesterday," answered Hamish, "and to-day is to-day. When the clans are crushed and confounded together, it is well and wise that their hatreds and their feuds should not survive their independence and their power. He that cannot execute vengeance like a man, should not harbour useless enmity like a craven. Mother, Young Barcaldine is true and brave; I know that MacPhadraick counselled him, that he should not let me take leave of you, lest you dissuaded me from my purpose; but he said, 'Hamish MacTavish is the son of a brave man, and he will not break his word.' Mother,

Barcaldine leads an hundred of the bravest of the sons of the Gael in their native dress, and with their fathers' arms—heart to heart—shoulder to shoulder. I have sworn to go with him—He has trusted me, and I will trust him."

At this reply, so firmly and resolvedly pronounced, Elspat remained like one thunderstruck, and sunk in despair. The arguments which she had considered so irresistibly conclusive, had recoiled like a wave from a rock. After a long pause, she filled her son's quaigh, and presented it to him with an air of dejected deference and submission.

"Drink," she said, "to thy father's roof-tree, ere you leave it for ever; and tell me,—since the chains of a new King, and of a new Chief, whom your fathers knew not save as mortal enemies, are fastened upon the limbs of your father's son,—tell me how many links you count upon them?"

Hamish took the cup, but looked at her as if uncertain of her meaning. She proceeded in a raised voice. "Tell me," she said, "for I have a right to know, for how many days the will of those you have made your masters permits me to look upon you?—In other words, how many are the days of my life? for when you leave me, the earth has nought besides worth living for!"

"Mother," replied Hamish MacTavish, "for six days I may remain with you, and if you will set out with me on the fifth, I will conduct you in safety to your new dwelling. But if you remain here, then will I depart on the seventh by day-break—then, as at the last moment, I MUST set out for Dunbarton, for if I appear not on the eighth day, I am subject to punishment as a deserter, and am dishonoured as a soldier and a gentleman."

"Your father's foot," she answered, "was free as the wind on the heath—it were as vain to say to him where goest thou, as to ask that viewless driver of the clouds, wherefore blowest thou. Tell me under what penalty thou must—since go thou must, and go thou wilt—return to thy thraldom?"

"Call it not thraldom, mother, it is the service of an honourable soldier—the only service which is now open to the son of MacTavish Mhor."

"Yet say what is the penalty if thou shouldst not return?" replied Elspat.

"Military punishment as a deserter," answered Hamish; writhing, however, as his mother failed not to observe, under some internal feelings, which she resolved to probe to the uttermost.

"And that," she said, with assumed calmness, which her glancing eye disowned, "is the punishment of a disobedient hound, is it not?"

"Ask me no more, mother," said Hamish; "the punishment is

nothing to one who will never deserve it."

"To me it is something," replied Elspat, "since I know better than thou, that where there is power to inflict, there is often the will to do so without cause. I would pray for thee, Hamish, and I must know against what evils I should beseech Him who leaves none unguarded, to protect thy youth and simplicity."

"Mother," said Hamish, "it signifies little to what a criminal may be exposed, if a man is determined not to be such. Our Highland chiefs used also to punish their vassals, and, as I have heard, severely—was it not Lachlan MacIan, whom we remember of old, whose head was struck off by order of his chieftain for shooting at the stag before him?"

"Ay," said Elspat, "and right he had to lose it, since he dishonoured the father of the people even in the face of the assembled clan. But the chiefs were noble in their ire—they punished with the sharp blade, but not with the batton. Their punishments drew blood, but they did not infer dishonour. Canst thou say the same for the laws under whose yoke thou hast placed thy free-born neck?"

"I cannot, mother—I cannot," said Hamish, mournfully. "I saw them punish a Sassenach for deserting, as they called it, his banner. He was scourged—I own it—scourged like a hound who has offended an imperious master. I was sick at the sight—I own it. But the punishment of dogs is only for men worse than dogs, who know not how to keep their faith."

"To this infamy, however, thou hast subjected thyself, Hamish," replied Elspat, "if thou shouldst give, or thy officers take, measure of offence against thee.—I speak no more to thee on thy purpose.— Were the sixth day from this morning's sun my dying day, and thou wert to stay to close mine eyes, thou wouldst run the risk of being lashed like a dog at a post—yes! unless thou hadst the gallant heart to leave me to die alone, and upon my desolate hearth, the last spark of thy father's fire, and of thy mother's life, forsaken to be extinguished together!"—Hamish traversed the hut with an impatient and angry pace.

"Mother," he said at length, "concern not yourself about such things. I cannot be subjected to such infamy, for never will I deserve it; and were I threatened with it, I should know how to die before I was so far dishonoured."

"There spoke the son of the husband of my heart!" replied Elspat; and she changed the discourse, and seemed to listen in melancholy acquiescence, when her son reminded her how short the time was which they were permitted to pass in each other's society, and entreated that it might be spent without useless and unpleasant recollections respecting the circumstances under which they must soon be separated.

Elspat was now satisfied that her son, with some of his father's other properties, preserved the haughty masculine spirit which rendered it impossible to divert him from a resolution which he had deliberately adopted. She assumed, therefore, an exterior of apparent submission to their inevitable separation; and if she now and then broke out into complaints and murmurs, it was either that she could not altogether suppress the natural impetuosity of her temper, or because she had the wit to consider, that a total and unreserved acquiescence might have seemed to her son constrained and suspicious, and induced him to watch and defeat the means by which she still hoped to prevent his leaving her. Her ardent, though selfish affection for her son, incapable of being qualified by a regard for the true interests of the unfortunate object of her attachment, resembled the instinctive fondness of the animal race for their offspring; and seeing little farther into futurity than one of the inferior creatures, she only felt, that to be separated from Hamish was to die.

In the brief interval permitted them, Elspat exhausted every art which affection could devise, to render agreeable to him the few days which they were apparently to spend with each other. Her memory carried her far back into former days, and her stores of legendary history, which furnish at all times a principal amusement of the Highlander in his moments of repose, were augmented by an unusual acquaintance with the songs of ancient bards, and traditions of the most approved Seannachies and tellers of tales. Her officious attentions to her son's accommodation, indeed, were so unremitted as almost to give him pain; and he endeavoured quietly to prevent her from giving herself so much personal toil in selecting the blooming heath for his bed, or preparing the meal for his refreshment. "Let me alone, Hamish," she would reply on such occasions; "you follow your own will in departing from your mother, let your mother have hers in doing what gives her pleasure while you remain."

So much she seemed to be reconciled to the arrangements which he had made in her behalf, that she could hear him speak to her of her removing to the lands of Green Colin, as the gentleman was called, on whose estate he had provided her an asylum. In truth, however, nothing could be farther from her thoughts. From what he had said during their first violent dispute, Elspat had gathered, that if Hamish returned not by the appointed time permitted by his furlough, he would incur the hazard of corporal punishment. Were he placed within the risk of being thus dishonoured, she was well aware that he would never submit to the disgrace, by a return to the regiment where it might be inflicted. Whether she looked to any farther probable consequences of her unhappy scheme, cannot be known; but the partner of MacTavish Mhor, in all his perils and his wanderings, was familiar with an hundred instances of resistance or escape, by which one brave man, amidst a land of rocks, lakes, and mountains, dangerous passes, and dark forests, might baffle the pursuit of hundreds. For the future, therefore, she feared nothing. Her sole engrossing object was to prevent her son from keeping his word with his commanding officer.

With this secret purpose, she evaded the proposal which Hamish repeatedly made, that they should set out together to take possession of her new abode; and she resisted it upon grounds apparently so natural to her character, that her son was neither alarmed nor displeased. "Let me not," she said, "in the same short week, bid farewell to my only son, and to the glen in which I have so long dwelt. Let my eye, when dimmed with weeping for thee, still look around, for a while at least, upon Loch Awe and on Ben Cruachan."

Hamish yielded the more willingly to his mother's humour in this particular, that one or two persons who resided in a neighbouring glen, and had given their sons to Barcaldine's levy, were also to be provided for on the estate of the chieftain, and it was apparently settled that Elspat was to take her journey along with them when they should remove to their new residence. Thus, Hamish believed that he had at once indulged his mother's humour, and insured her safety and accommodation. But she nourished in her mind very different thoughts and projects!

The period of Hamish's leave of absence was fast approaching, and more than once he proposed to depart, in such time as to insure his gaining easily and early Dunbarton, the town where were the headquarters of his regiment. But still his mother's entreaties, his own natural disposition to linger among scenes long dear to him, and, above all, his firm reliance in his own speed and activity, induced him to protract his departure till the sixth day, being the very last which he could possibly afford to spend with his mother, if indeed he meant to comply with the conditions of his furlough.

Chapter Eleven

But for your son, believe it—Oh, believe it—
Most dangerously you have with him prevailed,
If not most mortal to him.—
                              Coriolanus

ON THE EVENING which preceded his proposed departure, Hamish walked down to the river with his fishing-rod, to practise in the Awe, for the last time, a sport in which he excelled, and to find, at the same time, the means for making one social meal with his mother on something better than their ordinary cheer. He was as successful as usual, and soon killed a fine salmon. On his return homeward an incident befell him, which he afterwards related as ominous, though probably his heated imagination, joined to the universal turn of his countrymen for the marvellous, exaggerated into superstitious importance some very ordinary and accidental circumstance.

In the path which he pursued homeward, he was surprised to observe a person, who, like himself, was dressed and armed after the old Highland fashion. The first natural idea was that the passenger belonged to his own corps, who, levied by government, and bearing arms under royal authority, were not amenable for breach of the statutes against the use of the Highland garb or weapons. But he was struck on perceiving, as he mended his pace to make up to his supposed comrade, meaning to request his company for the next day's journey, that the stranger wore a white cockade, the fatal badge which was proscribed in the Highlands. The stature of the man was tall, and there was something shadowy in the outline, which added to his size; and his mode of motion, which rather resembled gliding than walking, impressed Hamish with superstitious fears concerning the character of the being which thus passed before him in the twilight. He no longer strove to make up with the stranger, but contented himself with keeping him in view, under the superstition common to the Highlanders, that you ought neither to intrude yourself on such supernatural apparitions as you may witness, nor fly from them or avoid their presence, but leave it to themselves to withhold or extend their communication, as their power may permit, or the purpose of their commission require.

Upon an elevated knoll by the side of the road, just where the pathway turned down to Elspat's hut, the stranger made a pause, and seemed to await Hamish's coming up. Hamish, on his part, seeing it was necessary he should pass the object of his suspicion, mustered up his courage, and approached the spot where the stranger had placed himself; who first pointed to Elspat's hut, and made, with arm and head, a gesture prohibiting Hamish to approach it, and then stretched his hand to the road which led to the southward, with a motion which seemed to enjoin his instant departure in that direction. In a moment afterwards the plaided form was gone—Hamish did not exactly say vanished, because there were rocks and stunted trees enough to have concealed him. But it was his own opinion that he had seen the spirit of MacTavish Mhor, warning him to commence his instant journey to Dunbarton, without waiting till morning, or again visiting his mother's hut.

In fact, so many accidents might arise to delay his journey, especially where there were many ferries, that it became his settled purpose, though he could not depart without bidding his mother adieu, that he neither could nor would abide longer than for that object; and that the first glimpse of next day's sun should see him many miles advanced towards Dunbarton. He descended the path, therefore, and entering the cottage, he communicated, in a hasty and troubled voice, which indicated his mental agitation, his determination to take his instant departure. Somewhat to his surprise, Elspat appeared not to combat his purpose, but she urged him to take some refreshment ere he left her for ever. He did so hastily, and in silence, thinking on the approaching separation, and scarce yet believing it would take place without a final struggle with his mother's fondness. To his surprise, she filled the quaigh with liquor for his parting cup.

"Go," she said, "my son, since such is thy settled purpose; but first stand once more on thy mother's hearth, the flame on which will be extinguished long ere thy foot shall again be placed there."

"To your health, mother!" said Hamish, "and may we meet again in happiness, in spite of your ominous words."

"It were better not to part," said his mother, watching him as he quaffed the liquor, of which he would have held it ominous to have left a drop.

"And now," she said, muttering the words to herself, "go—if thou canst go."

"Mother," said Hamish, as he replaced on the table the empty quaigh, "thy drink is pleasant to the taste, but it takes away the strength which it ought to give."

"Such is its first effect, my son," replied Elspat; "but lie down upon that soft heather couch, shut your eyes but for a moment, and, in the sleep of an hour, you shall have more refreshment than in the ordinary repose of three whole nights, could they be blended into one."

"Mother," said Hamish, upon whose brain the potion was now taking rapid effect, "give me my bonnet—I must kiss you and be gone

—Yet it seems as if my feet were nailed to the floor."

"Indeed," said his mother, "you will be instantly well, if you will sit down for half an hour—but half an hour; it is eight hours to dawn, and dawn were time enough for your father's son to make the a journey."

"I must obey you, mother—I feel I must," said Hamish, inarticulately; "but call me when the moon rises."

He sate down on the bed—reclined back, and almost instantly was fast asleep. With the throbbing glee of one who has brought to an end a difficult and troublesome enterprise, Elspat proceeded tenderly to arrange the plaid of the unconscious slumberer, to whom her extravagant affection was doomed to be so fatal, expressing, while busied in the office, her delight, in tones of mingled tenderness and triumph. "Yes," she said, "calf of my heart, the moon shall arise and set to thee, and so shall the sun; but not to light thee from the land of thy fathers, or tempt thee to serve the foreign prince or the feudal enemy! To no son of Dermid shall I be delivered, to be fed like a bondswoman; but he who is my pleasure and my pride shall be my guard and my protector. They say the Highlands are changed; but I see Ben Cruachan rear his crest as high as ever into the evening sky—no one hath yet herded his kine on the depth of Loch Awe—and yonder oak does not yet bend like a willow. The children of the mountains will be such as their fathers, until the mountains themselves shall be levelled with the strath. In these wild forests, which used to support thousands of the brave, there is still surely subsistence and refuge left for one aged woman, and one gallant youth, of the ancient race and the ancient manners."

While the misjudging mother thus exulted in the success of her stratagem, we may mention to the reader, that it was founded on the acquaintance with drugs and simples, which Elspat, accomplished in all things belonging to the wild life which she had led, possessed in an uncommon degree. With the herbs, which she knew how to select as well as how to distil, she could relieve more diseases than a regular medical person could easily believe. She applied some to dye the bright colours of the tartan—from others she compounded draughts of various powers, and unhappily possessed the secret of one which was strongly soporific. Upon the effects of this last concoction, as the reader doubtless has anticipated, she reckoned with security on delaying Hamish beyond the period for which his return was appointed; and she trusted to his horror for the apprehended punishment to which he was thus rendered liable, to prevent him from returning at all.

Sound and deep, beyond natural rest, was the sleep of Hamish MacTavish on that eventful evening, but not such the repose of his mother. Scarce did she close her eyes from time to time, but she awakened again with a start, in the terror that her son had arisen and departed; and it was only on approaching his couch, and hearing his deep-drawn and regular breathing, that she reassured herself of the security of the repose in which he was plunged.

Still, dawning, she feared, might awaken him, notwithstanding the unusual strength of the potion with which she had drugged his cup. If there remained a hope of mortal man accomplishing the journey, she was aware that Hamish would attempt it, though he were to die from fatigue upon the road. Animated by this new fear, she studied to exclude the light, by stopping all the crannies and crevices through which, rather than through any regular entrance, the morning beams might find access to her miserable dwelling; and this in order to detain amid its wants and wretchedness the being, on whom, if the world itself had been at her disposal, she would have joyfully conferred it.

Her pains were bestowed unnecessarily. The sun rose high above the heaven, and not the fleetest stag in Breadalbane, were the hounds at his heels, could have sped, to save his life, so fast as Hamish must have done to keep his appointment. Her purpose was fully attained —her son's return within the period assigned was impossible. She deemed it equally impossible, that he would ever dream of returning, standing, as he must now do, in the danger of an infamous punishment. By degrees, and at different times, she had gained from him a full acquaintance with the predicament in which he would be placed by failing to appear on the day appointed, and the very small hope he could entertain of being treated with lenity.

It is well known, that the great and wise Earl of Chatham prided himself on the scheme, by which he drew together for defence of the colonies those hardy Highlanders, who, until his time, had been the objects of doubt, fear, and suspicion, on the part of each successive administration. But some obstacles occurred, from the peculiar habit and temper of this people, to the execution of his patriotic project. By nature and habit, every Highlander was accustomed to the use of arms, but at the same time totally unaccustomed to, and impatient of, the restraints imposed by discipline upon regular troops. They were a species of militia, who had no conception of a camp as their only home. If a battle was lost, they dispersed to save themselves, and look out for the safety of their families; if won, they went back to their glens to hoard up their booty, and attend to their cattle and their farms. This privilege of going and coming at their pleasure, they would not be deprived of even by their Chiefs, whose authority was in most other respects so despotic.

It followed as a matter of course, that the new-levied Highland recruits could scarce be made to comprehend the nature of a military engagement, which compelled a man to serve in the army longer than he pleased; and perhaps, in many instances, sufficient care was not taken at enlisting to explain to them the permanency of the engagement which they came under, lest such a disclosure should induce them to change their mind. Desertions were therefore become numerous from the newly-raised regiment, and the veteran General who commanded at Dunbarton, saw no better way of checking them than by causing an unusually severe example to be made of a deserter from an English corps. The young Highland regiment was obliged to attend upon the punishment, which struck a people, peculiarly jealous of personal honour, with equal horror and disgust, and not unnaturally indisposed some of them to the service. The old General, however, who had been regularly bred in the German wars, stuck to his own opinion, and gave out in orders that the first Highlander who should either desert, or fail to appear at the expiry of his furlough, should be brought to the halberts, and punished like the culprit whom they had seen in that condition. No man doubted that General ———— would keep his word rigorously whenever severity was required, and Elspat, therefore, knew that her son, when he perceived that due compliance with his orders was impossible, must at the same time consider the degrading punishment denounced against his defection as inevitable, should he come within the General's power.

When noon was well passed, new apprehensions came on the mind of the lonely woman. Her son still slept under the influence of the draught; but what if, being stronger than she had ever known it administered, his health or his reason should be affected by its potency? For the first time, likewise, notwithstanding her high ideas on the subject of parental authority, she began to dread the resentment of the son, whom her heart told her she had wronged. Of late, she had observed that his temper was less docile, and his determinations, especially upon this late occasion of his enlistment, independently formed, and then boldly carried through. She remembered the stern wilfulness of his father when he accounted himself ill-used, and began to dread that Hamish, upon finding the deceit she had put upon him, might resent it even to the extent of casting her off, and pursuing his own course through the world alone. Such were the alarming and yet the reasonable apprehensions which began to crowd upon the unfortunate woman, after the apparent success of her ill-advised stratagem.

It was nigh evening that Hamish awoke, and then he was far from being in the full possession either of his mental or bodily powers. From his vague expressions and disordered pulse, Elspat at first experienced much apprehension; but she used such expedients as her medical knowledge suggested; and in the course of the night, she had the satisfaction to see him sink once more into a deep sleep, which probably carried off the greater part of the effects of the drug, for about sunrising she heard him arise, and call to her for his bonnet. This she had purposely removed, from a fear that he might awaken and depart in the night-time, without her knowledge.

"My bonnet—my bonnet," cried Hamish, "it is time to take fare-well. Mother, your drink was too strong—the sun is up—but with the next sun I will still see the double summit of the ancient Dun. My bonnet—my bonnet! Mother, I must be instant in my departure." These expressions made it plain that poor Hamish was unconscious that two nights and a day had passed since he had drained the fatal quaigh, and Elspat had now to venture on what she felt as the almost perilous, as well as painful task, of explaining her machinations.

"Forgive me, my son," she said, approaching Hamish, and taking him by the hand with an air of deferential awe, which perhaps she had not always used to his father, even when in his moody fits.

"Forgive you, mother—for what?" said Hamish, laughing; "for giving me a dram that was too strong, and which my head still feels this morning, or for hiding my bonnet to keep me an instant longer? Nay, do you forgive me. Give me the bonnet, and let that be done which now must be done. Give me my bonnet, or I go without it; surely I am not to be delayed by so trifling a want as that—I, who have gone for years with only a strap of deer's hide to tie back my hair. Trifle not, but give it me, or I must go bareheaded, since to stay is impossible."

"My son," said Elspat, keeping fast hold of his hand, "what is done cannot be recalled; could you borrow the wings of yonder eagle, you would arrive at the Dun too late for what you purpose,—too soon for what awaits you there. You believe you see the sun rising for the first time since you have seen him set, but yesterday beheld him climb Ben Cruachan, though your eyes were closed against his light."

Hamish cast upon his mother a wild glance of extreme terror, then instantly recovering himself, said—"I am no child to be cheated out of my purpose by such tricks as these—Farewell, mother, each moment is worth a lifetime."

"Stay," she said, "my dear—my deceived son! rush not on infamy and ruin—Yonder I see the priest upon the road on his white horse—ask him the day of the month and week—let him decide between us."

With the speed of an eagle, Hamish darted up the acclivity, and stood by the minister of Glenorquhy, who was pacing out thus early to administer consolation to a distressed family near Bunawe.

The good man was somewhat startled to behold an armed Highlander, then so unusual a sight, and apparently much agitated, stop his horse by the bridle, and ask him with a faltering voice the day of the week and month. "Had you been where you should have been yesterday, young man," replied the clergyman, "you would have known that it was God's Sabbath; and that this is Monday, the second day of the week, and twenty-first of the month."

"And this is true?" said Hamish.

"As true," answered the surprised minister, "as that I yesterday preached the word of God to this parish.—What ails you, young man? —are you sick?—are you in your right mind?"

Hamish made no answer, only repeated to himself the first expression of the clergyman—"Had you been where you should have been yesterday;" and so saying, he let go the bridle, turned from the road, and descended the path towards the hut, with the look and pace of one who was going to execution. The minister looked after him with surprise; but although he knew who was the inhabitant of the hovel, the character of Elspat had not invited him to open any communication with her, because she was generally reputed a Papist, or rather one indifferent to all religion, except some superstitious observances which had been handed down from her parents. On Hamish the Reverend Mr Tyrie had bestowed instructions when he was occasionally thrown in his way, and if the seed fell among the brambles and thorns of a wild and uncultivated disposition, it had not yet been entirely checked or destroyed. There was something so ghastly in the present expression of the youth's features, that the good man was tempted to go down to the hovel, and inquire whether any distress had befallen the inhabitants, in which his presence might be consoling, and his ministry useful. Unhappily he did not persevere in this resolution, which might have saved a great misfortune, as he would have probably become a mediator for the unfortunate young man. But recollection of the wild moods of such Highlanders as had been educated after the old fashion of the country, prevented his intruding himself on the widow and son of the far-dreaded robber MacTavish Mhor; and he thus missed an opportunity, which he afterwards sorely repented, of doing much good.

When Hamish MacTavish entered his mother's hut, it was only to throw himself on the bed he had left, and, exclaiming, "Undone, undone!" to give vent, in cries of grief and anger, to his deep sense of the deceit which had been practised on him, and of the cruel predicament to which he was reduced.

Elspat was prepared for the first explosion of her son's passion, and said to herself, "It is but the mountain torrent, swelled by the thunder shower. Let us sit and rest us by the bank; for all its present tumult, the time will soon come when we may pass it dry-shod." She suffered his complaints and his reproaches, which were, even in the midst of his agony, respectful and affectionate, to die away without returning any answer; and when, at length, having exhausted all the exclamations of sorrow which his language, copious in expressing the feelings of the heart, affords to the sufferer, he sunk into a gloomy silence, she suffered the interval to continue near an hour ere she approached her son's couch.

"And now," she said at length, with a voice in which the authority of the mother was qualified by its tenderness, "have you exhausted your idle sorrows, and are you able to place what you have gained against what you have lost? Is the false son of Dermid your brother, or the father of your tribe, that you weep because you cannot bind yourself to his belt, and become one of those who must do his bidding? Could you find in yonder distant country the lakes and the mountains that you leave behind you here? Can you hunt the deer of Breadalbane in the forests of America, or will the ocean afford you the silver-scaled salmon of the Awe? Consider, then, what is your loss, and, like a wise man, set it against what you have won."

"I have lost all, mother," replied Hamish, "since I have broken my word, and lost my honour. I might tell my tale, but who, Oh, who would believe me?" The unfortunate young man again clasped his hands together, and, pressing them to his forehead, hid his face upon the bed.

Elspat was now really alarmed, and perhaps wished the fatal deceit had been left unattempted. She had no hope or refuge saving in the eloquence of persuasion, of which she possessed no small share, though her total ignorance of the world as it actually existed, rendered its energy unavailing. She urged her son, by every tender epithet which a parent could bestow, to take care for his own safety.

"Leave me," she said, "to baffle your pursuers. I will save your life —I will save your honour—I will tell them that my fair-haired Hamish fell from the Corrie Dhu (black precipice) into the gulf, of which human eye never beheld the bottom. I will tell them this, and I will hang your plaid on the thorns which grow on the brink of the precipice, that they may believe my words. They will believe, and they will return to the Dun of the double-crest; for though the Saxon drum can call the living to die, it cannot recall the dead to their slavish standard. Then will we travel together far northward to the salt lakes of Kintail, and place glens and mountains betwixt us and the sons of Dermid. We will visit the shores of the dark lake, and my kinsmen—for was not my mother of the children of Kenneth, and will they not remember us with the old love?—Yes, they will receive us with the love of the olden time, which lives in those distant glens, where the Gael still dwell in their nobleness, unmingled with the churl Saxons, or with the base brood that are their tools and their slaves."

The energy of the language, somewhat allied to hyperbole, even in its most ordinary expressions, now seemed almost too weak to afford Elspat the means of bringing out the splendid picture which she presented to her son of the land in which she proposed to him to take refuge. Yet the colours were few with which she could paint her Highland paradise. "The hills," she said, "were higher and more magnificent than those of Breadalbane—Ben Cruachan was but a dwarf to Skooroora. The lakes were broader and larger, and abounded not only with fish, but with the enchanted and amphibious animal which gives oil to the lamp.* The deer were larger and more numerous—the white-tusked boar, the chase of which the brave loved best, was yet to be roused in these western solitudes—the men were nobler, wiser, and stronger, than the degenerate brood who lived under the Saxon banner. The daughters of the land were beautiful, with blue eyes and fair hair, and bosoms of snow, and out of these she would choose a wife for Hamish, of blameless descent, spotless fame, fixed and true affection, who should be in their summer bothy as a beam of the sun, and in their winter abode as the warmth of the needful fire."

Such were the topics with which Elspat strove to soothe the despair of her son, and to determine him, if possible, to leave the fatal spot, on which he seemed resolved to linger. The style of her rhetoric was poetical, but in other respects resembled that which, like other fond mothers, she had lavished on Hamish, while a child or a boy, in order to gain his consent to do something he had no mind to; and she spoke louder, quicker, and more earnestly, in proportion as she began to despair of her words carrying conviction.

On the mind of Hamish her eloquence made no impression. He knew far better than she did the actual situation of the country, and was sensible, that, though it might be possible to hide himself as a fugitive among more distant mountains, there was now no corner in the Highlands in which his father's profession could be practised, even if he had not adopted, from the improved ideas of the time when he lived, the opinion that the trade of the cateran was no longer the road to honour and distinction. Her words were therefore poured into regardless ears, and she exhausted herself in vain in the attempt to paint the regions of her mother's kinsmen in such terms as might tempt Hamish to accompany her thither. She spoke for hours, but she spoke in vain. She could extort no answer, save groans, and sighs, and

* The seals are considered by the Highlanders as enchanted princes.

ejaculations, expressing the extremity of despair.

At length, starting on her feet, and changing the monotonous tone in which she had chanted, as it were, the praises of the province of refuge, into the short, stern language of eager passion—"I am a fool," she said, "to spend my words upon an idle, poor-spirited unintelligent boy, who crouches like a hound to the lash. Wait here, and receive your task-masters, and abide your chastisement at their hands. But do not think your mother's eyes will behold it. I could not see it and live. My eyes have looked often upon death, but never upon dishonour. Farewell, Hamish!—We never meet again."

She dashed from the hut like a lapwing, and perhaps for the moment actually entertained the purpose which she expressed, of parting with her son for ever. She would have been a fearful sight that evening to those who met her wandering through the wilderness like a restless spirit, and speaking to herself in language which will endure no translation. She rambled for hours, seeking rather than shunning the most dangerous paths. The precarious track through the morass, the dizzy path along the edge of the precipice, or by the banks of the gulfing river, were the roads which, far from avoiding, she sought with eagerness, and traversed with reckless haste. But the courage arising from despair was the means of saving the life, which, (though deliberate suicide was rarely practised in the Highlands,) she was perhaps desirous of terminating. Her step on the verge of the precipice was firm as that of the wild goat. Her eye, in that state of excitation, was so keen as to discern, even amid darkness, the perils which noon would not have enabled a stranger to avoid.

Elspat's course was not directly forward, else she had soon been far from the bothy in which she had left her son. It was circuitous, for that hut was the centre to which her heart-strings were chained, and though she wandered around it, she felt it impossible to leave the vicinity. With the first beams of morning, she returned to the hut. Awhile she paused at the wattled door, as if ashamed that lingering fondness should have brought her back to the spot which she had left with the purpose of never returning; but there was yet more of fear and anxiety in her hesitation—of anxiety, lest her fair-haired son had suffered from the effects of her potion—of fear, lest his enemies had come upon him in the night. She opened the door of the hut gently, and entered with noiseless step. Exhausted with his sorrow and anxiety, and not entirely relieved perhaps from the influence of the powerful opiate, Hamish Bean again slept the stern sound sleep, by which the Indians are said to be overcome during the interval of their torments. His mother was scarcely sure that she actually discerned his form on the bed, scarce certain that her ear caught the sound of his breathing. With a throbbing heart, Elspat went to the fire-place in the centre of the hut, where slumbered, covered with a piece of turf, the glimmering embers of the fire, never extinguished on a Scottish hearth until the indwellers leave the mansion for ever.

"Feeble *greishogh*,"* she said, as she lighted, by the help of a match, a splinter of bog pine which was to serve the place of a candle; "weak *greishogh*, soon shalt thou be put out for ever, and may Heaven grant that the life of Elspat MacIan Macdonell have no longer duration than thine!"

While she spoke she raised the blazing light towards the bed, on which still lay the prostrate limbs of her son, in a posture that left it doubtful whether he slept or swooned. As she advanced towards him, the light flashed upon his eyes—he started up in an instant, made a stride forward with his naked dirk in his hand, like a man armed to meet a mortal enemy, and exclaimed, "Stand off!—on thy life, stand off!"

"It is the word and the action of my husband," answered Elspat; "and I know by his speech and his step the son of MacTavish Mhor."

"Mother," said Hamish, relapsing from his tone of desperate firmness into one of melancholy expostulation; "Oh, dearest mother, wherefore have you returned hither?"

"Ask why the hind comes back to the fawn," said Elspat—"why the cat of the mountain returns to her lodge and her young. Know you, Hamish, that the heart of the mother only lives in the bosom of the child."

"Then will it soon cease to throb," said Hamish, "unless it can beat within the bosom that lies beneath the turf.—Mother, do not blame me; if I weep, it is not for myself but for you, for my suffering will soon be over; but yours——O, who but Heaven shall set a boundary to it!"

Elspat shuddered and stepped backward, but almost instantly resumed her firm and upright position, and her dauntless bearing.

"I thought thou wert a man but even now," she said, "and thou art again a child. Hearken to me yet, and let us leave this place together. Have I done thee wrong or injury? if so, yet do not avenge it so cruelly —See, Elspat MacIan Macdonell, who never kneeled even to a priest, falls prostrate before her own son, and craves his forgiveness." And at once she threw herself on her knees before the young man, seized on his hand, and kissing it an hundred times, repeated as often, in heart-breaking accents, the most earnest entreaties for forgiveness. "Pardon," she exclaimed, "pardon, for the sake of your father's ashes— pardon for the sake of the pains with which I bore thee, the care with which I nurtured thee!—Hear it, Heaven, and behold it, Earth—the

* Greishogh, a glowing ember.

mother asks pardon of the child, and she is refused!"

It was in vain that Hamish endeavoured to stem this tide of passion, by assuring his mother, with the most solemn asseverations, that he forgave entirely the fatal deceit which she had practised upon him.

"Empty words," she said; "idle protestations, which are but used to hide the obduracy of your resentment. Would you have me believe you, then leave the hut this instant, and retire from a country which every hour renders more dangerous.—Do this, and I will believe you have forgiven me—refuse it, and again I call moon and stars, heaven and earth, to witness the unrelenting resentment with which you prosecute your mother for a fault, which, if it be one, arose out of love to you."

"Mother," said Hamish, "on this subject you move me not. I will fly before no man. If Barcaldine should send every Gael that is under his banner, here, and in this place, will I abide them. And when you bid me fly, you may as well command yonder mountain to be loosened from its foundations. Had I been sure of the road by which they are coming hither, I had spared them the pains of seeking me; but I might go by the mountain, while they perchance came by the lake. Here I will abide my fate; nor is there in Scotland a voice of power enough to bid me stir from hence, and be obeyed."

"Here, then, I also stay," said Elspat, rising up and speaking with assumed composure. "I have seen my husband's death—my eye-lids shall not grieve to look on the fall of my son. But MacTavish Mhor died as became the brave, with his good sword in his right hand; my son will perish like the bullock that is driven to the shambles by the Saxon owner who has bought him for a price."

"Mother," said the unhappy young man, "you have taken my life; to that you have a right, for you gave it. But touch not my honour!—it came to me from a brave strain of ancestors, and should be sullied neither by man's deed nor woman's speech. What I shall do, perhaps I myself yet know not; but tempt me no farther by reproachful words. You have already made wounds more than you can ever heal."

"It is well, my son," said Elspat, in reply. "Expect neither farther complaint nor remonstrance from me; but let us be silent, and wait the chance which Heaven shall send us."

The sun arose on the next morning, and found the bothy silent as the grave. The mother and son had arisen, and were engaged each in their separate task—Hamish in preparing and cleaning his arms with the greatest accuracy, but with an air of deep dejection. Elspat, more restless in her agony of spirit, employed herself in making ready the food which the distress of yesterday had induced them both to dispense with for an unusual number of hours. She placed it on the board before her son so soon as it was prepared, with the words of a Gaelic poet, "Without daily food, the husbandman's plough-share stands still in the furrow; without daily food, the sword of the warrior is too heavy for his hand. Our bodies are our slaves, yet they must be fed if we would have their service. So spoke in ancient day the Blind Bard to the warriors of Fion."

The young man made no reply, but he fed on what was placed before him, as if to gather strength for the scene which he was to undergo. When his mother saw that he had eaten what sufficed him, she again filled the fatal quaigh, and proffered it as the conclusion of the repast. But he started aside with a convulsive gesture, expressive at once of fear and abhorrence.

"Nay, my son," she said, "this time, surely, thou hast no cause of fear."

"Urge me not, mother," answered Hamish; "or put the leprous toad into a flagon, and I will drink; but from that accursed cup, and of that mind-destroying potion, never will I taste more!"

"At your pleasure, my son," said Elspat, haughtily, and began, with much apparent assiduity, the various domestic tasks which had been interrupted during the preceding day. Whatever was at her heart, all anxiety seemed banished from her looks and demeanour. It was but from an over activity of bustling exertion that it might have been perceived, by a close observer, that her actions were spurred by some internal cause of painful excitement; and such a spectator, too, might also have observed how often she broke off the snatches of songs or tunes which she hummed, apparently without knowing what she was doing, in order to cast a hasty glance from the door of the hut. Whatever might be in the mind of Hamish, his demeanour was directly the reverse of that adopted by his mother. Having finished the task of cleaning and preparing his arms, which he arranged within the hut, he sat himself down before the door of the bothy, and watched the opposite hill, like the fixed sentinel who expects the approach of an enemy. Noon found him in the same unchanged posture, and it was an hour after that period, when his mother, standing beside him, laid her hand on his shoulder, and said, in a tone indifferent, as if she had been talking of some friendly visit, "When dost thou expect them?"

"They cannot be here till the shadows fall long to the eastward," replied Hamish; "that is, even supposing the nearest party, commanded by Sergeant Allan Breack Cameron, has been commanded hither by express from Dunbarton, as it is most likely they will."

"Then enter beneath your mother's roof once more; partake the last time of the food which she has prepared; after this let them come, and thou shalt see if thy mother is an useless encumbrance in the day of strife. Thy hand, practised as it is, cannot fire these arms so fast as I can load them; nay, if it is necessary, I do not myself fear the flash or the report, and my aim has been held fatal."

"In the name of Heaven, mother, meddle not with this matter!" said Hamish. "Allan Breack is a wise man and a kind one, and comes of a good stem. It may be he can promise for our officers, that they will touch me with no infamous punishment; and if they offer me confinement in the dungeon, or death by the musket, to that I may not object."

"Alas, and wilt thou trust to their word, my foolish child? Remember the race of Dermid were ever fair and false, and no sooner shall they have gyves on thy hands, than they will strip thy shoulders for the scourge."

"Save your advice, mother," said Hamish, sternly; "for me, my mind is made up."

But though he spoke thus, to escape the almost persecuting urgency of his mother, Hamish would have found it, at that moment, impossible to say upon what course of conduct he had thus fixed. On one point alone he was determined, namely, to abide his destiny, be what it might, and not to add to the breach of his word, of which he had been involuntarily rendered guilty, by attempting to escape from punishment. This act of self-devotion he conceived to be due to his own honour, and that of his countrymen. Which of his comrades would in future be trusted, if he should be considered as having broken his word, and betrayed the confidence of his officers? and whom but Hamish Bean MacTavish would the regiment accuse, for having verified the suspicions which the Saxon General was well known to entertain against the good faith of the Highlanders? He was, therefore, bent firmly to abide his fate. But whether his purpose was to yield himself peaceably into the hands of the party who should come to apprehend him, or whether by resistance to provoke them to kill him on the spot, was a question which he could not himself have answered. His desire to see Barcaldine, and explain the cause of his absence at the appointed time, urged him to the one course; his fear of the degrading punishment, and of his mother's bitter upbraidings, strongly instigated the latter and the more dangerous purpose. He left it to chance to decide when the crisis should arrive; nor did he tarry long in expectation of the catastrophe.

Evening approached, the gigantic shadows of the mountains streamed in darkness towards the east, while their western peaks were still glowing with crimson and gold. The road which winds round Ben Cruachan was fully visible from the door of the bothy, when a party of five Highland soldiers, whose arms glanced in the sun, wheeled suddenly into sight from its most distant extremity, where it was lost behind the mountain. One walked a little before the other four, who marched regularly and in files, according to the rules of military discipline. There was no dispute, from the firelocks which they carried, and the plaids and bonnets which they wore, that they were a party of Hamish's regiment, under a non-commissioned officer; and there could be as little doubt of the purpose of their appearance on the banks of Loch Awe.

"They come briskly forward—" said the widow of MacTavish Mhor,—"I wonder how fast or how slow some of them will return again. But they are five, and it is too much odds for a fair field. Step back within the hut, my son, and shoot from the loophole beside the door. Two you may bring down ere they quit the high road for the footpath—and then they are but three; and your father, with my aid, has stood against that number."

Hamish Bean took the gun which his mother offered, but did not stir from the door of the hut. He was soon visible to the party on the high road, as was evident from their increasing their pace to a run; the files, however, still keeping together like coupled greyhounds, and advancing with great rapidity. In far less time than this would have been accomplished by men less accustomed to the mountains, they had left the high road, traversed the narrow path, and approached within pistol-shot of the bothy, at the door of which stood Hamish, fixed like a statue of stone, with his firelock in his hand, while his mother, placed behind him, and almost driven to frenzy by the violence of her passions, reproached him in the strongest terms which despair could invent, for his want of resolution and faintness of heart. Her words increased the bitter gall which was arising in the young man's own heart, as he observed the unfriendly speed with which his late comrades were eagerly making towards him, like hounds towards the stag when he is at bay. The untamed and angry passions which he inherited from father and mother, were awakened by the supposed hostility of those who pursued him; and the restraint under which they were held by his sober judgment, began gradually to give way. The sergeant now called him, "Hamish Bean MacTavish, lay down your arms and surrender."

"Do you stand, Allan Breack Cameron, and make your men stand, or it will be the worse for us all."

"Halt, men—" said the sergeant, but continuing himself to advance. "Hamish, think what you do, and give up your gun; you may spill blood, but you cannot escape punishment."

"The scourge—the scourge—my son, beware the scourge," whispered his mother.

"Take heed, Allan Breack," said Hamish. "I would not hurt you willingly,—but I will not be taken unless you can assure me against the Saxon lash."

"Fool!" answered Cameron, "you know I cannot—But I will do all I can. I will say I met you on your return, and the punishment will be light—but give up your musket—Come on, men."

Instantly he rushed forward, extending his arm as if to push aside the young man's levelled firelock—Elspat exclaimed, "Now, spare not your father's blood to defend your father's hearth!"—Hamish fired his piece, and Cameron dropped dead—all, it might be said, in the same moment of time. The soldiers rushed forward and seized Hamish, who, seeming petrified with what he had done, offered not the least resistance. Not so his mother, who, seeing the men about to put handcuffs on her son, threw herself on the soldiers with such fury, that it required two of them to hold her, while the rest secured the prisoner.

"Are you not an accursed creature," said one of the men to Hamish, "to have slain your best friend, who was contriving, during the whole march, how he could find some way of getting you off without punishment for your desertion?"

"Do you hear that, mother?" said Hamish, turning himself as much towards her as his bonds would permit. But the mother heard nothing, and saw nothing. She had fainted on the floor of her hut. Without waiting for her recovery, the party almost immediately began their homeward march towards Dunbarton, leading along with them their prisoner. They thought it necessary, however, to stay for a little space at the village of Dalmally, from which they dispatched a party of the inhabitants to bring away the body of their unfortunate leader, while they themselves repaired to a magistrate to state what had happened, and inquire his instructions as to the farther course to be pursued. The crime being of a military character, they were instructed to march the prisoner to Dunbarton without delay.

The swoon of the mother of Hamish lasted for a length of time; the longer perhaps that her constitution, strong as it was, must have been much exhausted by her previous agitation of three days' endurance. She was roused from her stupor at length by female voices, which cried the coronach, or lament for the dead, with clapping of hands and loud exclamation; while the melancholy note of a lament, appropriate to the clan Cameron, played on the bagpipe, was heard from time to time.

Elspat started up like one awakened from the dead, and without any accurate recollection of the scene which had passed before her eyes. There were females in the hut who were swathing the corpse in its bloody plaid before carrying it from the fatal spot. "Women," she said,

starting up and interrupting their chant at once and their labour—
"Tell me, women, why sing you the dirge of MacDhonuil Dhu in the
house of MacTavish Mhor?"

"She-wolf, be silent with thine ill-omened yell," answered one of
the females, a relation of the deceased, "and let us do our duty
to our beloved kinsman. There shall never be coronach cried, or
dirge played, for thee or thy bloody wolf-burd.* The ravens shall eat
him from the gibbet, and the foxes and wild cats shall tear thy corpse
upon the hill. Cursed be he that would sain your bones, or add a stone
to your cairn!"

"Daughter of a foolish mother," answered the widow of MacTavish
Mhor, "know that the gibbet, with which you threaten us, is no portion
of our inheritance. For thirty years the Black Tree of the Law, whose
apples are dead men's bodies, hungered after the beloved husband of
my heart; but he died like a brave man, with the sword in his hand, and
defrauded it of its hopes and its fruit."

"So shall it not be with thy child, bloody sorceress," replied the
female mourner, whose passions were as violent as those of Elspat
herself. "The ravens shall tear his fair hair to line their nests, before
the sun sinks beneath the Treshornish islands."

These words recalled to Elspat's mind the whole history of the last
three dreadful days. At first, she stood fixed as if the extremity of
distress had converted her into stone; but in a minute, the pride and
violence of her temper, out-braved as she thought herself on her own
threshold, enabled her to reply—"Yes, insulting hag, my fair-haired
boy may die, but it will not be with a white hand—it has been dyed in
the blood of his enemy, in the best blood of a Cameron—remember
that; and when you lay your dead in his grave, let it be his best epitaph,
that he was killed by Hamish Bean for essaying to lay hands on the son
of MacTavish Mhor on his own threshold. Farewell—the shame of
defeat, loss, and slaughter, remain with the clan that has endured it!"

The relative of the slaughtered Cameron raised her voice in reply;
but Elspat, disdaining to continue the objurgation, or perhaps feeling
her grief likely to overmaster her power of expressing her resentment,
had left the hut, and was walking forth in the bright moonshine.

The females who were arranging the corpse of the slaughtered
man, paused from their melancholy labour to look after her tall figure
as it glided away among the cliffs. "I am glad she is gone," said one of
the younger persons who assisted. "I would as soon dress a corpse
where the great Fiend himself—God sain us—stood visibly before us,
than where Elspat of the Tree is amongst us.—Ay—ay, even overmuch intercourse hath she had with the Enemy in her day."

* Wolf-brood, _i. e._ wolf-cub.

"Silly woman," answered the female who had maintained the dialogue with the departed Elspat, "thinkest thou that there is a worse fiend on earth, or beneath it, than the pride and fury of an offended woman, like yonder bloody-minded hag? Know that blood has been as familiar to her as the dew to the mountain-daisy. Many and many a brave man has she caused to breathe their last for little wrong they had done to her or hers. But her hough-sinews are cut, now that her wolf-burd must, like a murderer as he is, make a murderer's end."

Whilst the women thus discoursed together, as they watched the corpse of Allan Breack Cameron, the unhappy cause of his death pursued her lonely way across the mountain. While she remained within sight of the bothy, she put a strong constraint on herself, that by no alteration of pace or gesture, she might afford to her enemies the triumph of calculating the excess of her mental agitation, nay despair. She stalked, therefore, with a slow rather than a swift step, and, holding herself upright, seemed at once to endure with firmness that woe which was passed, and bid defiance to that which was about to come. But when she was beyond the sight of those who remained in the hut, she could no longer suppress the extremity of her emotion. Drawing her mantle wildly round her, she stopped at the first knoll, and climbing to its summit, extended her arms up to the bright moon, as if accusing heaven and earth for her misfortunes, and uttered scream on scream, like those of an eagle whose nest has been plundered of her brood. Awhile she vented her grief in these inarticulate cries, then rushed on her way with a hasty and unequal step, in the vain hope of overtaking the party which was conveying her son a prisoner to Dunbarton. But her strength, superhuman as it seemed, failed her in the trial, nor was it possible for her, with her utmost efforts, to accomplish her purpose.

Yet she pressed onwards, with all the speed which her exhausted frame could exert. When food became indispensable, she entered the first cottage: "Give me to eat," she said; "I am the widow of MacTavish Mhor—I am the mother of Hamish MacTavish Bean,—give me to eat, that I may once more see my fair-haired son." Her demand was never refused, though granted in many cases with a kind of struggle between compassion and aversion in some of those to whom she applied, which was in others qualified by fear. The share she had had in occasioning the death of Allan Breack Cameron, which must probably involve that of her own son, was not accurately known; but, from knowledge of her violent passions and former habits of life, no one doubted that in one way or other she had been the cause of the catastrophe; and Hamish Bean was considered, in the slaughter which he had committed, rather as the instrument than as the accomplice of his mother.

This general opinion of his countrymen was of little service to the unfortunate Hamish. As his captain, Green Colin, understood the manners and habits of his country, he had no difficulty in collecting from Hamish the particulars accompanying his supposed desertion, and the subsequent death of the non-commissioned officer. He felt the utmost compassion for a youth, who had thus fallen a victim to the extravagant and fatal fondness of a parent. But he had no excuse to plead which could rescue his unhappy recruit from the doom, which military discipline and the award of a court-martial denounced against him for the crime he had committed.

No time had been lost in their proceedings, and as little was interposed betwixt sentence and execution. General —— had determined to make a severe example of the first deserter who should fall into his power, and here was one who had defended himself by main force, and slain in the affray the officer sent to take him into custody. A fitter subject for punishment could not have occurred, and Hamish was sentenced to immediate execution. All that the interference of his captain in his favour could procure, was that he should die a soldier's death; for there had been a purpose of executing him upon the gibbet.

The worthy clergyman of Glenorquhy chanced to be at Dunbarton, in attendance upon some church courts, at the time of this catastrophe. He visited his unfortunate parishioner in his dungeon, found him ignorant indeed, but not obstinate, and the answers which he received from him, when conversing on religious topics, were such as induced him doubly to regret, that a mind naturally pure and noble should have remained unhappily so wild and uncultivated.

When he ascertained the real character and disposition of the young man, the worthy pastor made deep and painful reflections on his own shyness and timidity, which, arising from the evil fame that attached to the lineage of Hamish, had restrained him from charitably endeavouring to bring this strayed sheep within the great fold. While the good minister blamed his own cowardice in times past, which had deterred him from risking his person, to save, perhaps, an immortal soul, he resolved no longer to be governed by such timid counsels, but to endeavour, by application to his officers, to obtain a reprieve, at least, if not a pardon, for the criminal, in whom he felt so unusually interested, at once from his docility of temper and his generosity of disposition.

Accordingly the divine sought out Captain Campbell of Barcaldine at the barracks within the garrison. There was a gloom of melancholy on the brow of Green Colin, which was not lessened, but increased, when the clergyman stated his name, quality, and errand. "You cannot tell me better of the young man than I am disposed to believe," answered the Highland officer. "You cannot ask me to do more in his behalf than I am of myself inclined, and have already endeavoured to do. But it is all in vain. General ———— is half a Lowlander, half an Englishman. He has no idea of the high and enthusiastic character which in these mountains often brings exalted virtues in contact with great crimes, which, however, are less offences of the heart than errors of the understanding. I went so far as to tell him, that in this young man he was putting to death the best and the bravest of my company, where all are good and brave. I explained to him by what strange delusion the culprit's apparent desertion was occasioned, and how little his heart was accessary to the crime which his hand unhappily committed. His answer was, 'There are Highland visions, Captain Campbell, as unsatisfactory and vain as those of the Second Sight. An act of gross desertion may in any case be palliated under the plea of intoxication; the murder of an officer may be as easily coloured over with that of temporary insanity. The example must be made, and if it has fallen on a man otherwise a good recruit, it will have the greater effect.'—Such being the General's unalterable purpose," continued Captain Campbell, with a sigh, "be it your care, reverend sir, that your penitent prepare by break of day to-morrow for that great change which we shall all one day be subjected to."

"And for which," said the clergyman, "may God prepare us all, as I in my duty will not be wanting to this poor youth."

Next morning as the very earliest beams of sunrise saluted the grey towers which crown the summit of that singular and tremendous rock, the soldiers of the new Highland regiment appeared on the parade, within the Castle of Dunbarton, and having fallen into order, began to move downwards by steep staircases and narrow passages towards the external barrier-gate, which is at the very bottom of the rock. The wild wailings of the pibroch were heard at times, interchanged with the drums and fifes, which beat the Dead March.

The unhappy criminal's fate did not, at first, excite that general sympathy in the regiment which would probably have arisen had he been executed for desertion alone. The slaughter of the unfortunate Allan Breack had given a different colour to Hamish's offence; for the deceased was much beloved, and besides belonged to a numerous and powerful clan, of whom there were many in the ranks. The unfortunate criminal, on the contrary, was little known to, and scarcely connected with, any of his regimental companions. His father had been, indeed, distinguished for his strength and manhood; but he was of a broken clan, as those names were called, who had no chief to lead them to battle.

It would have been almost impossible in another case, to have turned out of the ranks of the regiment the party necessary for execution of the sentence; but the six individuals selected for that purpose, were friends of the deceased, descended, like him, from the race of MacDhonuil Dhu; and while they prepared for the dismal task which their duty imposed, it was not without a stern feeling of revenge. The leading company of the regiment began now to defile from the barrier-gate and was followed by the others, each successively moving and halting according to the orders of their Adjutant, so as to form three sides of an oblong square, with the ranks faced inwards. The fourth, or blank side of the square, was closed up by the huge and lofty precipice on which the Castle rises. About the centre of the procession, bare-headed, disarmed, and with his hands bound, came the unfortunate victim of military law. He was deadly pale, but his step was firm and his eye as bright as ever. The clergyman walked by his side—the coffin, which was to receive his mortal remains, was borne before him. The looks of his comrades were still, composed, and solemn. They felt for the youth, whose handsome form, and manly yet submissive deportment had, as soon as he was distinctly visible to them, softened the hearts of many, even of some who had been actuated by vindictive feelings.

The coffin destined for the yet living body of Hamish Bean was placed at the bottom of the hollow square, about two yards distant from the foot of the precipice, which rises in that place as steep as a stone wall to the height of three or four hundred feet. Thither the prisoner was also led, the clergyman still continuing by his side, pouring forth exhortations of courage and consolation, to which the youth appeared to listen with respectful devotion. With slow, and, it seemed, almost unwilling steps, the firing party entered the square, and were drawn up facing the prisoner, about ten yards distant. The clergyman was now about to retire—"Think, my son," he said, "on what I have told you, and let your hope be rested on the anchor which I have given. You will then exchange a short and miserable existence here, for a life in which you will experience neither sorrow nor pain.—Is there aught else which you can intrust me to execute for you?"

The youth looked at his sleeve buttons. They were of gold, booty perhaps which his father had taken from some English officer during the civil war. The clergyman disengaged them from his sleeves.

"My mother!" he said with some effort, "give them to my poor mother!—See her, good father, and teach her what she should think of all this—Tell her Hamish Bean is more glad to die than ever he was to rest after the longest day's hunting. Farewell, sir—farewell!"

The good man could scarce retire from the fatal spot—an officer afforded him the support of his arm. At his last look towards Hamish, he beheld him alive and kneeling on the coffin; the few that were around him had all withdrawn. The fatal word was given, the rock rang sharp to the sound of the discharge, and Hamish, falling forward with a groan, died, it may be supposed, without almost a sense of the passing agony.

Ten or twelve of his own company then came forward, and laid with solemn reverence the remains of their comrade in the coffin, while the Dead March was again struck up, and the several companies, marching in single files, passed the coffin one by one, in order that all might receive from the awful spectacle the warning which it was peculiarly intended to afford. The regiment was then marched off the ground, and reascended the ancient cliff, their music, as usual on such occasions, striking lively strains, as if sorrow, or even deep thought, should as short a while as possible be the tenant of the soldier's bosom.

At the same time the small party, which we before mentioned, bore the bier of the ill-fated Hamish to his humble grave, in a corner of the church-yard of Dunbarton, usually assigned to criminals. Here, among the dust of the guilty, lies a youth, whose name, had he survived the ruin of the fatal events by which he was hurried into crime, might have adorned the annals of the brave.

The minister of Glenorquhy left Dunbarton immediately after he had witnessed the last scene of this melancholy catastrophe. His reason acquiesced in the justice of the sentence, which required blood for blood, and he acknowledged that the ireful and vindictive character of his countrymen required to be powerfully restrained by the strong curb of social law. But still he mourned over the individual victim. Who may arraign the bolt of Heaven when it bursts among the sons of the forest; yet who can refrain from mourning, when it selects for the object of its blighting aim the fair stem of a young oak, that promised to be the pride of the dell in which it flourished? Musing on these melancholy events, noon found him engaged in the mountain passes, by which he was to return to his still distant home.

Confident in his knowledge of the country, the clergyman had left the main road, to seek one of those shorter paths, which are only used by pedestrians, or by men like the minister, mounted on the small, but sure-footed, hardy, and sagacious horses of the country. The place which he now traversed, was in itself gloomy and desolate, and tradition had added to it the terror of superstition, by affirming it was haunted by an evil spirit, termed *Cloght-dearg*, that is, Redmantle, who at all times, but especially at noon and at midnight, traversed the glen, in enmity both to man and the inferior creation, did such evil as her power was permitted to extend to, and afflicted with ghastly terrors those whom she had not license otherwise to hurt.

The minister of Glenorquhy had set his face in opposition to many of these superstitions, which he justly thought were derived from the dark ages of Popery, perhaps even from those of Paganism, and unfit to be entertained or believed by the Christians of an enlightened age. Some of his more attached parishioners considered him as too rash in opposing the ancient faith of their fathers; and though they honoured the moral intrepidity of their pastor, they could not avoid entertaining and expressing fears, that he would one day fall a victim to his temerity, and be torn to pieces in the glen of the Cloght-dearg, or some of those other haunted wilds, which he appeared rather to have a pride and pleasure in traversing, on the days and hours when the wicked spirits were supposed to have especial power over man and beast.

These legends came across the mind of the clergyman; and, alone as he was, a melancholy smile shaded his cheek, as he thought of the inconsistency of human nature, and reflected how many brave men, whom the yell of the pibroch would have sent headlong against fixed bayonets, as the wild bull rushes on his enemy, would have yet feared to encounter those visionary terrors, which he himself, a man of peace, and in ordinary perils no way remarkable for the firmness of his nerves, was now risking without hesitation.

As he looked round the scene of desolation, he could not but acknowledge, in his own mind, that it was not ill chosen for the haunt of those spirits, which are said to delight in solitude and desolation. The glen was so steep and narrow, that there was but just room for the meridian sun to dart a few scattered rays upon the gloomy and precarious stream which stole through its recesses, for the most part in silence, but occasionally murmuring sullenly against the rocks and large stones, which seemed determined to bar its further progress. In winter, or in the rainy season, this small stream was a foaming torrent of the most formidable magnitude, and it was at such periods that it had torn open and laid bare the broad-faced and huge fragments of rock, which, at the season of which we speak, hid its course from the eye, and seemed disposed totally to interrupt it. "Undoubtedly," thought the clergyman, "this mountain rivulet, suddenly swelled by a water-spout, or thunder-storm, has often been the cause of those accidents, which, happening in the glen called by her name, have been ascribed to the agency of the Cloght-dearg."

Just as this idea crossed his mind, he heard a female voice exclaim, in a wild and thrilling accent, "Michael Tyrie—Michael Tyrie!" He looked round in astonishment, and not without some fear. It seemed for an instant, as if the Evil Being, whose existence he had disowned, was about to appear for the punishment of his incredulity. This alarm did not hold him more than an instant, nor did it prevent his replying in a firm voice, "Who calls—and where are you?"

"One who journeys in wretchedness, between life and death," answered the voice; and the speaker, a tall female, appeared from among the fragments of rocks which had concealed her from view.

As she approached more closely, her mantle of bright tartan, in which the red colour much predominated, her stature, the long stride with which she advanced, and the writhen features and wild eyes which were visible from under her curch, would have made her no inadequate representative of the spirit which gave name to the valley. But Mr Tyrie instantly knew her as the woman of the Tree, the widow of MacTavish Mhor, the now childless mother of Hamish Bean. I am not sure whether the minister would not have endured the visitation of the Cloght-dearg herself, rather than the shock of Elspat's presence, considering the news with which he was charged. He drew up his horse instinctively, and stood endeavouring to collect his ideas, while a few paces brought her up to his horse's head.

"Michael Tyrie," said she, "the foolish women of the Clachan* hold thee as a God—be one to me, and say that my son lives. Say this, and I too will be of thy worship—I will bend my knee on the seventh day in thy house of worship, and thy God shall be my God."

"Unhappy woman," replied the clergyman, "man forms not pactions with his Maker as with a creature of clay like himself. Thinkest thou to chaffer with Him, who formed the earth, and spread out the heavens, or that thou canst offer aught of homage or devotion that can be worth acceptance in his eyes? He hath asked obedience, not sacrifice; patience under the trials with which he afflicts us, instead of vain bribes, such as man offers to his changeful brother of clay, that he may be moved from his purpose."

"Be silent, priest!" answered the desperate woman; "speak not to me the words of thy white book. Elspat's kindred were of those who crossed themselves and knelt when the sacring bell was rung; and she knows that atonement can be made on the altar for deeds done in the field. Elspat had once flocks and herds, goats upon the cliffs, and cattle in the strath. She wore gold around her neck and on her hair— thick twists as those worn by the heroes of old. All these would she have resigned to the priest—all these—and if he wished for the ornaments of the lady, or the sporran of the Chief, though they had been great as Maccallan Mhor himself, MacTavish Mhor would have procured them if Elspat had promised them. Elspat is now poor, and has

* i. e. The village, literally the stones.

anti Catholic

nothing to give. But the Black Abbot of Inchaffray would have bidden her scourge her shoulders, and macerate her feet by pilgrimage, and he would have granted his pardon to her when he saw that her blood had flowed, and that her flesh had been torn. These were the priests who had indeed power even with the most powerful—they threatened the great men of the earth with the word of their mouth, the sentence of their book, the blaze of their torch, the sound of their sacring bell. The mighty bent to their will, and unloosed at the word of the priests those whom they had bound in their wrath, and set at liberty, unharmed, him whom they had sentenced to death, and for whose blood they had thirsted. These were a powerful race, and might well ask the poor to kneel, since their power could humble the proud. But you!—against whom are ye strong, but against women who have been guilty of folly, and men who never wore sword? The priests of old were like the winter torrent which fills this hollow valley, and rolls these massive rocks against each other as easily as the boy plays with the ball which he casts before him—But you! you do but resemble the summer-shrunken stream, which is turned aside by the rushes, and stemmed by a bush of sedge—Woe worth you, for there is no help in you!"

Mr Tyrie was at no loss to conceive that Elspat had lost the Roman Catholic faith without gaining any other, and that she still retained a vague and confused idea of the composition with the priesthood, by confession, alms, and penance, and of their extensive power, which, according to her notion, was adequate, if duly propitiated, even to effecting her son's safety. Compassionating her situation, and allowing for her errors and ignorance, he answered her with mildness.

"Alas, unhappy woman! Would to God I could convince thee as easily where thou oughtest to seek, and art sure to find consolation, as I can assure you with a single word, that were Rome and all her priesthood once more in the plenitude of their power, they could not, for largesse or penance, afford to thy misery an atom of aid or comfort.—Elspat MacTavish, I grieve to tell you the news"—

"I know them without thy speech," said the unhappy woman—"My son is doomed to die."

"Elspat," resumed the clergyman, "he *was* doomed, and the sentence has been executed." The hapless mother threw her eyes up to heaven, and uttered a shriek so unlike the voice of a human being, that the eagle which soared in middle air answered it as she would have done the call of her mate.

"It is impossible!" she exclaimed, "it is impossible! Men do not condemn and kill on the same day! Thou art deceiving me. The people call thee holy—hast thou the heart to tell a mother she has murdered her only child?"

"God knows," said the minister, the tears falling fast from his eyes, "that were it in my power, I would gladly tell better tidings—But these which I bear are as certain as they are fatal—My own ears heard the death-shot, my own eyes beheld thy son's death—thy son's funeral.— My tongue bears witness to what my ears heard and my eyes saw."

The wretched female clasped her hands close together, and held them up towards heaven like a sibyl announcing war and desolation, while, in impotent yet frightful rage, she poured forth a tide of the deepest imprecations.—"Base Saxon churl!" she exclaimed, "vile hypocritical juggler! May the eyes that looked tamely on the death of my fair-haired boy be melted in their sockets with ceaseless tears, shed for those that are nearest and most dear to thee! May the ears that heard his death-knell be dead hereafter to all other sounds save the screech of the raven, and the hissing of the adder! May the tongue that tells me of his death and of my own crime, be withered in thy mouth—or better, when thou wouldst pray with thy people, may the Evil One guide it, and give voice to blasphemies instead of blessings, until men shall fly in terror from thy presence, and the thunder of heaven be launched against thy head, and stop for ever thy cursing and accursed voice! Begone! with this malison.—Elspat will never, never again bestow so many words upon living man."

She kept her word—from that day the world was to her a wilderness, in which she remained without thought, care, or interest, absorbed in her own grief, indifferent to everything else.

With her mode of life, or rather of existence, the reader is already as far acquainted as I have the power of making him. Of her death, I can tell him nothing. It is supposed to have happened several years after she had attracted the attention of my excellent friend Mrs Bethune Baliol. Her benevolence, which was never satisfied with dropping a sentimental tear, when there was room for the operation of effective charity, induced her to make various attempts to alleviate the condition of this most wretched woman. But all her exertions could only render Elspat's means of subsistence less precarious, a circumstance which, though generally interesting even to the most wretched outcasts, seemed to her a matter of total indifference. Every attempt to place any person in her hut to take charge of her miscarried, through the extreme resentment with which she regarded all intrusion on her solitude, or by the timidity of those who had been pitched upon to be inmates with the terrible woman of the Tree. At length, when Elspat became totally unable (in appearance at least) to turn herself on the wretched settle which served her for a couch, the humanity of Mr

Tyrie's successor sent two women to attend upon the last moments of the solitary, which could not, it was judged, be far distant, and to avert the shocking possibility that she might perish for want of assistance or food, before she sunk under the effects of extreme age, or mortal malady.

It was on a November evening, that the two women appointed for this melancholy purpose, arrived at the miserable cottage which we have already described. Its wretched inmate lay stretched upon the bed, and seemed almost already a lifeless corpse, save for the wandering of the fierce dark eyes, which rolled in their sockets in a manner terrible to look upon, and seemed to watch with surprise and indignation the motions of the strangers, as persons whose presence was alike unexpected and unwelcome. They were frightened at her looks; but, assured in each other's company, they kindled a fire, lighted a candle, prepared food, and made other arrangements for the discharge of the duty assigned them.

The assistants agreed they should watch the bedside of the sick person by turns; but, about midnight, overcome by fatigue, (for they had walked far that morning,) both of them fell fast asleep. When they awakened, which was not till after the interval of an hour or two, the hut was empty, and the patient gone. They rose in terror, and went to the door of the cottage, which was latched as it had been at night. They looked out into the darkness, and called upon their charge by her name. The night-raven screamed from the old oak tree, the fox howled on the hill, the hoarse waterfall replied with its echoes, but there was no human answer. The terrified women did not dare to make further search till morning should appear; for the sudden disappearance of a creature so frail as Elspat, together with the wild tenor of her history, intimidated them from stirring from the hut. They remained, therefore, in dreadful terror, sometimes thinking they heard her voice without, and at other times, that sounds of a different description were mingled with the mournful sigh of the night-breeze, or the dash of the cascade. Sometimes, too, the latch rattled, as if some frail and impotent hand were in vain attempting to lift it, and ever and anon they expected the entrance of their terrible patient, animated by supernatural strength, and in the company, perhaps, of some being more dreadful than herself. Morning came at length. They sought brake, rock, and thicket in vain. Two hours after daylight, the minister himself appeared, and on the report of the watchers, caused the country to be alarmed, and a general and exact search to be made through the whole neighbourhood of the cottage, and the oak tree. But it was all in vain. Elspat MacTavish was never found, whether dead or alive; nor could there ever be traced the slightest circumstance to indicate her fate.

The neighbourhood was divided concerning the cause of her dis-appearance. The credulous thought that the evil spirit, under whose influence she seemed to have acted, had carried her away in the body; and there are many who are still unwilling, at untimely hours, to pass the oak tree, beneath which, as they allege, she may still be seen seated according to her wont. Others less superstitious supposed, that had it been possible to search the gulf of the Corrie Dhu, the profound deeps of the lake, or the whelming eddies of the river, the remains of Elspat MacTavish might have been discovered; as nothing was more natural, considering her state of body and mind, than that she should have fallen in by accident, or precipitated herself intentionally into one or other of those places of sure destruction. The clergyman enter-tained an opinion of his own. He thought, that impatient of the watch which was placed over her, this unhappy woman's instinct had taught her, as it directs various domestic animals, to withdraw herself from the sight of her own race, that the death-struggle might take place in some secret den, where, in all probability, her mortal remains would never meet the eyes of mortals. This species of instinctive feeling seemed to him of a tenor with the whole course of her unhappy life, and most likely to influence her, when it drew to a conclusion.

Chapter Twelve

> Together both on the high lawns appeared.
> Under the opening eyelids of the morn
> They drove afield.
> *Elegy on Lycidas*

I HAVE SOMETIMES wondered why all the favourite occupations and pastimes of mankind go to the disturbance of that happy state of tranquillity, that *Otium*, as Horace terms it, which he says is the object of all men's prayers, whether preferred from sea or land; and that the undisturbed repose, of which we are so tenacious, when duty or necessity compels us to abandon it, is precisely what we long to exchange for a state of excitation, as soon as we may prolong it at our own pleasure. Briefly, you have only to say to a man, "remain at rest," and you instantly inspire the love of labour. The sportsman toils like his gamekeeper, the master of the pack takes as severe exercise as his whipper-in, the statesman or politician drudges more than the pro-fessional lawyer; and, to come to my own case, the volunteer author subjects himself to the risk of painful criticism, and the assured cer-tainty of mental and manual labour, just as completely as his needy brother, whose necessities compel him to assume the pen.

These reflections have been suggested by an annunciation on the part of Janet, "that the little Gillie-whitefoot was come from the printing office."

"Gillie-blackfoot you should call him, Janet," was my response, "for he is neither more nor less than an imp of the devil, come to torment me for *copy*, for so they call a supply of manuscript for the press."

"Now, Cot forgie your honour," said Janet; "for it is no like your ainsell to give such names to a faitherless bairn."

"I have got nothing else to give him, Janet—he must wait a little."

"Then I have got some breakfast to give the bit gillie," said Janet; "and he can wait by the fireside in the kitchen, till your honour's ready; and cood enough for the like of him, if he was to wait your honour's pleasure all day."

"But, Janet," said I to my little active superintendent, on her return to the parlour, after having made her hospitable arrangement, "I begin to find this writing our Chronicles is rather more tiresome than I expected, for here comes this little fellow to ask for manuscript—that is, for something to print—and I have got none to give him."

"Your honour can be at nae loss; I have seen you write fast and fast enough; and for subjects, you have the whole Highlands to write about, and I am sure you know a hundred tales better than that about Hamish MacTavish, for it was but about a young cateran and an auld carline, when all's done; and if they had burned the rudas quean for a witch, I am thinking, may be, they would not have tyned their coals— and her to gar her neer-do-weel son shoot a gentleman Cameron! I am third cousin to the Camerons mysell—my blood warms to them —And if you want to write about deserters, I am sure there were deserters enough on the top of Arthur's Seat, when the MacRaas broke out, and on that woeful day beside Leith Pier—Ohonari!—"

Here Janet began to weep, and to wipe her eyes with her apron. For my part, the idea I wanted was supplied, but I hesitated to make use of it. Topics, like times, are apt to become common by frequent use. It is only an ass like Justice Shallow, who would pitch upon the over-scutched tunes, which the carmen whistled, and try to pass them off as his *fancies* and his *good-nights*. Now, the Highlands, though formerly a rich mine for original matter, are, as my friend Mrs Bethune Baliol warned me, in some degree worn out by the incessant labour of modern romancers and novelists, who, finding in these remote regions primitive habits and manners, have vainly imagined that the public can never tire of them; and so kilted Highlanders are to be found as frequently, and nearly of as genuine descent, on the shelves of a circulating library, as at a Caledonian ball. Much might have been made at an earlier time out of the history of a Highland regiment, and the singular change of ideas which must have taken place in the minds of those who composed it, when exchanging their native hills for the battle fields of the Continent, and their simple, and sometimes indolent domestic habits, for the regular exertions demanded by modern discipline. But the market is forestalled. There is Mrs Grant of Laggan, has drawn the manners, customs, and superstitions of the mountains in their natural unsophisticated state, and my friend, General Stewart of Garth, in giving the real history of the Highland regiments, has rendered any attempt to fill up the sketch with fancy-colouring extremely rash and precarious. Yet I, too, have still a lingering fancy to add a stone to the cairn; and without calling in imagination to aid the impressions of juvenile recollection, I may just attempt to embody one or two scenes illustrative of the Highland character, and which belong peculiarly to the Chronicles of the Canongate, to the greyheaded eld of which they are as familiar as to Chrystal Croftangry. Yet I will not go back to the days of clanship and claymores. Have at you, gentle reader, with a tale of Two Drovers. An oyster may be crossed in love, says the gentle Tilburina—and a drover may be touched in point of honour, says the Chronicler of the Canongate.

The Two Drovers

IT was the day after the Doune Fair when my story commences. It had been a brisk market, several dealers had attended from the northern and midland counties in England, and the English money had flown so merrily about as to gladden the hearts of the Highland farmers. Many large droves were about to set off for England, under the protection of their owners, or of the topsmen whom they employed in the tedious, laborious, and responsible office of driving the cattle for many hundred miles, from the market where they had been purchased to the fields or farm-yards where they were to be fattened for the shambles.

The Highlanders in particular are masters of this difficult trade of driving, which seems to suit them as well as the trade of war. It affords exercise for all their habits of patient endurance and active exertion. They are required to know perfectly the drove-roads, which lie over the wildest tracts of the country, and to avoid as much as possible the highways, which distress the feet of the bullocks, and the turnpikes, which annoy the spirit of the drover; whereas on the broad green or grey track, which leads across the pathless moor, the herd not only move at ease and without taxation, but, if they mind their business, may pick up a mouthful of food by the way. At night, the drovers usually sleep along with their cattle, let the weather be what it will; and many of these hardy men do not once rest under a roof during a journey on foot from Lochaber to Lincolnshire. They are paid very highly, for the trust reposed is of the last importance, as it depends on their prudence, vigilance, and honesty, whether the cattle reach the final market in good order, and afford a profit to the grazier. But as they maintain themselves at their own expense, they are especially economical in that particular. At the period we speak of, a Highland drover was victualled for his long and toilsome journey with a few handfulls of oatmeal and two or three onions, renewed from time to time, and a ram's horn filled with whisky, which he used regularly, but sparingly, every night and morning. His dirk, or *skene-dhu*, (*i.e.* black knife,) so worn as to be concealed beneath the arm, or by the folds of the plaid, was his only weapon, excepting the cudgel with which he directed the movements of the cattle. A Highlander was never so happy as on these occasions. There was a variety in the whole journey, which exercised the Celt's natural curiosity and love of motion; there were the constant change of place and scene, the petty adventures incidental to the traffic, and the intercourse with the various farmers, graziers, and traders, intermingled with occasional merrymakings, not the less acceptable to Donald that they were void of expense; —and there was the consciousness of superior skill; for the Highlander, a child amongst flocks, is a prince amongst herds, and his natural habits induce him to disdain the shepherd's slothful life, so that he feels himself nowhere more at home than when following a gallant drove of his country cattle in the character of their guardian.

Of the number who left Doune in the morning, and with the purpose we have described, not a *Glunamie* of them all cocked his bonnet more briskly, or gartered his tartan hose under knee over a pair of more promising *spiogs*, (legs,) than did Robin Oig McCombich, called familiarly Robin Oig, that is Young, or the Lesser, Robin. Though small of stature, as the epithet Oig implies, and not very strongly limbed, he was as light and alert as one of the deer of his mountains. He had an elasticity of step, which, in the course of a long march, made many a stout fellow envy him; and the manner in which he busked his plaid and adjusted his bonnet, argued a consciousness that so smart a John Highlandman as himself would not pass unnoticed among the Lowland lasses. The ruddy cheek, red lips, and white teeth, set off a countenance which had gained by exposure to the weather a healthful and hardy rather than a rugged hue. If Robin Oig did not laugh, or even smile frequently, as indeed is not the practice among his countrymen, his bright eyes usually gleamed from under his bonnet with an expression of cheerfulness ready to be turned into mirth.

The departure of Robin Oig was an incident in the little town, in and near which he had many friends male and female. He was a topping person in his way, transacted considerable business on his own behalf, and was intrusted by the best farmers in the Highlands, in preference to any other drover in that district. He might have increased his business to any extent had he condescended to manage it by deputy; but except a lad or two, sister's sons of his own, Robin rejected the idea of assistance, conscious, perhaps, how much his reputation depended upon his attending in person to the practical discharge of his duty in every instance. He remained, therefore, contented with the highest premium given to persons of his description, and comforted himself with the hopes that a few journeys to England might enable him to conduct business on his own account, in a manner becoming his birth. For Robin Oig's father, Lachlan McCombich, (or, *son of my friend*, his actual clan-surname being MacGregor,) had been so called by the celebrated Rob Roy, because of the particular friendship which had subsisted between the grandsire of Robin and that renowned cateran. Some people even say, that Robin Oig derived his Christian name from a man, as renowned in the wilds of Lochlomond, as ever was his namesake Robin Hood, in the precincts of merry Sherwood. "Of such ancestry," as James Boswell says, "who would not be proud?" Robin Oig was proud accordingly; but his frequent visits to England and to the Lowlands had given him tact enough to know that pretensions, which still gave him a little right to distinction in his own lonely glen, might be both obnoxious and ridiculous if preferred elsewhere. The pride of birth, therefore, was like the miser's treasure, the secret subject of his contemplation, but never exhibited to strangers as a subject of boasting.

Many were the words of gratulation and good-luck which were bestowed on Robin Oig. The judges commended his drove, especially the best of them, which were Robin's own property. Some thrust out their snuff-mulls for the parting pinch—others tendered the *doch-an-dorrach*, or parting cup. All cried—"Good-luck travel out with you and come home with you.—Give you luck in the Saxon market—brave notes in the *leabhar-dhu*, (black pocket-book,) and plenty of English gold in the *sporran* (pouch of goatskin)."

The bonny lasses made their adieus more modestly, and more than one, it was said, would have given her best brooch to be certain that it was upon her that his eye last rested as he turned towards his road.

Robin Oig had just given the preliminary "*Hoo-hoo!*" to urge forward the loiterers of the drove, when there was a cry behind him.

"Stay, Robin—bide a blink. Here is Janet of Tomahourich—auld Janet, your father's sister."   *superstition*

"Plague on her, for an auld Highland witch and spaewife," said a farmer from the Carse of Stirling; "she'll cast some of her cantrips on the cattle."

"She canna do that," said another sapient of the same profession— "Robin Oig is no the lad to leave any of them, without tying Saint Mungo's knot on their tails, and that will put to her speed the best witch that ever flew over Dimayet upon a broomstick."

It may not be indifferent to the reader to know, that the Highland cattle are peculiarly liable to be *taken*, or infected, by spells and witchcraft, which judicious people guard against by knitting knots of peculiar complexity on the tuft of hair which terminates the animal's tail.

But the old woman who was the object of the farmer's suspicion seemed only busied about the drover, without paying any attention to the drove. Robin, on the contrary, appeared rather impatient of her presence.

"What auld-world fancy," he said, "has brought you so early from the ingle-side this morning, Muhme? I am sure I bid you good even, and had your God-speed, last night."

"And left me more siller than the useless old woman will use till you come back again, bird of my bosom," said the sibyl. "But it is little I would care for the food that nourishes me, or the fire that warms me, or for God's blessed sun itself, if aught but weal should happen to the grandson of my father. So let me walk the *deasil* round you, that you may go safe out into the far foreign land, and come safe home."

Robin Oig stopped, half embarrassed, half laughing, and signing to those around that he only complied with the old woman to soothe her humour. In the meantime, she traced around him, with wavering steps, the propitiation, which some have thought has been derived from the Druidical mythology. It consists, as is well known, in the person who makes the *deasil*, walking three times round the person who is the object of the ceremony, taking care to move according to the course of the sun. At once, however, she stopped short, and exclaimed, in a voice of alarm and horror, "Grandson of my father, there is blood on your hand."

"Hush, for God's sake, aunt," said Robin Oig; "you will bring more trouble on yourself with this Taishataragh (second sight) than you will be able to get out of for many a day."

The old woman only repeated, with a ghastly look, "There is blood on your hand, and it is English blood. The blood of the Gael is richer and redder. Let us see—let us——"

In the left margin, handwritten: *Removed off Macbeth*

Ere Robin Oig could prevent her, which, indeed, could only have been by positive violence, so hasty and peremptory were her proceedings, she had drawn from his side the dirk which lodged in the folds of his plaid, and held it up, exclaiming, although the weapon gleamed clear and bright in the sun, "Blood, blood—Saxon blood again. Robin Oig McCombich, go not this day to England!"

"Prutt, trutt," answered Robin Oig, "that will never do neither—it would be next thing to running the country. For shame, Muhme—give me the dirk. You cannot tell by the colour the difference betwixt the blood of a black bullock and a white one, and you speak of knowing Saxon from Gaelic blood. All men have their blood from Adam, Muhme. Give me my skene-dhu, and let me go on my road. I should have been half way to Stirling brig by this time—Give me my dirk, and let me go."

"Never will I give it to you," said the old woman—"Never will I quit my hold on your plaid, unless you promise me not to wear that unhappy weapon."

The women around him urged him also, saying few of his aunt's words fell to the ground; and as the Lowland farmers continued to look moodily on the scene, Robin Oig determined to close it at any sacrifice.

"Well, then," said the young drover, giving the scabbard of the weapon to Hugh Morrison, "you Lowlanders care nothing for these freats. Keep my dirk for me. I cannot give it you, because it was my father's; but your drove follows ours, and I am content it should be in your keeping, not in mine.—Will this do, Muhme?"

"It must," said the old woman—"that is, if the Lowlander is mad enough to carry the knife."

The strong westlandman laughed aloud.

"Goodwife," said he, "I am Hugh Morrison from Glenae, come of the Manly Morrisons of auld langsyne, that never took short weapon against a man in their lives. And neither needed they: They had their broadswords, and I have this bit supple (showing a formidable cudgel)—for dirking ower the board, I leave that to John Highlandman.—Ye needna snort, none of you Highlanders, and you in especial, Robin. I'll keep the bit knife, if you are feared for the auld spaewife's tale, and give it back to you whenever you want it."

Robin was not particularly pleased with some part of Hugh Morrison's speech; but he had learned in his travels more patience than belonged to his Highland constitution originally, and he accepted the service of the descendant of the Manly Morrisons, without finding fault with the rather depreciating manner in which it was offered.

"If he had not had his morning in his head, and been but a Dum-

fries-shire hog into the boot, he would have spoken more like a gentleman. But you cannot have more of a sow than a grumph. It's shame my
father's knife should ever slash a haggis for the like of him." *weakness*

Thus saying, (but saying it in Gaelic,) Robin drove on his cattle, *against*
and waved farewell to all behind him. He was in the greater haste, *English?*
because he expected to join at Falkirk a comrade and brother in
profession, with whom he proposed to travel in company.

Robin Oig's chosen friend was a young Englishman, Harry Wakefield by name, well known at every northern market, and in his way as
much famed and honoured as our Highland driver of bullocks. He
was nearly six feet high, gallantly formed to keep the rounds at Smithfield, or maintain the ring at a wrestling match; and although he might
have been overmatched, perhaps, among the regular professors of the
Fancy, yet, as a chance customer, he was able to give a bellyful to any
amateur of the pugilistic art. Doncaster races saw him in his glory,
betting his guinea, and generally successfully; nor was there a main
fought in Yorkshire, the feeders being persons of celebrity, at which
he was not to be seen, if business permitted. But though a *sprack* lad,
and fond of pleasure and its haunts, Harry Wakefield was steady, and
not the cautious Robin Oig McCombich himself was more attentive to
the main chance. His holidays were holidays indeed; but his days of
work were dedicated to steady and persevering labour. In countenance and temper, Wakefield was the model of Old England's merry
yeomen, whose clothyard shafts, in so many hundred battles, asserted
her superiority over the nations, and whose good sabres, in our own
time, are her cheapest and most assured defence. His mirth was
readily excited; for, strong in limb and constitution, and fortunate in
circumstances, he was disposed to be pleased with everything about
him; and such difficulties as he might occasionally encounter, were, to
a man of his energy, rather matter of amusement than serious annoy-
ance. With all the merits of a sanguine temper, our young English
drover was not without its defects. He was irascible, and sometimes to
the verge of being quarrelsome; and perhaps not the less inclined to
bring his disputes to a pugilistic decision, because he found few antagonists able to stand up to him in the boxing ring.

It is difficult to say how Henry Wakefield and Robin Oig first
became intimates; but it is certain a close acquaintance had taken
place betwixt them, although they had apparently few common topics
of conversation or of interest, so soon as their talk ceased to be
of bullocks. Robin Oig, indeed, spoke the English language rather
imperfectly upon any other topics but stots and kyloes, and Harry
Wakefield could never bring his broad Yorkshire tongue to utter a
single word of Gaelic. It was in vain Robin spent a whole morning,

during a walk over Minch-Moor, in attempting to teach his companion to utter, with true precision, the shibboleth *Llhu*, which is the
Gaelic for a calf. From Traquair to Murder-cairn, the hill rung with
the discordant attempts of the Saxon upon the unmanageable mono-
syllable, and the heartfelt laugh which followed every failure. They
had, however, better modes of awakening the echoes; for Wakefield
could sing many a ditty to the praise of Moll, Susan, and Cicely, and
Robin Oig had a particular gift at whistling interminable pibrochs
through all their involutions, and what was more agreeable to his
companion's southern ear, knew many of the northern airs, both lively
and pathetic, to which Wakefield learned to pipe a bass. Thus,
though Robin could hardly have comprehended his companion's
stories about horse-racing, cock-fighting, or fox-hunting, and
although his own legends of clan-fights and *creaghs*, varied with talk of
Highland goblins and fairy folk, would have been caviare to his companion, they contrived nevertheless to find a degree of pleasure in
each other's company, which had for three years back induced them to
join company and travel together, when the direction of their journey
permitted. Each, indeed, found his advantage in this companionship;
for where could the Englishman have found a guide through the
Western Highlands like Robin Oig McCombich? and when they were
on what Harry called the *right* side of the Border, his patronage, which
was extensive, and his purse, which was heavy, were at all times at the
service of his Highland friend, and on many occasions his liberality
did him genuine yeoman's service.

Chapter Thirteen

Were ever two such loving friends:—
How could they disagree?
O thus it was, he loved him dear,
    And thought how to requite him,
And having no friend left but he,
    He did resolve to fight him.
                Duke upon Duke

THE PAIR OF FRIENDS had traversed with their usual cordiality the
grassy wilds of Liddesdale, and crossed the opposite part of Cumberland, emphatically called The Waste. In these solitary regions, the
cattle under the charge of our drovers subsisted themselves cheaply,
by picking their food as they went along the drove-road, or sometimes
by the tempting opportunity of a *start and owerloup*, or invasion of the
neighbouring pasture, where an occasion presented itself. But now
the scene changed before them; they were descending towards a

fertile and enclosed country, where no such liberties could be taken
with impunity, or without a previous arrangement and bargain with
the possessors of the ground. This was more especially the case, as a
great northern fair was upon the eve of taking place, where both the
Scotch and English drover expected to dispose of a part of their cattle,
which it was desirable to produce in the market, rested and in good
order. Fields were therefore difficult to be obtained, and only upon
high terms. This necessity occasioned a temporary separation betwixt
the two friends, who went to bargain, each as he could, for the separate accommodation of his herd. Unhappily it chanced that both of
them, unknown to each other, thought of bargaining for the ground
they wanted on the property of a country gentleman of some fortune,
whose estate lay in the neighbourhood. The English drover applied to
the bailiff on the property, who was known to him. It chanced that the
Cumbrian Squire, who had entertained some suspicions of his manager's honesty, was taking occasional measures to ascertain how far
they were well founded, and had desired that any inquiries about his
enclosures, with a view to occupy them for a temporary purpose,
should be referred to himself. As, however, Mr Ireby had gone the day
before upon a journey of some miles' distance to the northward, the
bailiff chose to consider the check upon his full powers as for the time
removed, and concluded that he should best consult his master's
interest, and perhaps his own, in making an agreement with Harry
Wakefield. Meanwhile, ignorant of what his comrade was doing,
Robin Oig, on his side, chanced to be overtaken by a well-looked
smart little man upon a pony, most knowingly hogged and cropped, as
was then the fashion, the rider wearing tight leather breeches, and
long-necked bright spurs. This cavalier asked one or two pertinent
questions about markets and the price of stock. So Robin, seeing him
a well-judging civil gentleman, took the freedom to ask him whether
he could let him know if there was any grass-land to be let in that
neighbourhood, for the temporary accommodation of his drove. He
could not have put the question to more willing ears. The gentleman
of the buckskins was the proprietor, with whose bailiff Harry Wakefield had dealt, or was in the act of dealing.

"Thou art in good luck, my canny Scot," said Mr Ireby, "to have
spoken to me, for I see thy cattle have done their day's work, and I have
at my disposal the only field within three miles that is to be let in these
parts."

"The drove can pe gang two, three, four miles very pratty weel
indeed—" said the cautious Highlander; "put what would his honour
pe axing for the peasts pe the head, if she was to tak the park for twa or
three days?"

"We won't differ, Sawney, if you let me have six stots for winterers, in the way of reason."

"And which peasts wad your honour pe for having?"

"Why—let me see—the two black—the dun one—yon doddy—him with the twisted horn—the brockit—How much by the head?"

"Ah," said Robin, "your honour is a shudge—a real shudge—I couldna have set off the pest six peasts petter mysell, me that ken them as if they were my pairns, puir things."

"Well, how much per head, Sawney," continued Mr Ireby.

"It was high markets at Doune and Falkirk," answered Robin.

And thus the conversation proceeded, until they had agreed on the *prix juste* for the bullocks, the Squire throwing in the temporary accommodation of the enclosure for the cattle into the boot, and Robin making, as he thought, a very good bargain, providing the grass was but tolerable. The Squire walked his pony alongside of the drove, partly to show him the way, and see him put into possession of the field, and partly to learn the latest news of the northern markets.

They arrived at the field, and the pasture seemed excellent. But what was their surprise when they saw the bailiff quietly inducting the cattle of Harry Wakefield into the grassy Goshen which had just been assigned to those of Robin Oig McCombich by the proprietor himself. Squire Ireby set spurs to his horse, dashed up to his servant, and learning what had passed between the parties, briefly informed the English drover that his bailiff had let the ground without his authority, and that he might seek grass for his cattle wherever he would, since he was to get none there. At the same time he rebuked his servant severely for having transgressed his commands, and ordered him instantly to assist in ejecting the hungry and weary cattle of Harry Wakefield, which were just beginning to enjoy a meal of unusual plenty, and to introduce those of his comrade, whom the English drover now began to consider as a rival.

The feelings which arose in Wakefield's mind would have induced him to resist Mr Ireby's decision; but every Englishman has a tolerably accurate sense of law and justice, and John Fleecebumpkin, the bailiff, having acknowledged that he had exceeded his commission, Wakefield saw nothing else for it than to collect his hungry and disappointed charge, and drive them on to seek quarters elsewhere. Robin Oig saw what had happened with regret, and hastened to offer to his English friend to share with him the disputed possession. But Wakefield's pride was severely hurt, and he answered disdainfully, "Take it all, man—take it all—never make two bites of a cherry—thou canst talk over the gentry, and blear a plain man's eye—Out upon you, man—I would not kiss any man's dirty latchets for leave to bake in his oven."

Robin Oig, sorry but not surprised at his comrade's displeasure, hastened to entreat his friend to wait but an hour till he had gone to the Squire's house to receive payment for the cattle he had sold, and he would come back and help him to drive the cattle into some convenient place of rest, and explain to him the whole mistake they had both of them fallen into. But the Englishman continued indignant: "Thou hast been selling, hast thou? Ay, ay—thou is a cunning lad for kenning the hours of bargaining. Go to the devil with thyself, for I will ne'er see thy fause loon's visage again—thou should be ashamed to look me in the face."

"I am ashamed to look no man in the face," said Robin Oig, something moved; "and, moreover, I will look you in the face this blessed day, if you will bide at the Clachan down yonder."

"Mayhap you had as well keep away," said his comrade; and turning his back on his former friend, he collected his unwilling associates, assisted by the bailiff, who took some real and some affected interest in seeing Wakefield accommodated.

After spending some time in negotiating with more than one of the neighbouring farmers, who could not, or would not, afford the accommodation desired, Henry Wakefield at last, and in his necessity, accomplished his point by means of the landlord of the alehouse at which Robin Oig and he had agreed to pass the night, when they first separated from each other. Mine host was content to let him turn his cattle on a piece of barren moor, at a price little less than the bailiff had asked for the disputed inclosure; and the wretchedness of the pasture, as well as the price paid for it, were set down as exaggerations of the breach of faith and friendship of his Scottish crony. This turn of Wakefield's passions was encouraged by the bailiff, (who had his own reasons for being offended against poor Robin, as having been the unwitting cause of his falling into disgrace with his master,) as well as by the innkeeper, and two or three chance guests, who stimulated the drover in his resentment against his quondam associate,—some from the ancient grudge against the Scots, which, when it exists anywhere, is to be found lurking in the Border counties, and some from the general love of mischief, which characterizes mankind in all ranks of life, to the honour of Adam's children be it spoken. Good John Barleycorn also, who always heightens and exaggerates the prevailing passions, be they angry or kindly, was not wanting in his offices on this occasion; and confusion to false friends and hard masters, was pledged in more than one tankard.

In the meanwhile Mr Ireby found some amusement in detaining the northern drover at his ancient hall. He caused a cold round of beef to be placed before the Scot in the butler's pantry, together with a foaming tankard of home-brewed, and took pleasure in seeing the hearty appetite with which these unwonted edibles were discussed by Robin Oig McCombich. The Squire himself lighting his pipe, compounded between his patrician dignity and his love of agricultural gossip, by walking up and down while he conversed with his guest.

"I passed another drove," said the Squire, "with one of your countrymen behind them—they were something less beasts than your drove, doddies most of them—a big man was with them—none of your kilts though, but a decent pair of breeches—D'ye know who he may be?"

"Hout ay—that might, could, and would pe Hughie Morrison—I didna think he could hae peen sae weel up. He has made a day on us; put his Argyleshires will have wearied shanks. How far was he pehind?"

"I think about six or seven miles," answered the Squire, "for I passed them at the Christenbury Cragg, and I overtook you at the Hollan Bush. If his beasts be leg-weary, he will be maybe selling bargains."

"Na, na, Hughie Morrison is no the man for pargains—ye maun come to some Highland body like Robin Oig hersell for the like of these—put I maun pe wishing you goot night, and twenty of them let alane ane, and I maun down to the Clachan to see if the lad Henry Waakfelt is out of his humdudgeons yet."

The party at the alehouse were still in full talk, and the treachery of Robin Oig still the theme of conversation, when the supposed culprit entered the apartment. His arrival, as usually happens in such a case, put an instant stop to the discussion of which he had furnished the subject, and he was received by the company assembled with that chilling silence, which, more than a thousand exclamations, tells an intruder that he is unwelcome. Surprised and offended, but not appalled by the reception which he experienced, Robin entered with an undaunted and even a haughty air, attempted no greeting as he saw he was received with none, and placed himself by the side of the fire, a little apart from a table, at which Harry Wakefield, the bailiff, and two or three other persons, were seated. The ample Cumbrian kitchen would have afforded plenty of room even for a larger separation.

Robin, thus seated, proceeded to light his pipe, and call for a pint of twopenny.

"We have no twopence ale," answered Ralph Heskett the landlord; "but as thou find'st thy own tobacco, it's like thou may'st find thy own liquor too—it's the wont of thy country, I wot."

"Shame, goodman," said the landlady, a blithe bustling housewife, hastening herself to supply the guest with liquor—"Thou knowest well enow what the strange man wants, and it's thy trade to be civil, man. Thou shouldst know, that if the Scot likes a small pot, he pays a sure penny."

Without taking any notice of this nuptial dialogue, the Highlander took the flagon in his hand, and addressing the company generally, drank the interesting toast of "Good markets," to the party assembled.

"The better that the wind blew fewer dealers from the north," said one of the farmers, "and fewer Highland runts to eat up the English meadows."

"Saul of my pody, put you are wrang there, my friend," answered Robin, with composure; "it is your fat Englishmen that eat up our Scots cattle, puir things."

"I wish there was a summat to eat up their drovers," said another; "a plain Englishman canna make bread within a kenning of them."

"Or an honest servant keep his master's favour, but they will come sliding in between him and the sunshine," said the bailiff.

"If these pe jokes," said Robin Oig, with the same composure, "there is ower mony jokes upon one man."

"It is no joke, but downright earnest," said the bailiff. "Harkye, Mr Robin Ogg, or whatever is your name, it's right we should tell you that we are all of one opinion, and that is, that you, Mr Robin Ogg, have behaved to our friend Mr Harry Wakefield here, like a raff and a blackguard."

"Nae doubt, nae doubt," answered Robin, with great composure; "and you are a set of very feeling judges, for whose prains or pehaviour I wad not gie a pinch of sneeshing. If Mr Harry Waakfelt kens where he is wranged, he kens where he may be righted."

"He speaks truth," said Wakefield, who had listened to what passed, divided between the offence which he had taken at Robin's late behaviour, and the revival of his habitual habits of friendship.

He now rose, and went towards Robin, who got up from his seat as he approached, and held out his hand.

"That's right, Harry—go it—serve him out," resounded on all sides—"tip him the nailer—show him the mill."

"Hold your peace all of you, and be——," said Wakefield; and then addressing his comrade, he took him by the extended hand, with something alike of respect and defiance. "Robin," he said, "thou hast used me ill enough this day; but if you mean, like a frank fellow, to shake hands, and take a tussle for love on the sod, why I'll forgie thee, man, and we shall be better friends than ever."

"And would it not pe petter to be cood friends without more of the matter?" said Robin; "we will be much petter friendships with our panes hale than proken."

Harry Wakefield dropped the hand of his friend, or rather threw it from him.

"I did not think I had been keeping company for three years with a coward."

"Coward pelongs to none of my name," said Robin, whose eyes began to kindle, but keeping the command of his temper. "It was no coward's legs or hands, Harry Waakfelt, that drew you out of the fords of Frew, when you was drifting ower the plack rock, and every eel in the river expected his share of you."

"And that is true enough, too," said the Englishman, struck by the appeal.

"Adzooks!" exclaimed the bailiff—"sure Harry Wakefield, the nattiest lad at Whitson Tryste, Wooler Fair, Carlisle Sands, or Stagshaw Bank, is not going to show white feather? Ah, this comes of living so long with kilts and bonnets—men forget the use of their daddles."

"I may teach you, Master Fleecebumpkin, that I have not lost the use of mine," said Wakefield, and then went on. "This will never do, Robin. We must have a turn-up, or we shall be the talk of the country side. I'll be d——d if I hurt thee—I'll put on the gloves gin thou like. Come, stand forward like a man."

"To pe peaten like a dog," said Robin; "is there any reason in that? If you think I have done you wrong, I'll go before your shudge, though I neither know his law nor his language."

A general cry of "No, no—no law, no lawyer! a bellyful and be friends," was echoed by the bystanders.

"But," continued Robin, "if I am to fight, I have no skill to fight like a jackanapes, with hands and nails."

"How would you fight then?" said his antagonist; "though I am thinking it would be hard to bring you to the scratch anyhow."

"I would fight with proadswords, and sink point on the first plood drawn——like a gentlemans."

A loud shout of laughter followed the proposal, which indeed had rather escaped from poor Robin's swelling heart, than been the dictates of his sober judgment.

"Gentleman, quotha!" was echoed on all sides, with a shout of unextinguishable laughter; "a very pretty gentleman, God wot—Canst get two swords for the gentleman to fight with, Ralph Heskett?"

"No, but I can send to the armoury at Carlisle, and lend them two forks, to be making shift with in the meantime."

"Tush, man," said another, "the bonny Scots come into the world with the blue bonnet on their heads, and dirk and pistol at their belt."

"Best send post," said Mr Fleecebumpkin, "to the Squire of Corby Castle, to come and stand second to the *gentleman*."

In the midst of this torrent of general ridicule, the Highlander instinctively griped beneath the folds of his plaid.

"But it's better not," he said in his own language. "A hundred curses on the swine-eaters, who know neither decency nor civility!"

"Make room, the pack of you," he said, advancing to the door.

But his former friend interposed his sturdy bulk, and opposed his leaving the house; and when Robin Oig attempted to make his way by force, he hit him down on the floor, with as much ease as a boy bowls down a nine-pin.

"A ring, a ring!" was now shouted, until the dark rafters, and the hams that hung on them, trembled again, and the very platters on the *bink* clattered against each other. "Well done, Harry"—"Give it him home, Harry"—"Take care of him now—he sees his own blood!"

Such were the exclamations, while the Highlander, starting from the ground, all his coldness and caution lost in frantic rage, sprung at his antagonist with the fury, the activity, and the vindictive purpose, of an incensed tiger-cat. But when could rage encounter science and temper? Robin Oig again went down in the unequal contest; and as the blow was necessarily a severe one, he lay motionless on the floor of the kitchen. The landlady ran to offer some aid, but Mr Fleecebumpkin would not permit her to approach.

"Let him alone," he said, "he will come to within time, and come up to the scratch again. He has not got half his broth yet."

"He has got all I mean to give him, though," said his antagonist, whose heart began to relent towards his old associate; "and I would rather by half give the rest to yourself, Mr Fleecebumpkin, for you pretend to know a thing or two, and Robin had not art enough even to peel before setting to, but fought with his plaid dangling about him.— Stand up, Robin, my man! all friends now; and let me hear the man that will speak a word against you, or your country, for your sake."

Robin Oig was still under the dominion of his passion, and eager to renew the onset; but being withheld on the one side by the peace-making Dame Heskett, and on the other, aware that Wakefield no longer meant to renew the combat, his fury sunk into gloomy sullenness.

"Come, come, never grudge so much at it, man," said the brave-spirited Englishman, with the placability of his country, "shake hands, and we will be better friends than ever."

"Friends!" exclaimed Robin Oig with strong emphasis—"friends! —Never. Look to yourself, Harry Waakfelt."

"Then the curse of Cromwell on your proud Scots stomach, as the man says in the play, and you may do your worst, and be d——; for one man can say nothing more to another after a tussle, than that he is sorry for it."

On these terms the friends parted; Robin Oig drew out, in silence, a piece of money, threw it on the table, and then left the ale-house. But turning at the door, he shook his hand at Wakefield, pointing with his fore-finger upwards, in a manner which might imply either a threat or a caution. He then disappeared in the moonlight.

Some words passed after his departure, between the bailiff, who piqued himself on being a little of a bully, and Harry Wakefield, who, with generous inconsistency, was now not indisposed to begin a new combat in defence of Robin Oig's reputation, "although he could not use his daddles like an Englishman, as it did not come natural to him." But Dame Heskett prevented this second quarrel from coming to a head by her peremptory interference. "There should be no more fighting in her house," she said; "there had been too much already.—— And you, Mr Wakefield, may live to learn," she added, "what it is to make a deadly enemy out of a good friend."

"Pshaw, dame! Robin Oig is an honest fellow, and will never keep malice."

"Do not trust to that—you do not know the dour temper of the Scotch, though you have dealt with them so often. I have a right to know them, my mother being a Scot."

"And so is well seen on her daughter," said Ralph Heskett.

This nuptial sarcasm gave the discourse another turn; fresh customers entered the tap-room or kitchen, and others left it. The conversation turned on the expected markets, and the report of prices from different parts both of Scotland and England—treaties were commenced, and Harry Wakefield was lucky enough to find a chap for a part of his drove, and at a very considerable profit; an event of consequence more than sufficient to blot out all remembrances of the unpleasant scuffle in the earlier part of the day. But there remained one party from whose mind that recollection could not have been wiped away by possession of every head of cattle betwixt Esk and Eden.

This was Robin Oig McCombich.—"That I should have had no weapon," he said, "and for the first time in my life!—Blighted be the tongue that bids the Highlander part with the dirk—the dirk—ha! the English blood!—My muhme's word—when did her word fall to the ground?"

The recollection of the fatal prophecy confirmed the deadly intention which instantly sprang up in his mind.

"Ha! Morrison cannot be many miles behind; and if it were an hundred, what then!"

His impetuous spirit had now a fixed purpose and motive of action, and he turned the light foot of his country towards the wilds, through which he knew, by Mr Ireby's report, that Morrison was advancing. His mind was wholly engrossed by the sense of injury—injury sustained from a friend; and by the desire of vengeance on one whom he now accounted his most bitter enemy. The treasured ideas of self-importance and self-opinion—of ideal birth and quality, had become more precious to him, (like the hoard to the miser,) because he could only enjoy them in secret. But that hoard was pillaged, the idols which he had secretly worshipped had been desecrated and profaned. Insulted, abused, and beaten, he was no longer worthy, in his own opinion, of the name he bore, or the lineage which he belonged to— nothing was left to him—nothing but revenge; and, as the reflection added a galling spur to every step, he determined it should be as sudden and signal as the offence.

When Robin Oig left the door of the alehouse, seven or eight English miles at least lay betwixt Morrison and him. The advance of the former was slow, limited by the sluggish pace of his cattle; the last left behind him stubble-field and hedge-row, crag and dark heath, all glittering with frost-rhime in the broad November moonlight, at the rate of six miles an hour. And now the distant lowing of Morrison's cattle is heard; and now they are seen creeping like moles in size and slowness of motion on the broad face of the moor; and now he meets them—passes them, and stops their conductor.

"May good betide us," said the Southlander—"Is this you, Robin McCombich, or your wraith?"

"It is Robin Oig McCombich," answered the Highlander, "and it is not.—But never mind that, put pe giving me the skene-dhu."

"What! you are for back to the Highlands—The devil!—Have you selt all off before the fair? This beats all for quick markets."

"I have not sold—I am not going north—May pe I will never go north again.—Give me pack my dirk, Hugh Morrison, or there will pe words petween us."

"Indeed, Robin, I'll be better advised or I gie it back to you—it is a wanchancy weapon in a Highlandman's hand, and I am thinking you will be about some barns-breaking."

"Prutt, trutt! let me have my weapon," said Robin Oig impatiently.

"Hooly and fairly," said his well-meaning friend. "I'll tell you what will do better than these dirking doings—Ye ken Highlander and Lowlander, and Border-men, are a' ae man's bairns when you are over the Scots dyke. See, the Eskdale callants, and fighting Charlie of

Liddesdale, and the Lockerby lads, and the four Dandies of Lust-ruther, and a wheen mair grey plaids, are coming up behind; and if you are wranged, there is the hand of a Manly Morrison, we'll see you righted, if Carlisle and Stanwix baith took up the feud."

"To tell you the truth," said Robin Oig, desirous of eluding the suspicions of his friend, "I have enlisted with a party of the Black Watch, and must march off to-morrow morning."

"Enlisted! Were you mad or drunk?—You must buy yourself off— I can lend you twenty notes, and twenty to that, if the drove sell."

"I thank you—thank ye, Hughie; but I go with good will the gate that I am going,—so the dirk—the dirk!"

"There it is for you then, since less wunna serve. But think on what I was saying.—Wae's me, it will be sair news in the braes of Bal-quidder, that Robin Oig McCombich should have run an ill gate, and ta'en on."

"Ill news in Balquidder, indeed!" echoed poor Robin; "put Cot speed you, Hughie, and send you good marcats. Ye winna meet with Robin Oig again either at tryste or fair."

So saying, he shook hastily the hand of his acquaintance, and set out in the direction from which he had advanced, with the spirit of his former pace.

"There is something wrang with the lad," muttered the Morrison to himself; "but we will maybe see better into it the morn's morning."

But long ere the morning dawned, the catastrophe of our tale had taken place. It was two hours after the affray had happened, and it was totally forgotten by almost every one, when Robin Oig returned to Heskett's inn. The place was filled at once by various sorts of men, and with noises corresponding to their character. There were the grave, low sounds of men engaged in busy traffic, with the laugh, the song, and the riotous jest of those who had nothing to do but to enjoy themselves. Among the last was Harry Wakefield, who, amidst a grin-ning group of smock-frocks, hobnailed shoes, and jolly English physi-ognomies, was trolling forth the old ditty,

> What though my name be Roger,
> Who drives the plough and cart—

when he was interrupted by a well known voice, saying in a high and stern voice, marked by the sharp Highland accent, "Harry Waakfelt— if you be a man, stand up!"

"What is the matter?—what is it?" the guests demanded of each other.

"It is only a d—d Scotsman," said Fleecebumpkin, who was by this time very drunk, "whom Harry Wakefield helped to his broth to-day, who is now come to have *his cauld kail* het again."

"Harry Waakfelt," repeated the same ominous summons, "stand up, if you be a man!"

There is something in the tone of deep and concentrated passion, which attracts attention and imposes awe, even by the very sound. The guests shrunk back on every side, and gazed at the Highlander, as he stood in the middle of them, his brows bent, and his features rigid with resolution.

"I will stand up with all my heart, Robin, my boy, but it shall be to shake hands with you, and drink down all unkindness. It is not the fault of your heart, man, that you don't know how to clench your hands."

By this time he stood opposite to his antagonist; his open and unsuspecting look strangely contrasted with the stern purpose, which gleamed wild, dark, and vindictive in the eyes of the Highlander.

"'Tis not thy fault, man, that, not having the luck to be an Englishman, thou canst not fight more than a school-girl."

"I *can* fight," answered Robin Oig sternly, but calmly, "and you shall know it. You, Harry Waakfelt, showed me to-day how the Saxon churls fight—I show you now how the Highland Dunniewassal fights."

He seconded the word with the action, and plunged the dagger, which he suddenly displayed, into the broad breast of the English yeoman, with such fatal certainty and force, that the hilt made a hollow sound against the breast-bone, and the double-edged point split the very heart of his victim. Harry Wakefield fell, and expired with a single groan. His assassin next seized the bailiff by the collar, and offered the bloody poniard to his throat, whilst dread and surprise rendered the man incapable of defence.

"It were very just to lay you beside him," he said, "but the blood of a base pick-thank shall never mix on my father's dirk, with that of a brave man."

As he spoke, he cast the man from him with so much force that he fell on the floor, while Robin, with his other hand, threw the fatal weapon into the blazing turf-fire.

"There," he said, "take me who likes—and let fire cleanse blood if it can."

The pause of astonishment still continuing, Robin Oig asked for a peace-officer, and a constable having stepped out, he surrendered himself to his custody.

"A bloody night's work you have made of it," said the constable.

"Your own fault," said the Highlander. "Had you kept his hands off me twa hours since, he would have been now as well and merry as he was twa minutes since."

"It must be sorely answered," said the peace-officer.

"Never you mind that—death pays all debts; it will pay that too."

The horror of the bystanders began now to give way to indignation; and the sight of a favourite companion murdered in the midst of them, the provocation being, in their opinion, so utterly inadequate to the excess of vengeance, might have induced them to kill the perpetrator of the deed even upon the very spot. The constable, however, did his duty on this occasion, and with the assistance of some of the more reasonable persons present, procured horses to guard the prisoner to Carlisle, to abide his doom at the next assizes. While the escort was preparing, the prisoner neither expressed the least interest, nor attempted the slightest reply. Only, before he was carried from the fatal apartment, he desired to look at the dead body, which, raised from the floor, had been deposited upon the large table, (at the head of which Harry Wakefield had presided but a few minutes before, full of life, vigour, and animation,) until the surgeons should examine the mortal wound. The face of the corpse was decently covered with a napkin. To the surprise and horror of the bystanders, which displayed itself in a general *Ah!* drawn through clenched teeth and half-shut lips, Robin Oig removed the cloth, and gazed with a mournful but steady eye on the lifeless visage, which had been so lately animated, that the smile of good humoured confidence in his own strength, of conciliation at once, and contempt towards his enemy, still curled his lip. While those present expected that the wound, which had so lately flooded the apartment with gore, would send forth fresh streams at the touch of the homicide, Robin Oig replaced the covering, with the brief exclamation—"He was a pretty man!"

My story is nearly ended. The unfortunate Highlander stood his trial at Carlisle. I was myself present, and as a young Scottish lawyer, or barrister at least, and reputed a man of some quality, the politeness of the Sheriff of Cumberland offered me a place on the bench. The facts of the case were proved in the manner I have related them; and whatever might be at first the prejudice of the audience against a crime so un-English as that of assassination from revenge, yet when the rooted national prejudices of the prisoner had been explained, which made him consider himself as stained with indelible dishonour, when subjected to personal violence; when his previous patience, moderation, and endurance, were considered, the generosity of the English audience was inclined to regard his crime as the wayward aberration of a false idea of honour rather than as flowing from a heart naturally savage, or perverted by habitual vice. I shall never forget the charge of the venerable Judge to the jury, although not at that time liable to be much affected either by that which was eloquent or pathetic.

"We have had," he said, "in the previous part of our duty, (alluding to some former trials,) to discuss crimes which infer disgust and abhorrence, while they call down the well-merited vengeance of the law. It is now our still more melancholy duty to apply its salutary though severe enactments to a case of a very singular character, in which the crime (for a crime it is, and a deep one) arose less out of the malevolence of the heart, than the error of the understanding—less from any idea of committing wrong, than from an unhappily perverted notion of that which is right. Here we have two men, highly esteemed, it has been stated, in their rank of life, and attached, it seems, to each other as friends, one of whose lives has been already sacrificed to a punctilio, and the other is about to prove the vengeance of the offended laws; and yet both may claim our commiseration at least, as men acting in ignorance of each other's national prejudices, and unhappily misguided rather than voluntarily erring from the path of right conduct.

"In the original cause of the misunderstanding, we must in justice give the right to the prisoner at the bar. He had acquired possession of the inclosure, which was the object of competition, by a legal contract with the proprietor Mr Ireby; and yet, when accosted with reproaches undeserved in themselves, and galling doubtless to a temper at least sufficiently susceptible of passion, he offered notwithstanding to yield up half his acquisition, for the sake of peace and good neighbourhood, and his amicable proposal was rejected with scorn. Then follows the scene at Mr Heskett the publican's, and you will observe how the stranger was treated by the deceased, and I am sorry to observe, by those around, who seem to have urged him in a manner which was aggravating in the highest degree. While he asked for peace and for composition, and offered submission to a magistrate, or to a mutual arbiter, the prisoner was insulted by a whole company, who seem on this occasion to have forgotten the national maxim of 'fair play;' and while attempting to escape from the place in peace, he was intercepted, struck down, and beaten to the effusion of his blood.

"Gentlemen of the Jury, it was with some impatience that I heard my learned brother, who opened the case for the crown, give an unfavourable turn to the prisoner's conduct on this occasion. He said the prisoner was afraid to encounter his antagonist in fair fight, or to submit to the laws of the ring; and that therefore, like a cowardly Italian, he had recourse to his fatal stiletto, to murder the man whom he dared not meet in manly encounter. I observed the prisoner shrink from this part of the accusation with the abhorrence natural to a brave man; and as I would wish to make my words impressive, when I point his real crime, I must secure his opinion of my impartiality, by rebutting everything that seems to me a false accusation. There can be no doubt that the prisoner is a man of resolution—too much resolution—I wish to Heaven that he had less, or rather that he had had a better education to regulate it.

"Gentlemen, as to the laws my brother talks of, they may be known in the Bull-ring, or the Bear-garden, or the Cockpit, but they are not known here. Or, if they should be so far admitted as furnishing a species of proof, that no malice was intended in this sort of combat, from which fatal accidents do sometimes arise, it can only be so admitted when both parties are *in pari casu*, equally acquainted with, and equally willing to refer themselves to, that species of arbitrement. But will it be contended that a man of superior rank and education is to be subjected, or is obliged to subject himself, to this coarse and brutal strife, perhaps in opposition to a younger, stronger, or more skilful opponent? Certainly even the pugilistic code, if founded upon the fair play of Merry Old England, as my brother alleges it to be, can contain nothing so preposterous. And, gentlemen of the jury, if the laws would support an English gentleman, wearing, we will suppose, his sword, in defending himself by force against a violent personal aggression of the nature offered to this prisoner, they will not less protect a foreigner and a stranger, involved in the same unpleasing circumstances. If, therefore, gentlemen of the jury, when thus pressed by a *vis major*, the object of obloquy to a whole company, and of direct violence from one at least, and as he might reasonably apprehend, from more, the panel had produced the weapon which his countrymen, as we are informed, generally carry about their persons, and the same unhappy circumstance had ensued which you have heard detailed in evidence, I could not in my conscience have asked from you a verdict of murder. The prisoner's personal defence might indeed, even in that case, have gone more or less beyond the boundary of the *Moderamen inculpatæ tutelæ*, spoken of by lawyers, but the punishment incurred would have been that of manslaughter, not of murder. I beg leave to add, that I should have thought this milder species of charge was demanded in the case supposed, notwithstanding the statute of James I. cap. 8, which takes the case of slaughter by stabbing with a short weapon, even without malice prepense, out of the benefit of clergy. For this statute of stabbing, as it is termed, arose out of a temporary cause; and as the real guilt is the same, whether the slaughter be committed by the dagger, or by sword or pistol, the benignity of the modern law places them all on the same, or nearly the same footing.

"But, gentlemen of the jury, the pinch of the case lies in the interval of two hours interposed betwixt the reception of the injury and the fatal retaliation. In the heat of affray and *chaude mêlée*, law, compassionating the infirmities of humanity, makes allowance for the passions which rule such a stormy moment—for the sense of present pain, for the apprehension of further injury, for the difficulty of ascertaining with due accuracy the precise degree of violence which is necessary to protect the person of the individual, without annoying or injuring the assailant more than is absolutely necessary. But the time necessary to walk twelve miles, however speedily performed, was an interval sufficient for the prisoner to have recollected himself; and the violence with which he carried his purpose into effect, with so many circumstances of deliberate determination, could neither be induced by the passion of anger, nor that of fear. It was the purpose and the act of predetermined revenge, for which law neither can, will, nor ought to have sympathy or allowance.

"It is true, we may repeat to ourselves, in alleviation of this poor man's unhappy action, that his case is a very peculiar one. The country which he inhabits was, in the days of many now alive, inaccessible to the laws, not only of England, which have not even yet penetrated thither, but to those to which our neighbours of Scotland are subjected, and which must be supposed to be, and no doubt actually are, founded upon the general principles of justice and equity which pervade every civilized country. Amongst their mountains, as among the North American Indians, the various tribes were wont to make war upon each other, so that each man was obliged to go armed for his own protection, and for the offence of his neighbour. These men, from the ideas which they entertained of their own descent and of their own consequence, regarded themselves as so many cavaliers or men-at-arms, rather than as the peasantry of a peaceful country. Those laws of the ring, as my brother terms them, were unknown to the race of warlike mountaineers; that decision of quarrels by no other weapons than those which nature has given every man, must to them have seemed as vulgar and as preposterous as to the Noblesse of France. Revenge, on the other hand, must have been as familiar to their habits of society as to those of the Cherokees or Mohawks. It is, indeed, as described by Bacon, at bottom a kind of wild untutored justice; for the fear of retaliation must withhold the hands of the oppressor where there is no regular law to check daring violence. But though all this may be granted, and though we may allow that, such having been the case of the Highlands in the days of the prisoner's fathers, many of the opinions and sentiments must still continue to influence the present generation, it cannot, and ought not, even in this most painful case, to alter the administration of the law, either in your hands, gentlemen of the jury, or in mine. The first object of civilization is to place the general protection of the law, equally administered, in the room of that wild justice, which every man cut and carved for himself, according to the length of his sword and the strength of his arm. The law says to the subjects, with a voice only inferior to that of the Deity, 'Vengeance is mine.' The instant that there is time for passion to cool, and reason to interpose, an injured party must become aware, that the law assumes the exclusive cognizance of the right and wrong betwixt the parties, and opposes her inviolable buckler to every attempt of the private party to right himself. I repeat, that this unhappy man ought personally to be the object rather of our pity than our abhorrence, for he failed in his ignorance, and from mistaken notions of honour. But his crime is not the less that of murder, gentlemen, and, in your high and important office, it is your duty so to find. Englishmen have their angry passions as well as Scots; and should this man's action remain unpunished, you may unsheath, under various pretences, a thousand daggers betwixt the Land's-end and the Orkneys."

The venerable Judge thus ended what, to judge by his apparent emotion, and by the tears which filled his eyes, was really a painful task. The jury, according to his instructions, brought in a verdict of Guilty; and Robin Oig McCombich, *alias* MacGregor, was sentenced to death, and left for execution, which took place accordingly. He met his fate with great firmness, and acknowledged the justice of his sentence. But he repelled indignantly the observations of those who accused him of attacking an unarmed man. "I give a life for the life I took," he said, "and what can I do more?"

END OF VOLUME FIRST

this history catches up with him.

CHRONICLES
OF THE CANONGATE

VOLUME II

Chapter One

Indite, my muse, indite,
Subpœna'd is thy lyre,
The praises to requite
Which rules of court require.
Probationary Odes

THE CONCLUDING a literary undertaking, in whole or in part, is, to
the inexperienced at least, attended with an irritating titillation, like
that which attends on the healing of a wound—a prurient impatience,
in short, to know what the world in general, and friends in particular,
will say to our labours. Some authors, I am told, profess an oyster-like
indifference upon this subject; for my own part, I hardly believe in
their sincerity. Others may acquire it from habit; but in my poor
opinion, a neophyte like myself must be for a long time incapable of
such *sang froid*.

Frankly, I was ashamed to feel how childishly I felt on the occasion.
No person could have said prettier things than myself upon the
importance of stoicism concerning the opinion of others, when their
applause or censure refers to literary character only; and I had determined to lay my work before the public, with the same unconcern with
which the ostrich lays her eggs in the sand, giving herself no farther
trouble concerning the incubation, but leaving to the atmosphere to
bring forth the young, or otherwise, as the climate shall serve. But
though an ostrich in theory, I became in practice a poor hen, who has
no sooner made her deposit, but she runs cackling about, to call the
attention of every one to the wonderful work which she has performed.

As soon as I became possessed of my first volume, neatly stitched up and boarded, my sense of the necessity of communicating with some one became ungovernable. Janet was inexorable, and seemed already to have tired of my literary confidence; for whenever I drew near the subject, after evading it as long as she could, she made, under some pretext or other, a bodily retreat to the kitchen or the cockloft, her own peculiar and inviolate domains. My publisher would have been a natural resource; but he understands his business too well, and follows it too closely, to desire to enter into literary discussions, wisely considering, that he who has to sell books has seldom leisure to read them. Then my acquaintance, now that I have lost Mrs Bethune Baliol, are of that distant and accidental kind, to whom I had not face enough to communicate the nature of my uneasiness, and who probably would only have laughed at me had I made any attempt to interest them in my labours.

Reduced thus to a sort of despair, I thought of my friend and man of business Mr Fairscribe. His habits, it was true, were not likely to render him indulgent to light literature, and, indeed, I had more than once noticed his daughters, and especially my little songstress, whip into her reticule what looked very like a circulating library volume, as soon as her father entered the room. Still he was not only my assured, but almost my only friend, and I had little doubt that he would take an interest in the volume for the sake of the author, which the work itself might fail to inspire. I sent him, therefore, the book, carefully sealed up, with an intimation that I requested the favour of his opinion upon the contents, of which I affected to talk in the depreciatory style, which calls for point-blank contradiction, if your correspondent possess a grain of civility.

This communication took place on a Monday, and I daily expected (what I was ashamed to anticipate by volunteering my presence, however sure of a welcome) an invitation to eat an egg, as was my friend's favourite phrase, or a card to drink tea with Misses Fairscribe, or a provocation to breakfast, at least, with my hospitable friend and benefactor, and to talk over the contents of my inclosure. But the hours and days passed on from Monday till Saturday, and I had no acknowledgment whatever that my packet had reached its destination. "This is very unlike my good friend's punctuality," thought I; and having again and again vexed James, my male attendant, by a close examination concerning the time, place, and delivery, I had only to strain my imagination to conceive reasons for my friend's silence. Sometimes I thought that his opinion of the work had proved so unfavourable, that he was averse to hurt my feelings by communicating it—sometimes, that, escaping his hands to whom it was destined, it had found its way into his writing-chamber, and was become the subject of criticism to his smart clerks and conceited apprentices. "'Sdeath!" thought I, "if I were sure of this, I would——"

"And what would you do?" said Reason, after a few moments' reflection. "You are ambitious of introducing your book into every writing and reading chamber in Edinburgh, and yet you take fire at the thoughts of its being criticized by Mr Fairscribe's young people? Be a little consistent, for shame."

"I will be consistent," said I, doggedly; "but for all that, I will call on Mr Fairscribe this evening."

I hastened my dinner, donned my great-coat, (for the evening threatened rain,) and went to Mr Fairscribe's house. The old domestic opened the door cautiously, and before I asked the question, said, "Mr Fairscribe is at home, sir; but it is Sunday night." Recognizing, however, my face and voice, he opened the door wider, admitted me, and conducted me to the parlour, where I found Mr Fairscribe and the rest of his family engaged in listening to a sermon by the late Mr Walker of Edinburgh, which was read by Miss Catherine with unusual distinctness, simplicity, and judgement. Welcomed as a friend of the house, I had nothing for it but to take my seat quietly, and making a virtue of necessity, endeavour to derive my share of the benefit arising from an excellent sermon. But I am afraid Mr Walker's force of logic and precision of expression were somewhat lost upon me. I was sensible I had chosen an improper time to disturb Mr Fairscribe, and when the discourse was ended, I rose to take my leave, somewhat hastily, I believe. "A cup of tea, Mr Croftangry?" said the young lady. "You will wait and take part of a presbyterian supper," said Mr Fairscribe.—"Nine o'clock—I make it a point of keeping my father's hours on Sunday at e'en. Perhaps Dr —— (naming an excellent clergyman) may look in."

I made my apology for declining his invitation; and I fancy my unexpected appearance, and hasty retreat, had rather surprised my friend, since, instead of accompanying me to the door, he conducted me into his own apartment.

"What is the matter," he said, "Mr Croftangry? This is not a night for secular business, but if anything sudden or extraordinary has happened——"

"Nothing in the world," said I, forcing myself upon confession, as the best way of clearing myself out of the scrape,—"only—only I sent you a little parcel, and as you are so regular in acknowledging letters and communications, I—I thought it might have miscarried—that's all."

My friend laughed heartily, as if he saw into and enjoyed my motives and my confusion. "Safe?—it came safe enough," he said. "The wind of the world always blows its vanities into haven. But this is the end of the session, when I have little time to read anything printed except Inner-House papers;—yet if you will take your kail with us next Saturday, I will glance over your work, though I am sure I am no competent judge of such matters."

With this promise I was fain to take my leave, not without half persuading myself that if once the phlegmatic lawyer began my lucubrations, he would not be able to rise from them till he had finished the perusal, nor to endure an interval betwixt his reading the last page, and requesting an interview with the author.

No such marks of impatience displayed themselves. Time, blunt or keen, as my friend Joanna says, swift or leisurely, held his course; and on the appointed Saturday, I was at the door precisely as it struck four. The dinner hour, indeed, was five punctually; but what did I know but my friend might want half an hour's conversation with me before that time? I was ushered into an empty drawing-room, and, from a needlebook and work-basket, hastily abandoned, I had some reason to think I interrupted my little friend Miss Katie in some domestic labour more praiseworthy than elegant. In this critical age, filial piety must hide herself in a closet, if she has a mind to darn her father's linen.

Shortly after, I was the more fully convinced that I had been too early an intruder, when a wench came to fetch away the basket, and recommend to my courtesies a red and green gentleman in a cage, who answered all my advances by croaking out, "You're a fool—you're a fool, I tell you!" until, upon my word, I began to think the creature was in the right. At last my friend arrived, a little over-heated. He had been taking a turn at golf, to prepare him for "colloquy sublime." And wherefore not? since the game, with its variety of odds, lengths, bunkers, tee'd balls, and so on, may be no inadequate representation of the hazards attending literary pursuits. In particular, those formidable buffets, which make one ball spin through the air like a rifle shot, and strike another down into the very earth it is placed upon, by the maladroitness or the malicious purpose of the player—what are they but parallels to the favourable or depreciating notices of the reviewers, who play at golf with the publications of the season, even as Altisidora, in her approach to the gates of the infernal regions, saw the devils playing at racket with the new books of Cervantes' days.

Well, every hour has its end. Five o'clock came, and my friend, with his daughters, and his handsome young son, who, though fairly buckled to the desk, is every now and then looking over his shoulder at a smart uniform, set seriously about satisfying the corporeal wants of nature; while I, stimulated by a nobler appetite after fame, wished that the touch of a magic wand could, without all the ceremony of picking and choosing, carving and slicing, masticating and swallowing, have transported a *quantum sufficit* of the good things on my friend's hospitable board, into the stomachs of those who surrounded it, to be there at leisure converted into chyle, while their thoughts were turned on higher matters. At length all was over. But the young ladies sat still, and talked of the music of the Freischutz, for nothing else was then thought of; so we discussed the wild hunters' song, and the tame hunters' song, &c. &c. in all which my young friends were quite at home. Luckily for me, all this horning and hooping drew on some allusion to the Seventh Hussars, which gallant regiment, I observe, is a more favourite theme with both Miss Catherine and her brother than with my old friend, who presently looked at his watch, and said something significantly to Mr James about office hours. The youth got up with the ease of a youngster that would be thought a man of fashion rather than of business, and endeavoured, with some success, to walk out of the room, as if the locomotion was entirely voluntary; Miss Catherine and her sisters left us at the same time, and now, thought I, my trial comes on.

Reader, did you ever, in the course of your life, cheat the courts of justice and lawyers, by agreeing to refer a dubious and important question to the decision of a mutual friend? If so, you may have remarked the relative change which the arbiter undergoes in your estimation, when raised, though by your own free choice, from an ordinary acquaintance, whose opinions were of as little consequence to you as yours to him, into a superior personage, on whose decision your fate must depend *pro tanto*, as my friend Mr Fairscribe would say. His looks assume a mysterious if not a minatory expression; his hat has a loftier air, and his wig, if he wears one, a more formidable buckle.

I felt, accordingly, that my good friend Fairscribe, on the present occasion, had acquired something of a similar increase of consequence. But a week since, he had, in my opinion, been indeed an excellent-meaning man, perfectly competent to everything within his own profession, but immured at the same time among its forms and technicalities, and as incapable of judging of matters of taste as any mighty Goth whatsoever, of or belonging to the ancient Senate House of Scotland. But what of that? I had made him my judge by my own election; and I have often observed that an idea of declining such a reference, on account of his own consciousness of incompetency, is, as it perhaps ought to be, the last which occurs to the referee himself. He that has a literary work subjected to his judgement by the author, immediately throws his mind into a critical attitude, though the subject be one which he never before thought of. No doubt the author is well qualified to select his own judge, and why should the arbiter whom he has chosen doubt his own talents for condemnation or acquittal, since he has been doubtless picked out by his friend, from his indubitable reliance on their competence? Surely, the man who wrote the production is likely to know the person best qualified to judge of it.

Whilst these thoughts crossed my brain, I kept my eyes fixed on my good friend, whose motions appeared unusually tardy to me, while he ordered a bottle of particular claret, decanted it with scrupulous accuracy with his own hand, caused his old domestic to bring a saucer of olives, and chips of toasted bread, and thus, on hospitable thoughts intent, seemed to me to adjourn the discussion which I longed to bring on, yet feared to precipitate.

"He is dissatisfied," thought I, "and is ashamed to show it, afraid doubtless of hurting my feelings. What had I to do to talk to him about anything save charters and sasines?—Stay, he is going to begin."

"We are old fellows now, Mr Croftangry," said my landlord, "scarcely so fit to take a poor quart of claret between us, as we would have been in better days to take a pint, in the old Scottish liberal acceptation of the phrase. Maybe you would have liked me to have kept James to help us. But if it is not on a holiday or so, I think it is best he should observe office hours."

Here the discourse was about to fall. I relieved it by saying, Mr James was at the happy time of life, when he had better things to do than to sit over the bottle. "I suppose," said I, "your son is a reader?"

"Um—yes—James may be called a reader in a sense; but I doubt there is little solid in his studies—poetry and plays, Mr Croftangry, all nonsense—they set his head a-gadding after the army, when he should be minding his business."

"I suppose, then, that romances do not find much more grace in your eyes than dramatic and poetical compositions?"

"Deil a bit, deil a bit, Mr Croftangry, nor historical productions either. There is too much fighting in history, as if men only were brought into this world to send one another out of it. It nourishes false notions of our being, and chief and proper end, Mr Croftangry."

Still all this was general, and I became determined to bring our discourse to a focus. "I am afraid, then, I have done very ill to trouble you with my idle manuscripts, Mr Fairscribe; but you must do me the justice to remember, that I had nothing better to do than to amuse myself by writing the sheets I put into your hands the other day. I may truly plead—

I left no calling for this idle trade."

"I cry your mercy, Mr Croftangry," said my old friend, suddenly recollecting—"yes, yes, I have been very rude; but I had forgotten entirely that you had taken a spell yourself at that idle man's trade."

"I suppose," replied I, "you, on your side, have been too *busy* a man to look at my poor Chronicles?"

"No, no," said my friend, "I am not so bad as that neither. I have read them bit by bit, just as I could get a moment's time, and I believe I shall very soon get through them."

"Well, my good friend?" said I, interrogatively.

And "*Well*, Mr Croftangry," cried he, "I really think you have got over the ground very tolerably well. I have noted down here two or three bits of things, which I presume to be errors of the press, otherwise it might be alleged, perhaps, that you did not fully pay that attention to the grammatical rules which one would desire to see rigidly observed."

I looked at my friend's notes, which, in fact, showed that in one or two grossly obvious passages, I had left uncorrected such solecisms in grammar.

"Well, well, I own my fault; but, setting apart these casual errors, how do you like the matter and the manner of what I have been writing, Mr Fairscribe?"

"Why," said my friend, pausing, with more grave and important hesitation than I thanked him for, "there is not much to be said against the manner. The style is terse and intelligible, Mr Croftangry, very intelligible; and that I consider as the first point in everything that is intended to be understood. There are, indeed, here and there some flights and fancies, which I comprehended with difficulty; but I got to your meaning at last. There are people that are like ponies; their judgements cannot go fast, but they go sure."

"That is a pretty clear proposition, my friend; but then how did you like the meaning when you did get at it? or was that, like some ponies, too difficult to catch, and, when catched, not worth the trouble?"

"I am far from saying that, my dear sir, in respect it would be downright uncivil; but since you ask my opinion, I wish you could have thought about something more appertaining to civil policy, than all this bloody work about shooting, and dirking, and downright hanging. I am told it was the Germans who first brought in such a practice of choosing their heroes out of the Porteous Roll;* but, by my faith, we are like to be upsides with them. The first was, as I am credibly informed, Mr Scolar, as they call him; a scholar-like piece of work he has made of it, with his Robbers and thieves."

"Schiller," said I, "my dear sir, let it be Schiller."

* List of criminal indictments, so termed in Scotland.

"Shiller, or what you like," said Mr Fairscribe; "I found the book where I wish I had found a better one, and that is, in Kate's work-basket. I sat down, and, like an old fool, began to read; but there, I grant, you have the better of Shiller, Mr Croftangry."

"I should be glad, my dear sir, that you really think I have *approached* that admirable author; even your friendly partiality ought not to talk of my having *excelled* him."

"But I do say you have excelled him, Mr Croftangry, in a most material particular. For surely a book of amusement should be some-thing that one can take up and lay down at pleasure; and I can say justly, I was never at the least loss to put aside these sheets of yours when business came in the way. But, faith, this Shiller, sir, does not let you off so easily. I forgot one appointment on particular business, and I wilfully broke through another, that I might stay at home and finish his confounded book, which, after all, is about two brothers, the greatest rascals I ever heard of. The one, sir, goes near to murder his own father, and the other (which you would think still stranger) sets about to debauch his own wife."

"I find, then, Mr Fairscribe, that you have no taste for the romance of real life, no pleasure in contemplating those spirit-rousing impulses, which force men of fiery passions upon great crimes and great virtues?"

"Why, as to that, I am not just so sure. But then, to mend the matter," continued the critic, "you have brought in Highlanders into every story, as if you were going back again, *velis et remis*, into the old days of Jacobitism. I must speak my plain mind, Mr Croftangry. I cannot tell what innovations in Kirk and State may be now proposed, but our fathers were friends to both, as they were settled at the glori-ous Revolution, and liked a tartan plaid as little as they did a white surplice. I wish to Heaven, all this tartan fever bode well to the Prot-estant succession and the Kirk of Scotland."

"Both too well settled, I hope, in the minds of the subject," said I, "to be affected by old remembrances, on which we look back as on the portraits of our ancestors, without recollecting, while we gaze on them, any of the feuds by which the originals were animated while alive. But most happy should I be to light upon any topic to supply the place of the Highlands, Mr Fairscribe. I have been just reflecting that the theme is becoming a little exhausted, and your experience may perhaps supply"——

"Ha, ha, ha—*my* experience supply!" interrupted Mr Fairscribe, with a laugh of derision. "Why, you might as well ask my son James's experience to supply a case about thirlage. No, no, my good friend, I have lived by the law, and in the law, all my life; and when you seek the impulses that make soldiers desert and shoot their sergeants and corporals, and Highland drovers dirk English graziers, to prove themselves men of fiery passions, it is not to a man like me you should come. I could tell you some tricks of my own trade, perhaps, and a queer story or two of estates that have been lost and recovered. But, to tell you the truth, I think you might do with your Muse of Fiction, as you call her, as many an honest man does with his own sons in flesh and blood."

"And how is that, my dear sir?"

"Send her to India, to be sure. That is the true place for a Scot to thrive in; and if you carry your story fifty years back, as there is nothing to hinder you, you will find as much shooting and stabbing there as ever was in the wild Highlands. If you want rogues, as they are so much in fashion with you, you have that gallant caste of adventurers, who laid down their consciences at the Cape of Good Hope as they went out to India, and forgot to take them up again when they returned. Then, for great exploits, you have in the old history of India, before Europeans were numerous there, the most wonderful deeds, done by the least possible means, that perhaps the annals of the world can afford."

"I know it," said I, kindling at the ideas his speech inspired. "I remember in the delightful pages of Orme, the interest which mingles in his narratives, from the very small number of English which are engaged. Each officer of a regiment becomes known to you by name, nay, the non-commissioned officers and privates acquire an individual share of interest. They are distinguished among the natives like the Spaniards among the Mexicans. What do I say? they are like Homer's demigods among the warring mortals. Men, like Clive and Caillaud, influenced great events, like Jove himself. Inferior officers are like Mars or Neptune, and the sergeants and corporals might well pass for demigods. Then the various religious costumes, habits, and manners of the people of Hindustan,—the patient Hindhu, the warlike Rajahpoot, the haughty Moslemah, the savage and vindictive Malay—Glorious and unbounded subjects! The only objection is, that I have never been there, and know nothing at all about them."

"Nonsense, my good friend. You will tell us about them all the better that you know nothing of what you are saying; and come, we'll finish the bottle, and when Katie (her sisters go to the Assembly,) has given us tea, she will tell you the outline of the story of poor Menie Grey, whose picture you will see in the drawing-room, a distant relation of my father's, who had, however, a handsome part of cousin Menie's succession. There are none living that can be hurt by the story now, though it was thought best to smother it up at the time, as indeed even the whispers about it led poor cousin Menie to live very retired. I mind her well when a child. There was something very gentle, but rather tiresome, about poor cousin Menie."

When we came into the drawing-room, my friend pointed to a picture which I had before noticed, without, however, its having attracted more than a passing look; now I regarded it with more attention. It was one of those portraits of the middle of the eighteenth century, in which artists endeavoured to conquer the stiffness of hoops and brocades, by throwing a fancy drapery around the figure, with loose folds like a mantle or dressing gown, the stays, however, being retained, and the bosom displayed in a manner which shows that our mothers, like their daughters, were as liberal of their charms as the nature of their dress permitted. To this, the well-known style of the period, the features and form of the individual added, at first sight, little interest. It represented a handsome woman of about thirty, her hair wound simply about her head, her features regular, and her complexion fair. But on looking more closely, especially after having had a hint that the original had been the heroine of a tale, I could observe a melancholy sweetness in the countenance, that seemed to speak of woes endured, and injuries sustained, with that resignation which women can and do sometimes display under the insults and ingratitude of those on whom they have bestowed their affections.

"Yes, she was an excellent and an ill-used woman," said Mr Fairscribe, his eye fixed like mine on the picture—"She left our family not less, I dare say, than five thousand pounds, and I believe she died worth four times that sum; but it was divided among the nearest of kin, which was all fair."

"But her history, Mr Fairscribe," said I—"to judge from her look, it must have been a melancholy one."

"You may say that, Mr Croftangry. Melancholy enough, and extraordinary enough too—But," added he, swallowing in haste a cup of the tea which was presented to him, "I must away to my business—we cannot be gowffing all the morning, and telling old stories all the afternoon. Katie knows all the outs and the ins of cousin Menie's adventures as well as I do, and when she has given you the particulars, then I am at your service, to condescend more articulately upon dates or particulars."

Well, here was I, a gay old bachelor, left to hear a love tale from my young friend Katie Fairscribe, who, when she is not surrounded by a bevy of gallants, at which time, to my thinking, she shows less to advantage, is as pretty, well behaved, and unaffected a girl as you see tripping the new walks of Prince's Street or Heriot Row. Old bachelorship so decided as mine has its privileges in such a *tête-à-tête*, providing you are, or can seem for the time, perfectly good-humoured and attentive, and do not ape the manners of your younger years, in attempting which you will only make yourself ridiculous. I don't pretend to be so indifferent to the company of a pretty young woman as was desired by the poet, who wished to sit beside his mistress—

> — As unconcern'd, as when
> Her infant beauty could beget
> Nor happiness nor pain.

On the contrary, I can look on beauty and innocence, as something of which I know and esteem the value, without the desire or hope to make them my own. A young lady can afford to talk with an old stager like me without either artifice or affectation; and we may maintain a species of friendship, the more tender, perhaps, because we are of different sexes, yet with which that distinction has very little to do.

Now, I hear my wisest and most critical neighbour remark, "Mr Croftangry is in the way of doing a foolish thing. He is well to pass— Old Fairscribe knows to a penny what he is worth, and Miss Katie, with all her airs, may like the old brass that buys the new pan. I thought Mr Croftangry was looking very cadgy when he came in to play a rubber with us last night. Poor gentleman, I am sure I should be sorry to see him make a fool of himself."

Spare your compassion, dear madam, there is not the least danger. The *beaux yeux de ma cassette* are not brilliant enough to make amends for the spectacles which must supply the dimness of my own. I am a little deaf, too, as you know to your sorrow when we are partners; and if I could get a nymph to marry me with all these imperfections, who the deuce would marry Janet MacEvoy? and from Janet MacEvoy Chrystal Croftangry will not part.

Miss Katie Fairscribe gave me the tale of Menie Grey with much taste and simplicity, not attempting to suppress the feelings, whether of grief or resentment, which justly and naturally arose from the circumstances of the tale. Her father afterwards confirmed the principal outlines of the story, and furnished me with some additional circumstances, which Miss Katie had suppressed or forgotten. Indeed, I have learned on this occasion, what old Lintot meant when he told Pope, that he used to propitiate the critics of importance, when he had a work in the press, by now and then letting them see a sheet of the blotted proof, or a few leaves of the original manuscript. Our mystery of authorship hath something about it so fascinating, that if you admit any one, however little he may previously have been disposed to such studies, into your confidence, you will find that he considers himself as a party interested, and, if success follows, will think himself entitled to no inconsiderable share of the praise.

The reader has seen that no one could have been naturally less interested than was my excellent friend Fairscribe in my lucubrations, when I first consulted him on the subject; but since he has contributed a subject to the work, he has become a most zealous coadjutor; and half-ashamed, I believe, yet half-proud of the literary stock-company, in which he has got a share, he never meets me without jogging my elbow, and dropping some mysterious hints, as, "I am saying—when will you give us any more of yon?"—or, "Yon's not a bad narrative—I like yon."

Pray Heaven the reader may be of his opinion.

Chapter Two

The Surgeon's Daughter

> When fainting Nature call'd for aid,
>   And hovering Death prepared the blow,
> His vigorous remedy display'd
>   The power of Art without the show;
> In Misery's darkest caverns known,
>   His useful care was ever nigh,
> Where hopeless Anguish pour'd his groan,
>   And lonely Want retired to die;
> No summons mock'd by cold delay,
>   No petty gains disclaim'd by pride,
> The modest wants of every day
>   The toil of every day supplied.
>   SAMUEL JOHNSON

THE EXQUISITELY BEAUTIFUL portrait which the Rambler has painted of his friend Levett, well describes Gideon Grey, and many other village doctors, from whom Scotland reaps more benefit, and to whom she is perhaps more ungrateful, than to any other class of men, excepting her schoolmasters.

Such a rural man of medicine is usually the inhabitant of some petty borough or village, which forms the central point of his practice. But, besides attending to such cases as the village may afford, he is day and night at the service of every one who may command his assistance within a circle of forty miles in diameter, untraversed by roads in many directions, and including moors, mountains, rivers, and lakes. For late and dangerous journeys through an inaccessible country, for services of the most essential kind, rendered at the expense, or risk at least, of his own health and life, the Scottish village doctor receives at best a very moderate recompense, often one which is totally inadequate, and very frequently none whatsoever. He has none of the ample resources proper to the brothers of the profession in an English town. The burgesses of a Scottish borough are rendered, by their limited means of luxury, inaccessible to gout, surfeits, and all the comfortable chronic diseases, which are attendant on wealth and indolence. Four years, or so, of abstemiousness, enable them to stand an election dinner; and there is no hope of broken heads among a score or two of quiet electors, who settle the business over a table. There the mothers of the state never make a point of pouring, in the course of every revolving year, a certain quantity of doctor's stuff through the bowels of their beloved children. Every old woman, from the Townhead to the Townfit, can prescribe a dose of salts, or spread a plaster; and it is only when a fever or a palsy renders matters serious, that the assistance of the doctor is invoked by his neighbours in the borough.

But still the man of science cannot complain of inactivity or want of practice. If he does not find patients at his door, he seeks them through a wide circle. Like the ghostly lover of Leonora, he mounts at midnight, and traverses in darkness paths which, to those less accustomed to them, seem formidable in daylight, through straits where the slightest aberration would plunge him into a morass, or throw him over a precipice, on to cabins which his horse might ride over without knowing they lay in his way, unless he happened to fall through the roofs. When he arrives at such a stately termination of his journey, where his services are required, either to bring a wretch into the world, or prevent one from leaving it, the scene of misery is often such, that far from touching the hard-saved shillings which are gratefully offered to him, he bestows his medicines as well as his attendance— for charity. I have heard the celebrated traveller Mungo Park, who had experienced both courses of life, rather give the preference to travelling as a discoverer in Africa, than to wandering by night and day the wilds of his native land in the capacity of a country medical practitioner. He mentioned having once upon a time rode forty miles, sat up all night, and successfully assisted a woman under influence of the primitive curse, for which his sole remuneration was a roasted potato and a draught of butter-milk. But his was not the heart which grudged the labour that relieved human misery. In short, there is no creature in Scotland that works harder and is more poorly requited than the country doctor, unless perhaps it may be his horse. Yet the horse is, and indeed must be, hardy, active, and indefatigable, in spite of a rough coat and indifferent condition; and so you will often find in his master, under an unpromising and blunt exterior, professional skill and enthusiasm, intelligence, humanity, courage, and science.

Mr Gideon Grey, surgeon in the village of Middlemas, situated in one of the midland counties of Scotland, led the rough, active, and ill-rewarded course of life which we have endeavoured to describe. He was a man between forty and fifty, devoted to his profession, and of such reputation in the medical world, that he had been more than once, as opportunities occurred, advised to exchange Middlemas and its meagre circle of practice, for some of the larger towns in Scotland, or for Edinburgh itself. This advice he had always declined. He was a plain blunt man, who did not love restraint, and was unwilling to subject himself to that which was exacted in polite society. He had not himself found out, nor had any friend hinted to him, that a slight touch of the cynic, in manner and habits, gives the physician, to the common eye, an air of authority which greatly tends to enlarge his reputation. Mr Grey, or, as the country people called him, Doctor Grey, (he might hold the title by diploma for what I know, though he only claimed the rank of Master of Arts,) had few wants, and these were amply supplied by a professional income which generally approached two hundred pounds a-year, for which, upon an average, he travelled about five thousand miles on horseback in the course of the twelve months. Nay, so liberally did this revenue support himself and his ponies, called Pestle and Mortar, which he exercised alternately, that he took a damsel to share it, Jean Watson, namely, the cherry-cheeked daughter of an honest farmer, who being herself one of twelve children, who had been brought up on an income of fourscore pounds a-year, never thought there could be poverty in more than double the sum; and looked on Grey, though now termed by irreverent youth the Old Doctor, as a very advantageous match. For several years they had no children, and it seemed as if Doctor Grey, who had so often assisted the efforts of the goddess Lucina, was never to invoke her in his own behalf. Yet his domestic roof was, on a remarkable occasion, decreed to be the scene where the goddess's aid was required.

Late of an autumn evening three old women might be observed plying their aged limbs through the single street of the village at Middlemas towards the honoured door, which, fenced off from the vulgar causeway, was defended by a broken paling, partially inclosing two slips of ground, half arable, half overrun with an abortive attempt at shrubbery. The door itself was blazoned with the name of Gideon Grey, M.A. Surgeon, &c. &c. Some of the idle young fellows, who had been a minute or two before loitering at the other end of the street before the door of the alehouse, (for the pretended inn deserved no better name,) now accompanied the old dames with shouts of laughter, excited by their unwonted agility; and with bets on the winner, as loudly expressed as if they had been laid at the starting-post of Middlemas races. "Half-a-mutchkin on Luckie Simson!"—"Auld Peg Tamson against the field!"—"Mair speed, Alison Jaup, ye'll tak the wind out of them yet!"—"Canny against the hill, lasses, or we may have a brusten auld carline amang ye!" These, and a thousand such gibes rent the air, without being noticed, or even heard, by the anxious racers, whose object of contention seemed to be, which should first reach the Doctor's door.

"Guide us, Doctor, what can be the matter now?" said Mrs Grey, whose character was that of a good-natured simpleton; "Here's Peg Tamson, Jean Simson, and Alison Jaup, running a race on the hie street of the burgh!"

The Doctor, who had but the moment before hung his wet great-coat before the fire, (for he was just dismounted from a long journey,) hastened down stairs, auguring some new occasion for his services, and happy, that, from the character of the messengers, it was likely to be within burgh, and not landward.

He had just reached the door as Luckie Simson, one of the racers, arrived in the little area before it. She had got the start, and kept it, but at the expense, for the time, of her powers of speech; for when she came in presence of the Doctor, she stood blowing like a grampus, her loose toy flying back from her face, making the most violent efforts to speak, but without the power of uttering a single intelligible word. Peg Thomson whipped in before her.

"The leddy, sir, the leddy—"

"Instant help, instant help"—screeched, rather than uttered, Alison Jaup; while Luckie Simson, who had certainly won the race, found words to claim the prize which had set them all in motion. "And I hope, sir, you will recommend me to be the sick-nurse; I was here to bring you the tidings lang before ony o' thae lazy queans."

Loud were the counter protestations of the two competitors, and loud the laugh of the idle *loons* who listened at a little distance.

"Hold your tongue, ye flyting fools," said the Doctor; "and you, ye idle rascals, if I come out among you—" So saying, he smacked his long-lashed whip with great emphasis, producing much the effect of the celebrated *Quos ego* of Neptune, in the first Æneid. "And now," said the Doctor, "where, or who, is this lady?"

The question was scarce necessary; for a plain carriage, with four horses, came at a foot's-pace towards the door of the Doctor's house, and the old women, now more at their ease, gave the Doctor to understand, that the gentleman thought the accommodation of the Swan Inn totally unfit for his lady's rank and condition, and had, by their advice, (each claiming the merit of the suggestion,) brought her here, to experience the hospitality of the *west-room;*—a spare apartment, in which Doctor Grey occasionally accommodated such patients, as he desired to keep for a space of time under his own eye.

There were two persons only in the vehicle. The one, a gentleman in a riding dress, sprung out, and having received from the Doctor an assurance that the lady would receive tolerable accommodation in his house, he lent assistance to his companion to leave the carriage, and with great apparent satisfaction, saw her safely deposited in a decent sleeping apartment, and under the respectable charge of the Doctor and his lady, who assured him once more of every species of attention. To bind their promise more firmly, the stranger slipped a purse of twenty guineas (for this story chanced in the golden age) into the hand of the Doctor, as an earnest of the most liberal recompense, and requested he would spare no expense in providing all that was necessary or desirable for a person in the lady's condition, and for the helpless being to whom she might immediately be expected to give birth. He then said he would retire to the inn, where he begged a message might instantly acquaint him with the expected change in the lady's situation.

"She is of rank," he said, "and a foreigner; let no expense be spared. We designed to have reached Edinburgh, but were forced to turn off the road by an accident." Once more he said, "let no expense be spared, and manage that she may travel as soon as possible."

"That," said the Doctor, "is past my control. Nature must not be hurried, and she avenges herself of every attempt to do so."

"But art," said the stranger, "can do much," and he proffered a second purse, which seemed as heavy as the first.

"Art," said the Doctor, "may be recompensed, but cannot be purchased. You have already paid me more than enough to take the utmost care I can of your lady; should I accept more money, it could only be for promising, by implication at least, what is beyond my power to perform. Every possible care shall be taken of your lady, and that affords the best chance of her being speedily able to travel.—Now, go you to the inn, sir, for I may be instantly wanted, and we have not yet provided either an attendant for the lady, or a nurse for the child; but both shall be presently done."

"Yet a moment, Doctor—what languages do you understand?"

"Latin and French I can speak indifferently, and so as to be understood; and I read a little Italian."

"But no Portuguese or Spanish?" continued the stranger.

"No, sir."

"That is unlucky. But you may make her understand you by means of French. Take notice, you are to comply with her request in every thing—if you want means to do so, you may apply to me."

"May I ask, sir, by what name the lady is to be"——

"It is totally indifferent," said the stranger, interrupting the question; "you shall know it at more leisure."

So saying, he threw his ample cloak about him, turning himself half round to assist the operation, with an air which the Doctor would have found it difficult to imitate, and walked down the street to the little inn. Here he paid and dismissed the postilions, and shut himself up in an apartment, ordering no one to be admitted, till the Doctor should call.

The Doctor, when he returned to his patient's apartment, found his wife in great surprise, which, as is usual with persons of her character, was not unmixed with fear and anxiety.

"She cannot speak a word like a Christian being," said Mrs Grey.

"I know it," said the Doctor.

"But she threeps to keep on a black fause face, and skirls if we offer to take it away."

"Well then, let her wear it—What harm will it do?"

"Harm, Doctor! Was ever honest woman brought to bed with a fause face on?"

"Seldom, perhaps. But, Jean, my dear, those who are not quite honest must be brought to bed all the same as those who are, and we are not to endanger the poor thing's life by contradicting her whims at present."

Approaching the sick woman's bed, he observed that she indeed wore a thin silk mask, of the kind which do such uncommon service in the elder comedy; such as women of rank still wore in travelling, but certainly never in the situation of this poor lady. It would seem she had sustained importunity on the subject, for when she saw the Doctor, she put her hands to her face, as if she was afraid he would insist on pulling off the vizard. He hastened to say, in tolerable French, that her will should be a law to them in every respect, and that she was at perfect liberty to wear the mask till it was her pleasure to lay it aside. She understood him; for she replied, by a very imperfect attempt, in the same language, to express her gratitude for the permission, as she seemed to regard it, of retaining her disguise.

The Doctor proceeded to other arrangements; and, for the satisfaction of those readers who may love minute information, we record, that Luckie Simson, the first in the race, carried as a prize the situation of sick nurse beside the delicate patient; that Peg Thomson was permitted the privilege of recommending her good-daughter, Bet Jamieson, to be wet-nurse; and an *oe*, or grandchild, of Luckie Jaup was hired to assist in the increased drudgery of the family; the Doctor thus, like a practised minister, dividing among his trusty adherents such good things as fortune placed at his disposal.

About one in the morning the Doctor made his appearance at the Swan Inn, and acquainted the stranger gentleman, that he wished him joy of being the father of a healthy boy, and that the mother was, in the usual phrase, as well as could be expected.

The stranger heard the news with seeming satisfaction, and then exclaimed. "He must be christened, Doctor! he must be christened instantly!"

"There can be no hurry for that," said the Doctor.

"*We* think otherwise," said the stranger, cutting his argument short. "I am a Catholic, Doctor, and as I may be obliged to leave this place before the lady is able to travel, I desire to see my child received into the pale of the church. There is, I understand, a Catholic priest in this wretched place?"

"There is a Catholic gentleman, sir, Mr Goodriche, who is reported to be in orders."

"I commend your caution, Doctor," said the stranger; "it is dangerous to be too positive on any subject. I will bring that same Mr Goodriche to your house to-morrow."

Grey hesitated for a moment. "I am a Presbyterian Protestant, sir," he said, "a friend to the constitution as established in church and state, as I have a good right, having drawn his Majesty's pay, God bless him, for four years, as surgeon's mate in the Cameronian regiment, as my regimental Bible and commission can testify. But although I be bound especially to abhor all trafficking or trinketing with Papists, yet I will not stand in the way of a tender conscience. Sir, you may call with Mr Goodriche, when you please, at my house; and undoubtedly, you being, as I suppose, the father of the child, you will arrange matters as you please; only, I do not desire to be thought an abettor or countenancer of any part of the Popish ritual."

"Enough, sir," said the stranger bowing haughtily, "we understand each other."

The next day he appeared at the Doctor's house with Mr Goodriche, and two persons understood to belong to that reverend gentleman's communion. The party were shut up in an apartment with the infant, and it may be presumed that the solemnity of baptism was administered to the unconscious being, thus strangely launched upon the world. When the priest and witnesses had retired, the strange gentleman informed Mr Grey, that, as the lady had been pronounced unfit for travelling for several days, he was himself about to leave the neighbourhood, but would return thither in the space of ten days, when he hoped to find his companion able to leave it.

"And by what name are we to call the child and mother?"

"The infant's name is Richard."

"But it must have some sirname—so must the lady—She cannot reside in my house, yet be without a name."

"Call them by the name of your town here—Middlemas, I think it is?"

"Yes, sir."

"Well, Mrs Middlemas is the name of the mother, and Richard Middlemas of the child—and I am Matthew Middlemas, at your service. This," he continued, "will provide Mrs Middlemas in everything she may wish to possess—or assist her in case of accidents." With that he placed L.100 in Mr Grey's hand, who rather scrupled receiving it, saying, "He supposed the lady was qualified to be her own purse-bearer."

"The worst in the world, I assure you, Doctor," replied the stranger. "If she wished to change that piece of paper, she would scarce know how many guineas she should receive for it. No, Mr Grey, I assure you you will find Mrs Middleton—Middlemas—what did I call her—as ignorant of the affairs of this world as any one you have met with in your practice. So you will please to be her treasurer and administrator for the time, as for a patient that is incapable to look after her own affairs."

This was spoke, as it struck Dr Grey, in rather a haughty and supercilious manner. The words intimated nothing in themselves, more than the same desire of preserving incognito, which might be gathered from all the rest of the stranger's conduct; but the manner seemed to say, "I am not a person to be questioned by any one—What I say must be received without comment, how little soever you may believe or understand it." It strengthened Grey in his opinion, that he had before him a case either of seduction, or of private marriage, betwixt persons of the very highest rank; and the whole bearing, both of the lady and the gentleman, confirmed his suspicions. It was not in his nature to be troublesome or inquisitive, but he could not fail to see that the lady wore no marriage-ring; and her deep sorrow, and perpetual tremor, seemed to indicate an unhappy creature, who had lost the protection of parents, without acquiring a legitimate right to that of a husband. He was therefore somewhat anxious when Mr Middlemas, after a private conference of some length with the lady, bade him farewell. It is true, he assured him of his return within ten days, being the very shortest space which Grey could be prevailed upon to assign for any prospect of the lady being moved with safety.

"I trust in Heaven that he will return," said Grey to himself; "but there is too much mystery about all this, for its being a plain and well-meaning transaction. If he means to treat this poor thing, as many a poor girl has been used before, I hope that my house will not be the scene in which he chooses to desert her. The leaving the money has somewhat a suspicious aspect, and looks as if my friend were in the act of making some compromise with his conscience. Well—I must hope the best. Mean time my path is plainly to do what I can for the poor lady's benefit."

Mr Grey visited his patient shortly after Mr Middlemas's departure —as soon, indeed, as he could be admitted. He found her in violent agitation. Grey's experience dictated the best mode of procuring relief and tranquillity. He caused her infant to be brought to her. She wept over it for a long time, and the violence of her agitation subsided under the influence of parental feelings, which, from her appearance of extreme youth, she must have experienced for the first time.

The observant physician could, after this paroxysm, remark that his patient's mind was chiefly occupied in computing the passage of the time, and anticipating the period when the return of her husband —if husband he was—might be expected. She consulted almanacks, inquired concerning distances, though so cautiously as to make it evident she desired to give no indication of the direction of her companion's journey, and repeatedly compared her watch with those of others; exercising, it was evident, all that delusive species of mental arithmetic, by which mortals attempt to accelerate the passage of Time while they calculate his progress. At other times she wept anew over her child, which was by all judges pronounced as goodly an infant as needed to be seen; and Grey sometimes observed that she murmured sentences to the unconscious infant, not only the words, but the very sounds and accents of which were strange to him, and which, in particular, he knew not to be Portuguese.

Mr Goodriche, the Catholic priest, demanded access to her upon one occasion. She at first declined his visit, but afterwards received it, under the idea, perhaps, that he might have news from Mr Middlemas, as he called himself. The interview was a very short one, and the priest left the lady's apartment in displeasure, which his prudence could scarce disguise from Mr Grey. He never returned, although the lady's condition would have made his attentions and consolations necessary, had she been a member of the Catholic Church.

Mr Grey began at length to suspect his fair guest was a Jewess, who had yielded up her person and affections to one of a different religion; and the peculiar style of her beautiful countenance went to confirm this opinion. The circumstance made no difference to Grey, who saw only her distress and desolation, and endeavoured to remedy both to the utmost of his power. He was, however, desirous to conceal it from his wife, and the others around the sick person, whose prudence and liberality of thinking might be more justly doubted. He therefore so regulated her diet, that she could not be either offended, or brought under suspicion, by any of the articles forbidden by the Mosaic law being presented to her. In other respects than what concerned her health or convenience, he had but little intercourse with her.

The space passed within which the stranger's return to the borough had been so anxiously expected by his female companion. The disappointment occasioned by his non-arrival was manifested in the convalescent by anxiety, which was at first mingled with peevishness, and afterwards with fear. When two or three days had passed by without message or letter of any kind, Grey himself became anxious, both on his own account and the poor lady's, lest the stranger should have actually entertained the idea of deserting this defenceless and probably injured woman. He longed to have some communication with her, which might enable him to judge what inquiries could be made, or what else was most fitting to be done. But so imperfect was the poor young woman's knowledge of the French language, and perhaps so unwilling she herself to throw any light on her situation, that every attempt of this kind proved abortive. When Grey asked questions concerning any subject which appeared to approach the explanation, he observed she usually answered him by shaking her head, in token of not understanding what he said; at other times by silence and with tears, and sometimes by referring him to *Monsieur*.

For Monsieur's arrival, then, Grey began to become very impatient, as that which alone could put an end to a disagreeable species of mystery, which the good company of the borough began now to make the principal subject of their gossip; some blaming Grey for taking foreign *landloupers* into his house, on the subject of whose morals the most serious doubts might be entertained; others envying the "bonny hand" the Doctor was likely to make of it, by having disposal of the wealthy stranger's travelling funds; a circumstance which could not be well concealed from the public, when the honest man's expenditure for trifling articles of luxury came far to exceed its ordinary bounds.

The conscious probity of the honest Doctor enabled him to despise this sort of tittle-tattle, though the secret knowledge of its existence could not be agreeable to him. He went his usual rounds with his usual perseverance, and waited in patience until time should throw light on the subject and history of his lodger. It was now the fourth week after her confinement, and the recovery of the stranger might be considered as perfect, when Grey, returning from one of his ten-mile visits, saw a post-chaise and four horses at his door. "This man has returned," he said, "and my suspicions have done him less than justice." With that he spurred his horse, a signal which the trusty steed obeyed the more readily, as its progress was in the direction of the stable-door. But when, dismounting, the Doctor hurried into his own house, it seemed to him, that the departure as well as the arrival of this distressed lady was destined to bring confusion to his peaceful dwelling. Several idlers had assembled about his door, and two or three had impudently thrust themselves forward almost into the passage, to listen to a confused altercation which was heard from within.

Grey hastened forward, the foremost of the intruders retreating in confusion on his approach, while he caught the tones of his wife's voice, raised to a pitch which he knew, by experience, boded no good; for Mrs Grey, good-humoured and tractable in general, could sometimes perform the high part in a matrimonial duet. Having much more confidence in his wife's good intentions than her prudence, he lost no time in pushing into the parlour, to take the matter into his own hands. Here he found Mrs Grey at the head of the whole militia of the sick lady's apartment, that is, wet nurse, and sick nurse, and girl of all work, engaged in violent dispute with two strangers. The one was a dark-featured elderly man, with an eye of much sharpness and severity of expression, which now seemed partly quenched by a mixture of grief and mortification. The other, who appeared actively sustaining the dispute with Mrs Grey, was a stout, bold-looking, hard-faced person, armed with pistols, of which he made rather an unnecessary and ostentatious display.

"Here is my husband, sir," said Mrs Grey in a tone of triumph, for she had the grace to believe the Doctor one of the greatest men living, —"Here is the Doctor—let us see what you will say now."

"Why, just what I said before, ma'am," answered the man, "which is, that my warrant must be obeyed. It is regular, ma'am, regular."

So saying, he struck the forefinger of his right hand against a paper which he held towards Mrs Grey with his left.

"Address yourself to me, if you please, sir," said Dr Grey, seeing that he ought to lose no time in removing the cause into the proper court. "I am the master of this house, sir, and I wish to know the cause of this visit."

"My business is soon told," said the man. "I am a King's Messenger, and this lady has treated me, as if I was a baron-bailie's officer."

"That is not the question, sir," replied the Doctor. "If you are a King's Messenger, where is your warrant, and what do you propose to do here?" At the same time he whispered the little wench to call Mr Lawford, the town-clerk, to come thither as fast as he possibly could. The grandchild of Alison Jaup started off with an activity worthy of her grandmother.

"There is my warrant," said the official, "and you may satisfy yourself."

"The shameless loon dare not tell the Doctor his errand," said Mrs Grey exultingly.

"A bonny errand it is," said old Luckie Simson, "to carry awa' a lying-in woman, as a gled would do a clocking-hen."

"A woman no a month delivered—" echoed the nurse Jamieson.

"Twenty-four days eight hours and seven minutes to a second," said Mrs Grey.

The Doctor having looked over the warrant, which was regular, began to be afraid that the females of his family, in their zeal for defending the character of their sex, might be stirred up into some sudden fit of mutiny, and therefore commanded them to be silent.

"This," he said, "is a warrant for arresting the bodies of Richard Tresham, and of Zilia de Monçada, on account of High Treason. Sir, I have served his Majesty, and this is not a house in which traitors are harboured. I know nothing of any of these two persons, nor have I ever heard even their names."

"But the lady whom you have received into your family," said the Messenger, "is Zilia de Monçada, and here stands her father, Matthias de Monçada, who will make oath to it."

"If this be true," said Mr Grey, looking towards the alleged father, "you have taken a singular office on you. It is neither my habit to deny my own actions, nor to oppose the laws of the land. There is a lady in this house slowly recovering from confinement, having become under this roof the mother of a healthy child. If she be the person described in this warrant, and this gentleman's daughter, I must surrender her to the laws of the country."

Here the Esculapian militia were once more in motion.

"Surrender, Doctor Grey! It's a shame to hear you speak, and you that lives by women and weans, above your other means!" so exclaimed his fair better part.

"I wonder to hear the Doctor!"—said the younger nurse; "there's no a wife in the town would believe it o' him."

"I aye thought the Doctor was a man till this moment," said Luckie Simson; "but I believe him now to be an auld wife, little baulder than mysell; and I dinna wonder now that poor Mrs Grey"——

"Hold your peace, you foolish women," said the Doctor. "Do you think this business is not bad enough already, that you are making it worse with your senseless clavers?—Gentlemen, this is a very sad case. Here is a warrant for a high crime against a poor creature, who is little fit to be moved from one house to another, much more dragged to a prison. I tell you plainly, that I think the execution of this arrest may cause her death. It is your business, sir, if you be really her father, to consider what you can do to soften this matter, rather than to drive it on."

"Better death than dishonour," replied the stern-looking old man, with a voice as harsh as his aspect; "and you, Messenger," he continued, "look what you do, and execute the warrant at your peril."

"You hear," said the man, appealing to Grey himself, "I must have immediate access to the lady."

"In a lucky time," said Mr Grey, "here comes the town-clerk.— You are very welcome, Mr Lawford. Your opinion here is much wanted as a man of law, as well as of sense and humanity. I was never more glad to see you in all my life."

He then rapidly stated the case; and the Messenger, understanding the new-comer to be a man of some authority, again exhibited his warrant.

"This is a very sufficient and valid warrant, Dr Grey," replied the man of law. "Nevertheless, if you are disposed to make oath, that instant removal would be unfavourable to the lady's health, unquestionably she must remain here, suitably guarded."

"It is not so much the mere act of locomotion which I am afraid of," said the surgeon; "but I am free to depone, on soul and conscience, that the shame and fear of her father's anger, and the sense of the affront of such an arrest, with terror for its consequences, may occasion violent and dangerous illness—even death itself."

"The father must see the daughter, though they may have quarrelled," said Mr Lawford; "the officer of justice must execute his warrant, though it should frighten the criminal to death; these evils are only contingent, not direct and immediate consequences. You must give up the lady, Mr Grey, though your hesitation is very natural."

"At least, Mr Lawford, I ought to be certain that the person in my house is the party they search for."

"Admit me to her apartment," replied the man whom the Messenger termed Monçada.

"If it must be," said Grey,—"but I would rather face a cannon."

The Messenger, whom the presence of Lawford had made something more placid, began to become impudent once more. He hoped, he said, by means of this prisoner, to acquire the information necessary to apprehend the more guilty person. If more delays were thrown in his way, that information might come too late, and he would make all who were accessary to such delay responsible for the consequences.

"And I," said Mr Grey, "though I were to be brought to the gallows for it, protest, that this course may be the murder of my patient—Can bail not be taken, Mr Lawford?"

"Not in cases of high treason," said the official person; and then continued in a confidential tone, "Come, Mr Grey, we all know you to be a person well affected to our Royal Sovereign King George and to the Government; but you must not push this too far, lest you bring yourself into trouble, which everybody in Middlemas would be sorry for. The Forty-five has not been so far gone by, but we can remember enough of warrants of high-treason—ay, and ladies of quality committed upon such charges. But they were all favourably dealt with— Lady Ogilvy, Lady MacIntosh, Flora Macdonald, and all. No doubt this gentleman knows what he is doing, and has assurances of the young lady's safety—So you must just jouk and let the jaw gae by, as we say."—

"Follow me, then, gentlemen," said Gideon, "and you shall see the young lady;" and then, his strong features working with emotion at anticipation of the distress which he was about to inflict, he led the way up the small staircase, and opening the door, said to Monçada who had followed him, "This is your daughter's only place of refuge, in which I am, alas! too weak to be her protector. Enter, sir, if your conscience will permit you."

The stranger turned on him a scowl, into which it seemed as if he would willingly have thrown the power of the fabled basilisk. Then stepping proudly forwards, he stalked into the room. He was followed by Lawford and Grey, at a little distance. The Messenger remained in the doorway. The unhappy young woman had heard the disturbance, and guessed the cause too truly. It is possible she might even have seen the strangers on their descent from the carriage. When they entered the room, she was on her knees, beside an easy chair, her face in a silk wrapper that was hung over it. The man called Monçada uttered a single word; by the accent it might have been something equivalent to *Wretch;* but none knew its import. The female gave a convulsive shudder, such as that by which a dying soldier is affected on receiving a second wound. But without minding her emotion, Monçada seized her by the arm, and with little gentleness raised her to her feet, on which she seemed to stand only because she was supported by his strong grasp on her arm. He then pulled from her face the mask which she had hitherto worn. The poor creature still endeavoured to shroud her face, by covering it with her left hand, as the manner in which she was held prevented her from using the aid of the right. With little effort her father secured that hand also, which, indeed, was of itself far too little to serve the purpose of concealment, and showed her beautiful face, burning with blushes and covered with tears.

"You Alcalde, and you Surgeon," he said to Lawford and Grey, with a foreign action and accent, "this woman is my daughter, the same Zilia de Monçada who is signalled in that protocol. Make way, and let me carry her where her crimes may be atoned for."

"Are you that person's daughter?" said Lawford to the lady.

"She understands no English," said Grey; and addressing his patient in French, conjured her to let him know whether she was that man's daughter or not, assuring her of protection if the fact were otherwise. The answer was murmured faintly, but was too distinctly intelligible—"He was her father."

All farther title of interference seemed now ended. The Messenger arrested his prisoner, and, with some delicacy, required the assistance of the females to get her conveyed to the carriage in waiting.

Grey again interposed.—"You will not," he said, "separate the mother and the infant?" _man of reason + humility_

Zilia de Monçada heard the question, (which, being addressed to the father, Grey had inconsiderately uttered in French,) and it seemed as if it recalled to her recollection the existence of the helpless creature to which she had given birth, forgotten for a moment amongst the accumulated horrors of her father's presence. She uttered a shriek, expressing poignant grief, and turned her eyes on her father with the most intense supplication.

"To the parish with the bastard!"—said Monçada; while the helpless mother sunk lifeless into the arms of the females, who had now gathered round her.

"That will not pass, sir," said Mr Grey.—"If you are father to that lady, you must be grandfather to the helpless child; and you must settle in some manner for its future provision, or refer us to some responsible person."

Monçada looked towards Lawford, who expressed himself satisfied of the propriety of what Grey said.

"I object not to pay for whatever the wretched child may require," said he; "and if you, sir," addressing Grey, "choose to take charge of him, and breed him up, you shall have what will better your living."

Grey was about to refuse a charge so uncivilly offered; but after a moment's reflection, he replied, "I think so indifferently of the proceedings I have witnessed, and of those concerned in them, that if the mother desires that I should retain the care of this child, I will not refuse to do so."

Monçada spoke to his daughter, who was just beginning to recover from her swoon, in the same language in which he had first addressed her. The proposition which he made seemed highly acceptable, as she started from the arms of the females, and, advancing to Grey, seized his hand, kissed it, bathed it in her tears, and seemed reconciled, even in parting with her child, by the consideration, that the infant was to remain under his gu

"Good, kind man," she said in h
saved both mother and child."

The father, meanwhile, with mercantile
Lawford's hands notes and bills to the amoun
which he stated was to be vested for the child's
such portions as his board and education might req
of any correspondence on his account being necessar
death or the like, he directed that communication should
Seignior Matthias de Monçada, under cover to a certain b
house in London.

"But beware," he said to Grey, "how you trouble me about the
concerns, unless in case of absolute necessity."

"You need not fear, sir," replied Grey; "I have seen nothing to-day
which can induce me to desire a more intimate correspondence with
you than may be indispensable."

While Lawford drew up a proper minute of this transaction, by
which he himself and Grey were named trustees for the child, Mr
Grey attempted to restore to the lady the balance of the considerable
sum of money which Tresham (if such was his real name) had formerly deposited with him. With every species of gesture, by which
hands, eyes, and even feet, could express rejection, as well as in her
own broken French, she repelled the proposal of reimbursement,
while she entreated that Grey would consider the money as his own
property; and at the same time, forced upon him a ring set with
brilliants, which seemed of considerable value. The father then spoke
to her a few stern words, which she heard with an air of mingled agony
and submission.

"I have given her a few minutes to see and weep over the miserable
being which has been the seal of her dishonour," said the stern father.
"Let us retire, and leave her alone.—You, (to the Messenger,) watch
the outer door of the room."

Grey, Lawford, and Monçada, retired to the parlour accordingly,
where they waited in silence, each busied with his own reflections, till,
within the space of half an hour, they received information that the
lady was ready to depart.

"It is well," replied Monçada; "I am glad she has yet sense enough
left to submit to that which needs must be."

So saying, he ascended the stair, and again returned, leading down
his daughter, now again masked and closely veiled. As she passed
Grey, she uttered the words—"My child, my child!" in a tone of
unutterable anguish; then entered the carriage, which was drawn up
as close to the door of the Doctor's house as the little enclosure would

and accompanied by
hich drove furiously
ll who had witnessed
ieir conjectures, and
distributed among the
so much liberality, as
f the rights of woman-
patient.

eels of the carriage had
claims a share of human
:llous and affecting incid-

"Indeed, Doctor, y... ing out of the window till
some other patient calls for you, and then have to set off without your
dinner;—and I hope Mr Lawford will take pot-luck with us, for it is
past his own hour; and indeed we had something rather better than
ordinary for this poor lady—lamb and spinnage, and a veal Florentine."

The surgeon started as from a dream, and joined in his wife's
hospitable request, to which Lawford willingly assented.

We will suppose the meal finished, a bottle of old and generous
Antigua rum upon the table, and a modest little punch-bowl, judiciously replenished for the accommodation of the Doctor and his guest.
Their conversation naturally turned on the strange scene which they
had witnessed, and the Town-Clerk took considerable merit for his
presence of mind.

"I am thinking, Doctor," said he, "you might have brewed a bitter
browst to yourself if I had not come in as I did."

"Troth, and it might very well so be," answered Grey; "for, to tell
you the truth, when I saw yonder fellow vapouring with his pistols
among the women folk in my own house, the old Cameronian spirit
began to rise in me, and little thing would have made me cleek to the
poker."

"Hoot! hoot! that would never have done. Na, na," said the man of
law, "this was a case where a little prudence was worth all the pistols
and pokers in the world."

"And that was just what I thought when I sent to you, Clerk Lawford," said the Doctor.

"A wiser man he could not have called on to a difficult case," added

Mrs Grey, as she sat with her work at a little distance from the table.

"Thanks t'ye, and here's t'ye, my good neighbour," answered the scribe; "will you not let me help you to another glass of punch, Mrs Grey?" This being declined, he proceeded. "I am jalousing that the Messenger and his warrant were just brought in to prevent any opposition. Ye saw how quietly he behaved after I had laid down the law—I'll never believe the lady is in any risk from him. But the father is a dour chield; depend upon it, he has bred up the young filly on the curb-rein, and that has made the poor thing start off the course. I should not be surprised that he took her abroad, and shut her up in a convent."

"Hardly," replied Doctor Grey, "if it be true, as I suspect, that both the father and daughter are of the Jewish persuasion."

"A Jew!" said Mrs Grey; "and have I been taking a' this fyke about a Jew?—I thought she seemed to gie a scunner at the eggs and bacon that Nurse Simson spoke about to her. But I thought Jews had aye had lang beards, and yon man's face is just like one of our ain folks—I have seen the Doctor with a langer beard himsell, when he has not had leisure to shave."

"That might have been Mr Monçada's case," said Lawford, "for he seemed to have had a hard journey. But the Jews are often very respectable people, Mrs Grey—they have no territorial property, because the law is against them there, but they have a good hank in the money-market—plenty of stock in the funds, Mrs Grey; and, indeed, I think this poor young woman is better with her ain father, though he be a Jew and a dour chield into the bargain, than she would have been with the loon that wranged her, who is, by your account, Dr Grey, baith a papist and a rebel. The Jews are well attached to government; they hate the Pope, the Devil, and the Pretender, as much as ony honest man among ourselves."

"I cannot admire either of the gentlemen," said Dr Grey. "But it is but fair to say, that I saw Mr Monçada when he was highly incensed, and to all appearance not without reason. Now, this other man Tresham, if that be his name, was haughty to me, and I think something careless of the poor young woman, just at the time when he owed her most kindness, and me some thankfulness. I am, therefore, something of your opinion, Clerk Lawford, that the Christian is the worse bargain of the two."

"And you think of taking care of this wean yourself, Doctor? That is what I call being the good Samaritan."

"At cheap cost, Clerk; the child, if it lives, has enough to bring it up decently, and set it out in life, and I can teach it an honourable and useful profession. It will be rather an amusement than a trouble to me, and I want to make some remarks on the childish diseases which, with God's blessing, the child must come through under my charge; and since Heaven has sent us no children——"

"Hoot! hoot!" said the Town-Clerk, "you are in ower great a hurry now—you have na been sae lang married yet.—Mrs Grey, dinna let my daffing chase you away—we will be for a dish of tea belive, for the Doctor and I are nae glass-breakers."

Four years after this conversation took place, the event happened, at the possibility of which the Town-Clerk had hinted; and Mrs Grey presented her husband with an infant daughter. But good and evil are strangely mingled in this sublunary world. The fulfilment of his anxious longing for posterity was attended with the loss of his simple and kind-hearted wife; one of the most heavy blows which fate could inflict on poor Grey, and his house was made desolate even by the event which had promised for months before to add new comforts to its humble roof. Grey felt the shock as men of sense and firmness feel a decided blow, from the effects of which they never hope again fully to raise themselves. He discharged the duties of his profession with the same punctuality as ever, was easy, and even, to appearance, cheerful in his intercourse with society; but the sunshine of existence was gone. Every morning he missed the affectionate charges which recommended to him to pay attention to his own health, while he was labouring to restore that blessing to his patients. Every evening, as he returned from his weary round, it was without the consciousness of a kind and affectionate reception from one eager to tell, and interested to hear, all the little events of the day. His whistle, which used to arise clear and strong so soon as Middlemas steeple was in view, was now for ever silenced, and the rider's head drooped, while the tired horse, lacking the stimulus of his master's hand and voice, seemed to shuffle along as if it felt a share of his despondency. There were times when he was so much dejected as to be unable to endure even the presence of his little Menie, in whose infant countenance he could trace the lineaments of the mother, of whose loss she had been the innocent and unconscious cause. "Had it not been for this poor child"—he would think; but, instantly aware that the sentiment was sinful, he would snatch the infant to his breast, and load it with caresses—then hastily desire it to be removed from the parlour.

The Mahometans have a fanciful idea, that the true believer, in his passage to Paradise, is under the necessity of passing barefooted over a bridge composed of red-hot iron. But on this occasion, all the pieces of paper which the Moslem has preserved during his life, lest some holy thing being written upon them might be profaned, arrange themselves between his feet and the burning metal, and so save him from injury. In the same manner, the effects of kind and benevolent actions are sometimes found, even in this world, to assuage the pangs of subsequent afflictions.

Thus, the greatest consolation which poor Grey could find after his heavy deprivation, was in the frolic fondness of Richard Middlemas, the child who was in so singular a manner thrown upon his charge. Even at this early age he was eminently handsome. When silent, or out of humour, his dark eyes and striking countenance presented some recollections of the stern character imprinted on the features of his supposed father; but when he was gay and happy, which was much more frequently the case, these clouds were exchanged for the most frolicsome, mirthful expression, that ever dwelt on the laughing and thoughtless aspect of a child. He seemed to have a tact beyond his years in discovering and conforming to the peculiarities of human character. His nurse, one prime object of Richard's observance, was Nurse Jamieson, or as she was more commonly called for brevity, and *par excellence*, Nurse. This was the person who had brought him up from infancy. She had lost her own child, and soon after her husband, and being thus a lone woman, had, as used to be common in Scotland, remained a member of Dr Grey's family. After the death of his wife, she gradually obtained the principal superintendence of the whole household; and being an honest and capable manager, was a person of very great importance in the family.

She was bold in her temper, violent in her feelings, and, as often happens with those in her condition, was as much attached to Richard Middlemas, whom she had once nursed at her bosom, as if he had been her own son. This affection the child repaid by all the tender attentions of which his age was capable.

Little Dick was also distinguished by the fondest and kindest attachment to his guardian and benefactor, Dr Grey. He was officious in the right time and place, quiet as a lamb when his patron seemed inclined to study or to muse, active and assiduous to assist or amuse him whenever it seemed to be wished, and, in choosing his opportunities, he seemed to display an address far beyond his childish years.

As time passed on, this pleasing character seemed to be still more refined. In everything like exercise or amusement, he was the pride and the leader of the boys of the place, over the most of whom his strength and activity gave him a decided superiority. At school his abilities were less distinguished, yet he was a favourite with the master, a sensible and useful teacher.

"Richard is not swift," he used to say to his patron, Dr Grey, "but then he is sure; and it is impossible not to be pleased with a child who is so very desirous to give satisfaction."

Young Middlemas's grateful affection to his patron seemed to increase with the expanding of his faculties, and found a natural and pleasing mode of displaying itself in his attentions to little Menie Grey. Her slightest hint was Richard's law, and it was in vain that he was summoned forth by a hundred shrill voices to take the lead in hye-spye, or at foot-ball, if it was little Menie's pleasure that he should remain within, and build card-houses for her amusement. At other times, he would take the charge of the little damsel entirely under his own care, and be seen wandering with her on the borough common, collecting wild-flowers, or knitting caps made of bulrushes. Menie was attached to Dick Middlemas, in proportion to his affectionate assiduities; and the father saw with pleasure every new mark of atten-tion to his child on the part of his protegé.

During the time that Richard was silently advancing from a beauti-ful child into a fine boy, and approaching from a fine boy to the time when he must be termed a handsome youth, Mr Grey wrote twice a-year with much regularity to Mr Monçada, through the channel that gentleman had pointed out. The benevolent man thought, that if the wealthy grandfather could only see this relative, of whom any family might be proud, he would be unable to persevere in his resolution of treating as an outcast one so nearly connected with him in blood, and so interesting in person and disposition. He thought it his duty, there-fore, to keep open the slender and oblique communication with the boy's maternal grandfather, as that which might, at some fortunate period, lead to a closer connexion. Yet the correspondence could not, in other respects, be agreeable to a man of spirit like Mr Grey. His own letters were as short as possible, merely rendering an account of his ward's expenses, including a moderate board to himself, and of the state of his funds, attested by Mr Lawford, his co-trustee; and intim-ating Richard's state of health, and his progress in education, with a few words of brief but warm eulogy upon his goodness of head and heart. But the answers he received were still shorter. "Mr Monçada," such was their usual tenor, "acknowledges Mr Grey's letter of such a date, notices the contents, and requests Mr Grey to persist in the plan which he has hitherto prosecuted on the subject of their corres-pondence." On occasions where extraordinary expense seemed likely to be incurred, the remittances were made with readiness.

That day fortnight after Mrs Grey's death, fifty pounds were received, with a note, intimating that it was designed to put the child R.M. into proper mourning. The writer had added two or three words, desiring that the surplus should be at Mr Grey's personal disposal, to meet the additional expenses of this period of calamity; but Mr Monçada had left the phrase unfinished, apparently in despair

of turning it suitably in English. Dr Grey, without farther investigation, quietly added the sum to the account of his ward's little fortune,
contrary to the opinion of Mr Lawford, who, aware that he was rather
a loser than a gainer by the boy's residence in his house, was desirous
that his friend should not omit an opportunity of recovering some part
of his expenses on that score. But Grey was proof against all remonstrance.

As the boy advanced towards his fourteenth year, Dr Grey wrote a
more elaborate account of his ward's character, acquirements, and
capacity. He added, that he did this for the purpose of enabling Mr
Monçada to judge how the young man's future education should be
directed. Richard, he observed, was arrived at the point where education, losing its original and general character, branches off into different paths of knowledge, suitable to particular professions, and when it
was therefore become necessary to determine which of them it was his
pleasure that young Richard should be trained for; and he would, on
his part, do all he could to carry Mr Monçada's wishes into execution,
since the amiable qualities of the boy made him as dear to him, though
but a guardian, as he could have been to his own father.

The answer, which arrived in the course of a week or ten days, was
fuller than usual, and written in the first person.—"Mr Grey," such
was the tenor, "our meeting has been under such circumstances as
could not make us favourably known to each other at the time. But I
have the advantage of you, since, knowing your motives for entertaining an indifferent opinion of me, I could respect them, and you at the
same time; whereas you, unable to comprehend the motives—I
say, you, sir, being unacquainted with the infamous treatment I had
received, could not understand the reasons that I have for acting as I
have done. Deprived, sir, by the act of a villain, of my child, and she
despoiled of honour, I cannot bring myself to think of beholding the
creature, however innocent, whose look must always remind me of
hatred and of shame. Keep the poor child by you—educate him to
your own profession, but take heed that he looks no higher than to fill
such a situation in life as you yourself worthily occupy. For the condition of a farmer, a country lawyer, a medical practitioner, or some such
retired course of life, the means of outfit and education shall be amply
supplied. But I must warn him and you, that any attempt to intrude
himself on me further than I may especially permit, will be attended
with the total forfeiture of my favour and protection. So, having made
known my mind to you, I expect you will act accordingly."

The receipt of this letter determined Grey to have some explanation with the boy himself, in order to learn if he had any choice among
the professions thus opened to him; convinced, at the same time, from

his docility of temper, that he would refer the selection to his (Dr Grey's) better judgment.

He had previously, however, the unpleasing task of acquainting Richard Middlemas with the mysterious circumstances attending his birth, of which he presumed him to be entirely ignorant, simply because he himself had never communicated them, but had let the boy consider himself as the orphan child of a distant relation. But though the Doctor himself was silent, he might have remembered that Nurse Jamieson had the handsome enjoyment of her tongue, and was disposed to use it liberally.

From a very early period, Nurse Jamieson, amongst the variety of legendary lore which she instilled into her foster son, had not forgotten what she called the awful season of his coming into the world—the personable appearance of his father, a grand gentleman, who looked as if the whole world lay at his feet—the beauty of his mother, and the terrible blackness of the mask which she wore, her een that glanced like diamonds, and the diamonds she wore on her fingers, that could be compared to nothing but her own een, the fairness of her skin, and the colour of her silk rokelay, with much proper stuff to the same purpose. Then she expatiated on the arrival of his grandfather, and the awful man, armed with pistols, dirk, and claymore, (the last weapons existed only in Nurse's imagination,) the very Ogre of a fairy tale—then all the circumstances of the carrying off his mother, while bank-notes were flying about the house like screeds of brown paper, and gold guineas were as plenty as chuckie-stanes. All this, partly to please and interest the boy, partly to indulge her own talent for amplification, Nurse told with so many additional circumstances, and gratuitous commentaries, that the real transaction, mysterious and odd as it certainly was, sunk into tameness, like humble prose contrasted with the boldest flights of poetry.

To hear all this did Richard seriously incline, and still more was he interested with the idea of his valiant father coming for him unexpectedly at the head of a gallant regiment, with music playing and colours flying, and carrying his son away on the most beautiful pony eyes ever beheld; or his mother, bright as the day, might suddenly appear in her coach-and-six, to reclaim her beloved child; or his repentant grandfather, with his pockets stuffed out with bank-notes, would come to atone for his past cruelty, by heaping his neglected grandchild with unexpected wealth. Sure was Nurse Jamieson, "that it wanted but a blink of her bairn's bonny ee to turn their hearts, as Scripture sayeth; and as strange things had been, as they should come a'thegither to the town at the same time, and make such a day as had never been seen in Middlemas; and then her bairn would never be called by that lowland

name of Middlemas any more, which sounded as if it had been gathered out of the town gutter; but would be called Galatian, or Sir
William Wallace, or Robin Hood, or after some other of the great
princes named in story-books."

Nurse Jamieson's history of the past, and prospects of the future,
were too flattering not to excite the most ambitious visions in the mind
of a boy, who naturally felt a strong desire of rising in the world, and
was conscious of possessing the powers necessary to his advancement.
The incidents of his birth resembled those he found commemorated
in the tales which he read or listened to; and there seemed no reason
why they should not have a termination corresponding to those of
such veracious histories. In a word, while good Doctor Grey imagined
that his pupil was dwelling in utter ignorance of his origin, Richard
was meditating upon nothing else than the time and means by which
he was to be extricated from the obscurity of his present condition,
and enabled to assume the rank to which, in his own opinion, he was
entitled by birth.

So stood the feelings of the young man, when, one day after dinner,
the Doctor snuffing the candle, and taking from his pouch the great
leathern pocket-book in which he deposited particular papers, with a
small supply of the most necessary and active medicines, he took from
it Mr Monçada's letter, and requested Richard Middlemas's serious
attention, while he told him some circumstances concerning himself,
which it greatly imported him to know. Richard's dark eyes flashed
fire—the blood flushed his broad and well-formed forehead—the
hour of explanation was at length come. He listened to the narrative
of Gideon Grey, which, the reader may believe, being altogether
divested of the gilding which Nurse Jamieson's imagination had
bestowed upon it, and reduced to what mercantile men termed the
needful, exhibited little more than the tale of a child of shame,
deserted by its father and mother, and brought up on the reluctant
charity of a more distant relative, who regarded him as the living
though unconscious evidence of the disgrace of his family, and would
more willingly have paid for the expenses of his funeral, than that of
the food which was grudgingly provided for him. "Temple and
tower," a hundred flattering edifices of Richard's childish imagination, went to the ground at once, and the pain which attended their
demolition was rendered the more acute, by a sense of shame that he
should have nursed such reveries. He remained, while Dr Grey continued his explanation, in a dejected posture, his eyes fixed on the
ground, and the veins of his forehead swoln with contending passions.

"And now, my dear Richard," said the good surgeon, "you must
think what you can do for yourself, since your grandfather leaves you

the choice of three honourable professions, by any of which, well and wisely prosecuted, you may become independent if not wealthy, and respectable if not great. You will naturally desire a little time for consideration."

"Not a minute," said the boy, raising his head, and looking boldly at his guardian. "I am a free-born Englishman, and will return to England if I think fit."

"A free-born fool you are—" said Grey; "you were born, as I think no one can know better than I do, in the *west-room* of Stevenlaw's Land, in the Town-head of Middlemas, if you call that being a free-born Englishman."

"But Tom Hillary says that I am a true-born Englishman, notwithstanding, in right of my parents."

"Pooh, child! what do we know of your parents?—But what has your being an Englishman to do with the present question?"

"Oh Doctor!" answered the boy, bitterly, "you know we cannot scramble so hard as you do. The Scots are too moral, and too prudent, and too robust, for a poor pudding-eater to live amongst them, whether as a parson, or as a lawyer, or as a doctor—with your pardon, sir."

"Upon my life, Dick," said Dr Grey, "this Tom Hillary will turn your brain. What is the meaning of all this trash?"

"Tom Hillary says that the parson lives by the sins of the people, the lawyer by their distresses, and the doctor by their diseases—always asking your pardon, sir."

"Tom Hillary," replied the Doctor, "should be drummed out of the borough. A whipper-snapper of an attorney's apprentice, run away from Newcastle! If I hear him talking so, I'll teach him to speak with more reverence of the learned professions. Let me hear no more of Tom Hillary, whom you have seen far too much of lately. Think a little, like a lad of sense, and tell me what answer I am to give Mr Monçada."

"Tell him," said the boy, the tone of affected sarcasm laid aside, and that of injured pride substituted in its room, "tell him, that my soul revolts at the obscure lot he recommends to me. I am determined to enter my father's profession, the army, unless my grandfather chooses to receive me into his house, and place me in his own line of business."

"Yes, and make you his partner, I suppose, and acknowledge you for his heir?—" said Dr Grey; "a thing extremely likely to happen, no doubt, considering the way in which he has brought you up all along, and the terms in which he now writes concerning you."

"Then, sir, there is one thing which I can demand of you," replied the boy. "There is a large sum of money in your hands belonging to me; and since it is consigned to you for my use, I demand you should make the necessary advances to procure a commission in the army—account to me for the balance—and so, with thanks for past favours, I will give you no trouble in future."

"Young man," said the Doctor, gravely, "I am very sorry to see that your usual prudence and good humour are not proof against the disappointment of some idle expectations which you had not the slightest reason to entertain. It is very true that there is a sum, which, in spite of various expenses, may still approach to a thousand pounds or better, which remains in my hands for your behoof. But I am bound to dispose of it according to the will of the donor, and at any rate, you are not entitled to call for it until you come to years of discretion; a period from which you are six years absent according to law, and which, in one sense, you will never reach at all, unless you alter your present unreasonable crotchets. But come, Dick, this is the first time I have seen you in so absurd a humour, and you have many things, I own, in your situation, to apologize for impatience even greater than you have displayed. But you should not turn your resentment on me, that am no way in fault. You should remember, that I was your earliest and only friend, and took charge of you when every other person forsook you."

"I do not thank you for it," said Richard, giving way to a burst of uncontrolled passion. "You might have done better for me had you pleased."

"And in what manner, you ungrateful boy?" said Grey, whose composure was a little ruffled.

"You might have flung me under the wheels of their carriages as they drove off, and have let them trample on the body of their child, as they have done on his feelings."

So saying, he rushed out of the room, and shut the door behind him with great violence, leaving his guardian astonished at his sudden and violent change of temper and manner.

"What the deuce can have possessed him?—Ah, well. High-spirited, and disappointed in some follies which that Tom Hillary has put into his head—But his is a case for anodynes, and shall be treated accordingly."

While the Doctor formed this good-natured resolution, young Middlemas rushed to Nurse Jamieson's apartment, where poor Menie, to whom his presence always gave holiday feelings, hastened to exhibit, for his admiration, a new doll, of which she had made the acquisition. No one, generally, was more interested in Menie's amusements than Richard; but at present, Richard, like his celebrated namesake, was not i'the vein. He threw off the little damsel so carelessly, almost so rudely, that the doll flew out of Menie's hand, fell on the hearth-stone, and broke its waxen face. The rudeness drew from Nurse Jamieson a rebuke, even although the culprit was her darling.

"Hout awa', Richard—that wasna like yoursell, to guide Miss Menie that gate.—Haud your tongue, Miss Menie, and I'll soon mend the baby's face."

But if Menie cried, she did not cry for the doll; but while the tears flowed silently down her cheeks, she sat looking at Dick Middlemas with a childish face of fear, sorrow, and wonder. Nurse Jamieson was soon diverted from her attention to Menie Grey's distresses, especially as she did not weep aloud, and her attention became fixed on the altered countenance, red eyes, and swoln features, of her darling foster-child. She instantly commenced an investigation into the cause of his distress, after the usual inquisitorial manner of matrons of her class. "What is the matter wi' my bairn?" and "Wha has been vexing my bairn?" with similar questions, at last extorted this reply:

"I am not your bairn—I am no one's bairn—no one's son. I am an outcast from my family, and belong to no one. Dr Grey has told me so himself."

"And did he cast up to my bairn that he was a bastard?—troth he was na blate—my certie, your father was a better man than ever stood on the Doctor's shanks—a handsome grand gentleman, with an ee like a gled's, and a step like a Highland piper."

Nurse Jamieson had got on a favourite topic, and would have expatiated long enough, for she was a professed admirer of masculine beauty, but there was something which displeased the boy in her last simile; so he cut the conversation short, by asking whether she knew exactly how much money his grandfather had left with Dr Grey for his maintenance. "She could not say—didna ken—an awfu' sum it was to pass out of ae man's hand—She was sure it wasna less than ae hundred pounds, and it might weel be twa." In short, she knew nothing about the matter; but "she was sure Doctor Grey would count to him to the last farthing; for everybody kenned that he was a just man where siller was concerned. However, if her bairn wanted to ken mair about it, to be sure the Town-clerk could tell him all about it."

Richard Middlemas arose and left the apartment, without saying more. He went immediately to visit the old Town-clerk, to whom he had made himself acceptable, as, indeed, he had done to most of the dignitaries about the burgh. He introduced the conversation by the proposal which had been made to him for choosing a profession, and after speaking of the mysterious circumstances of his birth, and the doubtful prospects which lay before him, he easily led the Town-clerk into conversation as to the amount of the funds, and heard the exact state of the money in his guardians' hands, which corresponded with the information he had already received. He next sounded the worthy scribe on the possibility of his going into the army; but received a second confirmation of the intelligence Mr Grey had given him; being informed that no part of the money could be placed at his disposal without his guardians' especial consent. He then took leave of the Town-clerk, who, much approving the cautious manner in which he spoke, and his prudent selection of an adviser at this important crisis of his life, intimated to him, that should he choose the law, he would himself receive him into his office, upon a very moderate apprentice-fee, and would part with Tom Hillary to make room for him, as the lad was "rather pragmatical, and plagued him with speaking about his English practice, which they had nothing to do with on this side of the Border—the Lord be thanked!"

Middlemas thanked him for his kindness, and promised to consider his kind offer, in case he should determine upon following the profession of the law.

From Tom Hillary's master Richard went to Tom Hillary himself, who chanced then to be in the office. He was a lad about twenty, as smart as small, but distinguished for the accuracy with which he dressed his hair, and the splendour of a laced hat and embroidered waistcoat, with which he graced the church of Middlemas on Sundays. Tom Hillary had been bred an attorney's clerk in Newcastle-upon-Tyne, but, for some reason or other, had found it more convenient of late years to reside in Scotland, and was recommended to the Town-clerk of Middlemas, by the accuracy and beauty with which he transcribed the records of the burgh. It is not improbable that the reports concerning the singular circumstances of Richard Middlemas's birth, and the knowledge that he was actually possessed of a considerable sum of money, induced Hillary, though so much his senior, to admit the lad to his company, and enrich his youthful mind with some branches of information, which, in that retired corner, his pupil might otherwise have been some time in attaining. Amongst these were certain games at cards and dice, in which the pupil paid, as was reasonable, the price of initiation by his losses to his instructor. After a long walk with this youngster, whose advice, like the unwise son of the wisest of men, he probably valued more than that of his more aged counsellors, Richard Middlemas returned to his lodgings in Stevenlaw's Land, and went to bed sad and supperless.

The next morning Richard arose with the sun, and his night's rest appeared to have had its frequent effect, in cooling the passions and correcting the understanding. Little Menie was the first person to whom he made the *amende honorable;* and a much smaller propitiation than the new doll with which he presented her, would have been accepted as an atonement for a much greater offence. Menie was one of those pure spirits, to whom a state of unkindness is a state of pain, and the slightest advance of her friend and protector was sufficient to regain all her childish confidence and affection.

The father did not prove more inexorable than Menie had done. Mr Grey, indeed, thought he had good reason to look cold upon Richard at their next meeting, being not a little hurt at the treatment which he had received on the preceding evening. But Middlemas disarmed him at once, by frankly pleading that he had suffered his mind to be carried away by the supposed rank and importance of his parents, into a conviction that he was one day to share them. The letter of his grandfather, which condemned him to banishment and obscurity for life, was, he acknowledged, a very severe blow; and it was with deep sorrow that he reflected, that the irritation of his disappointment had led him to express himself in a manner far short of the respect and reverence of one who owed Mr Grey the duty and respect of a son, and ought to refer to his decision every action of his life. Grey, propitiated by an admission so candid, and made with so much humility, readily dismissed his resentment, and kindly inquired of Richard, whether he had bestowed any reflection upon the choice of a profession which had been subjected to him; offering, at the same time, to allow him all reasonable time to make up his mind.

On this subject, Richard Middlemas answered with the same promptitude and candour.—"He had," he said, "in order to forming his opinion more safely, consulted with his friend the Town-clerk." The Doctor nodded approbation. "Mr Lawford had, indeed, been most friendly, and had even offered to take him into his own office. But if his father and benefactor would permit him to study, under his instructions, the noble art in which he himself enjoyed such a deserved reputation, the mere hope that he might by-and-by be of some use to Mr Grey in his business, would greatly overbalance every other consideration. Such a course of education, and such a use of professional knowledge when he had acquired it, would be a greater spur to his industry, than the prospect even of becoming Town-clerk of Middlemas in his proper person."

As the young man expressed it to be his firm and unalterable choice, to study medicine under his guardian, and to remain a member of his family, Dr Grey informed Mr Monçada of the lad's determination; who, to testify his approbation, remitted to the Doctor the sum of L.100 as apprentice fee, a sum nearly three times as much as Grey's modesty had required.

Shortly after, when Dr Grey and the Town-clerk met at the small club of the burgh, their joint theme was the sense and steadiness of Richard Middlemas.

"Indeed," said the Town-clerk, "he is such a friendly and disinterested boy, that I could not get him to accept a place in my office, for fear he should be thought to be pushing himself forward at the expense of Tam Hillary."

"And, indeed, Clerk," said Grey, "I have sometimes been afraid that he kept too much company with that Tam Hillary of yours. But twenty Tam Hillarys would not corrupt Dick Middlemas."

Chapter Four

Dick was come to high renown
 Since he commenced physician;
Tom was held by all the town
 The better politician.
Tom and Dick

AT THE SAME PERIOD when Dr Grey took under his charge his youthful lodger Richard Middlemas, he received proposals from the friends of one Adam Hartley, to take him also as an apprentice. The lad was the son of a respectable farmer on the English side of the Border, who, educating his eldest son to his own occupation, desired to make his second a medical man, in order to avail himself of the friendship of a great man, his landlord, who had offered to assist his views in life, and represented a doctor or surgeon as the sort of person to whose advantage his interest could be most readily applied. Middlemas and Hartley were therefore associated in their studies. In winter they were boarded in Edinburgh, for attending the medical classes which were necessary for taking their degree. Three or four years thus passed on, and, from being mere boys, the two medical aspirants shot up into young men, who, being both very good-looking, well dressed, well bred, and having money in their pockets, became personages of some importance in the little town of Middlemas, where there was scarce anything that could be termed an aristocracy, but where beaux were scarce and belles were plenty.

Each of the two had his especial partisans; for though the young men themselves lived in tolerable harmony together, yet, as is usual in such cases, no one could approve of one of them, without at the same time comparing him with, and asserting his superiority over his companion.

Both were gay, fond of dancing, and sedulous attendants on the *practeezings*, as he called them, of Mr McFittie, a dancing-master, who, itinerant during the summer, afforded the youth of Middlemas in winter the benefit of his instructions at the rate of twenty lessons for five shillings sterling. On these occasions, each of Dr Grey's pupils had his appropriate praise. Hartley danced with more spirit—Middlemas with a better grace. Mr McFittie would have turned out Richard against the country-side in the minuet, and wagered the thing dearest to him in the world, (and that was his kit,) upon his assured success; but he admitted Hartley was superior to him in hornpipes, jigs, strathspeys, and reels.

In dress, Hartley was most expensive, perhaps because his father afforded him better means of being so; but his clothes were neither so tasteful when new, nor so well preserved when they began to grow old, as those of Richard Middlemas. Adam Hartley was sometimes fine, at other times rather slovenly, and on the former occasions looked rather too conscious of his splendour. His chum was at all times regularly neat and well dressed; while at the same time he had an air of good-breeding, which made him appear always at ease; so that his dress, whatever it was, seemed to be just what he ought to have worn at the time.

In their persons there was a still more strongly marked distinction. Adam Hartley was full middle size, stout, and well limbed; and an open English countenance, of the genuine Saxon mould, showed itself among chestnut locks, until the hair-dresser destroyed them. He loved the rough exercises of wrestling, boxing, leaping, and quarter-staff, and frequented, when he could obtain leisure, the bull-baitings, and foot-ball matches, by which the burgh was sometimes enlivened.

Richard, on the contrary, was dark, like his father and mother, with high features, beautifully formed, but exhibiting something of a foreign character; and his person was tall and slim, though muscular and active. His address and manners must have been natural to him, for they were, in elegance and ease, far beyond any example which he could have found in his native burgh. He learned the use of the small sword while in Edinburgh, and took lessons from a performer at the theatre, with the purpose of refining his mode of speaking. He became also an amateur of the drama, regularly attending the playhouse, and assuming the tone of a critic in that and other lighter departments of literature. To fill up the contrast, so far as taste was concerned, Richard was a dexterous and successful angler—Adam, a bold and unerring shot. Their efforts to surpass each other in supplying Dr Grey's table, rendered his housekeeping much preferable to what it had been on former occasions; and besides, small presents of fish and game are always agreeable amongst the inhabitants of a country town, and contributed to increase the popularity of the young sportsmen.

While the burgh was divided, for lack of better subject of disputa-
tion, concerning the comparative merits of Dr Grey's two apprentices,
he himself was sometimes chosen the referee. But in this, as on other
matters, the Doctor was cautious. He said the lads were both good
lads, and would be useful men in the profession, if their heads were
not carried with the notice which the foolish people of the burgh took
of them, and the parties of pleasure that were so often taking them
away from their business. No doubt it was natural for him to feel more
confidence in Hartley, who came of kenned folk, and was very near as
good as a born Scotsman. But if he did feel such a partiality, he blamed
himself for it, since the stranger child, so oddly cast upon his hands,
had peculiar good right to such patronage and affection as he had to
bestow; and truly the young man himself seemed so grateful, that it
was impossible for him to hint the slightest wish, that Dick Middlemas
did not hasten to execute.

There were persons in the burgh of Middlemas who were indis-
creet enough to suppose that Miss Menie Grey must be a better judge
than any other person of the comparative merits of these accomplished personages, respecting which the public opinion was generally
divided. No one even of her greatest intimates ventured to put
the question to her in precise terms; but her conduct was narrowly
observed, and the critics remarked, that to Adam Hartley her attentions were given more freely and frankly. She laughed with him,
chatted with him, and danced with him; while to Dick Middlemas her
conduct was more shy and distant. The premises seemed certain, but
the public were divided in the conclusions which were to be drawn
from them.

It was not possible for the young men to be the subject of such
discussions without being sensible that it was so; and thus contrasted
together by the little society in which they moved, they must have been
made of some better than ordinary clay, if they had not themselves
entered by degrees into the spirit of the controversy, and considered
themselves as rivals for public applause.

Nor is it to be forgotten, that Menie Grey was by this time shot up
into one of the prettiest young women, not of Middlemas only, but of
the whole county, in which the little burgh is situated. This, indeed,
had been settled by evidence, which could not be esteemed short of
decisive. At the time of the races, there were usually assembled in the
burgh some company of the higher classes from the country around,
and many of the sober burghers mended their incomes, by letting their
apartments, or taking in lodgers of quality for the busy week. All the
rural thanes and thanesses attended on these occasions; and such
was the number of cocked hats and silken trains, that the little town

seemed for a time totally to have changed its inhabitants. On this occasion, persons of a certain quality only were permitted to attend upon the nightly balls which were given in the old Town-house, and the line of distinction excluded Mr Grey's family.

The aristocracy, however, used their privileges with some feelings of deference to the native beaux and belles of the burgh, who were thus doomed to hear the fiddles nightly, without being permitted to dance to them. One evening in the race-week, termed the Hunters' Ball, was dedicated to general amusement, and liberated from the usual restrictions of etiquette. On this occasion all the respectable families in the town were invited to share the amusement of the evening, and to wonder at the finery, and be grateful for the condescension, of their betters. This was especially the case with the females, for the number of invitations to the gentlemen of the town was much more limited. Now, at this general muster, the beauty of Miss Grey's face and person had placed her, in the opinion of all competent judges, decidedly at the head of all the belles present, saving those with whom, according to the ideas of the place, it would hardly have been decent to compare her.

The Laird of the ancient and distinguished house of Loupenheight did not hesitate to engage her hand during the greater part of the evening; and his mother, renowned for her stern assertion of the distinctions of rank, placed the little plebeian beside her at supper, and was heard to say, that the surgeon's daughter behaved very prettily indeed, and seemed to know perfectly well where and what she was. As for the young Laird himself, he capered so high, and laughed so uproariously, as to give rise to a rumour, that he was minded to "shoot madly from his sphere," and to convert the village Doctor's daughter into a lady of his own ancient name.

During this memorable evening, Middlemas and Hartley, who had found room in the music gallery, witnessed the scene, and, as it would seem, with very different feelings. Hartley was evidently annoyed by the excess of attention which the gallant Laird of Loupenheight, stimulated by the influence of a couple of bottles of claret, and by the presence of a partner who danced remarkably well, paid to Miss Menie Grey. He saw from his lofty stand all the dumb show of gallantry, with the comfortable feelings of a famishing creature looking upon a feast which he is not permitted to share, and regarded every extraordinary frisk of the jovial Laird, as the same might have been regarded by a gouty person, who apprehended that the dignitary was about to descend on his toes. At length, unable to restrain his emotion, he left the gallery and returned no more.

Far different was the demeanour of Middlemas. He seemed gratified and elevated by the attention which was generally paid to Miss Grey, and by the admiration she excited. On the valiant Laird of Loupenheight he looked with indescribable contempt, and amused himself with pointing out to the burgh dancing-master, who acted *pro tempore* as one of the band, the frolicsome bounds and pirouettes, in which that worthy displayed a great deal more of vigour than of grace.

"But ye shouldna laugh sae loud, Maister Dick," said the master of capers; "he hasna had the advantage of a real gracefu' teacher, as ye have had; and troth, if he listed to tak some lessons, I think I could make some hand of his feet, for he is a souple chield, and has a gallant instep of his ain; and sic a laced hat hasna been seen on the causeway of Middlemas this mony a day.—Ye are standing laughing there, Dick Middlemas; I would have you be sure he does not cut you out with your bonny partner yonder."

"He be ——!" Middlemas was beginning a sentence which could not have concluded with strict attention to propriety, when the master of the band summoned McFittie to his post, by the following ireful expostulation:—"What are ye about, sir? Mind your bow-hand. How the deil d'ye think three fiddles is to keep down a bass, if yin o' them stands girning and gabbling as ye're doing? Play up, sir!"

Dick Middlemas, thus reduced to silence, continued, from his lofty station, like one of the gods of the Epicureans, to survey what passed below, without the gaieties which he witnessed being able to excite more than a smile, which seemed, however, rather to indicate a good-humoured contempt for what was passing, than a benevolent sympathy with the pleasures of others.

Chapter Five

Now, hold thy tongue, Billie Bewick, he said,
   Of peaceful talking let me be;
But if thou'rt a man, as I think thou art,
   Come ower the dike and fight with me.
        Northumberland Ballad

ON THE MORNING after this gay evening, the two young men were labouring together in a plot of ground behind Stevenlaw's Land, which the Doctor had converted into a garden, where he raised, with a view to pharmacy as well as botany, some rare plants, which obtained the place from the vulgar the sounding name of the Physic Garden. Mr Grey's pupils readily complied with his wishes, that they would take some care of this favourite spot, to which both contributed their labours, after which Hartley used to devote himself to the cultivation of the kitchen garden, which he had raised into this respectability from a spot not excelling a common kail-yard, while Richard Middlemas did his utmost to decorate with flowers and shrubs, a sort of arbour, usually called Miss Menie's bower.

At present, they were both in the botanic patch of the garden, when Dick Middlemas asked Hartley why he had left the ball so soon the evening before?

"I should rather ask you," said Hartley, "what pleasure you felt in staying there?—I tell you, Dick, it is a shabby low place this Middlemas of ours. In the smallest burgh in England every decent freeholder would have been asked if the Member gave a ball."

"What, Hartley!" said his companion, "are you, of all men, a candidate for the honour of mixing with the first-born of the earth? Mercy on us! How will canny Norrthumberrland (throwing a true northern accent upon the letter R,) acquit himself. Methinks I see thee in thy pea-green suit, dancing a jig with the Honourable Miss Maddie MacFudgeon, while chiefs and thanes around laugh as they would do at a hog in armour!"

"You don't, or perhaps you won't, understand me," said Hartley. "I am not such a fool as to desire to be hail-fellow-well-met with these fine folks—I care as little for them as they do for me. But as they do not choose to ask us to dance, I don't see what business they have with our partners."

"Partners, said you?" answered Middlemas; "I don't think Menie is very often yours."

"As often as I ask her," answered Hartley, rather haughtily.

"Ay? Indeed?—I did not think that.—And hang me, if I think so yet," said Middlemas, in the same sarcastic tone. "I tell thee, Adam, I will bet you a bowl of punch, that Miss Grey will not dance with you the next time you ask her. All I stipulate, is to know the day."

"I will lay no bets about Miss Grey," said Hartley; "her father is my master, and I am obliged to him—I think I should act very scurvily, if I were to make her the subject of any idle debate betwixt you and me."

"Very right," replied Middlemas; "you should finish one quarrel before you begin another. Pray, saddle your horse—Thou can ride up to the gate of Loupenheight Castle, and defy the Baron to mortal combat, for having presumed to touch the fair hand of Menie Grey."

"I wish you would leave Miss Grey's name out of the question, and take your defiances to your fine folks in your own name, and see what they will say to the surgeon's apprentice."

"Speak for yourself, if you please, Mr Adam Hartley. I was not born a clown, like some folks, and should care little, if I saw it fit, to talk to the best of them at the ordinary, and make myself understood too."

"Very likely," answered Hartley, losing patience; "you are one of themselves, you know—Middlemas of that Ilk."

"You scoundrel!" said Richard, advancing on him in fury, his taunting humour entirely changed into rage.

"Stand back," said Hartley, "or you will come by the worst; if you will break rude jests, you must put up with rough answers."

"I will have satisfaction for this insult, by Heaven!"

"Why, so you shall, if you insist on it," said Hartley; "but better, I think, to say no more about the matter. We have both spoken what would have been better left unsaid. I was in the wrong to say what I said to you, although you did provoke me—And now I have given you as much satisfaction as a reasonable man can ask."

"Sir," repeated Middlemas, "the satisfaction which I demand, is that of a gentleman—the Doctor has a pair of pistols."

"And a pair of mortars also, which are heartily at your service, gentlemen," said Mr Grey, coming forward from behind a yew hedge, where he had listened to the whole or greater part of this dispute. "A fine story it would be of my prentices shooting each other with my own pistols! Let me see either of you fit to treat a gunshot wound, before you think of inflicting one. Go, you are both very foolish boys, and I cannot take it kind of either of you to bring the name of my daughter into such disputes as these. Hark ye, lads, you both owe me, I think, some portion of respect, and even of gratitude—it will be a poor return, if, instead of living quietly with this poor motherless girl, like brothers with a sister, you should oblige me to increase my expense, and abridge my comfort, by sending my child from me, for the few months that you are to remain with me.—Let me see you shake hands, and let us have no more of this nonsense."

While their master spoke in this manner, both the young men stood before him in the attitude of self-convicted criminals. At the conclusion of his rebuke, Hartley turned frankly round, and offered his hand to his companion, who accepted it, but after a moment's hesitation. There was nothing further passed on the subject, but the lads never resumed the same sort of intimacy which had existed betwixt them in their earlier acquaintance. On the contrary, avoiding every connexion not absolutely required by their situation, and abridging as much as possible even their indispensable intercourse in professional matters, they seemed as much estranged from each other as two persons residing in the same small house had the means of being.

As for Menie Grey, her father did not appear to entertain the least anxiety upon her account, although from his frequent and almost daily absence from home, she was exposed to more constant intercourse with two handsome young men, both, it might be supposed, ambitious of pleasing her, than most parents would have deemed entirely prudent. Nor was Nurse Jamieson,—her menial situation, and her excessive partiality for her foster-son considered,—altogether such a matron as could afford her complete protection. Gideon Grey, however, knew that his daughter possessed, in its fullest extent, the upright and pure integrity of his own character, and that never father had less reason to apprehend that a daughter should deceive his confidence; and, justly secure of her principles, he overlooked the danger to which he exposed her feelings and affections.

The intercourse betwixt Menie and the young men seemed now of a guarded kind on all sides. Their meeting was only at meals, and Miss Grey was at pains, perhaps by her father's recommendation, to treat them with the same degree of attention. This, however, was no easy matter; for Hartley became so retiring, cold, and formal, that it was impossible for her to sustain any prolonged intercourse with him; whereas Middlemas, perfectly at his ease, sustained his part as formerly upon all occasions that occurred, and without appearing to press his intimacy assiduously, seemed nevertheless to retain the complete possession of it.

The time drew nigh at length when the young men, freed from the engagements of their indentures, must look to play their own independent part in the world. Mr Grey informed Richard Middlemas that he had written pressingly upon the subject to Monçada, and that more than once, but had not yet received an answer; nor did he presume to offer his own advice, until the pleasure of his grandfather should be known. Richard seemed to endure this suspense with more patience than the Doctor thought belonged naturally to his character. He asked no questions—stated no conjectures—showed no anxiety, but seemed to await with patience the turn which events should take. "My young gentleman," thought Mr Grey, "has either fixed on some course in his own mind, or he is about to be more tractable than some points of his character have led me to expect."

In fact, Richard had made an experiment on this inflexible relative, by sending Mr Monçada a letter full of duty, and affection, and gratitude, desiring to be permitted to correspond with him in person, and promising to be guided in every particular by his will. The answer to this appeal was his own letter returned, with a note from the bankers whose cover had been used, saying, that any future attempt to intrude on Mr Monçada, would put a final period to their remittances.

While things were in this situation in Stevenlaw's Land, Adam Hartley one evening, contrary to his custom for several months, sought a private interview with his fellow-apprentice. He found him in the little arbour, and could not omit observing, that Dick Middlemas, on his appearance, shoved into his bosom a small packet, as if afraid of its being seen, and snatching up a hoe, began to work with great devotion, like one who wished to have it thought that his whole soul was in his occupation.

"I wished to speak with you, Mr Middlemas," said Hartley; "but I fear I interrupt you."

"Not in the least," said the other, laying down his hoe; "I was only scratching up the weeds which the late showers have made rush up so merrily. I am at your service."

Hartley proceeded to the arbour, and seated himself. Richard imitated his example, and seemed to wait for the proposed communication.

"I have had an interesting communication with Mr Grey—" said Hartley, and there stopped, like one who finds himself entering upon a difficult task.

"I hope the explanation has been satisfactory?" said Middlemas.

"You shall judge.—Doctor Grey was pleased to say something to me very civil about my proficiency in the duties of our profession; and, to my great astonishment, asked me, whether, as he was now becoming old, I had any particular objection to continue in my present situation, but with some pecuniary advantages, for two years longer; at the end of which, he promised to me that I should enter into partnership with him."

"Mr Grey is an undoubted judge," said Middlemas, "what person will best suit him as a professional assistant. The business may be worth L.200 a-year, and an active assistant might go nigh to double it, by riding Strath-Devon and the Carse. No great subject for discussion after all, Mr Hartley."

"But," continued Hartley, "that is not all. The Doctor says—he proposes—in short, if I can render myself agreeable, in the course of these two years, to Miss Menie Grey, he proposes, that when they terminate, I should become his son as well as his partner."

As he spoke, he kept his eye fixed on Richard's face, which was for a moment strongly agitated; but instantly recovering, he answered, in a tone where pique and offended pride vainly endeavoured to disguise themselves under an affectation of indifference, "Well, Master Adam, I cannot but wish you joy of the patriarchal arrangement. You have served five years for your professional diploma—a sort of Leah, that privilege of killing and curing. Now you begin a new course of servitude for a lively Rachael. Undoubtedly—perhaps it is rude in me to ask —but undoubtedly you have accepted so flattering an arrangement?"

"You cannot but recollect there was a condition annexed," said Hartley, gravely.

"That of rendering yourself acceptable to a girl you have known for so many years?" said Middlemas, with a half-suppressed sneer. "No great difficulty in that, I should think, for such a person as Mr Hartley, with Doctor Grey's favour to back him. No, no—there could be no great obstacle there."

"Both you and I know the contrary, Mr Middlemas," said Hartley, very seriously.

"I know?—How should I know anything more than yourself about the state of Miss Grey's inclinations?" said Middlemas. "I am sure we have had equal access to know them."

"Perhaps so; but some know better how to avail themselves of opportunities.—Mr Middlemas, I have long suspected that you have had the inestimable advantage of possessing Miss Grey's affections, and"——

"I?—" interrupted Middlemas; "you are jesting, or you are jealous. You do yourself less, and me more, than justice; but the compliment is so great, that I am obliged to you for the mistake."

"That you may know," answered Hartley, "I do not speak either by guess, or from what you call jealousy, I tell you frankly, that Menie Grey herself told me the state of her affections. I naturally communicated to her the discourse I had with her father. I told her that I was but too well convinced that at the present moment I did not possess that interest in her heart, which alone might entitle me to request her acquiescence in the views which her father's goodness held out to me; but I entreated her not at once to decide against me, but give me an opportunity to make way in her affections, if possible; trusting that time, and the services which I should render to her father, might have an ultimate effect in my favour."

"A most natural and modest request. But what did the young lady say in reply?"

"She is a noble-hearted girl, Richard Middlemas; and for her frankness alone, even without her beauty and her good sense, deserves an emperor. I cannot express the graceful modesty with which she told me, that she knew too well the kindliness, as she was pleased to call it, of my heart, to expose me to the protracted pain of an unrequited passion. She candidly informed me that she had been long engaged to you in secret—that you had exchanged portraits;—and though, without her father's consent she would never become yours, yet she felt it impossible that she should ever so far change her senti-ments as to afford the most distant prospect of success to another."

"Upon my word," said Middlemas, "she has been extremely candid indeed, and I am very much obliged to her!"

"And upon *my* honest word, Mr Middlemas," returned Hartley, "you do Miss Grey the greatest injustice—nay, you are ungrateful to her, if you are displeased at her making this declaration. She loves you as a woman loves the first object of her affection—she loves you better—" He stopped, and Middlemas completed the sentence.

"Better than I deserve, perhaps?—Faith, it may well be so, and I love her dearly in return. But after all, you know, the secret was mine as well as hers, and it would have been better that she had consulted me before making it publ.c."

"Mr Middlemas," said Hartley, earnestly, "if the least of this feeling, on your part, arises from the apprehension that your secret is less safe because it is in my keeping, I can assure you that such is my grateful sense of Miss Grey's goodness, in communicating, to save me pain, an affair of such delicacy to herself and you, that wild horses should tear me limb from limb, before they forced a word of it from my lips."

"Nay, nay, my dear friend," said Middlemas, with a frankness of manner which indicated a cordiality that had not existed between them for some time, "you must allow me to be a little jealous in my turn. Your true lover cannot have a title to the name, unless he be sometimes unreasonable; and somehow, it seems odd she should have chosen for a confidant one whom I have often thought a formidable rival; and yet I am so far from being displeased, that I do not know that the dear sensible girl could after all have made a better choice. It is time that the foolish coldness between us should be ended, as you must be sensible that its real cause lay in our rivalry. I have much need of good advice, and who can give it to me better than the old companion, whose soundness of judgment I have always envied, even when some injudicious friends have given me credit for quicker parts?"

Hartley accepted Richard's proffered hand, but without any of the buoyancy of spirit with which it was offered.

"I do not intend," he said, "to remain many days in this place, perhaps not very many hours. But if, in the meanwhile, I can benefit you, by advice or otherwise, you may fully command me. It is the only way in which I can be of service to Menie Grey."

"Love my mistress, love me; a happy *pendant* to the old proverb, Love me, love my dog. Well, then, for Menie Grey's sake, if not for Dick Middlemas's, (plague on that vulgar tell-tale name,) will you, that are a stander-by, tell us, who are the unlucky players, what you think of this game of ours?"

"How can you ask such a question, when the field lies so fair before you? I am sure that Dr Grey would retain you as his assistant upon the same terms which he proposed to me. You are the better match, in all worldly respects, for his daughter, having some capital to begin the world with."

"All true—but methinks Mr Grey has showed no great predilection for me in this matter."

"If he has done injustice to your indisputable merit," said Hartley drily, "the preference of his daughter has more than atoned for it."

"Unquestionably, and dearly do I love her; otherwise, Adam, I am not a person to grasp at the leavings of other people."

"Richard," replied Hartley, "that pride of yours, if you do not check it, will render you both ungrateful and miserable. Mr Grey's ideas are most friendly. He told me plainly, that his choice of me as an assistant, and as a member of his family, had been long balanced by his early affection for you, until he thought he had remarked in you a decisive discontent with such limited prospects as his offer contained, and a desire to go abroad into the world, and push, as it is called, your fortune. He said, that although it was very probable that you might love his daughter well enough to relinquish these ambitious ideas for her sake, yet the demons of Ambition and Avarice would return after the exorciser Love had exhausted the force of his spells, and then he thought he would have just reason to be anxious for his daughter's happiness."

"By my faith, the worthy senior speaks scholarly and wisely," answered Richard—"I did not think he had been so clear-sighted. To say the truth, but for the beautiful Menie Grey, I should feel like a mill-horse, walking my daily round in this dull country, while other gay rovers are trying how the world will receive them. For instance, where do you yourself go?"

"A cousin of my mother's commands a ship in the Company's service. I intend to go with him as surgeon's mate. If I like the sea service, I will continue in it; if not, I will enter some other line."— This, Hartley said with a sigh.

"To India!" answered Richard; "happy dog—to India! You may well bear with equanimity all disappointments sustained on this side of the globe. Oh, Delhi! oh, Golconda! have your names no power to conjure down idle recollections?—India, where gold is won by steel; where a brave man cannot pitch his desire of fame and wealth so high, but that he may realize it, if he have fortune to his friend! Is it possible that the bold adventurer can fix his thoughts on you, and still be dejected at the thoughts that a bonny blue-eyed lass looked favourably on a less lucky fellow than himself?"

"Less lucky?" said Hartley. "Can you, the accepted lover of Menie Grey, speak in that tone, even though it be in jest?"

"Nay, Adam," said Richard, "don't be angry with me, because, being thus far successful, I rate my good fortune not quite so rapturously as perhaps you do, who have missed the luck of it. Your philosophy should tell you, that the object which we attain, or are sure of attaining, loses, perhaps even by that very certainty, a little of the extravagant and ideal value, which attached to it while the object of feverish hopes and aguish fears. But for all that, I cannot live without my sweet Menie. I would wed her to-morrow, with all my soul, without thinking a minute on the clog which so early a marriage would fasten on my heels. But to spend two additional years in this infernal wilderness, cruizing after crowns and half-crowns, when worse men are making lacs and crores of rupees—It is a sad falling off, Adam. Counsel me, my friend,—can you not suggest some mode of getting off from these two years of destined dulness?"

"Not I," replied Hartley, scarce repressing his displeasure; "and if I could induce Dr Grey to dispense with so reasonable a condition, I should be very sorry to do so. You are but twenty-one, and if such a period of probation was, in the Doctor's prudence, judged necessary for me, who am full two years older, I have no idea that he will dispense with it in yours."

"Perhaps not," replied Middlemas; "but do you not think that these two, or call them three, years of probation, had better be spent in India, where much may be done in a little while, than here, where nothing can be done save just enough to get salt to our broth, or broth to our salt? Methinks I have a natural turn for India, and so I ought. My father was a soldier, by the conjecture of all who saw him, and gave me a love of the sword, and an arm to use one. My mother's father was a rich trafficker, who loved wealth, I warrant me, and knew how to get it. This petty two hundred a-year, with its miserable and precarious possibilities, to be shared with the old gentleman, sounds in the ears of one like me, who have the world for winning, and a sword to cut my way through it, like something little better than a decent kind of beggary. Menie is in herself a gem—a diamond—I admit it. But then one would not set such a precious jewel in lead or copper, but in pure gold; ay, and add a circlet of brilliants to set it off with. Be a good fellow, Adam, and undertake the setting my project in proper colours before the Doctor. I am sure, the wisest thing for him and Menie both, is to permit me to spend this short term of probation in the land of cowries. I am sure my heart will be there at any rate, and while I am bleeding some bumpkin for an inflammation, I shall be in fancy relieving some nabob, or rajahpoot, of his plethora of wealth. Come—will you assist, will you be auxiliary? Ten chances but you plead your own cause, man, for I may be brought up by a sabre, or a bow-string, before I make my pack up; then your road to Menie will be free and open, and, as you will be possessed of the situation of comforter *ex officio*, you may take her 'with the tear in her ee,' as old saws advise."

"Mr Richard Middlemas," said Hartley, "I wish it were possible for me to tell you, in the few words which I intend to bestow on you, whether I pity you or despise you the most. Heaven has placed happiness, competence, and content within your power, and you are willing to cast them away, to gratify ambition and avarice. Were I to give an advice on this subject, either to Dr Grey or his daughter, it would be to break off all connexion with a man, who, however clever by nature, may soon show himself a fool, and however honestly brought up, may also, upon temptation, prove himself a villain.—You may lay aside the sneer, which is designed to be a sarcastic smile. I will not attempt to do this, because I am convinced that my advice would be of no use, unless it could come unattended with suspicion of my motives. I will hasten my departure from this house, that we may not meet again; and I will leave it to God Almighty to protect honesty and innocence against the dangers which must attend vanity and folly." So saying, he turned contemptuously from the youthful votary of ambition, and left the garden.

"Stop," said Middlemas, struck with the picture which had been held up to his conscience—"Stop, Adam Hartley, and I will confess to you——" But his words were uttered in a faint and hesitating manner, and either never reached Hartley's ear, or failed in changing his purpose of departure.

When he was out of the garden, Middlemas began to recall his usual boldness of disposition—"Had he stayed a moment longer," he said, "I would have turned Papist, and made him my ghostly confessor. The yeomanly churl!—I would give something to know how he has got such a hank over me. What are Menie Grey's engagements to him? She has given him his answer, and what right has he to come betwixt her and me? If old Monçada had done a grandfather's duty, and made suitable settlements on me, this plan of marrying the sweet girl, and settling here in her native place, might have done well enough. But to live the life of the poor drudge her father—to be at the command and call of every boor for twenty miles round!—why, the labours of a higgler, who travels scores of miles to barter pins, ribands, snuff and tobacco, against the housewife's private stock of eggs, mortskins, and tallow, is more profitable, less laborious, and faith, I think, equally respectable. No, no—unless I can find wealth nearer home, I will seek it where every one can have it for the gathering; and so I will down to the Swan Inn, and hold a final consultation with my friend."

Chapter Six

THE FRIEND whom Middlemas expected to meet at the Swan, was a person already mentioned in this history by the name of Tom Hillary, bred an attorney's clerk in the ancient town of Novum Castrum— *doctus utriusque juris*, as far as a few months in the service of Mr Lawford, Town-Clerk of Middlemas, could render him so. The last mention that we made of this gentleman, was when his gold-laced hat vailed its splendour before the fresher mounted beavers of the 'prentices of Dr Grey. That was now about five years since, and it was within six months that he had made his appearance in Middlemas, a very different sort of personage from that which he seemed at his departure.

He was now called Captain; his dress was regimental, and his language martial. He seemed to have plenty of cash, for he not only, to the great surprise of the parties, paid certain old debts, which he had left unsettled behind him, and that notwithstanding his having, as his old practice told him, a good defence of prescription, but even sent the minister a guinea, to the assistance of the parish poor. These acts of justice and benevolence were bruited abroad greatly to the honour of one, who, so long absent, had neither forgotten his just debts, nor hardened his heart against the cries of the needy. His merits were thought the higher, when it was understood he had served the honourable East India Company—that wonderful company of merchants, who may indeed, with the strictest propriety, be termed princes. It was about the middle of the eighteenth century, and the directors in Leadenhall Street were silently laying the foundation of that immense empire, which afterwards rose like an exhalation, and now astonishes Europe, as well as Asia, with its formidable extent, and stupendous strength. Britain had now begun to lend a wondering ear to the account of battles fought, and cities won, in the East; and was surprised by the return of individuals who had left their native country as adventurers, but now appeared surrounded by Oriental wealth and Oriental luxury, which dimmed even the splendour of the most wealthy of the British nobility. In this new-found El Dorado, Hillary had, it seems, been a labourer, and, if he told truth, to some purpose, though he was far from having completed the harvest which he meditated. He spoke indeed of making investments, and, as a mere matter of fancy, he consulted his old master, Clerk Lawford, concerning the purchase of a moorland farm, of three thousand acres, for which he would be content to give three or four thousand guineas, providing the game was plenty, and the trouting in the brook such as had been represented by advertisement. But he did not wish to make any extensive landed purchase at present. It was necessary to keep up his interest in Leadenhall Street; and in that view, it would be impolitic to part with his India stock and India bonds. In short, it was folly to think of settling on a poor thousand or twelve hundred a-year, when one was in the prime of life, and had no liver complaint; and so he was determined to double the Cape once again, ere he retired to the chimney corner of life. All he wished was, to pick up a few clever fellows for his regiment, or rather for his own company; and as in all his travels he had never seen finer fellows than about Middlemas, he was willing to give them the preference in completing his levy. In fact, it was making men of them at once, for a few white faces never failed to strike terror into these black rascals; and then, not to mention the good things that were going at the storming of a Pettah, or the plundering of a Pagoda, most of these tawny dogs carried so much treasure about their person, that a won battle was equal to a mine of gold to the victors.

The natives of Middlemas listened to the noble Captain's marvels with different feelings, as their temperaments were saturnine or sanguine. But none could deny that such things had been; and as he was known to be a bold dashing fellow, possessed of some abilities, and, according to the general opinion, not likely to be withheld by any peculiar scruples of conscience, there was no giving any good reason why Hillary should not have been as successful as others in the field, which India, agitated as it was by war and intestine disorders, seemed to offer to every enterprising adventurer. He was accordingly received by his old acquaintances at Middlemas rather with the respect due to his supposed wealth, than in a manner corresponding with his former humble pretensions.

Some of the notables of the village did indeed keep aloof. Among these, the chief was Dr Grey, who was an enemy of everything that approached to fanfaronade, and knew enough of the world to lay it down as a sort of general rule, that he who talks a great deal of fighting is seldom a brave soldier, and he who always speaks about wealth is seldom a rich man at bottom. Clerk Lawford was also shy, notwithstanding his *communings* with Hillary upon the subject of his intended purchase. The coolness of the Captain's old employer towards him was by some supposed to arise out of certain circumstances attending their former connexion; but as the Clerk himself never explained what these were, it is unnecessary to make any conjectures upon the subject.

Richard Middlemas very naturally renewed his intimacy with his former comrade, and it was from Hillary's conversation, that he had adopted that enthusiasm respecting India, which we have heard him express. It was indeed impossible for a youth, at once inexperienced in the world, and possessed of a most sanguine disposition, to listen without sympathy to the glowing descriptions of Hillary, who, though only a recruiting captain, had all the eloquence of a recruiting sergeant. Palaces rose like mushrooms in his descriptions; groves of lofty trees, and aromatic shrubs unknown to the chilly soils of Europe, were tenanted by every object of the chase, from the royal tiger down to the jackall. The luxuries of a Natch, and the peculiar Oriental beauty of the enchantresses who performed their voluptuous Eastern dances, for the pleasure of the haughty English conquerors, were no less attractive than the battles and sieges on which the Captain at other times expatiated. Not a stream did he mention but flowed over sands of gold, and not a palace that was inferior to that of the celebrated Fata Morgana. His descriptions seemed steeped in odours, and his every phrase perfumed in ottar of roses. The interviews at which these descriptions took place, often ended in a bottle of choicer wine than the Swan Inn afforded, with some other appendages of the table, which the Captain, who was a bon-vivant, had procured from Edinburgh. From this good cheer Middlemas was doomed to retire to the homely evening meal of his master, where not all the simple beauties of Menie were able to overcome his disgust at the coarseness of the provisions, or his unwillingness to answer questions concerning the diseases of the wretched peasants who were subjected to his inspection.

Richard's hopes of being acknowledged by his father had long since vanished, and the rough repulse and subsequent neglect on the part of Monçada, had satisfied him that his grandfather was inexorable, and that neither then, nor at any future time, did he mean to realize the visions which Nurse Jamieson's splendid figments had encouraged him to entertain. Ambition, however, was not lulled to sleep, though it was no longer nourished by the same hopes which had at first awakened it. The Indian Captain's lavish oratory supplied the themes which had been at first derived from the legends of the nursery; the exploits of a Lawrence and a Clive, as well as the magnificent opportunities of acquiring wealth to which these exploits opened the road, disturbed the slumbers of the young adventurer. There was nothing to counteract these except his love for Menie Grey, and the engagements into which it had led him. But his addresses had been paid to Menie as much for the gratification of his vanity, as from any decided passion for that innocent and guileless being. He was desirous of carrying off the prize, for which Hartley, whom he never loved, had the courage to contend with him. Then, Menie Grey had been beheld with admiration by men his superiors in rank and fortune, but with whom his ambition incited him to dispute the prize. No doubt, though urged to play the gallant at first rather from vanity than any other cause, the frankness and modesty with which his suit was admitted, made their natural impression on his heart. He was grateful to the beautiful creature, who acknowledged the superiority of his person and accomplishments, and fancied himself as devotedly attached to her, as her personal charms and mental merits would have rendered any one who was less vain or selfish than her lover. Still his passion for the surgeon's daughter ought not, he prudentially determined, to bear more than its due weight in a case so very important as the determining his line of life; and this he smoothed over to his conscience, by repeating to himself, that Menie's interest was as essentially concerned as his own, in postponing their marriage to the establishment of his fortune. How many young couples had been ruined by a premature union!

The contemptuous conduct of Hartley in their last interview, had done something to shake his comrade's confidence in the truth of this reasoning, and to lead him to suspect that he was playing a very sordid and unmanly part, in trifling with the happiness of this amiable and unfortunate young woman. It was in this doubtful humour that he repaired to the Swan Inn, where he was anxiously expected by his friend the Captain.

When they were comfortably seated over a bottle of Paxarete, Middlemas began, with characteristical caution, to sound his friend about the ease or difficulty with which an individual, desirous of entering the Company's service, might have an opportunity of getting a commission. If Hillary had answered truly, he would have replied, that it was extremely easy; for, at that time, the East India service presented no charms to that superior class of people who have since struggled for admittance under its banners. But the worthy Captain replied, that though, in the general case, it might be difficult for a young man to obtain a commission, without serving for some years as a cadet, yet, under his own protection, a young man entering his regiment, and fitted for such a situation, might be sure of an ensigncy, if not a lieutenancy, as soon as ever they set foot in India. "If you, my dear fellow," continued he, extending his hand to Middlemas, "would think of changing sheep-head broth and haggis for mulagatawny and curry, I can only say, that though it is indispensable that you should enter the service at first simply as a cadet, yet, by ——, you should live like a brother on the passage with me; and no sooner were we through the surf at Madras, than I would put you in the way of acquiring both wealth and glory. You have, I think, some trifle of money—a couple of thousands or so?"

"About a thousand or twelve hundred," said Richard, affecting the indifference of his companion, but feeling privately humbled by the scantiness of his resources.

"It is quite as much as you will find necessary for the outfit and passage," said his adviser; "and, indeed, if you had not a farthing, it would be the same thing; for if I once say to a friend, I'll help you, Tom Hillary is not the man to start for fear of the cowries. However, it is as well you have something of a capital of your own to begin upon."

"Yes," replied the proselyte—"I should not like to be a burden on any one. I have some thoughts, to tell you the truth, to marry before I leave Britain; and in that case, you know, cash will be necessary, whether my wife goes out with us, or remains behind, till she hear how luck goes with me. So, after all, I may have to borrow a few hundreds of you."

"What the devil is that you say, Dick, about marrying and giving in marriage?" replied his friend—"What can put it into the head of a gallant young fellow like you, just rising twenty-one, and six feet high on your stocking soles, to make a slave of yourself for life? No, no, Dick, that will never do. Remember the old song—

> Bachelor bluff, bachelor bluff,
> Hey for a heart that's rugged and tough!"

"Ay, ay, that sounds very well," replied Middlemas; "but then one must shake off a number of old recollections."

"The sooner the better, Dick; old recollections are like old clothes, and should be sent off by wholesale; they only take up room in one's wardrobe, and it would be old-fashioned to wear them.—But you look grave upon it. Who the devil is it has made such a hole in your heart?"

"Pshaw!" answered Middlemas, "I am sure you must remember—Menie—my master's daughter."

"What, Miss Green, the old pottercarrier's daughter?—a likely girl enough, I think."

"My master is a surgeon," said Richard, "not an apothecary, and his name is Grey."

"Ay, ay, Green or Grey—what does it signify? He sells his own drugs, I think, which we in the south call being a pottercarrier. The girl is a likely girl enough for a Scottish ballroom.—But is she up to anything?—Has she any *nouz*?"

"Why, she is a sensible girl, save in loving me," answered Richard; "and that, as Benedict says, is no proof of her wisdom, and no great argument of her folly."

"But has she spirit—spunk—dash—a spice of the devil about her?"

"Not a penny-weight—the kindest, simplest, and most manageable of human beings," answered the lover.

"She won't do then," said the monitor, in a decisive tone. "I am sorry for it, Dick; but she will never do. There are some women in the world that can bear their share in the bustling life we live in India—ay, and I have known some of them drag forward husbands that would otherwise have stuck fast in the mud till the day of judgment. Heaven knows how they paid the turnpikes they pushed them through! But these were none of your simple Susans, that think their eyes are good for nothing but to look at their husband, or sew baby-clothes. Depend on it, you must give up your matrimony, or your views of preferment. If you wilfully tie a clog round your throat, never think of running a race; and do not suppose that your breaking off with the lass will make any very terrible catastrophe. A scene there may be at parting; but you will soon forget her among the native girls, and she will fall in love with Mr Tapeitout, the minister's assistant and successor. She is not goods fitted for the Indian market, I assure you."

Among the capricious weaknesses of humanity, that one is particularly remarkable which inclines us to esteem persons and things not by their real value, so much as by the opinion of others, who are often very incompetent judges. Dick Middlemas had been urged forward, in his suit to Menie Grey, by his observing how much her partner, a booby laird, had been captivated by her; and she was now lowered in his esteem, because an impudent low-bred coxcomb had presumed to talk of her with disparagement. Either of these worthy gentlemen would have been as capable of enjoying the beauties of Homer, as judging of the merits of Menie Grey.

Indeed the ascendency which this bold-talking, promise-making soldier had acquired over Dick Middlemas, wilful as he was in general, was of a despotic nature; because the Captain, though greatly inferior in information and talent to the youth whose opinions he swayed, had skill in suggesting those tempting views of rank and wealth, to which Richard's imagination had been from childhood most accessible. One promise he exacted from Middlemas, as a condition of the services which he was to render him—It was absolute silence on the subject of his destination for India, and the views upon which it took place. "My recruits," said the Captain, "have been all marched off for the depot at the Isle of Wight; and I want to leave Scotland, and particularly this little burgh, without being worried to death, of which I must despair, should it come to be known that I can provide young griffins, as we call them, with commissions. Gad, I should carry off all the first-born of Middlemas as cadets, and none are so scrupulous as I am about making promises. I am as trusty as a Trojan for that; and you know I cannot do that for every one which I would for an old friend like Dick Middlemas."

Dick promised secrecy, and it was agreed that the two friends should not even leave the burgh in company, but that the Captain should set off first, and his recruit should join him at Edinburgh, where his enlistment might be attested; and then they were to travel together to town, and arrange matters for their Indian voyage.

Notwithstanding the definitive arrangement which was thus made for his departure, Middlemas thought from time to time with anxiety and regret about quitting Menie Grey, after the engagements which had passed between them. The resolution was taken, however; the blow was necessarily to be struck; and her ungrateful lover, long since determined against the life of domestic happiness, which he might have enjoyed had his views been better regulated, was now occupied with the means, not indeed of breaking off with her entirely, but of postponing all thoughts of their union until the success of his expedition to India.

He might have spared himself all anxiety on this last subject. The wealth of that India to which he was bound would not have bribed Menie Grey to have left her father's roof against her father's commands; still less when, deprived of his two assistants, he must be reduced to the necessity of continued exertion in his declining life, and therefore might have accounted himself altogether deserted, had his daughter departed from him at the same time. But though it would have been her unalterable determination not to accept any proposal of an immediate union of their fortunes, Menie could not, with all a lover's power of self-deception, succeed in persuading herself to be satisfied with Richard's conduct towards her. Modesty, and a becoming pride, prevented her from seeming to notice, but could not prevent her from bitterly feeling, that her lover was preferring the pursuits of ambition to the humble lot which he might have shared with her, and which promised content at least, if not wealth.

"If he had loved me as he pretended," such was the unwilling conviction that rose on her mind, "my father would surely not have ultimately refused him the same terms which he held out to Hartley. His objections would have given way to my happiness, nay, to Richard's importunity, which would have removed his suspicions of the unsettled cast of his disposition. But I fear—I fear Richard hardly thought the terms proposed were worthy of his acceptance. Would it not have been natural, too, that he should have asked me, engaged as we stand to each other, to have united our fate before his quitting Europe, when I might either have remained here with my father, or accompanied him to India, in quest of that fortune which he is so eagerly pushing for? It would have been wrong—very wrong—in me to have consented to such a proposal, unless my father had authorized it; but surely it would have been natural that Richard should have offered it? Alas! men do not know how to love like women. Their attachment is only one of a thousand other passions and predilections, —they are daily engaged in pleasures which blunt their feelings, and in business which distracts them. We—we sit at home to weep, and to think how coldly our affections are repaid!"

The time was now arrived at which Richard Middlemas had a right to demand the property vested in the hands of the Town-Clerk and Doctor Grey. He did so, and received it accordingly. His late guardian naturally inquired, what views he had formed in entering on life? The imagination of the ambitious aspirant saw in this simple question a desire, on the part of the worthy man, to offer, and perhaps press upon him, the same proposal which he had made to Hartley. He hastened, therefore, to answer drily, that he had some hopes held out to him which he was not at liberty to communicate; but that the instant he reached London, he would be sure to write to the guardian of his youth, and acquaint him with the nature of his prospects, which he was happy to say were rather of a pleasing character.

Grey, who supposed that at this critical period of his life, the father, or grandfather, of the young man might perhaps have intimated a disposition to open some intercourse with him, only replied,—"You have been the child of mystery, Richard; and as you came to me, so you leave me. Then, I was ignorant from whence you came, and now, I know not whither you are going. It is not, perhaps, a very favourable point in your horoscope, that everything connected with you is a secret. But as I shall always think with kindness on him whom I have known so long, so when you remember the old man, you ought not to forget that he has done his duty to you, to the extent of his means and power, and taught you that noble profession, by means of which, wherever your lot casts you, you may always gain your bread, and alleviate, at the same time, the distresses of your fellow-creatures." Middlemas was excited by the simple kindness of his master, and poured forth his thanks with the greater profusion, that he was free from the terror of the emblematical collar and chain, which a moment before seemed to glisten in the hand of his guardian, and gape to enclose his neck.

"One word more," said Mr Grey, producing a small ring-case. "This valuable ring was forced upon me by your unfortunate mother. I have no right to it, having been amply paid for my services; and I only accepted it with the purpose of keeping it for you till this moment should arrive. It may be useful, perhaps, should there occur any question about your identity."

"Thanks once more, my more than father, for this precious relic, which may indeed be useful. You shall be repaid, if India has diamonds left."

"India, and diamonds!" said Grey. "Is your head turned, child?"

"I mean," stammered Middlemas, "if London has any Indian diamonds."

"Pooh! you foolish la:l," answered Grey, "how should you buy diamonds, or what should I do with them, if you gave me ever so many? Get you gone with you while I am angry."—The tears were glistening in the old man's eyes.—"If I get pleased with you again, I shall not know how to part with you."

The parting of Middlemas with poor Menie was yet more affecting. Her sorrow revived in his mind all the liveliness of a first love, and he redeemed his character for sincere attachment, by not only imploring an instant union, but even going so far as to propose renouncing his more splendid prospects, and sharing Mr Grey's humble toil, if by doing so he could secure his daughter's hand. But though there was consolation in this testimony of her lover's faith, Menie Grey was not so unwise as to accept of sacrifices which might afterwards have been repented of.

"No, Richard," she said, "it seldom ends happily when people alter, in a moment of agitated feeling, plans which have been adopted under mature deliberation. I have long seen that your views were extended far beyond so humble a station as this place affords promise of. It is natural they should do so, considering that the circumstances of your birth seem connected with riches and with rank. Go, then, seek that riches and rank. It is possible your mind may be changed in the pursuit, and if so, think no more about Menie Grey. But if it should be otherwise, we may meet again, and do not believe for a moment that there can be a change in Menie Grey's feelings towards you."

At this interview, much more was said than it is necessary to repeat, much more thought than was actually said. Nurse Jamieson, in whose chamber it took place, folded her *bairns*, as she called them, in her arms, and declared that Heaven had made them for each other, and that she would not ask of Heaven to live beyond the day when she should see them bride and bridegroom.

At length, it became necessary that the parting scene should end; and Richard Middlemas, mounting a horse which he had hired for the journey, set off for Edinburgh, to which metropolis he had already forwarded his heavy baggage. Upon the road the idea more than once occurred to him, that even yet he had better return to Middlemas, and secure his happiness by uniting himself at once to Menie Grey, and to humble competence. But from the moment that he rejoined his friend

Hillary at their appointed place of rendezvous, he became ashamed even to hint at any change of purpose; and his late excited feelings were forgotten, unless in so far as they confirmed his resolution, that so soon as he had attained a certain portion of wealth and consequence, he would haste to share them with Menie Grey. Yet his gratitude to her father did not appear to have slumbered, if we may judge from the gift of a very handsome cornelian seal set in gold, and bearing engraved upon it Gules, a lion rampant within a bordure engrailed Or, which was carefully dispatched to Stevenlaw's Land, with a suitable letter. Menie knew the hand-writing, and watched her father's looks as he read it, thinking, perhaps, that it had turned on a different topic. Her father pshawed and poohed a good deal when he had finished the billet, and examined the seal.

"Dick Middlemas," he said, "is but a fool after all, Menie. I am sure I am not like to forget him, that he should send me a token of remembrance; and if he would be so absurd, could he not have sent me the improved lithotomical apparatus? And what have I, Gideon Grey, to do with the arms of my Lord Gray?—No, no—my old silver stamp, with the double G upon it, will serve my turn—But put the bonnie die away, Menie, my dear—it was kindly meant, at any rate."

The reader cannot doubt that the seal was safely and carefully preserved.

Chapter Seben

A lazar-house it seemed, wherein were laid
Numbers of all diseased.—
                                        MILTON

AFTER THE CAPTAIN had finished his business, amongst which he did not forget to have his recruit regularly attested, as a candidate for glory in the service of the Honourable East India Company, the friends left Edinburgh. From thence they got a passage by sea to Newcastle, where Hillary had also some regimental affairs to transact, before he joined his regiment. At Newcastle the Captain had the good luck to find a small brig, commanded by an old acquaintance and schoolfellow, which was just about to sail for the Isle of Wight. "I have arranged for our passage with him," he said to Middlemas—"for when you are at the depôt, you can learn a little of your duty, which cannot be so well taught on board of ship, and then I will find it easier to have you promoted."

"Do you mean," said Richard, "that I am to stay at the Isle of Wight all the time that you are jigging it away in London?"

"Ay, indeed do I," said his comrade, "and it's best for you too; whatever business you have in London, I can do it for you as well, or something better than yourself."

"But I choose to transact my own business myself, Captain Hillary," said Richard.

"Then you ought to have remained your own master, Cadet Middlemas. At present you are an enlisted recruit of the Honourable East India Company; I am your officer, and should you hesitate to follow me aboard, why, you foolish fellow, I could have you sent on board in handcuffs."

This was jestingly spoken; but yet there was something in the tone which hurt Middlemas's pride, and alarmed his fears. He had observed of late, that his friend, especially when in company of others, talked to him with an air of command or superiority, difficult to be endured, and yet so closely allied to the freedom often exercised betwixt two intimates, that he could not find any proper mode of rebuffing, or resenting it. Such manifestations of authority were usually followed by an instant renewal of their intimacy; but in the present case that did not so speedily ensue.

Middlemas, indeed, consented to go with his companion to the Isle of Wight, perhaps because if he should quarrel with him, the whole plan of his Indian voyage, and all the hopes built upon it, must fall to the ground. But he altered his purpose of intrusting his comrade with his little fortune, to lay out as his occasions might require, and resolved himself to overlook the expenditure of his money, which, in the form of Bank of England notes, was safely deposited in his travelling trunk. Captain Hillary, finding that some hint he had thrown out on this subject was disregarded, appeared to think no more about it.

The voyage was performed with safety and celerity; and having coasted the shores of that beautiful island, which he who once sees never forgets, through whatever part of the world his future path may lead him, the vessel was soon anchored off the little town of Ryde; and, as the waves were uncommonly still, Richard felt the sickness diminish, which, for a considerable part of the passage, had occupied his attention more than anything else.

The master of the brig, in honour to his passengers, and affection to his old schoolfellow, had formed an awning upon deck, and proposed to have the pleasure of giving them a little treat before they left his vessel. Lobscous, sea-pie, and other delicacies of a naval description, had been provided in a quantity far disproportionate to the number of the guests. But the punch which succeeded was of excellent quality, and portentously strong. Captain Hillary pushed it round, and insisted upon his companion taking his full share in the merry bout, the rather that, as he facetiously said, there had been some dryness between them, which good liquor would be sovereign in removing. He renewed, with additional splendours, the various panoramic scenes of India and Indian adventures, which had first excited the ambition of Middlemas, and assured him, that even if he should not be able to get him a commission instantly, yet a short delay would only give him time to become better acquainted with his military duties; and Middlemas was too much elevated by the liquor he had drunk, to see any difficulty which could oppose itself to his fortunes. Whether those who shared in the compotation were more seasoned topers—whether Middlemas drank more than they—or whether, as he himself afterwards suspected, his cup had been drugged, like those of Duncan's body-guard, it is certain, that on this occasion he passed, with unusual rapidity, through all the different phases of the respectable state of drunkenness,—laughed, sung, whooped, and hallooed, was maudlin in his fondness, and frantic in his wrath, and at length fell into a fast and imperturbable sleep.

The effect of the liquor displayed itself, as usual, in a hundred wild dreams of parched deserts, and of serpents whose bite inflicted the most intolerable thirst—of the suffering of the Indian on the death-stake—and the torments of the infernal regions themselves. When at length he awakened it appeared that the latter vision was in fact realised. The sounds which had at first influenced his dreams, and at length broken his slumbers, were of the most horrible, as well as the most melancholy description. They came from the ranges of pallet-beds, which were closely packed together in a species of military hospital, where a burning fever was the prevalent complaint. Many of the patients were under the influence of a high delirium, during which they shouted, shrieked, blasphemed, and uttered the most horrible imprecations. Others, sensible of their condition, bewailed it with low groans, and some attempts at devotion, which showed their ignorance of the principles, and even the forms of religion. Those who were convalescent talked ribaldry in a loud tone, or whispered to each other in canting language, upon schemes which, as far as a passing phrase could be understood by a novice, had relation to violent and criminal exploits.

Richard Middlemas's astonishment was equal to his horror. He had but one advantage over the poor wretches with whom he was classed, and it was in enjoying the luxury of a pallet to himself—most of the others being occupied by two unhappy beings. He saw no one who appeared to attend to the wants, or to heed the complaints, of the wretches around him, or to whom he could offer any appeal against his present situation. He looked for his clothes, that he might arise and extricate himself from this den of horrors; but his clothes were nowhere to be seen, nor did he see his portmanteau, or sea-chest. It was much to be apprehended that he would never see them more.

Then, but too late, he remembered the insinuations which had passed current respecting his friend the Captain, who was supposed to have been discharged by Mr Lawford, on account of some breach of trust in the Town-Clerk's service. But that he should have trepanned the friend who had reposed his whole confidence in him—that he should have plundered him of his fortune, and placed him in this house of pestilence, with the hope that death might stifle his tongue, were iniquities not to have been anticipated, even if the worst of these reports were true.

But Middlemas resolved not to be a-wanting to himself. This place must be visited by some officer, military or medical, to whom he would make an appeal, and alarm his fears at least, if he could not awaken his conscience. While he revolved these distracting thoughts, tormented at the same time by a burning thirst which he had no means of satisfying, he endeavoured to discover if, among those stretched upon the pallets nearest him, he could not discern some one likely to enter into conversation with him, and give him some information about the nature and customs of this horrid place. But the bed nearest him was occupied by two fellows, who, although to judge from their gaunt cheeks, hollow eyes, and ghastly looks, they were apparently recovering from the disease, and just rescued from the jaws of death, were deeply engaged in endeavouring to cheat each other of a few halfpence at a game of cribbage, mixing the terms of the game with oaths not loud but deep; each turn of luck being hailed by the winner as well as the loser with execrations, which seemed designed to blight both body and soul, now used as the language of triumph, and now as reproaches against fortune.

Next to the gamblers was a pallet, occupied indeed by two bodies, but only one of which was living—the other sufferer had been recently relieved from his agony.

"He is dead—he is dead!" said the wretched survivor.

"Then do you die too, and be d—d," answered one of the players, "and then there will be a pair of you, as Pugg says."

"I tell you he is growing stiff and cold," said the poor wretch—"the dead is no bedfellow for the living. For God's sake, help to rid me of the corpse."

"Ay, and get the credit of having done him—as may be the case with yourself, friend—for he had some two or three hoggs about him——"

"You know you took the last rap from his breeches pocket not an hour ago," expostulated the poor convalescent—"But help me to take the body out of the bed, and I will not tell the *jigger-dubber* that you have been before-hand with him."

"You tell the *jigger-dubber!*" answered the cribbage player. "Such another word, and I will twist your head round till your eyes look at the drummer's handwriting on your back. Hold your peace, and don't bother our game with your gammon, or I will make you as mute as your bedfellow."

The unhappy wretch, exhausted, sunk back beside his hideous companion, and the usual jargon of the game, interlarded with execrations, went on as before.

From this specimen of the most obdurate indifference, mingled with the last excess of misery, Middlemas became satisfied how little could be made of an appeal to the humanity of his fellow-sufferers. His heart sunk within him, and the thoughts of the happy and peaceful home, which he might have called his own, arose before his over-heated fancy, with a vividness of perception that bordered upon insanity. He saw before him the rivulet which wanders through the burgh-muir of Middlemas, where he had so often set little mills for the amusement of Menie while she was a child. One draught of it would have been worth all the diamonds of the East, which of late he had worshipped with such devotion; but that draught was denied to him as to Tantalus.

Rallying his senses from this passing illusion, and knowing enough of the practice of the medical art, to be aware of the necessity of preventing his ideas from wandering if possible, he endeavoured to recollect that he was a surgeon, and, after all, should not have the extreme fear for the interior of a military hospital, which its horrors might inspire into strangers to the profession. But though he strove, by such recollections, to rally his spirits, he was not the less aware of the difference betwixt the condition of a surgeon, who might have attended such a place in the course of his duty, and a poor inhabitant, who was at once a patient and a prisoner.

A footstep was now heard in the apartment, which seemed to silence all the varied sounds of woe that filled it. The cribbage party hid their cards, and ceased their oaths; other wretches, whose complaints had arisen to frenzy, left off their wild exclamations and entreaties for assistance. Agony softened her shriek, Insanity hushed its senseless clamours, and even Death seemed desirous to stifle his parting groan in the presence of Captain Seelencooper. This official was the superintendent, or, as the miserable inhabitants termed him, the Governor of the Hospital. He had all the air of having been originally a turnkey in some ill-regulated jail—a stout, short, bandy-legged man, with one eye, and a double portion of ferocity in that which remained. He wore an old-fashioned tarnished uniform, which did not seem to have been made for him; and the voice in which this minister of humanity addressed the sick, was that of a boatswain, shouting in the midst of a storm. He had pistols and a cutlass in his belt; for his mode of administration being such as provoked even hospital patients to revolt, his life had been more than once in danger amongst them. He was followed by two assistants, who carried hand-cuffs and strait-jackets.

As Seelencooper made his rounds, complaint and pain were hushed, and the flourish of the bamboo, which he bore in his hand, seemed powerful as the wand of a magician to silence all complaint and remonstrance.

"I tell you the meat is as sweet as a nosegay—and for the bread, it's good enough, and too good, for a set of lubbers, that lie shamming Abraham, and consuming the Right Honourable Company's victuals —I don't speak to them that are really sick, for God knows I am always for humanity."

"If that be the case, sir," said Richard Middlemas, whose lair the Captain had approached, while he was thus answering the low and humble complaints of those by whose bed-side he passed—"if that be the case, sir, I hope your humanity will make you attend to what I say."

"And who the devil are you?" said the governor, turning on him his single eye of fire, while a sneer gathered on his harsh features, which were so well qualified to express it.

"My name is Middlemas—I come from Scotland, and have been sent here by some strange mistake. I am neither a private soldier, nor am I indisposed, more than by the heat of this cursed place."

"Why then, friend, all I have to ask you is, whether you are an attested recruit or not?"

"I was attested at Edinburgh," said Middlemas, "but——"

"But what the devil would you have, then?—you are enlisted—the Captain and the Doctor sent you here—surely they know best whether you are private or officer, sick or well."

"But I was promised," said Middlemas, "promised by Tom Hillary——"

"Promised, were you? Why, there is not a man here that has not been promised something by somebody or another, or perhaps has promised something to himself. This is the land of promise, my smart fellow, but you know it is India that must be the land of performance. So good morning to you. The Doctor will come his rounds presently, and put you all to rights."

"Stay but one moment—one moment only—I have been robbed."

"Robbed! look you there now," said the Governor—"everybody

that comes here has been robbed.—Egad, I am the luckiest fellow in Europe—other people in my line have only thieves and blackguards upon their hands; but none come to my ken but honest, decent, unfortunate gentlemen, that have been robbed!"

"Take care how you treat this so lightly, sir," said Middlemas; "I have been robbed of a thousand pounds."

Here Governor Seelencooper's gravity was totally overcome, and his laugh was echoed by several of the patients, either because they wished to curry favour with the superintendent, or from the feeling which influences evil spirits to rejoice in the tortures of those who are sent to share their agony.

"A thousand pounds!" exclaimed Captain Seelencooper, as he recovered his breath,—"Come, that's a good one—I like a fellow that does not make two bites of a cherry—why, there is not a cull in the ken that pretends to have lost more than a few hoggs, and here is a servant to the Honourable Company that has been robbed of a thousand pounds! Well done, Mr Tom of Ten Thousand—you're a credit to the house, and to the service, and so good morning to you."

He passed on, and Richard, starting up in a storm of anger and despair, found, as he would have called after him, that his voice, betwixt thirst and agitation, refused its office. "Water, water!" he said, laying hold, at the same time, of one of the assistants who followed Seelencooper by the sleeve. The fellow looked carelessly round; there was a jug stood by the side of the cribbage players, which he reached to Middlemas, bidding him, "Drink and be d——d."

The man's back was no sooner turned, than the gamester threw himself from his own bed into that of Middlemas, and grasping firm hold of the arm of Richard, ere he could carry the vessel to his head, swore he should not have his booze. It may be readily conjectured, that the pitcher thus anxiously and desperately reclaimed, contained something better than the pure element. In fact, a large proportion of it was gin. The jug was broken in the struggle, and the liquor spilt. Middlemas dealt a blow to the assailant, which was amply and heartily repaid, and a combat would have ensued, but for the interference of the superintendent and his assistants, who, with a dexterity that showed them well acquainted with such emergencies, clapped a strait waistcoat upon each of the antagonists. Richard's efforts at remonstrance only procured him a blow from Captain Seelencooper's rat-tan, and a tender admonition to hold his tongue, if he valued a whole skin.

Irritated at once by sufferings of the mind and of the body, tormented by a raging thirst, and by the sense of his own dreadful situation, the mind of Richard Middlemas seemed again to be on the point of becoming unsettled. He felt an insane desire to imitate and reply to the groans, oaths, and ribaldry, which, so soon as the superintendent quitted the hospital, echoed around him. He longed, though he struggled against the impulse, to vie in curses with the reprobate, and in screams with the maniac. But his tongue clove to the roof of his mouth, his mouth itself seemed choked with ashes; there came upon him a dimness of sight, a rushing sound in his ears, and the powers of life were for a time suspended.

Chapter Eight

A wise physician, skill'd our wounds to heal,
Is more than armies to the common weal.
　　　　　POPE'S *Homer*

As RICHARD MIDDLEMAS returned to his senses, he was sensible that his blood felt more cool; that the feverish throb of his pulsation was diminished; that the ligatures on his person were removed, and his lungs performed their functions more freely. One assistant was binding up a vein, from which a considerable quantity of blood had been taken; another, who had just washed the face of the patient, was holding aromatic vinegar to his nostrils. As he began to open his eyes, the person who had just completed the bandage, said in Latin, but in a very low tone, and without raising his head, "Annon sis Ricardus ille Middlemas, ex civitate Middlemassiense? Responde in lingua Latina."

"Sum ille miserrimus," replied Richard, again shutting his eyes; for strange as it may seem, the voice of his comrade Adam Hartley, though his presence might be of so much consequence in this emergency, conveyed a pang to his wounded pride. He was conscious of unkindly, if not hostile, feelings towards his old companion; he remembered the tone of superiority which he used to assume over him, and thus to lie stretched at his feet, and in a manner at his mercy, aggravated his distress, by the feelings of the dying chieftain, "Earl Percy sees my fall." This was, however, too unreasonable an emotion to subsist above a minute. In the next, he availed himself of the Latin language, with which both were familiar, (for in that time the medical studies at the celebrated University of Edinburgh were, in a great measure, conducted in Latin,) to tell in a few words his own folly, and the villainy of Hillary.

"I must be gone instantly," said Hartley—"Take courage—I trust to be able to assist you. In the meantime, take food and physic from none but my servant, who you see holds the sponge in his hand. You are where a man's life has been taken for the sake of his gold sleeve-buttons."

"Stay yet a moment," said Middlemas—"Let me remove this temptation from my dangerous neighbours."

He drew a small packet from his under waistcoat, and put it into Hartley's hands.

"If I die," he said, "be my heir. You deserve her better than I."

All answer was prevented by the hoarse voice of Seelencooper.

"Well, Doctor, will you carry through your patient?"

"Symptoms are dubious yet," said the Doctor—"That was an alarming swoon. You must have him carried into the private ward, and my young man shall attend him."

"Why, if you command it, Doctor, needs must;—but I can tell you there is a man we both know, that has a thousand reasons at least for keeping him in the public ward."

"I know nothing of your thousand reasons," said Hartley; "I can only tell you that this young fellow is as well-limbed and likely a lad as the Company have among their recruits. It is my business to save him for their service, and if he dies by your neglecting what I direct, depend upon it I will not allow the blame to lie at my door. I will tell the General the charge I have given you."

"The General!" said Seelencooper, much embarrassed—"Tell the General?—ay, about his health. But you will not say anything about what he may have said in his light-headed fits. My eyes! if you listen to what feverish patients say when the tantivy is in their brain, your back will soon break with tale-bearing, for I will warrant you plenty of them to carry."

"Captain Seelencooper," said the Doctor, "I do not meddle with your department in the hospital—My advice to you is, not to trouble yourself with mine. I suppose, as I have a commission in the service, and have besides a regular diploma as a physician, I know when my patient is light-headed or otherwise. So do you let the man be carefully looked after, at your peril."

So saying, he left the hospital, but not till, under pretext of again consulting the pulse, he had pressed the patient's hand, as if to assure him once more of his exertions for his liberation.

"My eyes!" murmured Seelencooper, "this cockerel crows gallant, to come from a Scotch roost; but I would know well enough how to fetch the youngster off the perch, if it were not for the cure he has done on the General's pickaninies."

Enough of this fell on Richard's ear to suggest hopes of deliverance, which were increased when he was shortly afterwards removed to a separate ward, a place much more decent in appearance, and inhabited only by two patients, who seemed petty officers. Although sensible that he had no illness, save that weakness which succeeds violent agitation, he deemed it wisest to suffer himself still to be treated as a patient, in consideration that he should thus remain under his comrade's superintendence. Yet while preparing to avail himself of Hartley's good offices, the prevailing reflection of his secret bosom was the ungrateful sentiment, "Had Heaven no other means of saving me than by the hands of him I like least on the face of the earth?"

Meanwhile, ignorant of the ungrateful sentiments of his comrade, and indeed wholly indifferent how he felt towards him, Hartley proceeded in doing him such service as was in his power, without any other object than the discharge of his own duty as a man and as a Christian. The manner in which he became qualified to render his comrade assistance, requires some short explanation.

Our story took place at a period, when the Directors of the East India Company, with that hardy and persevering policy which has raised to such a height the British Empire in the East, had determined to send a large reinforcement of European troops to the support of their power in India, then threatened by the kingdom of Mysore, of which the celebrated Hyder Ali had usurped the government, after dethroning his master. Considerable difficulty was found in obtaining recruits for this service. Those who might have been otherwise disposed to be soldiers, were afraid of the climate, and of the species of banishment which the engagement implied; and doubted also how far the engagements of the Company might be faithfully observed towards them, when they were removed from the protection of the British laws. For these and other reasons, the military service of the King was preferred, and that of the Company could only procure the worst recruits, although their zealous agents scrupled not to employ the worst means. Indeed the practice of kidnapping, or crimping, as it is technically called, was at that time general, whether for the colonies, or even for the King's troops; and as the agents employed in such transactions must be of course entirely unscrupulous, there was not only much villainy committed in the direct prosecution of the trade, but it gave rise incidentally to remarkable cases of robbery, and even murder. Such atrocities were of course concealed from the authorities for whom the levies were made, and the necessity of obtaining soldiers for the Company's service made men, whose conduct was otherwise unexceptionable, averse to looking closely into the mode in which their recruiting service was conducted.

The principal depôt of the troops which were by these means assembled, was in the Isle of Wight, where the season proving unhealthy, and the men themselves being many of them of a bad habit of body, a fever of a malignant character broke out amongst them, and speedily crowded with patients the military hospital, of which Mr Seelencooper, himself an old and experienced crimp and kidnapper, had obtained the superintendence. Irregularities began to take place also among the soldiers who remained healthy, and the necessity of subjecting them to some discipline before they sailed was so evident, that several officers of the Company's naval service expressed their belief that otherwise there would be dangerous mutinies on the passage.

To remedy the first of these evils, the Court of Directors sent down to the island such of their medical servants whose ships were not ready to sail, amongst whom was Hartley, whose qualifications had been amply certified by a medical board, before which he had passed an examination, besides his possessing a diploma from the University of Edinburgh as M.D.

To enforce the discipline of their soldiers, the Court committed full powers to one of their own body, General Witherington. The General was an officer who had distinguished himself highly in their service. He had returned from India five or six years before, with a large fortune, which he had rendered much greater by an advantageous marriage with a rich heiress. The General and his lady went little into society, but seemed to live entirely for their infant family, three in number, being two boys and a girl. Although he had retired from the service, he willingly undertook the temporary charge committed to him, and taking a house at a considerable distance from the town of Ryde, he proceeded to enroll the troops into separate bodies, appoint officers of capacity to each, and by regular training and discipline, gradually to bring them into something resembling good order. He heard their complaints of ill usage in the articles of provisions and appointments, and did them upon all occasions the strictest justice, save that he was never known to restore one recruit to his freedom from the service, however unfairly or even illegally his attestation might have been obtained.

"It is none of my business," said General Witherington, "how you became soldiers—soldiers I found you, and soldiers I leave you. But I will take especial care, that as soldiers you shall have everything, to a penny or a pin's head, that you are justly entitled to." He went to work without fear or favour, reported many abuses to the Board of Directors, had several officers, commissaries, &c. removed from the service, and made his name as great a terror to the peculators at home, as it had been to the enemies of Britain in Hindostan.

Captain Seelencooper, and his associates in the Hospital department, heard and trembled, fearing that their turn should come next; but the General, who elsewhere examined all with his own eyes, showed a reluctance to visit the Hospital in person. Public report industriously imputed this to fear of infection. Such was certainly the motive; though it was not fear for his own safety that influenced General Witherington, but he dreaded lest he should carry the infection home to the nursery, on which he doated. The fears of his lady were yet more unreasonably sensitive; she would scarcely suffer the children to walk abroad, if the wind but blew from the quarter where the Hospital was situated.

But Providence baffles the precautions of mortals. In a walk across the fields, chosen as the most sheltered and sequestered, the children, with their train of Eastern and European attendants, met a woman who carried a child that was recovering from the small-pox. The anxiety of the father, joined to some religious scruples on the mother's part, had postponed inoculation, which was then scarcely in general use. The infection caught like a quick-match, and ran like wildfire through all those in the family who had not previously had the disease. One of the General's children, the second boy, died, and two of the Ayas, or black female servants, had the same fate. The hearts of the father and mother would have been broken for the child they had lost, had not their grief been suspended by anxiety for the fate of those who lived, and who were confessed to be in imminent danger. They were like persons distracted, as the symptoms of the poor patients seemed gradually to resemble more nearly that of the child already lost.

While the parents were in this agony of apprehension, the General's principal servant, a native of Northumberland like himself, informed him one morning that there was a young man from the same county among the Hospital doctors, who had publicly blamed the mode of treatment observed towards the patients, and spoken of another which he had seen practised with eminent success.

"Some impudent quack," said the General, "who would force himself into business by bold assertions. Doctor Tourniquet and Doctor Lancelot are men of high reputation."

"Do not mention their reputation," said the mother, with a mother's impatience; "did they not let my sweet Reuben die? What avails the reputation of the physician, when the patient perisheth?"

"If his honour would but see Doctor Hartley," said Winter, turning half towards the lady, and then turning back again to his master. "He is a very decent young man, who, I am sure, never expected what he said to reach your honour's ears—And he is a native of Northumberland."

"Send a servant with a led horse; let the young man come hither instantly."

It is well known, that the ancient mode of treating the small-pox was to refuse to the patient everything which Nature urged him to desire; and, in particular, to confine him to heated rooms, beds loaded with blankets, and spiced wine, when Nature called for cold water and fresh air. A different mode of treatment had of late been adventured upon by some practitioners, who preferred reason to authority, and Gideon Grey had followed it for several years with extraordinary success.

When General Witherington saw Hartley, he was startled at his youth; but when he heard him modestly, but with confidence, state the difference of the two modes of treatment, and the *rationale* of his practice, he listened with the most serious attention. So did his lady, her streaming eyes turning from Hartley to her husband, as if to watch what impression the arguments of the former were making upon the latter. General Witherington was silent for a few minutes after Hartley had finished his exposition, and seemed buried in profound reflection. "To treat a fever," he said, "in a manner which tends to produce one, seems indeed to be adding fuel to fire."

"It is—it is," said the lady. "Let us trust this young man, General Witherington. We shall at least give our darlings the comforts of the fresh air and cold water, for which they are pining."

But the General remained undecided. "Your reasoning," he said to Hartley, "seems plausible; but still it is only hypothesis. What can you show to support your theory, in opposition to the general practice?"

"My own observation," replied the young man. "Here is a memorandum book of medical cases which I have witnessed—it contains twenty cases of small-pox, of which eighteen were recoveries."

"And the two others?" said the General.

"Terminated fatally," replied Hartley: "we can as yet but partially disarm this scourge of the human race."

"Young man," continued the General, "were I to say that a thousand gold mohrs were yours in case my children live under your treatment, what have you to peril in exchange?"

"My reputation," answered Hartley, firmly.

"And you could warrant on your reputation the recovery of your patients?"

"God forbid I should be so presumptuous! But I think I could warrant my using those means, which, with God's blessing, afford the fairest chance of a favourable result."

"Enough—you are modest and sensible, as well as bold, and I will trust you."

The lady, on whom Hartley's words and manner had made a great impression, and who was eager to discontinue a mode of treatment which subjected the patients to the greatest pain and privation, and had already proved unsuccessful, eagerly acquiesced, and Hartley was placed in full authority in the sick room.

Windows were thrown open, fires reduced or discontinued, loads of bed-clothes removed, cooling drinks superseded mulled wine and spices. The sick-nurses cried out murder. Doctors Tourniquet and Lancelot retired in disgust, menacing something like a general pestilence, in vengeance of what they termed rebellion against the aphorisms of Hippocrates. Hartley proceeded quietly and steadily, and the patients got into a fair road of recovery.

The young Northumbrian was neither conceited nor artful; yet, with all his plainness of character, he could not but know the influence which a successful physician obtains over the parents of the children whom he has saved from the grave, and especially before the cure is actually completed. He resolved to use this influence in behalf of his old companion, trusting that the military tenacity of General Witherington would give way, in consideration of the obligation so lately conferred upon him.

On his way to the General's house, which was at present his constant place of residence, he examined the packet which Middlemas had put into his hand. It contained the picture of Menie Grey, plainly set, and the ring, with brilliants, which Doctor Grey had given to Richard, as his mother's last gift. The first of these tokens extracted from honest Hartley a sigh, perhaps a tear of sad remembrance. "I fear," he said, "she has not chosen worthily; but she shall be happy, if I can make her so."

Arrived at the residence of General Witherington, our Doctor went first to the sick apartment, and then carried to their parents the delightful account that the recovery of the children might be considered as certain. "May the God of Israel bless thee, young man!" said the lady, trembling with emotion; "thou hast wiped the tear from the eye of the despairing mother. And yet—alas! alas! still it must flow when I think of my cherub Reuben. Oh! Mr Hartley, why did we not know you a week sooner?—my darling had not then died."

"God gives and takes away, my lady," answered Hartley; "and you must remember, that two are restored to you out of three. It is far from certain, that the treatment I have used towards the convalescents would have brought through their brother; for the case, as reported to me, was of a very inveterate description."

"Doctor," said Witherington, his voice testifying more emotion than he usually or willingly gave way to, "you can comfort the sick in spirit, as well as the sick in body.—But it is time we settle our wager. You betted your reputation, which remains with you, increased by all the credit due to your eminent success, against a thousand gold mohrs, the value of which you will find in that pocket-book."

"General Witherington," said Hartley, "you are wealthy, and entitled to be generous—I am poor, and not entitled to decline whatever may be, even in a liberal sense, a compensation for my professional attendance. But there is a bound to extravagance, both in giving and accepting; and I must not hazard the newly acquired reputation with which you flatter me, by giving room to have it said, that I fleeced the parents, when their feelings were all afloat with anxiety for their children. Allow me to divide this large sum; one half I will thankfully retain, as a most liberal recompense for my labour; and if you still think you owe me anything, let me have it in the advantage of your good opinion and countenance."

"If I acquiesce in your proposal, Doctor Hartley," said the General, reluctantly receiving back a part of the contents of the pocket-book, "it is because I hope to serve you with my interest, even better than with my purse."

"And, indeed, sir," replied Hartley, "it was upon your interest that I am just about to make a small claim."

The General and his lady spoke both in the same breath, to assure him his boon was granted before asked.

"I am not so sure of that," said Hartley; "for it respects a point on which I have heard say, that your Excellency is rather inflexible—the discharge of a recruit."

"My duty makes me so," replied the General—"You know the sort of fellows that we are obliged to content ourselves with—they get drunk—grow pot-valiant—enlist over night, and repent next morning. If I were to dismiss all those who pretend to have been trepanned, we should have few volunteers remain behind. Every one has some idle story of the promises of a swaggering Sergeant Kite—It is impossible to attend to them.—But let me hear yours, however."

"Mine is a very singular case. The party has been robbed of a thousand pounds."

"A recruit for this service possessing a thousand pounds! Pshaw! My dear Doctor, depend upon it that the fellow has gulled you. Bless my heart, would a man who had a thousand pounds think of enlisting as a private sentinel?"

"He had no such thoughts," answered Hartley. "He was persuaded by the rogue whom he trusted, that he was to have a commission."

"Then this friend must have been Tom Hillary, or the devil; for no other could possess so much cunning and impudence. He will certainly find his way to the gallows at last. Still this story of the thousand pounds seems a touch even beyond Tom Hillary. What reason have you to think that this fellow ever had such a sum of money?"

"I have the best reason to know it for certain," answered Hartley; "he and I served our time together, under the same excellent master; and when he came of age, not liking the profession which he had studied, and obtaining possession of his little fortune, he was deceived by the promises of this same Hillary."

"Who has had him locked up in our well-ordered Hospital yonder?" said the General.

"Even so, please your Excellency," replied Hartley; "not, I think, to cure him of any complaint, but to give him the opportunity of catching one which will silence all inquiries."

"The matter shall be closely looked into. But how miserably careless the young man's friends must have been, to let a raw lad go out into the world with such a companion and guide as Tom Hillary, and such a sum as a thousand pounds in his pocket. His parents had better have knocked him on the head. It certainly was not done like canny Northumberland, as my servant Winter calls it."

"The youth must indeed have had strangely hard-hearted, or careless parents," said Mrs Witherington, in accents of pity.

"He never knew them, madam," said Hartley; "there was a mystery on the score of his birth. A cold, unwilling, and almost unknown hand, dealt him out his portion when he came of lawful age, and he was pushed into the world like a bark forced from shore, without rudder, compass, or pilot."

Here General Witherington involuntarily looked to his lady, while, guided by a similar impulse, her looks were turned upon him. They exchanged a momentary glance of deep and peculiar meaning, and then the eyes of both were fixed on the ground.

"Were you brought up in Scotland?" said the lady, addressing herself, in a faltering voice, to Hartley—"And what was your master's name?"

"I served my apprenticeship with Mr Gideon Grey of the town of Middlemas," said Hartley.

"Middlemas! Grey!" repeated the lady, and fainted away.

Hartley offered the succours of his profession; the husband flew to support her head, and the instant that Mrs Witherington began to recover, he whispered to her, in a tone betwixt entreaty and warning, "Zilia, beware—beware!"

Some imperfect sounds which she had begun to frame, died away upon her tongue.

"Let me assist you to your dressing-room, my love," said her obviously anxious husband.

She arose with the action of an automaton, which moves at the touch of a spring, and half hanging upon her husband, half dragging herself on by her own efforts, had nearly reached the door of the room, when Hartley following, asked if he could be of any service.

"No, sir," said the General sternly; "this is no case for a stranger's interference; when you are wanted I will send for you."

Hartley stepped back, on receiving a rebuff in a tone so different from that which General Witherington had used towards him in their previous intercourse, and disposed, for the first time, to give credit to public report, which assigned to that gentleman, with several good qualities, the character of a very proud and haughty man. Hitherto, he thought, I have seen him tamed by sorrow and anxiety, now the mind is regaining its natural tension. But he must in decency interest himself for this unhappy Middlemas.

The General returned into the apartment a minute or two afterwards, and addressed Hartley in his usual tone of politeness, though apparently still under an embarrassment, which he in vain endeavoured to conceal.

"Mrs Witherington is better," he said, "and will be glad to see you before dinner. You dine with us, I hope?"

Hartley bowed.

"Mrs Witherington is rather subject to this sort of nervous fit, and she has been much harassed of late by grief and apprehension. When she recovers from them, it is a few minutes before she can collect her ideas, and during such intervals—to speak very confidentially to you, my dear Doctor Hartley,—she speaks sometimes about imaginary events which have never happened, and sometimes about distressing occurrences in an early period of life. I am not, therefore, willing that any one but myself, or her old attendant Mrs Lopez, should be with her on such occasions."

Hartley admitted that a certain degree of light-headedness was often the consequence of nervous fits.

The General proceeded. "As to this young man—this friend of yours—this Richard Middlemas—did you not call him so?"

"Not that I recollect," answered Hartley; "but your Excellency has hit upon his name."

"That is odd enough—Certainly you said something about Middlemas?" replied General Witherington.

"I mentioned the name of the town," said Hartley.

"Ay, and I caught it up as the name of the recruit—I was indeed occupied at the moment by my anxiety about my wife. But this

Middlemas, since such is his name, is a wild young fellow, I suppose?"

"I should do him wrong to say so, your Excellency. He may have had his follies like other young men; but his conduct has, so far as I know, been respectable; but, considering we lived in the same house, we were not very intimate."

"That is bad—I should have liked him—that is—it would have been happy for him to have had a friend like you. But I suppose you studied too hard for him. He would be a soldier, ha?—Is he good-looking?"

"Remarkably so," replied Hartley; "and has a very prepossessing manner."

"Is his complexion dark or fair?" asked the General.

"Rather uncommonly dark," said Hartley,—"darker, if I may use the freedom, than your Excellency's."

"Nay, then he must be a black ouzel indeed!—Does he understand languages?"

"Latin and French tolerably well."

"Of course he cannot fence or dance?"

"Pardon me, sir, I am no great judge; but Richard is reckoned to do both with uncommon skill."

"Indeed!—Sum this up, and it sounds well. Handsome, accomplished in exercises, moderately learned, perfectly well-bred, not unreasonably wild. All this comes too high for the situation of a private sentinel. He must have a commission, Doctor—entirely for your sake."

"Your Excellency is generous."

"It shall be so; and I will find means to make Tom Hillary disgorge his plunder, unless he prefers being hanged, a fate he has long deserved. You cannot go back to the Hospital today. You dine with us, and you know Mrs Witherington's fears of infection; but to-morrow find out your friend. Winter shall see him equipped with everything needful. Tom Hillary shall repay advances, you know; and he must be off with the first detachment of the recruits, in the Middlesex India-man, which sails from the Downs on Monday fortnight; that is, if you think him fit for the voyage. I dare say the poor fellow is sick of the Isle of Wight."

"Your Excellency will permit the young man to pay his respects to you before his departure?"

"To what purpose, sir?" said the General, hastily and peremptorily; but instantly added, "You are right—I should like to see him. Winter shall let him know the time, and take horses to fetch him hither. But he must have been out of the Hospital for a day or two; so the sooner you can set him at liberty the better. In the meantime, take him to your own lodgings, Doctor; and do not let him form any intimacies with the officers, or any others, in this place, where he may light on another Hillary."

Had Hartley been as well acquainted as the reader with the circumstances of young Middlemas's birth, he might have drawn decisive conclusions from the behaviour of General Witherington, while his comrade was the topic of conversation. But as Mr Grey and Middlemas himself were both silent on the subject, he knew little of it but from general report, which his curiosity had never induced him to scrutinize minutely. Nevertheless, what he did apprehend interested him so much, that he resolved upon trying a little experiment, in which he thought there could be no great harm. He placed on his finger the remarkable ring intrusted to his care by Richard Middlemas, and endeavoured to make it conspicuous in approaching Mrs Witherington; taking care, however, that this occurred during her husband's absence. Her eyes had no sooner caught a sight of the gem, than they became riveted to it, and she begged a nearer sight of it, as strongly resembling one which she had given to a friend. Taking the ring from his finger, and placing it in her emaciated hand, Hartley informed her it was the property of the friend in whom he had just been endeavouring to interest the General. Mrs Witherington retired in great emotion, but next day summoned Hartley to a private interview, the particulars of which, so far as are necessary to be known, shall be afterwards related.

On the succeeding day after these important discoveries, Middlemas, to his great delight, was rescued from his seclusion in the Hospital, and transferred to his comrade's lodgings in the town of Ryde, of which Hartley himself was a rare inmate; the anxiety of Mrs Witherington detaining him at the General's house, long after his medical attendance might have been dispensed with.

Within two or three days a commission arrived for Richard Middlemas, as a lieutenant in the service of the East India Company. Winter, by his master's orders, put the wardrobe of the young officer on a suitable footing; while Middlemas, enchanted at finding himself at once emancipated from his late dreadful difficulties, and placed under the protection of a man of such importance as the General, obeyed implicitly the hints transmitted to him by Hartley, and enforced by Winter, and abstained from going into public, or forming acquaintances with any one. Even Hartley himself he saw seldom; and, deep as were his obligations, he did not perhaps greatly regret the absence of one, whose presence always affected him with a sense of humiliation and abasement.

Chapter Nine

THE EVENING before he was to sail for the Downs, where the Middlesex lay ready to weigh anchor, the new lieutenant was summoned by Winter to attend him to the General's residence, at once to be introduced to his patron, to thank him, and to bid him farewell. On the road, the old man took the liberty of schooling his companion concerning the respect which he ought to pay to his master, "who was, though a kind and generous man as ever came from Northumberland, extremely rigid in punctiliously exacting the degree of honour which was his due."

While they were advancing towards the house, the General and his wife expected their arrival with breathless anxiety. They were seated in a superb drawing-room, the General behind a large chandelier, which, shaded opposite to his face, threw all the light to the other side of the table, so that he could observe any person placed there, without becoming the subject of observation in turn. On a heap of cushions, wrapped in a glittering drapery of gold and silver muslins, mingled with shawls, a luxury which was then a novelty in Europe, sate, or rather reclined, his lady, who, past the full meridian of beauty, retained charms enough to distinguish her as a very fine woman, though her mind seemed occupied by the deepest emotion.

"Zilia," said her husband, "you are unable for what you have undertaken—take my advice—retire—you shall know all and everything that passes—but retire. To what purpose should you cling to the idle wish of beholding for a moment a being whom you can never again look upon?"

"Alas!" answered the lady, "and is not your declaration, that I shall never see him more, a sufficient reason that I should wish to see him now—should wish to imprint on my memory the features and the form which I am never again to behold while we are in the body? Do not, my Richard, be more cruel than was my poor father, even when his wrath was in its bitterness. He let me look upon my infant, and its cherub face dwelt with me, and was my comfort, among the years of unutterable sorrow in which my youth wore away."

"It is enough, Zilia—you have desired this boon—I have granted it —and, at whatever risk, my promise shall be kept. But think how much depends on this fatal secret—your rank and estimation in society—my honour interested that that estimation should remain uninjured. Zilia, the moment that the promulgation of such a secret gives prudes and scandal-mongers a right to treat you with scorn, will be fraught with unutterable misery, perhaps with bloodshed and death, should a man dare to take up the rumour."

"You shall be obeyed, my husband," answered Zilia, "in all that the frailness of nature will permit.—But oh, God of my fathers, of what clay hast thou fashioned us, poor mortals, who dread so much the shame which follows sin, yet repent so little for the sin itself!" In a minute afterwards steps were heard—the door opened—Winter announced Lieutenant Middlemas, and the unconscious son stood before his parents.

Witherington started involuntarily up, but immediately constrained himself to assume the easy deportment with which a superior receives a dependent, and which, in his own case, was usually mingled with a certain degree of hauteur. The mother had less command of herself. She too sprung up, as if with the intention of throwing herself on the neck of her son, for whom she had travailed and sorrowed. But the warning glance of her husband arrested her, as if by magic, and she remained standing, with her beautiful head and neck somewhat advanced, her hands clasped together, and extended forwards in the attitude of motion, but motionless, nevertheless, as a marble statue, to which the sculptor has given all the appearance of life, but cannot impart its powers. So strange a gesture and posture might have excited the young officer's surprise; but the lady stood in the shade, and he was so intent in looking upon his patron, that he was scarce even conscious of Mrs Witherington's presence.

"I am happy in this opportunity," said Middlemas, observing that the General did not speak, "to return my thanks to General Witherington, to whom they never can be sufficiently paid."

The sound of his voice, though uttering words so indifferent, seemed to dissolve the charm which kept his mother motionless. She sighed deeply, relaxed the rigidity of her posture, and sunk back on the cushions from which she had started up. Middlemas turned a look towards her at the sound of the sigh, and the rustling of her drapery. The General hastened to speak.

"My wife, Mr Middlemas, has been unwell of late—your friend, Mr Hartley, might mention it to you—an affection of the nerves."

Mr Middlemas was, of course, sorry and concerned.

"We have had distress in our family, Mr Middlemas, from the ultimate and heart-breaking consequences of which we have escaped by the skill of your friend, Mr Hartley. We will be happy if it is in our power to repay a part of our obligations in services to his friend and protegé, Mr Middlemas."

"I am only acknowledged as *his* protegé, then," *thought* Richard; but he *said*, "Every one must envy his friend, in having had the distinguished good fortune to be of use to General Witherington and his family."

"You have received your commission, I presume. Have you any particular wish or desire respecting your destination?"

"No, may it please your Excellency," answered Middlemas. "I suppose Hartley would tell your Excellency my unhappy state—that I am an orphan, deserted by the parents who cast me on the wide world, an outcast about whom nobody knows or cares, except to desire that I should wander far enough, and live obscurely enough, not to disgrace them by their connexion with me."

Zilia wrung her hands as he spoke, and drew her muslin veil closely around her head, as if to exclude the sounds which excited her mental agony.

"Mr Hartley was not particularly communicative about your affairs," said the General; "nor do I wish to give you the pain of entering into them. What I desire to know is, if you are pleased with your destination to Madras?"

"Perfectly, please your Excellency—anywhere, so that there is no chance of meeting the villain Hillary."

"Oh! Hillary's services are too necessary in the purlieus of Saint Giles's, the Lowlights of Newcastle, and such like places, where human carrion can be picked up, to be permitted to go to India. However, to show you the knave has some grace, there are the notes of which you were robbed. You will find them the very same paper which you lost, except a small sum which the rogue had spent, but which a friend has made up, in compassion for your sufferings." Richard Middlemas sunk on one knee, and kissed the hand which restored him to independence.

"Pshaw!" said the General, "you are a silly young man;" but he withdrew not his hand from his caresses. This was one of the occasions on which Dick Middlemas could be oratorical.

"O, my more than father," he said, "how much greater a debt do I owe to you than to the unnatural parents, who brought me into this world by their sin, and deserted me through their cruelty!"

Zilia, as she heard these cutting words, flung back her veil, raising it on both hands till it floated behind her like a mist, and then giving a faint groan, sunk down in a swoon. Pushing Middlemas from him with a hasty movement, General Witherington flew to his lady's assistance, and carried her in his arms, as if she had been a child, into the ante-room, where an old servant waited with the means of restoring suspended animation, which the unhappy husband too truly anticipated might be useful. These were hastily employed, and succeeded in calling the sufferer to life, but in a state of mental emotion that was terrible.

Her mind was obviously impressed by the last words which her son had uttered.—"Did you hear him, Richard!" she exclaimed, in accents terribly loud, considering the exhausted state of her strength —"Did you hear the words? It was Heaven speaking our condemnation by the voice of our own child. But do not fear, my Richard, do not weep! I will answer the thunder of Heaven with its own music."

She flew to a harpsichord which stood in the room, and, while the servant and master gazed on each other, as if doubting whether her senses were about to leave her entirely, she wandered over the keys, producing a wilderness of harmony, composed of passages recalled by memory, or combined by her own musical talent, until at length her voice and instrument united in one of those magnificent hymns in which her youth had praised her Maker, with voice and harp, like the Royal Hebrew who composed it. The tear ebbed insensibly from the eyes which she turned upwards—her vocal tones, combining with those of the instrument, rose to a pitch of brilliancy seldom attained by the most distinguished performers, and then sunk into a dying cadence, which fell, never again to arise,—for the songstress had died with her strain.

The horror of the distracted husband may be conceived, when all efforts to restore life proved totally ineffectual. Servants were dispatched for medical men—Hartley, and every other who could be found. The General precipitated himself into the apartment they had so lately left, and in his haste ran against Middlemas, who, at the sound of the music from the adjoining apartment, had naturally approached nearer to the door, and, surprised and startled by the sort of clamour, hasty steps, and confused voices which ensued, had remained standing there, endeavouring to ascertain the cause of so much disorder.

The sight of the unfortunate young man wakened the General's stormy passions to frenzy. He seemed to recognise his son only as the cause of his wife's death. He seized him by the collar, and shook him violently as he dragged him into the chamber of mortality.

"Come hither," he said, "thou for whom a life of lowest obscurity was too mean a fate—come hither, and look on the parents whom thou hast so much envied—whom thou hast so often cursed. Look at that pale emaciated form, a figure of wax, rather than flesh and blood— that is thy mother—that is the unhappy Zilia de Monçada, to whom thy birth was the source of shame and misery, and to whom thy ill-omened presence hath now brought death itself. And behold me—" he pushed the lad from him, and stood up erect, looking wellnigh in gesture and figure the apostate spirit he described—"Behold me—"

he said; "see you not my hair streaming with sulphur, my brow scathed with lightning?—I am the Arch-Fiend—I am the father whom you seek—I am the accursed Richard Tresham, the seducer of Zilia, and the father of her murderer!"

Hartley entered while this horrid scene was passing. All attention to the deceased, he instantly saw, would be thrown away; and understanding, partly from Winter, partly from the tenor of the General's frantic discourse, the nature of the disclosure which had occurred, he hastened to put an end, if possible, to the frightful and scandalous scene which had taken place. Aware how delicately the General felt on the subject of reputation, he assailed him with remonstrances on such conduct, in presence of so many witnesses. But the mind had ceased to answer to that once powerful key-note.

"I care not if the whole world hear my sin and my punishment," said Witherington. "It shall not be again said of me, that I fear shame more than I repent sin. I feared shame only for Zilia, and Zilia is dead!"

"But her memory, General—spare the memory of your wife, in which the character of your children is involved."

"I have no children!" said the desperate and violent man. "My Reuben is gone to Heaven, to prepare a lodging for the angel who has now escaped from earth in a flood of harmony, which can only be equalled where she is gone. The other two cherubs will not survive their mother. I shall be, nay, I already feel myself, a childless man."

"Yet I am your son," replied Middlemas, in a tone sorrowful, but at the same time tinged with sullen resentment—"Your son by your wedded wife. Pale as she lies there, I call upon you both to acknowledge my rights, and all who are present to bear witness to them."

"Wretch!" exclaimed the maniac father, "canst thou think of thine own sordid rights in the midst of death and frenzy? My son!—thou art the fiend who hast occasioned my wretchedness in this world, and who will share my eternal misery in the next. Hence from my sight, and my curse go with thee!"

His eyes fixed on the ground, his arms folded on his breast, the haughty and dogged spirit of Middlemas yet seemed to meditate reply. But Hartley, Winter, and other bystanders interfered, and forced him from the apartment. As they endeavoured to remonstrate with him, he twisted himself out of their grasp, ran to the stables, and seizing the first saddled horse that he found, out of many that had been in haste got ready to seek for assistance, he threw himself on its back, and rode furiously off. Hartley was about to mount and follow him; but Winter and the other domestics threw themselves around him, and implored him not to desert their unfortunate master, at a time when the influence which he had acquired over him might be the only restraint on the violence of his passions.

"He had a *coup de soleil* in India," whispered Winter, "and is capable of anything in his fits. These cowards cannot control him, and I am old and feeble."

Satisfied that General Witherington was a greater object of compassion than Middlemas, whom besides he had no hope of overtaking, and who he believed was safe in his own keeping, however violent might be his present emotions, Hartley returned where the greater emergency demanded his immediate care.

He found the unfortunate General contending with the domestics, who endeavoured to prevent his making his way to the apartment where his children slept, and exclaiming furiously—"Rejoice, my treasures—rejoice!—He has fled who would proclaim your father's crime, and your mother's dishonour!—He has fled, never to return, whose life has been the death of one parent, and the ruin of another! —Courage, my children, your father is with you—he will make his way to you through an hundred obstacles."

The domestics, intimidated and undecided, were giving way to him, when Adam Hartley approached, and placing himself before the unhappy man, fixed his eye firmly on the General's, while he said in a low but stern voice—"Madman, would you kill your children?"

The General seemed staggered in his resolution, but still attempted to rush past him. But Hartley, seizing him by the collar of his coat on each side, "You are my prisoner," he said; "I command you to follow me."

"Ha! prisoner and for high treason? Dog, thou hast met thy death!"

The distracted man drew a poniard from his bosom, and Hartley's strength and resolution might not perhaps have saved his life, had not Winter mastered the General's right hand, and contrived to disarm him.

"I am your prisoner, then," he said; "use me civilly—and let me see my wife and children."

"You shall see them to-morrow," said Hartley; "follow us instantly, and without the least resistance."

General Witherington followed like a child, with the air of one who is suffering for a cause in which he glories.

"I am not ashamed of my principles," he said—"I am willing to die for my King."

Without exciting his frenzy, by contradicting the fantastic ideas which occupied his imagination, Hartley continued to maintain over his patient the ascendency he had acquired. He caused him to be led to his apartment, and beheld him suffer himself to be put to bed.

Administering then a strong composing draught, and causing a servant to sleep in the room, he watched the unfortunate man till dawn of morning.

General Witherington awoke in his full senses, and apparently conscious of his real situation, which he testified by low groans, sobs, and tears. When Hartley drew near his bedside, he knew him perfectly, and said, "Do not fear me—the fit is over—leave me now, and see after yonder unfortunate. Let him leave Britain so soon as possible, and go where his fate calls him, and where we can never meet more. Winter knows my ways, and will take care of me."

Winter gave the same advice. "I can answer," he said, "for my master's security at present; but in Heaven's name, prevent his ever meeting again with that obdurate young man!"

Chapter Ten

Well, then, the world's mine oyster,
Which I with sword will open.
Merry Wives of Windsor

WHEN ADAM HARTLEY arrived at his lodgings in the sweet little town of Ryde, his first inquiries were after his comrade. He had arrived last night late, man and horse all in a foam. He made no reply to any questions about supper or the like, but snatching a candle, ran up stairs into his apartment, and shut and double-locked the door. The servants only supposed, that, being something intoxicated, he had ridden hard, and was unwilling to expose himself.

Hartley went to the door of his chamber, not without some apprehensions; and after knocking and calling more than once, received at length the welcome return, "Who is there?"

On Hartley announcing himself, the door opened, and Middlemas appeared, well dressed, and with his hair arranged and powdered; although, from the appearance of the bed, it had not been slept in on the preceding night, and Richard's countenance, haggard and ghastly, seemed to bear witness to the same fact. It was, however, with an affectation of indifference that he spoke.

"I congratulate you on your improvement in worldly knowledge, Adam. It is wise to desert the poor heir, and stick by him that is in immediate possession of the wealth."

"I staid last night at General Witherington's," answered Hartley, "because he is extremely ill."

"Tell him to repent of his sins, then," said Richard. "Old Grey used to say, a doctor had as good a title to give ghostly advice as a parson.

Do you remember Doctor Dulberry, the minister, calling him an interloper?"

"I am surprised at this style of language from one in your circumstances."

"Why, ay," said Middlemas, with a bitter smile,—"it would be difficult to most men to keep up their spirits, after gaining and losing father, mother, and a good inheritance, all in the same day. But I had always a turn for philosophy."

"I really do not understand you, Mr Middlemas."

"Why, I found my parents yesterday, did I not?" answered the young man. "My mother, as you know, had waited but that moment to die, and my father to become distracted; and I conclude both were contrived purposely to cheat me of my inheritance, as he has taken up such a prejudice against me."

"Inheritance?" repeated Hartley, bewildered by Richard's calmness, and half suspecting that the insanity of the father was hereditary in the family. "In Heaven's name, recollect yourself, and get rid of these hallucinations. What inheritance are you dreaming of?"

"That of my mother, to be sure, who must have inherited old Monçada's wealth—and to whom should it descend, save to her children?—I am the eldest of them—that fact cannot be denied."

"But consider, Richard—recollect yourself."

"I do," said Richard; "and what then?"

"Then you cannot but remember," said Hartley, "that unless there was a will in your favour, your birth prevents you from inheriting."

"You are mistaken, sir, I am legitimate.—Yonder sickly brats, whom you rescued from the grave, are not more legitimate than I am. —Yes! they could not allow the air of Heaven to breathe on them— me they committed to the winds and the waves—I am nevertheless their lawful child, as well as those puling offspring of advanced age and decayed health. I saw them, Adam—Winter showed the nursery to me while they were gathering courage to receive me in the drawing-room. There they lay, the children of predilection, the riches of the East expended that they might sleep soft, and wake to magnificence. I, the eldest brother—the heir—I stood beside their bed in the borrowed dress which I had so lately exchanged for the rags of an hospital. Their couches breathed the richest perfumes, while I was reeking from a pest-house; and I—I repeat it—the heir, the produce of their earliest and best love, was thus treated. No wonder that my look was that of a basilisk."

"You speak as if you were possessed with an evil spirit," said Hartley; "or else you labour under a strange delusion."

"You think those only are legally married over whom a drowsy parson has read the ceremony from a dog's-eared prayer-book? It may be so in your English law—but Scotland makes Love himself the priest. A vow betwixt a fond couple, the blue heaven alone witnessing, will protect a confiding girl against the perjury of a fickle swain, as much as if a Dean had performed the rites in the loftiest cathedral in England. Nay more; if the child of love be acknowledged by the father at the time when he is baptized—if he present the mother to strangers of respectability as his wife, the laws of Scotland will not allow him to retract the justice which has, in these actions, been done to the female whom he has wronged, or the offspring of their mutual love. This General Tresham, or Witherington, treated my unhappy mother as his wife before Grey and others, quartered her as such in the family of a respectable man, gave her the same name by which he himself chose to pass for the time. He presented me to the priest as his lawful offspring; and the law of Scotland, benevolent to the helpless child, will not allow him now to disown what he so formally admitted. I know my rights, and am determined to claim them."

"You do not then intend to go on board the Middlesex? Think a little—you will lose your voyage and your commission."

"I will save my birth-right," answered Middlemas. "When I thought of going to India, I knew not my parents, or how to make good the rights which I had through them. That riddle is solved. I am entitled to at least a third of Monçada's estate, which, by Winter's account, is considerable. But for you, and your mode of treating the small-pox, I should have had the whole. Little did I think, when old Grey was likely to have his wig pulled off, for putting out fires, throwing open windows, and exploding whisky and water, that the new system was to cost me so many thousand pounds."

"You are determined, then," said Hartley, "on this wild course?"

"I know my rights, and am determined to make them available," answered the obstinate youth.

"Mr Richard Middlemas, I am sorry for you."

"Mr Adam Hartley, I beg to know why I am honoured by your sorrow?"

"I pity you," answered Hartley, "both for the obstinacy of selfishness, which can think of wealth, after the scene you saw last night, and for the idle vision which leads you to believe that you can obtain possession of it."

"Selfish am I!" cried Middlemas; "why, I am a dutiful son, labouring to clear the memory of a calumniated mother—And am I a visionary?—Why, it was to this hope that I awakened, when old Monçada's letter to Grey, devoting me to perpetual obscurity, first roused me to a sense of my situation, and dispelled the dreams of my childhood. Do you think that I would ever have submitted to the drudgery which I shared with you, but that, by doing so, I kept in view the only traces of these unnatural parents, by means of which I proposed to introduce myself to their notice, and, if necessary, enforce the rights of a legitimate child? The silence and death of Monçada broke my plans, and it was then only I reconciled myself to the thoughts of India."

"You were very young, to have known so much of the Scottish law, at the time when we were first acquainted," said Hartley. "But I can guess your instructor."

"No less authority than Tom Hillary's," replied Middlemas. "His good counsel on that head is a reason why I do not now prosecute him to the gallows."

"I judged as much," replied Hartley; "for I heard him, before I left Middlemas, debating the point with Mr Lawford; and I recollect perfectly, that he stated the law to be such as you now lay down."

"And what said Lawford in answer?" demanded Middlemas.

"He admitted," replied Hartley, "that in circumstances where the case was doubtful, such presumptions of legitimacy might be admitted. But he said they were liable to be controlled by positive and precise testimony, as, for instance, the evidence of the mother declaring the illegitimacy of the child."

"But there can exist none such in my case," said Middlemas hastily, and with marks of alarm.

"I will not deceive you, Mr Middlemas, though I fear I cannot help giving you pain. I had yesterday a long conference with your mother, Mrs Witherington, in which she acknowledged you as her son, but a son born before marriage. This express declaration will, therefore, put an end to the suppositions on which you ground your hopes. If you please you may hear the contents of her declaration, which I have in her own handwriting."

"Confusion! is the cup to be for ever dashed from my lips?" muttered Richard; but recovering his composure, by exertion of the self-command of which he possessed so large a portion, he desired Hartley to proceed with his communication. Hartley accordingly proceeded to inform him of the particulars preceding his birth, and those which followed after it; while Middlemas, seated on a sea-chest, listened with inimitable composure to a tale which went to root up the flourishing hopes of wealth which he had lately so fondly entertained.

Zilia de Monçada was the only child of a Portuguese Jew of great wealth, who had come to London, in prosecution of his commerce. Among the few Christians who frequented his house, and occasionally his table, was Richard Tresham, a gentleman of a high Northumbrian family, deeply engaged in the service of Charles Edward during his short invasion, and though holding a commission in the Portuguese service, still an object of suspicion to the British government, on account of his well-known courage and Jacobitical principles. The high-bred elegance of this gentleman, together with his complete acquaintance with the Portuguese language and manners, had won the intimacy of old Monçada, and, alas! the heart of the inexperienced Zilia, who, beautiful as an angel, had as little knowledge of the world and its wickedness as the lamb that is but a week old.

Tresham made his proposals to Monçada, perhaps in a manner which too evidently showed that he conceived the high-born Christian was degrading himself in asking an alliance with the wealthy Jew. Monçada rejected his proposals, forbade him his house, but could not prevent the lovers from meeting in private. Tresham made a dishonourable use of the opportunities which the poor Zilia so incautiously afforded, and the consequence was her ruin. The lover, however, had every purpose of righting the injury which he had inflicted, and, after various plans of secret marriage, which were rendered abortive by the difference of religion, and other circumstances, flight for Scotland was determined on. The hurry of the journey, the fear and anxiety to which Zilia was subject, brought on her confinement several weeks before the usual time, so that they were compelled to accept of the assistance and accommodation offered by Mr Grey. They had not been there many hours ere Tresham heard, by the medium of some sharp-sighted or keen-eared friend, that there were warrants out against him for treasonable practices. His correspondence with Charles Edward had become known to Monçada during the period of their friendship; he betrayed it in vengeance to the British cabinet, and warrants were issued, in which, at Monçada's request, his daughter's name was included. This might be of use, he apprehended, to enable him to separate his daughter from Tresham, should he find the fugitives actually married. How far he succeeded the reader already knows, as well as the precautions which he took to prevent the living evidence of his child's frailty from being known to exist. His daughter he carried with him, and subjected her to severe restraint, which her own reflections rendered doubly bitter. It would have completed his revenge, had the author of Zilia's misfortunes been brought to the scaffold for his political offences. But Tresham skulked among friends in the Highlands, and escaped until the affair blew over.

He afterwards entered into the East India Company's service, under his mother's name of Witherington, which concealed the Jacobite and rebel, until these terms were forgotten. His skill in military affairs soon raised him to riches and eminence. When he returned to

Britain, his first enquiries were after the family of Monçada. His fame, his wealth, and the late conviction that his daughter never would marry any but him who had her first love, induced the old man to give that encouragement to General Witherington, which he had always denied to the poor and outlawed Major Tresham; and the lovers, after having been fourteen years separated, were at length united in wedlock.

General Witherington eagerly concurred in the earnest wish of his father-in-law, that every remembrance of former events should be buried, by leaving the fruit of the early and unhappy intrigue suitably provided for, but in a distant and obscure situation. Zilia thought far otherwise. Her heart longed, with a mother's longing, towards the object of her first maternal tenderness, but she dared not place herself in opposition at once to the will of her father, and the decision of her husband. The former, his religious prejudices much effaced by his long residence in England, had given consent that she should conform to the established religion of her husband and his country,—the latter, haughty as we have described him, made it his pride to introduce the beautiful convert among his high-born kindred. The discovery of her former frailty would have proved a blow to her respectability, which he dreaded like death; and it could not long remain a secret from his wife, that in consequence of a severe illness in India, even his reason became occasionally shaken by anything which violently agitated his feelings. She had, therefore, acquiesced in patience and silence in the course of policy which Monçada had devised, and which her husband anxiously and warmly approved. Yet her thoughts, even when their marriage was blessed with other offspring, anxiously reverted to the banished and outcast child, who had first been clasped to the maternal bosom.

All these feelings, "subdued and cherished long," were set afloat in full tide by the unexpected discovery of this son, redeemed from a lot of extreme misery, and placed before his mother's imagination in circumstances so disastrous.

It was in vain that her husband assured her that he would secure the young man's prosperity, by his purse and his interest. She could not be satisfied, until she had herself done something to alleviate the doom of banishment to which her eldest-born was thus condemned. She was the more eager to do so, as she felt the extreme delicacy of her health, which was undermined by so many years of secret suffering.

Mrs Witherington was, in conferring her maternal bounty, naturally led to employ the agency of Hartley, the companion of her son, and to whom, since the recovery of her younger children, she almost looked up as to a tutelar deity. She placed in his hands a sum of

L.2000, which she had at her own unchallenged disposal, with a request, uttered in the fondest and most affectionate terms, that it might be applied to the service of Richard Middlemas in the way Hartley should think most useful to him. She assured him of further support, as it should be needed; and a note to the following purport was also intrusted to him, to be delivered when and where the prudence of Hartley should judge it proper to confide to him the secret of his birth.

"Oh, Benoni! Oh, child of my sorrow!" said this interesting document, "why should the eyes of thy unhappy mother have been permitted to look on thee, since her arms were denied the right to fold thee to her bosom? May the God of Jews and of Gentiles watch over thee, and guard thee! May he remove, in his good time, the darkness which rolls between me and the beloved of my heart—the first fruit of mine unhappy, nay, unhallowed affection. Do not—do not, my beloved!—think thyself a lonely exile, while thy mother's prayers arise for thee at sunrise and at sunset, to call down every blessing on thy head—to invoke every power in thy protection and defence. Seek not to see me —Oh, why must I say so!—but let me humble myself in the dust, since it is my own sin, my own folly, which I must blame—but seek not to see or speak with me—it might be the death of both. Confide thy thoughts to the excellent Hartley, who hath been the guardian angel of us all— even as the tribes of Israel had each their guardian angel. What thou shalt wish, and he shall advise in thy behalf, shall be done, if in the power of a mother—And the love of a mother! is it bounded by seas, or can deserts and distance measure its limits? Oh, child of my sorrow! Oh, Benoni! let thy spirit be with mine, as mine is with thee.
"Z. W."

All these arrangements being completed, the unfortunate lady next insisted with her husband that she should be permitted to see her son in that parting interview which terminated so fatally. Hartley, therefore, now discharged as her executor, the duty intrusted to him as her confidential agent.

"Surely," he thought, as, having finished his communication, he was about to leave the apartment, "surely the demons of Ambition and Avarice will unclose the talons which they have fixed upon this man, at a charm like this."

And indeed Richard's heart had been formed of the nether millstone, had he not been duly affected by these first and last tokens of his mother's affection. He leant his head upon a table, and his tears flowed plentifully. Hartley left him undisturbed for more than an hour, and on his return found him in nearly the same attitude in which he had left him.

"I regret to disturb you at this moment," he said, "but I have still a part of my duty to discharge. I must place in your possession the deposit which your mother made in my hands—and I must also remind you that time flies fast, and that you have scarce an hour or two to determine whether you will prosecute your Indian voyage or no, under the new view of circumstances which I have opened to you."

Middlemas took the bills which his mother had bequeathed him. As he raised his head, Hartley could observe that his face was stained with tears. Yet he counted over the money with mercantile accuracy; and though he assumed the pen for the purpose of writing a discharge with an air of inconsolable dejection, yet he drew it up in good set terms, like one who had his senses much at his command.

"And now," he said, in a mournful voice, "give me my mother's narrative."

Hartley almost started, and answered hastily, "You have the poor lady's letter, which was addressed to yourself—the narrative is addressed to me. It is my warrant for disposing of a large sum of money—it concerns the rights of third parties, and I cannot part with it."

"Surely, surely it were better to deliver it into my hands, were it but to weep over it," answered Middlemas. "My fortune, Hartley, has been very cruel. You see what my parents intended would have made me their undoubted heir; yet their purpose was disappointed by accident. And now my mother comes with well-meant fondness, and while she means to advance my fortune, furnishes evidence to destroy it.—Come, come, Hartley—you must be conscious that my mother wrote those details entirely for my information. I am the rightful owner, and insist on having them."

"I am sorry I must insist on refusing your demand," answered Hartley, putting the papers in his pocket. "You ought to consider, that if this communication has destroyed the idle and groundless hopes which you have indulged in, it has, at the same time, more than trebled your capital; and that if there are some hundreds or thousands in the world richer than yourself, there are many millions not half so well provided. Set a brave spirit, then, against your fortune, and do not doubt your success in life."

His words seemed to sink into the gloomy mind of Middlemas. He stood silent for a moment, and then answered with a mild and insinuating voice,—

"My dear Hartley, we have long been companions—you can have neither pleasure nor interest in ruining my hopes—you may find some in forwarding them. Monçada's fortune will enable me to allow five thousand pounds to the friend who should aid me."

"Good morning to you, Mr Middlemas," said Hartley, endeavouring to withdraw.

"One moment—one moment," said Middlemas, holding him by the button at the same time, "I meant to say ten thousand—and—and —marry whomsoever you like—I will not be your hinderance."

"You are a villain!" said Hartley, breaking from him, "and I always thought you so."

"And you," answered Middlemas, "are a fool, and I never thought you better.—Off he goes—Let him—the game has been played and lost—I must hedge my bets; India must be my back-play."

All was in readiness for his departure. A small vessel and a favouring gale conveyed him and several other military gentlemen to the Downs, where the Indiaman which was to transport them from Europe, lay ready for their reception.

His first feelings were sufficiently disconsolate. But accustomed from his infancy to conceal his internal thoughts, he appeared in the course of a week the gayest and best bred passenger who ever dared the long and weary space betwixt Old England and her Indian possessions. At Madras, where the sociable feelings of the resident inhabitants give ready way to enthusiasm in behalf of any stranger of agreeable qualities, he experienced that warm hospitality which distinguishes the British character in the East.

Middlemas was well received in company, and in the way of becoming an indispensable guest at every entertainment in the place, when the vessel, on board of which Hartley acted as surgeon's mate, arrived at the same settlement. The latter would not, from his situation, have been entitled to expect much civility and attention; but this disadvantage was made up by his possessing the most powerful introductions from General Witherington, and from other persons of weight in Leadenhall Street, the General's friends, to the principal inhabitants in the settlement. He found himself once more, therefore, moving in the same sphere with Middlemas, and under the alternative of living with him on decent and distant terms, or of breaking off with him altogether.

The first of these courses might perhaps have been the wisest; but the other was most congenial to the blunt and plain character of Hartley, who saw neither propriety nor comfort in maintaining a show of friendly intercourse, to hide contempt, and mutual dislike.

The circle at Fort St George was much more restricted at that time than it has been since. The coldness of the young men did not escape notice; it transpired that they had been once intimates and fellow-students; yet it was now found that they hesitated at accepting invitations to the same parties. Rumour assigned many different and incompatible reasons for this deadly breach, to which Hartley gave no attention whatever, while Lieutenant Middlemas took care to coun-tenance those which represented the cause of the quarrel most favourably to himself.

"A little bit of rivalry had taken place," he said, when pressed by gentlemen for an explanation; "he had only had the good luck to get further in the good graces of a fair lady than his friend Hartley, who had made a quarrel of it, as they saw. He thought it very silly to keep up spleen, at such a distance of time and space. He was sorry, more for the sake of the strangeness of the appearance of the thing than any-thing else, although his friend had really some very good points about him."

While these whispers were working their effect in society, they did not prevent Hartley from receiving the most flattering assurances of encouragement and official promotion from the Madras government, as opportunity should arise. Soon after, it was intimated to him that a medical appointment of a lucrative nature in a remote settlement was conferred on him, which removed him for some time from Madras and its neighbourhood.

Hartley accordingly sailed on his distant expedition; and it was observed, that after his departure, the character of Middlemas, as if some check had been removed, began to display itself in disagreeable colours. It was noticed that this young man, whose manners were so agreeable and so courteous during the first months after his arrival in India, began now to show symptoms of a haughty and overbearing spirit. He had adopted, for reasons which the reader may conjecture, but which appeared to be mere whim at Fort St George, the name of Tresham, in addition to that by which he had hitherto been distin-guished, and in this he persisted with an obstinacy, which belonged more to the pride than the craft of his character. The Lieutenant-Colonel of the regiment, an old cross-tempered martinet, did not choose to indulge the Captain (such was now the rank of Middlemas) in this humour.

"He knew no officer," he said, "by any name save that which he bore in his commission," and he Middlemas'd the Captain on all occasions.

One fatal evening, the Captain was so much provoked, as to intim-ate peremptorily, "that he knew his own name best."

"Why, Captain Middlemas," replied the Colonel, "it is not every child that knows its own father, so how can every man be so sure of his own name?"

The bow was drawn at a venture, but the shaft found the rent in the armour, and stung deeply. In spite of all the interposition which could be attempted, Middlemas insisted on challenging the Colonel, who could be persuaded to no apology.

"If Captain Middlemas," he said, "thought the cap fitted, he was welcome to wear it."

The result was a meeting, in which, after the parties had exchanged shots, the seconds tendered their mediation. It was rejected by Middlemas, who, at the second fire, had the misfortune to kill his commanding officer. In consequence, he was obliged to fly from the British settlements; for, being universally blamed for having pushed the quarrel to extremity, there was little doubt that the whole severity of military discipline would be exercised upon the delinquent. Middlemas, therefore, vanished from Fort St George, and, though the affair had made much noise at the time, was soon no longer talked of. It was understood, in general, that he had gone to seek that fortune at the court of some native prince, which he could no longer hope for in the British settlements.

Chapter Eleven

THREE YEARS passed away after the fatal rencounter mentioned in the last Chapter, and Doctor Hartley returning from his appointed mission, which was only temporary, received encouragement to settle in Madras in a medical capacity; and, upon having done so, soon had reason to think he had chosen a line in which he might rise to wealth and reputation. His practice was not confined to his countrymen, but much sought after among the natives, who, whatever may be their prejudices against the Europeans in other respects, universally esteem their superior powers in the medical profession. This lucrative branch of practice rendered it necessary that Hartley should make the Oriental languages his study, in order to hold communication with his patients without the intervention of an interpreter. He had enough of opportunities to practise as a linguist, for, in acknowledgment, as he used jocularly to say, of the large fees of the wealthy Moslemah and Hindoos, he attended the poor of all nations gratis, whenever he was called upon.

It so chanced, that one evening he was hastily summoned by a message from the Secretary of the Government, to attend a patient of consequence. "Yet he is, after all, only a Fakir," said the message.

"You will find him at the tomb of Cara Razi, the Mahomedan saint and doctor, about one coss from the fort. Inquire for him by the name of Barak el Hadgi. Such a patient promises no fees; but we know how little you care about the pagodas; and, besides, the Government is your paymaster on this occasion."

"That is the last matter to be thought on," said Hartley, and instantly repaired in his palanquin to the place pointed out to him.

The tomb of the Owliah, or Mahomedan Saint, Cara Razi, was a place held in much reverence by every good Musselman. It was situated in the centre of a grove of mangos and tamarind trees, and was built of red stone, having three domes, and minarets at every corner. There was a court in front, as usual, around which were cells constructed for the accommodation of the Fakirs who visited the tomb from motives of devotion, and made a longer or shorter residence there as they thought proper, subsisting upon the alms which the Faithful never fail to bestow on them in exchange for the benefit of their prayers. These devotees were engaged day and night in reading verses of the Koran before the tomb, which was constructed of white marble, inscribed with sentences from the book of the Prophet, and with the various titles conferred by the Koran upon the Supreme Being. Such a sepulchre, of which there are many, is, with its appendages and attendants, respected during wars and revolutions, and no less by Feringis, (Franks, that is,) and Hindoos, than by Mahomedans themselves. The Fakirs, in return, act as spies for all parties, and are often employed in secret missions of importance.

Complying with the Mahomedan custom, our friend Hartley laid aside his shoes at the gates of the holy precincts, and avoiding to give offence by approaching near to the tomb, he went up to the principal Moullah, or priest, who was distinguishable by the length of his beard, and the size of the large wooden beads, with which the Mahomedans, like the Catholics, keep register of their prayers. Such a person, venerable by his age, sanctity of character, and his real or supposed contempt of worldly pursuits and enjoyments, is regarded as the head of an establishment of this kind.

The Moullah is permitted by his situation to be more communicative with strangers than his younger brethren, who in the present instance remained with their eyes fixed on the Koran, muttering their recitations without noticing the European, or attending to what he said, as he inquired at their superior for Barak el Hadgi.

The Moullah was seated on the earth, from which he did not arise, or show any mark of reverence; nor did he interrupt the tale of his beads, which he continued to count assiduously while Hartley was speaking. When he finished, the old man raised his eyes, and looking at him with an air of distraction, as if he was endeavouring to recollect what he had been saying, he at length pointed to one of the cells, and resumed his devotions like one who felt impatient of whatever withdrew his attention from his sacred duties, were it but for an instant.

Hartley entered the cell indicated, with the usual salutation of Salam Alaikum. His patient lay on a little carpet in a corner of the small white-washed cell. He was a man of about forty, dressed in the black robe of his order, very much torn and patched. He wore a high conical cap of Tartarian felt, and had round his neck the string of black beads belonging to his order. His eyes and posture indicated suffering, which he was enduring with stoical patience.

"Salam Alaikum," said Hartley; "you are in pain, my father?"—a title which he gave rather to the profession than to the years of the person he addressed.

"*Salam Alaikum bema sabastem*," answered the Fakir; "Well is it for you that you have suffered patiently. The Book saith, such shall be the greeting of the angels to those who enter paradise."

The conversation being thus opened, the physician proceeded to inquire into the complaints of the patient, and to prescribe what he thought advisable. Having done this, he was about to retire, when, to his great surprise, the Fakir tendered him a ring of some value.

"The wise," said Hartley, declining the present, and at the same time paying a suitable compliment to the Fakir's cap and robe,—"the wise of every country are brethren. My left hand takes no guerdon of my right."

"A Feringi can then refuse gold!" said the Fakir. "I thought they took it from every hand, whether pure as that of an Houri, or leprous like Gehazi's—even as the hungry dog recketh not whether the flesh he eateth be of the camel of the prophet Saleth, or of the ass of Degial —on whose head be curses!"

"The Book says," replied Hartley, "that it is Allah who closes and who enlarges the heart. Frank and Musselman are alike moulded by his pleasure."

"My brother hath spoken wisely," answered the patient. "Welcome the disease, if it bring thee acquainted with a wise physician. For what saith the poet—'It is well to have fallen to the earth, if while grovelling there thou shalt discover a diamond.'"

The physician made repeated visits to his patient, and continued to do so even after the health of el Hadgi was entirely restored. He had no difficulty in discerning in him one of those secret agents frequently employed by Asiatic Sovereigns. His intelligence, his learning, above all, his versatility and freedom from prejudices of every kind, left no doubt of Barak's possessing the necessary qualifications for conducting such delicate negotiations; while his gravity of habit and profession could not prevent his features from expressing occasionally a perception of humour, not usually seen in devotees of his class.

Barak el Hadgi talked often, amidst their private conversations, of the power and dignity of the Nawaub of Mysore; and Hartley had little doubt that he came from the Court of Hyder Ali, on some secret mission, perhaps for achieving a more solid peace betwixt that able and sagacious Prince and the East India Company's Government,—that which existed for the time being regarded on both parts as little more than a hollow and insincere truce. He told many stories to the advantage of this Prince, who certainly was one of the wisest that Hindoostan could boast; and amidst great crimes, perpetrated to gratify his ambition, displayed many instances of princely generosity, and, what was a little more surprising, of even-handed justice.

On one occasion, shortly before Barak el Hadgi left Madras, he visited the Doctor, and partook of his sherbet, which he preferred to his own, perhaps because a few glasses of rum or brandy were usually added to enrich the compound. It might be owing to repeated applications to the jar which contained this generous fluid, that the Pilgrim became more than usually frank in his communications, and not contented with praising his Nawaub with the most hyperbolic eloquence, he began to insinuate the influence which he himself enjoyed with the Invincible, the Lord and Shield of the Faith of the Prophet.

"Brother of my soul," he said, "do but think if thou needest aught that the all-powerful Hyder Ali Khan Bahauder can give; and then use not the intercession of those who dwell in palaces, and wear jewels in their turbans, but seek the cell of thy brother at the Great City, which is Seringapatam. And the poor Fakir, in his torn cloak, shall better advance thy suit with the Nawaub [for Hyder did not assume the title of Sultaun] than they who sit upon seats of honour in the Divan."

With these and sundry other expressions of regard, he exhorted Hartley to come into the Mysore, and look upon the face of the Great Prince, whose glance inspired wisdom, and whose nod conferred wealth, so that Folly or Poverty could not appear before him. He offered at the same time to requite the kindness which Hartley had evinced to him, by showing him whatever was worthy the attention of a sage in the land of Mysore.

Hartley was not reluctant to promise to undertake the proposed journey, if the continuance of good understanding betwixt their governments should render it practicable, and in reality looked forward to the possibility of such an event with a good deal of interest. The friends parted with mutual good wishes, after exchanging, in the Oriental fashion, such gifts as became sages, to whom knowledge was to be supposed dearer than wealth. Barak el Hadgi presented Hartley with a small quantity of the balsam of Mecca, very hard to be procured in an unadulterated form, and gave him at the same time a passport in a peculiar character, which he assured him would be respected by every officer of the Nawaub, should his friend be disposed to accomplish his visit to the Mysore. "The head of him who should disrespect this safe-conduct," he said, "shall not be more safe than that of the barley-stalk which the reaper has grasped in his hand."

Hartley requited these civilities by the present of a few medicines little used in the East, but such as he thought might, with suitable directions, be safely intrusted to a man so intelligent as his Moslem friend.

It was several months after Barak had returned to the interior of India, that Hartley was astonished by an unexpected rencounter.

The ships from Europe had but lately arrived, and had brought over their usual cargo of boys longing to be commanders, and young women, without any purpose of being married, but whom a pious duty to some brother, some uncle, or other male relative, brought to India to keep his house, until they should find themselves unexpectedly in one of their own. Doctor Hartley happened to attend a public breakfast given on this occasion by a gentleman high in the service. The roof of his friend had been recently enriched by a consignment of three nieces, whom the old gentleman, justly attached to his quiet hookah, and, it was said, to a pretty girl of colour, desired to offer to the public, that he might have the fairest chance to get rid of his new guests as soon as possible. Hartley, who was thought a fish worth casting a fly for, was contemplating this fair investment with very little interest, when he heard one of the company say to another in a low voice,——

"Angels and ministers! there is our old acquaintance, the Queen of Sheba, returned upon our hands like unsaleable goods."

Hartley looked in the same direction with the two who were speaking, and his eye was caught by a Semiramis-looking person, of unusual stature and amplitude, arrayed in a sort of riding habit, but so formed, and so looped and gallooned with lace, as made it resemble the upper tunic of a native chief. Her robe was composed of crimson silk, rich with flowers of gold. She wore wide trowsers of light blue silk, a fine scarlet shawl around her waist, in which was stuck a creeze, with a richly ornamented handle. Her throat and arms were loaded with chains and bracelets, and her turban, formed of a shawl similar to that worn around her waist, was decorated by a magnificent aigrette, from which a blue ostrich plume floated in one direction, and a red one in another. The brow, of European complexion, on which this tiara rested, was too lofty for beauty, but seemed made for command; the aquiline nose retained its form, but the cheeks were a little sunken, and the complexion so very brilliant, as to give strong evidence that the whole countenance had undergone a thorough repair since the lady had left her couch. A black female slave, richly dressed, stood behind her with a chowry, or cow's tail, having a silver handle, which she used to keep off the flies. From the mode in which she was addressed by those who spoke to her, this lady appeared a person of too much importance to be affronted or neglected, and yet one with whom none desired further communication than the occasion seemed in propriety to demand.

She did not, however, stand in need of attention. The well-known captain of an East Indian vessel lately arrived from Britain was sedulously polite to her; and two or three gentlemen, whom Hartley knew to be engaged in trade, tended upon her as they would have done upon the safety of a rich argosy.

"For Heaven's sake, what is that for a Zenobia?" said Hartley, to the gentleman whose whisper had first attracted his attention to this lofty dame.

"Is it possible you do not know the Queen of Sheba?" said the person of whom he inquired, no way loath to communicate the information demanded. "You must know, then, that she is the daughter of a Scotch emigrant, who lived and died at Pondicherry, a sergeant in Lally's regiment. She managed to marry a partizan officer named Montreville, a Swiss or Frenchman, I cannot tell which. After the surrender of Pondicherry, this hero and heroine—But hey—what the devil are you thinking of?—If you stare at her that way, you will make a scene; for she will think nothing of scolding you across the table."

But without attending to his friend's remonstrances, Hartley bolted from the table at which he sat, and made his way, with something less than the decorum which the rules of society enjoin, towards the place where the lady in question was seated.

"The Doctor is surely mad this morning—" said his friend Major Mercer to old Quarter-Master Calder.

Indeed Hartley was not perhaps strictly in his senses; for looking at the Queen of Sheba as he listened to Major Mercer, his eye fell on a light female form beside her, so placed as if she desired to be eclipsed by the bulky form and flowing robes we have described, and to his extreme astonishment, he recognised the friend of his childhood, the love of his youth—Menie Grey herself!

To see her in India was in itself astonishing. To see her apparently under such strange patronage, greatly increased his surprise. To make his way to her, and address her, seemed the natural and direct mode of satisfying the feelings which her appearance excited.

His impetuosity was however checked, when, advancing close upon Miss Grey and her companion, he observed that the former, though she looked at him, exhibited not the slightest token of recognition, unless he could interpret as such, that she slightly touched her upper-lip with her fore-finger, which, if it happened otherwise than by mere accident, might be construed to mean, "Do not speak to me just now." Hartley, adopting such an interpretation, stood stock still, blushing deeply; for he was aware that he made for the moment but a silly figure.

He was the rather convinced of this, when, with a voice which in the force of its accents corresponded with her commanding air, Mrs Montreville addressed him in English, which savoured slightly of a Swiss patois,—"You haave come to us very fast, sir, to say nothing at all. Are you sure you did not get your tongue stolen by de way?"

"I thought I had seen an old friend in that lady, madam," stammered Hartley, "but it seems I am mistaken."

"The good people do tell me that you are one Doctors Hartley, sir. Now, my friend and I do not know Doctor Hartley at all."

"I have not the presumption to pretend to your acquaintance, madam, but——"

Here Menie repeated the sign in such a manner, that though it was only momentary, Hartley could not misunderstand its purpose; he therefore changed the end of his sentence, and added, "But I have only to make my bow, and ask pardon for my mistake."

He retired back accordingly among the company, unable to quit the room, and inquiring at those whom he considered as the best news-mongers for such information as—"Who is that stately-looking woman, Mr Butler?"

"Oh, the Queen of Sheba, to be sure."

"And who is that pretty girl, who sits beside her?"

"Or rather behind her," answered Butler, a military chaplain; "faith, I cannot say—Pretty did you call her?" turning his opera-glass that way—"Yes, faith, she is pretty—very pretty—Gad, she shoots her glances as smartly from behind the old pile yonder, as Teucer from behind Ajax Telamon's shield."

"But who is she, can you tell me?"

"Some fair-skinned speculation of old Montreville's, I suppose, that she has got either to toady herself, or take in some of her black friends with.—Is it possible you have never heard of old Mother Montreville?"

"You know I have been so long absent from Madras—"

"Well," continued Butler, "this lady is the widow of a Swiss officer in the French service, who, after the surrender of Pondicherry, went off into the interior, and commenced soldier on his own account. He got possession of a fort, under pretence of keeping it for some simple Rajah or other; assembled around him a parcel of desperate vagabonds, of every colour in the rainbow; occupied a considerable territory, of which he raised the duties in his own name, and declared for independence. But Hyder Naig understood no such interloping proceedings, and down he came, besieged the fort and took it, though some pretend it was betrayed to him by this very woman. Be that as it may, the poor Swiss was found dead on the ramparts. Certain it is, she received large sums of money, under pretence of paying off her troops, surrendering of hill-forts, and Heaven knows what besides. She was permitted also to retain some insignia of royalty; and, as she was wont to talk of Hyder as the Eastern Solomon, she generally became known by the title of Queen of Sheba. She leaves her court when she pleases, and has been as far as Fort St George before now. In a word, she does pretty much as she likes. The great folks here are civil to her, though they look on her as little better than a spy. As to Hyder, it is supposed he has insured her fidelity by borrowing the greater part of her treasures, which prevents her from daring to break with him,—besides other causes that smack of scandal of another sort."

"A singular story," replied Hartley to his companion, while his heart dwelt on the question, How it was possible that the gentle and simple Menie Grey should be in the train of such a character as this adventuress?

"But Butler has not told you the best of it," said Major Mercer, who by this time came round to finish his own story. "Your old acquaintance, Mr Tresham, or Mr Middlemas, or whatever else he chooses to be called, has been complimented by a report, that he stood very high in the good graces of this same Boadicea. He certainly commanded some troops which she still keeps on foot, and acted at their head in the Nawaub's service, who craftily employed him in whatever could render him odious to his countrymen. The British prisoners were intrusted to his charge, and, to judge by what I felt myself, the devil might take a lesson from him in severity."

"And was he attached to, or connected with, this woman?"

"So Mrs Rumour told us in our dungeon. Poor Jack Ward had the bastinado for celebrating their merits in a parody on the play-house song,

> Sure such a pair were never seen,
> So aptly formed to meet by nature."

Hartley could listen no longer. The fate of Menie Grey, connected with such a man and such a woman, rushed on his fancy in the most horrid colours, and he was struggling through the throng to get to some place where he might collect his ideas, and consider what could be done for her protection, when a black attendant touched his arm, and at the same time slipt a card into his hand. It bore, "Miss Grey, Mrs Montreville's, at the house of Ram Sing Cottah, in the Black Town." On the reverse was written with a pencil, "Eight in the morning."

This intimation of her residence implied, of course, a permission, nay, an invitation, to wait upon her at the hour specified. Hartley's heart beat at the idea of seeing her once more, and still more highly at the thought of being able to serve her. At least, he thought, if there is danger near her, as is much to be suspected, she shall not want a counsellor, or, if necessary, a protector. Yet, at the same time, he felt the necessity of making himself better acquainted with the circumstances of her case, and the persons with whom she seemed connected. Butler and Mercer had both spoke to their disparagement: but Butler was a little of a coxcomb, and Mercer a great deal of a gossip. While he was considering what credit was due to their testimony, he was unexpectedly encountered by a gentleman of his own profession, a military surgeon, who had had the misfortune to have been in Hyder's prison, till set at freedom by the late pacification. Mr Esdale, for so he was called, was generally esteemed a rising man, calm, steady, and deliberate in forming his opinions. Hartley found it easy to turn the subject on the Queen of Sheba, by asking whether her Majesty was not somewhat of an adventuress.

"On my word, I cannot say," answered Esdale, smiling; "we are all upon the adventure in India, more or less; but I do not see that the Begum Montreville is more so than the rest."

"Why, that Amazonian dress and manner," said Hartley, "savour a little of the *picaresca*."

"You must not," said Esdale, "expect a woman who has commanded soldiers, and may again, to dress and look entirely like an ordinary person; but I assure you, that even at this time of day, if she wished to marry, she might easily find a respectable match."

"Why, I heard that she had betrayed her husband's fort to Hyder."

"Ay, that is a specimen of Madras gossip. The fact is, that she defended the place long after her husband fell, and afterwards surrendered it by capitulation. Hyder, who piques himself on observing the rules of justice, would not otherwise have admitted her to such intimacy."

"Yes, I have heard," replied Hartley, "that their intimacy was rather of the closest."

"Another calumny, if you mean any scandal," answered Esdale. "Hyder is too zealous a Mahomedan to entertain a Christian mistress; and besides, to enjoy the sort of rank which is yielded to a woman in her condition, she must refrain, in appearance at least, from all correspondence in the way of gallantry. Just so they said that the poor woman had a connexion with poor Middlemas of the ——— regiment."

"And was that also a false report?" said Hartley, in breathless anxiety.

"On my soul, I believe it was," answered Mr Esdale. "They were friends, Europeans in an Indian court, and therefore intimate; but I believe nothing more. By the by, though, I believe there was some quarrel between Middlemas, poor fellow, and you; yet I am sure that you will be glad to hear there is a chance of his affair being made up?"

"Indeed!" was again the only word which Hartley could utter.

"Ay, indeed," answered Esdale. "The duel is an old story now; and it must be allowed that poor Middlemas, though he was rash in that business, had provocation."

"But his desertion—his accepting of command under Hyder—his treatment of our prisoners—How can all these be passed over?" replied Hartley.

"Why, it is possible—I speak to you as a cautious man, and in confidence—that he may do us better service in Hyder's capital, or Tippoo's camp, than he could have done if serving with his own regiment. And then, for his treatment of prisoners, I am sure I can speak nothing but good of him in that particular. He was obliged to take the office, because those that serve Hyder Naig, must do or die. But he told me himself—and I believe him—that he accepted the office chiefly because, while he made a great bullying at us before the black fellows, he could privately be of assistance to us. Some fools could not understand this, and answered him with abuse and lampoons; and he was obliged to punish them, to avoid suspicion. Yes, yes, I and others can prove he was willing to be kind, if men would give him leave. I hope to thank him at Madras one day soon.—All this in confidence—Good morrow to you."

Distracted by the contradictory intelligence he had received, Hartley went next to question old Captain Capstern, the Captain of the Indiaman, whom he had observed in attendance upon the Begum Montreville. On inquiring after that commander's female passengers, he heard a pretty long catalogue of names, in which that he was so much interested in did not occur. On closer inquiry, Capstern recollected that Menie Grey, a young Scotchwoman, had come out under charge of Mrs Duffer, the master's wife. "A good decent girl," Capstern said, "and kept the mates and guinea-pigs at a respectable distance. She came out," he believed, "to be a sort of female companion, or upper-servant, in Madame Montreville's family. Snug birth enough," he concluded, "if she can find the length of the old girl's foot."

This was all that could be made of Capstern; so Hartley was compelled to remain in a state of uncertainty until the next morning, when an explanation might be expected with Menie Grey in person.

Chapter Twelve

THE EXACT HOUR assigned found Hartley at the door of the rich native merchant, who, having some reasons for wishing to oblige the Begum Montreville, had relinquished, for her accommodation and that of her numerous retinue, almost the whole of his large and sumptuous residence in the Black Town of Madras, as that district of the city is called which the natives occupy.

A domestic, at the first summons, ushered the visitor into an apartment, where he expected to be joined by Miss Grey. The room opened on one side into a small garden or parterre, filled with the brilliant-coloured flowers of eastern climates; in the midst of which the waters of a fountain rose upwards in a sparkling jet, and fell back again into a white marble cistern.

A thousand dizzy recollections thronged on the mind of Hartley, whose early feelings towards the companion of his youth, if they had slumbered during distance and the various casualties of a busy life, were revived when he found himself placed so near her, and in circumstances which interested from their unexpected occurrence and mysterious character. A step was heard—the door opened—a female appeared—but it was the portly form of Madame Montreville.

"What you do please to want, sir?" said the lady; "that is, if you have found your tongue this morning, which you had lost yesterday."

"I proposed myself the honour of waiting upon the young person, whom I saw in your excellency's company yesterday morning," answered Hartley, with assumed respect. "I have had long the honour of being known to her in Europe, and I desire to offer my services to her in India."

"Much obliged—much obliged; but Miss Grey is gone out, and

does not return for one or two days. You may leave your commands with me."

"Pardon me, madam," replied Hartley; "but I have some reason to hope you may be mistaken in this matter—And here comes the lady herself."

"How is this, my dear?" said Mrs Montreville, with unruffled front, to Menie, as she entered; "are you not gone out for two three days, as I tell this gentleman?—*mais c'est égal*—it is all one thing. You will say, How d'ye do, and goodbye, to Monsieur, who is so polite as to come to ask after our healths, and as he sees us both very well, he will go away home again."

"I believe, madam," said Miss Grey, with appearance of effort, "that I must speak with this gentleman for a few minutes in private, if you will permit us."

"That is to say, get you gone?—but I do not allow that—I do not like private conversation between young man and pretty young woman; *cela n'est pas honnête*. It cannot be in my house."

"It may be out of it, then, madam," answered Miss Grey, not pettishly or pertly, but with the utmost simplicity.—"Mr Hartley, will you step into that garden?—And you, madam, may observe us from the window, if it be the fashion of the country to watch so closely."

As she spoke this she stepped through a lattice-door into the garden, and with an air so simple, that she seemed as if she wished to comply with her patroness's ideas of decorum, though they appeared strange to her. The Queen of Sheba, notwithstanding her natural assurance, was disconcerted by the composure of Miss Grey's manner, and left the room, apparently in displeasure. Menie turned back to the door which opened into the garden, and said, in the same manner as before, but with less nonchalance,—

"I am sure I would not willingly break through the rules of a foreign country; but I cannot refuse myself the pleasure of speaking to so old a friend,—if, indeed," she added, pausing and looking at Hartley, who was much embarrassed, "it be as much pleasure to Mr Hartley as it is to me."

"It would have been," said Hartley, scarce knowing what he said— "it must be, a pleasure to me in every circumstance—But this extraordinary meeting—But your father——"

Menie Grey's handkerchief was at her eyes.—"He is gone, Mr Hartley. After he was left unassisted, his toilsome business became too much for him—he caught a cold, which hung about him, as you know he was the last to attend to his own complaints, till it assumed a dangerous, and, finally, a fatal character. I distress you, Mr Hartley, but it becomes you well to be affected. My father loved you dearly."

"Oh, Miss Grey!" said Hartley, "it should not have been thus with my excellent friend at the close of his useful and virtuous life—Alas, wherefore—the question bursts from me involuntarily—wherefore could you not have complied with his wishes? wherefore——"

"Do not ask me," said she, stopping the question which was on his lips; "we are not the formers of our own destiny. It is painful to talk on such a subject; but for once, and for ever, let me tell you that I should have done Mr Hartley wrong, if, even to secure his assistance to my father, I had accepted his hand, while my wayward affections did not accompany the act."

"But wherefore do I see you here, Menie?—Forgive me, Miss Grey, my tongue as well as my heart turns back to long-forgotten scenes—But why here?—why with this woman?"

"She is not, indeed, everything that I expected," answered Menie Grey; "but I must not be prejudiced by foreign manners, after the step I have taken—She is, besides, attentive, and generous in her way, and I shall soon—" she paused a moment, and then added, "be under better protection."

"That of Richard Middlemas?" said Hartley, with a faltering voice.

"I ought not, perhaps, to answer the question," said Menie; "but I am a bad dissembler, and those whom I trust, I trust entirely. You have guessed right, Mr Hartley," she added, colouring a good deal, "I have come hither to unite my fate to that of your old comrade."

"It is, then, just as I feared!" exclaimed Hartley.

"And why should Mr Hartley fear?" said Menie Grey. "I used to think you too generous—surely the quarrel which occurred long since ought not to perpetuate suspicion and resentment."

"At least, if the feeling of resentment remained in my own bosom, it would be the last I should intrude upon you, Miss Grey," answered Hartley. "But it is for you, and for you alone, that I am watchful.—This person—this gentleman whom you mean to intrust with your happiness—do you know where he is—and in what service?"

"I know both, more distinctly perhaps than Mr Hartley can do. Mr Middlemas has erred greatly, and has been severely punished. But it was not in the time of his exile and sorrow, that she who has plighted her faith to him should, with the flattering world, turn her back upon him. Besides, you have, doubtless, not heard of his hopes of being restored to his country and his rank?"

"I have," answered Hartley, thrown off his guard; "but I see not how he can deserve it, otherwise than by becoming a traitor to his new master, and thus rendering himself even more unworthy of confidence than I hold him to be at this moment."

"It is well that he hears you not," answered Menie Grey, resenting,

with natural feeling, the imputation on her lover. Then instantly soft-
ening her tone, she added, "My voice ought not to aggravate, but to
soothe your quarrel. Mr Hartley, I plight my word to you that you do
Richard wrong."

She said these words with affecting calmness, suppressing all
appearance of that displeasure, of which she was evidently sensible,
upon this depreciation of a beloved object.

Hartley compelled himself to answer in the same strain.

"Miss Grey," he said, "your actions and motives will always be
those of an angel; but let me entreat you to view this most important
matter with the eyes of worldly wisdom and prudence. Have you well
weighed the risks attending the course which you are taking in favour
of a man, who—nay, I will not again offend you—who may, I hope,
deserve your favour?"

"When I wished to see you in this manner, Mr Hartley, and
declined a communication in public, where we could have had less
freedom of conversation, it was with the view of telling you everything.
Some pain I thought old recollections might give, but I trusted it
would be momentary; and, as I desire to retain your friendship, it is
proper I should show that I still deserve it. I must then first tell you my
situation after my father's death. In the world's opinion, we were
always poor, you know; but in the proper sense I had not known what
real poverty was, until I was placed in dependence upon a distant
relation of my poor father, who made our relationship a reason for
casting upon me all the drudgery of her household, while she would
not allow that it gave me a claim to countenance, kindness, or anything
but the relief of my most pressing wants. In these circumstances I
received from Mr Middlemas a letter, in which he related his fatal
duel, and its consequence. He had not dared to write to me to share
his misery—Now, when he was in a lucrative situation, under the
patronage of a powerful prince, whose wisdom knew how to prize and
protect such Europeans as entered his service—now, when he had
every prospect of rendering our government such essential service by
his interest with Hyder Ali, and might eventually nourish hopes of
being permitted to return and stand his trial for the death of his
commanding officer—now, he pressed me to come to India, and share
his reviving fortunes, by accomplishing the engagement into which we
had long ago entered. A considerable sum of money accompanied this
letter. Mrs Duffer was pointed out as a respectable woman, who
would protect me during the passage. Mrs Montreville, a lady of
rank, having large possessions and high interest in the Mysore, would
receive me on my arrival at Fort St George, and conduct me safely to
the dominions of Hyder. It was further recommended, that, consider-

ing the peculiar situation of Mr Middlemas, his name should be concealed in the transaction, and that the ostensible cause of my voyage should be to fill an office in that lady's family.—What was I to do?—My duty to my poor father was ended, and my other friends considered the proposal as too advantageous to be rejected. The references given, the sum of money lodged, were considered as putting all scruples out of the question, and my immediate protectress and kinswoman was so earnest that I should accept of the offer made me, as to intimate that she would not encourage me to stand in my own light, by continuing to give me shelter and food, (she gave me little more,) if I was foolish enough to refuse compliance."

"Sordid wretch!" said Hartley, "how little did she deserve such a charge!"

"Let me speak a proud word, Mr Hartley, and then you will not perhaps blame my relations so much. All their persuasions, and even their threats, would have failed in inducing me to take a step, which has an appearance, at least, to which I found it difficult to reconcile myself. But I had loved Middlemas—I love him still—why should I deny it?—and I have not hesitated to trust him. Had it not been for the small still voice which reminded me of my engagements, I had maintained more stubbornly the pride of womanhood, and, as you would perhaps have recommended, I might have expected, at least, that my lover should have come to Britain in person, and might have had the vanity to think," she added, smiling faintly, "that if I were worth having, I was worth fetching."

"Yet now—even now," answered Hartley, "be just to yourself while you are generous to your lover.—Nay, do not look angrily, but hear me. I doubt the propriety of your being under the charge of this unsexed woman, who can no longer be termed a European. I have interest enough with females of the highest rank in the settlement— this climate is that of generosity and hospitality—there is not one of them, who, knowing your character and history, will not desire to have you in her society, and under her protection, until your lover shall be able to vindicate his title to your hand in the face of the world.—I myself will be no cause of suspicion to him, or of inconvenience to you, Menie. Let me but have your consent to the arrangement I propose, and the same moment that sees you under honourable and unsuspected protection, I will leave Madras, not to return till your destiny is in one way or other permanently fixed."

"No, Hartley," said Miss Grey. "It may, it must be, friendly in you thus to advise me; but it would be most base in me to advance my own affairs at the expense of your prospects. Besides, what would this be but taking the chance of contingencies, with the view of sharing poor

Middlemas's fortunes, should they prove prosperous, and casting him off, should they be otherwise? Tell me only, do you, of your own positive knowledge, aver that you consider this woman as an unworthy and unfit protectress for so young a person as I am?"

"Of my own knowledge I can say nothing; nay, I must own, that reports differ even concerning Mrs Montreville's character. But surely the mere suspicion——"

"The mere suspicion, Mr Hartley, can have no weight with me, considering that I can oppose to it the testimony of the man with whom I am willing to share my future fortunes. You acknowledge the question is but doubtful, and should not the assertion of him of whom I think so highly decide my belief in a doubtful matter? What, indeed, must he be, should this Madame Montreville be other than he represented her?"

"What must he be, indeed!" thought Hartley internally, but his lips uttered not the words. He looked down in a deep reverie, and at length started from it at the words of Miss Grey.

"It is time to remind you, Mr Hartley, that we must needs part. God bless and preserve you!"

"And you, dearest Menie," exclaimed Hartley, as he sunk on one knee, and pressed to his lips the hand which she held out to him, "God bless you!—you must deserve blessing. God protect you!—you must need protection.—Oh, should things prove different from what you hope, send for me instantly, and if man can aid you, Adam Hartley will!"

He placed in her hand a card containing his address. He then rushed from the apartment. In the hall he met the lady of the mansion, who made him a haughty reverence in token of adieu, while a native servant of the upper class, by whom she was attended, made a low and reverential salam.

Hartley hastened from the Black Town, more satisfied than before that some deceit was about to be practised towards Menie Grey— more determined than ever to exert himself for her preservation; yet more completely perplexed, when he began to consider the doubtful character of the danger to which she might be exposed, and the scanty means of protection which he had to oppose to it.

Chapter Thirteen

As Hartley left the apartment in the house of Ram Sing Cottah by one mode of exit, Miss Grey retired by another, to an apartment destined for her private use. She, too, had reason for secret and anxious reflection, since all her love for Middlemas, and her full confidence in his honour, could not entirely conquer her doubts concerning the character of the person whom he had chosen for her temporary protectress. And yet she could not rest these doubts upon anything distinctly conclusive; it was rather a dislike of her patroness's general manners, and a disgust at her masculine notions and expressions, that displeased her, than anything else.

Meantime, Madame Montreville, followed by her black domestic, entered the apartment where Hartley and Menie Grey had just parted. It appeared from the conversation which follows, that they had from some place of concealment overheard the dialogue we have narrated in the former chapter.

"It is good luck, Sadoc," said the lady, "that there is in this world the great fool."

"And the great villain," answered Sadoc, in good English, but in a most sullen tone.

"This woman, now," continued the lady, "is what in Frangistan you call angel."

"Ay, and I have seen those in Hindostan you may well call devil."

"I am sure that this—how you call him—Hartley, is a meddling devil. For, what has he to do? She will not have any of him. What is his business who has her? I wish we were well up the Ghauts again, my dear Sadoc."

"For my part," answered the slave, "I am half determined never to ascend the Ghauts more. Hark you, Adela, I begin to sicken of the plan we have laid. This creature's confiding purity—call her angel or woman, as you will—makes my practices appear too vile, even in my own eyes. I feel myself unfit to be your companion farther in the daring paths which you pursue. Let us part, and part friends."

"Amen, coward. But the woman remains with me," answered the Queen of Sheba.*

"With thee!" replied the seeming black—"never. No, Adela. She is under the shadow of the British flag, and she shall experience its protection."

"Yes—and what protection will it afford to you yourself?" retorted the Amazon. "What if I should clap my hands, and command a score of my black servants to bind you like a sheep, and then send word to the Governor of the Presidency that one Richard Middlemas, who had been guilty of mutiny, murder, desertion, and serving of the enemy against his countrymen, is here, at Ram Sing Cottah's house,

* In order to maintain uninjured the tone of passion throughout this dialogue, it has been judged expedient to discard, in the language of the Begum, the *patois* of Madame Montreville.

in the disguise of a black servant?" Middlemas covered his face with his hands, while Madame Montreville proceeded to load him with reproaches.—"Yes," she said, "slave, and son of a slave! Since you wear the dress of my household, you shall obey me as fully as the rest of them, otherwise,—whips, fetters—the scaffold, renegade, —the gallows, murderer! Dost thou dare to reflect on the abyss of misery from which I raised thee, to share my wealth and my affections? Dost thou not remember that the picture of this pale, cold, unimpassioned girl, was then so indifferent to thee, that you sacrificed it as a tribute due to the benevolence of her who relieved thee, to the affection of her who, wretch as thou art, condescended to love thee?"

"Yes, fell woman," answered Middlemas; "but was it I who encouraged the young tyrant's outrageous passion for a portrait, or who formed the abominable plan of placing the original within his power?"

"No—for to do so required brain and wit. But it was thine, flimsy villain, to execute the device which a bolder genius planned; it was thine to entice the woman to this foreign shore, under pretence of a love, which, on thy part, cold-blooded miscreant, never had existed."

"Peace, screech-owl!" answered Middlemas, "nor drive me to such madness as may lead me to forget thou art a woman."

"A woman, dastard! Is that thy pretext for sparing me?—what, then, art thou, who tremblest at a woman's looks, a woman's words?— I am a woman, renegade, but one who wears a dagger, and despises alike thy strength and thy courage. I am a woman, who has looked on more dying men than thou hast killed deer and antelopes. Thou must traffic for greatness?—thou hast thrust thyself like a five-years' child, into the rough sports of men, and wilt only be borne down and crushed for thy pains. Thou wilt be a double traitor, forsooth—betray thy betrothed to the Prince, in order to obtain the means of betraying the Prince to the English, and thus gain thy pardon from thy countrymen? But me thou shalt not betray. I will not be made the tool of thy ambition—I will not give thee the aid of my treasures and my soldiers, to be sacrificed at last to this northern icicle. No, I will watch thee as the fiend watches the wizard. Show but a symptom of betraying me while we are here, and I denounce thee to the English, who might pardon the successful villain, but not him who can only offer prayers for his life, in place of useful services. Let me see thee flinch when we are beyond the Ghauts, and the Nawaub shall know thy intrigues with the Nizam and the Mahrattas, and thy resolution to deliver up Banga-lore to the English, when the imprudence of Tippoo shall have made thee Killedar. Go where thou wilt, slave, thou shalt find me thy mis-tress."

"And a fair, though an unkind one," said the counterfeit Sadoc, suddenly changing his tone to an affectation of tenderness. "It is true, I pity this unhappy woman; true I would save her if I could—but most unjust to suppose I would in any circumstances prefer her to my Nourjehan, my light of the world, my Mootee Mahul, my pearl of the palace——"

"All false coin and empty compliment," said the Begum. "Let me hear, in two brief words, that you leave this woman to my disposal."

"But not to be interred alive under your seat, like the Circassian of whom you were jealous," said Middlemas, shuddering.

"No, fool; her lot shall not be worse than that of being the favourite of a prince. Hast thou, fugitive and criminal as thou art, a better fate to offer her?"

"But," replied Middlemas, blushing even through his base disguise at the consciousness of his abject conduct, "I will have no force on her inclinations."

"Such truce she shall have as the laws of the Zenana allow," replied the female tyrant. "A week is long enough for her to determine whether she will be the willing mistress of a princely and generous lover."

"Ay," said Richard, "and before that week expires——" He stopped short.

"What will happen before the week expires?" said the Begum Montreville.

"No matter—nothing of consequence. I leave the woman's fate with you."

"'Tis well—we march to-night on our return, so soon as the moon rises. Give orders to our retinue."

"To hear is to obey," replied the seeming slave, and left the apartment.

The eyes of the Begum remained fixed on the door through which he had passed. "Villain—double-dyed villain!" she said, "I see thy drift; thou wouldst betray Tippoo, in policy alike and in love. But me thou canst not betray.—Ho, there, who waits? Let a trusty messenger be ready to set off instantly with letters, which I will presently make ready. His departure must be a secret to every one.—And now shall this pale phantom soon know her destiny, and learn what it is to have rivalled Adela Montreville."

While the Amazonian Princess meditated plans of vengeance against her innocent rival and the guilty lover, the latter plotted as deeply for his own purposes. He had waited until such brief twilight as India enjoys rendered his disguise complete, then set out in haste for the part of Madras inhabited by the Europeans, or, as it is termed, Fort St George.

"I will save her yet," he said; "ere Tippoo can seize his prize, we will raise around his ears a storm which would drive the God of War from the arms of the Goddess of Beauty. The trap shall close its fangs upon this Indian tiger, ere he has time to devour the bait which enticed him into the snare."

While Middlemas cherished these hopes, he approached the Residency. The sentinel on duty stopped him, as of course, but he was in possession of the counter-sign, and entered without opposition. He rounded the building in which the President of the Council resided, an able and active, but unconscientious man, who, neither in his own affairs, nor in those of the Company, was supposed to embarrass himself much about the means which he used to attain his object. A tap at a small postern-gate was answered by a black slave, who admitted Middlemas to that necessary appurtenance of every government, a back stair, which, in its turn, conducted him to the office of the Bramin Paupiah, the Dubash, or steward of the great man, and by whose means chiefly he communicated with the native courts, and carried on many mysterious intrigues, which he did not communicate to his brethren at the council board.

It is perhaps justice to the guilty and unhappy Middlemas to suppose, that if the agency of a British officer had been employed, he might have been induced to throw himself on his mercy, might have explained the whole of his nefarious bargain with Tippoo, and, renouncing his guilty projects of ambition, might have turned his whole thoughts upon saving Menie Grey, ere she was transported beyond the reach of British protection. But the thin dusky form which stood before him, wrapped in robes of muslin embroidered with gold, was that of Paupiah, known as a master-counsellor of dark projects, an Oriental Machiavel, whose premature wrinkles were the result of many an intrigue, in which the existence of the poor, the happiness of the rich, the honour of men, and the chastity of women, had been sacrificed without scruple, to attain some private or political advantage. He did not even inquire by what means the renegade Briton proposed to acquire that influence with Tippoo which might enable him to betray him—he only desired to be assured that the fact was real.

"You speak at the risk of your head, if you deceive Paupiah, or make Paupiah the means of deceiving his master. I know, so does all Madras, that the Nawaub has placed his young son, Tippoo, as Vice-Regent of his newly-conquered territory of Bangalore, which Hyder hath lately added to his dominions. But that Tippoo should bestow the government of that important place on an apostate Feringi, seems more doubtful."

"Tippoo is young," answered Middlemas, "and to youth the temptation of the passions is what a lily on the surface of the lake is to childhood—they will risk life to reach it, though, when obtained, it is of little value. Tippoo has the cunning of his father and his military talents, but he lacks his cautious wisdom."

"Thou speakest truth—but when thou art Governor of Bangalore, hast thou forces to hold the place till thou art relieved by the Mahrattas, or by the British?"

"Doubt it not—the soldiers of the Begum Mootee Mahul, whom the Europeans call Montreville, are less hers than mine. I am myself her Bukshee, (General,) and her Sirdars are at my devotion. With these I could keep Bangalore for two months, and the British army may be before it in a week. What do you risk by advancing General Smith's army nearer to the frontier?"

"We risk a settled peace with Hyder," answered Paupiah, "for which he has made advantageous offers. Yet I say not but thy plan may be most advantageous. Thou sayest Tippoo's treasures are in the fort?"

"His treasures and his Zenana; I may even be able to secure his person."

"That were a goodly pledge—" answered the Hindoo minister.

"And you consent that the treasures shall be divided to the last rupee, as in this scroll?"

"The share of Paupiah's master is too small," said the Bramin; "and the name of Paupiah is unnoticed."

"The share of the Begum may be divided between Paupiah and his master," answered Middlemas.

"But the Begum will expect her proportion," answered Paupiah.

"Let me alone to deal with her," said Middlemas. "Before the blow is struck, she shall not know of our private treaty, and afterwards her disappointment will be of little consequence. And now, remember my stipulations—my rank to be restored—my full pardon to be granted."

"Ay," replied Paupiah, cautiously, "should you succeed. But were you to betray what has here passed, I will find the dagger of a Lootie which shall reach thee, wert thou sheltered under the folds of the Nawaub's garment. In the meantime, take this missive, and when you are in possession of Bangalore, dispatch it to General Smith, whose division shall have orders to approach as near the frontiers of Mysore as may be, without causing suspicion."

Thus parted this worthy pair; Paupiah to report to his principal the progress of these dark machinations, Middlemas to join the Begum on her return to the Mysore. The gold and diamonds of Tippoo, the importance which he was about to acquire, the ridding himself at once of the capricious authority of the irritable Tippoo, and the trouble-some claims of the Begum, were such agreeable subjects of contem-plation, that he scarcely thought of the fate of his European victim, unless to salve his conscience with the hope that the sole injury she could sustain might be the alarm of a few days, during the course of which he would acquire the means of delivering her from the tyrant, in whose Zenana she was to remain a temporary prisoner. He resolved, at the same time, to abstain from seeing her till the moment he could afford her protection, justly considering the danger which his whole plan might incur, if he again awakened the jealousy of the Begum. This he trusted was now asleep; and, in the course of their return to Tippoo's camp, near Bangalore, it was his study to soothe this ambi-tious and crafty female by blandishments, intermingled with the more splendid prospects of wealth and power to be opened to them both, as he pretended, by the success of his present enterprise.

It is scarce necessary to say, that such things could only be acted in the earlier period of our Indian settlements, when the check of the Directors was imperfect, and that of the Crown did not exist. My friend Mr Fairscribe is of opinion, that there is an anachronism in the introduction of Paupiah, the Bramin Dubash of the English governor.

Chapter Fourteen

IT APPEARS that the jealous and tyrannical Begum did not long suspend her purpose of agonizing her rival by acquainting her with her intended fate. By prayers or rewards, Menie Grey prevailed on a servant of Ram Sing Cottah, to deliver to Hartley the following dis-tracted note:—

"All is true your fears foretold—He has delivered me up to a cruel woman, who threatens to sell me to the tyrant Tippoo.—Save me if you can—if you have not pity, or cannot give me aid, there is none left upon earth.—M. G."

The haste with which Dr Hartley sped to the Fort, and demanded an audience of the Governor, was defeated by the delays interposed by Paupiah.

It did not suit the plans of this artful Hindhu, that any interruption should be opposed to the departure of the Begum and her favourite, considering how much the plans of the last corresponded with his own. He affected incredulity on the charge, when Hartley complained of an Englishwoman being detained in the train of the Begum against her consent, treated the complaint of Miss Grey as the result of some female quarrel unworthy of particular attention, and when at length he took some steps for examining further into the matter, he contrived they should be so tardy, that the Begum and her retinue were far beyond the reach of interruption.

Hartley let his indignation betray him into reproaches against Paupiah, in which his principal was not spared. This only served to give the impassible Bramin a pretext for excluding him from the Residency, with a hint, that if his language continued to be of such an imprudent character, he might expect to be removed from Madras, and stationed at some hill-fort or village among the mountains, where his medical knowledge would find full exercise in protecting himself and others from the unhealthiness of the climate.

As he retired, bursting with ineffectual indignation, Esdale was the first person whom Hartley chanced to meet with, and to him, stung with impatience, he communicated what he termed the infamous conduct of the Governor's Dubash, connived at, as he had but too much reason to suppose, by the Governor himself; exclaiming against the want of spirit which they betrayed, in abandoning a British subject to the fraud of renegades, and the force of a tyrant.

Esdale listened with that sort of anxiety which prudent men betray when they feel themselves like to be drawn into trouble by the discourse of an imprudent friend.

"If you desire to be personally righted in this matter," said he at length, "you must apply to Leadenhall Street, where I suspect—betwixt ourselves—complaints are accumulating fast, both against Paupiah and his master."

"I care for neither of them," said Hartley; "I need no personal redress—I desire none—I only want succour for Menie Grey."

"In that case," said Esdale, "you have only one resource—you must apply to Hyder himself——"

"To Hyder—to the usurper—the tyrant?"

"Yes, to this usurper and tyrant," answered Esdale, "you must be contented to apply. His pride is, to be thought a strict administrator of justice; and perhaps he may on this, as on other occasions, choose to display himself in the light of an impartial magistrate."

"Then I go to demand justice at his foot-stool," said Hartley.

"Not so fast, my dear Hartley," answered his friend; "first consider the risk. Hyder is just by reflection, and perhaps from political considerations; but by temperament, his blood is as unruly as ever beat under a black skin, and if you do not find him in the vein of judging, he is likely enough to be in that of killing. Stakes and bowstrings are as frequently in his head as the adjustment of scales of justice."

"No matter—I will instantly present myself at his Durbar. The Governor cannot for very shame refuse me letters of credence."

"Never think of asking them," said his more experienced friend; "it would cost Paupiah little to have them so worded as to induce Hyder to rid our sable Dubash, at once and for ever, of the sturdy free-spoken Dr Adam Hartley. A Vakeel, or messenger of government, sets out to-morrow for Seringapatam; contrive to join him on the road, his passport will protect you both. Do you know none of the chiefs about Hyder's person?"

"None, excepting his late emissary to this place, Barak el Hadgi," answered Hartley.

"His support," said Esdale, "although only a Fakir, may be as effectual as that of persons of more essential consequence. And, to say the truth, where the caprice of a despot is the question in debate, there is no knowing upon what it is best to reckon.—Take my advice, my dear Hartley, leave this poor girl to her fate. After all, by placing yourself in an attitude of endeavouring to save her, it is a hundred to one that you only insure your own destruction."

Hartley shook his head, and bade Esdale hastily farewell; leaving him in the happy and self-applauding state of mind proper to one who has given the best advice possible to a friend, and may conscientiously wash his hands of all consequences.

Having furnished himself with money, and with the attendance of three trusty native servants, mounted like himself on Arab horses, and carrying with them no tent, and very little baggage, the anxious Hartley lost not a moment in taking the road to Mysore, endeavouring, in the meantime, by recollecting every story he had ever heard of Hyder's justice and forbearance, to assure himself that he should find the Nawaub disposed to protect a helpless female, even against the future heir of his empire.

Before he crossed the Madras territory, he overtook the Vakeel, or messenger of the British Government, of whom Esdale had spoken. This man, accustomed for a sum of money to permit adventurous European traders who desired to visit Hyder's capital, to share his protection, passport, and escort, was not disposed to refuse the same good office to a gentleman of credit at Madras; and, propitiated by an additional gratuity, undertook to travel as speedily as possible. It was a journey which was not prosecuted without much fatigue and considerable danger, as they had to traverse a country frequently exposed to all the evils of war, more especially when they approached the Ghauts, those tremendous mountain-passes which descend from the table-land of Mysore, and through which the mighty streams that arise in the centre of the Indian peninsula, find their way to the ocean.

The sun had set ere the party reached the foot of one of these perilous passes, up which lay the road to Seringapatam. A narrow path, which now resembled an empty water-course, winding upwards among immense rocks and precipices, was at one time completely over-shadowed by dark groves of teak-trees, and at another, found its way beside impenetrable jungles, the habitation of jackals and tigers.

By means of this unsocial path the travellers threaded their way in silence,—Hartley, whose impatience kept him before the Vakeel, eagerly inquiring when the moon would enlighten the darkness, which, after the sun's disappearance, closed fast around them. He was answered by the natives according to their usual mode of expression, that the moon was in her dark side, and that he was not to hope to behold her bursting through a cloud to illuminate the thickets and strata of black and slaty rocks, amongst which they were winding. Hartley had therefore no resource, save to keep his eye steadily fixed on the lighted match of the *Sowar*, or horseman, who rode before him, which, for sufficient reasons, was always kept in readiness to be applied to the priming of the match-lock. The vidette, on his part, kept a watchful eye on the Dowrah, a guide supplied at the last village, who, having got more than half way from his own house, was much to be suspected of meditating how to escape the trouble of going further.* The Dowrah, on the other hand, conscious of the lighted match and loaded gun behind him, hollowed from time to time to show that he was on his duty, and to accelerate the march of the travellers. His cries were answered by an occasional ejaculation of Ulla from the black soldiers, who closed the rear, and who were meditating on former adventures, the plundering of a *Kaffila* (party of travelling mer-, chants) or some such exploit, or perhaps reflecting that a tiger, in the neighbouring jungle, might be watching patiently for the last of the party, in order to spring upon him, according to his usual practice.

The sun, which appeared almost as suddenly as it had left them, served to light the travellers in the remainder of the ascent, and called forth from the Mahomedans belonging to the party the morning prayer of Alla Akber, which resounded in long notes among the rocks and ravines, and they continued with better advantage their

---

* In every village the Dowrah, or Guide, is an official person, upon the public establishment, and receives a portion of the harvest or other revenue, along with the Smith, the Sweeper, and the Barber. As he gets nothing from the travellers whom it is his office to conduct, he never scruples to shorten his own journey and prolong theirs by taking them to the nearest village, without reference to the most direct line of route, and sometimes deserts them entirely. If the regular Dowrah is sick or absent, no wealth can procure a substitute.

forced march, until the pass opened upon a boundless extent of jungle, with a single high mud fort rising through the midst of it. Upon this plain rapine and war had suspended the labours of industry, and the rich vegetation of the soil had in a few years converted a fertile champaign country into an almost impenetrable thicket. Accordingly, the banks of a small nullah, or brook, were covered with the footmarks of tigers and other animals of prey.

Here the travellers stopped to drink, and to refresh themselves and their horses; and it was near this spot that Hartley saw a sight which forced him to compare the subject which engrossed his own thoughts, with the distress that had afflicted another.

At a spot not far distant from the brook, the guide called their attention to a most wretched-looking man, overgrown with hair, who was seated on the skin of a tiger. His body was covered with mud and ashes, his skin sun-burnt, his dress a few wretched tatters. He appeared not to observe the approach of the strangers, neither moving nor speaking a word, but remaining with his eyes fixed on a small and rude tomb, formed of the black slate-stones which lay around, and exhibiting a small recess for a lamp. As they approached the man, and placed before him a rupee or two, and some rice, they observed that a tiger's skull and bones lay beside him, with a sabre almost consumed by rust.

While they gazed on this miserable object, the guide acquainted them with his tragical history. Sadhu Sing had been a Sipahee, or soldier, and free-booter of course, the native and the pride of a half-ruined village which they had passed on the preceding day. He was betrothed to the daughter of a Sipahee, who served in the mud fort which they saw at a distance rising above the jungle. In due time, Sadhu, with his friends, came for the purpose of the marriage, and to bring home the bride. She was mounted on a Tatoo, a small horse belonging to the country, and Sadhu and his friends preceded her on foot, in all their joy and pride. As they approached the nullah near which the travellers were resting, there was heard a dreadful roar, accompanied by a shriek of agony. Sadhu Sing, who instantly turned, saw no trace of his bride, save that her horse ran wild in one direction, whilst in the other the long grass and reeds of the jungle were moving like the ripple of the ocean, when distorted by the course of a shark holding its way near the surface. Sadhu drew his sabre and rushed forward in that direction; the rest of the party remained motionless until roused by a short roar of agony. They then plunged into the jungle with their drawn weapons, where they speedily found Sadhu Sing holding in his arms the lifeless corpse of his bride, while a little farther lay the body of the tiger, slain by such a blow over the neck as desperation itself could alone have discharged.—The bride-less bridegroom would permit none to interfere with his sorrow. He dug a grave for his Mora, and erected over it the rude tomb they saw, and never afterwards left the spot. The beasts of prey themselves seemed to respect or dread the extremity of his sorrow. His friends brought him food and water from the nullah, but he neither smiled nor showed any mark of acknowledgment unless when they brought him flowers to deck the grave of Mora. Four or five years, according to the guide, had passed away, and there Sadhu Sing still remained among the trophies of his grief and his vengeance, exhibiting all the symptoms of advanced age, though still in the prime of youth. The tale hastened the travellers from their resting-place; the Vakeel because it reminded him of the dangers of the jungle, and Hartley because it coincided too well with the probable fate of his beloved, almost within the grasp of a more formidable tiger than that whose skeleton lay beside Sadhu Sing.

It was at the mud fort already mentioned that the travellers received the first accounts of the progress of the Begum and her party, by a Peon (or foot-soldier) who had been in their company, but was now on his return to the coast. They had travelled, he said, with great speed, until they ascended the Ghauts, where they were joined by a party of the Begum's own forces; and he and others, who had been brought from Madras as a temporary escort, were paid and dismissed to their homes. After this, he understood it was the purpose of the Begum Mootee Mahul, to proceed by slow marches and frequent halts, to Bangalore, the vicinity of which place she did not desire to reach until Prince Tippoo, with whom she desired an interview, should have returned from an expedition towards Vandicotta, in which he had lately been engaged.

From the result of his anxious inquiries, Hartley had reason to hope, that though Seringapatam was seventy-five miles more to the westward than Bangalore, yet, by using diligence, he might have time to throw himself at the feet of Hyder, and beseech his interposition, before the meeting betwixt Tippoo and the Begum should decide the fate of Menie Grey. On the other hand, he trembled as the Peon told him that the Begum's Bukshee, or General, who had travelled to Madras with her in disguise, had now assumed the dress and character belonging to his rank, and it was expected he was to be honoured by the Mahomedan Prince with some high office of dignity. With still deeper anxiety, he learned that a palanquin, watched with sedulous care by the slaves of Oriental jealousy, contained, it was whispered, a Feringi, or Frankish woman, beautiful as a Houri, who had been brought from England by the Begum, as a present to Tippoo. The deed of villainy was therefore in full train to be accomplished; it remained to see whether, by diligence on Hartley's side, its course could be interrupted.

When this eager vindicator of betrayed innocence arrived in the capital of Hyder, it may be believed that he consumed no time in viewing the temple of the celebrated Vishnoo, or in surveying the splendid Gardens called Loll-baug, which were the monument of Hyder's magnificence, and now hold his mortal remains. On the contrary, he was no sooner arrived in the city, than he hastened to the principal Mosque, having no doubt that he was there most likely to learn some tidings of Barak el Hadgi. He approached accordingly the sacred spot, and as to enter it would have cost a Feringi his life, he employed the agency of a devout Musselman to obtain information concerning the person whom he sought. He was not long in learning that the Fakir Barak was within the Mosque, as he had anticipated, busied with his holy office of reading passages from the Koran, and its most approved commentators. To interrupt him in his devout task was impossible, and it was only by a high bribe that he could prevail on the same Moslem whom he had before employed, to slip into the sleeve of the holy man's robe a paper containing his name, and that of the Khan in which the Vakeel had taken up his residence. The agent brought back for answer, that the Fakir, immersed, as was to be expected, in the holy service which he was in the act of discharging, had paid no visible attention to the symbol of intimation which the Feringi Sahib (European gentleman) had sent to him. Distracted with the loss of time, of which each moment was precious, Hartley next endeavoured to prevail on the Musselman to interrupt the Fakir's devotions with a verbal message; but the man was indignant at the very proposal.

"Dog of a Christian!" he said, "what art thou and thy whole generation, that Barak el Hadgi should lose a divine thought for the sake of an infidel like thee?"

Exasperated beyond self-possession, the unfortunate Hartley was now about to intrude upon the precincts of the Mosque in person, in hopes of interrupting the formal prolonged recitation which issued from its recesses, when an old man laid his hand on his shoulder, and prevented him from a rashness which might have cost him his life, saying, at the same time, "You are a Sahib Angrezie, (English gentleman;) I have been a Telinga, (a private soldier,) in the Company's service, and have eaten their salt. I will do your errand for you to the Fakir Barak el Hadgi."

So saying, he entered the Mosque, and presently returned with the Fakir's answer, in these enigmatical words:—"He who would see the sun rise must watch till the dawn."

With this poor subject of consolation, Hartley retired to his inn, to meditate on the futility of the professions of the natives, and to devise some other mode of finding access to Hyder than that which he had hitherto trusted to. On this point, however, he lost all hope, being informed by his late fellow-traveller, whom he found at the Khan, that the Nawaub was absent from the city on a secret expedition, which might detain him for two or three days. This was the answer which the Vakeel himself had received from the Dewan, with a farther intimation, that he must hold himself ready, when he was required, to deliver his credentials to Prince Tippoo, instead of the Nawaub; his business being referred to the former, in a way not very promising for the success of his mission.

Hartley was now nearly thrown into despair. He applied to more than one officer supposed to have credit with the Nawaub, but the slightest hint of the nature of his business seemed to strike all with terror. Not one of the persons he applied to would engage in the affair, or even consent to give it a hearing; and the Dewan plainly told him, that to engage in opposition to Prince Tippoo's wishes, was the ready way to destruction, and exhorted him to return to the coast. Driven almost to distraction by his various failures, Hartley betook himself in the evening to the Khan. The call of the Muezzins thundering from the minarets, had invited the faithful to prayers, when a black servant, about fifteen years old, stood before Hartley, and pronounced these words, deliberately, and twice over,—"Thus says Barak el Hadgi, the watcher in the Mosque. He that would see the sun rise, let him turn towards the east." He then left the caravanserai; and it may be well supposed that Hartley, starting from the carpet on which he had lain down to repose himself, followed his youthful guide with renewed vigour and palpitating hope.

Chapter Fifteen

'Twas the hour when rites unholy
    Call'd each Paynim voice to prayer,
And the star that faded slowly,
    Left to dews the freshen'd air.

Day his sultry fires had wasted,
    Calm and cool the moonbeams shone;
To the Vizier's lofty palace
    One bold Christian came alone.
            THOMAS CAMPBELL *Quoted from memory*

THE TWILIGHT DARKENED into night so fast, that it was only by his white dress that Hartley could discern his guide, as he tripped along the splendid Bazaar of the city. But the obscurity was so far favourable, that it prevented the inconvenient attention which the natives might otherwise have bestowed upon the European in his native dress, a sight at that time very rare in Seringapatam.

The various turnings and windings through which he was conducted, ended at a small door in a wall, which, from the branches that hung over it, seemed to surround a garden or grove.

The postern opened on a tap from his guide, and the slave having entered, Hartley prepared to follow, but stepped back as a gigantic African brandished at his head a scimitar three fingers broad. The young slave touched his countryman with a rod which he held in his hand, and it seemed as if the touch disabled the giant, whose arm and weapon sunk instantly. Hartley entered without farther opposition, and was now in a grove of mango trees, through which an infant moon was twinkling faintly amid the murmur of waters, the sweet song of the nightingale, and the odours of the rose, yellow jessamine, orange and citron flowers, and Persian Narcissus. Huge domes and arches, which were seen imperfectly in the quivering light, seemed to intimate the neighbourhood of some sacred edifice, where the Fakir had doubtless taken up his residence.

Hartley pressed on with as much haste as he could, and entered a side-door and narrow-vaulted passage, at the end of which was another door. Here his guide stopped, but pointed and made indications that the European should enter. Hartley did so, and found himself in a small cell, such as we have formerly described, wherein sate Barak el Hadgi, with another Fakir, who, to judge from the extreme dignity of a white beard, which ascended up to his eyes on each side, must be a man of great sanctity, as well as importance.

Hartley pronounced the usual salutation of Salam Alaikum in the most modest and deferential tone; but his former friend was so far from responding in their former strain of intimacy, that, having consulted the eye of his older companion, he barely pointed to a third carpet, upon which the stranger seated himself cross-legged after the country fashion, and a profound silence prevailed for the space of several minutes. Hartley knew the Oriental customs too well to endanger the success of his suit by precipitation. He waited an intimation to speak. At length it came, and from Barak.

"When the pilgrim Barak," he said, "dwelt at Madras, he had eyes and a tongue; but now he is guided by those of his father, the holy Scheik Hali ben Khaledoun, the superior of his convent."

This extreme humility Hartley thought inconsistent with the affectation of possessing superior influence, which Barak had shown while at the Presidency; but exaggeration of their own consequence is a foible common to all who find themselves in a land of strangers.

Addressing the senior Fakir, therefore, he told him in as few words as possible the villainous plot which was laid to betray Menie Grey into the hands of the Prince Tippoo. He made his suit for the reverend father's intercession with the Prince himself, and with his father the Nawaub, in the most persuasive terms. The Fakir listened to him with an inflexible and immovable aspect, similar to that with which a wooden saint regards his eager supplicants. There was a second pause, when, after resuming his pleading more than once, Hartley was at length compelled to end it for want of matter.

The silence was broken by the elder Fakir, who, after shooting a glance at his younger companion by a turn of the eye, without the least alteration of the position of the head and body, said, "The unbeliever has spoken like a poet. But does he think that the Nawaub Khan Hyder Ali Behauder will contest with his son Tippoo the Victorious, the possession of an infidel slave?"

Hartley received at the same time a side glance from Barak, as if encouraging him to plead his own cause. He suffered a minute to elapse, and then replied,—

"The Nawaub is in the place of the Prophet, a judge over the low as well as high. It is written, that when the Prophet decided a controversy between the two sparrows concerning a grain of rice, his wife Fatima said to him, 'Doth the Missionary of Allah well to bestow his time in distributing justice on a matter so slight, and betwixt such despicable litigants?'—'Know, woman,' answered the Prophet, 'that the sparrows and the grain of rice are the creation of Allah. They are not worth more than thou hast spoken; but justice is a treasure of inestimable price, and it must be imparted by him who holdeth power to all who require it at his hand. The Prince doth the will of Allah, who gives it alike in small matters as in great, and to the poor as well as the powerful. To the hungry bird, a grain of rice is as a chaplet of pearls to a sovereign.—I have spoken.'"

"Bismallah!—Praised be God! he hath spoken like a Moullah," said the elder Fakir, with a little more emotion, and some inclination of his head towards Barak, for on Hartley he scarcely deigned even to look.

"The lips have spoken it which cannot lie," replied Barak, and there was again a pause.

It was once more broken by Scheik Hali, who, addressing himself directly to Hartley, demanded of him, "Hast thou heard, Feringi, of aught of treason meditated by this Kafr (or infidel) against the Nawaub Behauder?"

"Out of a traitor cometh treason," said Hartley; "but, to speak after my knowledge, I am not conscious of such design."

"There is truth in the words of him," said the Fakir, "who accuseth not his enemy save on his knowledge. The things thou hast spoken shall be laid before the Nawaub; and as Allah and he will, so shall the issue be. Meantime, return to thy Khan, and prepare to attend the Vakeel of thy government, who is to travel with dawn to Bangalore, the strong, the happy, the holy city. Peace be with thee!—Is it not so, my son?"

Barak, to whom this appeal was made, replied, "Even as my father hath spoken."

Hartley had no alternative but to arise and take his leave with the usual phrase, "Salam—God's peace be with you!"

His youthful guide, who waited his return without, conducted him once more to his Khan, through by-paths which he could not have found out without pilotage. His thoughts were in the meantime strongly engaged on his late interview. He knew the Moslem men of religion were not implicitly to be trusted. The whole scene might be a scheme of Barak, to get rid of the trouble of patronizing a European in a delicate affair; and he determined to be guided by what should seem to confirm or discredit the intimation which he had received.

On his arrival at the Khan, he found the Vakeel of the British government in a great bustle, preparing to obey directions transmitted to him by the Nawaub's Dewan, or treasurer, directing him to depart the next morning with break of day for Bangalore.

He expressed great discontent at the order, and when Hartley intimated his purpose of accompanying him, seemed to think him a fool for his pains, hinting the probability that Hyder meant to get rid of them both by means of the freebooters, through whose countries they were to pass with such a feeble escort. This fear gave way to another, when the time of departure came, at which moment there rode up about two hundred of the Nawaub's native cavalry. The Sirdar who commanded these troops behaved with civility, and stated that he was directed to attend upon the travellers, and to provide for their safety and convenience on the journey; but his manner was reserved and distant, and the Vakeel insisted that the force was intended to prevent their escape, rather than for their protection. Under such unpleasant auspices, the journey between Seringapatam and Bangalore was accomplished in two days and part of a third, the distance being nearly eighty miles.

On arriving in view of this fine and populous city, they found an encampment already established within a mile of its walls. It occupied a tope or knoll, covered with trees, and looked full on the gardens which Tippoo had created in one quarter of the city. The rich pavilions of the principal persons flamed with silk and gold; and spears with gilded points, or poles supporting gold knobs, displayed numerous little banners, inscribed with the name of the Prophet. This was the camp of the Begum Mootee Mahul, who, with a small body of her troops, about two hundred men, was waiting the return of Tippoo under the walls of Bangalore. Their private motives for desiring a meeting the reader is acquainted with; to the public the visit of the Begum had only the appearance of an act of deference, frequently paid by inferior and subordinate princes to the patrons whom they depend upon.

These facts ascertained, the Sirdar of the Nawaub took up his own encampment within sight of that of the Begum, but at about half a mile's distance, dispatching to the city a messenger to announce to the Prince Tippoo, so soon as he should arrive, that he had come hither with the English Vakeel.

The bustle of pitching a few tents was soon over, and Hartley, solitary and sad, was left to walk under the shade of two or three mango trees, and looking to the displayed streamers of the Begum's encampment, to reflect that amid these insignia of Mahomedanism Menie Grey remained, destined by a profligate and treacherous lover to the fate of slavery to a heathen tyrant. The consciousness of being in her vicinity added to the bitter pangs with which Hartley contemplated her situation, and reflected how little chance there appeared of his being able to rescue her from it by the mere force of reason and justice, which was all he could oppose to the selfish passions of a voluptuary tyrant. A lover of romance might have meditated some means of effecting her release by force or address; but Hartley, though a man of courage, had no spirit of adventure, and would have regarded as desperate any attempt of the kind.

His sole gleam of comfort arose from the impression which he had apparently made upon the elder Fakir, which he could not help hoping might be of some avail to him. But on one thing he was firmly resolved, and that was, not to relinquish the cause he had engaged in whilst a grain of hope remained. He had seen in his own profession a quickening and a revival of life in the patient's eye, even when glazed apparently by the hand of Death; and he was taught confidence amidst moral evil by his success in relieving that which was physical only.

While Hartley was thus meditating, he was roused to attention by a heavy firing of artillery from the high bastions of the town; and turning his eyes in that direction, he could see advancing, on the northern side of Bangalore, a tide of cavalry, riding tumultuously forward, brandishing their spears in all different attitudes, and pressing their horses to a gallop. The clouds of dust which attended this vanguard, for such it was, combined with the smoke of the guns, did not permit Hartley to see distinctly the main body which followed; but the appearance of howdawed elephants and royal banners dimly seen through the haze, plainly intimated the return of Tippoo to Bangalore; while shouts and irregular discharges of musketry, announced the real or pretended rejoicing of the inhabitants. The city gates received the living torrent, which rolled towards them; the clouds of smoke and dust were soon dispersed, and the horizon was restored to serenity and silence.

The meeting between persons of importance, more especially of royal rank, is a matter of very great consequence in India, and generally much address is employed to induce the person receiving the visit, to come as far as possible to meet the visitor. From merely rising up, or going to the edge of the carpet, to advancing to the gate of the palace, to that of the city, or, finally, to a mile or two on the road, is all subject to negotiation. But Tippoo's impatience to possess the fair European induced him to grant on this occasion a much greater degree of courtesy than the Begum had dared to expect, and he appointed his garden, adjacent to the city walls, and indeed included within the precincts of the fortifications, as the place of their meeting; the hour noon, on the day succeeding his arrival; for the natives seldom move early in the morning, or before having broken their fast. This was intimated to the Begum's messenger by the Prince in person, as, kneeling before him, he presented the *nuzzur*, (a tribute consisting of three, five, or seven gold Mohurs, always an odd number,) and received in exchange a Khelaut, or dress of honour. The messenger, in return, was eloquent in describing the importance of his mistress, her devoted veneration for the Prince, the pleasure which she experienced on the prospect of their molakat, or meeting, and concluded with a more modest compliment to his own extraordinary talents, and the confidence which the Begum reposed in him. He then departed; and orders were given that on the next day all should be in readiness for the *Sowarree*, a grand procession, when the Prince was to receive the Begum as his honoured guest at his pleasure-house in the gardens.

Long before the appointed hour, the rendezvous of Fakirs, beggars, and idlers, before the gate of the palace, intimated the excited expectations of those who usually attend processions; while a more urgent set of mendicants, the courtiers, were hastening thither on horses or elephants, as their means afforded, always in a hurry to show their zeal, and with a speed proportioned to what they hoped or feared.

At noon precisely, a discharge of cannon, placed in the outer courts, as also of matchlocks and of small swivels, carried by camels, (the poor animals shaking their long ears at every discharge,) announced that

Tippoo had mounted his elephant. The solemn and deep sound of the nagara, or state drum, borne upon an elephant, was then heard like the distant discharge of artillery, followed by a long roll of musketry, and was instantly answered by that of numerous trumpets and tom-toms, (or common drums,) making a discordant, but yet a martial din. The noise increased as the procession traversed the outer courts of the palace in succession, and at length issued from the gates, having at their head the Chobdars, bearing silver sticks and clubs, and shouting, at the pitch of their voices, the titles and the virtues of Tippoo, the great, the generous, the invincible—strong as Rustan, just as Nou-shirvan—with a short prayer for his continued health.

After these came a confused body of men on foot, bearing spears, matchlocks, and banners, and intermixed with horsemen, some in complete shirts of mail, with caps of steel under their turbans, some in a sort of defensive armour, consisting of rich silk dresses, rendered sabre-proof by being stuffed with cotton. These champions preceded the Prince, as whose body-guards they acted. It was not till after this time that Tippoo raised his celebrated Tiger-regiment, disciplined and armed according to the European fashion. Immediately before the Prince came, on a small elephant, a hard-faced, severe-looking man, by office the distributor of alms, which he flung in showers of small copper money among the Fakirs and beggars, whose scrambles to collect them seemed to augment their amount; while the grim-looking agent of Mahomedan charity, together with his elephant, which marched with half angry eyes, and its trunk curled upwards, seemed both alike ready to chastise those whom poverty should render too importunate.

Tippoo himself next appeared, richly apparelled, and seated on an elephant, which, carrying its head above all the others in the proces-sion, seemed proudly conscious of superior dignity. The howdaw, or seat, which the Prince occupied, was of silver, embossed and gilt, having behind a place for a confidential servant, who waved the great chowry, or cow-tail, to keep off the flies; but who could also occasion-ally perform the task of spokesman, being well versed in all terms of flattery and compliment. The caparisons of the royal elephant were of scarlet cloth, richly embroidered with gold. Behind Tippoo came the various courtiers and officers of the household, mounted chiefly on elephants, all arrayed in their most splendid attire, and exhibiting the greatest pomp.

In this manner the procession advanced down the principal street of the town, to the gate of the royal gardens. The houses were orna-mented by broad cloth, silk shawls, and embroidered carpets of the richest colours, displayed from the verandahs and windows; even the meanest hut was adorned with some piece of cloth, so that the whole street had a singularly rich and gorgeous appearance.

This splendid procession having entered the royal gardens, approached, through a long avenue of lofty trees, a chabootra, or platform of white marble, canopied by arches of the same material, which occupied the centre. It was raised four or five feet from the ground, covered with white cloth and Persian carpets. In the centre of the platform was the musnud, or state cushion of the Prince, six feet square, composed of crimson velvet, richly embroidered. By especial grace, a small low cushion was placed on the right of the Prince, for the occupation of the Begum. In front of this platform was a square tank, or pond of marble, four feet deep, and filled to the brim with water as clear as crystal, having a large jet or fountain in the middle, which threw up a column of it to the height of twenty feet.

The Prince Tippoo had scarcely dismounted from his elephant, and occupied the musnud, or throne of cushions, when the stately form of the Begum was seen advancing to the place of rendezvous. The elephant being left at the gate of the gardens opening into the country opposite to that by which the procession of Tippoo had entered, she was carried in an open litter, richly ornamented with silver, and borne on the shoulders of six black slaves. Her person was as richly attired as silks and gems could accomplish.

Richard Middlemas, as the Begum's general or Buckshee, walked nearest to her litter, in a dress as magnificent in itself as it was remote from all European costume, being that of a Banka, or Indian courtier. His turban was of rich silk and gold, twisted very hard, and placed on one side of his head, its ends hanging down on the shoulder. His mustachoes were turned and curled, and his eyelids stained with antimony. The vest was of gold brocade, with a cummerband, or sash, around his waist, corresponding to his turban. He carried in his hand a large sword, sheathed in a scabbard of crimson velvet, and wore around his middle a broad embroidered sword-belt. What thoughts he had under this gay attire, and the bold bearing which corresponded to it, it would be fearful to unfold. His least detestable hopes were perhaps those which tended to save Menie Grey, by betraying the Prince who was about to confide in him, and the Begum, at whose intercession Tippoo's confidence was to be reposed.

The litter stopped as it approached the tank, on the opposite side of which the Prince was seated on his musnud. Middlemas assisted the Begum to descend, and led her, deeply veiled with silver muslin, towards the platform of marble. The rest of the retinue of the Begum followed in their richest and most gaudy attire, all males, however; nor was there a symptom of woman being in her train, except that a close litter, guarded by twenty black slaves, having their sabres drawn, remained at some distance in a thicket of flowering shrubs.

When Tippoo Saib, through the dim haze which hung over the waterfall, discerned the splendid train of the Begum advancing, he arose from his musnud, so as to receive her near the foot of his throne, and exchanged greetings with her upon the pleasure of meeting, and inquiries after their mutual health. He then conducted her to the cushion placed near to his own, while his courtiers anxiously showed their politeness in accommodating those of the Begum with places upon the carpets around, where they all sat down cross-legged—Richard Middlemas occupying a conspicuous situation.

The people of inferior note stood behind, and amongst them was the Sirdar of Hyder Ali, with Hartley and the Madras Vakeel. It would be impossible to describe the feelings with which Hartley recognised the apostate Middlemas, and the Amazonian Mrs Montreville. The sight of them worked up his resolution to make an appeal against them in full Durbar, to the justice which Tippoo was obliged to render to all who should complain of injuries. In the meanwhile, the Prince, who had hitherto spoken in a low voice, while acknowledging, it is to be supposed, the services and the fidelity of the Begum, now gave the sign to his attendant, who said, in an elevated tone, "Wherefore, and to requite these services, the mighty Prince, at the request of the mighty Begum, Mootee Mahul, beautiful as the moon, and wise as the daughter of Giamschid, hath decreed to take into his service the Buckshee of her armies, and to invest him, as one worthy of all confidence, with the keeping of his beloved capital of Bangalore."

The voice of the crier had scarce ceased, when it was answered by one as loud, which sounded from the crowd of by-standers, "Cursed is he who maketh the robber Leik his treasurer, or trusteth the lives of Moslemah to the command of an apostate!"

With unutterable satisfaction, yet with trembling doubt and anxiety, Hartley traced the speech to the elder Fakir, the companion of Barak. Tippoo seemed not to notice the interruption, which passed for that of some mad devotee, to whom the Moslem princes permit great freedoms. The Durbar, therefore, recovered from their surprise; and, in answer to the proclamation, united in the shout of applause which is expected to attend every annunciation of the royal pleasure.

Their acclamation had no sooner ceased than Middlemas arose, bent himself before the musnud, and, in a set speech, declared his unworthiness of such high honour as had now been conferred, and his zeal for the Prince's service. Something remained to be added, but his speech faltered, his limbs shook, and his tongue seemed to refuse its office.

The Begum started from her seat, though contrary to etiquette, and said, as if to supply the deficiency in the speech of her officer, "My slave would say, that in acknowledgment of so great an honour conferred on my Buckshee, I am so void of means, that I can only pray your Highness will deign to accept a lily from Frangistan, to plant within the recesses of the secret garden of thy pleasures. Let my Lord's guards carry yonder litter to the Zenana."

A female scream was heard, as, at a signal from Tippoo, the guards of his Seraglio advanced to receive the closed litter from the attendants of the Begum. The voice of the old Fakir was heard louder and sterner than before.—"Cursed is the prince who barters justice for lust! He shall die in the gate by the sword of the stranger."

"This is too insolent!" said Tippoo. "Drag forward that Fakir, and cut his robe into tatters on his back with your chabouks."*

But a scene ensued like that in the hall of Seyd. All who attempted to obey the command of the incensed despot fell back from the Fakir, as they would from the angel of death. He flung his cap and fictitious beard on the ground, and the incensed countenance of Tippoo was subdued in an instant, when he encountered the stern and awful eye of his father. A sign dismissed him from the throne, which Hyder himself ascended, while the officious menials hastily disrobed him of his tattered cloak, and flung on him a robe of regal splendour, and placed on his head a jewelled turban. The Durbar rung with acclamations to Hyder Ali Khan Behauder, "the good, the wise, the discoverer of hidden things, who cometh into the Divan like the sun bursting from the clouds."

The Nawaub at length signed for silence, and was promptly obeyed. He looked majestically around him, and at length bent his eyes upon Tippoo, whose downcast eyes, as he stood before the throne with his arms folded on his bosom, were strongly contrasted with the haughty look of authority which he had worn but a moment before. "Thou hast been willing," said the Nawaub, "to barter the safety of thy capital for the possession of a white slave. But the beauty of a fair woman caused Solomon ben David to stumble in his path; how much more, then, should the son of Hyder Naig remain firm under temptation?—That men may see clearly, we must remove the light which dazzles them. Yonder Feringi woman must be placed at my disposal."

"To hear is to obey," replied Tippoo, while the deep gloom on his brow showed what his forced submission cost his proud and passionate spirit. In the hearts of the courtiers present reigned the most eager curiosity to see the denouement of the scene, but not a trace of that wish was suffered to manifest itself on features accustomed to conceal

* Long whips.

all internal sensations. The feelings of the Begum were hidden under her veil; while, in spite of a bold attempt to conceal his alarm, the perspiration stood in large drops on the brow of Richard Middlemas. The next words of the Nawaub sounded like music in the ear of Hartley.

"Carry the Feringi woman to the tent of the Sirdar Belash Cassim, (the chief to whom Hartley had been committed.) Let her be tended in all honour, and let him prepare to escort her, with the Vakeel and the Hakim Hartley, to the Payeen-Ghaut, (the country beneath the passes,) answering for their safety with his head." The litter was on its road to the Sirdar's tents ere the Nawaub had done speaking. "For thee, Tippoo," continued Hyder, "I am not come hither to deprive thee of authority, or to disgrace thee before the Durbar. Such things as thou hast promised to this Feringi, proceed to make them good. The sun calleth not back the splendour which he lends to the moon; and the father obscures not the dignity which he has conferred on the son. What thou hast promised, that do thou proceed to make good."

The ceremony of investiture was therefore recommenced, by which the Prince Tippoo conferred on Middlemas the important government of the city of Bangalore, probably with the internal resolution, that since he was himself deprived of the fair European, he would take an early opportunity to remove the new Killedar from the charge; while Middlemas accepted it with the throbbing hope that he might yet outwit both father and son. The deed of investiture was read aloud —the robe of honour was put upon the newly-created Killedar, and an hundred voices, while they blessed the prudent choice of Tippoo, wished the governor good fortune, and victory over his enemies.

A horse was led forward, as the Prince's gift. It was a fine steed of the Cuttyawar breed, high-crested, with broad hind quarters; he was of a white colour, but had the extremity of his tail and mane stained red. His saddle was red velvet, the bridle and crupper studded with gilded knobs. Two attendants on lesser horses led this prancing animal, one holding the lance, and the other the long spear of their patron. The horse was shown to the applauding courtiers, and withdrawn, in order to be led in state through the streets, while the new Killedar should follow on the elephant, another present usual on such an occasion, which was next made to advance, that the world might admire the munificence of the Prince.

The huge animal approached the platform, shaking his large wrinkled head, which he raised and sunk, as if impatient, and curling upwards his trunk from time to time, as if to show the gulph of his tongueless mouth. Gracefully retiring with the deepest obeisance, the Killedar, well pleased the audience was finished, stood by the neck of the elephant, expecting the conductor of the animal would make him kneel down, that he might ascend the gilded howdah, which awaited his occupancy.

"Hold, Feringi," said Hyder. "Thou hast received all that was promised thee by the bounty of Tippoo. Accept now what is the fruit of the justice of Hyder."

As he spoke, he signed with his finger, and the driver of the elephant instantly conveyed to the animal the pleasure of the Nawaub. Curling his long trunk around the neck of the ill-fated European, the monster suddenly threw the wretch prostrate before him, and stamping his huge shapeless foot upon his breast, put an end at once to his life and to his crimes. The cry which the victim uttered was mimicked by the roar of the monster, and a sound like an hysterical laugh mingling with a scream, which rung from under the veil of the Begum. The elephant once more raised his trunk aloft, and gaped fearfully.

The courtiers preserved a profound silence; but Tippoo, upon whose muslin robe a part of the victim's blood had spirted, held it up to the Nawaub, exclaiming, in a sorrowful, yet resentful tone,— "Father—father—was it thus my promise should have been kept?"

"Know, foolish boy," said Hyder Ali, "that the carrion which lies there was in a plot to deliver Bangalore to the Feringis and the Mahrattas. This Begum (she started when she heard herself named) has given us warning of the plot, and hath so merited her pardon for having originally concurred in it,—whether altogether out of love to us we will not too curiously inquire.—Hence with that lump of bloody clay, and let the Hakim Hartley and the English Vakeel come before me."

They were brought forward, while some of the attendants flung sand upon the bloody traces, and others removed the crushed corpse.

"Hakim," said Hyder, "thou shalt return with the Feringi woman, and with gold to compensate her injuries, whereunto the Begum, as is fitting, shall contribute a share. Do thou say to thy nation, Hyder Ali acts justly." The Nawaub then inclined himself graciously to Hartley, and then turning to the Vakeel, who appeared much discomposed, "You have brought to me," he said, "words of peace, while your masters meditated a treacherous war. It is not upon such as you that my vengeance ought to alight. But tell the Kafr (or infidel) Paupiah, and his unworthy master, that Hyder Ali sees too clearly to suffer to be lost by treason the advantages he has gained by war. Hitherto I have been in the Carnatic as a mild prince—in future I will be a destroying tempest! Hitherto I have made inroads as a compassionate and merciful conqueror—hereafter I will be the messenger whom Allah sends to the kingdoms which he visits in judgment!"

It is well known how dreadfully the Nawaub kept this promise, and how he and his son afterwards sunk before the discipline and bravery of the Europeans. The scene of just punishment which he so faithfully exhibited might be owing to his policy, his internal sense of right, and to the ostentation of displaying it before an Englishman of sense and intelligence, or to all of these motives mingled together—but in what proportions it is not for us to distinguish.

Hartley reached the coast in safety with his precious charge, rescued from a dreadful fate when she was almost beyond hope. But the nerves and constitution of Menie Grey had received a shock from which she long suffered severely, and never entirely recovered. The principal ladies of the settlement, moved by the singular tale of her distress, received her with the utmost kindness, and exercised towards her the most attentive and affectionate hospitality. The Nawaub, faithful to his promise, remitted to her a sum of no less than ten thousand gold Mohurs, extorted, as was surmised, almost entirely from the hoards of the Begum Mootee Mahul, or Montreville. Of the fate of that adventuress nothing was known for certainty; but her forts and government were taken into Hyder's custody, and report said, that, her power being abolished and her consequence lost, she died by poison, either taken by herself, or administered by some other person.

It might be thought a natural conclusion of the history of Menie Grey, that she should have married Hartley, to whom she stood so much indebted for his heroic interference in her behalf. But her feelings were too much and too painfully agitated, her health too much shattered, to permit her to entertain thoughts of a matrimonial connexion, even with the acquaintance of her youth, and the champion of her freedom. Time might have removed these obstacles, but not two years after their adventures in Mysore, the gallant and disinterested Hartley fell a victim to his professional courage, in withstanding the progress of a contagious distemper, which he at length caught, and under which he sunk. He left a considerable part of the moderate fortune which he had acquired to Menie Grey, who, of course, did not want many advantageous offers of a matrimonial character. But she respected the memory of Hartley too much, to subdue in behalf of another the reasons which induced her to refuse the hand which he had so well deserved—nay, it may be thought, had so fairly won.

She returned to Britain—what seldom occurs—unmarried though wealthy; and, settling in her native village, appeared to find her only pleasure in acts of benevolence which seemed to exceed the extent of her fortune, had not her very retired life been taken into consideration. Two or three persons with whom she was intimate, could trace in her character that generous and disinterested simplicity and affection, which were the ground-work of her character. To the world at large her habits seemed those of the ancient Roman matron, which is recorded on her tomb in these four words,

DOMUM MANSIT—LANAM FECIT.

Chapter Sixteen

If you tell a good jest,
And please all the rest,
    Comes Dingley, and asks you, "What was it?"
And before she can know,
Away she will go
    To seek an old rag in the closet.
                    DEAN SWIFT

WHILE I WAS inditing the goodly matter which my readers have just perused, I might be said to go through a course of breaking-in to stand criticism, like a shooting-pony to stand fire. By some of those venial breaches of confidence, which always take place on the like occasions, my private flirtations with the Muse of Fiction became a matter whispered in Miss Fairscribe's circle, some ornaments of which were, I suppose, highly interested in the progress of the affair, while others "really thought Mr Chrystal Croftangry might have had more wit at his time of day." Then came the sly intimation, the oblique remark, all that sugar-lipped raillery which is fitted for the situation of a man about to do a foolish thing, whether it be to publish or to marry, and that accompanied with the discreet nods and winks of such friends as are in the secret, and the obliging eagerness of others to know all about it.

At length the affair became so far public, that I was induced to face a tea-party with my manuscript in my pocket, looking as simple and modest as any gentleman of a certain age need to do upon such an occasion. When tea had been carried round, handkerchiefs and smelling bottles prepared, I had the honour of reading the Surgeon's Daughter, for the entertainment of the evening. It went off excellently; my friend Mr Fairscribe, who had been seduced from his desk to join the literary circle, only fell asleep twice, and readily recovered his attention by help of his snuff-box. The ladies were politely attentive, and when the cat, or the dog, or a next neighbour, tempted an individual to relax, Katie Fairscribe was on the alert, like an active whipper-in, with look, touch, or whisper, to recall them to a sense of what was going on. Whether Miss Katie was thus active merely to enforce the literary discipline of her coterie, or whether she was really interested by the beauties of the piece, and desirous to enforce them on others, I will not venture to ask, in case I should end in liking the girl—and she is really a pretty one—better than wisdom would warrant, either for my sake or hers.

I must own, my story here and there flagged a good deal; perhaps there were faults in my reading, for while I should have been attending to nothing but how to give the words effect as they existed, I was feeling the chilling consciousness, that they might have been, and ought to have been, a great deal better. However, we kindled up at last, when we got to the East Indies, although on the mention of tigers, an old lady, whose tongue had been impatient for an hour, broke in with, "I wonder if Mr Croftangry ever heard the story of Tiger Tullideph?" and had nearly inserted the whole narrative as an episode in my tale. She was, however, brought to reason, and the subsequent mention of shawls, diamonds, turbans, and cummerbands, had their usual effect in awakening the imaginations of the fair auditors. At the extinction of the faithless lover in a way so horribly new, I had, as indeed I expected, the good fortune to excite that expression of painful interest, which is produced by drawing in the breath through the compressed lips; nay, one Miss of fourteen actually screamed.

At length my task was ended, and the fair circle rained odours upon me, as they pelt beaux at the Carnival with sugar-plums, and drench them with scented spices. There was "Beautiful," and "Sweetly interesting," and "O Mr Croftangry," and "How much obliged," and "What a delightful evening," and "O Miss Katie, how could you keep such a secret so long!" While the dear souls were thus smothering me with rose-leaves, the merciless old lady carried them all off by a disquisition upon shawls, which she had the impudence to say, arose entirely out of my story. Miss Katie endeavoured to stop the flow of her eloquence in vain; she threw all other topics out of the field, and from the genuine Indian, she made a digression to the imitation shawls now made at Paisley, out of real Thibet wool, not to be known from the actual Country shawl, except by some inimitable cross-stitch in the border. "It is well," said the old lady, wrapping herself up in a rich Kashmire, "that there is some way of knowing a thing that cost fifty guineas from an article that is sold for five; but I venture to say there are not one out of ten thousand that would understand the difference."

The politeness of some of the fair ladies would now have brought back the conversation to the forgotten subject of our meeting. "How could you, Mr Croftangry, collect all these hard words about India?— you were never there."—"No, madam, I have not had that advantage;

but like the imitative operatives of Paisley, I have composed my shawl by incorporating into the woof a little Thibet wool, which my excellent friend and neighbour, Colonel MacKerris, one of the best fellows who ever trod a Highland moor, or dived into an Indian jungle, had the goodness to supply me with."

My rehearsal, however, though not absolutely and altogether to my taste, has prepared me in some measure for the less tempered and guarded sentence of the world. So a man must learn to encounter a foil before he confronts a sword; and to take up my original simile, a horse must be accustomed to a *feu de joie* before you can ride him against a volley of balls. Well, Corporal Nym's philosophy is not the worst that has been preached, "Things must be as they may." If my lucubrations give pleasure, I may again require the attention of the courteous reader; if not, here end the

CHRONICLES OF THE CANONGATE.

EXPLANATORY NOTES

In these notes a comprehensive attempt is made to identify Scott's sources, and all quotations, references, historical events, and historical personages, to explain proverbs, and to translate difficult or obscure language. (Phrases are explained in the notes while single words are treated in the glossary.) The notes are brief; they offer information rather than critical comment or exposition. Gaelic phrases are first transliterated into modern Gaelic, and then translated. When a quotation has not been recognised this is stated: any new information from readers will be welcomed. References are to standard editions, or to the editions Scott himself used. Books in the Abbotsford Library are identified by reference to the appropriate page of the *Catalogue of the Library at Abbotsford*. When quotations reproduce their sources accurately, the reference is given without comment. Verbal differences in the source are indicated by a prefatory 'see', while a general rather than a verbal indebtedness is indicated by 'compare'. Biblical references are to the Authorised Version. Plays by Shakespeare are cited without authorial ascription, and references are to *William Shakespeare: The Complete Works*, edited by Peter Alexander (London and Glasgow, 1951, frequently reprinted).

The following publications are distinguished by shortened forms of reference; all manuscripts referred to in the Explanatory and Historical Notes are in the National Library of Scotland.

Bonser   K. J. Bonser, *The Drovers* (London, 1970).
Boxiana   Pierce Egan, *Boxiana: or Sketches of Antient and Modern Pugilism*, 2 vols (London, 1818): *CLA*, 135.
Brewer   *Brewer's Dictionary of Phrase and Fable*, rev. Ivor H. Evans (London, 1970).
Brittlebank   Kate Brittlebank, *Tipu Sultan's Search for Legitimacy* (Delhi, 1997).
Burt   Edmund Burt, *Letters from a Gentleman in the North of Scotland*, 2 vols (1754): *CLA*, 19.
CLA   [J. G. Cochrane], *Catalogue of the Library at Abbotsford* (Edinburgh, 1838).
CSD   *The Concise Scots Dictionary*, ed. Mairi Robinson (Aberdeen, 1985).
Dobie   M. R. Dobie, Manuscript notes on *Chronicles of the Canongate*, MS 23065.
EEWN   The Edinburgh Edition of the Waverley Novels (Edinburgh, 1993–).
Ferguson   James Ferguson's sketches of India, MS 913, ff. 167r–84r.
Haldane   A. R. Haldane, *The Drove Roads of Scotland*, 2nd edn (Edinburgh, 1968).
Harris   Stuart Harris, *The Place Names of Edinburgh: Their Origins and History* (Edinburgh, 1996).
Hobson-Jobson   Henry Yule and A. C. Burnell, *Hobson-Jobson: A Glossary of Colloquial Anglo-Indian Words and Phrases* (Calcutta, 1990). First published 1886.
Journal   *The Journal of Sir Walter Scott*, ed. W. E. K. Anderson (Oxford, 1972).
Khair-Ullah   Frank S. Khair-Ullah, 'Orientalism in the Romantics: A Study

in Indian Material' (unpublished Ph.D. thesis, University of Edinburgh, 1953).

The Koran   *The Koran: commonly called the Alkoran of Mohammed. Translated into English from the Original Arabic . . . to which is prefixed A Preliminary Discourse by George Sale* (London, [1887]): first published 1734.

Krishnaswami   P. R. Krishnaswami, 'Sir Walter Scott's Indian Novel "The Surgeon's Daughter" ', *The Calcutta Review*, n.s. 7 (1919), 431–52.

Language of Walter Scott   Graham Tulloch, *The Language of Walter Scott* (London, 1980).

Letters   *The Letters of Sir Walter Scott*, ed. H. J. C. Grierson and others, 12 vols (London, 1932–37).

Life   J. G. Lockhart, *Memoirs of the Life of Sir Walter Scott, Bart.*, 7 vols (Edinburgh, 1837–38).

Magnum   *The Waverley Novels*, 48 vols (Edinburgh, 1829–33).

Minstrelsy   *Minstrelsy of the Scottish Border*, ed. T. F. Henderson, 4 vols (Edinburgh, 1902).

Narrative Sketches   *Narrative Sketches of the Conquest of the Mysore*, 2nd edn (London, 1800): *CLA*, 312.

Normand   W. G. Normand, Lord Normand, Manuscript notes on points of law in *Chronicles of the Canongate*, MSS 23091 and 23092.

Orme   Robert Orme, *A History of the Military Transactions of the British Nation in Indostan, from the year MDCCXLV*, 2 vols (London, 1775–78): *CLA*, 253.

ODEP   *The Oxford Dictionary of English Proverbs*, 3rd edn, rev. F. P. Wilson (Oxford, 1970).

OED   *The Oxford English Dictionary*, 2nd edn (Oxford, 1989).

Poetical Works   *The Poetical Works of Sir Walter Scott, Bart.*, [ed. J. G. Lockhart], 12 vols (Edinburgh, 1833–34).

Prose Works   *The Prose Works of Sir Walter Scott, Bart.*, 28 vols (Edinburgh, 1834–36).

Ramsay   Allan Ramsay, *A Collection of Scots Proverbs* (1737), in *The Works of Allan Ramsay*, 6 vols, ed. Alexander M. Kinghorn and Alexander Law (Edinburgh and London: Scottish Text Society, 1972), 5.59–133: see *CLA*, 169.

Scurry   *Captivity, Sufferings, and Escape of James Scurry, who was detained a prisoner during ten years, in the Dominions of Hyder Ali and Tippoo Saib* (London, 1824): *CLA*, 238.

SND   *The Scottish National Dictionary*, ed. William Grant and David Murison, 10 vols (Edinburgh, 1931–76).

Stewart   David Stewart, *Sketches of the Character, Manners, and Present State of the Highlanders of Scotland with details of the Military Service of the Highland Regiments*, 2 vols (Edinburgh, 1822): *CLA*, 19.

Traditions of Edinburgh   Robert Chambers, *Traditions of Edinburgh*, 2 vols (Edinburgh, 1825): *CLA*, 332.

Tulloch   Sir Walter Scott, *The Two Drovers and Other Stories*, ed. Graham Tulloch (Oxford, 1987).

EXPLANATORY NOTES TO THE INTRODUCTION

title page   Author of "Waverley" soubriquet for Scott. His first novel, *Waverley*, was published anonymously in 1814; his second novel, *Guy Mannering*, appeared the following year with 'By the Author of "Waverley" ' on the title-page, and this attribution was used for all Scott's later novels except *Tales of my Landlord*.

title-page   motto   sic itur ad astra   *Latin* 'this is the path to the stars': Virgil, *Aeneid* (29–19 BC), 9.641. This was the motto on the arms of the Burgh of the Canongate; see also notes to 13.7 and 13.12–14.

3.5 Arlechino servant character in the Italian commedia dell'arte, known in English as Harlequin.

3.9 Touchstone, with quips, and cranks the clown in *As You Like It*; for 'quips, and cranks' see John Milton, 'L'Allegro' (1631), line 27. A *crank* is a fanciful turn of speech.

3.15 Foire de St Germain from the late 16th century travelling players erected their booths at the fairs held in the St Germain quarter of Paris. Italian players were expelled from France in 1697 but returned in 1716.

3.22 attic wit Attica was the area of Greece which included Athens; 'attic' carried implications of cultural sophistication and refinement.

3.28 played Harlequin barefaced an Italian actor, Giovanni Bissoni (1666–1723), playing the part of another servant character, Scapin or Finocchio, in Paris on 21 September 1716, discarded his mask at the behest of the audience (Antoine-Jean-Baptiste-Abraham d'Origny, *Annales du Théatre Italien*, 3 vols (Paris, 1788), 1.36). The French audience's desire to see the actor's face is an incident in the history of the discarding of the mask in 18th-century theatre.

4.1 the Author of Waverley see note to title-page.

4.5 the original manuscripts were carefully preserved in 1823 Scott gave the manuscripts of all the novels then published to his publisher Archibald Constable (1774–1827). When Constable & Co. failed in 1826 the manuscripts were claimed by the trustees of his creditors, to whom they were adjudged in 1831. They were sold at auction in London shortly after Scott's death for £317 (Dobie). Later manuscripts were retained by Scott and given to Robert Cadell in 1831.

4.11 my mask, like my Aunt Dinah's Laurence Sterne, *The Life and Opinions of Tristram Shandy, Gentleman*, 9 vols (1759–67), Vol. 8, Ch. 3.

4.17 Lord Meadowbank Alexander Maconochie (1777–1861), raised to the bench with the title Lord Meadowbank in 1819.

4.19–20 public meeting ... Theatrical Fund a Theatrical Fund for the support of actors in sickness and old age is particularly associated with David Garrick (1717–79) who founded such a fund at Drury Lane theatre in London. A Theatrical Fund was instituted in Edinburgh in 1819 but fell into abeyance, and the dinner held on 23 February 1827, at which Scott presided, was intended to revive it. Scott includes a long newspaper report of the proceedings at the dinner in the Magnum (41.[xxxv]–lxxiii).

5.5 Joseph Train (1779–1852), exciseman and antiquary from Galloway. He began a correspondence with Scott in 1814, and supplied information used in *The Lord of the Isles* (1815). His conversation with Scott in May 1816 is one of the sources of inspiration for the novel published as *Old Mortality* in 1816 (*The Tale of Old Mortality*, ed. Douglas Mack, EEWN 4b, 359–60). Train was gratified by this public acknowledgement of what Scott owed to him (letter from Train to Scott, 14 November 1827, MS 3905, f. 152r), but Scott's indebtedness to Train was more limited than his mention here might imply: see *Guy Mannering*, ed. P. D. Garside, EEWN 2, 361–62.

5.9 that celebrated wanderer Scott describes his meeting with Robert Paterson (c. 1715–1801) known as Old Mortality, in the Introduction to the Magnum *Old Mortality* (1830), 9.222–27.

5.11 Covenanters Scottish Presbyterians of the period 1660–88 whose name came from the National Covenant (1638), a manifesto designed to consolidate opposition to Charles I's religious innovations, and from the Solemn League and Covenant (1643), a treaty between Scotland and England which was to extend Presbyterianism to England in return for the help of a Scottish army in the Parliamentary cause in the Civil War (1642–49). After the Restoration of the monarchy in 1660, Charles II repudiated Prebyterianism and the

National Covenant, and attempted to force Episcopalianism on Scotland, using laws enforced by military persecution, particularly in SW Scotland. Ministers who did not comply with various enactments were removed from their charges and they and many in their congregations worshipped in the open air in conventicles. The persecution continued in the short reign (1685–88) of his Roman Catholic brother, James VII and II.

5.11   died while imprisoned in the Castle of Dunnottar   from May to July 1685 about 160 Covenanters from SW Scotland were incarcerated in Dunnottar in appalling conditions in what came to be known as the Whigs' Vault. Most of those who died did so while trying to escape. Dunnottar is a castle on the NE coast of Scotland, S of Stonehaven. Scott visited Dunottar in 1796.

5.13   Argyle's rising   Archibald Campbell, 9th Earl of Argyll (1629–85), raised a rebellion in 1685 against the accession of James VII and II to the throne.

5.14   the Whigs' Vault   see note to 5.11. The term 'Whig' was originally a nickname for the supporters of the National Covenant but came to be applied in England to those who in 1679 opposed the succession of James to the throne because he was a Roman Catholic. At the Revolution of 1688, when James was deposed, the word was used of those who favoured the Protestant succession, and thus it became the name of the dominant political party of the 18th century.

5.18   Closeburn   18 km NW of Dumfries in SW Scotland.

5.23   Lockerby   Lockerbie in Dumfriesshire. Scott received this account of Robert Paterson's death from Joseph Train (Magnum, 9.227–28, 233–35). Another tradition claims that Old Mortality died at Caerlaverock, S of Dumfries, where he is buried (J. H. Thomson, *The Martyr Graves of Scotland* (Edinburgh, [1903]), 387–88).

5.28   an unknown correspondent   Scott received the story of Helen Walker, the model for Jeanie Deans, the heroine of *The Heart of Mid-Lothian* (1818), in an anonymous communication in 1817.

5.40–41   I am unable to present to the public   Scott felt unable to publish the 'original sketch' on which *The Heart of Mid-Lothian* was based because he still did not know who had sent it, and because he made it 'a kind of rule not to publish even anonymous letters for fear of giving offence' (*Letters*, 10.298). However, this very passage in *Chronicles* may have led the wife of Scott's lawyer, John Gibson, to identify his correspondent as Mrs Helen Goldie of Dumfriesshire (*Letters*, 10.297–98), and Scott revealed her name and published her letter in 1830 in the Introduction to the Magnum edition of *The Heart of Mid-Lothian* (11.142–47).

6.3–4   in a Scottish family of rank   that of James Dalrymple, first Viscount Stair (1619–95); see *The Bride of Lammermoor*, ed. J. H. Alexander, EEWN 7a, 333.

6.4   female relative   Scott had heard the story from his maternal great-aunt, Margaret Swinton (d. 1780), and also from his mother; see *The Bride of Lammermoor*, ed. J. H. Alexander, EEWN 7a, 333.

6.31   Jonathan Oldbuck   the antiquary who supplies the title of Scott's *The Antiquary* (1816). The character was based on George Constable (1719–1803), a friend of Scott's family whom he first met in Prestonpans in 1777 (Scott's 'Memoirs', in *Scott on Himself*, ed. David Hewitt (Edinburgh, 1981), 17–18).

6.38–39   one of the few surviving friends of my father   Scott added a note to the Magnum edition (41.xvii) identifying this friend as 'James Chalmers, Esq. solicitor at law, London, who died during the publication of the present edition of these Novels. (Aug. 1831.)'.

7.1–2   the Baron of Bradwardine and Colonel Talbot   characters in *Waverley* (1814). In the novel the 'exchange of gallantry' is in fact between the hero, Edward Waverley, and Colonel Talbot (*Waverley*, ed. Claire Lamont

(Oxford, 1981), 225–26, 260–61, 312–13); Scott's failure of memory suggests that subconsciously he recognised that the Baron of Bradwardine would have been a better representation of the Jacobite Stewart of Invernahyle than the wavering hero.

7.4 Alexander Stewart of Invernahyle Stewart of Invernahyle in Argyllshire (d.1795) had been a client of Scott's father and Scott always remembered him with affection. The facts of his life are explored in Lorn M. Macintyre, 'Scott's Story of Invernahyle', *Blackwood's Magazine*, 316 (1974), 142–53.

7.7–8 the troubles of 1745 the Jacobite rising against the Hanoverian government, known as 'the '45'.

7.8 the battle of Preston the battle of Prestonpans, in East Lothian, 21 September 1745, in which the Jacobites defeated a Hanoverian army.

7.15–16 Lochaber axe weapon combining an axe and a spear with a hook behind for laying hold of the victim of an assault, named after a district of the Highlands SW of Inverness.

7.18 Lieutenant Colonel Allan Whitefoord this should have been Lt. Col. Charles Whitefoord (d.1753), as was pointed out to Scott by his grandson, Caleb Whitefoord, in a letter of 23 November 1827 (MS 3095, f. 166r–66v). Whitefoord's family came from Ballochmyle in Ayrshire.

7.23 John Roy Stewart Jacobite soldier and poet (1700–52). He fought at Prestonpans, and after the defeat of the '45 escaped to France.

7.27 the Chevalier Prince Charles Edward Stewart (1720–88), 'Bonnie Prince Charlie', who led the Jacobite rising of 1745 in the right of his father, James (1688–1766), the Jacobite claimant to the throne of Britain.

7.30 Whig see note to 5.14.

7.31 the battle of Culloden in which the Jacobites were finally defeated; fought on 16 April 1746, near Inverness.

7.41 the mark of the Beast Revelation 16.2.

7.43 the Duke of Cumberland William Augustus, Duke of Cumberland (1721–65), third son of George II, commander of the Hanoverian forces at Culloden.

8.3 the House of Hanover named after George, Elector of Hanover (1660–1727) who became George I of Britain in 1714 on the death of the Stewart Queen Anne without issue.

8.25 proscription ... the Act of Indemnity after the 1745 rising an Act of Attainder listed the most prominent Jacobites, and required them to surrender by 12 July 1746. Failure to do so rendered them liable to be attainted of high treason. (Attainted persons were put to death; their estates could not be inherited by their heirs and fell to their feudal superior; and their titles and honours were forfeit.) A general Act of Indemnity (passed June 1747) ended the liability of most ordinary Jacobite supporters.

8.30 William Erskine (1769–1822), a close friend of Scott. Sources for the early novels are given in a review of the first series of *Tales of my Landlord* in *The Quarterly Review*, 16 (1817), 430–80, the manuscript of which, owned by the publishers John Murray, is entirely in Scott's hand in spite of what he says here. Further information on sources is given here; and his last word appeared in the Introductions he wrote for each novel in the Magnum edition.

8.36 Meg Merrilees the gipsy in *Guy Mannering* (1815). For Scott's sources for the character see *Guy Mannering*, ed. P. D. Garside, EEWN 2, 505–06.

8.39–40 the Legend of Montrose for Scott's knowledge of the clan legend relating to the Stewarts of Ardvoirlich in Perthshire, which he uses in the novel published as *A Legend of Montrose* (1819): see *A Legend of the Wars of Montrose*, ed. J. H. Alexander, EEWN 7b, 39–41, 221–23; for 'the wager about the candlestick' see 30–33.

9.5   Wolf's Hope   the name of the village in *The Bride of Lammermoor*, which
Scott has here confused with Wolfscrag, the name of Edgar Ravenswood's
castle. Wolfscrag has often been identified with Fast Castle; but see J. H.
Alexander's note in *The Bride of Lammermoor*, E.E.W.N 7a, 338. In the Magnum
Chronicles of the Canongate Scott added a note intimating 'the Kaim of Urie, on
the eastern coast of Scotland, as having suggested an idea for the tower called
Wolf's-Crag, which the public more generally identified with the ancient tower
of Fast-Castle' (41.xxiv).

9.6   Tillietudlem   Lady Margaret Bellenden's castle in *The Tale of Old
Mortality* (1817), which Lockhart claimed was inspired by Craignethan Castle,
visited by Scott in 1799 (*Life*, 1.306–07). Draffane, or Draffan, is an old name
for Craignethan and survives as a place-name in the area.

9.7   valley in the Monastery   the fictitious Glendearg in *The Monastery*
(1820) is associated with the valley of the Allan Water which flows south into the
Tweed a couple of miles above Melrose. The river flows near the Pavilion, a
hunting-lodge belonging to John Lord Somerville (1765–1819), a friend of
Scott's with whom he shared interests in sport and agriculture.

9.26–27   by snowing brown   the source of this anecdote has not been
found. Ambitious weather effects were achieved on the 18th-century stage as
Alexander Pope indicates when describing the creator of pantomimes, John
Rich, 'Mid snows of paper, and fierce hail of pease' (*The Dunciad* (1728),
3.258).

9.34–35   Corporal Nym . . . the humour or caprice of the time   alluding to Nym's repeated use of phrase 'that's the humour of it' in *Henry V*. In the
context of a refusal to answer a question a nearer Shakespearean source is
Shylock's 'I'll not answer that, / But say it is my humour' (*The Merchant of Venice*,
4.1.42–43).

9.41   the age of thirty years   Scott was born in 1771; he published poems
and translations from 1796 but his first major work was his *Minstrelsy of the
Scottish Border*, 2 vols (Kelso, 1802). What follows, however, applies more
appropriately to his verse romance *The Lay of the Last Minstrel* (1805) which
established his fame as a poet.

10.11   with triple brass   see Horace's *Odes* (23 BC), 1.3.9, referring to the
protective clothing worn by the first person to put to sea in a boat.

10.20   circumstances which gave rise to them   sentiments similar to
Byron's 'One hates an author that's *all author*' (*Beppo* (1818), stanza 75). In the
next stanza Byron commends Scott as one of those writers 'who know the world
like men' and 'think of something else beside the pen'.

10.28   frankly told my motives for concealment   the frankness of this
account of Scott's motives has been investigated by Seamus Cooney in 'Scott's
Anonymity—Its Motives and Consequences', *Studies in Scottish Literature*, 10
(1973), 207–19.

11.1   twenty persons at least   Lockhart endeavoured to list these people in
his biography of Scott (*Life*, 7.20–21).

11.8   meditated, and in part printed   *Chronicles of the Canongate* was
started in May 1826, and was printed as it was written. The text up to 98.19 had
been printed before Scott's avowal of authorship on 23 February 1827.

11.9–11   declaration . . . introduction nor preface   in the manuscript
the opening chapter, written in June 1826, starts: 'As no preface introduction or
preliminary adverstizement of any kind is intended the work itself must
necessary commencen commence with some account of its author ⟨and⟩ his
pretensions and his purpose in appearing before the public. The gentle reader
therefore . . .' (f. 4r). After the public acknowledgement of his authorship, Scott
added the Introduction and altered the beginning of his text.

11.26   Abbotsford   Scott's home near Melrose in the Scottish Borders.

13.6 **Sic itur ad astra** see note to title-page.

13.7 **path to heaven** an example of the Christian use of a pre-Christian quotation, to which Virgil's works in particular lent themselves: see Virgil, *Aeneid* (29–19 BC), 9.641, where the words are spoken by Apollo to Ascanius and are more literally translated 'this is the path to the stars'.

13.8 **armorial bearings of the Canongate** the Canongate, or 'way of the canons', derives its name from the Augustinian canons whose monastery at Holyrood was founded by David I in 1128. According to legend King David (1084–1153; king from 1124), against the advice of his confessor, went hunting on the Feast of the Exaltation of the Holy Cross. In the course of the hunt he was pinned down by a stag and on attempting to clutch its antlers found himself holding a cross. That night he was told in a dream to found an abbey dedicated to the Holy Rood or Cross.

13.10 **from the church to the pillory** the figure of the stag's head with the cross stands at the apex of the south gable of the Canongate church (built in 1688); it is also visible on the Canongate Tolbooth (1591). The stocks of the Canongate, perhaps the pillory referred to, now in the Museum of Scotland in Edinburgh, are illustrated in James Grant, *Old and New Edinburgh*, 3 vols (London, 1882), 2.31; they bear no arms or motto.

13.11 **the Good Town** a soubriquet for Edinburgh

13.12–14 **Westminster ... nobility and gentry** the Royal Palace of Holyrood is in the Canongate, outside the old burgh of Edinburgh, as in London St James's Palace is in Westminster, outside the city of London. When Holyrood became the chief residence of the Scottish kings in the early 16th century the Canongate became a fashionable residential area, and several of the noble families of Scotland established town houses there. The street declined later as a result of the removal of first the Scottish Court to London in 1603, and then the Scottish Parliament in 1707, and finally the building of the New Town of Edinburgh from 1767. The Canongate was administered by the Town Council of Edinburgh from 1636; it became part of the city of Edinburgh in 1856, but the name is retained for the area between the site of the old Netherbow Port (see note to 52.25) and Holyrood.

13.16 **Chrystal** a Scots diminutive of Christopher (*The Penguin Dictionary of Surnames*, ed. Basil Cottle, 2nd edn (London, 1978), 91).

13.18 **the gentle reader** a compliment to the reader common in the 18th-century novel, implying that he or she is of good birth, and therefore of refined taste.

13.19 **Captain Bobadil's humour** Ben Jonson, *Every Man In His Humour* (1598), 1.5.35–37: 'by the heart of valour in me (except it be to some peculiar and choice spirits, to whom I am extraordinarily engaged, as yourself, or so) I could not extend thus far'.

13.22 **with a fortune ... rather the worse for wear** Lockhart claims that in Scott's portrait of Chrystal Croftangry 'there can be no doubt that a good deal was taken from nobody but himself' (*Life*, 7.82).

13.28 **laced coats and triple ruffles** alluding to male dress of the 18th century.

13.28–29 **blows of the Forty-five** the rising of the Jacobites against the Hanoverian government in 1745.

14.4 **Grand Climacteric** astrologers believed that the seventh and ninth years, with their multiples, were critical points in life; 63, the product of multiplying 7 and 9, was known as the Grand Climacteric, which few would survive (*Brewer*, 235). If Croftangry was 62 when he started to write in 1826 (53.43) he would have been born in 1764. Those who were sexagenarians in his youth would have been born in about 1720.

14.6 the Parliament-House the building where the Scottish Parliament met before the Union of the Parliaments of Scotland and England in 1707. In Scott's day the hall was used as a meeting place for young advocates hoping to be offered a brief. Lockhart quotes this sentence, applying it to Scott himself as a young advocate in 1793–94 (*Life*, 1.215). Croftangry, however, was a young laird and studied law, as the sons of Scottish landowners frequently did, more as an appropriate education than with the specific intention of making a career at the bar.

14.9–10 Bayle's... the Covenant Close John Bayle's tavern was in Shakespeare Square (near the Edinburgh theatre, at the N end of the North Bridge); Fortune's tavern at the Cross Keys was in Stamp Office Close on the N side of the High Street and was where Edinburgh's literati met as the Poker Club; the premises of Charles Walker, vintner, were in Writer's Court on the N side of the High Street. Covenant Close is on the S side of the High Street, and is so called because a copy of the National Covenant (1638) was signed there. Oysters were a common delicacy in 18th-century Edinburgh: see *Traditions of Edinburgh*, 2.268–70.

14.28 out to nurse *literally*, to be suckled by someone other than the mother; here the reference is to a financial agent.

14.32 near the Abbey of Holyrood although in ruins by the late 18th century, the Abbey retained its status as a sanctuary for debtors. The ancient custom of sanctuary, or the right of safety from legal pursuit, gave the debtor time to seek relief or accommodation with creditors. Many people had occasion to seek sanctuary at Holyrood until imprisonment for debt was abolished in 1880: see Hugh Hannah, 'The Sanctuary of Holyrood', *The Book of the Old Edinburgh Club*, 15 (Edinburgh, 1927), 55–98.

The manuscript shows that Scott had considered as possible titles 'Chronicles of the Canongate Or Traditions of the Sanctuary' and 'The Canongate Miscellany Or Traditions of the Sanctuary' (f. 4). Lockhart comments that 'the choice of the hero's residence, the original title of the book, and a world of minor circumstances, were suggested by the actual condition and prospects of the author's affairs' (*Life*, 7.82–83). The subject of sanctuary could never have been far from Scott's mind: his publisher Robert Cadell took sanctuary in Holyrood on 4 February 1826 (*Journal*, 76), and in the autumn of 1827 (a year after writing this passage), under pressure from a creditor, Abud and Co., Scott confronted the possibility of himself taking shelter in the sanctuary of Holyrood, and asked Cadell to arrange a lodging for him (*Journal*, 370–71; *Letters*, 10.302).

14.35 magnificent wilds the open and mountainous ground which was once a royal hunting park and known as the King's (or Queen's) park.

14.38–39 John Doe and Richard Roe the names given to fictitious litigants in various (often complex) actions to recover real property (i.e. land and buildings) under English law; in a more general sense, as here, these are the supposed parties in a hypothetical legal argument. Thus Croftangry means that as he was now in the sanctuary of Holyrood he was free of the threat of legal action. In the Magnum Scott added a sentence here: 'In short, the precincts of the palace are now best known as being a place of refuge at any time from all pursuit for civil debt' (41.6). See also *ODEP*, 413.

15.8 the accurate Maitland this description of the boundary of the sanctuary of Holyrood is abbreviated from William Maitland, *The History of Edinburgh*, (Edinburgh, 1753), 153. The sanctuary was an area five miles in circumference which included Holyrood Park. It had been walled by James V (1512–42; king from 1513) and Scott and Maitland trace its boundary in a clockwise direction starting from a gate in the NW of the park. A description of the sanctuary published in 1819 refers to 'the north gate of the King's Park at Croftangrie' (Hugh Hannah, 'The Sanctuary of Holyrood', *The Book of the Old Edinburgh Club*, 15 (Edinburgh, 1927), 66). The 'gutter, or kennel' went up the middle of Horse Wynd and crossed the foot of the Canongate to the Watergate. The tennis court was a building for 'royal tennis', which Maitland notes was 'now converted into a Linnen Manufactory' (156); the physic garden was the ancestor of the Edinburgh Botanic Garden. The church-yard is that of Holyrood Abbey church; St Ann's Yards were to the E and S of Holyrood and in Scott's day there were houses there (Hannah, 74). Clackmill-house (on modern maps, Clockmill), to the east of Holyrood, gets its name from 'clack', the noisy clapper of a mill which by striking the hopper shakes the corn into the millstones (*OED*, *clack*, substantive 3). The boundary of the sanctuary continued S so as to take in Arthur's Seat and Salisbury Crags, both prominent features on the Edinburgh sky-line. The turnstyle, known as the tirless or tirlies, was at the foot of Holyrood Park Road.

15.9 the Girth a legally sanctioned place of safety (*OED*, *grith*, substantive 3); a circle of cobbles in the middle of the street at the foot of the Canongate marks the site of the Girth Cross which was removed in 1767 (Harris, 292).

15.17–18 Sunday...walk without limitation 'Under Roman Law, in the time of the Christian emperors, Sunday was consecrated not only from all labours but from all legal proceedings. Scots Law borrowed this feature from Roman Law, and consequently no diligence could go out against anyone on Sunday' (Hugh Hannah, 'The Sanctuary of Holyrood', *The Book of the Old Edinburgh Club*, 15 (Edinburgh, 1927), 82). Another consideration was that since the roof of what remained of the Abbey Church at Holyrood, which after the Reformation was used as a Protestant church, had collapsed in 1768 it was necessary to leave the sanctuary to attend a church.

15.24–25 the old town of Edinburgh...fresh air Edinburgh was notorious for its foul smells. The buildings of the old town were tall tenements, each housing several families. Drainage and the disposal of refuse from these houses was by the expedient of flinging it out on to the street after nightfall, accompanied by shouts to alert unwary passers-by.

15.27 the portico which surrounds the palace the palace at Holyrood grew out of the Abbey guest house extended first by James IV in 1498–1501; the largest part of it was built at the instigation of Charles II by Sir William Bruce starting in 1671. Bruce's building forms a square with an inner courtyard in an Italianate style. A portico is a covered walk or arcade, and Scott refers to the arcaded loggia in the inner courtyard. Its accessibility is clear from James Boswell's account of his farewell to Edinburgh in 1762 in *Boswell's London Journal*, ed. Frederick A. Pottle (New Haven, 1950), 41.

15.32 the brook Kidron was to Shimei see 1 Kings 2.36–46; Shimei had cursed David in 2 Samuel 16.5–13.

15.38 Elysium the habitation of the blessed after death in Greek mythology; a place of perfect happiness.

16.14–15 no other alternative Sir Herbert Grierson comments that Scott's friend R. P. Gillies (1788–1858), 'a fellow victim of the depression, is in part the model of the spendthrift Chrystal' (*Sir Walter Scott, Bart.* (London, 1938), 282). Gillies had lost a fortune and made an uncertain livelihood by writing.

16.24 hornworks, and covered ways terms from the art of fortification. A hornwork was a projecting part of a fortification added to occupy additional ground; a covered way, or covert way, was a hidden passage in a fortification (*OED*, *covert*, adjective 1b).

16.38–39 Styx...from Limbo Lake in classical mythology the Styx is a river in the underworld of which Pluto is the ruler. Limbo is the habitation of unbaptized infants and of the just who died before Christ's coming. It is a lake in

Spenser, *The Faerie Queene*, 1.2.32: 'What voyce of damned Ghost from *Limbo* lake'.

16.42 Leith smack Leith, on the Firth of Forth, is the port for Edinburgh. Regular sailings of smacks, light single-masted sailing vessels, from Leith to London were first established in 1791 (Sue Mowat, *The Port of Leith* (Edinburgh, [1994]), 315–21).

16.42 standing down sailing with the wind or tide (*OED*, *stand*, verb 92c).

17.4 as befell the sheep in the fable see Robert Henryson (1429?–1508?), 'The Sheep and the Dog' and 'The Wolf and the Wether' (*The Poems of Robert Henryson*, ed. Denton Fox (Oxford, 1981), 47–54 and 92–97).

17.7 always life for living folk *proverbial* 'There is ay a Life for a living Man' (Ramsay, 114).

17.11 like liberty to Virgil's shepherd see Publius Vergilius Maro (Virgil: 70–19 BC), *Eclogues* (*c.* 37 BC), 1.27–30.

17.20 ipsa corpora *Latin, literally* the bodies themselves; here the physical reality of the money in the form of coins.

17.21–22 Rundell and Bridge the jewellers Rundell, Bridge and Rundell in Ludgate Hill, London. Scott saw Bridge in London on 8 May 1828 (*Journal*, 471).

17.24 in —— Square the Magnum (41.11) supplies the name 'Brown's Square'. This was a development to the south of the Old Town begun by James Brown in 1763, and gradually destroyed to allow the building of George IV Bridge, Chambers Street, and the new extension to the Royal Museum of Scotland (Harris, 124).

17.27 the congregation of the just see Psalm 1.5: 'the congregation of the righteous'; the metrical version of the Psalm has 'th' assembly of the just'.

17.33 mail-coach the mail-coach was dedicated to the fast distribution of mail, but often carried a few passengers as well. The service was introduced in 1784; the first Scottish service, between Edinburgh and Glasgow, began in 1788, and spread rapidly to other routes.

17.38 Mr—— the Magnum (41.12) supplies the name 'Sommerville'.

17.42 he is not in euphemism implying that the person does not want to acknowledge callers.

19.20 the same benevolent Samaritan see Luke 10.30–37.

19.20–21 went about doing good Acts 10.38 (Peter speaking of Jesus).

19.39 Mezentius the tyrannical king of Agylla: see Virgil, *Aeneid*, 8.481–88.

20.4 Juvenal Decimus Junius Juvenalis (AD *c.* 60–130), Roman poet known for the bitterness and ironic humour of his *Satires*.

20.5–7 omni... amici worse than any bodily loss is the failing mind, which remembers neither the names of servants nor the face of a friend: Juvenal (AD *c.* 60–130), *Satires*, 10.232–34.

20.12 ex capite lecti *Latin* from the head of the bed, i.e one's death bed. Normand explains that 'Till 1871 all deeds affecting heritage if granted on death bed, i.e. after contracting the illness which ended in death, were ineffectual if they affected adversely the heir's rights of succession'.

20.13 morbus sonticus *Latin* a serious disease, sickness so serious as to form an excuse for not appearing in a court of law.

20.18 Harry—poor Harry Dobie suggests that this may be a reference to Henry Erskine (1746–1817), Lord Advocate 1783, and Dean of the Faculty of Advocates 1785–96. He was noted for his eloquence and wit.

21.15 until all is over this scene draws on the last illness and death of Scott's father in 1799. Lockhart records, 'When the first Chronicles of the Canongate appeared, a near relation of the family said to me—"I had been out of Scotland for some time, and did not know of my good friend's illness, until I reached Edinburgh, a few months before his death. Walter carried me to visit him, and warned me that I should see a great change. I saw the very scene that is here painted of the . . . sickroom—not a feature different—poor Anne Scott [Scott's sister], the gentlest of creatures, was treated by the fretful patient precisely like this niece"' (*Life*, 1.301). Scott's lawyer, John Gibson, recalled a conversation on the subject of death with Scott who remarked, 'I am not afraid to die, but I dread the death of the mind before the body: that happened to my father' (John Gibson, *Reminiscences of Sir Walter Scott* (Edinburgh, 1871), 42).

21.15 **The whole Faculty** of medical doctors.

21.35-36 **Many a lad . . . many a lass grown old** Charles Morris (1745–1838), 'The Toper's Apology', lines 33–34. See *Letters*, 4.31, and 9.501 where Scott gives the whole verse.

22.1 **played small game than sat out** *proverbial* played for low stakes rather than giving up gaming entirely. See Ramsay, 126: 'Ye'll play at sma' Game before ye stand out'.

22.5-6 **bits of painted pasteboard** playing cards.

22.12 **mentioned by Cicero** Marcus Tullius Cicero (106–43 BC), Roman orator and statesman, who wrote an essay, *De Senectute* (46–44 BC), on old age.

22.15 **Beau Nash** Richard Nash (1674–1762), known for his fashionable dress and manners. He made a living as a gambler but in 1704 was made master of ceremonies at Bath where he conducted public balls with great splendour. He died in poverty.

22.16 **thrust aside by tittering youth** see Alexander Pope, 'The Second Epistle of the Second Book of Horace' (1737), lines 324–25: 'before a sprightlier Age/ Comes titt'ring on, and shoves you from the stage'.

22.17 **went into devotion** devoted themselves to religion; alluding to the French phrase *être dévot*, to be overly religious. The phrase got its pejorative sense in French from its use in 18th-century anti-religious writing.

22.19-20 **peeped into microscopes** as a result of improvements in microscopes 'between 1800 and 1830 observers and observations multiplied' (William Coleman, *Biology in the Nineteenth Century* (Cambridge, 1977), 24). Scott's friend Sir David Brewster (1781–1868) contributed to the theory of microscope lenses as well as publishing papers on optics and many other scientific subjects.

22.20 **fashionable experiments** by the end of the 18th century the work of Antoine-Laurent Lavoisier (1743–94), the father of modern chemistry, had become fashionable, and by 1826 there were in Edinburgh many societies interested in chemistry, natural history and physical science in general.

22.29-30 **man of business** lawyer.

23.9 **the Upper Ward of Clydesdale** Lanarkshire was divided into three wards, the Upper Ward, the furthest up the river Clyde, being administered from Lanark.

23.12 **of that Ilk** of the same, meaning that the name of the family was the same as that of their land, here Croftangry.

23 motto Alexander Pope, 'The Second Satire of the Second Book of Horace Paraphrased' (1734), lines 167–68.

23.19 **Croftangry** the house known as Croftangry, dating from the early 17th century, stands to the north of Holyrood (David MacGibbon and Thomas Ross, *The Castellated and Domestic Architecture of Scotland*, 5 vols (Edinburgh, 1887–92), 4.434–37; *The Buildings of Scotland: Edinburgh*, ed. John Gifford (Harmondsworth, 1984), 147). The name is also used for the road leading south from Abbey Hill on which the house stands. The name appears on a map of 1647 and in records of the 18th and early 19th centuries spelled Croftangrie, Croftangry, Croft Angery, Croft Angry (Harris, 212).

23.21–22 King Milcolumb, or Malcolm *Gaelic Mael Coluim,* a follower of St Columba, the 6th-century Irish monk who played a leading part in bringing Christianity to Scotland; the name is anglicised as Malcolm. Malcolm III (1058–93), known as Malcolm Canmore, moved from his base in Dunfermline to Edinburgh. His wife Margaret died in Edinburgh Castle in 1093.

23.22 quha *Scots* who; the Old Scots spelling *quh* for English *wh* survived in documents into the 18th century. Another example in this passage is *quhilk* for 'which': *Language of Walter Scott,* 198.

23.26 Croft-an-ri a *croft* in Scotland and elsewhere is a smallholding, a piece of arable land adjacent to a house; Gaelic *righ* means king. This explanation of the name 'Croftangry' is a false derivation. Stuart Harris notes that Croftangry is 'a field name widely recorded in the Lowlands from 1497 onwards, deriving from Anglian *croft angr,* a fenced grazing in the croft or arable infield, as distinct from unfenced grazings on the outby land. The pseudo-Gaelic spelling 'Croft an righ' appears only at Holyrood and only since the 1820s, when the progressive change in map spellings from *-angry* and *-anry* to *an'rhi* and *an righ* shows that it was deliberately altered to suit a notion that it was Gaelic for 'king's croft'.' (Harris, 212). The change in spelling predates *Chronicles of the Canongate*: Dobie notes that '*The Edinburgh Directory* gives Croftangrie till 1824 inclusive, and Croft-an-Righ from 1826 on'.

23.33 to cultivate the earth see Genesis 3.17–19, 23.

23.35–36 prophets have been taken from the pleugh Elisha was ploughing when he received the mantle of Elijah in 1 Kings 19.19.

23.37 Cincinnatus Lucius Quinctius Cincinnatus, a legendary Roman hero who was called from the plough to be dictator in 458 BC at a time of military emergency. Having defeated the enemy he resigned the dictatorship and returned to his farm.

24.6 Virgilius Roman poet, Publius Vergilius Maro (Virgil: 70–19 BC).

24.6–7 subduing the soil see Virgil, *Georgics* (29 BC), 1.99.

24.14 seed sown on the naked rocks see Matthew 13.5.

24.15 the flitting and faithless sands see Matthew 7.26.

24.17 the inditer of this goodly matter see Psalm 45.1.

24.17–18 rather lengthy, as our American friends say before the 19th century the word was used only by American writers. Scott, referring to Southey, wrote in a letter of 22 April 1813, 'He is *lengthy* as the Americans say' (*Letters*, 3.255).

24.19 the Bannatyne club club formed in 1823 for the purpose of publishing works of Scottish literature and history of which Scott was president. It was named after George Bannatyne (1545–1608?), an important early collector of Scottish poetry, and lasted until 1861.

24.19 throw off publish.

24.23 Haec nos novimus esse nihil *Latin* we understood these things of ours to be nothing: Martial, *Epigrams* (AD 86–101), 13.2.8.

24.23 Vix ea nostra voco *Latin* I hardly call these things ours (referring to families and inheritances which the speaker has not created for himself): Ovid, *Metamorphoses* (AD 2–9), 13.141.

24.28 Tib Tibb, or Tibbie, is a Scots diminutive of the name Isabella and, less commonly, of Elizabeth.

24.28–29 Somerville...that noble house the Somervilles, a family of Norman origin, had estates in both southern Scotland and Gloucestershire. Scott knew John, 14th Lord Somerville (1765–1819); see note to 9.7.

24.30 the wrong side of the blanket *proverbial* outside marriage (*ODEP*, 924).

24.31 Inquisitio post mortem *Latin* inquest after death; a legal procedure by which the identity of the heir to a property was established on the death of the owner of lands or other heritable property (Normand).

24.31–32   sub vexillo regis . . . Branxton, lie Floddenfield   *Latin* under the king's standard, at the battle near Branxton, otherwise known as Floddenfield. James IV of Scotland (1473–1513) was defeated and killed by the English at Flodden in Northumberland in 1513. 'Lie' appears in charters before a vernacular translation in a passage of Latin.

24.33   were forfeited   i.e. their lands and estates were forfeited.

24.34   Sir John Colville of the Dale   who gave this account of himself when charged as a rebel, 'I am, my lord, but as my betters are/ That led me hither' (*2 Henry IV*, 4.3.64–65).

24.34–35   the field of Langside   where Mary Queen of Scots was defeated in 1568, now in the district of Glasgow of that name.

24.35   contentious times of the last Stuarts   the Stewart kings Charles II (1630–85; reigned 1660–85) and James VII and II (1633–1701, reigned 1685–88), during whose reigns Covenanters (see notes to 5.11) suffered persecution. Stuart is a variant spelling of Stewart showing French influence (see note to 63.43–64.1 below).

24.36–37   harbouring and resetting intercommuned ministers   letters of intercommuning were issued in August 1675, forbidding people from contact with those who had been outlawed (see note to 77.39) for persistent attendance at conventicles (open-air services). The royal proclamation commands subjects not to 'reset, supply, or intercommune with any of the foresaid Persons or Rebels, . . . nor furnish them with Meat, Drink, House, Harbour, Victual, nor no other Thing useful or comfortable to them, nor have Intelligence with them by Word, Writ, or Message' (Robert Wodrow, *The History of the Sufferings of the Church of Scotland*, 2 vols (Edinburgh, 1721–22), 1.Ap.168: *CLA*, 11).

24.37–38   the Calendar of the Covenant   a list of saints and martyrs of the Covenant (*OED*, *calendar*, substantive 4b), i.e. Covenanters and those who suffered or died in the cause of the Presbyterian Church of Scotland: see notes to 5.11.

24.38–39   took the sheaf from the mare   *proverbial* got back what was about to be consumed (see Ramsay, 88).

25.4   belly-gods   *Scots* gluttons; see Philippians 3.19: 'enemies of the cross of Christ . . . whose God is their belly'.

25.7   the prodigal son . . . swine-trough   see Luke 15.16.

25.8   such unnatural Neroes   reference to the Roman Emperor Lucius Domitius Nero (AD 37–68), notorious for extravagance and vanity.

25.10   Epicurishnesse   fastidious extravagance, voluptuousness; a popular allusion to the doctrines of the Greek philosopher Epicurus (341–271 BC).

25.31–32   fifty or sixty years before I was born   this is, if Chrystal Croftangry was about 62 in 1826, in about the first decade of the 18th century.

25.39–40   an upright walk in life   see, for instance, Psalm 15.2; Proverbs 28.18.

26.18–19   natale solum, if Swift be right   Jonathan Swift, 'Whitshed's Motto on his Coach/ *Libertas et natale Solum*/ Liberty and my native Country' (1735), lines 6–7: '*Natale Solum*: My Estate:/ My dear Estate, how well I love it'.

26.32   to throw their feet   of a horse, to lift the feet well in moving, especially over rough ground (*OED*, *throw*, verb 25, where this passage is the first instance cited).

26.32–33   Minion-burn   the name may allude to the Scots word 'minnon', a minnow or small fresh-water fish.

26.33   yellow trout   the non-migratory trout found in streams, usually known as the brown trout.

26.33   **Seggy-cleuch**   i.e. sedgy gorge.

27.13   **the number of new bridges**   Thomas Telford (1757–1834) built four bridges in the Lanark area, of which the most celebrated is the Cartland Crags bridge built over the Mouse Water near Lanark in 1821–23.

28.4   **Glentanner with L.200**   L. is the sign for a pound in money, rendered nowadays as £. 'Glen' is a Scots term for a valley; 'tanner' is the slang name for a sixpence, recorded by *OED* since 1811.

28.11   **circumduce the term**   *Scots law* declare the time for adducing evidence to have elapsed (Normand).

28.12   **condescendence**   *Scots law* the statement of facts relied on by the pursuer in a legal action (Normand).

28.27   **the Lords of Council and Session**   the Judges of the Court of Session, the supreme civil court in Scotland.

28.28   **the New Sessions House**   new accommodation built for the Court of Session adjacent to the Parliament House in 1817–19.

28.29   **25th November 18——**   as Croftangry is writing in 1826 (53.43), the year is probably unstated here to save Scott the trouble of looking up a calendar for 1824 or 1825.

28.30   **Castle–Treddles**   the name alludes to the fact that the owner made his fortune through weaving. The treddle or treadle was a lever worked by the foot on a weaver's loom.

28.31–32   **parsonage and vicarage**   originally tiends or tithes due to a parson and a vicar respectively. In Scotland in the early 19th century both were a tax upon certain lands payable in kind (wheat, barley, oats, and peas in the case of parsonage teinds, and grass, kale, carrots, calves, lambs, butter, cheese and fish in the case of vicarage teinds), and since 1633 both had been used to maintain the parish minister, but could be purchased, thus constituting a kind of property.

28.38   **freehold qualifications**   property qualifications allowing the owner to vote in Parliamentary elections. Only those who owned land of a certain value qualified as 'freeholders' and were entitled to vote. The estate of Glentanner is large enough to be divided into four and qualify the holder of each section as a 'freeholder'. The votes would be valuable in a hotly contested election.

28.39   **upset price**   price at an auction below which bids will not be accepted.

28.41   **the proven rental**   aggregate of all feudal dues, and rents from farms, cottages, etc., as proved to the satisfaction of the Court for the purposes of a sale on behalf of creditors. The sale price was thirty times that sum.

29.1   **improvable character of the land**   in the late 18th and early 19th centuries land was often sold at prices far beyond what the current rent justified when it seemed probable that investment in drainage, lime, walls, hedges etc. would improve yields of crops and thus in time justify higher rentals to tenant farmers.

29.13   **Dives**   a rich man, alluding to Luke 16.19, rendered in the Vulgate *dives*, the Latin adjective meaning 'rich', 'wealthy'.

29   **motto**   George Farquhar, *The Stage Coach* (1704), 1.304–10.

29.30   **stout Indian cane**   bamboo cane.

29.40   **Welsh wigs**   worsted caps.

30.2   **Mr Piper**   Edward Piper, whom Scott calls 'the Great Contractor for the Mail coaches, one of the sharpest men in his line' after receiving a visit from him on 29 May 1830 (*Journal*, 592). The contractor hired mail-coaches from the builders, Besant and Vidler, supplied horses and drivers, and worked the coaches over the roads covered by their contracts.

30.3   **frampal jades**   mettlesome horses; Tulloch (362) points out that Scott borrowed the phrase from Thomas Middleton and Thomas Dekker, *The Roaring Girl* (1611), 3.1.10.

30.5 Johnie Groat's house ... Cornhill Bridge Johnie Groat's house, now known as John o' Groats, is the most northerly point of the Scottish mainland; Ladykirk is on the Anglo-Scottish border in Berwickshire. Compare Robert Burns, 'On the Late Captain Grose's Peregrinations thro' Scotland' (1789), lines 1–2: 'Hear, Land o' Cakes, and brither Scots,/ Frae Maidenkirk to Johny Groats!' (Maidenkirk is the most southerly part of Scotland, on the Mull of Galloway). Cornhill Bridge crosses the River Tweed at Coldstream in Berwickshire, where mail-coaches to London crossed the border; Cornhill is just S, in Northumberland.

30.16 Vanity Fair the fair visited by Pilgrim in John Bunyan, *The Pilgrim's Progress* (1678): 'it beareth the name of *Vanity-Fair*, because the Town where tis kept, *is lighter than* Vanity; and also, because all that is there sold, or that cometh thither, is *Vanity*' (*The Pilgrim's Progress*, ed. Roger Sharrock (Oxford, 1960), 88).

30.19 knows the road, like the English postilion not identified.

30.20–21 carriers at Gadshill see *1 Henry IV*, 2.1.

30.21 from the death of John Ostler see *1 Henry IV*, 2.1.9–10: 'this house is turned upside down since Robin Ostler died'.

30.24 save the time for an account of the speeds mail-coaches were expected to maintain in Scotland see A. R. B. Haldane, *Three Centuries of Scottish Posts* (Edinburgh, 1971), 78–85.

30.29 in terrorem *Latin* to the terror of. See Horace, *Epistles* (*c*. 20 BC), 1.17, lines 6–8.

30.36 twenty minutes the length of breaks was determined by the length of time required to change horses between stages.

30.39 on our front facing us.

31.6–7 like a Lei'stershire clown bolting bacon compare *ODEP*, 718–19, where Leicestershire men have a proverbial reputation for eating beans.

31.10–11 to help the tea-kettle to serve the tea (*OED*, *help*, verb 8b).

31.11 an Old Stager one qualified by experience, a veteran.

31.17 Amatus and Amata *Latin* lovers, male and female.

31.17–18 the Peri Bathous satirical work by Pope, Swift and others, and attributed to the fictitious Martin Scriblerus entitled Περι βαθους: or, *Martinus Scriblerus his Treatise of the Art of Sinking in Poetry* (1727). The lines quoted here (of which the original source is unknown) are given in Chapter 11 as an example of hyperbole and described as 'that modest Request of two absent Lovers' (*The Art of Sinking in Poetry*, ed. Edna Leake Steeves (New York, 1952), 52).

31.21 give Mr P. his full revenge for Mr P. see note to 30.2. Mr Piper will have his revenge when the narrator explains the disadvantages of travel by steam-boat; this humorous intention is not fulfilled.

31.21–22 more recent enormity of steam-boats the first commercial steam-boat service was in 1789, and there were steam-boats on the Clyde by 1813. For a writer in Edinburgh the most remarkable development was the newly-formed London and Edinburgh Steam Packet Company which began sailings of its first steam vessel, the *City of Edinburgh*, in 1821 (Sue Mowat, *The Port of Leith* (Edinburgh, [1994]), 331).

31.24 no living with them or without them Martial, *Epigrams* (AD 86–101), 12.47.2.

31.27 his Majesty's carriage indicating that the coach carried mail. The right to carry mail derived from that of the Postmaster General, which was a Royal appointment.

31.31 cue ... called military straight, thin pigtail, often false.

31.36 pull them up reprove them.

32.4 shabby genteels people trying to keep up a genteel appearance, aspirers to be considered gentlemen.

32.14 These were thy gods, O Israel said by the Israelites at the sight of the golden calf: see Exodus 32.4, 8.

32.21 the crack of the whip a chance to take control, or be of importance, especially in the exercise of a former profession.

32.22 the brow of a hill . . . Glentanner Lockhart claims that 'The scenery of [Croftangry's] patrimonial inheritance was sketched from that of Carmichael, the ancient and now deserted mansion of the noble family of Hyndford' (*Life*, 7.87). Carmichael House was designed on an ambitious plan but never finished; it was surrounded by fine plantations. The title of the Carmichaels, Earls of Hyndford, became dormant on the death of Andrew, the 6th Earl, in 1817. Scott had made several visits to Clydesdale, the first in 1799, and used the area between Bothwell and Craignethan for the setting of *The Tale of Old Mortality* (1816): see Douglas S. Mack, Introduction to *The Tale of Old Mortality* (London, 1999), xiv–xix. The location of the fictitious Glentanner is further upstream, in the area of Clydesdale a few miles above Lanark.

32.30 as bare as my nail *proverbial* as naked as my nail: see *Proverbs, Sentences and Proverbial Phrases from English Writings before 1500*, ed. Bartlett Jere Whiting (Harvard, 1968), 423.

32.38 acute Gothic arches the pointed Gothic arch was typical of ecclesiastical rather than castle architecture.

33.6 Corehouse Linn Corra Linn, one of a series of spectacular waterfalls on the river Clyde, near the estate of Corehouse two miles S of Lanark.

33.20–21 hot closets cupboards or ovens for keeping food and plates warm; Scott had such arrangements at Abbotsford.

33.21 might not cool, as our Scotch phrase goes the use of 'cool' intransitively is not recorded as particularly Scottish in *OED*, *SND*, or *CSD*.

33.23 these temples of Comus Comus is a figure personifying revelry, sometimes presented as a deity. Tulloch (362–63) points out that this reference alludes to the Comus in Ben Jonson's masque *Pleasure Reconciled to Virtue* (1618) who is described in the opening stage direction as 'the god of cheer, or the belly'.

33.25 some feudal Bastille the notorious prison in Paris burst open during the French Revolution; Scott describes the confining of prisoners in iron cages in the reign of Louis XI of France (1423–83) in a note in the Magnum *Quentin Durward* (32.219n–220n).

34.12 the beasts that perish Psalm 49.12, 20.

34.13 bread to the labourer see Alexander Pope, 'Epistle to Burlington' (1731), lines 169–71: 'Yet hence the Poor are cloath'd, the Hungry fed;/ Health to himself, and to his Infants bread/ The Lab'rer bears'.

34.17 panders . . . horse-jockeys see Samuel Johnson, 'A Short Song of Congratulation' (1780), line 19.

34.25–28 Nunc ager Umbreni . . . pectora rebus Horace, *Satires* (30 BC), 2.2, lines 133–36: 'To-day the land bears the name of Umbrenus; of late it had that of Ofellus; to no one will it belong for ever, but the good of it will pass, now to me and now to another. Live, then, as brave men, and with brave hearts oppose adversity'. Alexander Pope's imitation, quoted in Scott's note, is in 'Second Satire of the Second Book of Horace Paraphrased' (1734), lines 167–70, 175–80.

35.3 the town of—— probably Lanark.

35.24 Fairntosh whisky from Ferintosh in the Black Isle, N of Inverness. This distillery had a particular reputation because it was owned by Duncan Forbes of Culloden (1685–1747), whose family for some years were exempted from paying tax on it in recompense for what they had lost supporting the government cause in 1745 (see Scott's review of the *Culloden Papers* (1816), in *Prose Works*, 20.86n).

35.38–39 **in service** employed in domestic service.

35.39–40 **ganging back in the world** going down in the world.

39.40 **victualling office** office concerned with the provisioning of ships, or other circumstances in which food was supplied without lodging.

35.42 **Eppie** Scots diminutive of Elizabeth or Elspeth.

35.43 **in her offer** *Scots* at her disposal, for her to choose.

36.3 **again the hair** *Scots* rubbed against the hair, rubbed up the wrong way.

36.10 **Odd's mercy** *oath* God's mercy.

36.14 **bad steps** *Scots* awkward bits of the road; *SND* cites this passage.

36.15–16 **Horace and Prior** the Roman poet Quintus Horatius Flaccus (Horace: 65–8 BC) praises his Sabine farm in various passages; Matthew Prior (1664–1721) published celebrated lines on the rural and literary life: 'GREAT MOTHER, let me Once be able/ To have a Garden, House, and Stable;/ That I may Read, and Ride, and Plant,/ Superior to Desire, or Want' ('Written at Paris, 1700. In the beginning of Robe's Geography' (1700), lines 8–11).

36.19–20 **Which sloping hills ... brown oak grows** Thomas Warton (1728–90), 'On the Approach of Summer' (1753), lines 296–97.

36.33–34 **Covenanter ... Captain Crichton** David Steele, a leading Covenanter (see note to 5.11) from Lesmahagow, SW of Lanark, was killed by a party of dragoons led by Captain John Creichton in 1686. The episode is described in *Memoirs of Captain John Creichton* (1731), in *The Works of Jonathan Swift*, ed. Walter Scott, 19 vols (Edinburgh, 1814), 10.154–56.

36.34 **the times of the persecution** see note to 5.11.

37.21–22 **predestinated child of perdition** refers to the doctrine of predestination whereby a person's ultimate salvation or damnation is preordained; the phrase 'son of perdition' occurs in John 17.12 and 2 Thessalonians 2.3.

37.31 **Christians of the first age** see Acts 4.34–37.

37.33 **let byganes be byganes** *proverbial* let bygones be bygones: see Ramsay, 96; *ODEP*, 96.

38 **motto** John Gay, 'A True Story of an Apparition' (1720), lines 57–58.

38.13–14 **gentlemen trustees on the highways** from 1663 under the Turnpike Acts building and maintaining such roads were financed by tolls and managed by boards of trustees.

38.33 **Appian or Flaminian highways** in Roman Italy the Via Appia was the main road leading S from Rome and the Via Flaminia the main road leading N.

38.25 **"almost too small" for sight** *King Lear*, 4.6.20.

38.32–34 **three shuttles in a field diapré ... a weaver's beam proper** this satirical coat of arms unites terms associated with weaving and the language of heraldry. Shuttles are instruments for carrying thread from one side of the loom to the other; in heraldry the 'field' is the background to whatever appears on the shield; 'diapre' ('diapered') is a heraldic term frequently applied to cloth, meaning ornamented with a pattern of intersecting lines. A heraldic crest appears above the shield; a web is a whole piece of cloth as it comes from the loom. Supporters are figures appearing on either side of the shield; the weaver's beam is a wooden cylinder or roller on which thread or cloth is wound; in heraldry the term 'proper' means in its natural colour. The 'giants for supporters' were probably suggested by the description of Goliath in 1 Samuel 17.7: 'And the staff of his spear was like a weaver's beam'.

39.18 **pays the lawing maun choose the lodging** *proverbial* he who pays the bill must choose the lodging: *ODEP*, 615, which cites this passage.

39.33–34 a barometer and thermometer the thermometer came into use in the first half of the 17th century, and the barometer in the second half of the century.

39.39–40 though he never wore it it is not unusual for men to appear in portraits of the 17th and 18th centuries in armour which they never wore.

40.16 the cotton mill the most famous cotton mill on the Clyde was that founded at New Lanark by David Dale (1739–1806) and later managed by his son-in-law Robert Owen (1771–1858). New Lanark, which was sited to exploit the water power of the Clyde, was a cotton-spinning mill and remained in operation until 1968. Mr Treddles's failed enterprise seems, from his name and coat of arms, to be associated with handloom weaving, which suffered economic difficulties in the early decades of the 19th century.

40.18 five years auld David Dale employed children as young as six at New Lanark; Robert Owen raised the age to ten. The Factory Act of 1819, applying only to cotton-mills, prohibited the employment of children under nine.

40.29 air and exercise Robert Owen in particular favoured fresh air and dancing.

40.30 their carritch catechism, Christian doctrine set out in the form of questions and answers used to instruct children.

40.30 Reediemadeasy alluding to text-books for children with that title. A copy of *Guy's British Primer or Reading Made Easy*, 10th edition (London, 1826), is in the Bodleian Library and a copy of *Reading Made Easy*, 4th edition (Berwick, 1835), is in the British Library. There was debate about the conditions under which children were employed at New Lanark. Sir John Carr records, 'they are employed from six in the morning until eight at night; and after that hour, when they are exhausted and desirous of rest, an affectation of humane attention is displayed by many of their masters, in having them instructed till ten in reading and writing' (*Caledonian Sketches, or a Tour through Scotland in 1807* (London, 1809), 539).

40.32 to beat the wood for cocks employed to raise the game, here woodcocks, for sportsmen.

40.33 broken bread left-overs.

40.42–41.1 an honest walk before God and man echoing phrases found in several places in the Bible: e.g. Psalm 116.9, 'walk before the Lord'; 1 Thessalonians 4.12, 'walk honestly toward them that are without'.

41.4 as black as sin proverbial: see *OED*, *sin*, where this use is cited; and *ODEP*, 63. Lockhart comments: 'Christie Steele's brief character of Croftangry's ancestry ... appears to suit well all that we have on record concerning [Scott's] own more immediate progenitors of the stubborn race of Raeburn' (*Life*, 7.87). Scott's great-grandfather, Walter Scott known as 'Beardie' (1653–1729), was the second son of Walter Scott of Raeburn.

41.18 a hundred pund sterling stressing that it is to be paid in British money, and not the old Scottish coinage in which a pound was worth much less.

41.23 its lawfulness that is, from a religious point of view.

41.29 of my own fee from my own wages.

42.12 necessity has no law proverbial *ODEP*, 557–58.

42.18–19 Dunlap cheese sweet-milk cheese, taking its name from Dunlop in Ayrshire.

42.19 at a' hands on all hands, on all sides.

42.22–25 For he did spend ... auld gudeman from 'The Auld Goodman', lines 13–16, published in Allan Ramsay, *The Tea-Table Miscellany*, 4 vols (Edinburgh, 1723–37); Scott owned the 13th edition (Edinburgh, 1762) in which the quotation is on p. 111: *CLA*, 171.

42.26 **it is a long lane that has no turning** *proverbial* implying that every calamity has an ending (*ODEP*, 480).

42.28 **sown his wild oats** *proverbial* grown out of youthful dissipation (*ODEP*, 889).

42.40 **to make gude her shame** by marrying her if she became pregnant.

43.18 **looked ower his nose at** looked down his nose at.

43.18 **lang syne** long ago.

43.32 **L——** Lanark.

43.39 **like the deluge** the Flood in Genesis 7.4.

43.41 **the Corso in Rome** a street, originally one in which horse races were run. Scott made a reference to 'the Italian race-horses . . . which instead of riders have spurs tied to their sides' in his *Journal* for 21 January 1826, as his financial collapse became certain (*Journal*, 64).

44.6 **walking matches** pedestrian contests, the ancestor of modern athletics, were popular in the 18th century and drew crowds of spectators (Dennis Brailsford, *British Sport: A Social History* (Cambridge and Lanham, Maryland, 1992), 56–57).

44.12 **en bagatelle** *French* as a joke or a trifle, flippantly.

44.21 **with the morning cool reflection came** see Nicholas Rowe, *The Fair Penitent* (1703), 1.1.162: 'at length the morn and cold indifference came'.

44.38 **my misfortunes** Lockhart comments, 'for his strongly Scottish feelings about parting with his land, and stern efforts to suppress them, the author had not to go so far a-field' (*Life*, 8.87). At one of the lowest points in his fortunes Scott had anticipated the loss of Abbotsford: 'I have walkd my last on the domains I have planted, sate the last time in the halls I have built' (22 January 1826, *Journal*, 65). In fact as Abbotsford had been settled on Scott's son, Walter, on his marriage in 1825 the house and estate could not be sold.

44.41 **as young Norval does Glenalvon's** see John Home, *Douglas* (1757), 4.1.376–77: 'Therefore I thank Glenalvon for his counsel,/ Altho' it sounded harshly'.

45 **motto** *As You Like It*, 3.5.73–74.

45.12–13 **commissioner of supply** person appointed by Parliament to levy the land-tax in their county (*OED*, *supply*, substantive 10b).

45.13 **the magisterial functions of the bench** as a Justice of the Peace, a lay magistrate (often a landowner in this period) appointed to try lesser offences within a county.

45.15–16 **small subscription library** lending library financed by the subscriptions of the members. The first subscription or circulating library in Scotland was founded by Allan Ramsay in Edinburgh in 1725.

45.18 **the Scottish metropolis** Edinburgh.

45.24 **Cape Wrath** the NW point of the Scottish mainland.

45.25 **Auld Reekie** *Scots* 'Old Smoky', a name for Edinburgh from the number of smoking chimneys in the tightly-packed tenements of the Old Town.

45.26 **exploring in all directions** the italics recognise that *explore* was usually used transitively, rather than intransitively as here.

45.28 **And whare trew ye I gaed?** asked by Sir Pertinax MacSycophant in Charles Macklin, *The Man of the World* (1781), 3.1: 'Where do you think I ganged?'.

45.29–30 **George's Square . . . the Calton Hill** George's Square, to the south of the Old Town, was begun in 1766 by James Brown and named after his brother George Brown of Elliston; the modern form George Square came into use after 1816 (Harris, 287). Charlotte Square is in the New Town, developed after 1767 to the north of the Old Town which was confined to a narrow volcanic ridge between the Castle and Holyrood. The 'old New Town' is the original plan of three major thoroughfares running east-west, Princes Street, George

Street and Queen Street, with intersecting streets and squares at each end. The 'new New Town' is the development north of Queen Street begun in 1802 (Harris, 467–68). In 1818–19 the New Town began to expand to the east (Harris, 144–45), round Calton Hill. Scott comments on these features of Edinburgh in his 'Essay on Border Antiquities' (1814), in *Prose Works*, 7.231–37.

45.32–35 the errant knight . . . obstacle to his free passage the 'wall of air' is found in French Arthurian romances: e.g. Chrétien de Troyes, *Eric and Enide* (c. 1170), lines 5739–45, in Chrétien de Troyes, *Arthurian Romances*, trans. D. D. R. Owen (London, 1987), 76; and *Lancelot of the Lake* (early 13th century), trans. Corin Corley (Oxford, 1989), 387. See Roger Sherman Loomis, *Arthurian Tradition & Chrétien de Troyes* (New York, 1949), 178–80.

45.36 pitching my tent settling down; a humorous allusion to the patriarchs in Genesis 12.8, 26.27, 31.25.

46.1 D—n the parade *The Monastery*, ed. Penny Fielding, EEWN 9, 6.17, where the same story is attributed to the fictitious Captain Clutterbuck, a retired soldier.

46.3 rus in urbe Martial, *Epigrams*, 12.57.21: 'the country in the town'.

46.6–7 my mind being at ease . . . more delicate see *King Lear*, 3.4.11–12: 'When the mind's free/ The body's delicate'.

46.8 like the trade of Pompey Pompey admits of his trade of bawd, 'Indeed, it does stink in some sort, sir' (*Measure for Measure*, 3.2.25).

46.9 an ounce of civet *King Lear*, 4.6.129–30.

46.20 Shanet this spelling reproduces the pronunciation of a Gaelic speaker. The sound [dz] is not found initially in Gaelic, yielding 'Shanet' for 'Janet', and later in the text 'shentleman' for 'gentleman' (*Language of Walter Scott*, 255–56).

46.26 inclining to sixty see *1 Henry IV*, 2.4.10.

46.28 honi soit qui mal y pense *French* shame on him who thinks evil of it: the motto of the Order of the Garter.

47.1 Cot bless us God bless us, an example of the substitution of one consonant by another, especially initially, to represent Gaelic-influenced pronunciation (*Language of Walter Scott*, 255–56). The substitution of *c* for *g* is seen again in 'cood', 'creat' and 'craze' in the following lines.

47.5 the chapel there was a Roman Catholic chapel in Broughton Street, at the head of Leith Walk, in 1826.

47.5–6 you may be do not think it would do you cood Protestants, unlike Catholics, do not usually pray for the souls of the dead.

47.15–16 frae Glenshee, that came down for the haarst poor Highlanders would come down to work in the Lowlands during harvest. Glenshee is in NE Perthshire.

47.24 think lang *Scots* think longingly, grieve.

47.27 your mother's son stressing relationships especially through the female line is a feature of the imitation of Gaelic speech in English or Scots.

47.33 messengers and sheriff-officers messengers at arms were appointed by the Lord Lyon King of Arms to execute the orders of the Court of Session; sheriff-officers were appointed by the sheriff to execute the orders of the Sheriff Court. In cases of debt the crown would demand (using messengers and sheriff-officers to execute the summons) that debtors satisfy their creditors.

47.36 his ped his bed, another example of the substitution of one initial consonant for another to indicate the pronunciation of a Gaelic speaker. There are many other examples in the text of the voiceless Gaelic *b* being represented by *p* (see the Glossary under P).

48.6–7 although a Scotchwoman, her cleanliness the Scots had a reputation, at least among travellers, for lack of cleanliness in domestic matters.

48.19 Tomanthoulich fictitious place name; the form 'Tomna', from *Gaelic* hill of, occurs in some Scottish place-names: see note to 127.2.

49.3 town tail i.e. end of the town; a *tail* is a long bit of land jutting out from a larger piece, and Holyrood is the eastern extremity of the Old Town of Edinburgh.

49.3 the King's cows referring to 'Croft-an-ri'; see note to 23.26.

49.7–8 her nainsell her own self, a phrase common in the literary representation of Highland speech. It is sometimes used as an emphatic *I*; but Janet seldom uses a first-person pronoun, referring to herself instead in the third person.

49.14–15 kirk or chapel Presbyterian or Catholic church.

49.16 Och, Ohellany, Ohonari Gaelic expressions of lamentation. In his 'Glenfinlas; or Lord Ronald's Coronach' Scott glossed the cry 'O hone a rie'!' as 'Alas for the prince or chief' (*Poetical Works*, 4.169). Gaelic *righ*, king, gives the last element in Ohonari.

49.16 the glen is desolate referring to the depopulation of the Highlands, whether through emigration or the clearances, resulting from changing patterns of social organisation and agricultural practice in the decades following the defeat of the Jacobite rising of 1745, and particularly in the late 18th and early 19th centuries. In many places factors from lowland Scotland were brought in to run Highland estates, and so 'the Saxon's house stands tall' when the rest of the population has gone. *Saxon* is a form of 'Sassenach', a word used of a non-Gaelic-speaking lowlander or Englishman.

49.19 the heath-bird frae the glen for metaphorical references to the natural world in the representation of Highland speech see note to 82.33–35.

49.20 of imagination all compact *A Midsummer Night's Dream*, 5.1.8.

49.27 tenement in the Abbey-yard there were tenements within the sanctuary, buildings let out in flats and rooms, where debtors seeking sanctuary could stay. Most have since been demolished.

49.36–37 I care not … the cabin is convenient Ben Jonson, *Every Man In His Humour* (1598), 1.5.31–32.

49.38–39 newer phraseology … self-contained Scott uses the old term 'house within itself' in his 'General Account of Edinburgh' (1821) in *The Provincial Antiquities and Picturesque Scenery of Scotland* (2 vols, London, 1826, 1.74) to indicate architecture different from the tenements with their shared staircases which were typical of the Old Town of Edinburgh (*Prose Works*, 7.231; see also *Guy Mannering* (1815), ed. P. D. Garside, EEWN 2, 201.10 and note).

49.41–42 the hill and crags of the King's Park see note to 14.35. The hill is Arthur's Seat and the crags the Salisbury Crags.

50.2–3 Little Croftangry in his review of *Chronicles of the Canongate* John Wilson claimed that Croftangry's house was 'the late Mr Paton's house, on the edge of the King's Park' (*Blackwood's Edinburgh Magazine*, 22 (November 1827), 557). This was the antiquary George Paton (1721–1807), who lived in Lady Stair's Close off the Lawnmarket in 1793–1800. *The Edinburgh Directory* does not list him thereafter, and since in 1800 he lost his money in the failure of a bank it is probable that he took up residence in the sanctuary of Holyrood.

50.8 Portobello sands on the Firth of Forth, east of Edinburgh. Scott's reference to cavalry drill is probably a recollection of his drills with the Edinburgh Light Dragoons in 1797 (*Life*, 1.258–60).

50.26 theatre the Theatre Royal, in Shakespeare Square at the N end of the North Bridge from 1769. It was demolished in 1859 to make room for the General Post Office.

50.27 one or two public societies the societies in Edinburgh in the early 19th century are described in Hugo Arnot, *The History of Edinburgh … to which has been added, A Sketch of the Improvements of the City, from 1780 to 1816*

(Edinburgh, 1816), 548–52. They included the Royal Society of Edinburgh and the Society of Antiquaries, both of which obtained royal charters in 1783, as well as societies promoting medicine, natural history and horticulture.

50.31 Bonassus the Greek and Latin word for the bison, but probably used here as a pun: 'I must have been the great ass himself to have mistaken myself for a genius'.

50.35 fading traces of antiquity … daily vanishing compare the conclusion to Scott's Introduction to *Minstrelsy of the Scottish Border* (1802–03): 'By such efforts, feeble as they are, I may contribute somewhat to the history of my native country; the peculiar features of whose manners and character are daily melting and dissolving into those of her sister and ally' (*Minstrelsy*, 1.175).

50.36 a modern instance see *As You Like It*, 2.7.156.

50.37–44 What ails me … Caledonian wood Joseph Hall, *Virgidemiarum. Sixe Bookes. The three last Bookes of byting Satyrs* (1599), 6.1.217–24 (*CLA*, 107).

50.42 Brute's first arrival in the mythological history of England the first king of the Britons. He was great-grandson of Æneas, the Roman hero; having inadvertently killed his father he took refuge in Britain.

50.43 Saint George's sorrel and his cross of blood George, patron saint of England, is usually depicted on a horse as he kills the dragon; tradition holds that he suffered martyrdom under the Roman emperor Diocletian around AD 303, hence the red cross in St George's flag.

50.44 Arthur's round board … wood according to medieval romance, 150 knights of the 6th-century Romano-British king, Arthur, sat at a round table, made by the magician Merlin. The precise reference of the phrase 'Caledonian wood' has not been identified, but Arthur was associated with Brittany, Cornwall, Wales and Scotland.

51.5 penny ballads and broadsides popular songs printed on a single sheet of paper and sold for 1*d*. (0.4p).

51.7–8 a little picking and stealing 'To keep my hands from picking and stealing': 'A Catechism', printed before 'The Order of Confirmation', in *The Book of Common Prayer*.

51.10 clean conveyance *Law* legal transfer of property clear of encumbrance or restriction.

51.16 Sentiment, and Dialogues, and Disquisition different sorts of writing to be found in collections of periodical essays like those mentioned in the following paragraph.

51.25–26 the Spectator … the Lounger *The Spectator* (1711–14) and *The Guardian* (1713) were periodical papers published in London by Joseph Addison and Richard Steele; *The Mirror* (1779) and *The Lounger* (1785–87) in Edinburgh by Henry Mackenzie.

51.27–29 Johnson … many of whose Ramblers Samuel Johnson's papers for *The Rambler* (1750–52) contain some of his most magisterial utterances and established his reputation as a moralist. Croftangry's disparaging view of Johnson's style and seriousness is not that usually expressed by Scott.

51.37 throwing stones … windows of my own *proverbial* those who live in glass houses should not throw stones. See *OED*, *glass*, substantive 1 (1633); and *Brewer*, 456.

51.43 the full tide of existence see Samuel Johnson's verdict that 'the full tide of human existence is at Charing-cross' (*Boswell's Life of Johnson* (1791), ed. George Birkbeck Hill and L. F. Powell, 6 vols (London, 1934–50), 2.337).

52.5 the modern Comus and Mammon Comus here is the god of feasting as at 33.23 above, with the addition of the worldly seducer from John Milton,

Comus (1634). Mammon means riches, personified in Matthew 6.24, Luke 16.13, and in Milton's *Paradise Lost* (1667), 2.228–83.

52.8 Genius of feudal times Arthur's Seat, the 'misty and lonely mountain', evokes an older, feudal structure of society and values, which, according to the sociological theory of the Scottish Enlightenment, had been superseded by the industrial and urban society of Edinburgh.

52.14 Zimmerman the Swiss doctor Johann Georg Zimmerman (1728–95) who published *Über die Einsamkeit* ('On Solitude') in 1756, and a revised edition in 1784.

52.17 Veamos—Caracco! *Spanish: veamos* means 'let's see'; *caracco* is probably *carajo*, an emphatic expletive, almost a swear word. A rough translation might be 'Let's see, damn it'.

52.21 printer's devil printer's errand boy; originally the boy who lifted the printed sheets from the press, who got blackened with ink.

52.25 Netherbow the site of the old gate pulled down in 1764 which divided the Canongate from the city of Edinburgh. Brass setts in the road where St Mary's Street and Jeffrey Street meet the Canongate indicate where it stood.

52.26 Prince's Street the most southerly of the streets of the New Town, and hence the first to be reached from the Old Town. The ascent was social. The street was named after the Prince of Wales, son of George III; Harris observes that the spelling 'was indifferently *Prince's*, *Princes'* or *Princes* until the last became the settled form in the late 1830s' (464).

52.27–28 Valley of Holyrood see note to 14.35.

52.30 the Long Town of Kirkaldy Kirkcaldy on the N shore of the Firth of Forth, opposite Edinburgh; the town consisted of little more than one street 3½ miles (5 km) long, which gave it its soubriquet.

52.30–31 the skippers and coalliers of the East of Fife coal was dug in Fife from the 13th century, and was exported by ship from the small ports of the county.

52.31 the classical arcades of St Andrews there were arcades in the courts of St Mary's and St Salvator's Colleges of the University of St Andrews, which were destroyed later in the 19th century (R. G. Cant, *The University of St Andrews* (Edinburgh, 1946), 63, 91, 104–06).

52.32–33 breath ... will carry their sails see the Epilogue to *The Tempest* (11–12): 'Gentle breath of yours my sails/ Must fill'.

52.34–35 Scotch whisky ... prohibitory duty an Act to Eliminate Illicit Distilling passed in 1823 put a tax on the distilling of whisky at the rate of 2s. 3d. (11p) per gallon of proof spirit. Its popularity was not increased when the rate was raised to 2s. 4d. (12p) in 1825 and 2s. 10d. (14p) in 1826.

53.2–3 begging-box ... an ass's a charity-box inviting donations from passers-by. There is a photograph of an 18th-century begging-box from the Edinburgh Infirmary in *The Book of the Old Edinburgh Club*, 15 (Edinburgh, 1927), opposite p. 144. It is metal and ornamented with fruit and flowers rather than an animal's head.

53.7 Galashiels grey grey, or grey and white, woollen cloth woven in the town of Galashiels, near Abbotsford, and worn by Borderers.

53.10–11 Let every herring ... his own head 'Every man must stand by his own endeavour, industry and interest' (James Kelly, *A Complete Collection of Scotish Proverbs* (London, 1721), 240; *ODEP*, 370).

53.14 her friendship in Scots the word can include the idea of kinship, as well as friendship in the English sense.

53.17 Mrs Martha Bethune Baliol in the Magnum Introduction to *Chronicles of the Canongate* Scott acknowledges that Mrs Bethune Baliol 'was designed to shadow out in its leading points the interesting character of a dear friend of mine, Mrs Murray Keith' (41.xxxii). Lockhart adds that in the portrait

'I am assured he has mixed up various features of his own beloved mother' (*Life*, 7.82). Mrs Anne Murray Keith (1736–1818) was unmarried, but the title Mrs was often used as a mark of age or respect as well as of marriage.

54.9–10 Perhaps...sermon Robert Burns, 'Epistle to a Young Friend' (1786), lines 7–8.

54.12 Molière's recipe Jean-Baptiste Poquelin (1622–73), known as Molière, the great French comic dramatist who 'adopted the well-known practice of reading his pieces, while in manuscript, to his housekeeper, La Foret, and observing the effect they produced on so plain, but shrewd and sensible a mind, before bringing them on the stage' (Scott's review article, 'Molière', in *Prose Works*, 17.213–14).

54.14–15 Wilkie or Allan Sir David Wilkie (1785–1841) was famous for painting scenes of lower-class life in Scotland; his friend Sir William Allan (1782–1850), who spent much of his career abroad, painted scenes from Scottish history as well as scenes from humble life.

54.23 seriously incline *Othello*, 1.3.146: describing how Desdemona attended to Othello's account of his travels.

54.37 sweet word Mesopotamia the land 'between the rivers', in modern Iraq, is mentioned several times in the Bible. The origin of 'the story of the old woman who told her pastor that she "found great support in that blessed word *Mesopotamia*"' is not known (*Brewer*, 705).

54.40–43 Timmerman...Carpenter 'Timberman', Janet's mistake for Zimmerman (see note to 52.14). The name MacIntyre, in Gaelic *Mac an t-saoir*, means 'son of a carpenter'.

55.8 delilahs of the imagination Delilah is the woman whom Samson loved and who betrayed him in Judges 16; her ornaments were added by John Milton in *Samson Agonistes* (1671), lines 710–24. John Dryden refers to ranting passages in his earlier plays as 'those Dalilahs of the theatre' in his Dedication to *The Spanish Friar* (1681), and he speaks of 'tropes and figures' twice in his 'Apology for Heroic Poetry, and Poetic Licence' (1677) (*The Works of John Dryden*, ed. Walter Scott, 18 vols (Edinburgh, 1808), 6.377, 5.111 and 116). Scott used the phrase of his childhood love of ballads in his 'Memoirs' (*Scott on Himself*, ed. David Hewitt (Edinburgh, 1981), 28), and of Abbotsford in *Letters*, 5.60.

55.9 caviar to the multitude delicacy the multitude cannot appreciate: see *Hamlet*, 2.2.430.

55.10–11 paying back—it is a double labour *1 Henry IV*, 3.3.179.

55.14 applaud it done see *Macbeth*, 3.2.45–46: 'Be innocent of the knowledge, dearest chuck,/ Till thou applaud the deed'.

55.19 Know that I alone am king of me John Dryden, *Almanzor and Almahide, or, the Conquest of Granada* (1672), Part I, 1.1.206 (*The Works of John Dryden*, ed. Walter Scott, 18 vols (Edinburgh, 1808), 4.40).

55 motto *Coriolanus*, 2.1.91.

55.30 ship-shape and Bristol fashion everything stowed and the ship ready for sea, deriving from the reputation of the port of Bristol (*Brewer*, 23–24).

55.34 our ancient consorts ships sailing in company (*OED*, consort, substantive 1, 2). This paragraph is where Scott started to write *Chronicles of the Canongate* in May 1826, and the elegiac reference to 'our ancient consorts' recalls the death of his wife earlier in the same month.

56.5 to buy a ring Scott was given a ring in memory of Mrs Murray Keith (see note to 53.17). His letter of thanks addressed to the Hon. Mrs Lindsay on 13 June 1818 is in *Letters*, 5.161–63.

56.10 in the vaward of youth see *2 Henry IV*, 1.2.165.

56.17–18 person of quality and fortune, as these are estimated in

Scotland i.e. in Scotland she was recognised as being from an old family and as being well-off, although by English standards she was not rich.

56.21 the eventful year 1745 when the Jacobites, including many High-landers, took Edinburgh (apart from the Castle) and Prince Charles Edward Stewart held court at Holyrood between September and his setting out for England in November 1745. If Mrs Bethune Baliol can be assumed to have been about five years old in 1745 she would have been about 86 when she died in 1826.

56.23–24 her father's bequest … more than one brave brother Anne Murray Keith's father was Robert Keith of Craig, who became Ambassador in Vienna and St Petersburg and died in 1774. She had two brothers, neither of whom died in active service. Lieutenant-General Sir Robert Murray Keith (1730–95) followed his father as Ambassador in Vienna and Sir Basil Keith (d. 1777) served in the navy and became Governor of Jamaica.

56.27 My intimacy … with the excellent lady Scott probably got to know Anne Murray Keith after 1793–94 when she settled in George Street with her cousin the Dowager Countess of Lady Balcarres (*The Edinburgh Directory, from July 1793 to July 1794* (Edinburgh, 1793)). The two ladies lived at 'no. 51, south side' until 1811–12 when they moved to 110 George Street. Mrs Murray Keith was living at the latter address at her death in 1818.

56.29 when in Edinburgh Robert Chambers notes the numbers of un-married women of good family who lived in Edinburgh in the 18th century and set the tone of social life there (*Traditions of Edinburgh*, 2.23–52), and Henry Cockburn recalled 'a singular race of excellent Scotch old ladies' in the Edin-burgh of his youth (*Memorials of His Time* (Edinburgh, 1856), 57–67).

56.30–32 one of those old hotels … Canongate Florence MacCunn points out that Mrs Bethune Baliol's house was reminiscent of the house occupied by Dugald Stewart (1753–1828), Professor of Moral Philosophy at Edinburgh University, whose classes Scott attended (*Sir Walter Scott's Friends* (Edinburgh, 1909), 29). It was Lothian House, also known as Lothian Hut, built by the Marquess of Lothian in about 1750, in Horse Wynd on the south side of the Canongate not far from Holyrood. Dugald Stewart lived there from 1797–98 until 1809–10 (*The Edinburgh Directory*).

56.31–32 Palace of Holyrood-house the proper, extended name of Holyrood Palace.

56.36–37 pulled her house down … building and burning Lothian House was pulled down in 1825 and replaced by a brewery (James Grant, *Old and New Edinburgh*, 3 vols (London, 1882), 2.38–39), which was in its turn demolished in 1998 to make way for the Scottish Parliament building. There were many changes in the Old Town of Edinburgh in the early 19th century: e.g. the old Tolbooth which gave its name to Scott's *The Heart of Mid-Lothian* (1818) was demolished in 1817; in Parliament Square, the 17th-century build-ing which had housed the Scottish Parliament was given a classical front in 1808, and the Signet Library and new court buildings were constructed. A fire in November 1824 destroyed much of the S side of the High St from Parliament Square to the Tron Kirk.

57.3–4 porte cochère *French* carriage entrance.

57.9 Garrick in the character of Lusignan the celebrated actor David Garrick (1717–79) played the part of Lusignan, 'King of Palestine', in *Zara* (1736), adapted by Aaron Hill from Voltaire's *Zaire* (1732).

57.11–13 hackney-coach … ticketed presence coach kept for hire, and *ticketed* either because it displayed its licence or because it carried a notice displaying its hire charges.

57.20 knitting his stocking it was not uncommon for men to knit in the 18th century, as a way of eking out a poor livelihood.

57.31–33 two gable ends . . . half circular tower Dobie remarks that 'Baliol's Lodging is a typical mansion of the 17th and early 18th centuries, built on an L-plan, with the entrance and turnpike stair in the angle, having crow-stepped (notched) gables and ornament on the windows. The plan derived from the previous fortified towers'. Architecturally Mrs Bethune Baliol's house is more like Croftangry House than what is known of Lothian House.

57.41 the South Back of the Canongate now called Holyrood Street.

58.4 the arms of Bethune and Baliol Scott gives his fictitious character names from two ancient Scottish families. Bethune (from Béthune in Picardy) is often anglicised as Beaton; members of the family played leading roles in church and state in pre-Reformation Scotland. The Baliol family descended from Guy de Baliol (from Bailleul also in Picardy) who came to England at the Norman Conquest and gained lands in N England. John Baliol (1249–1315) became King of Scotland in 1292 with the support of Edward I of England. The Baliol family disappear from the historical record after the 14th century.

58.6 iron rasp Scottish predecessor of the door knocker. Chambers describes it as 'a small rod of iron, twisted or notched, which was placed perpendicularly, starting out a little from the door, and bore a small ring of the same metal, which an applicant for admittance drew rapidly up and down the *nicks*, so as to produce a grating sound . . . These were almost all disused about sixty years ago, when knockers were generally substituted as more genteel' (*Traditions of Edinburgh*, 1.236–37).

58.9–10 Mount Baliol probably fictitious; Baliol is not a place-name in Scotland.

58.12 Beauffet from French *buffet*, a side-board.

58.21–22 He's sad and civil . . . my fortunes Olivia speaking of Malvolio: *Twelfth Night*, 3.4.5–6.

58.24–25 his old-fashioned wages in 1770 a manservant's wage was £4 a year besides board and lodging; in 1800 it was £16 or £18 (Thomas Somerville, *My Own Life and Times 1741–1814*, (Edinburgh, 1861), 340–41).

58.39–40 windows . . . save the tax window-tax was first imposed in England in 1696–97, and extended to Scotland in 1710; it was eventually abolished in 1851–52 (Normand).

59.3–4 collected the income tax income tax of 10% was imposed in 1798 to help pay for the war against France, and was collected from the payer. By an Act of 1803 it was reduced to 5% and collected at source, and in 1815 it was abolished. Croftangry must therefore be referring to a time before 1803 (Dobie). In *Traditions of Edinburgh* (2.18–19), Chambers attributes a willingness to pay taxes to Lady Lovat (1710–96).

59.8 James the Sixth's time James VI of Scotland (1566–1625; king from 1567).

59.9 Jameson George Jameson (1588–1644), a distinguished Scottish portrait painter who painted many members of the Scottish nobility and gentry.

59.12 Holyrood-house see note to 56.31–32.

59.22 cabinets of japan and or moulu 'japan' is a varnish or lacquer originally from Japan, especially a hard black varnish which left a shiny surface; '*or moulu*', literally 'ground gold' in French, is a gold or bronze varnish. Both were used to decorate furniture and other wooden objects. Florence MacCunn notes that 'Mrs Bethune Baliol's characteristic treasures were certainly possessions of Anne Keith' (*Sir Walter Scott's Friends* (Edinburgh and London, 1909), 29).

59.30 the fortunes of Britain in 1715 in the unsuccessful Jacobite rising of that year. Scott had symbolised the defeat of the Jacobite cause by the hanging of weapons on the wall in *Waverley*, ed. Claire Lamont (Oxford, 1981), 338.

59.30 spontoon kind of half-pike carried by infantry officers and used for signalling orders to the regiment.

59.31–32 the Black Watch at Fontenoy the name of the 42nd regiment, the first corps raised for the royal service in the Highlands, which fought at Fontenoy, in modern Belgium, where the British were defeated by the French in 1745. See notes to 77.13 and 85.34.

59.42 Flanders lace Flanders, now divided between Belgium, Holland and France, is famous for lace-making.

60.10–11 the morning...four at the utmost morning was the time before dinner, the main meal of the day. The time of dinner was getting later in Scott's lifetime, moving from about two to six o'clock (Henry Cockburn, *Memorials of His Time* (Edinburgh, 1856), 33–34).

60.15 blue stocking female pedant; the phrase, which had French antecedents, comes from the society for intellectual discussion between both men and women founded by Elizabeth Montagu in about 1750, one of whose members wore blue worsted instead of the more formal silk stockings (*Brewer*, 127).

60.22–23 matched in mouth...under each *A Midsummer Night's Dream*, 4.1.120–21, referring to the cry of hounds. Theseus's hounds varied in deepness of 'mouth', so that 'A cry more tuneable/ Was never holla'd to, nor cheer'd with horn'.

60.24–25 one mighty Tom of a fellow see the catch about the bells at Christ Church, Oxford, ending 'But there's never a man/ Will leave his can/ Till he hears the mighty *Tom*' (Henry Bold, *Latine Songs with their English: and Poems* (London, 1685), 124, lines 12–14). Large bells elsewhere are also called Tom (*Brewer*, 1089).

60.26–27 chère exquise *French* choice fare, excellent food.

60.29 vins extraordinaires *French* fine wines; in contrast to *vins ordinaires*, wines for daily use.

60.34 chasse café *French* 'chase coffee', a liqueur or other spirit-based drink taken after coffee; an after-dinner drink (*OED*, *chasse*, 2).

60.36 the unnatural hour of eight as dinner became later it pushed the serving of other meals later as well. Cockburn indicates that 'supper' was served after nine o'clock (*Memorials of His Time* (Edinburgh, 1856), 42).

61.4 preparing for tea on the 'new meal' of tea, served after dinner and before supper, see Marion Lochhead, *The Scots Household in the Eighteenth Century* (Edinburgh, 1948), 46–49.

61.23 in Carthusian silence the monastic Order of Carthusians was founded by St Bruno in 1084 in the valley of Chartreuse north of Grenoble. The monks combine the solitary life of hermits with communal life and periods of conversation are rare.

62.13 the battle of Ramillies a victory of the Duke of Marlborough over the French in 1706.

62.18 raised a little at heel Dobie comments that heels were high in the middle of the 18th century, low in the 1820s. Chambers, in describing Lady Lovat as a '*last-century* person', mentions her 'high-heeled shoes' (*Traditions of Edinburgh*, 2.3–4).

62.43–63.1 a brother...national importance see note to 56.23–24.

63.4 during the last war during the war against revolutionary France (1793–1802) and particularly the Napoleonic War that followed (1803–15), except during the short-lived peace of 1802–03, it was impossible for ordinary British travellers to visit France.

63.21–22 Susannah, Countess of Eglinton Susannah Kennedy (1689–1780), who married the 9th Earl of Eglinton and survived him by 51 years (*Traditions of Edinburgh*, 1.260–71).

63.22 Allan Ramsay poet, dramatist, editor (1684–1758). Ramsay was the most important literary figure in Scotland in the first part of the 18th century. His first volume of poetry in Scots and English was published in 1721. In 1723 he published *The Tea-Table Miscellany*, a selection of Scots songs that was repeatedly expanded over the next 14 years, and *The Ever Green*, a selection of older Scottish poetry, in 1724. His play, *The Gentle Shepherd*, dedicated to the Countess of Eglinton (see note above), followed in 1725.

63.23 the Hon. Mrs Colonel Ogilvy wife of the Hon. Patrick Ogilvie of Longmay and Inchmartin, d. 1753; she was 'supposed to be the *best-bred* woman of her time in Scotland' (*Traditions of Edinburgh*, 2.129).

63.24 Auld Reekie see note to 45.25.

63.24 were required to dress themselves see *2 Henry IV*, 2.3.21–22.

63.26–27 great folk lived within little space in the tenements of the Old Town of Edinburgh, where richer families lived in the first and second floors, with the poor above and below and sharing the same staircase.

63.31 Scottish, decidedly Scottish this has become a celebrated assertion of the survival of an upper-class Scots speech in Scott's day, particularly among women. The deliberate attempt to write standard written English and to adopt an English pronunciation by many educated Scots in the 18th century had led to Scots being perceived as vulgar. Scott put the contrary view in a letter to Archibald Constable on 25 February [1822]: 'Scotch was a language which we have heard spoken by the learnd and the wise & witty & the accomplishd and which had not a trace of vulgarity in it but on the contrary sounded rather graceful and genteel. You remember how well Mrs. Murray Keith—the late Lady Dumfries—my poor mother & other ladies of that day spoke their native language' (*Letters*, 7.83; see also *Life*, 1.75).

63.34–35 the accent of St James's…Billingsgate St James's Palace was the London residence of the monarch; Billingsgate was the London fish-market, notorious for colourful language.

63.38 the ancient court of Scotland the Scottish court moved to England in 1603 when James VI became also James I of England. The 'royal halls of Holyrood' had been little used since, except for the Duke of York's residence there in 1679–82 and Prince Charles Edward Stewart's short stay in 1745 (see notes to 56.21, 64.14–15, 65.17).

63.43–64.1 Scottish court…that of France French influence on the Scottish court was particularly strong after 1554 when Mary of Guise became Queen Regent on behalf of her daughter, Mary Queen of Scots, whom she married to the French Dauphin (see note to 65.23). Scott wrote of the song-writer, Mrs Alison Cockburn (1712?–94), a friend of his mother, 'her conversation brought her much nearer to a Frenchwoman than to a native of England; and, as I have the same impression with respect to ladies of the same period and the same rank in society, I am apt to think that the *vieille cour* of Edinburgh rather resembled that of Paris than that of St James's' (Robert Chambers, *The Scottish Songs*, 2 vols (Edinburgh, 1829), lxiii).

64.7 Fletcher of Salton Andrew Fletcher of Saltoun (1655–1716), Scottish politician and patriot, an opponent of the Union of 1707, and famous for his oratory.

64.7–8 Graham of Claverhouse John Graham of Claverhouse, first Viscount Dundee (?1649–89), soldier and politician. He was notorious for his campaign against the Covenanters in south-west Scotland and died supporting the Jacobite cause at Killiecrankie. Scott celebrated him in a song usually known as 'Bonny Dundee' (*Poetical Works*, 12.194–97).

64.9 the famous Duchess of Lauderdale Elizabeth Murray, Duchess of Lauderdale (d. 1697), was prominent in the court of Charles II; her name was associated with scandal, political intrigue and greed.

64.10 some fairy alluding either to the longevity of fairies, or to the belief that humans were sometimes taken by fairies and returned to earth many years later. For the supernatural lapse of time in fairyland, such that years seem days, see Alexander Carmichael, *Carmina Gadelica*, 6 vols (Edinburgh, 1928–71), 2.23, 356.

64.14–15 Mary of Este ... banishment Mary of Modena (1658–1718), wife of James, Duke of York (later James VII and II). He was sent to Edinburgh as the King's Commissioner to the Scottish Parliament, 1679–82, to remove him from England where his Catholicism caused trouble for his brother, Charles II.

64.16–18 Charles the Second ... beyond the Forth Charles II, having been proclaimed King by the Estates (Parliament) of Scotland on the death of his father in 1649, landed in northern Scotland in 1650. Oliver Cromwell (1599–1658), 'the bold usurper', invaded Scotland, defeated the Scots at Dunbar in September 1650, and gradually extended his power over the country. Charles escaped across the Forth to England in 1651.

64.19 Beau cousin *French* handsome cousin. The phrase has a mock-heroic tone because *cousin* is the term with which French kings would compliment people who were not necessarily in that relation to them; the relationship between Mrs Bethune Baliol and the narrator is described at 53.13–16.

64.32 the Empress Queen, or Frederick of Prussia Maria Theresa, Empress of the Holy Roman Empire and Queen of Hungary and Bohemia (1717–80); Frederick II, the Great, King of Prussia (1712–86).

64.35 the Revolution of 1688 when James VII of Scotland and II of England (1633–1701) fled from London leaving the throne to his daughter Mary and her husband William of Orange.

64.38–39 the riding of the last Scottish Parliament the last Scottish Parliament before the Treaty of Union of 1707 was opened on 3 October 1706. The Riding of the Parliament was the procession, attended with pageantry, in which the sovereign's High Commissioner was conducted from Holyrood to the Parliament House for the opening of Parliament.

64.40–41 Lord Moray's Lodging Moray House, built in the early 17th century on the S side of the Canongate, was the home of the earls of Moray from 1643 to 1845; some of the negotiations connected with the Union of 1707 took place in its premises. It is now Edinburgh University's Moray House Institute of Education. The original corbelled balcony on the first floor is still visible from the street.

65.1 vile seducer of youth compare *1 Henry IV*, 2.4.446 ('That villainous abominable misleader of youth, Falstaff'); and *2 Henry VI*, 4.7.35 ('Thou hast most traitorously misled the youth of the realm in erecting a grammar school').

65.3 the wandering Jew in late medieval legend, a Jew who insulted Christ on the way to Calvary and was condemned to wander over the face of the earth until Judgment Day (*Brewer*, 1138).

65.6 ma belle cousine *French* my fair cousin: see note to 64.19.

65.12 the battle of Flodden see note to 24.31–32.

65.13–14 Bruce and Wallace ... my Baliol blood Robert the Bruce (1274–1329), who reigned as Robert I from 1306, and William Wallace (?1272–1305) were both heroes in the struggle for Scottish independence from England. Members of the Bruce and Baliol families were rival claimants to the Scottish throne, see notes to 58.4 and 71.35–38.

65.17 the accession of James ... Britain James VI of Scotland (1566–1625) united the crowns of Scotland and England when he succeed to the throne of England in 1603 on the death of Queen Elizabeth. Britain is the name of the island containing Scotland, England and Wales and was adopted as the name of the political entity created in 1603.

65.21 bag and baggage military phrase signifying the soldier with all his belongings, or the whole of the equipment and stores of an army (*Brewer*, 68).

65.22 Cockenzie village to the E of Edinburgh.

65.22 the Earl of Winton James VI made Robert, 7th Lord Seton, the Earl of Winton in 1600. The Earl's funeral took place on 5 April 1603, the day on which James VI left Edinburgh for England; the King halted at the orchard of Seton, a few miles E of Edinburgh, so as not to draw mourners away from the funeral of his 'good, faithful, and loyal subject' (John Nichols, *The Progresses, Processions, and Magnificent Festivities, of King James the First*, 4 vols (London, 1828), 3.306).

65.23 poor Mary James VI and I's mother was Mary Queen of Scots (1542–87), who after many misfortunes was imprisoned and subsequently beheaded at the behest of Queen Elizabeth of England.

66.7–8 the Cross... the Assembly-Rooms the Mercat (Market) Cross, a shaft surmounted by a unicorn on an octagonal platform in the High Street near St Giles' Cathedral, was a social meeting place as well as a place of trade. It was demolished in 1756 as Scott laments in *Marmion* (1808), 5.25 (*Poetical Works*, 7.274–75), and replaced in 1885. In the 18th century assemblies, social occasions usually involving dancing, were held in Assembly Close off the High Street, until the social venues of the Old Town were superseded by the Assembly Rooms built in George Street in the New Town in 1783.

66.9 in his Journal Jonathan Swift (1667–1745), poet and satirist, was Dean of St Patrick's Cathedral, Dublin. Swift noted in his *Journal to Stella* (written 1710–13), addressed to Esther Johnson and Rebecca Dingley, that on 12 March 1712 he had dined with 'two gentlemen of the Highlands of Scotland; yet very polite men' (*The Works of Jonathan Swift*, ed. Walter Scott, 19 vols (Edinburgh, 1814), 3.306).

66.25 confess and be hanged cited as a proverb in Christopher Marlowe, *The Jew of Malta* (1592), 4.1.148–49, 'Blame not us but the proverb, Confes and be hang'd' (M. P. Tilley, *A Dictionary of the Proverbs in England in the Sixteenth and Seventeenth Centuries* (Ann Arbor, Michigan, 1950), C.587.)

66.26–35 old Birrel... a Highlandman's promise Robert Birrel (*fl.* 1567–1605), burgess of Edinburgh, kept a diary of current events which is printed in Sir John Graham Dalzell, *Fragments of Scotish History* (Edinburgh, 1798): *CLA*, 4. The incident concerning Allaster MacGregor of Glenstrae took place in 1603 and occurs on pp. 60–61.

66.30 Maccallan Mhor of the day *Gaelic MacCailein Mór*, son of Colin the Great, the title of the chiefs of the clan Campbell, who claim descent from Colin Campbell of Lochow who died in 1294. They became Earls and then Dukes of Argyll.

66.30 word of promise... the ear see *Macbeth*, 5.8.21–22: Macbeth recognises the witches 'keep the word of promise to our ear, / And break it to our hope!'.

66.32 the other side of the Tweed by implication, to England. Since the town of Berwick had been English since 1482, there was no need to take them across Tweed, and in his review of the *Culloden Papers* Scott, following Birrel, takes the prisoners to Berwick only (*Prose Works*, 20.50).

66.37 brought up in France probably because they were Jacobites and had taken refuge in France after the failure of the Jacobite risings of 1715 and 1745.

66.43 John Highlandman generic name for a Highlandman.

67.7–8 The Highlands... fairly wrought out by Scott himself and his imitators. In his *Journal* for 8 July 1826, however, Scott noted that 'The highlanders have been off the field now for some time' (169).

67.25–26 between Glencroe and Inverary the road from Tarbet on Loch Lomond by Glen Croe and Glen Kinglas to Inverary was the usual approach to the Western Highlands.

67.31–32 Let that be done... but not to-day Matthew Prior puts these words in the mouth of Robert Harley, Earl of Oxford (1661–1724) in his poem

'Erle Robert's Mice' (1712), lines 60–61.

67.34   the Abbey clock   there is no clock on the ruined Abbey at Holyrood; but a clock dated 1680 is on the cupola above the entrance to the Palace.

HISTORICAL NOTE TO 'THE HIGHLAND WIDOW'

The date of the story. *Chronicles of the Canongate* is a collection of tales introduced and linked by a fictitious compiler and narrator, Chrystal Croft-angry, who is writing in 1826, as he tells us himself (53.42–43). He received the memorandum on which 'The Highland Widow' is based from his friend, Mrs Martha Bethune Baliol, who in turn is nominally recounting experiences from her highland tour which took place 'five and thirty, or perhaps nearer forty years' (68.13) before. That suggests that she made her tour between 1786 and 1791.

The historical context. The tale of the deserter and his mother takes place after the defeat of the Jacobite rising of 1745–46 (77.38–39), and probably in 1758 (see below).

After the so-called Glorious Revolution of 1688–89 in which James VII and II lost his throne, the Highlands of Scotland remained, for the most part, sympathetic to him and his descendants; but only a minority of clan chiefs were prepared to involve themselves and their followers (called Jacobites, from the Latin word for James, *Jacobus*) in the armed struggle to restore the Stewart monarchy in 1689, 1708, 1715, 1719 and finally in 1745. After 1715 it was recognised that turbulence in the Highlands posed a threat to the Hanoverian dynasty (George, Elector of Hanover, became King of Great Britain and Ireland in 1714), and to the Whig politicians who had established it, but the measures the government adopted were not effectual. For example, the principal participants in the rising of 1715 had their estates forfeited, but forfeited estates were very often administered by relatives; the government passed a disarming act in 1716, and tightened it in 1725, but steps to ensure disarmament were never taken.

That such measures did not bring the Highlands within the control of the British government is illustrated by the career of the celebrated Rob Roy Mac-Gregor (1671–1734) from whom MacTavish Mhor, Hamish's father, derives his characteristics (see note to 76.40–41). Rob Roy was originally a cattle-dealer, failed financially, and then 'earned a living' by levying protection money on tenants of the Duke of Montrose in Menteith within thirty miles of Glasgow, and by stealing from all those who neglected or refused to pay. In such circumstances there was a kind of 'wild-west' law, but it was not the law of the land (see note to 77.4–5).

The rising of 1745–46 changed everything. After the defeat of the Jacobites at the Battle of Culloden in April 1746, military repression in the Highlands was brutal and savage: those found in arms were to be shot on the spot, and the homes of those who had absconded were to be burned, and their cattle driven away; in practice search-and-destroy tactics were used indiscriminately. Some 3000 people were taken prisoner: many died in custody; many were deported; about 120 were judicially executed. Garrisons were extended, and Fort George, one of the great military bastions of Europe, was built near Inverness. The disarming act of 1746 provided much stiffer penalties for possessing arms, and this time soldiers were empowered to search for weapons. Wearing tartan was proscribed (see note to 79.39). Most important of all, the Heritable Jurisdictions Act (20 George II. c. 43), passed in 1747 and effective from 1748, abolished the hereditary right of landowners and clan chiefs to try persons accused of all crimes committed in the area of their jurisdiction except murder, fire-raising, rape, and robbery with violence. The Act was of the greatest significance in reducing the power of landowners and chiefs over their feudal vassals, and in giving control of the administration of justice to anti-Jacobite lawyers and politicians in lowland Scotland.

If the aftermath of Culloden involved savage repression, there were also moves towards assimilation. General Wade, Commander-in-Chief in Scotland from 1725, had begun a programme of road-building in the Highlands, and between 1726 and 1737 some 260 miles of military road were constructed; the process continued after the '45 (see notes to 68.17; 72.3–4). The nominal aim was to supply Highland garrisons and to allow troops to be deployed rapidly, but the actual effect was to bring the Highlands closer to lowland Britain. In addition, Wade also established a series of independent companies to patrol, or 'watch', areas of the Highlands, primarily to prevent the activities of those such as Rob Roy. In 1739 these companies were brought together to form the first Highland regiment in the British Army, named the Black Watch or (from 1751) the 42nd Regiment of Foot (see note to 77.13). Soldiers in the Black Watch wore 'their native tartan' (see note to 85.34), unlike civilians who were prevented by law from doing so.

Hamish is thus in a real quandary: by enlisting in a regiment of the British army he betrays his father; but by enlisting he wears the tartan and maintains the military tradition of his forbears. The tragedy of 'The Highland Widow' arises from this conflict in symbolic loyalties.

The date of the action. The date of the main action is determined principally by historical evidence. Hamish enlists in 'one of the new regiments' which was to be sent to fight the French in America (88.24–25) during the Seven Years' War (1756–63), and it is clearly a newly-embodied corps which Hamish joins. During the war ten new Highland Regiments were raised (including the second battalion of the Black Watch), but not all of them participated in the campaign in North America (see note to 88.24–25). Of the three that did, two, namely Montgomerie's Highlanders and Fraser's Highlanders, were recruited in the north of Scotland. The first battalion of the Black Watch was not a 'new regiment' at the outset of the Seven Years' War; so attention is thrown on to the second battalion, which was raised between July and October 1758, drawing largely on men from the southern Highlands.[1]

The only date mentioned in the narrative is the minister's information 'this is Monday, the second day of the week, and twenty-first of the month' (101.5–6). It is clearly summer. The only date during that part of the Seven Years' War when Highland regiments were being sent to America which was simultaneously summer, Monday and the 21st is Monday 21 August 1758.[2] It is probable, therefore, that the main events of 'The Highland Widow' take place in August 1758. Scott's reticence about specifying dates like this too precisely may arise from his habitual use of historical material which does not strictly belong to the year which he has in mind. For instance, desertion is the pivotal issue of 'The Highland Widow', but the material upon which Scott draws actually belongs to 1743 (see notes to 99.6–7, and 116.13). Another piece of historical material which is adapted for the use of the narrative is the name of the recruiter, 'Barcaldine's son' (89.31). Alexander Campbell, younger of Barcaldine, was an officer in the first battalion the Black Watch prior to the Seven Years' War.[3] In 'The Highland Widow' he appears only recently 'made a leader' (89.31–32), enabling Scott to create a fictitious body of troops, raised by a Campbell in Argyllshire, to join the second battalion of the Black Watch in 1758.

Although the historical evidence points to 1758 as the date of the main action the time references in the tale as a whole do not entirely cohere. The problem concerns Hamish's date of birth. It appears that Elspat gave birth to Hamish during her husband's 'evil days' (78.1), which, the context implies, come after the battle of Culloden in April 1746. He was an 'infant child', who was 'a considerable encumbrance' to his parents as they lived the lives of fugitives (78.1–3). As Elspat reminds her son, 'I bore you away on my back, through the fire of six of the Saxon soldiers, and you a wailing child' (81.1–3). To be so young a child Hamish must have been born in about 1746, which would make him only 12 in 1758. This is too young an age for enlisting in the army, and an age incompatible with the fact that it is a young man, not a child, who takes decisive action to assert his independence from his mother. Scott makes Hamish a man of the new post-feudal, post-Jacobite era; to fit his story and its symbolic import to history requires an extension of the historical years between 1746 and 1758, a necessity which both explains and justifies Scott's reluctance to specify precise dates.

Sources. Scott had told the story of 'The Highland Widow' orally before using it in *Chronicles of the Canongate*. Maria Edgeworth, in thanking Scott for a copy of the tales, wrote:

> We are in the midst of Elspat's history—most interesting it is!—I never can forget the impression your first relating it to us (in the open carriage when we were travelling) made on my mind.[4]

But the tale was not Scott's own. On 27 May 1826, the day he started to write *Chronicles of the Canongate*, he noted in his *Journal*: 'Mrs. M. K.'s tale of the Deserter with her interview with the lad's mother may be made most affecting but will hardly endure much expansion'.[5] When he came to describe its origin for the Magnum he explained that 'The Highland Widow'

> was derived from Mrs. Keith and was told with a few additional circumstances exactly as Mrs Murray Keith herself told the story and neither the highland Cicerone MacLeish nor the demure waiting woman were ideal[6] characters. There were indeed some imaginary circumstances which I rather regret for on reconsidering the tale with a view to the present Edition I am convinced I have injured the simplicity of the narrative which in Mrs Keiths narration was extremely affecting.[7]

Anne Murray Keith (1736–1818) was the daughter of Robert Keith of Craig (d. 1774). She was a friend of Scott's maternal aunt, Christian Rutherford,[8] and he probably got to know her after 1793–94 when she settled in George Street, Edinburgh, with her cousin the Dowager Countess of Balcarres (see note to 56.27). On her death Scott described her as 'one who lived among us with the recollections of a former generation, yet, with all the warmth of heart, and clearness of intellect, which enabled her to enter into the events and interests of our own.[9] Scott acknowledged that the character of Mrs Martha Bethune Balliol, the fictitious source and narrator of 'The Highland Widow', is based on Mrs Murray Keith.[10]

Although Scott twice attributes the tale of 'The Highland Widow' to Mrs Murray Keith he had another source, which perhaps he had forgotten. A tale similar to that of 'The Highland Widow' is recounted in Sir John Carr's *Caledonian Sketches, or a Tour through Scotland in 1807* (London, 1809).[11] Scott had reviewed this book unflatteringly in the *Quarterly Review*, where he had summed it up as 'a short description of the exterior of the country, a few trite anecdotes of ancient history and manners, and an account of local customs and laws neither remarkable for value nor accuracy'.[12] Nonetheless the similarities between Scott's story, and that in Carr, are striking:

> The Highlanders are remarkable for their filial affection and obedience. An undutiful son or daughter, in the Highlands, is ranked amongst those who blemish human nature. To show to what extremity this submission to parental will is occasionally carried, I lay before my reader the following

affecting instance, which occurred a few years since:—An English lady, who was travelling in a solitary part of the Highlands, remarked an old woman, dressed in black, sitting upon a stone, by the road side, and weeping. The lady directed her guide to go to her, and inquire who she was; he accordingly asked her for some account of herself. After a conversation which lasted some time, he informed the lady that the poor woman was very unhappy, and had good cause to be so, for she had an only son, who enlisted in the army against her will, though she suppressed her feelings, that he might follow his inclinations; that soon afterwards he obtained a furlough, and came back to her, when, from excess of fondness, she would not allow him to leave her, though the time appointed for his return had expired. His commanding-officer sent a message to him, ordering him to return; he still remained with his mother: another and peremptory order followed; it was alike disregarded. At length a file of soldiers was dispatched to the cottage, to seize him as a deserter. When, with anguish in his heart, he was preparing to submit, his mother called out, "What, Sandy, will you spare your blood upon your enemies?" The youth, wrought up almost to phrenzy by the horror of his situation and this appeal, seized his musket, and discharged it at his comrades, upon which they fired, and shot him instantly dead. When the story was finished, the lady went up to console this venerable object of her sympathy, upon which she just raised her grey head, and sobbed, "My beautiful, my brave!" an exclamation which she had borrowed from the play of *Douglas*, and which so closely applied to her feelings.[13]

Sir John Carr (1772–1832) was an Englishman who had published accounts of travels in several European countries before visiting Scotland. As Scott pointed out in his review, his *Caledonian Sketches* show him incorporating material from previous accounts into his text without acknowledgement.[14] Carr spent some days in Edinburgh on his tour of Scotland, but there is no evidence that he met Mrs Murray Keith. Scott, in his *Journal*, implies that Mrs Murray Keith had been the traveller who had met the Highland widow, having an 'interview with the lad's mother'; Carr says that the traveller was an 'English lady'. In the light of this discrepancy one cannot but notice that Scott is not explicit on this point in his Magnum Introduction. 'The Highland Widow', he claims,

> was derived from Mrs Murray Keith, and is given, with the exception of a few additional circumstances—the introduction of which I am rather inclined to regret—very much as the excellent old lady used to tell the story. Neither the Highland cicerone Macturk, nor the demure washing-woman,[15] were drawn from imagination: and on re-reading my tale, after the lapse of a few years, and comparing its effect with my remembrance of my worthy friend's oral narration, which was certainly extremely affecting, I cannot but suspect myself of having marred its simplicity by some of those interpolations, which, at the time when I penned them, no doubt passed with myself for embellishments.[16]

It looks as if this story recounting the experience of an unnamed traveller had some currency and Mrs Murray Keith was a particularly fine narrator of it.

There are several differences between Carr's version of the tale and 'The Highland Widow'; one of the most striking is that Carr's version does not mention the drugged drink. Whether elements of 'The Highland Widow' which are not in Carr's version were present in Mrs Murray Keith's narration, or whether they were part of Scott's creative process in writing his tale, can only be conjectured. But the conjecture that Scott interpolated the drugged drink can be assisted by noticing other material which he added and for which there are identifiable sources.

Scott's Elspat MacTavish is an altogether tougher proposition than the mother in Carr's narrative. She is in the tradition of Scott's earlier strong-minded mothers and Highland women, in particular Helen MacGregor in *Rob Roy*. Another source for details of Elspat's life and death is the account of a solitary Highland woman, Catherine Cameron, which Scott received from Robert Scott Moncrieff.[17] After her husband's death at Culloden Catherine Cameron retired to a remote spot in Perthshire with a few goats and was found sitting in front of her miserable hut; she refused the offer of better accommodation and had 'no anxiety' at the thought that she might die alone and remain unburied.

The details of military discipline, such as corporal punishment and the conduct of a firing squad, which are such an important part of 'The Highland Widow' are missing from Carr's tale, but are described in a book which Scott admired, David Stewart of Garth's *Sketches of the Character, Manners, and Present State of the Highlanders of Scotland with details of the Military Service of the Highland Regiments* (Edinburgh, 1822).

Carr does not say in which part of the Highlands his tale took place.[18] The setting beside the River Awe in Argyllshire must therefore come from either Mrs Murray Keith or Scott. Scott had made the journey through Argyllshire to Oban on his way to the Hebrides in 1810.[19] Argyllshire indicated to Scott the country of the Campbells and enabled him to give a political edge to his tale. His Elspat MacTavish is the loyal widow of a vanquished and dispossessed Jacobite, and her son in enlisting is not merely leaving his mother but is pledging loyalty to the Hanoverian government and the Whig clan Campbell. Scott took the setting in Gaelic-speaking Scotland seriously, to the extent that he did at least some work on his own knowledge of Gaelic, for Robert Cadell wrote to him shortly before *Chronicles* was published: 'About twelvemonths ago I sent to you for the use of the "*Highland Widow*" a Gaelic Grammar—the person from whom I got it wishes it return[ed]'.[20]

Scott indicates in his Magnum Introduction to 'The Highland Widow' that he had added some circumstances to Mrs Murray Keith's tale. There is little doubt that one of them is the Minister's journey home at the end of the tale through a glen haunted by the *Cloght-dearg* (116.36–117.15). The name of the evil spirit derives from a tale told to Scott by Mrs Hepburne, and subsequently repeated in a letter from her husband, J. Stewart Hepburne.[21] The tale is set in Perthshire, just north of Aberfeldy, and concerns '"Fear a' cloc dhearg"—the Man in the Red Cloak'. According to the legend the Man in the Red Cloak lived in a cave, which opened in the Rock of Weem and terminated under the water of Loch Glassie,[22] into which he seduced young girls. The tale, which was apparently a song, was gathered by Stewart Hepburne's sister-in-law, Miss Stewart, from an old woman at Cluny, called Girzein Alaster (1734–*c*. 1827).

The title of the tale. The title comes from a song called 'The Highland Widow's Lament' which was first published in eight stanzas in James Johnson's *Scots Musical Museum* in 1796.[23] It is a Jacobite lament in which the singer bewails her reduced condition since the death of her husband at Culloden. It was contributed to the collection by Robert Burns and it is thought that Burns wrote at least part of it (probably the specifically Jacobite stanzas).[24] Scott uses stanzas 1 and 5 of Burns's text as the motto to the second chapter of his tale (76).

The same song with three additional stanzas is printed in R. H. Cromek, *Remains of Nithsdale & Galloway Song* (London, 1810), 198. The additional stanzas (enclosed in square parentheses and said by Cromek to be 'now first printed') are between stanzas 7 and 8 of Burns's text; they are significant in the present context because they give the Highland Widow two sons whose future vengeance is her consolation:

I hae nocht left me ava,
   Ochon, ochon, ochrie!
But bonny orphan lad-weans twa,
   To seek their bread wi' me.

I hae yet a tocher-band,
   Ochon, ochon, ochrie!
My winsome Donald's durk and brand,
   Into their hands to gie.

There's only ae blink o' hope left,
   To lighten my auld e'e;
To see my bairns gie bluidy crowns
   To them gart Donald die.

Cromek either collected these stanzas in Galloway, or wrote them himself.[25] They may have suggested to Scott the theme of a mother bringing up her son to avenge the death of his father, which is not present in Burns's version of the song.

When Scott started to write the tale the manuscript (f. 30) shows the title 'The Highland Widow' followed by one stanza of 'The Highland Widow's Lament' as a motto (stanza 5 of Burns's text). That motto was deleted in the manuscript and replaced with four lines from Coleridge's 'Christabel' (68). The motto from 'The Highland Widow's Lament', increased to two stanzas, was moved to the beginning of the second chapter (76) where its connection with the title of the tale is less obvious.

NOTES

For shortened forms of reference see 289–90.

1   Stewart, 1.291.
2   Detailed examination of the chronology of the Waverley Novels has demonstrated that Scott must have used an almanac: see for example *Guy Mannering*, ed. P. D. Garside, EEWN 2, 496–500.
3   [Neil McMicking], *Officers of the Black Watch 1725 to 1752* (Perth, [1952]), 24.
4   Letter from Maria Edgeworth to Scott, 9–15 November 1827, MS 3905, f. 145r. This probably took place on the Edgeworths' visit to Scott in 1823.
5   *Journal*, 150.
6   Meaning here, imaginary or fictitious.
7   From Scott's manuscript of the Magnum Introduction to *Chronicles of the Canongate*, in the Huntington Library, California (MS HM 1982). The passage was revised before publication in the Magnum, 41.xxxiii–xxxiv.
8   *Letters*, 8.39.
9   *Letters*, 5.162.
10 Magnum, 41.xxxii; see also notes to 53.17, 56.23–24, and 56.27 above.
11 I am grateful to Professor Ina Ferris for drawing Carr's version of the tale to my attention.
12 *Prose Works*, 19.160–84 (166).
13 Sir John Carr, *Caledonian Sketches, or a Tour through Scotland in 1807* (London, 1809), 439–41.
14 *Prose Works*, 19.168.
15 The cicerone is MacLeish, and the woman a waiting-woman.
16 Magnum, 41.xxxiii–xxxiv.
17 The story of Catherine Cameron is recounted in a letter from 'A. S.' to Robert Scott Moncrieff, which has been endorsed by Scott 'Highland Anecdote respecting a Solitary female' (MS 874, ff. 307r–308v). The letter is undated; but the paper has a watermark dated 1806.

18 Carr travelled up the River Awe from Taynuilt to Dalmally (505–06), but his tale is not associated with any particular place in the Highlands. It occurs in Chapter 23 of his *Caledonian Sketches*, the theme of which is 'the Highland character elucidated'.

19 *Life*, 2.310. Scott wrote to the painter David Wilkie on 2 August 1817, 'Pray do not omit to visit the head of Loch Awe, which I look upon as equal to any thing in the Highlands' (*Letters*, 4.484).

20 24 August 1827, MS 3904, f. 236r.

21 20 July 1825, MS 874, ff. 317r–18r.

22 John Wilson, reviewing *Chronicles of the Canongate*, located the Cloght-Dearg on 'the moors of Glen-Falloch' (*Blackwood's Edinburgh Magazine*, 22 (November 1827), 556). Glenfalloch is N of Loch Lomond and was described by Wordsworth as 'the Vale of Awful Sound' (*Journals of Dorothy Wordsworth*, ed. E. de Selincourt, 2 vols (London, 1959), 1.372).

23 James Johnson, *The Scots Musical Museum*, 6 vols (Edinburgh, 1787–1803), 5, no. 498.

24 *The Poems and Songs of Robert Burns*, ed. James Kinsley, 3 vols (Oxford, 1968), 2.877–78 and note on 3.1515.

25 See Claire Lamont, 'Jacobite Songs as Intertexts in *Waverley* and *The Highland Widow*' in *Scott in Carnival*, ed. J. H. Alexander and David Hewitt (Aberdeen, 1993), 110–21.

EXPLANATORY NOTES TO 'THE HIGHLAND WIDOW'

For shortened forms of reference see 289–90.

68 motto Samuel Taylor Coleridge, 'Christabel' (1797), lines 39–42.

68.13 five and thirty ... years ago i.e 1786–91; see Historical Note, 319.

68.15–16 the short Highland tour see John Knox, *A Tour through the Highlands of Scotland, and the Hebride Isles, in MDCCLXXXVI* (London, 1787), 9: 'Strangers who come to this place from motives of health or amusement, generally visit Glasgow, Loch Lomond, and Inveraray, on the west; or Perth, Dunkeld, Blair, and Taymouth, on the north. Many gentlemen visit all these places; and this is called The Short Tour of SCOTLAND.' Tourists had been attracted to the Highlands at least since the publication of Thomas Pennant's *A Tour in Scotland; MDCCLXIX* (Chester, 1771) and his *A Tour in Scotland, and Voyage to the Hebrides; MDCCLXXII*, 2 vols (Chester, 1774–76). Mrs Bethune Baliol's route was Stirling–Tyndrum–Dalmally–round Ben Cruachan and down the River Awe–Oban.

68.17 the military roads a programme of military road-building in the Highlands was started in 1725 by General George Wade (1673–1748) and continued until 1789. The interest of the army in Highland communications was a consequence of the Jacobite risings of 1715 and 1719. See Historical Note, 320.

68.20 King George George III, reigned 1760–1820.

68.21 the insurrection of 1745 the rising of the Jacobites (from Latin *Jacobus*, meaning James), supporters of the claim of the Stewarts to the throne of Britain, in 1745–46. At that time the Stewart claimant was James Edward Francis (1688–1766), son of James VII and II who had fled the throne in 1688. The Jacobite army, led by his son Prince Charles Edward (1720–88), was supported by many of the Highland clans. Its initial defeat of the Hanoverian forces, and its march into England as far south as Derby, had given a frightening impression of the Scottish highlanders to those living in the south.

68.31–32 Greatheart in the Pilgrim's Progress Christiana's guide in Part II of John Bunyan, *The Pilgrim's Progress* (1684).

68.37 mail-coaches and steam-boats see notes to 17.33 and 31.21–22.

69.12   first ready   the first postilion to be ready to set off, whose readiness may be his only merit.

69.30   would "be killing" lamb   Tulloch (378) points out that the use of *will* (here *would*) with a continuous form of the verb is a literary device to indicate a Highland speaker.

69.30   Tyndrum   an important junction 60 km NW of Stirling, where the road divides to go N to Fort William and W to Oban.

69.30   Glenuilt   not listed in gazeteers of Scotland. It is tempting to suggest that Scott meant Taynuilt, at the mouth of the River Awe (except that at 71.18–19 Donald MacLeish hints that 'there was no good halting place between Dalmally and Oban').

69.32–33   wheaten loaf ... the Land of Cakes   many travellers lamented the scarcity of wheat bread in the Highlands. On 20 July 1818 Keats found on Loch Awe 'we have lost the sight of white bread entirely ... but no oat Cake wanting' (*The Letters of John Keats*, ed. Hyder Edward Rollins, 2 vols (Cambridge, Mass., 1958), 1.338). Scotland got the name 'the Land of Cakes' from one of its staple foods, unleavened oat or barley-meal cakes. The first instance of the phrase describing Scotland cited by the *OED* is in 1669 (*cake*, substantive 1b).

69.35   which side of a Highland bridge was passable   insufficient attention was given to maintenance of military roads in the Highlands. In *New Ways through the Glens* (London, 1962), 9, A. R. B. Haldane quotes a report of 1784–85: 'The number of bridges upon these roads amount to 938. Many of them are insufficient, some ruinous, and other of those that were first built, injudiciously constructed and ill-executed.' Scott does not confine such bridges to the Highlands: 'the brigg ower Warroch burn is safe eneugh, if he haud to the right side' (*Guy Mannering*, ed. P. D. Garside EEWN 2 (Edinburgh, 1999), 60–61).

69.39–40   piques himself on being a maize-eater   takes pride in eating maize, which was poor man's food.

70.9   Gil Blas   Alain-René Lesage, *Histoire de Gil Blas de Santillane* (1715–35).

70.9   Don Quixote   Miguel de Cervantes, *Don Quixote* (Part 1, 1605; Part 2, 1615).

70.14   at Falkirk or Preston   victories of the Jacobite army during the '45. The Jacobites defeated the Hanoverian forces at Prestonpans, not far from Edinburgh, at the beginning of the campaign on 21 September 1745. The victory at Falkirk on 17 January 1746 was a stand in the course of retreat.

70.14–15   the frail yet faithful record of times which had passed away   alluding to the Gaelic phrase *na làithean a dh'aom*, 'times which had passed away'.

70.21–22   as good gentlemen as the king   see *Don Quixote*, Part 2 (1615), Chapter 48: Dona Rodriguez says of her late husband 'he was as noble as the king, for he came from La Montana', alluding to a mountainous region in the N of Spain.

70.31   mountain dew   whisky, especially if illicitly distilled.

70.31–32   like Gideon's fleece   see Judges 6.37: Gideon's fleece was wet with dew while the surrounding earth remained dry, a sign that God would save Israel.

70.41   the family of MacLeish   an early bearer of the name MacLeish 'was one of the laird of Glenurquhay's vassals in 1638', thus associating the name with Argyllshire (George F. Black, *The Surnames of Scotland* (New York, 1946), 537).

71.12   Dalmally   32 km E of Oban.

71.13 incumbent at Glenorquhy in the Magnum Scott noted: 'This venerable and hospitable gentleman's name was MacIntyre' (41.128). This identification had already been guessed by John Wilson, reviewing *Chronicles of the Canongate* for *Blackwood's Edinburgh Magazine*, 22 (November 1827), 558n. The Rev. Joseph MacIntyre (1735–1823) was minister of the parishes of Glenorchy and Inishail from 1765 until his death. Many travellers acknowledged his hospitality at the church and manse at Dalmally.

71.14 the stern chiefs of Lochawe the Campbells who gained possession of Lochawe (often spelled Lochow) from Robert the Bruce (1274–1329) and whose power spread from there until they were the most powerful clan in Argyll. As part of this expansion Duncan Campbell, 4th of Lochow (d. 1453), obtained the lands of Glenorchy from the MacGregors in the early 15th century. Duncan's son, Sir Colin Campbell (d. 1475), was the first of the Campbells of Glenorchy.

71.14–15 Duncan with the thrum bonnet i.e. wearing a cap made of waste yarn; probably Duncan Campbell, 7th of Glenorchy (1545–1631), '*Donacha dhu na curich*, as he is called from the *cowl* in which he is represented in his picture at Taymouth' (William Bowie, *The Black Book of Taymouth*, ed. Cosmo Innes (Edinburgh, 1855), iv). A cowl in Scots is a close-fitting woollen cap (*SND*). At Taymouth Castle, which Scott visited in 1797, there was a celebrated genealogy of the Campbells of Glenorchy painted in 1635 by George Jameson (1588–1644). It is reproduced in Duncan Thomson, *The Life and Art of George Jamesone* (Oxford, 1974), plate 94.

71.15–16 mouldering towers of Kilchurn at the east end of Loch Awe; said to have been built *c.* 1450 by Margaret, wife of Colin Campbell of Glenorchy (d. 1475: see note to 71.14) while her husband was on a crusade. Kilchurn Castle became of less importance to the Campbells of Glenorchy and their descendants the earls and marquises of Breadalbane as their power increased in Perthshire. Kilchurn was garrisoned during the '45 but was subsequently abandoned; Pennant remarks that it is 'now a ruin, having lately been struck by lightening' (*A Tour in Scotland; MDCCLXIX*, 3rd edn (Warrington, 1774), 216). The striking appearance of the 'mouldering towers' caused Wordsworth to write his 'Address to Kilchurn Castle' after visiting it in 1803.

71.21–22 Cruachan Ben Ben Cruachan (1126m), 21 km E of Oban.

71.24–25 clan of MacDougal of Lorn … Robert the Bruce Robert the Bruce, who reigned as Robert I, 1306–29, consolidating his position on the throne, defeated John MacDougall of Lorn in the Pass of Brander in 1308. Lorn is the area of Argyllshire between the River Awe and the sea. Subsequently Bruce drove John of Lorn out of the country and gave 'great part of his possessions to his own nephew Sir Colin Campbell, who became the first of the great family of Argyll, which afterwards enjoyed such power in the Highlands' (Walter Scott, *Tales of a Grandfather*, first series, 3 vols (Edinburgh, 1828), 1.235; *Prose Works*, 22.192).

71.25–26 the Wellington of his day Arthur Wellesley, Duke of Wellington (1769–1852), the victorious British general during the Napoleonic wars.

71.29–30 great number of cairns yet visible cairns (piles of stones) were visible on the W side of the River Awe in the 19th century. John Leyden saw them in 1800 and was told that 'they covered the ancient MacGregors' (*Journal of a Tour in the Highlands*, ed. James Sinton (Edinburgh, 1903), 85). Scott writes as if he had seen them himself, probably on his journey to Oban in 1810. They are fully described in Archibald Smith, 'Traditions of Glenurchay', in *The Proceedings of the Society of Antiquaries of Scotland*, 7 (1870), 222–41. Little is visible now, and there is no mention of cairns beside the River Awe in the Royal Commission on the Ancient and Historical Monuments of Scotland's volume *Argyll: An Inventory of the Ancient Monuments*, Volume 2, *Lorn* (Edinburgh, 1975). John Dunbar, head of the Commission, has confirmed that any cairns that survive are not monuments, but the result of field clearances. There is a local recollection that the stones were used in the building of the barrage over the River Awe in connection with the Cruachan Hydro–Electric scheme.

71.32–33   the sister of soldiers   see note to 56.23–24.

71.34   Bonaparte   Napoleon Bonaparte (1769–1821), a Corsican soldier who rose to power in France after the Revolution of 1789 and led the French in a major European war of conquest until his defeat by Wellington at Waterloo in 1815. The campaigns of Bonaparte and Wellington were on Scott's mind as he wrote *Chronicles of the Canongate* in the intervals of writing his nine-volume *Life of Napoleon* (Edinburgh, 1827).

71.35–38   even a Baliol . . . with whom he contended   Robert Bruce, Earl of Annandale, 'the Competitor' (1210–95) failed in his claim to the throne of Scotland against John Baliol (1249–1315) in 1292. His grandson Robert the Bruce (1274–1329), who became King Robert I in 1306, was always opposed by Baliol's descendants (see note to 58.4). Professor G. W. S. Barrow has pointed out to me that the competition for the throne is dealt with at some length in the first volume of Patrick Fraser Tytler's *History of Scotland*, 9 vols (Edinburgh, 1828–43). Although the volume was not published until 1828 Scott knew the author, and was well placed to hear of the latest historical reassessments.

72.1–2   things which are long enough a-gone   an allusion to an Irish song sung by Sophia Edgeworth (1803–37), step-sister of Maria Edgeworth, during their stay at Abbotsford in the summer of 1823. Scott quotes two stanzas of the song in a letter to Maria Edgeworth of 22 September 1823 (*Letters*, 8.90). James C. Corson notes that 'In Mrs Hope-Scott's MS. Music Book at Abbotsford this song is included with the music' (*Notes and Index to Sir Herbert Grierson's Edition of the Letters of Sir Walter Scott* (Oxford, 1979), 225).

72.3–4   General Wade's military road   the road from Dalmally round Ben Cruachan and down the River Awe was built 1750–51 not by Wade but by his successor, William Caulfeild, Inspector of Roads 1732–67: see William Taylor, *The Military Roads in Scotland* (Newton Abbot, 1976), 24, 69, 151. The original road was not at the edge of the loch, as is the present A85, but was higher up the mountain side where traces of it may still be seen.

72.7   Roman engineers   under the Emperor Severus in AD 208–10. Scott wrote of the attempted conquest of the Caledonians: 'He cut down forests, made roads through marshes and over mountains, and endeavoured to secure the districts which he overran' (*The History of Scotland*, which Scott contributed to *The Cabinet Cyclopaedia*, ed. Dionysius Lardner, 2 vols (London, 1830), 1.5–6.

72.9–10   our sister kingdom   i.e. England.

72.12   the second sight   the facility of 'seeing' things distant in time or place, particularly associated with the Scottish Highlanders.

72.133–14   Had you but seen these roads . . . General Wade   attributed to William Caulfeild, but evidence for the attribution is lacking: see William Taylor, *The Military Roads in Scotland* (Newton Abbot, 1976), 25.

72.20–21   victories of Bonaparte have been without results   in view of his final defeat at Waterloo (1815).

72.21   his road over the Simplon   Napoleon built a carriage road in 1800–07 through the mountain pass over the Alps in southern Switzerland.

72.27   the majestic lake   Loch Awe, which the travellers leave to enter the Pass of Brander through which runs the River Awe.

72.32   the iron founderies at Bunawe   in 1753 an iron furnace was founded by ironmasters from Cumbria at Bonawe, where the River Awe flows into Loch Etive. The forests of birch and oak in the area supplied charcoal for the furnace; iron ore was brought in by sea from Lowland Scotland and Cumbria. The furnace was in operation until 1876; the site is now laid out for visitors. Thomas Pennant describes the wooded sides of Ben Cruachan and mentions the 'considerable iron-foundery, which I fear will soon devour the beautiful woods of the country' (*A Tour in Scotland; MDCCLXIX*, 3rd edn (Warrington, 1774), 217).

72.39 in a fall of sixty feet Allt Cruachan, the stream which descends from Ben Cruachan into the River Awe. The fall is hidden for the modern visitor by the railway line, built in 1880, which is carried on a stone viaduct in front of it; and by the Ben Cruachan Hydro-Electric Scheme, opened in 1965, which has put buildings on 'the spot of clear ground' in front of it. There are, however, still oak trees in the area.

73.22 the whilst in the meantime.

73.35 The ne'er a bit not a bit, absolutely not (see *CSD*, *never*).

73.35 clean aff the road wholly off the road, i.e. quite wrong.

74.11 browsing on the roof of the hut Burt notes: 'When the Hut has been built some Time, it is cover'd with Weeds and Grass; and, I do assure you I have seen Sheep, that had got up from the Foot of an adjoining Hill, feeding upon the Top of the House' (Burt, 2.41).

74.29–30 as Judah is represented in the Syrian medals under the Emperor Vespasian, after the fall of Jerusalem in AD 70, brass coins were struck at Antioch in Syria marking the Roman conquest of the Jews. One type, known as the Judaea Capta type from the inscription on it, shows a weeping woman sitting under a palm tree. See Seth William Stevenson, C. Roach Smith and Frederic W. Madden, *A Dictionary of Roman Coins* (London, 1889), 490–91.

75.7–8 MacTavish see note to 76.40–41.

75.9 pursued by the Furies spirits of punishment in Ancient Greece avenging in particular wrongs done to kindred.

75.11 Orestes and Oedipus Orestes, hero of the plays known as the *Oresteia* (458 BC) by Aeschylus, killed his mother and her lover, who had murdered his father, and was pursued by the Furies. Oedipus, the hero of plays by Sophocles (c. 496–406 BC), unwittingly killed his father and married his mother; the horror of his deeds drove him to blind himself and go into exile.

76.23 My beautiful—my brave! Lady Randolph's lament for her son in John Home's tragedy *Douglas* (1757), 5.1.283. Mrs Bethune Baliol shares friendship with the Rev. John Home (1722–1808) with Scott (*Life*, 1.22, 139).

76 motto see 'The Highland Widow's Lament', lines 1–4, 17–20, collected and partly written by Burns: *The Poems and Songs of Robert Burns*, ed. James Kinsley, 3 vols (Oxford, 1968), no. 590, 2.877–78. See also Historical Note, 323–24.

76.40–41 MacTavish Mhor Gaelic *mór*, meaning the great, or strong. 'MacTavish' is from Gaelic *MacTamhais*, 'son of Thomas'. The MacTavishes are said to have lived near the mouth of the River Awe: see Archibald Smith, 'Traditions of Glenurchay', in *Proceedings of the Society of Antiquaries of Scotland*, 7 (1870), 229. The characteristics of MacTavish Mhor derive from the MacGregors, and especially from the celebrated Rob Roy MacGregor (1671–1734).

77.2 the Lowland line Scotland is commonly divided into Highland (northern, western, and Gaelic-speaking) and Lowland (southern, eastern, and Scots-speaking). The idea of a 'line' came into currency in the late 18th century as a result of legislation concerning the distilling of whisky. The 'imaginary line' (*Prose Works*, 20.16) runs diagonally across the country roughly between Dumbarton and Stonehaven, but the coastal plain of Aberdeenshire and Moray is not considered to be in the Highlands.

77.4–5 **protection-money** the payment of money to depredators for protection was illegal, but hard to prevent while law-enforcement in the Highlands was uncertain: see David Marshall, *Sir Walter Scott and Scots Law* (Edinburgh, 1932), 34, 107; and Historical Note, 319.

77.6 **fleech the deil than fight him** *proverbial* 'Better flatter a Fool than fight wi' him' (Ramsay, 71). *Fleech* is Scots, to cajole, flatter; *deil* is Scots, the devil.

77.11 **Monteith . . . Ballybught** Monteith, or Menteith, is a fertile district of W Stirlingshire. 'Ballybught' is probably fictitious.

77.13 **the Highland Watch** in 1725 Independent Companies of soldiers were raised to keep the peace in the Highlands. In 1739 they became the first Highland Regiment in the British army, and were known as the Black Watch or 43rd Regiment of Foot. They subsequently became the 42nd, and in 1758 the Royal Highland Regiment. See also note to 85.34 below.

77.30–35 **My sword, my spear . . . have is mine** see 'The Cretan Warrior', lines 7–12, trans. John Leyden from Hybrias the Cretan: *The Poetical Remains of the late Dr. John Leyden*, ed. James Morton (London, 1819) 205. For the Greek original see *Greek Lyric*, ed. David A. Campbell, 5 vols (Cambridge, Mass., 1993), 5.294.

77.37–38 **the expedition of Prince Charles Edward** see Historical Note, 319–20, and note to 68.21. The Jacobite rising of 1745 was finally defeated at Culloden in 1746.

77.39 **outlawed** put outside the law and deprived of its benefit and protection, i.e. made subject to summary justice. After the '45 all Jacobites who had participated in the rising were required to surrender themselves and their weapons; those who failed to do so were outlawed. MacTavish Mhor has also been outlawed because of his failure to surrender himself to a sheriff on account of his activities as cattle thief.

77.40–41 **Garrisons . . . never before been seen** see Historical Note, 319–20.

77.41 **red coat** i.e. a British soldier, from the scarlet uniform worn by British soldiers up to the end of the 19th century.

78.1 **evil days** days of misfortune or misery. Ecclesiastes 12.1: 'Remember now thy Creator in the days of thy youth, while the evil days come not'.

78.6 **the Sidier Roy** *Gaelic* red soldiers, alluding to the scarlet uniform of the Hanoverian army.

78.10–11 **the silver buttons from his waistcoat** David Stewart of Garth, in his account of Highlanders' dress, records that 'silver buttons were frequently found among the better and more provident of the lower ranks,—an inheritance often of long descent' (Stewart, 1.75). They would defray the funeral expenses should the wearer die far from home.

78.31 **great change which had taken place** after the '45 the government took steps to prevent a recurrence by measures to disarm the Highlands (1746), and to break the spirit of clanship by removing the heritable jurisdictions of the chiefs (1748); see Historical Note, 319–20.

78.34 **the stormy sons of the sword** see 'sons of the sword', and 'stormy son of war', in *Fingal* (1762), one of the works which James Macpherson (1736–96) claimed to have translated from Ossian, a legendary Gaelic poet of the 3rd century (James Macpherson, *The Poems of Ossian*, ed. Howard Gaskill (Edinburgh, 1996), 82, 83).

79.3 **had been burned** that is, as a witch. The first capital punishment for witchcraft in Scotland was in 1479, the last was in Dornoch in 1727. The crime of witchcraft was removed in Scotland in 1736, although it remained a crime to pretend to be a witch.

79.39 **the long-skirted Lowland coat** after the '45 the wearing of Highland dress, tartan and the plaid, was forbidden and remained proscribed until 1782.

79.42   the belted-plaid and short hose   the 'belted plaid', the ancestor of the kilt, was the characteristic dress of the Highland man. 'This was a piece of tartan two yards in breadth, and four in length, which surrounded the waist in large plaits, or folds, adjusted with great nicety, and confined by a belt, buckled tight round the body. While the lower part came down to the knees, the other was drawn up and adjusted to the left shoulder, leaving the right arm uncovered, and at full liberty' (Stewart, 1.74). 'Short hose' were made from tartan cloth with a seam up the back of the leg, and held in place with a garter. Burt records that the stocking 'rises no higher than the Thick of the Calf' (Burt, 2.186).

80.43   distaff and spindle   the *distaff* was a cleft stick about 3 ft long on which the flax was wound. It was held under the left arm and the fibres of the flax were drawn from it through the fingers of the left hand, and twisted by the right, with the aid of the spindle round which the thread was wound. The *spindle* was a hooked rod which was made to revolve and to draw the fibres into thread. For a description and illustration see Robert Chambers, *The Book of Days*, 2 vols (Edinburgh and London, 1883), 1.68–69.

81.6–7   wrapped up in my plaid   Highland women wore the plaid as a cloak which could be brought up over the head.

81.22   the calf of her heart   *Gaelic laogh mo chridhe*; *laogh*, calf, is a common term of endearment for a child.

81.27   Taymouth Castle   belonging to the Marquis of Breadalbane at Balloch where Loch Tay flows into the River Tay in Perthshire; it was extensively rebuilt in the early 19th century.

81.28   Two days passed   the manuscript reads 'Days after days passed' (f. 47r). It seems that when he first wrote this paragraph Scott envisaged a longer interval before anyone again visited Elspat. The opening phrase was later changed to accord with the opening phrase of the next paragraph.

82.18   MacPhadraick   *Gaelic* son of Patrick.

82.20–21   tacksman   superior tenant of a clan chief, often one of his close kin, who acted as a kind of agent for the chief in dealings with clansmen (see *Prose Works*, 20.20–21, 24–25).

82.33–35   the Bard hath spoken ... the thrush's song   Scott gives Elspat an elevated language drawing on the wisdom of Gaelic bards and making frequent use of references to the natural world which are charged with metaphorical meaning. Few of her observations derive directly from James Macpherson's translations of Ossian, but they reflect 18th-century ideas of primitive language as expressed by Hugh Blair in *A Critical Dissertation on the Poems of Ossian* (1763): see for instance *The Poems of Ossian*, ed. Howard Gaskill (Edinburgh, 1996), 345–46, 384.

83.18   book sealed   Revelation 5.1.

83.18   fountain closed   see Song of Solomon 4:12: 'a spring shut up, a fountain sealed'.

83.19   those whom they called Saxons   that is Lowland Scots, as well as English.

83.26–27   barbarous conduct ... after the battle of Culloden   after the defeat of the Jacobites at Culloden in 1746, the victorious Hanoverian forces massacred prisoners and the wounded, and laid waste areas of the Highlands sympathetic to the Jacobites.

83.31   a combined government   that is, the government of both Scotland and England. Scott refers to 'the complicated and combined constitution of Great Britain' in *Prose Works*, 20.10.

84.14–15   on a bed of rotten straw, like an over-worn hound   Burt records a Highland woman talking about her three husbands: 'the two first were honest Men, and very careful of their Family, for they both *died for the Law*: That is, were hang'd for Theft. Well, but as to the last? *Hout!* says she, *a fulthy Peast! He dy'd at Hame, lik an auld Dug, on a Puckle o' Strae'* (Burt, 2.232–33).

84.24–25 she arose . . . and was refreshed the actions of David, after hearing that his sick child had died and anxiety was therefore over: see 2 Samuel 12.20.

85.5–6 the Feast of the Tabernacles see Leviticus 23.33–44; 'boughs of goodly trees' are mentioned in verse 40.

85.10 the cloud-berry *Rubus Chamaemorus*, an orange-red fruit of the bramble family found on high moorland in Scotland.

85.10 the emblem of his family the cloudberry is claimed as the emblem of the clan Macfarlane.

85.34 in their native tartan Stewart, referring to the 42nd Highland Regiment, the Black Watch, comments on the Highlanders' dress: 'This, as it consisted so much of the black, green, and blue tartan, gave them a dark and sombre appearance in comparison with the bright uniform of the regulars who at that time had coats, waistcoats, and breeches, of scarlet cloth. Hence the term Dhu, or Black, as applied to this corps' (1.223–24).

86 motto last stanza of 'Jemmy Dawson', a ballad about a young man executed for joining the 'rebel clans' in 1745, by William Shenstone (1714–63).

86.23 the red light of the harvest-moon Professor Donald Meek has pointed out that the Gaelic phrase *gealach an ruadhain*, 'the moon of red hue', was used in Tiree of one of the moons around harvest time.

86.28 Hope deferred . . . the heart sick Proverbs 13.12; the 'royal sage' is Solomon (see 1 Kings 4.29–34) to whom the Proverbs are attributed (1.1).

86.35–36 the plume . . . gentle birth Samuel Johnson observes of the young Laird of Coll that he 'did not endeavour to dazzle them [his clansmen] by any magnificence of dress: his only distinction was a feather in his bonnet' (*A Journey to the Western Islands of Scotland*, ed. J. D. Fleeman (Oxford, 1985), 106). The bonnet, the characteristic Scottish male headdress, was a flat woollen cap, usually dark blue.

86.38 sporran mollach *Gaelic, literally* hairy purse; 'A large purse of goat's or badger's skin, answering the purpose of a pocket, and ornamented with a silver or brass mouth-piece, and many tassels, hung before' (Stewart, 1.74–75).

87.19 the gate of Fort-Augustus military barracks at Kilcumein at the head of Loch Ness founded by General Wade in 1727. As it was named after the second son of George I, William Augustus, Duke of Cumberland (1721–65), the victor at Culloden in 1746, and as it acted as his headquarters after the battle, there is no better symbol of Hanoverian power in Scotland.

87.23 take odds of take advantage of.

87.27 Breadalbane, and broad Lorn Breadalbane ('broad Albyn') is an area of NW Perthshire, surrounding Loch Tay; Lorn is the part of Argyll between Loch Awe and Loch Etive. Both districts belonged to Campbell families.

87.31 Silver he left me i.e. the bounty paid to Hamish on enlisting, which Highlanders often gave to the families they left behind.

87.41..without value i.e. without expecting something in return.

88.16 the impenetrable deserts of Y Mac Y Mhor title of Lord Reay, chief of the Mackays, who come from Sutherland in NW Scotland; it means 'Iye, son of Iye the Great'. The name Mackay is the usual English rendering of Gaelic *MacAoidh*; Scott here alludes to another spelling of it, MacIye: see Margaret O. Macdougall, *The Clan Mackay* (Edinburgh, 1953) 29.

88.22–23 the Sound of Mull . . . rocks of Harris respectively, the passage between the island of Mull and the Scottish mainland; small islands to the west of Mull; and the S half of the main island in the Outer Hebrides.

88.24–25   one of the new regiments ... the French in America   probably the 2nd battalion, the Black Watch: see Historical Note, 320. Montgomerie's Highlanders (77th Regiment of Foot), and Fraser's Highlanders (78th) were raised in 1757; the second battalion of the Black Watch in 1758. All three were sent to North America during the Seven Years' War (1756–63) where they fought against the French. Four other Highland regiments, three of which fought in Germany and one in India, were raised in 1759 and 1760, and four more in 1761.

89.10   from MacAllan Mhor   chief of the Macdonalds of Clanranald, whose family descended from Allan Macdonald or Macranald, who distinguished himself at the battle of Harlaw in 1411 and died in 1419. The heir of Macdonald of Clanranald had been a staunch Jacobite during the '45. See Alexander Mackenzie, *History of the Macdonalds and Lords of the Isles* (Inverness, 1881), 368, 430–34.

89.11   from Caberfae   chief of the clan Mackenzie, the Earl of Seaforth, whose crest is the stag's head, in Gaelic *cabar feidh*.

89.14–15   Glengary, Lochiel, Perth, Lord Lewis   Jacobite leaders. Aeneas, son of Macdonald of Glengarry, led his father's clan in the '45 and was accidentally shot after the battle of Falkirk in 1746. Donald Cameron, younger of Lochiel (*c.* 1695–1748), was one of the most staunch supporters of Prince Charles and after Culloden escaped to France with him. James Drummond, Duke of Perth (1713–47), one of the commanders of the Jacobite army, was rescued by a French ship in 1746. Lord Lewis Gordon who raised a Jacobite regiment in Aberdeenshire died in France in 1754.

89.18   Drummossie-muir   the Jacobite's name for the battle of Culloden, from the moor near Inverness on which it took place.

89.31   Barcaldine's son   Alexander Campbell of Barcaldine, in Benderloch 10 km N of Loch Etive, descended from Colin Campbell (1644–1726). He was an officer in the first battalion, the Black Watch (see Historical Note, 320). In 'The Highland Widow' Elspat's enemies are not only the 'Saxon', but also the Campbells, the most powerful clan in Argyll. The Campbells were a Whig clan and had fought on the Hanoverian side in the '45. Scott, in giving his fictional 'MacTavish Mhor' features of the MacGregors, alludes to the fact that the MacGregors had been dispossessed of their lands in Glenorchy by the Campbells.

89.37   Letter-findreight   probably imaginary. Dobie suggests the name may be composed of *leitir*, 'a hillside' (generally running down to water), and *fionn traigh*, 'white strand'.

90.17   Him of Hanover   King George II (reigned 1727–60), who was also Elector of Hanover. The use of George II's lesser title implies that for Elspat the true king of Britain is the Jacobite claimant.

90.18   the royal Stuart   the Jacobite heir, James Edward Francis (1688–1766), son of James VII and II. 'Stuart' is the French spelling of Stewart and both forms are used.

90.21   the race of Dermid   Clan Campbell, so called from their reputed ancestor, Diarmid O'Duibhne.

90.22–26   murdered ... at Glencoe ... friendship   Elspat's paternal ancestry was from the Macdonalds who were massacred in Glencoe in 1692. One aspect of the outrage was that the Campbells who perpetrated the massacre were entertained by the Macdonalds on the evening preceding it.

90.30–31   the unhappy house of Glenlyon   the leader of the Campbells at the Massacre of Glencoe was Robert Campbell of Glenlyon (1632–96). He and his descendants suffered various misfortunes which they came to attribute to a curse on them for their actions in 1692: see Duncan Campbell, *The Lairds of Glenlyon*, (1886), 274, 276, 284–85. Stewart gives an example of a tragedy befalling a Campbell of Glenlyon in 1771 which the protagonist attributes to the 'curse of God and Glenco' (Stewart, 1.100n–01n).

91.3   shoulder to shoulder   Donald Macintosh describes the 'Clans of the Gael, shoulder to shoulder!' as 'a favourite health among the Gael, when called on for a toast': *Mackintosh's Collection of Gaelic Proverbs, and Familiar Phrases*, ed. Alexander Campbell (Edinburgh, 1819), 79.

91.25   Dunbarton   Dumbarton, on the N side of the Firth of Clyde, where the river Leven joins the Clyde. Dumbarton rock had been an important fortress since the Roman occupation and was repaired and garrisoned in the 18th century against the Jacobite threat. In recent years the name of the town and the castle has been spelled Dumbarton, and the name of the former county Dunbarton. That distinction is modern (see I. M. M. MacPhail, *Dumbarton Castle*, (Edinburgh, 1979), 202–03), and the first edition of *Chronicles of the Canongate* spells the name of the town and castle Dunbarton throughout.

91.29   where goest thou   see John 3.8.

92.9   to punish their vassals   exercised by virtue of the heritable jurisdictions abolished in 1748.

93.29–30   the blooming heath for his bed   'In their houses also they lye upon the ground, laying betwixt them and it, brakens, or hadder, the rootes thereof downe, and the tops up, so prettily layed together, that they are as soft as feather-beds, and much more wholsome': 'A true Description and Division of the whole Countrey of Scotland', from 'Monipenny's Chronicle' (1597), in *A Collection of Scarce and Valuable Tracts (The Somers Tracts)*, ed. Walter Scott, 13 vols (1809–15), 8.388.

93.36   Green Colin   a name of a Campbell of Dunstaffnage who attacked the ancestor of Scott's friend Alexander Stewart of Invernahyle. The story is contained in 'The History of Donald the Hammerer' which Scott contributed to Robert Jamieson's edition of Edmund Burt's *Letters from a Gentleman in the North of Scotland*, 5th edn, 2 vols (London, 1818), 1.lxiv–lxxvi. Scott used the episode again in *Tales of a Grandfather*, second series, in *Prose Works*, 23.312, where he refers to 'Cailen Uaine, or Green Colin, from the green colour which predominated in his tartan'.

95   motto   *Coriolanus*, 5.3.187–89.

95.24   white cockade   knot of ribbon worn on a military hat. White was the colour of the Jacobites, and black that of the Hanoverians, during the '45.

98.27   the great and wise Earl of Chatham   William Pitt (1708–78), created Earl of Chatham in 1766. As secretary of state 1756–61 in charge of the conduct of the Seven Years' War with France he raised regiments of Highlanders to fight in the British army; their first task was to serve in the American colonies (see Historical Note, 320). In a famous speech of 1766 he claimed, 'I sought for merit wherever it was to be found; it is my boast that I was the first minister who looked for it and found it in the mountains of the north' (Stewart, 2.63).

99.6–7   desertions were . . . numerous   this was a marked feature after the formation of the first battalion of the Black Watch. It served in the Highlands until 1743, but on being moved to London a number of soldiers absconded. The three ring-leaders were executed by firing squad at the Tower of London on 18 July 1743: see note to 116.13.

99.11–12   the punishment . . . horror and disgust   Stewart more than once comments on the horror with which Highlanders regarded corporal punishment. 'To the young Highlanders the dread of corporal punishment not only checks their military propensity, and prevents their entering the army, but it conveys to their minds a greater degree of horror and shame than even death itself. When a Highlander is brought to the halberts, he considers himself as having lost his caste. He becomes, in his own estimation, a disgraced man, and is no longer fit for the society of his friends' (Stewart, 2. 213–14). Liberal opinion against military flogging spread during the Napoleonic wars: for instance an article entitled 'One Thousand Lashes' was published in the *Examiner* (2 September 1810), 557–58. The publishers, Leigh and John Hunt, were put on trial for seditious libel but were acquitted. The *Examiner* article puts most stress on the physical cruelty of the punishment, but it adds: 'Besides, what is a man good for after he has had the cat-o'nine-tails across his back? Can he ever hold up his head among his fellows?' (558). Military flogging was not abolished until 1906.

99.14   regularly bred in the German wars   the War of the Austrian Succession (1740–48). Stewart, talking about a severe commanding officer, remarks: 'In the system of the officer in question, which was formed on the old Prussian model, fear was the great principle of action' (Stewart, 2.214).

100.10   the double summit of the ancient Dun   the twin volcanic rock at Dumbarton; see note to 91.25. *Dun* is Gaelic for 'hill', hence a fort on a hill.

101.5–6   Monday, the second day of the week, and twenty-first of the month   probably Monday 21 August 1758: see Historical Note, 320.

101.22–23   seed fell among the brambles and thorns   the Parable of the Sower: see Matthew 13.7; Mark 4.7; and Luke 8.7.

102.33   Corrie Dhu   'the mountains exhibit vast yawning chasms, like the sides of a volcano suddenly torn asunder. This appearance is expressed by the name Corry, which is given to one of the great rents in the north-eastern extremity of Cruachan' (John Stoddart, *Remarks on Local Scenery & Manners in Scotland during the Years 1799 and 1800*, 2 vols (London, 1801), 1.269, on the scenery of Loch Awe).

102.39   the salt lakes of Kintail   the sea lochs, Loch Alsh, Loch Long and Loch Duich, in Kintail, an area in the south of Wester Ross.

102.41   the dark lake   Dobie suggests Loch Duich, 'confused in popular etymology with loch dubhach, which means "dark lake"; or perhaps a phrase for the sea'.

102.41–42   was not my mother of the children of Kenneth   was not my mother a Mackenzie. The Mackenzies, who had lands in Kintail, got their name 'the children of Kenneth' from an ancestor said to have died in 1304.

103.11   Skooroora   Sgurr Fhuaran (sometimes written Scour Ouran), the highest of the Five Sisters, which run east from the head of Loch Duich. It is 1068m, however, as against Ben Cruachan's 1126.

103.13   animal which gives oil to the lamp   Burt records that 'every grown Seal is worth to them about forty Shillings Sterling, which arises from the Skin and the Oil' (Burt, 1.50).

103.14   the white-tusked boar   the wild boar was hunted in Scotland in the Middle Ages but 'in spite of the fact that its chase was strictly preserved to the royal court and the great landed nobles, it was exterminated in Scotland probably in the early years of the seventeenth century' (James Ritchie, *The Influence of Man on Animal Life in Scotland* (Cambridge, 1920), [184]). Elspat may be recalling the boar-hunting in Ossian, for instance in 'Sul-Malla of Lumon: A Poem' (James Macpherson, *The Poems of Ossian*, ed. Howard Gaskill (Edinburgh, 1996), 301–02).

103.17–18   beautiful, with blue eyes and fair hair   Dobie comments that their 'fairness may have been due to Norse descent. There are early Norse settlements on parts of the western mainland about the sea-lochs.'

103.18   and bosoms of snow   compare 'Her breast was like the snow of one night', in James Macpherson's *Fragments of Ancient Poetry* (1760): James Macpherson, *The Poems of Ossian*, ed. Howard Gaskill (Edinburgh, 1996),

14.

103.22   needful fire   perhaps echoing 'needfire' (Gaelic *teine éiginn*), fire produced by the friction of dry wood, having reputed magical or prophylactic properties (*CSD*).

103   foot-note   for the Highland belief in the royal ancestry of seals see A. M. Macfarlane, 'Sea Myths and Lore of the Hebrides', in *Transactions of the Inverness Scientific Society and Field Club*, 9 (1918–25), 384–85. 'A certain King of Norway had a family of sons and daughters, all of whom were of incomparable beauty; so greatly so, indeed, as to excite the jealousy of their stepmother, who, learning magic for the purpose, put them under a spell that they would be neither fish nor animal for ever; when on land their desire would be to the sea, and vice-versa when on the sea' (384).

103.41–42   spoke for hours, but she spoke in vain   see George Crabbe, *The Parish Register* (1807), Part 2, line 130: 'I preach for ever; but I preach in vain!', repeated, slightly varied, at line 246.

104.11   like a lapwing   see *Much Ado About Nothing*, 3.1.24–25: 'look where Beatrice, like a lapwing runs/ Close by the ground'.

104.21–22   deliberate suicide   Stewart cites an instance: 'A few years ago, an unfortunate girl in Breadalbane became so bewildered in her imagination by the picture drawn of the punishment of unbelievers, that she destroyed herself in a fit of desperation, a rare, and I may almost say, the only instance of this crime in the Highlands' (Stewart, 1.130).

104.41–42   sleep by which Indians . . . interval of their torments   see William Robertson, *The History of America*, 4th edn, 3 vols (London, 1783), 2.138–42, 145–47 (see *CLA*, 204), which describes the torments inflicted on prisoners and on young warriors among the American Indians. The sleep which occupies the intervals between torments is not explicitly referred to but is perhaps implied by the fact that 'they often prolong this scene of anguish for several days' (2.141).

105.6   splinter of bog pine   'To supply the Want of Candles, when they have Occasion for more Light than is given by the Fire, they provide themselves with a Quantity of Sticks of Fir, the most resinous that can be procured' (Burt, 2.127–28).

105.8   Elspat MacIan Macdonell   it has already been established that Elspat's father was a Macdonald of Glencoe, sometimes spelled Macdonell (see note to 90.22–26). The Macdonalds of Glencoe were known as 'Clann Ian Abraich', after their progenitor, John Og, a natural son of Angus Og of the Isles (d. 1329). See Alexander Mackenzie, *History of the Macdonalds and Lords of the Isles* (Inverness, 1881), 524.

105.33   the cat of the mountain   the wild cat.

107.2–6 the words of a Gaelic poet, . . . to the warriors of Fion   Fion is the warrior hero of ancient Irish and Scottish poetry, whom Macpherson (see note to 78.34) usually calls Fingal; he was father of the blind bard Ossian. It is traditional for bards, from Homer onwards, to be blind, indicating a mind receptive to inspiration.

107.15–16   leprous toad   the toad is a traditional emblem of something loathsome.

107.39   Allan Breack Cameron   *Gaelic breac* freckled. Stewart mentions a 'freebooter, Alexander Stewart, (commonly called Alister Breac from his being marked with the small-pox)' (Stewart, 1.42).

111.2   MacDhonuil Dhu   the chief of the Clan Cameron is called Mac-Dhomhnuill duibh, son of Donald the dark-haired, after the first chief of the clan who fought at Harlaw in 1411.

111.9–10   add a stone to your cairn   'A heap of stones was thrown over the spot where a person happened to be killed or buried. Every passenger added a stone to this heap, which was called a *Cairn*. Hence the Highlanders have a saying, when one person serves another, or shows any civility, "I will add a stone to your cairn;" in other words, I will adorn your grave, or respect your memory' (Stewart, 1.93n.).

111.13   the Black Tree of the Law   the gallows. A similar conceit describing a tree in which a body was hanging is found in *Quentin Durward*, 3 vols (Edinburgh, 1823), 1.54–55: 'I love not the Castle when the covin-tree bears such acorns as I see yonder'.

111.19   ravens...hair to line their nests   compare 'The Two Corbies', lines 15–16: *Minstrelsy*, 2.417.

113.33   this strayed sheep within the great fold   see Matthew 18.12–13; Luke 15.4, and 6.

114.16   gross desertion may, in any case, be palliated   the General speaks sceptically: in any legal case the accused could plead intoxication or temporary insanity. I am grateful to Professor John Cairns for pointing out that intoxication is unlikely to have provided a defence in Scots law of the time for an act of gross desertion; 'temporary insanity' might have provided a defence to a charge of murder, but the claim would have had to be proved. Scott had had occasion to consider the question of drunkenness as a defence in cases of bad behaviour among soldiers in a letter of paternal remonstrance, written on 18 May 1821, addressed to his son, Walter, who was a cornet in the 18th Hussars (*Letters*, 6.437–40).

114.27   grey towers   the buildings on the rock are visible in Paul Sandby's view of Dumbarton Castle from the west (*c.* 1745), reproduced in I. M. M. MacPhail, *Dumbarton Castle* (Edinburgh, 1979), plate 12.

114.30–31   steep staircases...external barrier-gate   steep stairs descend from the place where the rock divides; the gate is in King George's Battery on the south side of the castle.

114.33–34   the Dead March   solemn music played at a funeral procession, especially at a military funeral.

115.40   the civil war   the Jacobite rising of 1745.

116.13   the awful spectacle   Stewart describes the execution of three deserters from the Black Watch in London in 1743 and quotes from the *St James's Chronicle* of 20 July 1743: 'three of the Highland deserters, were shot upon the parade within the Tower, pursuant to the sentence of the court-martial. The rest of the Highland prisoners were drawn out to see the execution, and joined in their prayers with great earnestness. They behaved with perfect resolution and propriety. Their bodies were put into three coffins by three of the prisoners, their clansmen and namesakes, and buried in one grave, near the place of execution' (Stewart, 1.243).

116.26–27   blood for blood   compare Genesis 9.6.

116.42   Cloght-dearg, that is Redmantle   the name of the evil spirit derives from a supernatural tale told to Scott by Mrs Hepburne and repeated in a letter of 20 July 1825 from her husband (MS 874, ff. 317r–18r). See Historical Note, 323.

117.17   by the Christians of an enlightened age   many clergy in the Highlands in the 18th century tried to combat superstition among their parishioners. In his letter to Scott about 'the Man in the Red Cloak' (see note above) J. Stewart Hepburn adds that the machinations of evil spirits 'are now under due restraint in consequence, (as the people say) "of the Gospel having grown sae rife" ' (f. 317r).

117.12   be torn to pieces   in the Hepburnes' tale 'The poor victims of delusion returned no more:—but thereafter some mangled fragments of their bodies (their lungs) were seen floating on the dark water of Loch Glassy' (f. 317v).

117.27   glen was so steep and narrow   this appears to be a description of

Glen Croe, which runs north from Loch Long and is a shorter path (116.37) on the route between Dunbarton and Dalmally. Travel writers frequently mentioned its rocky desolation: e.g. Henry Skrine, *Three Successive Tours in the North of England, and great part of Scotland* (London, 1795), 45, and John Stoddart, *Remarks on Local Scenery & Manners in Scotland during the Years 1799 and 1800*, 2 vols (London, 1801), 1.245–51.

118.22–23   the seventh day the Jewish Sabbath.

118.23   and thy God shall be my God echoing Ruth's words to Naomi, 'thy people shall be my people, and thy God my God' (Ruth 1.16).

118.25   creature of clay compare Job 10.9, 13.12, and 33.6.

118.28   worth acceptance in his eyes compare 1 Timothy 2.3: 'For this is good and acceptable in the sight of God our Saviour'.

118.28–29   He has asked obedience, not sacrifice see 1 Samuel 15.22: 'Behold, to obey is better than sacrifice, and to hearken than the fat of rams'.

118.29   patience under the trials compare James 1.3: 'the trying of your faith worketh patience'.

118.33   thy white book *Gaelic an Leabhar Bàn*, the white book, a name for the Bible.

118.34   the sacring bell a small bell rung at the elevation of the host in the Roman Catholic Mass.

118.37–38   gold... thick twists as those worn by the heroes of old Scott describes 'the *Torques*, or chain, formed of twisted gold, worn by the Celtic chiefs of rank' in his 'Essay on Border Antiquities' (1814), in *Prose Works*, 7.16.

119.1   the Black Abbot of Inchaffray head of the abbey of Augustinian canons ('Black Canons') founded at Inchaffray in Perthshire by Gilbert, Earl of Strathearn, in 1200. Its Abbot celebrated Mass in sight of the Scottish army at Bannockburn (1314), as Scott records in a note to *The Lord of the Isles* (1815), Canto 6, stanza 21 (*Poetical Works*, 10.249). An abbot with something like Elspat's view of his calling occurs in *The Lord of the Isles*, Canto 2, stanza 28 (*Poetical Works*, 10.87–88).

119.13–14   against women who have been guilty of folly an indictment of the presbyterian clergy for their concern with sexual transgression.

119.19   Woe worth you *Scots* may ill betide you (*CSD, worth*).

119.19–20   no help in you see Psalm 146.3: 'Put not your trust in ... man, in whom there is no help'.

119.42–43   Men do not condemn and kill on the same day the sentiment is not of legal origin. The most famous protest in literature at too quick an application of capital punishment after conviction is Isabella's in *Measure for Measure*: 'To-morrow! O, that's sudden!' (2.2.83).

120.40   pitched upon fixed upon, appointed.

122.13   places of sure destruction a death which echoes that of Lady Randolph in John Home's *Douglas*, 5.327–42; see note to 76.23.

HISTORICAL NOTE TO 'THE TWO DROVERS'

Cattle-droving. Cattle-droving over long distances in Britain was at its peak in the eighteenth and nineteenth centuries, after the growth of urban populations beyond the number that could be fed from the surrounding countryside, and before the coming of mechanised transport. In particular cattle were driven from the north and west of Scotland and Wales into England where they were fattened for the London market. The Highlands of Scotland bred cattle, but lacked the rich pastures required to fatten them. Cattle were therefore driven from Scotland to England, especially to Lincolnshire and East Anglia, where they were fattened before being taken to the London market at Smithfield.[1]

The export of Scottish cattle into England was taking place as early as the fourteenth century.² The trade came into importance after the Union of the Parliaments of Scotland and England in 1707, and increased throughout the eighteenth century. It has been estimated that by the end of the century 100,000 cattle left Scotland annually.³ Herds of cattle were brought south on foot, tended by drovers, and using routes that have come to be known as drove roads. Traces of the old drove roads can still be found in the countryside and on maps.

Large-scale cattle-droving started to decline in the nineteenth century with the coming of railways and the cattle-truck, and had largely died out by the early twentieth century. At the peak of the trade there were well-known markets, known as trysts or fairs, at which cattle were bought and sold and prepared for their further journey. Important trysts took place on the border between the Highlands and Lowlands of Scotland, during the summer and autumn which were the favoured seasons for droving. Scott's tale of 'The Two Drovers' starts at the tryst at Doune in Perthshire. Drovers were needed both to bring cattle from the north and west to these trysts, and to take the herds south into England. The Scots drover, often a Highlander, became a recognised figure in the English countryside through which he travelled, as is clear from John Clare's description of Scottish drovers in Northamptonshire in *The Shepherd's Calendar*.⁴ 'The Two Drovers' tells of an incident which took place in the eighteenth century on a cross-border cattle drove that had entered England in the west of the country. The incident takes place in the county of Cumberland; Cumberland was united with Westmorland in 1974 to form the modern English county of Cumbria.

The route of the drovers in 'The Two Drovers'. The route south followed by the two drovers with their cattle is as follows: Doune Fair, Stirling Bridge, Falkirk, Traquair, Minch Moor, Murder Cairn, Liddesdale, 'The Waste' of Cumberland, Christianbury Crag, ending in 'fertile and enclosed country' in which is the Hollan Bush, Squire Ireby's Hall and Ralph Heskett's inn.⁵ Of these places Squire Ireby's Hall and Ralph Heskett's inn are fictitious, and Murder Cairn and the Hollan Bush, although typical names, are probably fictitiously sited.

The incidents of the tale take place on Squire Ireby's land and in the neighbouring inn, which are in enclosed country. There are some other indications of location: Squire Ireby had just returned from the north and had passed Hugh Morrison 'at the Christenbury Cragg' (134.18), which is in the north-east of Cumberland three miles south of the Border. He met Robin Oig six or seven miles further south 'at the Hollan Bush' (134.18–19). Squire Ireby's land and the inn are south of the Hollan Bush, and when Robin Oig left the inn 'seven or eight English miles at least lay betwixt Morrison and him' (139.18–19). The inn should, therefore, be about ten miles south of Christianbury Crag. There are some other indications of the locality of the inn: when the people are teasing Robin they ask if he would like a sword brought from the armoury at Carlisle (136.40), or whether a second might be sought at Corby Castle (137.1–2), which is near Wetheral. Allowing for the exaggeration of mockery those two references seem to indicate that the inn is within range of Carlisle. This view is strengthened by the fact that the squire and the landlord both take their names —Ireby and Heskitt—from places in the orbit of Carlisle.

The source of 'The Two Drovers'. 'The Two Drovers' is based on an account Scott had heard many years earlier of a Highland cattle-drover condemned to death in Carlisle for the murder of an English drover. Scott's source for this tale was George Constable (1719–1803), a friend of his father on whom he had already drawn for the character of Jonathan Oldbuck in *The Antiquary* (1816).⁶ In the passage which he added to the end of the Introduction in the Magnum edition of *Chronicles of the Canongate* Scott acknowledged his debt:

> The next tale, entitled "The Two Drovers," I learned from another old friend, the late George Constable Esq. of Wallace-Craigie, near Dundee, whom I have already introduced to my reader as the original Antiquary of Monkbarns. He had been present, I think, at the trial at Carlisle, and seldom mentioned the venerable judge's charge to the jury, without shedding tears,—which had peculiar pathos, as flowing down features, carrying rather a sarcastic or almost a cynical expression.[7]

George Constable, a native of Dundee, was born in 1719 and practised as a writer (solicitor) in Edinburgh. In 1789 he settled at Wallace-Craigie near Dundee and he died in 1803.[8] Scott met him first in 1777 at Prestonpans and got to know him well in succeeding years:

> He used always to dine at my father's house of a Sunday and was authorized to turn the conversation out of the austere and calvinistic tone which it usually maintained on that day, upon subjects of history or auld lang syne. He remembered the forty-five and told many excellent stories, all with a strong dash of peculiar caustic humour.[9]

Scott had appropriate experience for making use of Constable's tale of the two drovers. His grandfather, Robert Scott, had been 'one of the first who was active in the cattle trade afterwards carried to such extent between the Highlands of Scotland and the feeding counties in England, and by his droving transactions acquired a considerable sum of money.[10] Scott had drawn on that way of life in *Rob Roy* (1817), whose outlaw hero counted cattle-droving as his legitimate trade. 'The Two Drovers' starts in Doune, which Scott visited in 1793,[11] and ends in Carlisle. Scott had already described a Carlisle courtroom in *Waverley* (1814), Volume 3, Chapter 21. As to his knowledge of Cumberland, Scott met his future wife at Gilsland in 1797, and drew on that area in *Guy Mannering* (1815).[12] The route the two drovers take from Liddesdale into Cumberland is probably to the west of that followed by Brown travelling north from Mump's Ha' in *Guy Mannering*, Volume 2, Chapters 1 and 2. The Border was, of course, associated with ballads. Scott's *Minstrelsy of the Scottish Border* (1802–03) contains, besides rieving ballads set in Cumberland like 'Hobbie Noble' (*Minstrelsy*, 2.115–29), a ballad on a fight between two friends, one from each side of the Border, 'Graeme and Bewick' (*Minstrelsy*, 3.75–87).

Date of the action. When Scott uses the incident derived from Constable as the source of 'The Two Drovers' he gives it to his fictitious narrator, Chrystal Croftangry. Croftangry claims to have been present at the trial 'as a young Scottish lawyer' (142.30). Croftangry, who is described as approaching sixty-three in 1826,[13] would have been born in 1763 or 1764 and would have been a young lawyer in the mid to late 1780s.

There are other elements of the tale as Croftangry tells it, besides the narrator's presence at the trial, which make it plausible that the tale should be set in the late 1780s. Croftangry says that his tale 'will not go back to the days of clanship and claymores' (124.16–17), both of which were curtailed by legislation passed after the Jacobite rising of 1745. Robin Oig is described as wearing Highland dress (125.30–40), which was proscribed between 1746 and 1782 following the '45. The Judge's address to the jury at the end of the tale occurs long enough after 1745 for the jury to need to be reminded about the social organisation of the Highlands of Scotland under clanship, and for that way of life to be associated with 'the prisoner's fathers' rather than with Robin himself (144.43–145.40). Robin Oig's grandfather had been a friend of Rob Roy, who died in 1734 (126.17–21). Christopher Johnson has pointed out that boxing, which is an issue in the quarrel between the drovers, was particularly popular in the 1780s.[14]

Is Constable's narrative historically verifiable? Scott's account of the origin of 'The Two Drovers' implies that the incident on which the tale was based was historical, and that George Constable in describing the speech of the judge was doing so from a recollection of being present at the trial. If these two claims are true we have some guide to the date of the incident: as Constable was born in 1719 it is unlikely to have taken place much before 1740, and it must have taken place before 1803, the date of his death, and probably before 1789, the year in which he retired to Wallace-Craigie. That leaves quite a wide spectrum of dates. The fictitious narrator, Croftangry, who takes on Constable's role as the source of the story, attended the trial as a young lawyer (142.30). We are not told Constable's age when he attended the trial; but it is possible that in making Croftangry a young man at the time of the trial Scott carried over a memory of Constable's having been a young man, which would push the date to the early end of the spectrum. On the other hand Scott may have made Croftangry (who was born in 1763 or 64) attend the trial as a young man to make the date of the trial fit with Constable's experience if he had attended it as a mature man, which draws the date of the trial towards the late end of the spectrum.

Attempts to corroborate the story and to fix the date of the incident have proved unsuccessful. The Highland drover was tried at the Carlisle Assizes for a murder committed in the county of Cumberland (142.10). The Assize Records for the English Northern Circuit are in the Public Record Office in London; but they are hard to use if one does not have a date to start from.[15] In an attempt to establish a date a survey was undertaken of the local newspapers as the Assizes were usually reported in them. The earliest newspaper published in Cumberland was *The Cumberland Pacquet; Or, Ware's Whitehaven Advertiser* which started publication on 20 October 1774. The Carlisle Assizes took place in the summer (usually August) each year, and *The Cumberland Pacquet* reported them giving the names of those who were tried, a brief description of the crime, and the verdict, especially in the case of capital charges which were usually few. For the period before 1774 it was necessary to turn to the Newcastle newspapers. The Assize judges on the Northern Circuit were in Newcastle upon Tyne before they proceeded to Carlisle, and in some years *The Newcastle Courant* (founded 1711) and *The Newcastle Journal* (1739) reported the Carlisle Assizes.[16] Unfortunately this search, which was necessarily incomplete, did not supply a date with which to approach the Assize records.

A search in the Public Record Office concentrated on the Crown Minute Books (ASSI 41 and 42), the Gaol Book (ASSI 42), and an attempt to read the Indictments (ASSI 44) for the years for which the newspapers had supplied no information. Dr Sheena Sutherland, who assisted with this search, looked for Scottish names in the index to ASSI 45, Criminal Depositions and Case Papers. It is disappointing to report that no case matching that in 'The Two Drovers' was found.

The fact that the case of the Highland drover has not been corroborated will provoke the suggestion that perhaps the setting of the trial in Carlisle is part of the fiction rather than a constituent part of the source story of 'The Two Drovers'. Scott, having portrayed the trial of Fergus Mac-Ivor and Evan Dhu at Carlisle in *Waverley*, may have chosen Carlisle as the appropriate place for a Highlander to confront an alien judicial system. That leaves the possibility that the case which lies behind 'The Two Drovers', assuming it to have an historical basis, was heard somewhere other than Carlisle.

There is one more tantalising reference. In his review of *Chronicles of the Canongate* in *Blackwood's* John Wilson wrote:

"The Two Drovers" is a mere evolvement or developement of what may be supposed to have been the real circumstances of a melancholy case of murder, which many years ago was tried at Carlisle; and the very charge of the judge to the jury, almost "*in totidem verbis*," is given, with some few touches of more solemn and pathetic eloquence than are to be found in the real and original charge, fine as it was, and coming as it did from the lips of a most eminent and remarkable man.[17]

The striking thing about this passage is that Wilson seems to know who the judge was, and even suggests that he knew the 'real and original charge' and recognised the extra touches of eloquence which Scott had added to it. Wilson (1785–1854) was rather young to have heard the story from Constable. He did, however, settle in Westmorland, at Elleray on Windermere, in 1807 and retained his house there when he moved to Edinburgh in 1815.[18] Was the story of the remarkable judge current in the Lake District? If Wilson had heard it there his testimony would confirm that the original trial took place in Carlisle. It cannot be discounted, however, that Wilson may have heard the story from Scott, perhaps on his visit to Elleray in 1825.[19] The historical source of the tale of 'The Two Drovers' remains a mystery.

NOTES

For shortened forms of reference see 289–90.

1   This trade is described in A. R. B. Haldane, *The Drove Roads of Scotland* (Edinburgh, 1952), and K. J. Bonser, *The Drovers* (London, 1970).

2   Haldane, 11.

3   Bonser, 75, 81.

4   John Clare, *The Shepherd's Calendar* (1827), 'July', lines 187–218 (*John Clare: Poems of the Middle Period 1822–1837*, ed. Eric Robinson, David Powell and P. M. S. Dawson, 2 vols (Oxford, 1996), 1.91–92).

5   The route of the drovers in southern Scotland may be followed in Haldane, 151–58 and map.

6   See *The Antiquary*, ed. David Hewitt, EEWN 3, 448.

7   Magnum, 41.xxxiv.

8   W. S. Crockett, *The Scott Originals* (London and Edinburgh, 1912), 123–27.

9   From Scott's 'Memoirs', in *Scott on Himself*, ed. David Hewitt (Edinburgh, 1981), 17. The passage was written in 1826.

10   *Scott on Himself*, ed. David Hewitt (Edinburgh, 1981), 4.

11   *Life*, 1.207.

12   See Walter Scott, *Guy Mannering*, ed. P. D. Garside, EEWN 2, 502–03.

13   13.23–14.4, 53.42–43.

14   Christopher Johnson, 'Anti-pugilism: Violence and Justice in Scott's "The Two Drovers"', *Scottish Literary Journal*, 22 (1995), 47.

15   For a brief history of the English Northern Circuit see J. S. Cockburn, 'The Northern Assize Circuit', *Northern History*, 3 (1968), 118–30; a more popular history is Dick Hamilton, *Foul Bills and Dagger Money* (London, 1979).

16   In a search covering the years 1739–1800 the names and brief details of those tried at the Carlisle Assizes were found in either the Newcastle or the Carlisle newspapers for all the years except 1741, 1743–44, 1747, 1749, 1756–57, 1761–65, 1768–69, 1774, 1776, 1796. In some of these years the details of those tried at the Carlisle Assizes were not printed; in others the August issues of the newspapers have not survived. It will be noted that there are significant omissions in the middle of the period covered, which might be regarded as the most likely for the trial which Constable attended.

17   *Blackwood's Edinburgh Magazine*, 22 (November 1827), 570.

18 Mary Wilson Gordon, 'Christopher North': A Memoir of John Wilson, 2 vols (Edinburgh, 1862), 1.119–83.
19 Life, 6.78. Mary Wilson Gordon describes Scott's visit to Elleray, which lasted three days, in her biography of her father (2.91–93).

EXPLANATORY NOTES TO 'THE TWO DROVERS'

For shortened forms of reference see 289–90.

122 motto John Milton, 'Lycidas' (1637), lines 25–27, a pastoral elegy in which a shepherd laments the death of a friend.

122.29 that Otium, as Horace terms it ease, tranquillity; see *Odes* (23 BC), 2.16.1–8 by the Roman poet Quintus Horatius Flaccus (Horace: 65–8 BC).

123.2 Gillie-whitefoot from Gaelic *gillecasfliuch*, 'gillie-wetfoot', a boy with wet feet, the servant of a Highland chief who 'Carries him, when on Foot, over the Fords' (Burt, 2.158). Tulloch points out that the word 'sometimes appeared in Scots in forms such as *gilliewitfitt*, and the middle element was mistaken for *whit* "white" as Scott does here' (395).

123.5 imp of the devil child of the devil (*OED*, *imp*, substantive 4c). A 'devil' is the name for a printer's errand-boy: see note to 52.21.

123.8 Cot God. The pronunciation indicates that the speaker is a Highlander: see note to 47.1.

123.8–9 your ainsell your own self, translating the Gaelic emphatic pronoun adjuncts; another indication that the speaker is a Highlander (*Language of Walter Scott*, 255).

123.20–21 fast and fast enough quickly and with facility.

123.23 Hamish MacTavish hero of the previous tale, 'The Highland Widow'.

123.24–25 burned...for a witch see note to 79.3.

123.27 third cousin to the Camerons Burt remarks about Highlanders, 'They have a Pride in their Family, as almost every one is a Genealogist' (Burt, 2.115).

123.29–30 Arthur's Seat, when the MacRaas broke out in 1778 the 78th Highland regiment, raised by Kenneth Mackenzie, Earl of Seaforth, which included Macraes who were traditional followers of the Mackenzies, mutinied over conditions and occupied the hill in Edinburgh called Arthur's Seat for several days. After negotiation they returned to duty (Stewart, 2.lxxxiv; John Prebble, *Mutiny: Highland Regiments in Revolt 1743–1804* (London, 1975), 109–36).

123.30 woeful day beside Leith pier in 1779 when Highlanders belonging to the 42nd and 71st regiments, about to embark for America, were told they were to be transferred to Lowland regiments. The Highlanders refused and a fight broke out between them and the soldiers sent to apprehend them (Stewart, 2.lxxxiv). Scott recounted seeing as a boy the dead bodies of the Highlanders 'laid there wrapt in their plaids' in a letter to Maria Edgeworth, 23 July 1839 (*Letters*, 11.378).

123.30 Ohonari! *Gaelic* a lamentation; see note to 49.16.

123.34–35 Justice Shallow...overscutched tunes Falstaff, resigning Shallow to 'the rearward of the fashion', says that he 'sung those tunes to the overscutch'd huswifes that he heard the carmen whistle, and sware they were his fancies or his good-nights' (2 *Henry IV*, 3.2.312–16). 'Overscutch'd huswifes' are worn out whores, literally 'well-whipped'; Scott transfers the adjective to the tunes, meaning well-worn.

123.38–39 modern romancers and novelists of whom Walter Scott was the most celebrated; 'kilted Highlanders' figure particularly in *Waverley* (1814),

Rob Roy (1818), and *The Legend of the Wars of Montrose* (1819). Mrs Bethune Baliol's warning is at 67.7–8.

123.43   circulating library   lending or subscription library, see note to 45.15–16.

123.43   a Caledonian ball   a ball where Highland dress is worn.

124.1   a Highland regiment   for the raising of the Highland regiments see the Historical Note to 'The Highland Widow', 320, and notes to 88.24–25 and 98.27.

124.4   the battle fields of the Continent   three Highland regiments, raised in 1759 and 1760, were deployed in Europe during the Seven Years' War (1756–63).

124.4–5   sometimes indolent domestic habits   a standard criticism of Highlanders, which Johnson explains: 'Having little work to do, they are not willing, nor perhaps able to endure a long continuance of manual labour, and are therefore considered as habitually idle' (Samuel Johnson, *Journey to the Western Islands of Scotland*, ed. J. D. Fleeman (Oxford, 1985), 69).

124.6   Mrs Grant of Laggan   Anne Grant (1755–1838), widow of the minister of Laggan, who wrote several books inspired by her life in the Highlands: *Poems on Various Subjects* (Edinburgh, 1803), which contains a long poem entitled 'The Highlanders'; *Letters from the Mountains*, 3 vols (London, 1806); *Essays on the Superstitions of the Highlanders of Scotland*, 2 vols (London, 1811). Scott got to know her after she settled in Edinburgh in 1810.

124.8–9   General Stewart of Garth   Major General David Stewart of Garth (1772–1829), author of *Sketches of the Character, Manners, and Present State of the Highlanders of Scotland with details of the Military Service of the Highland Regiments*, 2 vols (Edinburgh, 1822). After a lifetime of military service he became Governor of St Lucia in 1828 and died there the following year. He was involved with Scott in organising the visit of George IV to Edinburgh in 1822.

124.12   add a stone to the cairn   see note to 111.9–10.

124.15   the greyheaded eld   compare *The Merry Wives of Windsor*, 4.4.35: 'idle-headed eld'.

124.17   the days of clanship and claymores   before the defeat of the Jacobite rising of 1745–46. Measures taken to prevent a repetition included disarming the Highlands (1746) and abolishing heritable jurisdictions through which clan chiefs exercised legal power over their feudal vassals (1748): see the Historical Note to 'The Highland Widow', 319–20, and note to 78.31. A *claymore*, from Gaelic, *claidheamh-mór*, great sword, was originally a large two-handed sword but by the 18th century was a basket-hilted Highland broadsword.

124.17   Have at you   an imperative announcing the speaker's intention to attack or get going (*OED*, *have*, verb 20).

124.18–19   An oyster ... the gentle Tilburina   see Tilburina's mad song in Richard Brinsley Sheridan, *The Critic* (1779), 3.1.298.

124.23   the Doune Fair   on the river Teith in Perthshire, on the principal route for cattle coming S from Skye and NW Scotland. The fair, or tryst, at Doune, which was new in the 1760s, was held in November and was the last important cattle sale of the year on the border between the Highlands and Lowlands of Scotland (Haldane, 83, 147–48).

124.24–25   the northern and midland counties in England   English dealers started to come to the cattle markets in Scotland in the second half of the 18th century; among the earliest were dealers from the Craven district of Yorkshire (Haldane, 121, 179–80).

124.38–39   highways ... turnpikes   the stone surface of a made road was damaging to the hooves of the cattle; cattle which were to be driven on hard roads were sometimes shod for the purpose (Haldane, 32–35). A turnpike is a stretch of road maintained from the tolls paid by those using it. Cattle were charged per head as they passed the toll-gate, and, in addition to the cost, the drover would be annoyed by the time it took for the herd to be counted through it (Haldane, 209; Bonser, 66–68).

125.1   sleep along with their cattle Haldane quotes a journal from 1723 describing this (Haldane, 35–36).

125.3–4   from Lochaber to Lincolnshire respectively a district of the Scottish Highlands SW of Inverness, and one of the counties of England where cattle from Scotland were fattened for the London market (Bonser, 73, 83).

125.4   paid very highly Haldane comments on this passage: 'The wages of the leading drovers or "topsmen" may have been considerable and commission on the outcome of a successful drove was not uncommon, but from such information as is available it seems that the ordinary working drover was not highly paid' (Haldane, 53).

125.5–7   the trust reposed … a profit to the grazier there were different ways of financing a drove. If the drover had the money to purchase the cattle from the farmer (grazier) he might do so; otherwise he would have to take the drove on credit from the farmer, a cattle-dealer, or a bank. In the latter case it was particularly important that the drover was reliable and returned with money sufficient to pay off the debt (Bonser, 77–78).

125.13   His dirk according to Burt 'The Blade is straight, and generally above a Foot long … They pretend they can't well do without it, as being useful to them in cutting Wood, and upon many other Occasions; but it is a conceal'd Mischief hid under the Plaid, ready for secret stabbing, and in a close Encounter, there is no Defence against it' (Burt, 2.174).

125.22   Donald here a generic name for a Highlander.

125.24   amongst flocks … amongst herds a contrast is drawn between flocks (of sheep) and herds (of cattle). Sheep-farming was practised in the Highlands but did not become extensive until the second half of the 18th century. To Highlanders black cattle were a more natural form of property.

125.27   his country cattle West Highland cattle, small, with long hair and curved horns.

125.30   Glunamie Lowland name for a Highlander. Scott has a note on its origin in the Magnum *The Fair Maid of Perth*, 42.74; it appears to come from Gaelic *glùineanach* meaning 'gartered', referring to the hose of a Highlander (*CSD*).

125.31   his tartan hose see note to 79.42.

125.39–40   a John Highlandman … Lowland lasses *John Highlandman* is another generic name for a Highlander; the idea of the Highlander attracting a Lowland girl is a common motif in 18th-century Scottish songs.

126.10   sister's sons of his own see note to 47.27.

126.17–18   McCombich (or, son of my friend) Scott gives the same surname to Evan Dhu, the foster-brother of the Highland chieftain, Fergus Mac-Ivor, in *Waverley*, ed. Claire Lamont (Oxford, 1981), 74–75. The derivation 'son of my friend' may come from Gaelic *mac*, a son, and *companach*, a companion. George F. Black derives the name, however, from the Gaelic 'MacThomaidh, "son of Tommie" (diminutive of Thomas)': *The Surnames of Scotland* (New York, 1946), 474.

126.19   Rob Roy Rob Roy MacGregor (1671–1734), celebrated Highland outlaw: see Historical Note to 'The Highland Widow', 319.

126.23–24   Robin Hood … Sherwood the comparison between Rob Roy and the English outlaw hero Robin Hood was not uncommon. Dorothy Wordsworth at Glengyle on the banks of Loch Katrine remarked that 'Rob Roy [is] as famous here as ever Robin Hood was in the Forest of Sherwood': 'Recollections of a Tour made in Scotland A.D. 1803', *Journals of Dorothy Wordsworth*, ed. E.

de Selincourt, 2 vols (London, 1959), 1.268.

126.23 **the wilds of Lochlomond** Rob Roy came from Inversnaid on the E bank of Loch Lomond and had property and influence in the area.

126.24–25 **such ancestry ... be proud?** James Boswell (1748–96), the biographer of Samuel Johnson, made this comment after claiming descent from Robert the Bruce (*Boswell's Life of Johnson*, ed. George Birkbeck Hill and L. F. Powell, 6 vols (Oxford, 1934–50), 5.25n).

127.2 **Tomahourich** probably Tomnahurich, a small hill near Inverness; its name comes from Gaelic *tom na h'iubhraich*, 'hillock with the junipers' (James B. Johnston, *Place-Names of Scotland* (London, 1934), 312).

127.5 **the Carse of Stirling** 'carse' is a Scots word for a stretch of fertile, alluvial land on both sides of a river; the 'Carse of Stirling' is the name given to the part of the Carse of Forth near Stirling.

127.8–9 **Saint Mungo's knot** St Mungo (d. *c.* 612), also known as St Kentigern, founded the church in Glasgow and is said to be buried on the site of the Cathedral. Legend claims that he was led to Glasgow by two bulls, hence perhaps his association with cattle. I am grateful to the late Alan Bruford for the comment that 'Tying knotted threads (often red) with charms said over each knot, round the tails of cattle to protect them from the Evil Eye, is certainly Highland practice, and has survived to the [twentieth] century: tying knots in the actual hair of the tail is presumably a misunderstanding of this'; Dr Bruford had not heard this practice attributed to St Mungo. Saints commonly invoked to protect cattle in the Highlands are the Virgin Mary, St Bridget, and St Columba (Alexander Carmichael, *Carmina Gadelica*, 6 vols (Edinburgh, 1928–71), 4.40–47).

127.10 **Dimayet** Dumyat, an outlying summit of the Ochil Hills near Stirling. It is just N of Logie, of which Charles Roger records: 'About the second decade of the last century, there lived, in the parish of Logie, several ill-favoured old women, to whom the reputation of witchcraft was confidently attached' (*A Week in Bridge of Allan* (Edinburgh, 1852), 16).

127.23 **bird of my bosom** an expression found in songs addressed to children, for instance in John Leyden, 'Finland Song. Addressed by a Mother to her Child', line 5 (*The Poetical Remains of the late Dr. John Leyden*, ed. James Morton (London, 1819), 192).

127.26 **walk the deasil round you** Gaelic *deiseal*, towards the south or the sun; here the name for a propitious ceremony involving walking round a person or building in the direction of the sun to avert evil fortune. The practice is described in Martin Martin, *A Description of the Western Islands of Scotland*, 2nd edn (London, 1716), 116–19, 277–78 (*CLA*, 5): 'Some of the poorer sort of People in these Islands retain the Custom of performing these Rounds Sun-ways, about the Persons of their Benefactors three times, when they bless them, and wish good success to all their Enterprizes' (118). Scott describes the *deasil* in *Waverley*, ed. Claire Lamont (Oxford, 1981), 118, to which he adds a Magnum note (1.255).

127.27 **the far foreign land** meaning here England.

127.32 **the Druidical mythology** alluding to the ancient order of priestly officials in pre-Roman Britain. There was interest in the Druids in the 18th century, and a tendency to attribute to them pre-Christian beliefs like sun-worship.

127.39 **this Taishataragh (second sight)** Gaelic *taibhsearachd*, the facility of seeing things distant in time or place, particularly associated with the Scottish Highlanders.

128.8 **running the country** fleeing the country, usually to evade arrest.

128.11 **all men have their blood from Adam** proverbial 'We are all Adam's children' (*ODEP*, 3).

128.13 Stirling brig i.e. Stirling bridge, on the route S from Doune, crossing the river Forth at Stirling.

128.18–19 few of his aunt's words fell to the ground came to nothing (*OED*, *ground*, substantive 8b).

128.29–30 westlandman...Glenae Hugh Morrison comes from Glenae in Dumfriesshire, in SW Scotland, 'the male inhabitants of which were long famed for broils, battles, and feats of activity' (Robert Chambers, *The Popular Rhymes of Scotland* (Edinburgh, 1826), 111–112).

128.31 the Manly Morrisons of auld langsyne Robert Chambers notes of 'The Manly Morisons': 'This is, or was, especially applicable to a family, which had been settled for a long period at Woodend, in the parish of Kirkmichael, in Dumfries-shire, and become remarkable for the handsomeness of its cadets' (*The Popular Rhymes of Scotland*, 209). *Auld langsyne* means literally 'old long ago', old times; the expression is famous from the Scottish song of that title.

128.31 never took short weapon implying the treachery of a short weapon as against the long sword.

128.34 dirking ower the board stabbing across the table.

128.36 feared for *Scots* afraid of, apprehensive because of.

129.2 more of a sow than a grumph *proverbial* see *ODEP*, 234: 'What can you expect from a hog but a grunt'. Scott uses the expression in his *Journal* for 10 April, 1827: 'But what can be expected of a *Sow* but a *grumph*?' (*Journal*, 295).

129.3 knife should ever slash a haggis see Robert Burns, 'To a Haggis' (1787), lines 13–14: 'His knife see Rustic-labour dight,/ An' cut you up wi' ready slight'.

129.6 Falkirk town S of the River Forth famous for its cattle fairs.

129.8–9 Harry Wakefield his name implies his place of origin: Wakefield is a town in Yorkshire.

129.11–12 keep the rounds at Smithfield *pugilism* a 'round' is a single bout in a fight or a boxing-match (*OED*, *round*, substantive 23b). Smithfield is an ancient market-place in London formally established as a cattle market in 1638; its space was also used for sporting events.

129.12 maintain the ring space, originally defined by a circle of spectators, for a boxing or wrestling match (*OED*, *ring*, substantive 14a).

129.13–14 professors of the Fancy professionals, experts at boxing. 'The fancy' is a name for the art of boxing (*OED*, *fancy*, A, substantive 12c).

129.14 chance customer sporting opponent who chances to present himself.

129.14 bellyful see *bellyful* in Francis Grose, *A Classical Dictionary of the Vulgar Tongue*, 3rd edn (London, 1796): 'A hearty beating, sufficient to make a man yield or give out' (*CLA*, 156).

129.15 Doncaster races horse-races have been held at Doncaster in Yorkshire since at least the 17th century; the classic race, the St Leger, is run there each September.

129.21 the main chance the course of action most likely to produce advantage or profit.

129.24 clothyard shafts arrows a cloth-yard in length, alluding to the measure for cloth which differed slightly from the ordinary yard (*Brewer*, 236). The long-bow gave England military superiority over France in the late 14th and early 15th centuries.

129.25–26 good sabres, in our own time referring in particular to the defence of the country during the Napoleonic wars. Pierce Egan, writing in 1812 in the dedicatory letter to his *Boxiana; or, Sketches of Antient and Modern Pugilism*, 2 vols (London, 1818), attributes to boxing 'the alacrity of the TAR in serving his gun, and the daring intrepidity of the BRITISH SOLDIER in mounting the breach, producing those brilliant victories which have reflected so much honour on the English Nation' (1.v). Scott had paid tribute to the pugilistic champion, John Shaw, who fought heroically before being killed at Waterloo in 1815 (*Paul's Letters to his Kinsfolk* (Edinburgh, 1816), 155).

130.1 over Minch-Moor the first of a series of place-names which indicate the drovers' route south from Falkirk towards the Anglo-Scottish border. Minch-Moor is SE of Innerleithen in the Scottish Borders.

130.2 the shibboleth Llhu *Gaelic laogh*, a calf. Edward Dwelly notes that an 'l' before an 'a' in Gaelic 'has no sound in English exactly like it' (*The Illustrated Gaelic-English Dictionary*, 8th edn (Glasgow, 1973), ix–x). A shibboleth is a word which non-native speakers of a language have difficulty in pronouncing, hence used for detecting enemies or foreigners; from Judges 12.6, where the fleeing Ephraimite pronounced 'Shibboleth' as 'Sibboleth', 'for he could not frame to pronounce it right'.

130.3 Traquair to Murder-cairn Traquair is on the S side of the River Tweed opposite Innerleithen. Haldane has traced this drove road through the Borders 'south-east from Traquair, crossing the hills by Minch Moor and Broomylaw to the top of Long Philip Burn to reach the Ettrick Valley to the west of Selkirk' (Haldane, 155 and map). The drove-road from Traquair over Minch Moor is marked as such on modern maps.

130.8 interminable pibrochs music for the bagpipes, chiefly martial but also used for dirges.

130.15 caviare to his companion see *Hamlet*, 2.2.431–32, implying that Robin's tales were a delicacy which his companion would not appreciate.

130.25 yeoman's service a phrase used by the prince in *Hamlet*, 5.2.36.

130 motto 'Duke upon Duke. An excellent new ballad' is printed in Scott's edition of *The Works of Jonathan Swift*, 19 vols (Edinburgh, 1814), 13.333–38, in a section entitled 'Miscellanies in Verse, by Mr Pope, Dr Arbuthnot, Mr Gay, &c. collected by Dr Swift and Mr Pope, 1727'; the lines quoted may be found in *The Poems of Alexander Pope*, ed. John Butt, 11 vols (London, 1939–69), 6.219.39–44.

130.35–36 Liddesdale … The Waste Scott picks up the drovers' route again in Liddesdale, the valley of the Liddel Water running SW in the western Scottish Borders; they would probably have crossed the Kershope Burn into England (Haldane, 157). The drove would enter the parish of Bewcastle in north Cumberland of which William Hutchinson comments, 'There are two great drove-roads through the parish, one from Scotland to the southern parts of England … by which many thousands of cattle and sheep pass yearly' (William Hutchinson, *The History of the County of Cumberland*, 2 vols (Carlisle, 1794), 1.95–96).

A *waste* is in legal usage a piece of uncultivated common land; more generally it implies land sparsely-inhabited and untilled. In his Introduction to the ballad 'Hobbie Noble' Scott refers to 'that mountainous and desolate tract of country, bordering upon Liddesdale, emphatically termed the Waste of Bewcastle' (*Minstrelsy*, 2.116). In 18th-century maps of Cumberland the name 'Waste' is applied to a more limited area bounded by Bewcastle in the N, Gilsland in the S, and the border with Northumberland in the E; in *Guy Mannering* the Waste is directly north of Gilsland (*Guy Mannering*, ed. P. D. Garside, EEWN 3, 120.36, 40 and 42, 124.9, 39). The Waste was also known as Spadeadam Waste, a name that survives in local usage although modern maps, referring to its partial afforestation, call it Spadeadam Forest (*The Place-Names of Cumberland*, ed. A. M. Armstrong, and others, 3 vols (Cambridge, 1950–52), 1.96–97; Hutchinson, map between 1.42 and 43).

130.39 start and owerloup *Scots* 'sudden rush and leap over'; trespass by animals on neighbouring land (*CSD*, *start*).

131.1   fertile and enclosed country   Hutchinson observes of the parish of Bewcastle, 'scarce one-third of the parish consists of inclosed lands' (*The History of the County of Cumberland*, 1.95). Bonser points out the nuisance to droving of the gradual process of enclosure, whereby unfenced common lands were enclosed with hedges or dykes (Bonser, 71–73).

131.4   a great northern fair   Scott may have had in mind the fair at Carlisle. Although the chief fairs of the year in Carlisle were held on 26 August and 19 September, fairs for horses and cattle took place until Christmas (Bonser, 133–34). The other big fair in the area was at Rosley, near Wigton, SW of Carlisle, where was 'held yearly a great fair on Whitsun Monday, and also every fortnight day after till All saints day, for horses, cattle, sheep, cloth, and many other kinds of goods' (Joseph Nicholson and Richard Burn, *The History and Antiquities of the Counties of Westmorland and Cumberland*, 2 vols (London, 1777), 2.142).

131.19   Mr Ireby   Ireby is a market-town SW of Carlisle, on the road to Whitehaven.

131.26   knowingly hogged and cropped   with its mane cut and its ears clipped in a stylish fashion.

131.28   long-necked bright spurs   the neck of the spur is the part which connects the sides, which clip over the rider's boot, to the rowel, the pricking device. Long-necked spurs were a 15th-century invention designed to accommodate a horse's body-armour, which would place the rider's foot at a distance from the horse's side. By the 18th century long-necked spurs were a matter of fashion. See Charles De Lacy Lacy, *The History of the Spur* (London, 1911), 41–42, 72.

131.40   pe gang   be going; an example of the substitution of one initial consonant for another to indicate the pronunciation of a Gaelic speaker. There are further examples in Robin Oig's speech of the voiceless Gaelic *b* being represented by *p* (*The Language of Walter Scott*, 255). Tulloch points out that 'the otiose use of the verb *to be*' is another indicator of Highland speech (398).

131.42   if she was   the use of 'she' as a general-purpose pronoun, meaning here 'I', is another feature of the literary representation of Highland speech. It is found as early as Richard Holland's *The Buke of the Howlat* (c. 1450). Tulloch comments that 'it seems to have no basis in reality' (*Language of Walter Scott*, 255).

132.1   Sawney   see *sawney* in Francis Grose, *A Classical Dictionary of the Vulgar Tongue*, 3rd edn (London, 1796): 'A general nick-name for a Scotchman ... Sawny or Sandy being the familiar abbreviation or diminutive of Alexander, a very favourite name among the Scottish nation'.

132.2   in the way of reason   in recompense.

132.4–5   the two black ... the brockit   West Highland cattle, often referred to as 'black cattle', were 'in colour black, white, dun, red and brindled' (Bonser, 50); 'brockit' is Scots for an animal with a white streak down its face.

132.6   a shudge   a judge; this imitates the pronunciation of a Gaelic speaker as [dz] is not found initially in Gaelic (*Language of Walter Scott*, 255–56).

132.7   set off   mark off, identify from others.

132.12   prix juste   *French* fair price.

132.13   into the boot   in addition, into the bargain.

132.21   Goshen   the fertile land in Egypt given to Jacob and his sons during a famine; see Genesis 45.10–47.6.

132.35   Fleecebumpkin   the name implies one who deprives the country people of their money by unscrupulous dealing.

132.42   two bites of a cherry   proverbial: *ODEP*, 849.

132.43   blear a plain man's eye   deceive a plain man (*CSD*, *blear*).

132.43   out upon you   expression of reproach.

133.1   kiss any man's dirty latchets   *proverbial* to kiss the dust, to grovel. Compare *ODEP*, 429, and *Macbeth*, 5.8.28–29: 'I will not yield/ To kiss the ground before young Malcolm's feet'. See also next note.

133.1–2   to bake in his oven   to make a living. Wakefield is saying that he will not grovel before anyone to make a living. See note to 135.16.

133.11   thy fause loon's visage   the Englishman is apparently quoting a Scots expression here: a *fause loon* is a treacherous or deceitful fellow.

133.25   Mine host   the innkeeper; *mine* (instead of *my*) is an archaic or poetic usage before a vowel or *h* (*OED*).

133.38   Adam's children   see note to 128.11.

133.38–39   Good John Barleycorn   the personification of malt whisky, which is made from barley, frequently celebrated in song.

134.13   Hout ay   indeed, certainly (*CSD*, *hoot*).

134.15   Argyleshires   West Highland cattle bred in Argyllshire in western Scotland (Haldane, 236–37).

134.18–19   Christenbury Cragg ... the Hollan Bush   Christianbury Crag (487m) is prominent in NE Cumberland, near the border with Northumberland. The 'Hollan Bush' is 'six or seven miles' (10 km) S of it. The Hollan Bush is a typical name for a farm which gave hospitality to travellers. 'Hollan' or 'hollin', meaning holly, is common in place-names in northern England. M. A. Atkin has pointed out that farms with 'hollin' names usually stand alone, on a boundary for instance between settled land and moor. She suggests that 'they were resting places along the route which offered shelter and fodder for travellers and their animals, and were accordingly signposted with a branch of holly to indicate their significance' (M. A. Atkin, 'Hollin Names in North-West England', *Nomina*, 12 (1988–89), 77). Holly was sometimes a winter food for cattle (Martin Spray, 'Holly as a fodder in England', *Agricultural History Review*, 29 (1981), 97–110).

134.22   Robin Oig hersell   himself; gender confusion of this sort is a feature of the representation of Highland speech, see note to 49.7–8.

134.41   Ralph Heskett   the parish of Hesket is 14 km SE of Carlisle, on the route to Penrith.

135.16   canna make bread   make a livelihood (*OED*, *bake*, verb 6).

135.18   sliding in between him and sunshine   the expression has not been found, but *sunshine* here means 'source of happiness or prosperity' (*OED*, *sunshine*, 2a).

135.35–36   go it—serve him out ... tip him the nailer—show him the mill   series of slang expressions: 'go it' dates from *c.* 1820 and means 'keep at it! fight hard!' (Eric Partridge, *A Dictionary of Slang and Unconventional English*, ed. Paul Beale, 8th edn (New York and London, 1984), 475); 'serve him out' is boxing slang from *c.* 1815 meaning 'take revenge on him' or 'punish him' (Partridge, 1036); a 'nailer' is a 'marvellously good thing' (*OED*, *nailer*, slang 3a), and 'tip him the nailer' means 'give him a good one' (see *OED*, *tip*, verb⁴ 1); a 'mill' is a fight with fists (*OED*, *mill*, substantive 8a, from *c.* 1819), and the phrase 'show him the mill' probably means 'show him what a fist fight looks like'.

135.41   tussle for love   fight without stakes, playing a competitive game for the pleasure of playing (*OED*, *love*, substantive 10a).

135.41   on the sod   on the ground. The term comes originally from cockfighting alluding to the grass on which the fight took place, but Pierce Egan uses the term 'anecdotes belonging to the *sod*' for descriptions of boxing (*Boxiana*, 1.224).

136.9–10   the fords of Frew   on the River Forth near Kippen 10 km upstream from Stirling. In dry seasons drovers avoided the toll on Stirling Bridge by crossing the Forth at the Ford of Frew (Haldane, 83), but in *Rob Roy* they are said to be 'at all times deep and difficult of passage, and often altogether unfordable' (*Rob Roy*, 3 vols (Edinburgh, 1818), 3.7.24–8.1).

136.15–16 Whitson Tryste … Stagshaw Bank Whitsun Tryste was a fair held at Whitsuntide at Wooler in Northumberland. The cattle market in Carlisle was held on land beside the river Eden called the Sands, 'the river being divided into two branches, or channels, by a small island called the Sands, where the market for cattle is held' (William Hutchinson, *The History of the County of Cumberland*, 2 vols (Carlisle, 1794), 2.577 and map between 584–85). The Eden has since been directed into one channel, and the name the Sands is retained in the modern Sands Centre. Stagshaw Bank is on the Roman Wall in Northumberland, just north of Corbridge; fairs were held there at Whitsun and Midsummer (Bonser, 134–35).

136.16 show the white feather an accusation of cowardice. See *white* in Francis Grose, *A Classical Dictionary of the Vulgar Tongue*, 3rd edn (London, 1796): 'He has a white feather; he is a coward: an allusion to a game cock, where having a white feather is a proof that he is not of the true game breed'.

136.17 with kilts and bonnets the characteristic dress of the Scottish Highlander; the bonnet is a flat woollen hat worn by men, typically blue in colour.

136.21 I'll put on the gloves Pierce Egan refers to 'The *gloves*, stuffed with wool, whereby instruction is received by the *novice*, without any hurt or injury, and from the frequent use of which, the more experienced boxer obtains practice and improvement' (*Boxiana*, 3.18).

136.29 with hands and nails this may echo the slang expression 'tip him the nailer', and implies an undignified scrap which is not what Harry Wakefield is proposing. It follows Robin's acknowledgement that he does not know the language of the country.

136.31 bring you to the scratch the scratch is the line drawn across the ring, to which boxers are brought for an encounter (*OED*, *scratch*, substantive 5).

136.32–33 sink point on the first plood drawn drop or lower swords on the first blood drawn ('point' is short for 'point of the sword'); the suggestion is for a symbolic encounter rather than for a fight to the death.

136.33 like a gentlemans Robin's difficulty with English is indicated by his confusing the singular and plural of gentleman. His proposal of fighting with swords like gentlemen implies social disdain for the idea of fighting with the fists. Defenders of boxing, however, stressed its advantages over the '*genteel* mode' of fighting with swords or pistols as fewer deaths ensued from encounters with the fist (*Boxiana*, 1.11–13).

136.40 the armoury at Carlisle in Carlisle Castle.

136.40–41 lend them two forks probably two pitchforks, used in farming, a suggestion made in mockery.

137.1–2 Corby Castle Corby Castle, overlooking the River Eden near Wetheral, 7 km E of Carlisle, was the home of a branch of the Howard family. Scott visited Corby in 1815 (*Life*, 3.380–81).

137.2 stand second to term from duelling, meaning to act as representative of one of the participants in a duel by carrying the challenge, arranging the locality, and preparing the weapons.

137.5–6 A hundred curses on the swine eaters translation of Gaelic *ceud mallachd air luchd-ithe nam muc*; Scott used a similar expression in the speech of a Highlander in *Waverley*, ed. Claire Lamont (Oxford, 1981), 118.

137.6 the swine-eaters Highlanders did not eat pork.

137.12 A ring, a ring! an invitation to form a circle in which an impromptu fist-fight could take place.

137.14–15 Give it him home effectively, thoroughly (*OED*, *home*, adverb 4a).

137.15 he sees his own blood! *proverbial* 'The Scot will not fight till he sees his own blood'; described as a proverb against the Scots in *The Fortunes of Nigel*, 3 vols (Edinburgh, 1822), 1.26, and quoted from there in *ODEP*, 705.

137.19   when could rage encounter science   Egan repeatedly stresses that 'BOXING, the first principles of which are, most unquestionably, derived from NATURE ... ultimately, produced the *Science* of SELF-DEFENCE' (*Boxiana*, 1.253–54).

137.25   half his broth   half what he deserves.

137.30   setting to   *pugilism* beginning to fight (*OED*, *set*, verb 152f (*b*)).

137.40   better friends than ever   Egan gives an Englishman's view of the outcome of a boxing encounter: 'The fight done, the hand is given, in token of peace; resentment vanishes; and the cause generally buried in oblivion' (*Boxiana*, 1.14).

137.43–138.1   the curse of Cromwell ... in the play   an Irish curse; see Thomas Carlyle, *Oliver Cromwell's Letters and Speeches*, 4 vols (London, 1897), 2.165: 'Such is what the Irish common people still call the "Curse of Cromwell" '. Oliver Cromwell (1599–1658) was leader of the Parliamentary army during the English Civil War and Protector of England (1653–58). He led campaigns of conquest and repression in Ireland (1649–50) and Scotland (1650–51); in consequence his name is hated in both countries and is used here as a hostile taunt by an Englishman. The play has not been identified.

138.14   an Englishman ... not come natural to him   Egan remarks that 'Pugilism is in perfect unison with the feelings of Englishmen' (*Boxiana*, 1.3), and refers to 'the old intuitive English spirit of Boxing' (1.302).

138.25   well seen on   *Scots* visible or apparent in (*SND*, *see*, verb 9).

138.35–36   betwixt Esk and Eden   the Esk flows S through Dumfriesshire into the Solway Firth; the Eden flows N through Cumberland and joins the Irthing E of Carlisle.

138.40–41   when did her word fall to the ground   when was what she said of no consequence. See note to 128.18–19.

139.18–19   English miles   of 1760 yards, distinguished from the longer Scots mile of 1984 yards though the exact length varied from place to place (*SND*).

139.27   May good betide us   may good befall us, may God help us.

139.31   you are for back to the Highlands   *Scots* you want to go back to the Highlands (*CSD*, *for*).

139.40   Hooly and fairly   *Scots* slowly and gently, but steadily (*CSD*, *huilie*).

139.42   are a' ae man's bairns   are all one man's children, that is children of Adam (see note to 128.11).

139.43   over the Scots dyke   a turf bank that marked the line of the Anglo-Scottish border in an area N of Carlisle where the boundary was disputed. It runs between the River Esk, just below its confluence with the Liddel Water, and the River Sark.

139.43–140.2   the Eskdale ... Lustruther   Eskdale in southern Scotland is the valley of the River Esk which flows south through Dumfriesshire into the Solway; *callant* is Scots meaning 'young man'. Scott describes an 'old and sturdy yeoman belonging to the Scottish side, by surname an Armstrong or Elliot, but well known by his soubriquet of Fighting Charlie of Liddesdale' in a note in the Magnum *Guy Mannering* (3.228–30). Lockerby is Lockerbie in Dumfriesshire, but the fame of its 'lads' has not survived. In another note in the Magnum *Guy Mannering* (3.271) Scott records: 'In the small village of Lustruther, in Roxburghshire, there dwelt, in the memory of man, four inhabitants, called Andrew, or Dandie, Oliver. They were distinguished as Dandie Eassil-gate, Dandie Wassil-gate, Dandie Thumbie, and Dandie Dumbie. The two first had their names from living eastward and westward in the street of the village; the third from something peculiar in the conformation of his thumb; the fourth from his taciturn habits.'

140.2   grey plaids   referring to the grey mantles worn by Scottish borderers.

140.4   Stanwix   an ancient settlement on the N bank of the River Eden opposite Carlisle, now a suburb of Carlisle.

140.6–7   enlisted...the Black Watch   see Historical Note to 'The Highland Widow', 320, and note to 77.13.

140.13–14   the braes of Balquidder   the hills of Balquidder in SW Perthshire, the particular haunt of Rob Roy.

140.15   ta'en on   enlisted.

140.23   the morn's morning   *Scots* tomorrow morning.

140.24   the catastrophe of our tale   an unhappy event which brings about the conclusion of a play or story.

140.34–35   What though...plough and cart   'Hodge of the Mill and buxome Nell', lines 35–36, in Allan Ramsay, *The Tea-Table Miscellany*, 4 vols (Edinburgh, 1723–37); Scott owned the 13th edn (Edinburgh, 1762) in which the quotation is on p. 380: *CLA*, 171.

140.42   helped to his broth   see note to 137.25.

140.43   his cauld kail het again   *proverbial* cold broth hot again (see 137.25 and 140.42), literally cold cabbage hot again: see *ODEP*, 132.

141.1–2   stand up, if you be a man   *Romeo and Juliet*, 3.3.87.

141.9   drink down all unkindness   *The Merry Wives of Windsor*, 1.1.178.

141.10–11   how to clench your hands   'If a man designs to strike a hard blow, let him shut his fist as firm as possible; the power of his arm will then be considerably greater than if but slightly closed, and the velocity of his blow greatly augmented by it' (*Boxiana*, 1.38).

141.34   blazing turf-fire   peat fire.

142.2   death pays all debts   proverbial: *ODEP*, 174.

142.10   to abide his doom   await the verdict or pronouncement of the court.

142.10   assizes   courts held periodically in each English county and attended by travelling judges of the High Court of Justice. In the 18th century the Cumberland assizes were held annually in Carlisle, usually in August. All serious cases, like charges of murder, were held over to the next assizes. *Assize* is a legal term meaning literally 'a session'.

142.26   at the touch of the homicide   the belief that a corpse bleeds at the approach of the murderer. Compare *Richard III*, 1.2.55–61; *The Fair Maid of Perth*, ed. A. D. Hook and Donald Mackenzie, EEWN 21, 218.18–28. Scott writes on the subject in a note to 'Earl Richard', in *Minstrelsy*, 3.241–45.

142.30   I was myself present   the fictitious narrator, Chrystal Croftangry, claims to have been at the trial; in fact the person who was present was Scott's source for the tale, George Constable; see Historical Note, 339–40.

142.32   the Sheriff of Cumberland   it was the Sheriff's job to oversee the proper conduct of the assizes.

143.20   at the bar   in the court, referring to a wooden bar which separated the judge and the accused.

143.33   national maxim of 'fair play'   upright conduct in a game, hence equitable actions generally (*OED*, *fair*, adjective 10c).

143.40   the laws of the ring   the first attempt to draw up rules for pugilism, or bareknuckle fighting, was made by the champion Jack Broughton in 1743 (*Boxiana*, 1.51–52; Dennis Brailsford, *Bareknuckles: A Social History of Prize-Fighting* (Cambridge, 1988), 8–9).

143.40–41   a cowardly Italian   'scarcely any person in Italy is without the stiletto...but, in England, the FIST only is used' (*Boxiana*, 1.13).

144.7–9   the laws...are not known here   pugilism itself was of uncertain legal status after 1750; despite that, its popularity increased in the 1780s and during the Napoleonic wars, and it had the patronage of royalty. The use of a pugilistic encounter to settle personal disagreements, even supposing the 'laws of the ring' to be observed, was a popular vestige of the ordeal or trial by combat and its results were not sanctioned by the law.

144.8   the Bull-ring, or the Bear-garden, or the Cockpit   for bull or bear-baiting and cock-fighting. Maintaining bull-rings, bear-gardens and cockpits became illegal in 1835 in England, and 1850 in Scotland; the activities were not explicitly made illegal until 1911 in England and 1912 in Scotland.

144.12   in pari casu   *Latin* in an equal situation.

144.18   Merry Old England   Hazlitt, in his essay on 'Merry England' (1825) comments: 'the noble science of boxing is all our own. Foreigners can scarcely understand how we can squeeze pleasure out of this pastime; the luxury of hard blows given or received; the joy of the ring; nor the perseverance of the combatants' (*The Complete Works of William Hazlitt*, ed. P. P. Howe, 21 vols (London, 1930–34), 17.154).

144.20   English gentleman . . . his sword   although boxing in England had a following among the upper classes its practitioners were usually from the lower classes. Egan commends boxing as a means of settling differences by claiming 'it is an inherent principle—the impulse of a moment—acted upon by the most ignorant and inferior ranks of the people' (*Boxiana*, 1.14).

144.24   vis major   *Latin* stronger force.

144.32–33   Moderamen inculpatæ tutelæ   *Latin* mitigating circumstances of unimpugnable defence.

144.34   manslaughter, not of murder   *law* manslaughter is criminal homicide of a lower degree of criminality than murder; homicide committed in the heat of passion, or without previous intention, are examples of manslaughter.

144.36   the statute of James I. cap. 8   law passed in the English Parliament in 1604, the 2nd year of the reign of James I (James VI and I: see note to 65.17), which became known as the statute of stabbing. It enacted 'That every person and persons which . . . shall stab or thrust any person or persons that hath not then any weapon drawn, or that hath not then first stricken the party which shall so stab or thrust, so as the person or persons so stabbed or thrust shall thereof die within the space of six months then next following, although it cannot be proved that the same was done of malice forethought, yet the party so offending, and being thereof convicted by verdict of twelve men, confession or otherwise according to the law of this realm, shall be excluded from the benefit of his or their clergy, and suffer death as in case of wilful murder' (*The Statutes at Large*, ed. Danby Pickering, Vol. 8 (Cambridge, 1763), 85).

144.38   malice prepense   *French* malice aforethought, a legal term meaning a wrongful act carried out intentionally.

144.38   benefit of clergy   the exemption accorded to clergy in the Middle Ages from trial in a secular court, later extended to anyone who could read. The 'benefit' lay largely in the incapacity of the ecclesiastical courts to condemn to death. The more serious crimes were gradually excluded from it, but benefit of clergy lasted in England until 1827.

144.39   a temporary cause   Sir Michael Foster comments on the statute of stabbing: 'This statute was made at a critical time, and, as tradition hath it, upon a very special occasion. It is supposed to have been principally intended to put an effectual stop to outrages then frequently committed by persons of inflammable spirits and deep resentment; who, wearing short daggers under their cloaths, were too well prepared to do quick and effectual execution upon provocations extremely slight' (*A Report of Some Proceedings on the Commission for the Trial of the Rebels in the Year 1746, in the county of Surry . . . to which are added Discourses* *upon a few Branches of the Crown Law*, 3rd edn (London, 1792), 297–98): see *CLA*, 298.

145.2   chaude mêlée   *French* hot encounter.

145.18   in the days of many now alive   i.e. before the defeat of the Jacobite rising of 1745–46 (see note to 124.17, and Historical Note to 'The Highland Widow', 319–20); for the date of the action see Historical Note, 340–41.

145.19–20   not only of England...of Scotland   the laws of England did not obtain in Scotland, although laws enacted by the combined Parliament of Great Britain after 1707 did. Perhaps those are what the judge refers to. Before the defeat of the '45 even Scottish law did not reach the Highlands.

145.24   the North American Indians   it was common among 18th-century Scottish historians and philosophers to liken the Scottish Highlanders to the natives of North America. In *The History of America*, 4th edn, 3 vols (London, 1783), 2.129 (see *CLA*, 204) William Robertson says that 'the incessant hostilities among rude nations' must be 'imputed to the passion of revenge, which rages with such violence in the breast of savages, that eagerness to gratify it may be considered as the distinguishing characteristic of men in their uncivilized state... When the right of redressing his own wrongs is left in the hands of every individual, injuries are felt with exquisite sensibility, and vengeance exercised with unrelenting rancour. No time can obliterate the memory of an offence, and it is seldom that it can be expiated but by the blood of the offender.'

145.33   the Noblesse of France   Scott gives a short history of duelling, emphasising its origin and importance among the French aristocracy, in his Introduction to 'The Duel of Wharton and Stuart', in *Minstrelsy*, 3.88–99.

145.35   the Cherokees or Mohawks   Iroquois tribes in North America; in the 18th century the Cherokees lived in Georgia, eastern Tennessee, and the western Carolinas, and the Mohawks in what is now New York State. The Iroquois had a particular reputation for warfare and for maintaining a warrior code of honour.

145.36   as described by Bacon   Francis Bacon (1561–1626). 'Revenge is a kind of wild justice' is the opening of the essay 'Of Revenge', published in his *Essayes or Covnsels, Civill and Morall* (London, 1625), 19–21.

146.5–6   Vengeance is mine   Romans 12.19: 'Vengeance is mine; I will repay, saith the Lord'.

146.17   the Land's end and the Orkneys   respectively the southernmost tip of England, and islands N of the mainland of Scotland.

146.21   alias   *Latin* otherwise known as.

146.22   execution   the infliction of punishment following a judicial sentence, in this case hanging.

146.25–26   I give a life for the life I took   see Exodus 21.23: 'And if any mischief follow, then thou shalt give life for life'.

HISTORICAL NOTE TO 'THE SURGEON'S DAUGHTER'

Scott once observed 'Our younger children are as naturally exported to India as our black cattle were sent to England'.[1] The three tales in *Chronicles of the Canongate* are linked by the theme of exports from Scotland, be they cattle to England or young men to America or India. 'The Surgeon's Daughter' introduces an additional element, the illicit export of a young woman. In the first hint of *Chronicles of the Canongate* Scott promised an 'Eastern Tale'.[2] In the end his Indian tale, 'The Surgeon's Daughter', was the last of the three to be written, and he was engaged on it in the summer of 1827.

Joseph Train's narrative. The main source of 'The Surgeon's Daughter' is acknowledged in a short note Scott prepared for the Magnum edition:

The Author has nothing to say now in reference to this little Novel, but that the principal incident on which it turns, was narrated to him one morning at breakfast by his worthy friend, Mr Train, of Castle Douglas, in Galloway.[3]

Joseph Train (1779–1852) was an excise officer in Galloway who supplied Scott with legendary and antiquarian material which he used in several novels (see text, 5, and note to 5.5). Train recorded that he had 'related to Sir Walter at his table in North Castle Street, the story of a Fifeshire Surgeon's daughter, which pleased him so much that he said, "Well, Mr Train you never run out of excellent stories"'.[4] While preparing material for the Magnum volume Scott asked Train if he would 'give him in writing the story as nearly as possible in the shape in which he had told it'. Train did so, and it was published in the Magnum.[5]

Train's narrative starts in Fife and concerns a dissolute young man named D******* for whom a relation, Davie Duff, a prosperous manufacturer and councillor of his burgh popularly called 'The Thane of Fife', obtained an appointment in the civil service of the East India Company. D******* was courting Emma, the daughter of a neighbouring surgeon, and before he left for India the lovers exchanged miniatures. D******* arrived in India and took up his post 'in a large frontier town of the Company's dominions'. He prospered and was able to write to the surgeon in Fife asking for the hand of his daughter. It was arranged that Emma should sail out to India to join her lover, and on the voyage she has the protection of C******, the ship's captain who was an old school friend of her brother.

On the arrival of the fleet at the appointed port, D*******, with a large cavalcade of mounted Pindarees,[6] was, as expected, in attendance, ready to salute Emma on landing, and to carry her direct into the interior of the country. C******, who had made several voyages to the shores of Hindostan, knowing something of Hindoo manners and customs, was surprised to see a private individual in the Company's service with so many attendants; and when D******* declined having the marriage ceremony performed, according to the rites of the Church, till he returned to the place of his abode, C******, more and more confirmed in his suspicion that all was not right, resolved not to part with Emma, till he had fulfilled, in the most satisfactory manner, the promise he had made before leaving England, of giving her duly away in marriage. Not being able by her entreaties to alter the resolution of D*******, Emma solicited her protector C****** to accompany her to the place of her intended destination, to which he most readily agreed, taking with him as many of his crew as he deemed sufficient to ensure the safe custody of his innocent protegée, should any attempt be made to carry her away by force.

Both parties journeyed onwards till they arrived at a frontier town, where a native Rajah was waiting the arrival of the fair maid of Fife, with whom he had fallen deeply in love, from seeing her miniature likeness in the possession of D*******, to whom he had paid a large sum of money for the original, and had only intrusted him to convey her in state to the seat of his government.

No sooner was this villainous action of D******* known to C******, than he communicated the whole particulars to the commanding officer of a regiment of Scotch Highlanders that happened to be quartered in that part of India, begging at the same time, for the honour of Caledonia, and protection of injured innocence, that he would use the means in his power, of resisting any attempt that might be made by the native chief to wrest from their hands the virtuous female who had been so shamefully decoyed from her native country by the worst of mankind. Honour occupies too large a space in the heart of the Gael to resist such a call of humanity.

The Rajah, finding his claim was not to be acceded to, and resolving to enforce the same, assembled his troops, and attacked with great fury the place where the affrighted Emma was for a time secured by her countrymen, who fought in her defence with all their native valour, which at length so overpowered their assailants, that they were forced to retire in every direction, leaving behind many of their slain, among whom was found the mangled corpse of the perfidious D*******.

C****** was immediately afterwards married to Emma, and my informant assured me he saw them many years afterwards, living happily together in the county of Kent, on the fortune bequeathed by the "Thane of Fife."

This story has not been verified historically. A correspondent to *Notes and Queries* in 1933 asked if there was any truth in Train's story and if the parties in it could be identified, and received no reply.[7]

The tale as Train recounts it contains more details than one imagines would have been included in an oral narrative at the breakfast table; but perhaps the salient elements can be identified. Scott probably got from Train a tale set partly in Scotland and partly in India, involving a surgeon's daughter and an unscrupulous young man who decoys her to India with the intention of handing her over to an Indian ruler who has fallen in love with her on seeing her portrait in miniature. In turning this tale into 'The Surgeon's Daughter' Scott selects and adds. He makes no use of the character of the Thane of Fife, and greatly expands that of the surgeon. In the character of Dr Gideon Grey it has been thought that he drew on the character of his own doctor, Dr Ebenezer Clarkson of Selkirk.[8]

Train's narrative gives no explanation of the perfidious behaviour of D*******. Scott offers some scope for the study of motive in the account of the birth and childhood of the bastard child whose family refuses to acknowledge him. In an article on 'Scott and Hoffman', Frederick E. Pierce pointed out that the account of the arrival and reception of Zilia at Dr Grey's, her wearing a mask even during childbirth, and the introduction of a Roman Catholic priest echo incidents in 'Das Gelübde' ('The Vow'), a story by E. T. A. Hoffmann, whose works Scott had reviewed in May 1827.[9] The episode leading to the death of Zilia is indebted to Scott's recollection of a lady who rushed to a pianoforte and played 'in a sort of frenzy' on being asked by her eldest son why he was not his supposed father's heir.[10]

There is little in Train's tale to indicate date, except that his informant had met the surgeon's daughter in Kent,[11] nor to suggest in which part of India it took place. Scott sets his tale at a specific period of Indian history, during the Mysore wars, and that determines his setting. As is his usual method of writing historical fiction, he inserts a narrative of fictitious characters into an historical setting and allows important historical figures, in this case Haidar Ali, ruler of Mysore, to make brief but significant appearances.

The British setting. 'The Surgeon's Daughter' is set in the Scottish village of Middlemas, the Isle of Wight, Madras, Seringapatam (Srirangapattana), and Bangalore. Middlemas is the only one of these which is fictitious. Middlemas has long been associated with Selkirk, perhaps only because of the likeness between Dr Gideon Grey and Dr Ebenezer Clarkson. There are certainly aspects of the tale which imply that Scott conceived of Middlemas as being in the Scottish Borders, despite the fact that Train's narrative starts in Fife. When it is first mentioned the little town is described as 'situated in one of the midland counties of Scotland' (159.42–43). This does not settle the question between the Borders and Fife, since the *OED* allows the word *midland* to mean both the middle of a country and 'inland'. When Richard Tresham and Zilia de Monçada, travelling north from London, arrive in Middlemas Tresham offers this explanation to Dr Grey, '"We designed to have reached Edinburgh, but were forced to turn off the road by an accident"' (162.18–19). This argues for the Borders. After the introduction of Adam Hartley from Northumberland and Tom Hillary from Newcastle there are several references to the two sides of the Border which would have less point if Middlemas were in Fife. Adam Hartley, for instance, is described as 'the son of a respectable farmer on the English side of the Border' (187.20). There are, however, other passages which are at odds with a Border setting. Richard Middlemas, estimating the worth of Dr Grey's practice, comments that 'an active assistant might go nigh to double it, by riding Strath-Devon and the Carse' (195.25–26). These place-names suit Fife better than the Borders.[12] Another indication that Scott sometimes has Fife in mind is the reference to 'rural thanes and thanesses' (189.42) and 'chiefs and thanes' (192.16). The title 'thane' is appropriate to the east of Scotland north of the Forth, and would be widely associated with Fife through the title of Macduff, Thane of Fife, in *Macbeth*.

The other setting in Britain is in the military hospital in the Isle of Wight. The tone of the hospital scene in 'The Surgeon's Daughter' is probably indebted to Smollett. Tobias Smollett (1721–71), who had served as a surgeon's mate in the Navy, drew on his experiences in *The Adventures of Roderick Random* (1748), Chapters 24–38.

The Indian setting: the British in south India. The presence of the British in India originated in the activities of the British East India Company. The East India Company was founded in 1600 with a view to developing trade with India, the East Indies and China. Its earliest trading objective was to bring back to Europe by the sea route round Africa the spices which came from the islands of the East Indies. For this purpose trading stations were established on the Indian coast and Indian textiles, especially cotton, were bought both to sell in the East Indies and to bring back to Europe. In the first 150 years of the Company's existence its ambitions were confined to trade, and any territorial interest it had in India was the consequence of the need to defend its trading stations as they grew in wealth and consequence. By the eighteenth century the East India Company had three main trading stations in India, Madras, Bombay and Calcutta. Each of these was known as a Presidency, and was governed by a President with a court of governors. The Company employed not only traders but its own armed forces and civil service.[13]

In the mid-eighteenth century the role of the East India Company in India started to grow from being concerned primarily with trade to having a territorial interest in the country. Several reasons have been adduced for this. The power of the Mughal Emperors, who had dominated north India since the sixteenth century and had made increasing claims on the south, was weakened after the death of Aurangzeb in 1707. Under his successors the autonomy of the Indian states increased, leading to power struggles in which the British became involved. East India Company agents in India had to reckon also with European rivals. The French East India Company also sought trading privileges in India, and when wars broke out between the two countries in Europe in the mid-eighteenth century their forces fought each other in India. One result of these battles was to increase the size of the British army in India beyond what was necessary to defend trading factories. Another was that the Indian states became involved as allies of one side or other. The issues were economic as well as political and military. As time went on the increasing wealth of the East India

Company's trading stations had a destabilising effect on the states with which it traded, driving them into a client relationship with the Company. There were two main theatres of war, in southern India and Bengal. After a long struggle the British gained the upper hand over the French in southern India, destroying their most important fort at Pondicherry in 1761. In Bengal Robert Clive won a victory at Plassey in 1757 which led to the British gaining supremacy over the whole of Bengal, and to Calcutta becoming the chief centre of British government in India.

In southern India, however, the growing territorial power of the British met determined opposition. The East India Company's power base was their Fort at Madras. The Madras Presidency extended its influence over the region known as the Carnatic, the territory between the Coromandel coast and the Eastern Ghats, the mountains bounding Mysore. The Indian ruler, the Nawab of Arcot, became an ally and client of the East India Company. Other powers in the area were the Nizam of Hyderabad, whose influence increased in the south as that of his Mughal superiors waned, and the Marathas, a warlike Hindu confederacy in the centre and west of India. The most formidable opponent of the British, however, was Mysore. Haidar Ali (1721–82), a Muslim who had in 1761 usurped the power of the Hindu Rajah of Mysore, challenged the power exercised by the British in the Carnatic from Madras. There followed a series of campaigns known as the Mysore Wars.[14]

The first was in 1767–69 when Haidar Ali defeated the British, threatening Madras itself. Under the terms of the truce the British undertook to come to the aid of Mysore in the event of war. The British failed to honour this agreement when the Marathas invaded Mysore in 1771, earning the lasting resentment of Haidar Ali. There was an uneasy peace in the 1770s which was broken in 1780 when Haidar Ali invaded the Carnatic with a huge army and defeated the British, taking many prisoners. The horror of this attack was impressed on those at home by Edmund Burke's description in the course of a speech in Parliament in 1785 on the mismanagement of affairs in the Presidency of Madras:

> and compounding all the materials of fury, havock, and desolation, into one black cloud, he [Haidar Ali] hung for a while on the declivities of the mountains. Whilst the authors of all these evils [the British] were idly and stupidly gazing on this menacing meteor, which blackened all their horizon, it suddenly burst, and poured down the whole of its contents upon the plains of the Carnatic... A storm of universal fire blasted every field, consumed every house, destroyed every temple. The miserable inhabitants flying from their flaming villages, in part were slaughtered; others, without regard to sex, to age, to the respect of rank, or sacredness of function, fathers torn from children, husbands from wives, enveloped in a whirlwind of cavalry, and amidst the goading spears of drivers, and the trampling of pursuing horses, were swept into captivity, in an unknown and hostile land.[15]

The second Mysore War lasted between 1780 and 1784. Haidar Ali died in 1782 and was succeeded by his son Tipu Sultan (c. 1750–99). Tipu continued his father's hostility towards the British, and gained French support. After initial success he was defeated in the third Mysore War (1790–92), and finally destroyed in the fourth. Tipu's body was found by the British who stormed his capital at Seringapatam[16] in 1799.

The date of the action. Train's narrative does not tell us the name of the 'native Rajah' who fell in love with Emma on seeing her portrait. In 'The Surgeon's Daughter' Scott makes the bold move of attributing this to an historical character: it is Tipu who wishes to possess Menie Grey on seeing her portrait. In the tale Richard Middlemas's unscrupulous actions are presented as taking place at a time of uneasy truce between the British and Mysore (248.7–11), and their discovery causes Haidar Ali to take vengeance on Madras (284.20–285.3). The incidents in the tale and the historical record conform quite neatly if the climax of 'The Surgeon's Daughter' is reckoned to take place in the mid to late 1770s.

The tale takes place in the lifetime of Haidar Ali, Nawab of Mysore, who died in 1782. Richard Middlemas was born some time after the Jacobite rising of 1745 (171.6, 238.43–239.1: see Historical Note to 'The Highland Widow', 319–20). Menie Gray was born four years later (176.8). Middlemas is not allowed to take his fortune into his own hands until he is twenty-one (182.12–13). If one assumes that Richard was born in the late 1740s he would have gone to India in about 1770. That is just after the first Mysore war (1767–69), hence the truce. At the end of the tale Haidar Ali threatens vengeance on the British for Richard's treachery. That vengeance was exacted when Haidar Ali descended on the Carnatic in 1780 at the beginning of what is known as the second Mysore War (1780–84).

Scott and India. Scott never went to India, and so was in an obvious sense ill-equipped to set a tale there. However, there were many links between Scott and the British in India.[17]

Family and Friends. For a start Scott's family had Indian connections. His eldest brother Robert (1767–87) died young in the East India Company service.[18] India was a land of opportunity for young men, if they survived. Scott even considered going himself,[19] and thought seriously of it for his younger son, Charles (1805–41).[20] One who did go was his nephew Walter (1807–76), whom Scott was supporting during the writing of *Chronicles of the Canongate*.[21] It was his wider family, however, which supplied him with information about India. His uncle, Colonel William Russell of Ashestiel (1738–1803) served with both the army and the East India Company in Madras, and his cousin, James Russell, was born there. James Russell (1781–1859) served in the 3rd Madras Native Cavalry from 1795–1824 and returned to Scotland in 1825.[22] Scott's brother-in-law, Charles Carpenter (1772–1818), was 'commercial Resident at Salem in India' and sent letters and gifts to his sister.[23] Salem is in south India and within the area of influence of the Madras Presidency. Another relation who contributed, unknowingly, to *Chronicles of the Canongate* was David Haliburton (Scott's paternal grandmother was a Haliburton), who served in the Madras Civil Service from 1770 until *c.* 1797.[24]

Margaret Tait has pointed out how many of Scott's neighbours in his childhood in George Square, Edinburgh, had connections with India.[25] Among his Border friends who went to India was the poet John Leyden (1775–1811), who had helped Scott gather ballads for *Minstrelsy of the Scottish Border*. He went to Madras as an Assistant Surgeon (like Adam Hartley) in 1803 and never returned, succumbing to illness in Java in 1811. Leyden spent two years in south India, in Madras and Mysore. Few of his letters reached home but some did and Scott knew them.[26] In Seringapatam Leyden met a native of Dumfriesshire, John Malcolm (1769–1853), who was Resident at the Court of Mysore. Scott knew Sir John Malcolm, who later became Governor of Bombay.[27] In the Borders, in addition to his cousins, Scott's neighbour Colonel James Ferguson was retired from the Indian service, and in the event played a significant part in 'The Surgeon's Daughter'. The number of Anglo-Indians in Scott's circle makes one understand his complaint, when he wanted help with Indian details for the tale:

Colonel Fergusson's absence is unlucky. So is Maxpopple and half a dozen Qui His besides, willing to write chitts, eat Tiffing and vent all their pagan jargon when one does not want to hear it and now that I want a touch of their slang, lo! there is not one near me.[28]

India and the Mysore Wars in Scott's Experience. In considering Scott's preparedness to write about India one cannot ignore the influence of growing up in the late eighteenth century. India was never out of the news in Scott's youth. Debates over the India Bill, finally passed in 1784 bringing the East India Company under Crown control, were important enough to bring down governments.[29] The impeachment of Warren Hastings for improper conduct as Governor-General in India began in 1788 and went on until his acquittal in 1795. Party politics and the eloquence of Burke and Sheridan ensured that it was fully reported. And then there were the Mysore Wars. These were well reported in newspapers, journals, histories and less formal narratives, particularly after the outbreak of the third Mysore war.[30] Scott observed in 1808 in his Introduction to Dryden's *Aureng-zebe* (1676) that 'so much has our intimacy increased with the Oriental world, that the transactions of Delhi are almost as familiar to us as those of Paris'.[31]

Two aspects of the conduct of Haidar Ali and Tipu Sultan in the Mysore wars, in addition to the military threat they posed to the British, were particularly resented in Britain and clearly made an impression on Scott. One was their treatment of prisoners. British prisoners were held by both Haidar and Tipu and the severity with which they were treated was recorded, in particular in autobiographical accounts by survivors.[32] The most famous Scots prisoner was David Baird (1757–1829), imprisoned for almost four years after being wounded at Pollilur in 1780.[33] Baird survived to lead the storming of Seringapatam in 1799. Many years later, when Scott's elder son Walter (1801–47) was serving with the 18th Hussars in Ireland the commander was Sir David Baird. Scott wrote to Walter 'I shall be glad to hear that you have seen Sir David Baird. His fate was a singular one in seeing Tippoo Sa[h]ib lie dead at his feet after the said Tippoo had kept him so many months in a dungeon at Bangalore'.[34]

The other cause of particular resentment was Tipu's alliance with the French during the period before and after the French Revolution. This allegiance might arise naturally from the pattern of alliances between the Indian states and Europeans in India, but there was added danger in a prince who allowed himself to be referred to as 'Citizen Tipu'.[35] The association of the rulers of Mysore with the French threat in Scott's mind is apparent from this letter concerning the fall of Napoleon in 1814:

> I never thought nor imagined that he would have given in as he has done. I always considered him as possessing the genius and talents of an Eastern conqueror; and although I never supposed that he possessed, allowing for some differences of education, the liberality of conduct and political views which were sometimes exhibited by old Hyder Ally, yet I did think he might have shown the same resolved and dogged spirit of resolution which induced Tippoo Saib to die manfully upon the breach of his capital city with his sabre clenched in his hand.[36]

Events in the Mysore wars were recorded in paintings and prints and in the theatre. Tipu in particular became a celebrated bogeyman in British popular culture.[37] Indian artefacts were brought to Britain and Scott, who was a collector, had many, including a sword said to have belonged to Tipu.[38]

It is an artefact exported to India, the miniature portrait, that is crucial to the action of 'The Surgeon's Daughter'. A miniature of a young woman which attracts an unidentified Rajah is part of the story which Scott received from Joseph Train, but Scott makes it Tipu who is attracted to the young woman portrayed on it. It is possible, but unproven, that a strange coincidence may have influenced Scott in making that change. Margaret Tait has drawn attention to an entry in the catalogue of an exhibition of *Portrait Drawings by Scottish Artists* held in Edinburgh in 1955:

> A miniature of Elizabeth Welwood, wife of Allan Maconochie, 1st Lord Meadowbank, by John Brown (1752–87); pencil; drawn in 1786; was found after the capture of Seringapatam in Tippoo Sahib's bedroom by Sir David Baird, whose wife was Mrs Maconochie's cousin german. It had been taken by Tippoo from a relation. Lent by L. Maconochie Welwood, Esq.[39]

This story has not been confirmed, but Elizabeth Welwood was the wife of Allan Maconochie, Lord Meadowbank (1748–1816), the father of the friend who precipitated Scott's acknowledgement of the authorship of the Waverley Novels in 1827.

'The Surgeon's Daughter' is the only work by Scott to have scenes set in India. In *Guy Mannering* (1815) both Colonel Mannering and the hero, Brown or Bertram, have served in south India. In *The Antiquary* (1816) Oldbuck's brother-in-law had lost his life in India on a military expedition against Haidar Ali. In *Saint Ronan's Well* (1824) Captain MacTurk had been a prisoner of Tipu in Bangalore, and in the character of Touchwood Scott introduces the humorous figure of the Scottish 'Nabob'. In all of these novels the historical reference is to south India and the Mysore wars. Scott was clearly well prepared for the setting of 'The Surgeon's Daughter'. By choosing the 1770s, however, he avoided the incidents most celebrated in paintings and popular accounts, like the handing over of Tipu's young sons as hostages to the British in 1792, and Tipu's death in 1799. 'The Surgeon's Daughter' is set at an early stage in Tipu's life, when Scott could contrast him with his father, a contrast which is itself pervasive in the literature of the wars.[40]

Indian sources: books. Scott was, of course, also indebted to books. In his 'Memoirs' Scott recalled a book which he had read avidly during a boyhood illness, Robert Orme's *History of the Military Transactions of the British Nation in Indostan, from the year MDCCXLV* (London, 1763, 1778).[41] In deciding to write an Indian tale Scott's narrator, Chrystal Croftangry, recalls 'the delightful pages of Orme' (155.22). Orme's book could supply, however, only a background to 'The Surgeon's Daughter' as it deals with the military campaigns of the British army in India between 1745 and 1761. In 'The Surgeon's Daughter' the surrender of Pondicherry in 1761, with which Orme's *History* ends, is mentioned as an event which took place before the beginning of the tale (250.24). The first volume of Orme's work starts with 'A Dissertation on the Establishments made by Mahomedan Conquerors in Indostan' which together with the maps in the book would have supplied the young Scott with some account of India.

Events in India in the late eighteenth century brought forth a vast literature, with a considerable amount devoted to the events in the south. There were serious histories like Orme and Mark Wilks, *Historical Sketches of the South of India, in an attempt to trace the History of Mysoor*, 3 vols (London, 1810–17). There were also many accounts of the Mysore wars, based on the writers' experiences in battle and in imprisonment.[42] The less scholarly of these repeat each other, and in such a way that certain topics come to be expected, like, for instance, the cruelty of an oriental despot, or the catalogue of riches found in Tipu's palace.

Besides Orme Scott seems to have owned only two books on southern India. One is the *Captivity, Sufferings, and Escape of James Scurry, who was detained a prisoner during ten years, in the Dominions of Hyder Ali and Tippoo Saib* (London, 1824).[43] This is based on the personal experience in India between 1781 and *c.*

1791 of James Scurry (c. 1766–1822). It illustrates the process of incorporating material from previous accounts which is typical of the literature of the Mysore wars in that Scurry, who seldom gives dates, includes a description of the storming of Seringapatam (1799), which took place after his return to England. The other work which Scott possessed was *Narrative Sketches of the Conquest of the Mysore, effected by the British Troops and their Allies, in the Capture of Seringapatam, and the Death of Tippoo Sultaun* (London, 1800).⁴⁴ This is a different sort of book from Scurry's, being put together to illustrate the large panorama of the storming of Seringapatam painted by Robert Ker Porter (1777–1842) and exhibited in 1800.⁴⁵ It is admittedly part-narrative and part-compilation, and it acknowledges substantial quotations from other publications.

This small harvest from the *Catalogue of the Library at Abbotsford* shows that Scott was not consciously collecting Indian material. If he wished to refresh his memory of incidents which were news in his youth he could have consulted the volumes of *The Annual Register*, which he possessed, and which perhaps because of its connection with Edmund Burke gave serious attention to India.⁴⁶ No doubt Scott saw other books which he did not possess; but it may be a mistake to put too much stress on reading. It appears that there was in Scotland an oral culture among those connected with the British in India which meant that information, however it originated, was widely communicated even to those who did not actively seek it.

An example of what was probably based largely on oral information in 'The Surgeon's Daughter' is the character of the Brahmin dubash, Paupiah. There is in the text a surprising passage (266.20–22) in which Mr Fairscribe suggests that the introduction of this character is an anachronism, which seems to imply that Fairscribe was aware of a historical source. This puzzle was solved by P. R. Krishnaswami in an article in *The Calcutta Review* in 1919. Krishnaswami wrote:

> We have the most interesting and illuminating account of Paupiah and his times in a little book printed at Madras in 1825, called "The Trial of Avadhanum Paupiah, Brahmin Dubash to John Holland, Esq., at the Quarter Sessions held at Fort St. George, July, 1792." As it was only two years later than the publication of this book that the "Surgeon's Daughter" was written, and from the details mentioned by Scott exactly corresponding to those of the Trial, we cannot but conclude that Scott must have read this interesting book. Paupiah was charged with, and convicted of, conspiring against Mr. Haliburton, member of the Board of Revenue and Persian Translator, and bringing about his being sent away from these high offices to be paymaster of the forces at the unhealthy frontier station, Chanderghirry, where Mr. Haliburton complained that no medical officer was stationed. It was only in the time of the successor to the Hollands that Mr. Haliburton was able to get redress.⁴⁷

Krishnaswami did not realise that Haliburton was a relation of Scott's.⁴⁸ Scott may have read about Paupiah; but he must certainly have heard the story, probably from Haliburton himself. Scott's *Journal* for 28 July 1826 certainly records an appropriately Indian occasion: 'Old Mr. Haliburton dined with us also Colonel Russell. What a man for four score or thereby is old Haly, an Indian too.'⁴⁹

In the Explanatory Notes priority in citing sources and analogues is given to books which Scott is known to have possessed. A few others are cited where they appear to shed light on 'The Surgeon's Daughter' and reveal Scott's acquaintance with the general pool of knowledge about India. An instance of this is a couple of references to *Narrative of a Journey through the Upper Provinces of India, from Calcutta to Bombay, 1824–1825* (London, 1828) by Reginald Heber (1783–1826). Scott knew Heber (and his half-brother Richard), but the book was published too late to have a direct influence on 'The Surgeon's Daughter'. It is likely, however, that Heber picked up material in north India which was available also to Scott's friend, James Ferguson.

As we have seen Scott had his plot from Train, and he had access to written and oral sources concerning the British in India. What he did not have was a first-hand knowledge of the country, its appearance, and the manners of its people. As a consequence when he got his tale to India he found he needed specific help, and he turned to his neighbour Colonel James Ferguson.

Indian sources: *Colonel James Ferguson*. James Ferguson (1778–1859) was a son of the philosopher Adam Ferguson and younger brother of Scott's friend from youth, Adam Ferguson. James Ferguson was born in 1778, entered the East India Company as a cadet at the age of twenty, and served with the 23rd Bengal Native Infantry. In 1808 he was a member of the military escort which accompanied Charles Metcalfe on a mission to the Rajah of Lahore. He spent ten years in Delhi, 1812–22, first as commander of the escort to Metcalfe when he was Resident, and then as his assistant. Ferguson's last appointment in India was in 1822 when he was sent as assistant to the Resident at the Court of Malwa and Rajputana.[50] He returned to Scotland in 1823 and came to live with his sisters at Huntlyburn, the house on the Abbotsford estate where they had lived since 1818. Scott's *Journal* records many social visits between them, and it is clear that Colonel Ferguson's experiences in India often featured in the conversation.

By 22 August 1827 Scott had got the tale of 'The Surgeon's Daughter' to India and realised that he needed further information for the descriptive parts: 'I cannot go on with the tale without I could speak a little Hindhanee, a small seasoning of curry powder—Fergusson will do it if I can screw it out of him'.[51] Ferguson obliged with some sketches of Indian life and manners which Scott found 'capitally good' and 'highly picturesque'.[52] The sketches, which survive in the National Library of Scotland,[53] are on the following topics: a description of a European in the service of a native, describing the ceremonies when he is raised to higher rank—in this sketch it is stated that 'to be trampled to death by an Elephant is a common punishment among the natives' (ff. 167r–67v); 'Tomb of an Owliah, or Mohummedan Saint' (ff. 169r–170r); the Begum and her court (ff. 171r–72r); ceremonies to be observed on the arrival of a person of distinction from another country, the Begum's durbar, and a description of a procession to greet a visitor (ff. 173r–76v); 'Dress of a Banka or Dandy' (f. 176v–77v); the Begum's history and the government of her state (f. 179r–80r); a journey up a mountain pass and the story of Sadhu Sing (ff. 181r–84v).

Ferguson does not mention Haidar Ali or Tipu, nor does he name any places. He supplies an account of a journey through a mountain pass, not specifically one up the Eastern Ghats to Mysore. The sketches seem to indicate that Scott had put certain requests to him: how might a European in the service of an Indian be treated, and dressed? and what formalities are observed at a durbar? It appears also that in supplying the information Ferguson entered creatively into what he was writing. This is especially so in the case of the Begum; Ferguson filled out a possible narrative for her as the ruler of a state which Scott did not use.

Where Scott found a sketch useful he made extensive use of it, quoting some passages almost verbatim. The description of the 'Tomb of an Owliah' is used with little alteration, as is the account of the journey up a mountain pass and the story of Sadhu Sing. Scott's Begum gets details of her dress from Ferguson, and Middlemas in Mysore is given the dress of a 'Banka or Dandy'. The account of the ceremonies marking the arrival of a person of distinction are used in 'The

Surgeon's Daughter' for the arrival of Tipu at Bangalore. Only in the last two sketches listed above are there substantial passages for which Scott found no use in 'The Surgeon's Daughter'.

The Begum Montreville. The manuscript of 'The Surgeon's Daughter' shows (f. 134r) that the character of the Begum, Madame Montreville, had been introduced into the tale before Ferguson's sketches arrived, and that they added descriptive detail to a character who had already been conceived. There have been various suggestions as to Scott's source for the Begum. The most persuasive, made by P. R. Krishnaswami, is that she was based on the Begum Samru or Sumru (c. 1748–1836) an Indian woman, widow of an Austrian military officer, Walter Reinhart, who had been given land in Meerut, north of Delhi, by the Mughal emperor. She ruled the territory and gave military support to the East India Company. She was an exotic figure, renowned for lavish dress and entertainment and for intrigues and autocratic behaviour.[54]

Denys Forrest makes another suggestion, one that has the advantage of being connected with Haidar Ali: 'the Begum derives almost certainly from de la Tour's description of a certain Madame Mequinez, to whom Haidar gave the colonelcy of her late husband's regiment'.[55] A contemporary, Edward Moor, diffuses the search for a source by noting: 'In Tippoo's, the Mahratta's, and the Nizam's services, it is not unfrequent, on the death of a commandant of respectability, for the widow to be considered the superior of the corps, and to receive its emoluments'. And he goes on to cite an Italian woman who gained charge of a battalion in Hyderabad.[56]

These references do, at least, demonstrate that the type of the female military adventuress, sometimes a European or widow of a European, was not unknown in India. What is persuasive about the Begum Sumru's claim to contribute to the character of Scott's Begum is that to her is attributed the atrocity of punishing a servant girl who had displeased her by immuring her until she died, which is said of Begum Montreville at 263.10–11. Heber records this of Begum Sumru:

> One of her dancing girls had offended her, how I have not heard. The Begum ordered the poor creature to be immured alive in a small vault prepared for the purpose, under the pavement of the saloon where the nâtch was then celebrating, and, being aware that her fate excited much sympathy and horror in the minds of the servants and soldiers of her palace, and apprehensive that they would open the tomb and rescue the victim as soon as her back was turned, she saw the vault bricked up before her own eyes, then ordered her bed to be placed directly over it, and lay there for several nights, till the last faint moans had ceased to be heard, and she was convinced that hunger and despair had done their work.[57]

Death by Elephant. Scott wanted an Indian death for his traitor, Middlemas. It appears that he raised with Ferguson the appropriateness of using an elephant as the means of death, as in his first sketch Ferguson wrote:

> The Elephant may be a male often very unruly, may have been taught by the use of an effigy dressed in the costume of the European, on a signal from his Mohawut or driver to treat the unlucky Feringee in the manner desired. To be trampled to death by an Elephant is a common punishment among the natives.[58]

This is confirmed from other contemporary writers. Scurry says of Tipu 'his most common mode of punishment was, that of drawing to death by the elephant's feet'[59] and Moor, in the course of a comparison between the power to punish in Europe and India, writes 'We read with horror and indignation of a subject, at the nod of an imperious tyrant, being dragged from his family and trodden to pieces at the foot of an elephant'.[60]

Anglo-Indian language. Ferguson uses a lot of Indian words in his sketches, many of which find their way into 'The Surgeon's Daughter'. One can assume that Scott took them from Ferguson, except that all but a few had already appeared in print and were common enough in the appropriate literature, that of Indian warfare and ceremonial. It would be more accurate to say, therefore, that Ferguson's sketches probably brought certain expressions to Scott's mind as he wrote 'The Surgeon's Daughter'. Such expressions include: banka, bukshee, chabootra, chobdars, chowry, coss, dowrah, Feringi, howdah, kaffila , khelaut, killedar, molakat, musnud, nagara, nuzzur, nullah, Owliah, Sahib Angrezie, sipahee, sirdar, sowar, sowarree, tatoo, Telinga, tom-toms, vakeel.[61]

There are other Anglo-Indian or Eastern terms in the text which are not in Ferguson's sketches, and therefore must have come from Scott's general know-ledge of matters Indian. Some are from Arabic and Persian, the languages of Islam and of the Mughal conquerors of India: divan, hadgi, houri, khan, muez-zin, ottar (of roses), sultaun, zenana. This vocabulary Scott had drawn on in his fiction before, particularly in *The Talisman* (1825). Other expressions are more exclusively Anglo-Indian, deriving from Indian languages with or without the mediation of another European language. These are, from Hindi and Urdu, bahauder, cowries, dubash, hookah, 'lacs and crores of rupees', lootie, nabob, natch, naig, pagoda, Rajah, Rajahpoot; and from Tamil, the chief language of south India: curry, mulagatawny, pettah (which Scott probably got from Orme), and tope. In addition Scott gives us 'griffin', an Anglo-Indian term of unknown derivation, and the Anglo-Indian usage 'mates and guinea-pigs'.[62]

Scott finished 'The Surgeon's Daughter' on 16 September 1827:

> The Ladies went to church. I God forgive me finishd the *Chronicles* with a good deal assistance from Colonel Fergusson's notes about Indian affairs. The patch is I suspect too glaring to be pleasing.[63]

The claim that the 'patch' was noticeable was repeated by Lockhart[64] and so became an orthodoxy. But those who have not had the sugggestion made to them do not always notice it. A different criticism is that, since Ferguson's experience was in north India, his sketches do not give a convincing impression of south India.[65] That would have been more serious if Scott's settings had been in the Hindu south. They were, however, in the East India Company's Fort at Madras, a Muslim tomb, and at Seringapatam and Bangalore at the courts and ritual occasions of Muslim rulers. It was Mysore under its Muslim rulers, Haidar Ali and Tipu Sultan, that put up such a resistance to the territorial expansion of the British in south India and Scott's tale is set in the confrontation between the two.

In 'The Surgeon's Daughter' Scott uses Indian history as a setting for an historical tale or short novel.[66] It tells a tragic tale against the background of the confrontation between Christian British and Muslim Indians. Both sides have their heroes and their villains. It does not question the presence of the British in India—the imperial question—although it questions their conduct when there. It does not describe ordinary Indian life. Perhaps more surprising is the fact that Scott shows no debt to the writings of one of the greatest British writers on India of the eighteenth century, Sir William Jones (1746–94). Jones's work created sympathy for Hinduism and for Hindu poetry. Scott seems to have been tem-peramentally unable to respond to writing in the Jones tradition,[67] and, being a generation later, seems to have missed that window in Indo-European relations when the cultures of the two continents were seen as ultimately linked rather than ultimately alien from each other.

NOTES

For shortened forms of reference see 289–90.

1 *Letters*, 7.185; letter to Lord Montagu, [June 1822].
2 MS 21016, f. 26r.

3 Magnum, 48.[149]–59.

4 Joseph Train, 'Brief Sketch of a Correspondence with Sir Walter Scott, Commencing in the year 1814', MS 3277, pp. 178–79. The date on which Train told his story is not certain, being 'In the Spring of the year following my visit to Abbotsford'. He says that he visited Abbotsford after the publication of *Old Mortality* to insist that he had not disclosed the secret of Scott's authorship, but, as Scott sent him a complimentary copy of *Old Mortality* on 21 December 1816 (*Letters*, 4.323–24), Train's breakfast meeting with Scott could have been in either 1817 or 1818.

5 Magnum, 48.151–57. Train's manuscript has not come to light.

6 Pindaris were bands of irregular cavalry or marauders in central India; they were suppressed by the British in 1817.

7 *Notes and Queries*, 164 (25 March 1933), 207.

8 *Life*, 7.88.

9 Frederick E. Pierce, 'Scott and Hoffman' in *Modern Language Notes*, 45 (1930), 457–60. Scott's review was published in the *Foreign Quarterly Review*, 1 (July 1827) and is reprinted in *Prose Works*, 18.270–332.

10 *Life*, 6.94. This story was told to Lockhart by Thomas Moore who heard it from Scott when a guest at Abbotsford in 1825. Frederick C. White drew attention to it in *Notes and Queries*, 158 (14 June 1930), 422.

11 The presence of Highland soldiers in India limits the possible date of Train's story. The first Highland regiment to go to India, the 89th Highland Regiment, arrived in 1762; the 71st Highland Regiment of Foot (Macleod's) arrived in Madras in 1780, while the 73rd (formerly the 2nd battalion of the Black Watch) and the 72nd (Seaforth's) both arrived in India in 1782.

12 The river Devon flows south from Perthshire into the Forth.

13 For brief histories of the East India Company see John Keay, *The Honourable Company: A History of the English East India Company* (London, 1991) and Philip Lawson, *The East India Company: A History* (London and New York, 1993).

14 For histories of the British in southern India and the Mysore Wars see P. J. Marshall, 'The British in Asia: Trade to Dominion, 1700–1765', in *The Oxford History of the British Empire*, Vol. 2, *The Eighteenth Century*, ed. P. J. Marshall (Oxford, 1998), 487–507; L. B. Bowring, *Haidar Ali and Tipu Sultan* (Oxford, 1893); B. Sheik Ali, *British Relations with Haidar Ali (1760–1782)* (Mysore, 1963); N. K. Sinha, 'Mysore: Haidar Ali and Tipu Sultan', in *The History and Culture of the Indian People*, Vol. 8, *The Maratha Supremacy*, ed. R. C. Majumdar (Bombay, 1977), 452–71; Kate Brittlebank, *Tipu Sultan's Search for Legitimacy* (Delhi, 1997).

15 Edmund Burke, 'Speech on the Nabob of Arcot's Debts', 28 February 1785, in *The Writings and Speeches of Edmund Burke*, Vol. 5, *India: Madras and Bengal 1774–1785*, ed. P. J. Marshall (Oxford, 1981), 519.

16 'To substitute for the well known name Seringapatam the true orthography of Sreerung-puttun, would not only have the appearance of affectation, but would produce real confusion': Mark Wilks, *Historical Sketches of the South of India, in an attempt to trace the History of Mysoor*, 3 vols (London, 1810–1817), 1.[vii].

17 Iain Gordon Brown, 'Griffins, Nabobs and a Seasoning of Curry Powder: Walter Scott and the Indian Theme in Life and Literature', in *The Tiger and the Thistle: Tipu Sultan and the Scots in India 1760–1800*, ed. Anne Buddle (Edinburgh: National Gallery of Scotland, 1999), 71–79 and notes on 91–92.

18 Scott's 'Memoirs', in *Scott on Himself*, ed. David Hewitt (Edinburgh, 1981), 9.

19 *Letters*, 7.452; letter to Thomas Scott, 1 November [1810].

20 *Letters*, 6.109; letter to Thomas Scott, 10 January 1820.

21 *Journal*, 78, entry for 6 February 1826.

22 *Journal*, 22, entry for 30 November 1825.

23 *Letters*, 1.74; letter to Miss C. Rutherford [October 1797].

24 *Letters*, 8.332n. David Haliburton is listed as a 'Senior Merchant' and member of the Board of Revenue in 'the Company's Civil Establishment at Fort St. George

[Madras]' in *The East India Kalendar; or, Asiatic Register . . . For the Year 1791* (London, 1791), 89.

25 Margaret Tait, 'The Surgeon's Daughter', *The Scott Newsletter*, 5 (1984), 6.

26 Scott printed one of Leyden's letters describing his time in Madras and Mysore in his memoir, 'John Leyden, M.D.' first published in *The Edinburgh Annual Register* for 1811 and reprinted in *Prose Works*, 4.137–98 (the letter is on 178–85).

27 *Journal*, 240, entry for 17 November 1826. Scott indicates his acquaintance with Anglo-Indian gossip by referring to Malcolm as 'Bahauder Jah', for 'Bahadur Jaw', meaning that he was a champion talker (*Hobson-Jobson*, 48–49).

28 *Journal*, 342, entry for 22 August 1827. 'Maxpopple' (for Maxpoffle, the name of his farm) is Scott's cousin William Scott of Raeburn (1773–1855). Scott uses three Anglo-Indian terms: 'Qui His' are Anglo-Indians, from the words used in India to summon a servant; 'chitts' are letters or notes; 'Tiffing' is a light midday meal.

29 Lucy S. Sutherland, *The East India Company in Eighteenth-century Politics* (Oxford, 1952), 365–414.

30 P. J. Marshall, ' "Cornwallis Triumphant": War in India and the British Public in the Late Eighteenth Century', in *War, Strategy and International Politics*, ed. Lawrence Freedman and others (Oxford, 1992), 58.

31 *The Works of John Dryden*, ed. Walter Scott, 18 vols (London, 1808), 5.170.

32 There is a collection of three such accounts in *Captives of Tipu*, ed. A. W. Lawrence (London, 1929).

33 Anne Buddle, 'The Tiger and the Thistle', in *The Tiger and the Thistle: Tipu Sultan and the Scots in India 1760–1800*, ed. Anne Buddle (Edinburgh: National Gallery of Scotland, 1999), 15–17.

34 *Letters*, 6.271; letter of 5 October [1820]. Baird was imprisoned at Seringapatam, not Bangalore.

35 Denys Forrest, *Tiger of Mysore: The Life and Death of Tipu Sultan* (London, 1970), 250–52.

36 *Letters*, 3.451; letter to Robert Southey, 17 June 1814.

37 Denys Forrest, *Tiger of Mysore: The Life and Death of Tipu Sultan* (London, 1970), 315–37, 346–61; Pauline Rohatgi, 'From Pencil to Panorama: Tipu in Pictorial Perspective', and Anne Buddle, 'Myths, Melodrama and the Twentieth Century', in *The Tiger and the Thistle: Tipu Sultan and the Scots in India 1760–1800* (Edinburgh: National Gallery of Scotland, 1999), 39–53, 58–69.

38 *Letters*, 9.103, 104n.; letter to David MacCulloch, 3 May [1825]. A considerable number of Indian weapons is listed in M. M. Maxwell-Scott's *Catalogue of the Armour & Antiquities at Abbotsford* (Edinburgh, 1888).

39 Margaret Tait, '*The Surgeon's Daughter*: Possible Sources?', *The Scott Newsletter*, 9 (1986), 9. The catalogue is *Portrait Drawings by Scottish Artists: 1750–1850* (Edinburgh: Scottish National Portrait Gallery, 24 July–11 September 1955). Most of the accounts of Tipu's death list the objects found in his palace. This particular discovery is not recorded, nor is it mentioned in Theodore Hook, *The Life of General, the Right Honourable Sir David Baird, Bart.*, 2 vols (London, 1832), 2.352. Baird married Miss Campbell Preston of Valleyfield in 1810.

40 Outside fiction Scott seldom had occasion to write about India. He wrote a short article on the burning of widows (*sati*) after a conversation with his cousin James Russell in 1825 (*Journal*, 22–23). It was sent to J. G. Lockhart on 17 February 1826 for publication but is not known to have appeared.

41 *Scott on Himself*, ed. David Hewitt (Edinburgh, 1981), 34–35. The book is in two volumes, the first published in 1763 and the second in two parts in 1778. Scott possessed the first volume in the 2nd edn of 1775 and the second volume in the 1st edn (*CLA*, 253).

42 There is a description of these in Kate Teltscher, *India Inscribed: European and British Writing on India 1600–1800* (Oxford, 1995), chapter 7, ' "Vocabularies of Vile Epithets": British Representations of the Sultans of Mysore'.

43 *CLA*, 238.

44 *CLA*, 312. Scott owned the 2nd edn (London, 1800).

45 The panorama is reproduced in Pauline Rohatgi, 'From Pencil to Panorama: Tipu in Pictorial Perspective', in *The Tiger and the Thistle: Tipu Sultan and the Scots in India 1760–1800*, ed. Anne Buddle (Edinburgh: National Gallery of Scotland, 1999), 51–53.

46 *CLA*, 329.

47 P. R. Krishnaswami, 'Sir Walter Scott's Indian Novel: "The Surgeon's Daughter"', *The Calcutta Review*, n.s. 7 (1919), 431–52 (445–46).

48 A copy of *The Trial of Avadhanum Paupiah* (Madras, 1825) has not been located. The story can, however, be corroborated elsewhere. John Hollond was Governor of Fort St George, Madras, in 1789–90, and his brother Edward was Governor in 1790. The financial improprieties of the Hollond brothers and their dubash Paupiah are mentioned in *Correspondence of Charles, First Marquis Cornwallis*, ed. Charles Ross, 3 vols (London, 1859), 2.64, 66, 493–95, 499. According to a note on 2.66 'Avadanum Paupiah Braminy' died in 1809. David Haliburton is not mentioned by Cornwallis, but he is mentioned in David Leighton's account of Paupiah and his employers in *Vicissitudes of Fort St. George* (Madras & Bombay, 1902) where he is described as resisting the financial chicanery 'and other sinister proposals of the Hollonds' (223). Leighton adds 'He appears to have been a man of some spirit, and probably had interest with the Directors'.

49 *Journal*, 178. Scott says here that Haliburton returned home in 1785; the correct date is *c.* 1797.

50 V .C. P. Hodson, *List of the Officers of the Bengal Army 1758–1834* (London, 1928), Part II, 173; James Ferguson and Robert Menzies Fergusson, *Records of the Clan and Name of Fergusson, Ferguson and Fergus* (Edinburgh, 1895), 12, 185–88.

51 *Journal*, 342–43, entries for 22 and 25 August 1827. By 'Hindhanee' Scott meant Hindustani, which was the usual 18th-century term for Urdu.

52 *Journal*, 352 and 354, entries for 16 and 23 September 1827.

53 MS 913, ff. 165r–84v. Ferguson's sketches and Scott's use of them have been studied by Frank S. Khair-Ullah in 'Orientalism in the Romantics: A Study in Indian Material' (unpublished Ph.D. thesis, University of Edinburgh, 1953), Chapter 6.

54 Krishnaswami, 440–43; W. H. Sleeman, *Rambles and Recollections of an Indian Official*, 2 vols (London, 1844), 2.377–99; *The Raj: India and the British 1600–1947*, ed. C. A. Bayly (London: National Portrait Gallery, 1990), 171.

55 Denys Forrest, *Tiger of Mysore: The Life and Death of Tipu Sultan* (London, 1970), 324–25; M. M. D. L. T. [Maistre de la Tour], *The History of Ayder Ali Khan*, 2 vols (Dublin, 1774), 1.111.

56 Edward Moor, *A Narrative of the Operations of Captain Little's Detachment . . . during the Late Confederacy in India, against Nawab Tippoo Sultan Bahadur* (London, 1794), 117–18.

57 Reginald Heber, *Narrative of a Journey through the Upper Provinces of India, from Calcutta to Bombay, 1824–1825*, 2nd edn (London, 1828), 2.278–79: see *CLA*, 317.

58 MS 913, ff. 167r–67v.

59 Scurry, 113.

60 Moor, 194.

61 All these words are in the *OED*, though sometimes in different spellings, except for: Angrezie, banka, dowrah, molakat, and Owliah.

62 All the Anglo-Indian words in the text are explained in the Glossary; for 'mates and guinea-pigs' see note to 255.4.

63 *Journal*, 352.

64 *Life*, 6.82.

65 Edgar Johnson, *Sir Walter Scott: The Great Unknown*, 2 vols (London, 1970), 2.1070.

66 There had been other novels set in India, of which the best known are perhaps Phebe Gibbes, *Hartly House, Calcutta*, 3 vols (London, 1789), Elizabeth Hamilton, *Transla-*

tion of the Letters of a Hindoo Rajah, 2 vols (London, 1796), and Sydney Owenson, Lady Morgan, *The Missionary, an Indian Tale*, 3 vols, 2nd edn (London, 1811). None of these is in Scott's library, although he knew Elizabeth Hamilton. On the day he finished 'The Surgeon's Daughter' he noted in his *Journal*, 'I understand too there are one or two East Indian novels which have lately appeard—Naboclish' (352). He may be referring to two novels by William Hockley, *Pandurang Hari; or, Memoirs of a Hindoo*, 3 vols (London, 1826) and *The Zenana; or, A Nuwab's Leisure Hours*, 3 vols (London, 1827).

67 See for instance his review of Robert Southey's *The Curse of Kehama*, in *The Quarterly Review* for February 1811, reprinted in *Prose Works*, 17.301–37.

EXPLANATORY NOTES TO 'THE SURGEON'S DAUGHTER'

For shortened forms of reference see 289–90.

147 motto see [Joseph Richardson and others], *Probationary Odes, by the various Candidates for the Office of Poet Laureat to his Majesty, in the room of William Whitehead, Esq. deceased* (London, 1785), 35: no. 8, lines 1–2.

147.19 sang froid *French* dispassion.

147.25 the ostrich lays her eggs in the sand the ostrich was believed to neglect its eggs: 'ova sua fovere neglegit; sed proiecta tantummodo fotu pulveris animantur': 'it does not incubate its eggs; but they are kept alive only by the warmth of sand thrown over them' (Isidore of Seville (*c.* 560–636), *Etymologies*, XII. vii. 20). But it is less neglectful than tradition implies: 'the cock does most of the incubating and sits on the eggs faithfully each night. The Ostrich hen also incubates, always by day when her duller colour has a protective advantage. Often the eggs are left partly covered with sand in the daytime for the sun to keep warm' (Oliver L. Austin, Jr, *Birds of the World*, (London, 1962), 16).

148.1–2 stitched up and boarded printed sheets are folded and sewn to form a gathering, and the gatherings are sewn together to form a book; before the advent of cloth for the purpose in the late 1820s books were sold 'in boards', a stout paper binding.

148.7–9 My publisher ... follows it too closely possibly an allusion to Robert Cadell (1788–1849), the publisher of *Chronicles of the Canongate*, who was a cautious businessman.

148.20 circulating library volume volume from a lending library operating by private subscription: see note to 45.15–16. Such libraries were the usual means by which young ladies obtained novels, and reluctance to be seen reading a novel is common in 18th-century literature: compare Richard Brinsley Sheridan, *The Rivals* (first performed 1775), 1.2.

148.31 to eat an egg, as was my friend's favourite phrase expression indicating a modest or hurried meal: 'The devill cannot stay her, sh'le ont,/ Eate an egge now, and then we must away' (John Fletcher, *Wit Without Money* (1639), 3.2.1–2).

149.6 take fire at become ignited or angry (*OED, fire*, substantive 2b).

149.14 it is Sunday night as the text indicates, Sunday evenings in this period in Scotland were often used for religious edification, and casual visiting for social purposes was unusual. Scott describes the reading of a sermon on a Sunday evening in his childhood in *Letters*, 8.399; see also Henry Cockburn's description of Sir Henry Moncreiff's Sunday evenings, in *Memorials of His Time* (Edinburgh, 1856), 42.

149.17–18 the late Mr Walker of Edinburgh the Rev. Robert Walker (1716–83), Minister of St Giles, Edinburgh, 1754–83. His *Sermons on Practical Subjects* appeared in 4 volumes (1765–96), and were very popular: e.g. a 5th edition of the first volume was published in Edinburgh and London in 1785.

149.27 presbyterian supper Sunday supper. The phrase was current in

Edinburgh at the end of the 18th century (*SND*), and alludes to the Church of Scotland which is presbyterian in organisation.

150.3 the end of the session the Court of Session in Edinburgh, the supreme civil law-court in Scotland, sat for three terms in the year, 12 November–24 December, 15 January–11 March, and 12 May–11 July.

150.4 Inner-House papers documents required for the hearing of a case before the Inner House of the Court of Session. Cases were first heard in the Outer House and came to the Inner House on appeal. The Inner House sat in an inner chamber of Parliament House in Edinburgh.

150.4 take your kail with us have dinner with us. Curled kail is a cabbage-like plant once grown widely in Scotland whose particular advantage is that it can be harvested in winter; it features in many Scottish recipes. Annette Hope comments that it was 'so ubiquitous that the word became a synonym for soup and even for the main meal of the day' (*A Caledonian Feast* (Edinburgh, 1987), 192).

150.7 fain to take my leave glad under the circumstances, content to leave since nothing better was offered (*OED, fain,* adverb 2).

150.12–13 Time, blunt or keen see Joanna Baillie, *Rayner* (1804), 3.2. Scott knew Baillie (1762–1851) and lines from the same song were in his mind as he confronted his financial crash on 21 January 1826 (*Journal*, 62).

150.15 five punctually for the times of dinner see note to 60.10–11.

150.21 a mind to darn her father's linen this was a sensitive matter: Jane Austen wrote of a young woman, Miss Armstrong, 'Like other young Ladies she is considerably genteeler then her Parents; Mrs Armstrong sat darning a pr of Stockings the whole of my visit—' (To Cassandra Austen, 14 September 1804; *Jane Austen's Letters*, ed. Deidre La Faye (Oxford, 1995), 94).

150.28–29 colloquy sublime John Milton, *Paradise Lost* (1667), 8.455.

150.29–30 odds, lengths, bunkers, tee'd balls golfing terms: *odds* refers to the allowance given to a weaker player, a handicap (*SND, odd* III, noun 1); *bunkers* are sandy hollows which are perilous to the player (*SND, bunker* 7); a ball is *tee'd* when it is placed on the tee, the small heap of sand or earth from which it is driven at the start of each hole (*SND, tee* I, noun 1 and II, verb 1). *Lengths* appear to refer to the holding of the club: Olive M. Geddes quotes verses on golf written by Thomas Kincaid in 1687 which include the lines 'At such lenth hold the club as fitts your strenth/ The lighter head requires the longer lenth' (*A Swing through Time: Golf in Scotland 1457–1743* (Edinburgh, 1992), [41]).

150.34 the malicious purpose of the player playing the adversary's ball appears to have been traditional practice in golf. The practice is forbidden in the rules (1744) for the Silver Club competition of the Honourable Company of Edinburgh Golfers, but it was lawful in the game as played by the Royal Burgess Club which laid down in 1790 that 'every person shall have it in his power to play his Ball in any direction he chuses, either upon his Adversary's Ball or otherwise', and which reasserted this position in its rules of 1814. See C. B. Clapcott, 'Some Comments on the Articles and Laws in Playing the Golf' (1945), in *The Clapcott Papers*, ed. Alastair J. Johnston (Edinburgh, 1985), 485–507. See also [John Cundell], *Rules of the Thistle Golf Club, with Some Historical Notices Relative to the Progress of the Game of Golf* (Edinburgh, 1824), which was printed by James Ballantyne and Co., and to which Scott contributed (*CLA*, 300). Rule XIV (50) forbids 'playing on your adversary's ball, not lying in your way to the hole', which implies it was legal to play the opponent's ball on the green.

150.37 Altisidora see Miguel de Cervantes, *Don Quixote* (Part 1, 1605; Part 2, 1615), Part 2, Ch. 70.

150.41–42 looking over his shoulder at a smart uniform i.e. he hankered after the army. Scott recalls his own feelings at having to study law when he would have preferred, had his lameness allowed it, to be a soldier.

151.3   a quantum sufficit   *Latin* a sufficient quantity.

151.7   the music of the Freischutz   the opera *Der Freischütz* (*The Marksman*) by the German romantic composer, Carl Maria Friedrich Ernst von Weber (1786–1826). It was first performed in Berlin in 1821, and in Edinburgh in 1824 (James C. Dibdin, *Annals of the Edinburgh Stage* (Edinburgh, 1888), 310).

151.10   horning and hooping   blowing of horns and shouting (whooping) as by the foresters and huntsmen in the opera.

151.11   the Seventh Hussars   cavalry regiment taking its name from the light horsemen of 15th-century Hungary. They were stationed in Edinburgh and Perth from April 1826 to March 1827, having already been in Scotland 1819–20 (Dobie).

151.27   pro tanto   *Latin* as far as this matter is concerned. Normand comments 'though this is not a legal term, it is still a term more often used by lawyers than by others. It is a minor example of the influence of Scott's legal training on his writing.'

151.37–38   Senate House of Scotland   the Court of Session, whose judges are known as Senators.

152.12–13   on hospitable thoughts intent   John Milton, *Paradise Lost* (1667), 5.332.

152.19–21   quart … pint, in the old Scottish liberal acceptation   two imperial pints (1.14 litres) and 3 imperial pints (1.7 litres).

152.33   Deil a bit   *Scots* not a bit; *deil* is the Scots form of 'devil'.

152.36   chief and proper end   alluding to the Catechism, a list of questions and answers which teach the doctrines of Christianity. The first question in the Westminster Larger Catechism (1648) is 'What is the chief and highest end of man?': Thomas F. Torrance, *The School of Faith: The Catechisms of the Reformed Church* (London, 1959), [185].

152.43   I left no calling for this idle trade   Alexander Pope, 'An Epistle from Mr Pope to Dr Arbuthnot' (1734), line 129.

153.38   Porteous Roll   *Scots law* list of persons drawn up by the Justice Clerk for indictment before the High Court of Justiciary (Scotland's highest criminal court) when on circuit (*CSD*).

153.42   Schiller   the German dramatist Johann Christoph Friedrich Schiller (1759–1805) whose tragedy *Die Räuber* (1781) started a fashion for tragic heroes at war with society. A translation by Alexander Fraser Tytler entitled *The Robbers* appeared in 1792.

154.15–16   two brothers, the greatest rascals   Franz Moor tries to kill his father, and his brother Karl, in disguise, makes love to his own betrothed.

154.24–25   Highlanders into every story   Fairscribe is referring to the two stories in the first volume of *Chronicles of the Canongate*, 'The Highland Widow' and 'The Two Drovers'.

154.25   velis et remis   *Latin* with sails and oars, a proverbial expression meaning with all resources.

154.25–26   the old days of Jacobitism   see the Historical Note to 'The Highland Widow', 319–20.

154.27   innovations in Kirk and State   perhaps referring to the movement towards parliamentary and burgh reform which led to the Reform Act of 1832; and to the opposition in the Scottish church to lay patronage, the right of certain landowners to appoint ministers to parishes, which led to the Veto Act of 1834 which declared that no minister should be placed in a church against the wishes of the congregation.

154.28–29   the glorious Revolution   the events of 1688–89 which brought the Protestant William III and Queen Mary to the throne in place of the

Catholic James VII and II, and which established the Presbyterian church (the Kirk) as the national church of Scotland.

154.29–30   tartan plaid ... white surplice   characteristic dress of a Scottish highlander and of an Episcopalian clergyman, both regarded with suspicion by a lowland Presbyterian.

154.38   Highlands ... the theme is becoming a little exhausted   see note to 67.7–8.

155.10–11   India ... Scot to thrive in   Henry Dundas, 1st Viscount Melville (1742–1811), was accused, as President of the Board of Control of the East India Company, of giving undue preference to Scots in appointing to Indian posts. In March 1787 James Gillray produced a cartoon entitled 'The Board of Control or the Blessings of a Scotch Dictator' which depicted ragged Scots waiting for posts in India. See Holden Furber, *Henry Dundas* (London, 1931), 31–34.

155.11   fifty years back   Chrystal Croftangry started his *Chronicles* in 1826 (53.43). The story to follow is set fifty years earlier, in the 1770s: see the Historical Note, 359–60.

155.15   the Cape of Good Hope   the most southerly point of the African continent, rounded by ships from Britain on the sea route to India.

155.22   the delightful pages of Orme   *A History of the Military Transactions of the British Nation in Indostan, from the year MDCCXLV* (1763, 1778) by Robert Orme (1728–1801). Orme served with the East India Company in Calcutta until 1754 when he was appointed to the Council in Madras, where he remained until his return to Britain in 1758. He was appointed official historian of the East India Company in 1769. Scott records that during an illness in adolescence he amused himself by re-enacting battles with the aid of shells, seeds and pebbles. One of the books which inspired such play was 'Orme's interesting and beautiful history of Indostan, where copious plans aided by the clear and luminous explanations of the author rendered my imitative amusement peculiarly easy' (*Scott on Himself*, ed. David Hewitt (Edinburgh, 1981), 34–35).

155.27   like the Spaniards among the Mexicans   the Spanish conquered Mexico in 1518–21. Comparison between the British in India and the Spanish in America was not uncommon. A striking instance is Richard Brinsley Sheridan's *Pizarro* (1799), a play about the Spanish conquest of Peru which was recognised as alluding to the impeachment of Warren Hastings for his conduct in India (Sara Suleri, *The Rhetoric of English India* (Chicago and London, 1992), 68–74).

155.28   like Homer's demigods among the warring mortals   Homer (*c.* 8th century BC) the Greek poet to whom the epic poems the *Iliad* and the *Odyssey* are attributed. Gods from the Greek pantheon play a part in the narratives. Demigods are either inferior gods, or the result of a union between a god and a mortal (*OED*).

155.28–29   Clive and Caillaud   Robert Clive (1725–74), Lord Clive, was the hero of British military campaigns in India in the 18th century. He started his career in south India where he distinguished himself at the siege of Arcot in 1751. He was sent to Bengal after the fall of Calcutta in 1756 and defeated the Nawab of Bengal at the battle of Plassey (1757), leading to the British gaining control of Bengal and the beginning of the British territorial empire in India. Clive returned to England in 1767; his conduct in India, and the source of the wealth with which he returned, were subsequently investigated by Parliament. Brigadier-General John Caillaud (d. 1810), who like Clive is frequently mentioned by Orme, was active in south India against the French until 1759 when he was sent to Bengal.

155.29–30   Jove ... Mars or Neptune   Jove, or Jupiter, is the supreme god of the Roman pantheon, in which Mars is the god of war, and Neptune the god of the sea.

155.32–34 Hindustan...Malay Hindustan is the name for Hindi-speaking north India, but is frequently used for the whole peninsula. Of the character of the Hindus Orme explains 'The sway of despotic government has taught them the necessity of patience' (Robert Orme, *Historical Fragments of the Mogul Empire* (London, 1805), 431). Rajputs were Hindus of north and central India distinguished for their warrior spirit and for their resistance to the Mughal conquerors. The Moslemah (Muslims) are the descendants of the Mughal invaders who entered northern India from Persia in the 16th century and founded an extensive empire. (The *OED* points out that 'Moslemah' is an erroneous plural form of Moslem; Scott's use of the term in *The Talisman* (1825) is the only instance cited.) Malays had a particular reputation for violent behaviour in the 18th century.

155.38 to the Assembly to dance in the Assembly Rooms in George Street, Edinburgh (see note to 66.7–8).

155.39–40 the story of poor Menie Grey for Scott's source for this tale see Historical Note, 355–57.

156.15 woman of about thirty for Menie to be about thirty the painting would have to date from the 1780s, rather than 'the middle of the eighteenth century' (see Historical Note, 360), but perhaps Scott refers to the style of portraiture.

156.36 to condescend more articulately upon to specify, to give detail; *articulately* probably does not refer to clarity of utterance, but to addressing the topic article by article (*OED*, *articulately* 4).

156.42 the new walks of Prince's Street or Heriot Row Princes Street was completed in 1805 (see notes to 45.29–30 and 52.26). The ground W of the Mound was enclosed and planted as gardens in about 1820, the lay-out being superintended by Scott's friend James Skene of Rubislaw. The gardens belonged to the proprietors of Princes Street, who presented Scott with a key in May 1827 (*Letters*, 10.216); they were made over to the City in 1876. Heriot Row, a handsome residential street with private gardens, N of Queen Street, was built in 1803–08 (A. J. Youngson, *The Making of Classical Edinburgh* (Edinburgh, 1966), 208).

156.43 tête-à-tête *French* face to face, intimate conversation.

157.6–8 As unconcern'd...happiness nor pain Sir Charles Sedley (1639?–1701), 'Child and Maiden', lines 2–4.

157.11 an old stager a veteran, an old hand (*OED*).

157.16 well to pass well-to-do, well-off (*OED*, *pass*, verb 3b).

157.18 the old brass that buys the new pan *proverbial* 'His old brass will buy you a new pan', said to a young woman marrying a rich old man: James Kelly, *Complete Collection of Scottish Proverbs* (London, 1721), 163; Ramsay, 87.

157.33 beaux yeux de ma cassette *French* 'the bright eyes of my money-box'; said by the miser Harpagon in Molière (Jean-Baptiste Poquelin), *L'Avare* (1668), 5.3.

157.25 we are partners at a game of cards.

157.26–27 who the deuce exclamation of impatience, who the devil?

157.35 what old Lintot meant the publisher Bernard Lintot (1675–1736) who published the poems of Alexander Pope (1688–1744). The story is told in John Nichols, *Literary Anecdotes of the Eighteenth Century*, 9 vols (London, 1812–15), 8.172.

158 motto Samuel Johnson, 'On the Death of Dr Robert Levet' (1782), lines 13–24. Levet was a humble doctor who had tended the poor with so little reward that he was glad of shelter in Johnson's house.

158.26 the Rambler Samuel Johnson (1709–84); he was often referred to by the name of his periodical paper *The Rambler* (1750–52) which was admired for its morality and practical wisdom.

158.27 Gideon Grey Lockhart records that 'many things in the character and manners of Mr Gideon Gray of Middlemas . . . were considered at the time by Sir Walter's neighbours on Tweedside as copied from Dr Ebenezer Clarkson of Selkirk' (*Life*, 7.88); see also 'Our Gideon Grays', in John Brown, *Horae Subsecivae* (Edinburgh, 1858), [439]–54 and W. S. Crockett, *The Scott Originals* (London and Edinburgh, 1912), 369–[72].

159.4–5 Four years the average length of a Parliament.

159.6–7 a score or two of quiet electors representatives of the royal burghs in Parliament were chosen by delegates called 'electors', whose dinners were a common subject of satire.

159.10–11 from the Townhead to the Townfit from the top to the bottom (Townfoot) of the town.

159.11 a dose of salts short for Epsom salts, a preparation of magnesium sulphate given as a medicine for digestive disorders.

159.16 the ghostly lover of Leonora see *Lenore* (1774), a ballad by Gottfried August Bürger (1747–94), in which a dead lover comes on horseback in response to the heroine's grieving. Scott translated it as *William and Helen* in 1796, and published it as his first literary achievement.

159.27 Mungo Park (1771–1806), the explorer of the river Niger, who practised as a surgeon in Peebles 1801–05. Scott knew Park, whose brother was his Sheriff's officer, and heard at first hand his views on travelling in Africa and in the Scottish Border (*Life*, 2.10–13).

159.32–33 the primitive curse childbirth, from Genesis 3.16: 'Unto the woman he said, I will greatly multiply thy sorrow and thy conception; in sorrow thou shalt bring forth children'.

159.42 the village of Middlemas on the location of Middlemas see the Historical Note, 357–58.

160.13 by diploma from the Incorporation of Surgeons in Edinburgh, founded early in the 16th century. Many practised without obtaining it.

160.19 Pestle and Mortar named after implements used in preparing medicines. A pestle is used to pound ingredients placed in the bowl called the mortar, and they became the unofficial insignia of the apothecary's profession.

160.27 the goddess Lucina the Roman goddess of childbirth.

160.32 the honoured door Andrew Lang pointed out that Gideon Grey's house does not appear to be modelled on that of Dr Clarkson, which was on the N side of the market-place in Selkirk (*The Waverley Novels*, Border Edition, 48 vols (London, 1892–94), 46.[225]).

160.40 on the winner compare the bets on the race between two old women in Fanny Burney, *Evelina* (1778), Letter 68.

161.6 Guide us expression of surprise or consternation, short for 'God guide us' (*CSD*).

161.1 Canny against take care on, proceed cautiously on.

161.33 Quos ego of Neptune 'Whom I . . .', the unfinished threat of Neptune to the winds in Virgil, *Aeneid* (29–19 BC), 1.135.

162.9 in the golden age before the disappearance of the gold guinea coin. In 1663 the Royal Mint was authorised to issue gold coins of the value of 20s. (£1) for the use of traders to Africa. They were popularly known as *guineas* because they were used in the trade to the Guinea coast, and made of gold from Guinea. In 1717 their value was fixed at 21s. (£1.05); the last coinage of guineas was in 1813. See *OED*, *guinea* 3a.

163.12 a fause face *Scots* a false face, a mask (*CSD*).

163.15 brought to bed in childbirth.

163.22–23 in the elder comedy the phrase usually refers to Greek comedy produced in Athens during the 5th century BC, in which the actors wore grotesque masks. Zilia's 'thin silk mask' makes it more likely that Scott is referring to English Restoration drama (1660–1700) in which women wore masks out of doors and in the course of intrigues.

164.13 reported to be in orders 'reported' because it was against the law for a priest to perform the services of the Roman Catholic church from the Reformation until the Catholic Emancipation Act of 1829.

164.18 established in church and state see note to 154.28–29.

164.20 the Cameronian regiment or 26th of Foot, formed in 1689 to support the cause of the Protestant succession from among the Cameronians, Presbyterian Covenanters who were followers of Richard Cameron (d. 1680).

165.26 private marriage i.e. a clandestine marriage effected without the proclamation of banns (public proclamation in the parish church of the parties' intention to marry). This would have been a permissible form of marriage in England prior to the passing of the Marriage Act of 1753 (26 George II, c. 33).

166.43 articles forbidden by the Mosaic law in Leviticus Ch. 11, of which the most important to a Scottish household was pork in any form.

167.26–27 the "bonny hand" the fine profit (*OED, hand*, substantive 27).

168.34 King's Messenger or messenger at arms: officer appointed by the Lord Lyon King of Arms to execute the orders of the Court of Session and the High Court of Justiciary.

168.35 baron-bailie's officer minor official in a barony, similar to a constable, who acted on the orders of the *baron-bailie*, the legal representative of the baron. A *barony* was an estate held directly from the crown whose owner, the baron, had a heritable jurisdiction to try all offences committed within the barony; heritable jurisdictions were abolished in 1748 (see Historical Note to 'The Highland Widow', 319–20).

169.13 Moncada the name of the Spanish monk in Charles Robert Maturin's *Melmoth the Wanderer* (1820).

169.13 High Treason violation of a subject's allegiance to the sovereign, particularly in circumstances where civil and political disorder might follow.

169.27 the Esculapian militia the cohorts of Aesculapius, the classical god of healing.

169.30 better part better half, wife.

170.3 stern-looking old man the inflexible character of Zilia's father may be influenced by Scott's experience of harassment for debt by a Jewish money-lender, William Abud, over the winter of 1826–27 (*Life*, 7.83–87).

170.43 bail not be taken capital crimes (which included treason) were not bailable.

171.3 King George George II (reigned 1727–60).

171.6 The forty-five has not been so far gone by the Jacobite rising of 1745–46: see note to 68.21.

171.9 Lady Ogilvy, Lady MacIntosh, Flora Macdonald Margaret (*c.*1724–57), wife of David, Lord Ogilvy (Jacobite Earl of Airlie): she assisted her husband in 1745–46, was arrested after Culloden but escaped and died in France. Anne (d. 1787), wife of Aeneas Mackintosh of Mackintosh: while her husband raised men for the Government she raised many of the clan for Prince Charles Edward; arrested after Culloden she was released six weeks later: see Sir Bruce Gordon Seton and Jean G. Arnot, *The Prisoners of the '45*, Scottish History Society, 3 vols (Edinburgh, 1928–29), 1.212–17. Flora Macdonald (1722–90) is the Jacobite heroine famous for helping Prince Charles Edward to escape to Skye in 1746 disguised as her maid; she was arrested and taken to London but was released under the Act of Indemnity of 1747.

171.11–12 jouk and let the jaw gae by *proverbial literally* bend (or stoop) and let the wave (or torrent) pass, i.e: bend to the storm: see James Kelly,

Complete Collection of Scottish Proverbs (London, 1727), 189; Ramsay, 91; *ODEP*, 414.

172.21 To the parish with the bastard! i.e. committing the child to being brought up by local charity or poor-relief, organised by parish.

174.1 led horse spare horse, led by an attendant.

174.16 take pot-luck take one's chance as to what is in the pot, used in cases of impromptu hospitality.

174.18–19 lamb and spinnage, and a veal Florentine lamb and spinach is a common combination in Scottish cookery: 'Lamb-Cutlets with Spinage' appears in *The Cook and Housewife's Manual ... by Mistress Margaret Dods* [Mrs Johnston], 5th edn (Edinburgh, 1833), 254. Veal Florentine is a pastry-covered pie of veal and spices, thought to have been introduced into Scotland from France: see F. Marian McNeill, *The Scots Kitchen* (London and Glasgow, 1929), 136–37. Annette Hope points out that 'whereas the French invariably use "florentine" to denote the presence of spinach in a dish, Scots usage signifies that one of the ingredients is pastry' (*A Caledonian Feast* (Edinburgh, 1987), 308).

174.23 Antigua rum rum from Antigua in the West Indies, used as the base for punch, a drink composed of spirits, lemon and spices.

174.28–29 brewed a bitter browst *proverbial* brewed a bitter brew (*ODEP*, 85).

174.33 cleek to seize, snatch.

175.22 they have no territorial property Jews, regarded as aliens, were not allowed to own land in Britain. Jews were banished from England in 1290, and although some returned, especially from Spain and Portugal fleeing the Spanish Inquisition, they had no legal protection until 1655. The first organised Jewish community in Scotland was established in Edinburgh in 1816. Jews were not given full rights as citizens until 1890: see *Encyclopaedia Judaica*, 16 vols (Jerusalem, 1971), 6.751–56, 14.1035–36.

175.29 the Pope 18th-century Popes sanctioned several measures against Jews in the name of protecting Catholic orthodoxy (*Encyclopaedia Judaica*, 13.859).

175.29 the Pretender a name for the Jacobite claimant to the throne of Britain, from French *prétendant*, claimant, but usually used disparagingly. Jews were loyal to the Hanoverian goverment, and the Jewish financier Samson Gideon helped the maintenance of financial stability during the Jacobite rising of 1745–46 (*Encyclopaedia Judaica*, 7.560).

175.40 the good Samaritan see Luke 10.25–37.

176.32 Menie the Magnum notes that the name Menie is a diminutive of Marion (48.219).

176.40 bridge composed of red-hot iron reference to al-Sirat, the narrow bridge over hell in Muslim belief (*The Encyclopaedia of Islam New Edition* (Leiden, 1960–), Vol. 8, ed. C. E. Bosworth and others (Leiden, 1997), 670–71. The bridge is usually described like a sharp blade rather than red-hot; Scott mentions 'a bar of red-hot iron, stretched across a bottomless gulph' in his Introduction to 'A Lyke-Wake Dirge' (*Minstrelsy*, 3.164), where he gives his source as 'D'Herbelot, *Bibliothèque Orientale*', i.e. Barthelemi D'Herbelot, *Bibliothèque Orientale; ou Dictionnaire Universel, contenant Tout ce qui fait connoître les Peuples d l'Orient* (La Haye, 1777–79): see *CLA*, 267. The reference in D'Herbelot has not been traced.

176.40–41 all the pieces of paper in the version in the *Minstrelsy* the 'good works of each true believer, assuming a substantial form, will then interpose betwixt his feet and this "*Bridge of Dread*"' (3.164).

177.17 par excellence *French* pre-eminently.

179.8 fourteenth year in Scots law a boy came out of pupillarity on his 14th birthday, at which point a guardian ceased to have legal control of the person of his ward, although he controlled his property during the years of minority, i.e. until the ward's 21st birthday.

180.19   with much proper stuff   *Macbeth*, 3.4.60.

180.31   hear . . . incline   like Desdemona listening to Othello's account of his adventures: see *Othello*, 1.3.145–46.

180.40   to turn their hearts, as Scripture sayeth   see Malachi 4.6; Luke 1.17.

181.2–3   Galatian, or Sir William Wallace, or Robin Hood   the Magnum notes: 'Galatian is a name of a person famous in Christmas gambols' (48.224). He was the hero of a folk-play performed by 'guizards', or maskers, who went from house to house on New Year's Day in Scotland: see Robert Chambers, *Popular Rhymes, Fireside Stories, and Amusements of Scotland* (Edinburgh, 1842), 68–69; the source of this version seems to have been Scott. Sir William Wallace (d. 1305) was the Scottish leader in the wars against Edward I; his story was told in Blind Harry's *Wallace* (*c*. 1460), which appeared in a modernised version by William Hamilton of Gilbertfield in 1722, and was recounted in ballads and chapbooks. Robin Hood is the legendary Nottinghamshire outlaw celebrated in many ballads and songs, who was thought in Scott's day to have lived in the late 12th-century.

181.35–37   Temple and tower . . . went to the ground   John Milton, 'Captain or colonel, or knight in arms' (1642), lines 11–12.

182.7   if I think fit   Middlemas was legally free to do so after his 14th birthday: see note to 179.8.

182.9–10   Stevenlaw's Land   in Scots *land* means 'building' or 'tenement'.

182.18   pudding-eater   nickname for an Englishman recorded from 1726 (*OED*, *pudding* 11). A pudding, which could be savoury or sweet, was cooked by boiling or steaming. Scott, in a letter to Maria Edgeworth, writes: 'eggs and flour and suet put together *compose* a pudding that is are [*sic*] united into that generous and nutritious mass which we Scotchmen upbraid the English with being so partial to' (*Letters*, 9.80).

182.26–27   drummed out of the borough   expelled publicly to the accompaniment of the beating of a drum, heightening the disgrace (*OED drum*, verb 7).

183.12   years of discretion   the time of life at which a person is presumed to be capable of exercising discretion or prudence; i.e. the age of twenty-one. See note to 179.8.

183.43   was not i' the vein   *Richard III*, 4.2.122.

184.5   Hout awa'   expression of remonstrance or regret, Oh dear, Oh no.

184.22   my certie   expression of surprise or emphasis, assuredly.

185.14   they had nothing to do with   English law differs from Scots law.

185.37–38   the unwise son of the wisest of men   Rehoboam, son of Solomon, in 1 Kings 12.8, who 'forsook the counsel of the old men, which they had given him, and consulted with the young men that were grown up with him'.

186.1   the amende honorable   *French* an apology, honourable recompense.

187   motto   these lines are probably Scott's own, written in allusion to Charles Dibdin (1768–1833), 'Tom and Dick. An Urbiad, or Town Eclogue', which compares 'Tom the carman' and 'cooper Dick' (*Comic Tales and Lyrical Fancies* (London, 1825), 25–36).

187.27–28   Edinburgh . . . taking their degree   it was usual for students to enter Edinburgh University at Richard Middlemas's age of 14 (179.8); Scott himself attended his first classes there at 12.

188.9–10   hornpipes, rigs, strathspeys, and reels   Robert Burns, 'Tam o' Shanter' (1790), line 117.

188.32–33 small sword light sword, tapering gradually from the hilt to the point, used in fencing.

188.33–34 lessons from a performer at the theatre in the 1760s it was common for actors to give elocution lessons to literary and fashionable people who wished to acquire an educated, southern English pronunciation. For example, James Boswell received lessons from an actor named Love, and in 1761 attended the lectures of Thomas Sheridan (1719–88), the Irish actor-manager: see *Boswell's London Journal 1762–1763*, ed. Frederick A. Pottle (London, 1950), 8–9. See also Henry Grey Graham, *The Social Life of Scotland in the Eighteenth Century*, 4th edn (London, 1937), 118–21.

188.35 the playhouse the first theatre to be built in Edinburgh operated 1746–67 in Playhouse Close, off the S side of the Canongate; the most famous play to receive its first production there was John Home's *Douglas* in 1756. The first licensed theatre in Scotland, the new Theatre Royal in Shakespeare Square at the N end of the North Bridge, opened in 1769.

189.38 the races perhaps alluding to the races at Selkirk where the race-course is reputed to date from the 17th century; the more celebrated races are, however, at Kelso where a new race-course was established in 1822.

190.20 Loupenheight in Scots *loup* means 'leap', 'bound', or 'dance'.

190.27–28 shoot madly from his sphere see *A Midsummer Night's Dream*, 2.1.153–54: 'And certain stars shot madly from their spheres/ To hear the sea-maid's music'.

191.4–5 pro tempore *Latin* for the time.

191.19 keep down a bass keep their end up against bass instruments in the band.

191.22 the gods of the Epicureans Epicureans were followers of the Greek philosopher Epicurus (341–270 BC). In his *De Rerum Natura* the Epicurean poet Lucretius (94–55 BC) speaks of the abode of the gods where nothing disturbs their peace of mind (3.18–24), and of the pleasure the wise derive from looking down on the wandering and striving of others (2.7–10).

191 motto see 'Graeme and Bewick', stanza 27, in *Minstrelsy*, 3.83.

191.37 the Physic Garden a garden specialising in medicinal plants.

192.13 canny Norrthumberrland the term *canny*, meaning 'good', 'pleasant', 'worthy', is regularly applied to Northumberland and Newcastle.

192.14 northern accent on the letter R Northumbrians pronounce the letter R with a burr, technically an uvular trill, rather like the French pronunciation: see *The Oxford Companion to the English Language*, ed. Tom McArthur (Oxford, 1992), 168.

192.16 chiefs and thanes mocking reference to the local gentry: *chiefs* implies the chiefs of Highland clans; *thane* is a Scots title, mostly found N of the Forth, for someone holding land of the king (see Historical Note, 358).

192.17 a hog in armour *proverbial* an expression for an awkward person embarrassed in his movements by fine clothing (*ODEP*, 376).

192.35–36 mortal combat fight which does not end until one of the participants is killed.

193.1 Middlemas of that Ilk the phrase *of that Ilk* means 'of the same place' where the patronymic and the territorial designation are the same (see note to 23.12). The usage is usually confined to landed families, and this is an insulting reminder to Richard that his name is simply that of the town in which he was born.

193.14 pair of mortars there is a submerged pun here: pistols suggest pestles and hence mortars; see note to 160.19.

195.26 Strath-Devon and the Carse the river Devon runs S from Perthshire into the Forth; its higher reaches are in Glendevon. A *strath* is a wide valley; a *carse* is low-lying land beside a river, here perhaps the Carse of Forth, which extends E from the river Devon on both sides of the Forth. These names imply that Scott at this point envisaged Middlemas to be N of the Forth: see Historical Note, 357–58.

195.37–39 **a sort of Leah . . . a lively Rachael** like Jacob in Genesis 29.16–30.

197.34 **a happy pendant to** to make a pair with; *pendant* is French, meaning 'match', 'fellow'.

197.35 **Love me, love my dog** proverbial Ramsay, 98; *ODEP*, 492.

198.13–14 **push . . . your fortune** engage actively in making one's fortune (*OED, push*, verb 11b).

198.20 **speaks scholarly and wisely** see *The Merry Wives of Windsor*, 1.3.2.

198.26–27 **the Company's service** the East India Company, which had the monopoly of trade with the East (see Historical Note, 358). It was granted its charter in 1600 and survived until 1858.

198.32 **Oh, Delhi! oh, Golconda!** Delhi was the capital of the Mughal empire. Golconda was a sultanate in central India which succumbed to the Mughals in 1636; it was famous for its diamond mines and its name came to signify wealth.

198.35 **he may realize it** Scott had been given precise information about prize-money awarded to soldiers in India in a letter of 6 August 1800 by his brother-in-law, Charles Carpenter, in south India: 'The picking among the military in the way of prize money has been nearly in the following proportions— a general Pags. 27000—Colonel, 10,000—Lt Col. 7000—Major 5000—Captain 2200; a Subaltern 1080' (MS 3874, f. 76r–76v). *Pags.* are pagodas, gold coins of south India. It appears that this was the distribution of money after the storming of Seringapatam in 1799, and Carpenter adds 'every cash of which they fully deserved'. There is a table showing 'Distribution of Prize Money, and Gratuity to the several Ranks of the Main Army in India', in Alexander Dirom, *A Narrative of the Campaign in India which terminated the war with Tippoo Sultan, in 1792* (London, 1793), 269–70.

199.9 **lacs and crores of rupees** the rupee was the silver coin of the Mughal empire and became the standard coin of India. The Anglo-Indian terms *lac* and *crore* mean respectively one hundred thousand and ten million (i.e. 100 lacs) and are commonly applied to quantities of money.

199.30 **a diamond** until diamonds were found in Brazil in 1725 and South Africa in 1867 Indian diamonds supplied the world (*Arts of India: 1550–1900*, ed. John Guy and Deborah Swallow (London: Victoria and Albert Museum, 1990), 110). The compliment to Menie, therefore, likens her to the riches of India.

199.35–36 **the land of cowries** India. Cowries are small, translucent shells found in the Indian Ocean and used as money in some parts of Africa and south Asia; cowries were in use as very small denomination coins in NE India until the second decade of the 19th century. See Radha Kamal Mukherjee and K. K. Datta, 'Economic and Social Conditions in India in the Eighteenth Century', in *The Maratha Supremacy*, ed. R. C. Majumdar, *The History and Culture of the Indian People*, Vol. 8 (Bombay, 1977), 747.

199.38 **nabob** an Anglo-Indian spelling (from Portuguese *nababo* from Urdu *nawwab*) of the title of an official or governor of a province under the Mughal empire, otherwise rendered as Nawab or Nawaub. Orme notes that 'the title of Nabob . . . signifies Deputy' (Orme, 1.36).

199.40 **bow-string** string of a bow, used for strangling offenders.

199.42 **ex officio** *Latin* by virtue of office.

199.43 **with the tear in her ee** proverbial with the tear in her eye (*ODEP*, 442).

201.4 **Novum Castrum** *Latin* new castle referring to Newcastle upon Tyne, whose castle was founded in 1080.

201.5 **doctus utriusque juris** *Latin* learned in both kinds of law, ecclesiastical and civil, and so qualified to practise.

201.21 **hardened his heart against the cries of the needy** see e.g. Deuteronomy 15.7, 11: 'thou shalt not harden thine heart', and 'Thou shalt open thine hand wide unto thy brother, to thy poor and to thy needy, in thy land'.

201.22–23 **the honourable East India Company** see note to 198.26–27.

201.23–24 **wonderful company of merchants ... be termed princes** the full name of the East India Company was the 'Company of Merchants of London Trading into the East Indies'. From being a trading company the East India Company in the 18th century gained political control over large areas of India.

201.25–26 **the directors in Leadenhall Street** the Company was governed by a Court of Directors whose office was in Leadenhall Street, London. East India House was demolished in 1862 and the Lloyd's building now occupies the site: see *The London Encyclopaedia*, ed. Ben Weinreb and Christopher Hibbert (London, 1983), 250.

201.27 **rose like an exhalation** a description of one of the buildings of Hell in John Milton, *Paradise Lost* (1667), 1.711.

201.28 **its formidable extent** by 1827 most of India was ruled either directly by Britain under a Governor-General or by Indian rulers in British protectorates.

201.30 **the account of battles fought** the most important battles of 'the middle of the eighteenth century' were at Arcot (1751) and Wandiwash (1760) which checked French ambitions in India and gave the British control over the Coromandel Coast in south India, Plassey (1757) which led to British control of Bengal, and Buxar (1764) where Sir Hector Munro defeated the Nawab of the northern state of Oudh (Awadh). Sara Suleri observes that 'before the 1780s, India had largely functioned in the British imagination as an area beyond the scope of cartography, a space most inviting to European wills to plunder and to the flamboyant entrepreneurship of such a figure as Robert Clive' (*The Rhetoric of English India* (Chicago and London, 1992), 26).

201.32–33 **Oriental wealth and Oriental luxury** large fortunes were made by the Company's employees by trade and by war. Salaries were not high but were supplemented by perquisites and sinecures and by opportunities to undertake private trading ventures, in which accusations of corruption and extortion were not infrequent. 'Luxury' was always part of the Western perception of the East; the portable sort which an adventurer might bring home would include gold, gems and fine textiles.

201.34 **wealthy of the British nobility** the most famous example was that of Robert Clive (see note to 155.28–29) who was given the title Baron Clive of Plassey in 1762, and who spent the money he gained in India buying land, particularly in his native Shropshire. In response to a Parliamentary enquiry into the sources of his wealth he is said to have declared, 'By God, Mr. Chairman, at this moment I stand astonished at my own moderation!' The threat of new Indian money to the old landed families of Britain is one of the themes of Samuel Foote's satirical comedy *The Nabob* (1772).

201.34 **El Dorado** *Spanish* the land of gold imagined by the Spanish conquerors of America.

202.5 **India stock and India bonds** the East India Company was a joint-stock company and Hillary could invest in it by purchasing either variably priced stock or fixed price bonds.

202.7 **no liver complaint** a common health risk of Europeans in India. William Mackintosh comments: 'The English in Hindostan are universally subject to the bile, which almost always terminates in the liver and becomes dangerous. This disorder they denominate *the liver'* (*Travels in Europe, Asia, and Africa*, 2 vols (London 1782), 1.352n).

202.15 the storming of a Pettah or the plundering of a Pagoda a *pettah* is a town or village outside a fort and sometimes itself fortified; a *pagoda* is a temple or sacred building. Orme refers to 'a large pettah, by which name the people on the coast of Coromandel call every town contiguous to a fortress' (1.147). An extreme example of what could be seized as the result of military conquest were the treasures captured after the taking of Seringapatam in 1799, and listed by many writers, e.g. 'The Captured Treasures', in *Narrative Sketches*, 96–108, and Scurry, 236–43.

202.16 treasure about their persons a spectacular example is the treasure found on the body of Tipu Sultan at Seringapatam and described in Scurry, 230–231, and *Narrative Sketches*, 87.

202.25 war and intestine disorders after the death of the Emperor Aurangzeb in 1707 the Mughal empire began to lessen its hold. The Nawabs of provinces asserted their independence and the Marathas extended their conquests. That these developments led to 'uncontrolled violence and endemic warfare' is questioned by modern historians: see P. J. Marshall, 'The British in Asia: Trade to Dominion', in *The Oxford History of the British Empire*, Vol. 2, *The Eighteenth Century*, ed. P. J. Marshall (Oxford, 1998), 495.

202.36 communings not a technical term of law, but it is used to denote communications and negotiations which precede a concluded agreement or contract (Normand).

203.5–6 recruiting captain . . . recruiting sergeant commissioned and non-commissioned officers respectively, in charge of getting recruits for the service. T. A. Heathcote writes about recruiting for the East India Company army: 'Not until 1799 was the Company granted power to recruit and train recruits in England and subject them to military law there. Permanent recruiting offices were set up, manned by recruiting officers and sergeants of the Company's service, in London, Edinburgh, Dublin, and Liverpool' (*The Indian Army: The Garrison of British Imperial India, 1822–1922* (Newton Abbot, 1974), 156).

203.6 Palaces rose like mushrooms a common image for the sudden appearance of wealth in India. In Henry Mackenzie's periodical paper *The Lounger* John Homespun describes how 'my neighbour Mushroom's son, who had sent out to India about a dozen years ago, returned home with a fortune' (*The Lounger*, 17 (28 May 1785)).

203.8–9 from the royal tiger down to the jackall the former is the tiger of Bengal, regarded as the biggest and noblest kind. The howling of jackals was remarked by travellers in India. *Hobson-Jobson* notes that the 'jackal takes the place of the fox as the object of hunting "meets" in India; the indigenous fox being too small for sport' (443).

203.9 The luxuries of a Natch or nautch, Indian dancing performed by professional dancing-girls, regarded by travellers as one of the 'luxuries' of India. William Mackintosh gives this account: 'One particular class of women are allowed to be openly prostituted: these are the famous dancing girls. Their attitudes and movements are very easy, and not ungraceful. Their persons are delicately formed, gaudily decorated, and highly perfumed. By the continuation of wanton attitudes, they acquire, as they grow warm in the dance, a frantic lasciviousness themselves, and communicate, by a natural contagion, the most voluptuous desires to the beholders' (*Travels in Europe, Asia, and Africa*, 2 vols (London, 1782), 1.331).

203.13–14 a stream . . . flowed over sands of gold in many parts of the world gold is found on the surface, in the sand of rivers.

203.14–15 Fata Morgana *Italian* Fairy Morgan, known in French as

Morgan le Fay, a character in Arthurian legend. Fata Morgana appears in *Orlando Innamorato* (1487) by Matteo Maria Boiardo (1441?–94) and *Orlando Furioso* (1532) by Ludovico Ariosto (1474–1533) where she lives at the bottom of a lake and dispenses the treasures of the earth.

203.16   ottar of roses   or *attar*, a very fragrant, volatile oil derived from rose petals. John Homespun finds in the conversation of the Mushrooms, newly returned from India, 'such accounts of Nabobs, Rajahs, and Rajah-Pouts, elephants, palanquins, and processions; so stuck full of gold, diamonds, pearls, and precious stones, with episodes of dancing girls, and otter of roses!' (Henry Mackenzie, *The Lounger*, 17 (28 May 1785)).

203.35   the exploits of a Lawrence and a Clive   Stringer Lawrence (1697–1775) was the commander of the East India Company's forces against the French on the Coromandel Coast between 1748 and 1759. His reorganisation of the Company's forces earned him the title 'the Father of the Indian Army'. Robert Clive (1725–74) started his military career under Lawrence in south India (see note to 155.28–29).

204.12   line of life   career, alluding to 'the thread fabled to be spun by the Fates, determining the duration of a person's life' (*OED, line*, 1g and 27).

204.24   Paxarete   mixture of fortified wine and boiled-down grape juice, formerly drunk as a sherry, now used primarily for colouring or sweetening sherry or whisky; Paxarete is a small town in the Jerez district of Spain (*OED*, where this is the first instance cited).

204.30   that superior class of people   during the 18th century India tended to attract unscrupulous fortune-seekers; after Pitt's India Act of 1784 much of the power of the Court of Directors of the East India Company was transferred to a Board of Control appointed by the Crown and oversight of all aspects of the Indian service started to be strengthened.

204.33–34   for some years as a cadet   an officer entering the East India Company's army went out as a cadet, without a commission, while he learned the service. Hillary is no doubt exaggerating his influence in these matters. Scott wrote to his brother Thomas about getting a cadetship in the East India Company's service for his nephew Walter (1807–76) in 1821 (*Letters*, 6.393–94).

204.38–39   sheep-head broth and haggis for mulagatawny and curry   characteristic dishes of Scotland and India. There is a recipe for 'Powsowdie, or Sheep's Head Broth' in F. Marian McNeill, *The Scots Kitchen* (London and Glasgow, 1929), 87–89; haggis is made from minced liver and other offal, oatmeal, onion and pepper stuffed in a sheep's stomach. Mulagatawny (mulligatawny) is a highly-seasoned Indian soup, and curry is a spiced sauce or stew as a relish for or accompaniment to rice.

204.42   the surf at Madras   Madras does not have a natural harbour and the approach to the beach was made dangerous by lines of surf. John Leyden described his arrival thus: 'We landed after passing through a very rough and dangerous surf, and being completely wetted by the spray, and were received on the beach by a number of natives who wanted to carry us from the boat on their naked, greasy shoulders, shining with cocoa oil. I leaped on shore with a loud huzza, tumbling half a dozen of them on the sand' (*The Poetical Remains of the late Dr. John Leyden*, ed. James Morton (London, 1819), lxxxviiin).

205.16–17   marrying and giving in marriage   see Mark 12.25; Luke 20.35.

205.21–22   Bachelor bluff... tough   not identified.

205.40   as Benedict says   see *Much Ado About Nothing*, 2.3.216–18.

206.15   Mr Tapeitout, the minister's assistant   presumably referring to the measured length of his sermons.

206.37   the depot at the Isle of Wight   the 'Company's United Kingdom Depot was first established at Newport, on the Isle of Wight, in 1801. It moved to Brompton Barracks, Chatham, in 1815, and then to Warley Barracks, Brent-wood, Essex in 1843' (T. A. Heathcote, *The Indian Army: The Garrison of British Imperial India, 1822–1922* (Newton Abbot, 1974), 156). The depot on the Isle of Wight was established too late for the story of Richard Middlemas, but Scott may have recalled that John Leyden waited on the Isle of Wight for a favourable wind before sailing to India (Letters from John Leyden to Richard Heber, ?6 and ?7 April 1803, transcribed in MS 939, ff. 46–54).

206.42–43 as trusty as a Trojan *OED* gives the colloquial sense of the term Trojan as 'a vague term of commendation or familiarity: a good fellow (often with the alliterative epithet *true* or *trusty*)' and among its examples cites this passage.

207.5–6 travel together to town i.e. to London.

208.4 only one of a thousand other passions a sentiment most memorably stated for Scott's generation by Byron: 'Man's love is of his life a thing apart,/ 'Tis woman's whole existence' (*Don Juan*, canto 1 (1819), stanza 194).

210.8–9 Gules, a lion rampant within a bordure engrailed Or similar to the arms of Lord Gray, whose title was created in 1445 when Andrew Gray of Foulis (born *c.* 1390) became Lord Gray. The arms of Lord Gray are 'Gules, *a Lion* rampant within *a Bordure ingrailed* Argent' (Alexander Nisbet, *A System of Heraldry Speculative and Practical*, 2 vols (Edinburgh, 1722), 1.172–73: see *CLA*, 11; *The Scottish Peerage*, ed. Sir James Balfour, 9 vols (Edinburgh, 1904–14), 4.273, 296). In non-heraldic language the shield is red (gules), with a lion rampant within a scalloped border in gold (or) or silver (argent) on it. A lion rampant stands on one hind leg with the others pawing the air.

210.17 the improved lithotomical apparatus equipment for perform-ing a lithotomy, an operation to remove a stone in the bladder; this apparatus appears to be Scott's invention.

210 motto John Milton, *Paradise Lost* (1667), 11.479–80.

211.30–31 beautiful island ... never forgets on a visit to Hampshire in 1807 Scott spent 'a day in the dockyard of Portsmouth, and two or three more in the Isle of Wight' (*Life*, 2.119).

211.32 Ryde small town on the NE coast of the Isle of Wight, developed in the 18th century as a seaside resort. John Leyden waited here for the *Hugh Inglis* Indiaman to sail taking him to India (see Historical Note, 360).

212.12–13 Duncan's body-guard see *Macbeth*, 1.7.63–67; 2.2.6.

212.20–21 the Indian on the death-stake a reference to the American Indians whose treatment of prisoners taken in battle is described by William Robertson: 'The prisoners are tied naked to a stake ... Every species of torture is applied that the rancour of revenge can invent ... Nothing sets bounds to their rage but the dread of abridging the duration of their vengence [*sic*] by hastening the death of the sufferers' (*The History of America*, 4th edn (London, 1783), 2.129: see *CLA*, 204).

212.21 the infernal regions i.e. Hell.

212.26–27 military hospital the most famous military hospital in the area was Haslar, the Royal Naval Hospital at Gosport, founded in 1746. For horrify-ing descriptions of a military hospital Scott had the model of Tobias Smollett, in *Roderick Random* (1748), Chs 24–38.

213.13 a-wanting to himself wanting in looking after his own interest.

213.26–27 oaths not loud but deep see *Macbeth*, 5.3.27: 'Curses not loud but deep'.

213.36 Pugg character in Ben Jonson, *The Devil is an Ass* (1616). The allusion has not been identified.

213.40 having done him *slang* having killed him (*OED*, *do*, verb, B.I.11e).

214.2 been before-hand with him anticipated, forestalled him (*OED*, *beforehand*, A.1c).

214.5 drummer's handwriting weals from flogging. Drummers carried out corporal punishment in the army.

214.22 Tantalus a king in Greek mythology who was punished for an offence against the gods by being made to stand in water which receded when he tried to drink.

214.39 Seelencooper *Dutch* zielenkooper, soul-purchaser.

215.14–15 shamming Abraham *nautical slang* malingering, feigning sickness (*OED, sham*, verb, 6).

215.26 private soldier ordinary soldier without rank or distinction of any kind (*OED, private*, substantive, 2b).

216.14 two bites of a cherry proverbial: *ODEP*, 849.

216.14 cull in the ken *slang* fellow in the house.

216.17 Tom of Ten thousand a name originally applied to Thomas Thynne of Longleat (1648–82): his 'wealth, attested by the popular sobriquet "Tom of Ten Thousand," seems to have been almost his sole claim to consideration' (*Dictionary of National Biography*).

216.31 the pure element i.e. water.

216.5–7 his tongue clove to the roof of his mouth i.e. he was unable to speak: the phrase is used in several places in the Old Testament, e.g. Psalm 137.6; Ezekiel 3.26.

217 motto Homer, *The Iliad*, trans. Alexander Pope (1715–20), 11.636–37.

217.21–23 Annon sis Ricardus ... in lingua Latina *Latin* are you not Richard Middlemas, from the town of Middlemas? Answer in Latin.

217.24 Sum ille miserrimus *Latin* I am that most wretched man.

217.31–32 Earl Percy sees my fall said by the dying Douglas in the ballad of 'Chevy Chase': see *The English and Scottish Popular Ballads*, ed. Francis James Child, 5 vols (Boston and New York, 1882–98), 162B, stanza 37.

217.34–36 medical studies ... conducted in Latin all exercises, both oral and written, in the study of medicine at Edinburgh University were conducted in Latin until 1834 when the first theses in English were accepted (Sir Alexander Grant, *The Story of the University of Edinburgh During its first 300 Years*, 2 vols (London, 1884), 1.332).

218.9 carry through bring safely through a crisis.

218.13 needs must it is necessary, it must be done (*OED, needs*, adverb, d).

218.24 My eyes! vulgar expression of astonishment or asseveration (*OED, eye*, substantive, I.2h).

218.31 diploma see note to 160.13.

219.1 petty officers low-ranking officers in the navy.

219.15–16 Directors of the East India Company see notes to 198.26–27 and 201.25–26.

219.17 British Empire in the East see notes to 201.28 and 201.30.

219.20 the celebrated Hyder Ali Haidar Ali (1721–82), a Muslim soldier of humble birth who came to prominence in the army of Mysore in south India during the 1750s when Mysore was threatened from the north by the Marathas. By the 1760s he had usurped the power of the Hindu Rajah of Mysore and was fully involved in the campaigns and alliances of the area, in which he tended to support the French rather than the British. The first Anglo-Mysore War broke out in 1767 when Haidar Ali and the Nizam of Hyderabad invaded the territory of the Nawab of Arcot who was supported by the British. In the confrontation with the forces of the East India Company that followed Madras itself was threatened. The peace-treaty which ended the war in 1769 agreed an alliance between Haidar Ali and the British; violations of its terms were so frequent that the Madras Government came to expect a renewal of hostilities, which broke out in 1780. See N. K. Sinha, 'Mysore: Haidar Ali and

Tipu Sultan', in *The History and Culture of the Indian People*, Vol. 8, *The Maratha Supremacy*, ed. R. C. Majumdar (Bombay, 1977), 452–71.

219.28 military service of the King i.e. the British army, as distinct from the army of the East India Company. The first British army regiments were sent to India during the Seven Years' War; the regular army garrison was permanent from 1780.

219.29 the worst recruits writing of the 1750s Orme calls the East India Company's soldiers 'as usual, the refuse of the vilest employments in London' (1.265). After the reforms introduced by the India Act of 1784 the situation started to change (see note to 204.30), and in 1821 Scott refused his son Walter's request to go to India with the army in these terms: 'If you had been to go there I could have got you a good appointment in civil service or indeed I would greatly have preferd your going in the Companys military to your going there as an officer in the Kings service by which you can get neither experience in your profession nor credit nor wealth nor anything but an obscure death in storming the hill fort of some Rajah with an unpronounceable name' (*Letters*, 6.433). The Company's European Regiments were a haven for soldiers of fortune, adventurers, rogues, and petty criminals, where few questions were asked about a recruit's background, and where the authorities were not too fussy about the answers: see T. A. Heathcote, *The Indian Army: The Garrison of British Imperial India 1822–1922* (Newton Abbot, 1974), 156.

220.16 as M.D. regulations for the degree of Doctor of Medicine were enacted in the University of Edinburgh in 1767; before that students studying medical subjects took the degree of Master of Arts (Sir Alexander Grant, *The Story of the University of Edinburgh During its first 300 Years*, 2 vols (London, 1884), 1.330–32).

221.16 inoculation widely practised in the East, inoculation against small-pox was introduced to Britain from Turkey by Lady Mary Wortley Montagu in 1721–22. It remained in use until Edward Jenner introduced vaccination in 1796. Dobie comments that he could not find any record of Jews having scruples against inoculation.

221.34–35 Doctor Tourniquet and Doctor Lancelot the names make satirical reference to their profession: a 'tourniquet' is a tight bandage to staunch bleeding; 'lance a lot' refers to the technique of lancing, making a surgical incision.

222.1 led horse spare horse, led by an attendant for Hartley to ride on the return journey.

222.3 the ancient mode of treating the small-pox stimulating and heating measures used to be taken to promote the eruption of the pustules, in the belief that they would rid the body of the disease. The cooling method of treating smallpox was introduced by Thomas Sydenham (1624–80), and was regarded as unorthodox for a long time.

222.20 fuel to fire proverbial: see *ODEP*, 293.

223.10–11 the aphorisms of Hippocrates sayings of the ancient Greek doctor (5th century BC) to whom several works on medicine are attributed. The *Aphorisms* was a collection of pithy summaries of Hippocratic practice, in use as a textbook at least until 1800, but, as smallpox was unknown at the time of Hippocrates, it does not support the doctors' appeal to authority.

223.37 God gives and takes away see Job 1.21: 'the Lord gave, and the Lord hath taken away; blessed be the name of the Lord', a passage frequently used in funeral services.

224.34 swaggering Sergeant Kite character in George Farquhar, *The Recruiting Officer* (1706).

224.39 private sentinel private soldier, an ordinary soldier without rank (*OED*, sentinel, 4).

225.19–20 canny Northumberland see note to 192.13.

227.15 a black ouzel indeed like the daughter of Silence in *2 Henry IV*, 3.2.7. Ouzel is an old name for a blackbird.

227.34 the Downs naval anchorage off Deal on the SE coast of England.

229.17 gold and silver muslins translucent cotton fabrics with an open weave, decorated with gold and silver thread. They were exported from Burhanpur in central India: see Vernonica Murphy, 'Europeans and the Textile Trade', in *Arts of India: 1550 to 1900*, ed. John Guy and Deborah Swallow (London: Victoria and Albert Museum, 1990), 156. Henry Mackenzie mentions 'gold muslins' from India in *The Lounger*, 17 (28 May 1785).

229.18 shawls . . . novelty in Europe Kashmir shawls, finely woven from goat's wool, became fashionable in Europe from about 1700. In India they had mostly been worn by men, though women wore them as wraps in the cold season; in Europe they were regarded as a female accessory: see Veronica Murphy, 'Europeans and the Textile Trade', in *Arts of India: 1550 to 1900*, ed. John Guy and Deborah Swallow (London: Victoria and Albert Museum, 1990), 169.

230.1–2 bloodshed and death the result of an ensuing duel.

230.4 God of my fathers Daniel 2.23; in a variety of forms a common Old Testament phrase. Zilia has learned English in the intervening years and Scott gives her a language drawn from the Old Testament.

230.5 clay . . . fashioned us compare Job 10.9; Isaiah 45.9.

231.17 destination to Madras the affairs of the East India Company in India in the 18th century were administered through three Presidencies, at Madras, Bombay and Calcutta. The settlement at Madras, founded in 1639, was the centre for trade with south India.

231.20–21 the purlieus of Saint Giles's the area round the church of St Giles in the Fields in St Giles High Street, London, formerly notorious for poverty and crime.

231.21 the Lowlights of Newcastle a disreputable area of North Shields, downriver from Newcastle upon Tyne, named after the Low Light, the lower of two lighthouses marking the entrance to the Tyne.

232.8 flew to a harpsichord the poet Thomas Moore remembered a conversation with Scott about music during his visit to Abbotsford in 1825: 'I was much struck by his description of a scene he had once with Lady —— (the divorced Lady ——) upon her eldest boy, who had been born before her marriage with Lord ——, asking why he himself was not Lord —— (the second title). "Do you hear that?" she exclaimed wildly to Scott; and then rushing to the pianoforte, played, in a sort of frenzy, some hurried airs, as if to drive away the dark thoughts then in her mind' (*Life*, 6.94).

232.14 voice and harp there are several references to singing with a harp in the Psalms: 'unto thee will I sing with the harp, O thou Holy One of Israel' (71.22).

232.14–15 the Royal Hebrew King David, to whom the Psalms are attributed.

234.3 a coup de soleil *French* sunstroke; there is a description of the *coup de soleil*, 'of all others, the most fatal attack', in *Narrative Sketches*, 39n.

234 motto *The Merry Wives of Windsor*, 2.2.4–5; see *ODEP*, 519 (Mayor of Northampton). Pistol implies that the world offers opportunities for profit to the bold.

236.18–19 inheritance . . . of my mother Middlemas's rhetorical argument about rights to his mother's estate ('to whom should it descend, save to her children?') is moral rather than legal and reflects considerable legal uncertainty. English common law in this period gave a widower the life-rent of his deceased wife's real property (land and buildings); were she intestate her legitimate

children (see note to 236.26 on Middlemas's legitimacy) might have a claim to
her moveable estate but such common-law rights were being eroded in the 18th
century and could in any case be frustrated by the provisions of a will.

236.25 your birth prevents you from inheriting Hartley is English and
assumes English law: an illegitimate child could not be heir-in-law to real estate
and so could not inherit unless, as Hartley says, there is a will in his favour.

236.26 I am legitimate Middlemas's arguments depend on his parents
being married. In England those under the age of 21 had to have their father's
consent to their marriage. As Zilia did not have that consent, she and her lover
eloped to Scotland (see text, 239.18–19) where parental consent was not
required. Unfortunately, Richard was born prematurely (239.21), before the
marriage took place. However, at 236.43–237.17 he argues that the marriage of
his parents was effected prior to his birth by one of the Scots forms of irregular
(but perfectly valid) marriage: either by the mutual consent of both parties, or
by the promise of future marriage followed by sexual intercourse on the basis of
that promise. If contested, proof of marriage would be found in documentary
evidence such as letters, or in the public acknowledgement of the marriage
before witnesses; Middlemas's reference to baptism relates to the circumstances of his own birth (see text, 164) rather than to any legal procedure, but
would have been acceptable as public acknowledgment. See Patrick Irvine,
Considerations on the Expediency of the Law of Marriage in Scotland (Edinburgh,
1828), 9–10, 45–70, and Frederick Parker Walton, *A Handbook of Husband
and Wife according to the Law of Scotland* (Edinburgh, 1893), 16–19, 25–32.
Middlemas's use of Scots law, the jurisdiction most favourable to his circumstances, is not wholly specious for in Scott's day it had not been clearly established which law would apply in cases of this kind: see Walton, 420–25.

236.28 allow the air of Heaven compare *Hamlet*, 1.2.141–42.

236.35 the heir i.e. the heir-in-law; according to the law of both Scotland
and England the heir-in-law was the eldest son who was entitled to inherit all the
real property of his parents. See also note to 237.22–23.

236.43 legally married from the Marriage Act of 1753 (26 George II, c.
33) marriages in England and Wales had to be performed after the proclamation
of banns (public proclamation in the parish church of the parties' intention to
marry) in one of the churches in which the banns had been read.

237.3 vow betwixt a fond couple see note to 236.26.

237.11 Tresham, or Witherington *Tresham* is the name of a Catholic
family in Northamptonshire; *Witherington* is the name of the heroic Northumbrian in the ballad of 'Chevy Chase' (*The English and Scottish Popular Ballads*, ed.
F. J. Child, 5 vols (New York, 1882–98), 162b, stanza 50). A Captain Witherington, 'a strange unaccountable man', died in 1756 in the Black Hole of
Calcutta (John Keay, *The Honourable Company: A History of the English East
India Company* (London, 1991), 301–02).

237.22–23 I am entitled to at least a third as a Jew Monçada could not
own real property (see note to 175.22), and Middlemas assumes that his mother
has kept her inheritance as moveable property of which he claims one third as
one of three surviving children. Her husband would have life-rent of any real
property she had bought with her inheritance, which, as a convert to the Church
of England (see text, 240.17), she would have been entitled to do.

238.20–21 declaring the illegitimacy of the child Scottish marriage
law was based upon the consent of the parties involved rather than upon performing a ceremony, and so Zilia's declaring that she was not married when she
gave birth to Richard invalidates his arguments for his legitimacy (see text,
236.43–37.17, and note to 236.26).

238.42–43 Tresham . . . a high Northumbrian family see note to
237.11.

238.43–239.1   Charles Edward . . . invasion   Prince Charles Edward Stewart (1720–88), son of the Jacobite claimant to the throne of Britain, landed in Scotland in August 1745, to lead the Jacobite rising of 1745–46. See Historical Note to 'The Highland Widow', 319–20, and note to 68.21.

239.1–2   a commission in the Portuguese service   it was not unusual for Jacobites to serve in armies in Continental Europe while they were under suspicion at home.

239.17 secret marriage   see note to 165.26.

239.18–19   flight for Scotland   under Scots law Zilia could have married without her father's consent, which she could not do in England until she was twenty-one. This was the usual reason why lovers eloped from England to Scotland.

239.38   in the Highlands   many, though not all, of the Highland clans were Jacobite.

239.40   the East India Company   Dr John Riddy comments that many Jacobites came to Hanoverian respectability in the service of the East India Company.

239.41   name of Witherington   see note to 237.11.

240.5   outlawed   see note to 77.39.

240.17   the established religion of her husband and his country   at the beginning of the tale her husband was a Catholic (164.8); the religion established by law in England was Episcopalian Protestant.

240.30   subdued and cherished long   Samuel Taylor Coleridge, 'Love' (1799), line 76.

241.9   Oh, Benoni, Oh, child of my sorrow   see Genesis 35.18 and marginal gloss. *Benoni*, son of my sorrow, is the name given by the dying Rachel to her son Benjamin.

241.24   tribes of Israel . . . guardian angel   in the Old Testament there is no mention of angels protecting the several tribes; but in John's vision of the new Jerusalem the city 'had a wall great and high, and had twelve gates, and at the gates twelve angels, and names written thereon, which are the names of the twelve tribes of the children of Israel' (Revelation 21.12).

241.38–39   the nether millstone   Job 41.24, referring to the lower, fixed millstone, against which the upper one moved to grind corn etc.

242.15   in good set terms   *As You Like It*, 2.7.17.

243.14   hedge my bets   compensate for loss in placing bets by making transactions which balance it (*OED*, *hedge*, verb, 8a).

243.22   the long and weary space   the time taken by a voyage to India would be anything from three months to a year.

243.34   Leadenhall-street   see note to 201.25–26.

243.43   Fort St George   the fortified centre of the British settlement in Madras whose earliest buildings were consecrated on St George's Day, 1640. Orme says of it, 'none but the English, or other Europeans under their protection, resided in this division, which contained about 50 good houses, an English and a Roman Catholic church, together with the residence of the factory, and other buildings belonging to the company' (1.65). Some of these buildings and extensive 18th-century fortifications are still visible.

244.19   the Madras government   the Presidency was governed by a President or Governor appointed by the Court of Directors in London and a Council.

244.43–245.1   not every child that knows its own father   proverbial: see Ramsay, 83; *ODEP*, 899.

245.3   at a venture   at random, without thought (*OED*, *venture*, substantive, 1c).

245.7   the cap fitted . . . wear it   proverbial: see *ODEP*, 101.

245.9   a meeting   to fight a duel. Duelling was illegal in Britain except between soldiers where it was permitted until 1844. In two other novels which mention India, *Guy Mannering* and *Saint Ronan's Well*, Scott refers to the tragic outcome of duelling between soldiers. Krishnaswami comments: 'The duel which Middlemas fought with his commanding officer reflects a characteristic feature of the early Anglo-Indian life. We have, from the instance of the famous one between Warren Hastings and Sir Philip Francis downwards, quite a long list of duels recorded in the annals of the British settlements in India' (444).

245.13-14 having pushed the quarrel to extremity duels often had a symbolic element and participants sought to avoid killing their opponents. Middlemas is to blame for refusing a resolution of the quarrel and insisting on a second round of fire.

246.1-2 Cara Razi, the Mahomedan saint and doctor ar-Rāzī, a Persian physician, philosopher and alchemist. Abu Bakr ar-Razi (AD 850–925), known in the West under his Latinized name of Rhazes, was the author of several influential books on medicine.

246.3 Barak El Hadgi Barak the Pilgrim; Hadgi (Hadji) is the title given to one who has made the pilgrimage to Mecca.

246.8 The tomb of the Owliah Arabic *awliyā*, saints or holy men (the word is plural; the singular is *walī*). John Gilchrist, *A Dictionary, English and Hindoostanee*, 2 vols (Calcutta, 1787–90), under *saint* has *wulee*, and under *saints* has *oulee,a* (2.772). Saints' tombs are common in the Islamic world. Krishnaswami identifies this with the tomb of Tipu Mastan Auliah at Arcot, in the Carnatic, after whom Tipu Sultan was named (439).The first edition greatly expands the manuscript here (see Appendix 2, 376), drawing for the first time in the tale on James Ferguson's sketches of India (see Historical Note, 364–66). The description of the tomb, the fakir and the moullah come from Ferguson's second sketch (ff. 169r–70r).

246.10 mangos and tamarind trees the mango (*mangifera indica*) is extensively cultivated in India, yielding fruit eaten either raw or in pickles and conserves; the tamarind (*tamarindus indica*), known as 'the date of India', is valued for the acid pulp of its pod which has culinary and medicinal uses.

246.11 three domes, and minarets at every corner domed buildings in a court-yard marked at each corner with a minaret is a style of Mughal tomb architecture, of which the most celebrated example is the Taj Mahal near Agra, completed in 1648. The sphere of the dome in such architecture symbolises heaven.

246.19 the book of the Prophet the Koran, dictated to the Prophet Muhammad by the Angel Gabriel.

246.23 Feringis Arabic and Persian *feringhee*, an eastern term for a European. The word comes from Frank, the name of the Germanic people who conquered Gaul in the 6th century and gave their name to France. It was first used of the crusaders by the nations bordering on the Levant and became a general term for a European.

246.30 large wooden beads the chain of beads, or rosary, used to assist concentration in prayer and the counting of the ninety-nine Names of God, the list of divine attributes.

246.39 inquired at Scots inquired of.

247.7 Salam Alaikum Arabic *salam'alai-kum* peace be upon you.

247.9 black robe of his order, very much torn and patched Khair-Ullah points out that Ferguson describes the dress of the 'Devotees' as 'a shirt of patch work or black blanket' (f. 170r) and adds 'Scott, however, makes a compromise and thus falsifies the description' (123). Scott had introduced the 'khirkah', the torn robe of the dervise, in *The Talisman*, in *Tales of the Crusaders*, 4 vols (Edinburgh, 1825), 4.71.

247.9–10 high conical cap of Tartarian felt Scott added the phrase 'of Tartarian felt' to Ferguson's 'a high cap in the shape of a cone' (f. 170r). Tartars, or Tatars, are nomadic peoples of the Asian steppes and deserts. Felt is a kind of cloth made by compacting and matting fibres rather than by weaving, and was often used by the Tatars for carpets and clothing.

247.16 Salam Alaikum bema sabastem *Arabic salam' alai-kum bimā sabartum*, peace be upon you, because you have endured with patience (*The Koran*, 13, p. 183).

247.25–26 left hand takes no guerdon of my right takes no recompense from someone whom I regard as part of myself, altering the significance of the proverb, 'To refuse with the right hand and take with the left' (*ODEP*, 669).

247.28–29 leprous like Gehazi's Gehazi is the servant of Elisha, in 2 Kings Ch. 5, who was punished with leprosy for obtaining payment by deception from Naaman whom the prophet had cured of the disease.

247.30 the camel of the prophet Saleth, or of the ass of Degial 'When a ravenous cur gets meat, he enquires not whether the flesh is of Saleh's camel or of the ass of Dujal (*The Gûlistân, or Rose Garden. By Musle-Huddeen Shaik Sâdy, of Sheeraz*, trans. Francis Gladwin (London, 1808), 250). The Persian poet Sa'di died in 1292. The story of the prophet Sâleh who gave the people a camel as a sign from God is in *The Koran*, 7, pp. 112–13; Al Dajjâl, an imposter, is a false prophet who will arrive on an ass before the end of the world (see George Sale, 'The Preliminary Discourse', prefixed to his translation of *The Koran*, 62–63).

247.33 enlarges the heart common phrase in *The Koran*, e.g. 94, p. 449.

247.37–38 the poet ... discover a diamond not identified.

248.6 Mysore Indian state 500 km W of Madras, in the modern state of Karnataka.

248.7 Hyder Ali see note to 219.20.

248.11 a hollow and insincere truce the truce of 1769 which ended the first Anglo-Mysore War. 'The war with Mysore was waged without skill or judgment, and Haidar Ali dictated peace on his own conditions in 1769, almost under the walls of Madras. The Peace laid an obligation upon Madras to aid the ruler of Mysore if attacked by another Power. This engagement the English were unable to fulfil when Mysore was invaded by a Maratha army in 1771, and they earned by their default the undying hate of a formidable and relentless foe' (P. E. Roberts, 'Clive and Warren Hastings', in *The Cambridge Modern History*, Vol. 6 (Cambridge, 1909), 567).

248.15 even-handed justice *Macbeth*, 1.7.10. This is similar in tenor to the obituary of Haidar Ali in *The Annual Register* which concluded: 'He had been ... a bitter, and very nearly a fatal enemy, to the English East India company; but it would be disgraceful and mean, on that account, to suppress his virtues, or endeavour to conceal his great qualities' (*The Annual Register ... For the Year 1783* (London, 1785), 89–90).

248.18 rum or brandy the Muslim fakir would not usually drink alcohol.

248.24 the Invincible, the Lord and Shield of the Faith of the Prophet titles of a Muslim ruler.

248.26 Hyder Ali Khan Bahauder *Persian and Arabic khan* means lord or prince; *Hindi bahauder* (bahadur), meaning hero or champion, was a title conferred in the Mughal empire and by Indian rulers and was conferred on Haidar Ali by the Rajah of Mysore in 1759. Mark Wilks says that 'Hyder was always more gratified by the single appellation of Bahauder than by any other title' (*Historical Sketches of the South of India, in an attempt to trace the History of Mysoor*, 3 vols (London, 1810–17), 1.372n–73n).

248.29 Seringapatam capital of Mysore; modern Srirangapattana, but always spelled Seringapatam in 18th and early 19th-century sources and often in later histories.

248.30 the Nawaub *Urdu nawwab, Portuguese nabob,* a Muslim official acting as deputy or governor in the Mughal empire. Haidar Ali was invested with the title in 1761, 'and the title of *Nabob,* and the name *Hyder Ali Khan Behauder,* by which he was designated in those deeds, were certainly henceforth assumed by Hyder' (Mark Wilks, *Historical Sketches of the South of India, in an attempt to trace the History of Mysoor,* 3 vols (London, 1810–17), 1.439).

248.30–31 Hyder did not assume the title of Sultaun *from Arabic via French sultan,* the sovereign or chief ruler of a Muslim country. Haidar Ali never openly assumed a royal title, preferring the more modest title Nawab. His son Tipu dethroned the Rajah of Mysore and assumed the title of Sultan in 1786 (N. K. Sinha, 'Mysore: Haidar Ali and Tipu Sultan', in *The Maratha Supremacy,* ed. R. C. Majumdar, *The History and Culture of the Indian People,* Vol. 8 (Bombay, 1977), 466–67).

248.34 the Mysore this is not the usual usage, and Scott probably got it from *Narrative Sketches of the Conquest of the Mysore* which he owned. It seems to be analogous to the Anglo-Indian usage 'the Carnatic' (*Hobson-Jobson,* 164).

249.4 the balsam of Mecca an aromatic resin used medicinally, usually externally to heal wounds or soothe pain; also called Balm of Gilead.

249.19 without any purpose of being married young unmarried women were sent to India in the expectation that they would find husbands there. A writer in *The New Monthly Magazine,* referring to India as 'that land of husbands', noted 'Amongst our female passengers there were several who were carrying out a tolerable assortment of charms for the Madras market' ('Society in India.—No. I', 22 (1828), 229).

249.25 hookah... colour *Urdu hookah,* an Indian pipe in which tobacco and spices are smoked through water. Daniel Terry bought for Scott a 'handsome East Indian Hookay for £2.10s.' (Wilfred Partington, *Sir Walter Scott's Post-Bag* (London, 1932) 134). The two consolations of a hookah and a native woman reconciled many Europeans to India.

249.31 Angels and ministers! *Hamlet,* 1.4.39.

249.31–32 the Queen of Sheba according to Jewish and Islamic tradition the Queen of Saba, or Sheba, in SW Arabia in the 10th century BC; a nickname for a woman of regal dress and bearing.

249.34 a Semiramis-looking person Semiramis was Queen of Assyria in the late 9th century BC; she became a legendary heroine.

249.37–38 robe was composed of crimson silk the description of the Begum's robe, trousers, shawl and turban derive from Ferguson (f. 176v).

249.39 a creeze *Malay kris or creese,* a Malay dagger with a blade of a wavy form. Khair-Ullah (139) points out that the dagger is like the one sent by Leyden to Scott (*Letters,* 2.533).

249.42 aigrette jewelled ornament for the head resembling or containing feathers, named after the French for the Lesser White Heron which has a crest of feathers on its head including two long ones hanging behind. The word is used for a jewelled turban ornament resembling a tuft of feathers, of which fine examples were made by the craftsmen of the Mughal court. The wearing of a large bird's feather in the turban was a sign of high status. See Susan Stronge, 'The Age of the Mughals', in *Arts of India: 1550–1900,* ed. John Guy and Deborah Swallow (London: Victoria and Albert Museum, 1990) 94, 103, 106.

250.3 retained its form the surviving manuscript ends after this phrase.

250.7 chowry, or cow's tail *Hindi* fly-whisk often made of the bushy tail of the Tibetan yak, commonly called a cow's tail by Europeans. With a costly decorated handle it was one of the insignia of Asiatic royalty. This detail comes from Ferguson (f. 175r).

250.18 **what is that for** *Scots* the English form is 'how is that for' (*CSD, what*).

250.18 **Zenobia** Queen of Palmyra in Syria who fought the Roman Emperor Aurelian and was defeated by him in AD 272.

250.24–25 **Pondicherry, a sergeant in Lally's regiment** Pondicherry was the chief French fort on the Coromandel coast which fell to the British after a long siege in 1761. The commander of the French forces at Pondicherry was Thomas Arthur, Comte de Lally (1702–66).

251.38 **as Teucer from behind Ajax Telamon's shield** Teucer, an archer, took shelter behind the huge shield of Ajax, son of Telamon, King of Salamis, in Homer (*c.* 8th century BC), *Iliad*, 8.266–72.

251.42–43 **old Mother Montreville** 'mother' is a term of address for an elderly woman of the lower class, here used disparagingly (*OED, mother*, 4a); it is also slang for a procuress or female brothel-keeper (Eric Partridge, *A Dictionary of the Underworld*, 3rd edn (London, 1968), 451).

252.2 **this lady is the widow** for sources of the character of Madame Montreville see Historical Note, 365.

252.9 **Hyder Naig** *Urdu naik*, a leader, a title used in India in various senses; in military contexts it denotes a rank corresponding to that of corporal. Before he was made Bahadur in 1759 (see note to 248.26) Haidar Ali's title was Naik, which he retained thereafter in a manner analogous to the use of '*le petit caporal*' (the little corporal) for Napoleon (*Encyclopaedia Britannica*, 11th edn).

252.9 **the Eastern Solomon ... Queen of Sheba** King Solomon was distinguished for his wisdom; the visit of the Queen of Sheba to Solomon is recounted in 1 Kings 10.1–13 and 2 Chronicles 9.1–12.

252.34 **Boadicea** or Boudicca (d. AD 60), ancient British queen who led a revolt against Roman rule.

252.35 **on foot** in active employment or operation (*OED, foot*, substantive, 32c).

252.35–36 **in the Nawaub's service** Edward Moor deplored the fact that 'from dissatisfaction, pecuniary distresses, caprice possibly, and other causes, some [British officers] are induced to forget their duty, and to enter the service of a foreign power' (*A Narrative of the Operations of Captain Little's Detachment ... against Nawab Tippoo Sultan Bahadur* (London, 1794), 120).

252.37–38 **British prisoners were intrusted to his charge** Scurry suffered under a British guard while a prisoner of Haidar Ali: 'an European made his appearance, clad in the Mohammedan dress, with a large red turban, and a formidable pair of mustaches' (60). He was one Dempster, 'a base wretch, and a deserter from the Bengall Artillery' (67–68, 107).

253.1–2 **Sure such a pair were never seen** see Richard Brinsley Sheridan, *The Duenna* (1775), 2.2, the first two lines of the final song in the scene.

253.9 **Ram Sing Cottah** apparently fictitious. Singh, meaning lion, was a title borne by several military castes of north India.

253.9–10 **the Black Town** to the N of Fort St George was 'another division, much larger and worse fortified, in which were many very good habitations belonging to the Armenian and to the richest of the Indian merchants, who resided in the company's territory: this quarter was called the Black Town' (Orme, 1.65). The area is now called George Town.

253.25–26 **Hyder's prison ... the late pacification** by the treaty of 1769 (see note to 248.11) prisoners were restored on both sides.

254.9 **Just so** precisely in that way; here, 'in a similar calumny' (*OED, just*, adverb, 1c).

245.26–27 **in Hyder's capital, or Tippoo's camp** Haidar Ali's capital was Seringapatam; Tipu (*c.* 1750–99) was his son and successor.

254.39 **the contradictory intelligence** the British at Madras were frequently accused of gossip, of which the chapter just ending gives examples.

254.40 Capstern variant spelling of capstan, a mechanism on board ship for winding cable, especially the anchor cable.

255.3 Mrs. Duffer the name means pedlar, especially one who sells trashy goods as valuable, under false pretences (*OED*, *duffer*, I.1 and 2).

255.4 mates and guinea-pigs 'mates' were assistants to functionaries on board ship; 'guinea-pigs' were midshipman in the East India service, alluding to the fees paid to the captain with whom they embarked (see note to 162.9). The two terms were linked in a quotation of 1779: 'I promise you, to me it was no slight penance to be exposed during the whole voyage to the half sneering, satirical looks of the mates and guinea-pigs' (*Hobson-Jobson*, 401).

255.7–8 find the length of the old girl's foot *proverbial* get to know the woman's disposition or inclinations (see Ramsay, 124; *ODEP*, 456).

256.7 two three *Scots* two or three, several.

256.8 mais c'est égal *French* but it's all the same.

256.17 cela n'est pas honnête *French* that is not proper behaviour.

259.8–9 accept of the offer made to me probably drawing on the situation of the Miss Erskines, daughters of Scott's friend William Erskine, Lord Kinneder (1768–1822), who planned to go to India after a hostile reception by their aunt (*Letters*, 10.326–28, 339n).

259.9–10 to stand in my own light *proverbial* to prejudice my chances (see *ODEP*, 770).

259.19–20 the small still voice in which God appeared to Elijah in 1 Kings 19.12; often used to signify conscience.

261.17 in Frangistan the land of the seringis, Europe, by analogy with Hindustan, the land of the Hindus. The term is not in *OED* or *Hobson-Hobson*, but 'Franguestan' is used by Byron in *The Giaour* (1813), line 506.

261.22 the Ghauts *Anglo-Indian from Hindi* the passes leading to Mysore. The word *ghat* means a path of descent from a mountain, a mountain pass; 'the Ghats' is the name applied by Europeans to two mountain ranges bounding the plateau of Mysore on the east and west; the Begum is referring to the Eastern Ghats. See *Hobson-Jobson*, 369.

261.38 Governor of the Presidency see notes to 231.17 and 244.19.

262.13 the young tyrant Tipu, Haidar Ali's son.

262.34–35 I will watch thee as the fiend watches the wizard this expression has not been identified. Wizards and witches were thought to derive their power from a contract with the devil, who might therefore be supposed to keep them under surveillance.

262.39–40 thy intrigues with the Nizam and the Mahrattas *Urdu and Turkish Nizam*, governor, the hereditary title of the rulers of Hyderabad, the southern part of the Mughal empire, who gained independence in the 18th century. The Marathas are a Hindu people from west India, with their capital at Poona (Pune), whose power and territorial influence increased as the authority of the Mughal empire waned. Orme says of the Marathas: 'It is now a century that they have made a figure as the most enterprizing soldiers of Indostan, and as the only nation of Indians, which seems to make war an occupation by choice; for the Rajpouts are soldiers by birth' (1.40). Leagues and hostilities among the East India Company at Madras, the Nizam of Hyderabad, the Marathas, and Haidar Ali of Mysore were a feature of south Indian politics in the late 18th century.

262.40–41 Bangalore fortified town in Mysore, founded in 1537, 130 km NE of Seringapatam.

263.5–6 my Nourjehan, my light of the world, my Mootee Mahul, my pearl of the palace these names derive from Ferguson (f. 171r). Nurjahan (*Arabic nūr*, light; *Persian jāhān*, world) was the name of the wife of the Mughal emperor Jahangir (ruled 1605–27). John Gilchrist gives *motee* for *pearl* and *muhul* for *palace* in his *A Dictionary, English and Hindoostanee*, 2 vols (Calcutta, 1787–90), 2.627, 613.

263.10–11 Circassian native of Circassia, a region in the northern Caucasus. Circassian women were regarded as particularly beautiful and were sold as slaves. Byron describes the sale of a Circassian slave in *Don Juan*, Canto 4 (1821), stanzas 113–14. For the probable source of this incident see the Historical Note, 365.

263.18 the laws of the Zenana *Persian and Hindustani zenana*, part of a house in which the women of the family were secluded, hence wives and concubines, a harem. It is not clear what 'the laws of the Zenana' were—and they may be an invention of Scott's—except that the context implies that they allowed a week's respite before a new entrant became the mistress of the prince.

263.30 To hear is to obey *Arabic sam'an wa ta'atan* proverbial.

264.4–5 God of War ... Goddess of Beauty Mars the Roman god of war loved Venus, the goddess of love, whose name means 'beauty'.

264.6 this Indian tiger an appropriate description of Tipu Sultan who used the tiger as his badge: 'The Tiger being the figurative Royal animal in the nations of India, as the Lion is in the British dominions, its representative badge was found upon almost every article of the late Sultaun's princely property—whether in his palace, in his fortresses, or in the field' (*Narrative Sketches*, 78n).

264.8–9 the Residency Scott makes it clear below that he means the house of the President or Governor. In the terminology of the East India Company, however, Resident was the name of the head of a lesser trading station, or a representative at an Indian court.

264.18 the Bramin Paupiah, the Dubash *Sanskrit Brahmin*, a member of the highest or priestly cast among the Hindus, though by the 18th century likely to be involved in secular occupations; *Hindi dubash*, an interpreter (literally one who speaks two languages), an Indian manager for a European administrator or merchant. For the origin of this character see Historical Note, 363.

264.18 the great man whose activities are reminiscent of those of John and Edward Hollond, successively Governors of Madras in 1789–90, see Historical Note, 363.

264.29 in robes of muslin embroidered with gold see note to 229.18.

264.31 Machiavel a wily and unscrupulous politician, from Niccolo Machiavelli (1469–1527), Italian statesman and political theorist whose book *The Prince* (1513) gained him a reputation for the cynical subordination of morality to the needs of government.

264.41–42 Vice-Regent ... Bangalore Haidar Ali had gained possession of Bangalore in 1757 from the Rajah of Mysore; it does not appear that Tipu had the office of 'Vice-Regent'.

265.13 her Bukshee ... her Sirdars *Persian and Urdu bukshi*, paymaster and commander-in-chief of the army of an Indian state; *Urdu sirdar*, in India a military leader or officer. Scott got these terms from Ferguson (ff. 179r–179v).

265.13 at my devotion entirely devoted to me (*OED, devotion*, 6).

265.15–16 General Smith's army Joseph Smith (?1733–90), who distinguished himself in the war of 1767–69 against Haidar Ali and was promoted Major-General shortly after the peace.

265.21 his Zenana Tipu's zenana was found after the fall of Seringapatam (1799) to contain 333 women, including servants; although most of them came from south India others came from as far afield as Istanbul (Brittlebank, 24, 97, 119, 136).

265.36 Lootie *Anglo-Indian from Hindi*, a term applied in India to irregular forces whose chief object in warfare was plunder, marauder. *Narrative Sketches* refers to 'parties of the enemy's Looties, or irregular cavalry, which continually infested the line of march' (33).

266.19–20 check of the Directors ... of the Crown before 1773 the Governors and Councils of the three Presidencies in India were answerable only to the Court of Directors in London. The Regulating Act of that year sought to reform the operation of the Court of Directors and to enforce its authority on its servants in India, creating the office of Governor-General, first held by Warren Hastings (1732–1818), based in Bengal and with authority over the other British Presidencies in India. The authority of the Crown over the Company's activities was increased by Pitt's India Act of 1784 which created a ministerial Board of Control in London to superintend all matters concerning British territorial possessions in India.

266.21–22 an anachronism in the introduction of Paupiah Scott's tale is set in the 1770s; Paupiah's activities seem to date from the years preceding his trial in 1792. Andrew Lang claimed that 'The critical part here ascribed to Fairscribe was really played by Colonel James Ferguson' (*The Waverley Novels*, Border Edition, 48 vols (1892–94), 46.486).

267.12 removed from Madras the fate of Scott's relation, David Haliburton, who displeased the historical Paupiah, see Historical Note, 360, 363.

267.34 to the usurper referring to Haidar Ali's usurpation of the Wodeyar Rajahs of Mysore; see note to 219.20.

267.43 in the vein of judging in the mood for judging (*OED*, *vein*, 14c).

268.1 stakes and bowstrings impaling with stakes and strangling with bowstrings were known methods of punishment.

268.4 letters of credence letters of recommendation or introduction (*OED*, *credence*, 4b).

268.26 Arab horses the Mughals imported Arab horses from Iran. As they were needed in warfare the East India Company built up its own stock by importing Arab horses from Europe, the Middle East and South Africa (*The Raj: India and the British 1600–1947*, ed. C. A. Bayly (London: National Portrait Gallery, 1990) 45).

268.42 Ghauts see note to 261.22. 'The following passage indicates that the great Sir Walter, with this usual sagacity, saw the true sense of the word in its geographical use, though misled by books to attribute to the (so called) "Eastern Ghauts" the character that belongs to the Western only' (*Hobson-Jobson*, 369).

269.2–270.7 The sun had set ... animals of prey the details of the journey up the pass derive from Ferguson (ff. 181r–82v); Scott may also have recalled the description of passes ascending from the Carnatic to Mysore in *Narrative Sketches*, [17n].

269.7 dark groves of teak-trees Ferguson does not name the trees. Teak (*tectona grandis*) is indigenous in south India; its fine and durable wood was used for ship-building, and domestic and temple architecture.

269.14 the moon was in her dark side Ferguson supplies this expression (f. 181r).

269.20 match-lock the matchlock musket, in which a lighted match was inserted to fire the gunpowder (priming), was introduced into India by the Mughals in the 16th century and continued in use until the 19th (*The Raj: India and the British 1600–1947*, ed. C. A. Bayly, (London: National Portrait Gallery, 1990) 237). Scott has amplified Ferguson's statement that the Sowar's 'match, for good & sufficient reasons, was kept in a proper state of illumination' (f. 181r).

269.21 the Dowrah *Hindustani dowra*, a village runner or guide. The word is not in *OED* but is in *Hobson-Jobson* where this passage is the only example cited (326). Ferguson is the source of the information in the text and the footnote (ff. 181r–81v).

269.35–36 the morning prayer of Alla Akber *Arabic*, 'God is Great'.

270.1 forced march one in which the capacity to march is forced or exerted beyond the ordinary limit (*OED, forced*, participial adjective, 3a).

270.2 a single high mud fort Mark Wilks comments: ' "Mud Fort," from the usually imperfect construction of the village defences, is a term of contempt in India, although the substance itself (kneaded clay) resists the effects of cannon-shot better than any other material' (*Historical Sketches of the South of India, in an attempt to trace the History of Mysoor*, 3 vols (London, 1810–17), 1.439n).

270.12–271.11 At a spot not far distant ... the prime of youth the tale of Sadhu Sing comes from Ferguson with little alteration (ff. 182v–83v). Sadhu is a Sanskrit word meaning 'holy man'; Sing, usually Singh, is a name from north India meaning 'lion'.

270.24 Sipahee *Persian and Urdu sepoy,* an Indian employed as a soldier in the British army (Ferguson f. 183r). Orme notes: 'The Indian natives, and Moors [Muslims], who are trained in the European manner, are called Sepoys: in taking our arms and military exercise, they do not quit their own dress or any other of their customs' (1.80).

271.3 his Mora Khair-Ullah notes that 'The girl's name "Mora" was a byword at the time of Ferguson's stay in India: she was a favourite dancing girl of Ranjit Singh whom he later married' (112). Ranjit Singh was the Rajah of Lahore whose court Ferguson visited in 1808.

271.19 Peon *Portuguese* in India, a foot soldier, footman or messenger. Orme distinguishes a peon and a sepoy by the fact that peons supplied their own arms: 'on the coast of Coromandel the Europeans distinguish all these undisciplined troops, whether armed with swords and targets, with bows and arrows, with pikes and lances, with match-locks, or even with muskets, by the general name of Peons' (Orme, 1.80).

271.28 towards Vandicotta unless this is fictitious it probably refers to the fortress town of Gandikota, N of Bangalore and NW of Cuddapah, which was taken by the British in 1791. 'Ganjecotta' is N of Bangalore on the map in Edward Moor, *A Narrative of the Operations of Captain Little's Detachment ... against Nawab Tippoo Sultan Bahadur* (London, 1794), opposite p.[1]; 'Gandicottah' is NE of Benguluru (Bangalore) in a map in Orme (1. opposite p.[33]).

272.6 the temple of the celebrated Vishnoo the temple of Sri Ranganatha, a name of the Hindu god Vishnu, from which Srirangapattana, or Seringapatam, gets its name. The temple complex is within the Fort at the west end of the island in the river Kaveri on which Seringapatam stands, and its sanctuary contains an image of Vishnu. It was extensively restored in the late 19th century.

272.7 the splendid Gardens called Loll-baug the Lal Bagh or Red Garden. There is a description of the garden in *Narrative Sketches*: 'The Loll-Baug, or Garden of Rubies, fills the eastern end of the island of Seringapatam; it was the work of Tippoo Sultaun, and laid out by himself. The taste was the strait-lined rows of vast cypress trees of most refreshing shade, with parterres filled with fruit trees, flowers and vegetables of every variety ... In this garden stands the magnificent Mausoleum in which is deposited the body of Hyder Ally: it is a building indescribably rich in the Moorish composition of its architecture, with minarets and turrets of elegant but fantastic forms' (46n–47n). Tipu was buried beside his father and the tomb, known as the Gumbaz, is still preserved in its formal garden.

272.10 the principal Mosque the large mosque which now stands within the Fort of Seringapatam was built by Tipu Sultan in 1787–88; Hartley would have visited its predecessor.

272.29 Dog of a Christian a particular insult since dogs were unclean animals in Islam.

272.37 a Sahib Angrezie the term and its definition 'English gentleman' come from Ferguson (f. 184v). *Angrezie*, which is not in *OED* or *Hobson-Jobson*, appears to be a rendering of Arabic and Persian *Ingilizi*, English.

272.38 Telinga the name of a people and a language in south India. It came to be used in north India for an Indian soldier disciplined and dressed in the European fashion (a sepoy) because the first such soldiers were sent to Bengal from Madras. The term is in Ferguson (f. 184r).

272.39 eaten their salt enjoyed their hospitality, with the implication of some degree of dependency (*OED*, *salt*, 2b); the expression is in Ferguson (f. 184r).

273.5 the Khan *Persian and Arabic khan*, a building for the accommodation of travellers. *The New Monthly Magazine* commented: 'What Anglo-Indian could read without a stare of the wildest astonishment, of [Hartley's] journey to Seringapatam, to obtain an audience of that very accommodating person, Hyder Ali Sahib? It was indeed very provident in Sir Walter Scott to send the poor fellow to a comfortable inn, when he got there . . . But unluckily there are no inns or khans (the Persian word for the same thing) in any part of Hyder's dominions' ('Society in India.— No.I', 22 (1828), 225–26).

273 motto see Thomas Campbell, 'The Turkish Lady' (1804), lines 1–8; the last three lines are entirely Scott's.

274.8–9 a gigantic African slavery and slave-trading was not uncommon in India in the 18th century and Africans were sometimes employed as domestic slaves. Orme mentions slaves brought from Africa and Madagascar (1.81, 93). See Radha Kamal Mukherjee and K. K. Datta, 'Economic and Social Conditions in India in the Eighteenth Century', in *The Maratha Supremacy*, ed. R. C. Majumdar, *The History and Culture of the Indian People*, Vol. 8 (Bombay, 1977), 743, 764.

274.16 Persian Narcissus Ferguson mentions all the flowers listed (ff. 171v–72r). The Persian narcissus may be *fritillaria Persica*, a fritillary known in northern India.

274.39 the holy Scheik Hali ben Khaledoun *Arabic sheikh*, a head of a Muslim religious order.

275.21 the two sparrows concerning a grain of rice not identified.

275.21 his wife Fatima the first wife of Muhammad and mother of his children was Khadija (d. 619); Fatima (*c.* 606–32) was his daughter.

275.30–31 chaplet of pearls to a sovereign 'a pearl rosary was a continual ornament of [Tipu's] person; the pearls of which it consisted were of uncommon size and beauty; they had been the collection of many years, and were the pride of his dress. Whenever he could purchase a pearl of extraordinary size, he never omitted the opportunity, and made it supply on his rosary the place of another, of inferior form and beauty' (*Narrative Sketches*, 87). In India pearls are associated with royalty; in Islam the pearl represents the divine word and individual large pearls and pearl necklaces were frequently worn by Mughal rulers: see Brittlebank, 138–39.

275.32 Bismallah! *Arabic bi'smillah*, in the name of Allah. It occurs at the beginning of each sura (chapter) of the Koran and is a common exclamation among Muslims.

275.40 this Kafr (or infidel) *Arabic kaffir*, an infidel. Ferguson uses the term spelling it 'Kafir' (f. 181v). The spelling *Kafr* is recorded in 1790 (*OED*, *kaffir*, 1; see also *caffre* 1) so it is likely that Scott retained the memory of an earlier acquaintance with the word.

276.41–42 the gardens which Tippoo had created the most extensive gardens in Bangalore, also called Lal Bagh, were established by Haidar Ali; both father and son planted gardens and Tipu in particular took trouble to obtain rare trees and plants: see Brittlebank, 118–19.

276.42–43 pavilions stately tents or marquees. Mughal rulers made use of tents when travelling through their territories; a chintz tent which belonged to Tipu Sultan is preserved in the Clive Collection at Powis Castle: see Mildred Archer and others, *Treasures from India: The Clive Collection at Powis Castle* (London: The National Trust, 1987), 95–96, [98].

278.8–33   The meeting... in the gardens the description of the formalities observed before the meeting of Tipu and the Begum are indebted to Ferguson (ff. 173r–74r), and probably draw on his experiences in Lahore and Delhi.

278.11–13   as far as possible... a mile or two on the road 'In Islam the predominate spatial metaphor to describe power relationships is horizontal, rather than vertical as it is in the West. Accordingly, in the language of government and power, the imagery is of nearness to or distance from a ruler' (Bernard Lewis, *The Political Language of Islam* (Chicago and London, 1988), 11).

278.22–23   the nuzzur... Mohurs *Urdu nazar*, in India a present made by an inferior to a superior; *Persian mohur* is a gold coin of the Mughal empire. Khair-Ullah points out that the reference to gold mohurs indicates that the source of Ferguson's information (f. 174r) was north India, as the gold coin of south India was the pagoda (112). Reginald Heber presented 'a nuzzur of fifty-one gold mohurs' when he visited the 'Emperor of Delhi' (*Narrative of a Journey through the Upper Provinces of India, from Calcutta to Bombay, 1824–1825*, 2nd edn, 3 vols (London, 1828), 2.298). Kate Brittlebank comments that offerings 'made in the coin of the realm, as was usually the case, acknowledged the legitimacy of the ruler' (Brittlebank, 92).

278.24   Khelaut *Urdu* robe of honour. Indian society reinforced social relations by means of gift-giving. *Khelaut* comes from Arabic *khil'at* meaning a garment cast off, implying that the recipient was receiving something previously worn by the donor and transferring some of his essence: see Brittlebank, 95–96, 101.

278.27   their molakat, or meeting the first edition read 'motakul'. Scott got this word, which is not in *OED*, from Ferguson who wrote 'moolakal' (f. 174r). Khair-Ullah points out that Ferguson frequently did not cross t's or close the tops of his small a's (104), and the 't' was put in the wrong place. *Arabic mulaqah* and *Persian mulaqat* mean a meeting or encounter, and John Gilchrist's *A Dictionary, English and Hindoostanee*, 2 vols (Calcutta, 1787–90), under *meeting* has *mōōlaqat* (2.543).

278.34–280.2   Long before... gorgeous appearance the details of Tipu's procession derive from Ferguson's description of the procession of his Begum (ff. 174r–75v). For the function of such processions in Indian concepts of kingship see Brittlebank, 133.

278.43   their long ears it was Scott who gave the camels long ears; Ferguson has 'the poor animals shaking their ears at every discharge' (f. 174v).

279.2   nagara kettle-drum. The word (which Scott got from Ferguson) is from Arabic and Persian *naqara*: see the etymology of *naker* in the *OED*. The term *naker*, also meaning kettle-drum, came into English from Old French but the *OED* comments that in English 'the word seems to have had real currency only in the 14th century'. Curiously the first citation after 1440 is in *Ivanhoe* (ed. Graham Tulloch, EEWN 8, 245.10). It appears that Scott did not recognise the link between 'naker' and his Anglo-Indian word for a drum.

279.10–11   strong as Rustan, just as Noushirvan similes supplied by Ferguson, originally to describe the Begum: 'bold as Roostum & just as Nosheerivan' (f. 179r). Rustem is the hero of the Persian epic *Shahnameh*, the 'Book of Kings', by Firdawsi (940–1020). Noushirvan, or Chosroes, an ancient king of Persia known as Anushirvan, 'the blessed', is famed in Persian literature for his justice: compare *The Gûlistân, or Rose Garden. By Musle-Huddeen Shaik Sâdy, of Sheeraz*, trans. Francis Gladwin (London, 1808), 37–38.

279.14 with caps of steel under their turbans see Ferguson (ff. 174v–75r).

279.15–16 rendered sabre-proof by being stuffed with cotton this detail is not in Ferguson.

279.18 his celebrated Tiger-regiment when Tipu was ruler of Mysore he surrounded himself with tiger imagery. 'The grenadier battalions of Tippoo's Sepoys, or regular infantry, are composed of Moormen [Muslims], or Hindoos of large stature, who carry firelocks chiefly of French manufacture, with long and indented bayonets. They are, by our troops, called Tiger Grenadiers, or Tiger men, from their dress, which is a short bannian [jacket] of purple woollen stuff, transversely striped, or speckled with white irregular spots of a lozenge form, and thence named the Tiger Jacket' (*Narrative Sketches*, 52n). His ordnance was cast in the form of tigers and his armour and weapons were ornamented with the tiger motif: see Veronica Murphy, 'The Later Provincial Courts and British Expansion', in *Arts of India: 1550 to 1900*, ed. John Guy and Deborah Swallow (London: Victoria and Albert Museum, 1990), 187. For the origin of the tiger motif see Brittlebank, 140–46.

279.33 chowry, or cow-tail see note to 250.7.

280.4 chabootra *Hindustani* paved or plastered platform, attached to a house or in a garden; this is the first instance of the word cited in *OED* (see *chabutra*). The description of the setting for the *Durbar* derives from Ferguson (f. 171r).

280.7 Persian carpets the manufacture of pile carpets was introduced into India from Persia in the 16th century by the Mughal Emperor Akbar: see Veronica Murphy, 'Europeans and the Textile Trade', in *Arts of India: 1550 to 1900*, ed. John Guy and Deborah Swallow (London: Victoria and Albert Museum, 1990), 156.

280.25 Banka, or Indian courtier the details of Middlemas's appearance come from Ferguson's description of the 'Dress of a Banka or Dandy' (ff. 176v–177r). The word *banka* is not in *OED* or *Hobson-Jobson* but John Gilchrist translates the word *fop* as *banka* in *A Dictionary, English and Hindoostanee*, 2 vols (Calcutta, 1787–90), 1.350. Khair-Ullah comments: 'The "Bankah" or as Ferguson correctly glosses it, Dandy, was a phenomenon peculiar to Delhi. In Urdu literature the phrase commonly used is "Dilli ka Bankah" (a fop of Delhi) and refers to that class of dandies that were the result of the declining Mughal court' (99).

280.40 silver muslin see note to 229.18.

280.43–281.1 close litter Orme notes: 'Women of rank in Indostan never appear in public; and travel in covered carriages, which are very rarely stopped or examined even in times of suspicion' (1.50).

281.17 in full Durbar *Persian and Urdu durbar*, the court or public audience of an Eastern ruler. Kate Brittlebank comments that it was 'a visual display of the order of things' (Brittlebank, 97–98). The description of Tipu's durbar owes something to Ferguson (ff. 173v–74r), in particular the sense that 'The Darbar is held for the despatch of business. Petitions . . . are presented, and answers dictated' (f. 173v).

281.24 daughter of Giamschid the exploits of Jemshid, the legendary hero of Persia, are related by Firdawsi (940–1020) in his epic *Shahnameh*, the 'Book of Kings'. There is no mention of a daughter.

281.29 the robber Leik see 'The History of the Robber of Seistan', in *Tales of the East*, ed. Henry Weber (Edinburgh, 1812), 2.686–87: *CLA*, 43. A robber called Leich was struck by remorse while robbing the king's treasury and was subsequently installed as his treasurer.

282.5 deign to accept a lily there are a few accounts of European women being taken as concubines of Indians. Orme records that after the Black Hole of

Calcutta (1756) 'an English woman, the only one of her sex among the sufferers, was reserved for the seraglio of the general Meer Jaffier' (2.77). Margaret Tait cites a case of a young European woman being sold by her parents to Haidar Ali: see 'The Surgeon's Daughter: Possible Sources?', The Scott Newsletter, 9 (Winter, 1986), 8.

282.12   in the gate   an expression common in the Old Testament, implying 'in public'.

282.15   the hall of Seyd   Arabic Saqīfat Banī Sā'ida the Hall of the Clan of Sā'ida, where an assembly was held after the death of Muhammad (AD 632) and where after some strife Abū Bakr was chosen as his successor. See Wilferd Madelung, The Succession to Muhammad: A Study of the Early Caliphate (Cambridge, 1997), 28.

282.17   the angel of death   Azraël, the angel of death, who in Muslim tradition separates men's souls from their bodies: see George Sale, 'The Preliminary Discourse' prefixed to his translation of The Koran (London, [1887]: first published 1734), 56).

282.17–18   He flung his cap and fictitious beard   Mark Wilks records that Tipu once assumed 'the guise of one who had renounced the world . . . a travelling mendicant, the son of a holy fakir' (Historical Sketches of the South of India, in an attempt to trace the History of Mysoor, 3 vols (London, 1810–17), 2.145). See also Khair-Ullah, 132.

282.34–35   a fair woman caused Solomon ben David to stumble   see 1 Kings 11.1–6. Solomon, son of King David, 'loved many strange women' and 'did evil in the sight of the Lord'. The story of Solomon and Jerâda, daughter of the King of Sidon, is told in a note to George Sale's translation of The Koran, 342n.

282.39   To hear is to obey   Arabic sam'an wa ta'atan proverbial.

282.43–283.1   to conceal all internal sensations   this was remarked by Europeans in India. Orme gives this example: 'The young Seid Mahomed was taught to conceal the emotions he naturally felt at seeing the murderer of his father named in the list of his friends as a guest invited with his approbation. Such are the manners of a court in Indostan' (1.56).

283.6   the Sirdar Belash Cassim   apparently fictitious.

283.9   Payeen-Ghaut   Persian and Hindi, the coastal or low country between the Eastern Ghats and Madras (Hobson-Jobson, 690; see also note to 261.22).

283.25   the robe of honour   this was the Khelaut: see note to 278.24.

283.29   the Cuttyawar breed   Kathiawar, a peninsula in Gujerat in NW India was famous for breeding horses. The details come from Ferguson's description of the horse of his 'Banka or Dandy' (ff. 177r–77v).

283.36–37   present usual on such an occasion   the details of the ceremony in which someone is raised to higher rank come from Ferguson (f. 167r).

283.42   his tongueless mouth   an elephant's tongue is not easily seen.

284.11   shapeless foot upon his breast   for this method of death see Historical Note, 365.

284.25–26   that lump of bloody clay   clay, or earth, as a term for the material part of a person, the body without the soul, derives from Genesis 2.7. The phrase 'lump of clay' is used in accounts of the death of Tipu: 'He, who had left his palace in the morning, a powerful imperious Sultaun, full of vast ambitious projects, was brought back a lump of clay' (Narrative Sketches, 79).

284.40   the Carnatic   the Anglo-Indian name for the coastal area of south India, E of the Eastern Ghats, between Mysore and Madras (Hobson-Jobson).

284.40–41   in future I will be a destroying tempest   the second Anglo-Mysore War broke out in 1780: 'The Madras government by its tactlessness then induced a coalition of the usually hostile Marathas, the Nizam of Hyderabad, and Haidar Ali of Mysore, without preparing any means for meeting it. In

1780 the Carnatic was overrun to the walls at Madras and two armies defeated' (Percival Spear, *A History of India*, 2 vols (London, 1965), 2.91). The British forces defeated by Haidar Ali at Pollilur in 1780 were led by Scots and included David Baird who many years later became Scott's son's commanding officer: see Historical Note, 361.

285.2   he and his son afterwards sunk   Haidar Ali died in 1782; Tipu was killed in the storming of his capital at Seringapatam by the British in 1799.

285.5   Domum Mansit—Lanam Fecit   *Latin* she stayed at home and spun wool: an epitaph from 150 BC. 'The original was an inscription "Lanam feci, domum servavi"' (J. F. Gronovius, note on the *Aulularia*, 1.2, line 3, in Plautus, *Comoedia* (Leyden, 1664), 120). Scott quotes it in his *Journal*, 375, 515.

285   motto   Jonathan Swift, 'Dingley, and Brent' (1724), lines 13–18.

286.14   inditing the goodly matter   see Psalm 45.1.

286.32   smelling bottles   phials or small bottles containing smelling-salts or perfume, used as a restorative in cases of faintness or headache.

287.11   the East Indies   i.e. India and adjacent regions and islands, to be distinguished from the West Indies: see R. E. Hawkins, *Common Indian Words in English* (Delhi, 1984), 42.

287.13   the story of Tiger Tullideph   not identified. *Tiger* may be the slang usage, 'vulgarly or obtrusively overdressed person' (*OED*, tiger, 7a). The earliest citation is from Scott's *Journal*: 'Our young men . . . have one capital name for a fellow that outres and outroars fashion . . . They hold him a vulgarian and call him a tiger' (285). Tullideph appears to be a rare Scots surname: William Tullideph became Principal of St Leonard's College in the University of St Andrews in 1739 and of the United College in 1747 (R. G. Cant, *The University of St Andrews* (Edinburgh, 1946), 88, 91).

287.22   rained odours   *Twelfth Night*, 3.1.81.

287.23   the Carnival   street festivities which take place in Roman Catholic countries in the last days before Lent, of which those in Rome were the most celebrated.

287.32–33   the imitation shawls now made at Paisley   Kashmir shawls were coveted possessions and so expensive that they were imitated in Britain. Paisley, near Glasgow, was one of the centres of manufacture, and the characteristic feathery cone or palmette motif common on the shawls became known as 'paisley', even in India: see Veronica Murphy, 'Europeans and the Textile Trade', in *Arts of India: 1550 to 1900*, ed. John Guy and Deborah Swallow (London: Victoria and Albert Museum, 1990), 169.

287.33   real Thibet wool   shawls were made from the wool of the Kashmir goat and the wild goat of Tibet; as these were scarce and expensive cheaper imitations came to be made with wool from other sources.

287.34   the actual Country shawl   in Anglo-Indian usage *country* means Indian, as opposed to European (*OED*, country, 13b).

287.34–35   inimitable cross-stitch in the border   this detail is probably a satirical invention of Scott's.

287.35–36   a rich Kashmire   a shawl from Kashmir in northern India; in the 19th century the spelling *cashmere* became common.

287.36–37   a thing that cost fifty guineas   Henry Mackenzie's John Homespun felt the cost of an Indian shawl: 'My wife said a shawl was a decent comfortable wear for a middle-aged woman like her . . . which she got a monstrous bargain, tho' I am ashamed to tell, that it stood me in two fat oxen and a year-old cow' (*The Lounger*, 17 (28 May 1785)).

288.3   friend and neighbour, Colonel MacKerris   from *Gaelic Mac-Fhearghuis*, son of Fergus, 'in Gaelic pronounced like "Mac-Kerrash"' (James Ferguson and Robert Menzies Fergusson, *Records of the Clan and Name of Fergusson, Ferguson and Fergus* (Edinburgh, 1895), 11; also George F. Black, *The*

Surnames of Scotland (New York, 1946), 526 under Mackerras). In the short Introduction which Scott added to 'The Surgeon's Daughter' in the Magnum edition (1833) he acknowledged that 'the military friend who is alluded to as having furnished him with some information as to Eastern matters, was Colonel James Ferguson of Huntly Burn ... which name he took the liberty of concealing under its Gaelic form' (48.150). For Ferguson's contribution to 'The Surgeon's Daughter' see Historical Note, 364–66.

288.10   a feu de joie   *French* a friendly or ceremonial discharge of firearms, a salute.

288.12   Things must be as they may   see *Henry V*, 2.1.20.

GLOSSARY

The glossary offers definitions of single and hyphenated words; phrases are explained in the Explanatory Notes. The glossary includes all words in Scots, Gaelic and in foreign languages, and English words which might be difficult to the modern reader. The term *Gaelic English* indicates the pronunciation of English by a Gaelic speaker. Variant spellings of a single word are listed together, with the most common use first. For each word (or sense of a word) up to four occurrences are listed; where a word occurs more than four times in the text only the first is given, followed by 'etc.'. Sometimes the reader is directed to the Explanatory Notes for fuller information.

The Glossary is compiled from the *Oxford English Dictionary*, 2nd edition (Oxford, 1989), *The Concise Scots Dictionary*, ed. Mairi Robinson (Aberdeen, 1985), and Edward Dwelly, *The Illustrated Gaelic-English Dictionary*, 7th edition (Glasgow, 1971). Anglo-Indian terms in 'The Surgeon's Daughter' are identified from the *OED* where possible; where that is not possible the reader is directed to a note. Where the spelling of such words is not the spelling preferred in the *OED* that spelling is given in parentheses. The indication of language of origin in the case of the Anglo-Indian words is given, often in abbreviated form, from the *OED*.

a' *Scots* all 19.8 etc.

a'body *Scots* everybody 46.19

aboon *Scots* above 40.27

abide *wait* 142.10

accessary *law* not the chief actor in an offence but concerned in it 114.13, 170.39

acclivity upward slope of a hill 100.40

accoutred equipped 58.11

accuracy precision 185.21

active *Scots* effective 181.21

adjutant *military* officer in the army who receives and communicates orders from superior officers 115.11

Adzooks *oath* God's hooks, i.e. God's nails 136.14

ae *Scots* one 139.42, 184.31, 184.31

æra era 65.16

aff *Scots* off 41.4, 73.35

again *Scots* against 36.3

a-gone ago, past 72.2

aguish burning, feverish 199.4

aigrette spray of gems worn on the head 249.42 (see note)

ain *Scots* own 23.37 etc.

ainsell *Scots* own self 123.9

alane *Scots* alone 134.24

alcalde *Spanish* magistrate or official with judicial power in Spain and Portugal 171.42

alias *Latin* otherwise known as 146.21

Allah, Alla *Arabic* name of the Deity among Muslims 247.32 etc.

almanack annual publication containing a calendar, astronomical data, tables and other calculations 166.14

amang *Scots* among 161.2

Amazon warlike woman, from the race of female warriors alleged by the Greek historian, Herodotus, to exist in Scythia 261.36

Amazonian resembling an Amazon 253.34, 263.40, 281.15

ambient surrounding 45.33

amenable answerable 95.20

an' *Scots* and 46.29, 73.31

an *Scots* if 48.19

ance *Scots* once 43.14

anchorite hermit, religious recluse 52.2

ane *Scots* one, a, an 23.20 etc.

anent *Scots* concerning 24.13

angelica aromatic herb whose stem is frequently candied 63.19

Angrezie English 272.37 (see note)

anodyne medicine or treatment that alleviates pain and soothes the feelings 183.35

antediluvians those existing before the Old Testament Flood, the very old 65.12

antimony brittle metallic substance used in powdered form to darken the eye-lids, kohl 280.29

apostate one who forsakes religious faith or moral allegiance 232.43, 265.1, 281.15, 281.30

apothecary one who prepares and sells medicinal drugs, a general practitioner 46.10, 205.33

apout *Gaelic English* about 48.15

arch-fiend Satan 233.2

argosy large merchant vessel, especially from Ragusa or Venice 250.17

arraign accuse, indict 116.30

articulately article by article, specifically 156.36

assizes session of the criminal court for a county 142.10 (see note)

a'thegither *Scots* altogether 180.41

attestation administration of an oath of allegiance to a military recruit 220.33

attested sworn, certified (see attestation) 207.5, 210, 28, 215.29, 215.30

attic refined, delicate, poignant 3.23 (see note)

attorney lawyer; sometimes used reproachfully to imply a knave or swindler 182.27, 185.24, 201.4

aught anything 39.1 etc.

auld *Scots* old 23.29 etc.

automaton machine whose movement is caused by a hidden spring or clock-work 226.3

aver declare true, assert 28.14

awa' *Scots* away 169.3, 184.5 (see note)

awfu' *Scots* awful 184.30

awmous *Scots* alms 40.41

awn *Scots* own 40.18

axing *Gaelic English* asking 131.42

ay *Scots* yes 19.6 etc.

aya (ayah) *Anglo-Indian from Portuguese* native nurse or maidservant, children's nurse 221.20

aye *Scots* always 19.8 etc.

back-play reply, response 243.14

backsliding falling away, apostacy 24.42

baffle confuse, defeat 102.31

bahauder see behauder

bailiff officer of justice who executes writs, debt-collector 49.16; agent, estate-manager 131.14 etc.

bairn *Scots* child 40.17 etc.

baith *Scots* both 43.19, 140.4, 175,28

baiting-place place for food and refreshment 71.10

ball missile projected from a firearm, bullet 288.11

banka *Urdu* fop, courtier 280.25 (see note)

bannet *Scots* bonnet, cap 41.4

bannock flat unleavened loaf 69.15

bar rail in a court at which prisoners stand for trial 143.20

bard Highland minstrel and poet 67.23, 82.33, 93.25, 107.6

bark small ship 225.26

bar-keeper person at the counter of a tavern 14.11

baron-bailie *Scots* baron's deputy in legal matters 168.35 (see note)

barony estate held by feudal tenure directly from the crown 28.29, 28.40, 36.23

barns-breaking *Scots* idle frolic, mischievous action 139.38

basilisk fabulous serpent whose look was fatal 171.21, 236.40

basket-hilt hilt in which the swordsman's hand is protected by narrow plates of steel curved like a basket 84.9

bass bass-viol, viola da gamba 191.19

bastinado eastern method of punishment by beating the soles of the feet with a stick 252.42

bastion projecting part of a fortification, rampart 277.38

battery pieces of artillery placed together for combined action 7.10

batton stick, rod 92.16

bauld *Scots* bold 169.35

bazaar *from Turkish via Italian* Eastern market-place or street of shops 273.43

bead-roll list of people, originally to be prayed for 47.20

beam parts of a loom on which the warp is wound before weaving, and the cloth as it is woven 38.34

bean *Gaelic bàn* fair-haired, fair 78.38 etc.

bearing *heraldry* that which is borne on an escutcheon 13.9

beau, beaux *French noun* fashionable young man, lover, escort 22.15 etc.

beaver hat made of beaver fur 201.8

begum *Urdu* princess or lady of high rank in India 253.33 etc.

behauder, bahauder (bahadur) *Hindi* hero, champion, often affixed to an officer's name 248.26, 275.14, 275.41, 282.24

behoof benefit, advantage 183.105

belive *Scots* soon, at once 176.6

belle *French* beautiful or fashionable young woman 187.34, 190.6, 190.17

bellicous bellicose, warlike 23.39

belly-gods *Scots* gluttons 25.4

bellyful hearty beating 129.14 (see note), 136.26

belted-plaid *Scots* male Highland dress consisting of a tartan plaid with one end pleated like a kilt and held round the waist by a belt and the other end thrown over the shoulder 86.34

ben *Gaelic beinn* mountain 71.22 etc.

bethink consider, reflect 47.23

betwixt between 131.8, 139.19, 146.8

bide *Scots* remain, live, wait, endure 41.11 etc.

bien *Scots* well-to-do 40.40

bigged *Scots* built 49.11

bigging *Scots* building 23.27

biggit *Scots* built 24.15

bill written order for the payment of money 173.5, 242.10

billet short letter, note 210.13

billie *Scots* friend, comrade 191.28

bink *Scots* kitchen dresser, shelf 137.14

birling *Scots* rowing-boat or galley used in the West Highlands 88.22

bit *Scots* spot, place 73.37; 'bit of' indicating smallness, endearment or contempt 123.11, 128.33, 128.36

bittock *Scots* bit 35.5

Bismallah (bi'smillah) *Arabic* in the name of Allah, common Muslim exclamation 275.32

blabber swollen 18.21

blackguard rogue, scoundrel 15.39, 135.25, 216.2

blate *Scots* timid, reticent 184.22

blear *verb* dim, blind 132.43

bleeding drawing blood for medicinal purposes 199.37

blink *Scots* short time, moment 35.9, 127.2

bluff frank, blunt, plain-spoken 205.21, 205.21

bodach *Gaelic* old man, spectre or ghost 73.34

bodle *Scots* coin worth two pence Scots (0.16p), hence something of little value 48.23

body *Scots* person, individual 40.17, 40.40, 134.22

bogle *Scots* phantom, spectre 73.34

bohea a black tea 44.28

bolting *colloquial* swallowing hastily, gulping down 31.6

bonbonnière *French* box for sweets 63.18, 64.33

bondswoman serf, slave 97.16

bonnet *Scots* flat woollen cap worn by men 49.13 etc.

bonny *Scots* beautiful, handsome, pretty 30.14 etc.

bon-vivant *French* gourmand, one fond of good living 203.19

boot bargain 129.1, 132.13

bordure *heraldry* border within the shield of a coat of arms 210.8

bothy *Scots* hut, cottage 103.20 etc.

boudoir small room for a lady's personal use 33.26, 60.8, 61.15

bout drinking session 211.43

bower-maiden maid, waiting-woman 68.29

bow-string, bowstring string of a bow used to strangle an offender 199.40, 268.1

box *Scots verb* cover with boards 39.30

brae *Scots* bank, hill 24.2, 73.7, 73.13; in plural, an upland mountainous district 140.13

brake clump of bushes 121.38

Bramin (Brahmin) *Sanskrit* member of the highest or priestly caste among the Hindus 264.18, 265.26, 266.22, 267.10

brass money 157.18

braw *Scots* handsome, fine 49.13, 49.16

breacan *Gaelic* tartan 87.19, 89.14

breack *Gaelic breac* freckled, pitted with small-pox 107.39 etc.

bread livelihood, means of subsistence 135.16

brig *Scots* bridge 128.13

brig merchant ship with two masts 38.39, 210.33, 211.36

brilliants diamonds of the finest cut and brilliancy 173.26, 199.32, 223.24

brisk lively 124.24

briskly smartly 125.31

broad-cloth fine, plain-wove cloth 49.10, 279.42

broadside sheet of paper printed on one side, with proclamations, dying speeches, ballads, etc. 51.5

broadsword sword with a broad blade 59.29 etc.

brockit *Scots* animal with a white streak down its face 132.5

broken injured, bruised 159.6

broth *figurative and ironical* hot soup 137.25

brownie goblin, household spirit 73.33

browst *Scots* brew 174.29

bruited rumoured 201.18

brusten *Scots* bursting, breathless from overexertion 161.2

buckle curl, set, said of hair or a wig 151.30

buckler shield, protection 146.9

buckshee, bukshee (bukshi) *Persian and Urdu* paymaster and commander-in-chief of the army of an Indian state 265.13 etc.

buckskins leather breeches 131.34

buffet stroke, blow 150.32

bullock castrated bull, more generally cattle 124.38 etc.

bunker sandy hollow on a golf course 150.30

burgess *Scots* citizen, freeman of a burgh 32.41, 159.2

burgh *Scots* town 161.9 etc.

burgher *Scots* inhabitant of a town 189.40

burgh-muir *Scots* town moor, untilled land belonging to a burgh 214.18

busked set in order 125.38

but only 123.23, 128.43, 133.8; except, than 129.2

byganes *Scots* bygones 37.33

ca' *Scots* call 35.24, 41.30, 41.37

cabin hut, hovel 159.20

cadet gentleman who entered the army without a commission to learn the military profession 204.33, 204.40, 206.41, 211.6

cadgy *Scots* cheerful, in good spirits 157.19

cairn *Scots* heap of stones raised as a memorial of a battle, death or burial 71.30, 111.10, 124.12

cairn-gorum *Scots* cairngorm, stone or crystal of a yellow or rust colour, named after the Highland mountains where it is found 27.10

cake *Scots* thin, hard-baked bread of oatmeal 69.16, 69.33 (see note to 69.32–33)

callants *Scots* youths, fellows 139.43

callit *Scots* called 23.26, 23.28

canna *Scots* cannot 41.19, 42.19, 127.7, 135.16

canny *Northern English adjective* good, worthy 225.19, 192.13

canny *Scots adjective* cautious, shrewd 131.36; of good omen 73.32

canny *Scots adverb* carefully, cautiously 161.1

canting thieves' or vagabonds' jargon 212.34

cantrip *Scots* spell, charm, magic 127.5

caparison ornamented cloth or covering for a saddle or harness 279.35

caracco *Spanish carajo* emphatic expletive 52.17

caravan company of people travelling together 63.7

caravanserai *Persian* inn in eastern countries especially for the accommodation of parties of merchants 273.26

card-house house or structure made of playing-cards 178.7

carline *Scots* old woman 79.3,

123.24, 161.2

carmen carters, carriers 15.29, 123.35

Carthusian of the Carthusian monastic order, known for the austerity of its rule 61.23 (see note)

carried Scots carried away, transported 46.33, 189.6

carrion carcass 284.20; contemptuous reference to a person, 231.22

carritch Scots catechism 40.30

cashiered dismissed from service 51.3

castor hat, probably of rabbit's fur 29.31

catastrophe event which produces the conclusion, dénouement 140.24

catechise question 65.12

cateran highland fighting man, robber, marauder 77.14 etc.

cattle horses 45.22

cauld Scots cold 140.43

cause law subject of litigation, case 168.31

cavalier horseman, knight, gentleman trained to arms 131.28, 145.28

certie Scots see note to 184.22

chabootra (chabutra) Hindustani platform attached to a house or in a garden 280.4 (see note)

chabouk Persian and Urdu horsewhip 282.14

chaffer bargain, haggle 118.26

chaise carriage 67.25, 73.7

chaise-and-four carriage drawn by four horses 32.9

chambering lewdness 25.6

champaign level, open country without hills or trees 270.5

chap buyer 138.30

chapel Scots Roman Catholic church 47.5, 49.15

chaplet ornament for the head or neck 275.30

chappit Scots struck 19.7

chieftain head of a Highland clan 8.9

chield Scots fellow 36.11 etc.

chobdar Persian and Urdu staffbearer, attendant carrying a staff overlaid with silver as a sign of office 279.8

chowry Hindi fly-whisk 250.7 (see note), 279.33

chuckie-stanes Scots pebbles or marbles, used in a game 180.25

churl base fellow, boor 82.38 etc.

chyle fluid in the intestines, part of the digestive process 151.5

cicerone Italian guide 35.9 etc.

circumduce Scots law declare to have elapsed 28.11

citizen civilian 67.37

citron fruit like a lemon grown in the East 274.16

civet perfume obtained from the civet cat 46.9

clachan Gaelic hamlet, village, village inn 118.20, 133.15, 134.24

clackmill mill 15.5 (see note to 15.8)

clanship social organisation by clan and the spirit of loyalty attaching to it 124.17

classical of the standard set by the civilisations of Greece and Rome 3.23, 69.38

clavers Scots gossip, chatter 169.39

clay earth as the material of the human body 118.25, 118.30, 189.31, 230.5, 284.26 (see note)

claymore Scots from Gaelic highland sword 84.9, 86.37, 124.17 (see note), 180.21

cleek Scots seize, snatch 174.33

climacteric critical stage in human life 14.4 (see note)

clocking-hen clucking hen, hen sitting on eggs 169.4

clog heavy piece of wood attached to the leg or neck of a man or beast to impede motion 199.6, 206.11

cloght-dearg Gaelic cleòc dearg red mantle or cloak 116.42, 117.12, 117.40, 118.16

clombe climbed 24.2

clothyard yard by which cloth was measured 129.24 (see note)

cloud-berry berry like a raspberry growing on high ground in northern Europe 85.10 (see note)

clove past tense of cleave stuck, adhered 217.5 (see note)

clown peasant, country person 192.41

coach-and-six coach drawn by six horses 180.36

coadjutor assistant, helper 158.4

coallier collier, supplier of coal 52.30

cockade knot of ribbon worn on a

soldier's cap 95.24

cocked worn jauntily 125.30, 189.43

cockloft small loft, room under the roof reached by a ladder 148.6

cock woodcock 40.32

cognizance *law* jurisdiction, the hearing and trying of a cause 146.8

colours flag, standard 180.33; aspect, appearance, 199.33

commissaries *military* officers in charge of supplies 220.40

commission warrant by which officers in the army from the ensign upwards are appointed 164.21 etc.

commodity collection of goods for sale 51.2

communing *Scots* debate, discussion 202.36

communion church, religious fellowship 164.32

company *military* sub-division of an infantry regiment commanded by a captain 59.31, 115.9, 116.9, 202.10

compassionating pitying 119.26, 145.2

competence adequate means for living 200.4, 209.43

composing sedative 235.1

composition compounding, compromise, mutual agreement for settling differences 119.23, 143.31

compotation drinking together, carouse 212.10

compounded compromised 134.5

condescend *Scots* enter into particulars, specify 156.36

condescendence *Scots law* legal statement of facts 28.12 (see note)

conducteur *French* driver, guide 69.3

confinement child-birth 169.23, 239.20

conjured appealed to, charged 172.5

connexion relationship by marriage rather than blood 56.19

contingencies uncertainty of outcome 259.43

contingent incidental 170.27

controlled *law* overruled 238.19

conversazione *Italian* evening assembly for conversation 60.33

conveyance *law* transference of property from one person to another 51.10

cood *Gaelic English* good 47.7, 123.13, 135.43

coodman *Gaelic English* see gudeman 47.17

copy manuscript prepared for printing 123.6

coronach *Gaelic corranach* funeral song, dirge 84.7, 110.36, 111.6

corn *Scots verb* give a horse a feed of oats 73.30

cornelian dull, red, semi-transparent quartz 210.7

corrie *Scots* hollow on a mountainside surrounded by steep slopes 102.33, 122.8

coss *Hindi* measure of distance in India, varying in different parts between one and three miles 246.2

Cot *Gaelic English* God 47.1 (see note) etc.

coterie select social group 287.1

cottar *Scots* tenant occupying a cottage 40.17

couldna *Scots* could not 48.23, 132.7

counter-sign pass-word 264.10

country *Anglo-Indian* Indian, as opposed to European; native 287.34

covenanter *Scottish history* adherent of the seventeenth-century covenants on matters of church and state, extreme Protestant 5.11, 36.33

coverit *Scots* covered 23.28

cowrie *Hindi and Urdu* shells used as money in Africa and southern Asia 199.36, 205.8

cracks *Scots* tales, gossip 39.16

crank fanciful turn of speech 3.16

craze *Gaelic English* graze 49.4

creagh *Gaelic creach* raid, incursion for plunder 77.9, 130.14

creat *Gaelic English* great 47.24

creeze (creese) *Malay* Malay dagger with a wavy blade 249.39

crest *heraldry* device placed above the shield and helmet in a coat of arms 38.33

cribbage card game played by two to four players 213.26, 214.3, 214.34, 216.24

crimping procuring men for service by seducing, decoying or entrapping them 219.31, 220.4

croft *Scots* smallholding 23.25, 23.27

crony associate, friend 133.29

cropped trimmed, cut 131.26

crore *Hindi* ten millions 199.9

crupper strap to keep a saddle in place 283.31

crown coin worth five shillings (25p) 36.7, 47.17, 199.8

cruizing wandering on the look-out for business 199.8

cudgel club , short thick stick used as a weapon 125.15, 128.33

cue plait of hair worn hanging behind 31.31

cull *slang* fellow, simpleton 216.14

cummerband (cummerbund) *Persian and Urdu* sash, girdle, waist-belt 280.29, 287.16

curb-rein rein used to check an unruly horse 175.9

curch *Scots* kerchief, woman's cap 49.14, 118.11

curry *Tamil* spiced sauce or stew served with rice 204.39

cushion escutcheon, coat of arms 41.36, 41.36

cutlass short sword, particularly used by sailors 215.4

dae *Scots* do 42.15

daddles *low* hands, fists 136.17, 138.14

daffing *Scots* joking, acting playfully or foolishly 176.6

dainty *Scots* pleasant, agreeable 43.22

deal thin piece of wood, usually pine 33.15

dean chief officer of a cathedral 237.5

deasil *Gaelic deiseal* southward, towards the sun 127.26 (see note)

decoring *Scots* decorating, adorning 39.33

defile *verb* march in a line or in files 115.9

deil *Scots* devil 44.16 etc.

demigod minor or inferior deity 155.28

denouement *French* outcome or unravelling of a plot 282.42

denounced proclaimed, declared against 15.32, 99.22

depone *Scots* declare upon oath 170.20

depreciating disparaging 128.42, 150.35

depreciation lowering of estimation, disparagement 258.7

depreciatory belittling 148.26

derogation loss of honour or reputation 38.30

deuce devil 157.27 (see note), 183.33

devoted doomed 15.34

devotee one zealously devoted to religion or religious observance 54.36, 246.17, 248.4, 281.34

dewan *Arabic and Persian* in India, financial minister or treasurer of a Muslim state 273.8, 273.17, 276.22

dhu *Gaelic dubh* black, dark 85.34 etc.

diapason rich, deep burst of sound 60.26

diapré *heraldry* diapered, checked 38.32

didna *Scots* did not 41.39, 134.13, 184.30

die *Scots* toy, trinket 210.19

dike *Scots* wall 191.31

dilation expansion 18.22

dinna *Scots* do not 39.14 etc.

dirk *Scots noun* highlander's short dagger 86.38 etc.

dirk *Scots verb* stab with a dirk 155.2

dirking stabbing 128.34, 139.41, 153.36

disclamation disclaimer, repudiation 24.22

discuss try the quality of, consume 134.4

disinterested free from self-seeking 48.29, 187.4, 285.30, 286.1

disinterestedly without self-seeking 30.27

disquisition writing in which a subject is investigated or discussed 51.16, 287.29

distaff staff used in the spinning of wool and flax to hold the unspun fibres 80.43, 81.1

distemper disease 285.32

divan *Persian* council, council-chamber 248.32, 282.25

Dives *Latin* rich man 29.13 (see note)

divot slice of earth with grass growing on it, turf 74.4

doch-an-dorrach *Gaelic deoch-an-doruis* drink at parting, stirrup-cup 70.34, 126.36

doddy *Scots* bull or cow without horns 132.4, 134.10

doer *Scots* agent 14.40, 16.23

dollar crown (25p), five-shilling

piece 48.18, 82.15, 89.43

domiciliation settling in a home 45.14

done *slang* killed 213.40

doom condemnation, sentence of punishment 142.10

door-cheek *Scots* door-post, doorway 43.22

dour *Scots* unyielding, stern, sullen 138.22, 175.8, 175.26

dowrah *Hindustani* village runner, guide 269.21 (see note), 269.24, 269.38, 269.43

dram measure of spirits 46.36, 57.17, 100.20

drap *Scots* drop 35.23

draught potion, medicine 97.34, 235.1

dreid *Scots* dread 25.8

drive urge animals forward 122.25, 124.29, 124.35

drove *noun* number of animals moving together 77.11 etc.

drover person superintending the movement of large numbers of cattle 124.18 etc.

drove-road road used and established by droves of animals 124.36, 130.38

dubash *Hindi* interpreter, in India agent employed by a European in transacting business with natives 264.18, 266.22, 267.19, 268.7

duenna *Spanish* elderly woman companion or servant 68.34

dun *noun* debt-collector 52.20

dun *Gaelic dùn* fortified hill 100.10, 100.29, 102.37

dun *adjective* dull brown 132.4

dunniewassal *Gaelic duin'uasal* gentleman 141.19

durbar *Persian and Urdu* court kept by an Indian ruler; public audience or levee held by a native prince 268.3 etc.

duties rents, taxes, dues 252.8

earnest foretaste, instalment 162.10

éclat *French* brilliance 63.28

ee *Scots* eye 180.40, 184.23

een *Scots* eyes 180.16, 180.18

e'en evening 41.19, 149.29; *Scots* even 47.14

Egad *oath* God, or by God 216.1

eld old people 124.15

Elysium abode of the blessed after death in Greek mythology, place of perfect happiness 15.38

emblazonry depiction of heraldic devices 24.21

embrasure aperture, bay 61.23

enclosed fenced, as opposed to open land 131.1

enclosure, inclosure field, land marked off by boundaries 131.18, 132.13, 133.27, 143.21

enemy the enemy of man, the devil 111.43

engrailed *heraldry* indented with a series of curvilinear notches, scalloped 210.9

enow *Scots* enough 135.3

Epicurishnesse luxury, sensuality 25.10 (see note)

ere before 80.40 etc.

Esculapian belonging to Aesculapius god of medicine 169.27

even *noun* evening 127.20

even *Scots, verb* impute, make out 42.38

evidents *Scots law* documents establishing a right or title 24.12

excise tax on goods, customs 5.5

excitation excitement, stimulus 122.33

exotic exotic tree, hence delicate 132.31

exploding discrediting 237.27

extempore *Latin* without premeditation or preparation 3.11

eyes see note to 218.24

factor *Scots* agent for a landlord 46.43

fancy caprice, imagination 201.38

fain gladly 21.10; glad under the circumstances 150.7

faitherless *Scots* fatherless 123.9

fakir *Arabic, literally* poor man, Muslim religious mendicant 245.40 etc.

fancies songs, impromptu musical compositions 123.36

fancy boxing, pugilism 129.14

fanfaronade ostentation, fanfare 202.32

fash trouble 19.6, 35.22

fat wealthy 14.28

fause *Scots and English dialect* false 41.24, 133.11, 163.12, 163.16

faut *Scots* fault 41.30, 41.30

fauteuil *French* armchair 61.22

fearfu' *Scots* fearful 74.34

fee *Scots* servant's wages 41.29

feeder trainer 14.16, 129.17

feeling sympathetic, compassionate 135.27

fell ruthless, savage 262.12

feringi (feringhee) *Arabic and Persian* Indian term for a European, oriental adoption of the word Frank 246.23 (see note) etc.

fery *Gaelic English* very 54.39, 55.1

fey *Scots* fated to die, behaving as if doomed 46.41

figments invented stories, fictions 203.30

fife small wind instrument used to accompany the drum in military music 114.33

filigree delicate ornament made of silver threads 59.41

firelock musket or gun ignited by a spark 109.3, 109.23, 110.7

fleech *Scots* flatter 77.6

flit *Scots* shift, move house 24.15, 41.19

flyting *Scots* quarrelling 161.30

forfeited suffered confiscation of estates for treasonable activity 24.33

forfeiture punishment of confiscation of lands and titles 25.2

foil light sword used in fencing, with a blunt edge and a button at the point 288.9

for as an example of 123.24, 127.4

fore-stair *Scots* outside staircase leading to the first floor of a building 46.15

foretauld *Scots* foretold 43.24

forgie *Scots* forgive 123.8, 135.41

formalist stickler for forms and rules 22.38

forthink *Scots* regret, have second thoughts 47.25

Forty-five *Scottish history* the Jacobite rising of 1745 13.29

fourscore eighty 160.22

frae *Scots* from 40.18 etc.

frampal mettlesome, spirited 30.3

Frangistan country of the seringi, or European 261.17 (see note), 282.5

Frank European 246.23 (see note), 247.33

Frankish see previous entry 271.42

freat fret, agitation of the mind, passion 128.24

free-booter, freebooter adventurer in search of plunder 270.25, 276.27

free-holder owner of property 192.9

freestone fine-grained sandstone or limestone that can be easily cut 32.30, 33.1

fresher freshly, newly 201.8

friends *plural* relations, kin 187.19, 225.16, 259.4, 270.31

front face, forehead 256.6

fuff *Scots* outburst of temper 48.8

fugitive *adjective* ephemeral, occasional 52.24, 52.38

fule *Scots* foolish 41.9

furlough leave of absence granted to a soldier for a stated time 93.40, 94.35, 99.15

fyke *Scots* trouble, bother 175.14

Gad *oath* God 206.40, 251.36

gae *Scots* go 40.41 etc.

Gael *noun* Scottish highlander 67.20 etc.

Gaelic *noun* the Gaelic language 129.4, 129.43, 130.3

Gaelic *adjective* highland 128.11

gallooned beribboned, trimmed 249.36

game-cock cock bred and trained for cock-fighting 14.16

gamester gambler, one who habitually plays at games of chance for money 21.43

gammon *slang* chatter 214.6

gang *Scots* go 35.39 etc.

gane *Scots* gone 42.8, 49.17

gar *Scots* cause 123.26

gartered tied with a band 125.31

gate *Scots* route, way, manner 36.10 etc.

gauger *Scots* exciseman 46.43

gear *Scots* possessions, property 42.23, 47.28

genteels *noun* aspirers to be considered gentlemen 32.4

gentle having the status of a gentleman 13.18, 13.20.124.19

gentrice *Scots* people of good birth or breeding, gentry 41.37

ghostly spiritual 200.25, 235.40

gibbet gallows 111.8, 111.12, 113.21

gie *Scots* give 48.26, 135.28, 138.36, 175.15

gied *Scots* gave 40.30, 48.26

gien *Scots* given 47.4

gillie *Gaelic gille* attendant, lad, servant 88.9, 123.11

gillie-whitefoot barefoot highland lad 123.2 (see note)

gin *Scots and English dialect* if 136.21

girdle-cake bread or cake cooked on a flat iron plate 70.28

girning *Scots* grinning 191.20

girth grith, place of protection or sanctuary 15.9

glass-breaker *Scots* hard-drinker 176.7

gled *Scots* kite, bird of prey 169.4, 184.24

glen *Scots* highland valley, narrow, mountainous valley 48.17 etc.

glowering *Scots* staring, gazing intently 174.14

glunamie *Scots* lowland name for a highlander 125.30 (see note)

God-speed parting wish for success, 'God speed you' 127.21

good-daughter *Scots* daughter-in-law 163.37, 168.40

goodman see gudeman

goodnights compositions improvised while going to sleep, or last thing at night 123.36

goodwife, gudewife *Scots* hostess of an inn, wife, old woman 35.24 etc.

gossip woman friend 50.16

goot *Gaelic English* good 134.23

Goth person devoid of culture and taste 151.37

governante mistress of a household, housekeeper 36.30, 48.6

gowffing *Scots* golfing 156.33

gracefu' *Scots* graceful 191.8

grampus whale, person puffing and blowing 161.18

grandsire grandfather 24.16, 24.29, 24.42, 26.20

gratis *Latin* for nothing, freely 245.36

gratulation compliment, congratulation 126.32

grazier one who grazes or feeds cattle for the market 21.43, 125.7, 125.21, 155.2

greishogh *Gaelic griosach* burning ember 105.5, 105.43, 105.7

griffin *Anglo-Indian* European newly arrived in India, novice, newcomer 206.40

grinded ground 67.9

griped groped, sought to clutch something 137.4

grit *Scots* great 23.21

grudge be troubled, vexed 137.38

grumph *Scots* grunt 129.2

gude *Scots* good 19.8 etc.

gudeman, goodman *Scots* husband, host, owner or tenant of a small farm 35.25, 42.25, 135.1

gudewife see goodwife

guerdon reward, recompense 247.25

guide *Scots verb* take care of, handle, 161.6 (see note), 184.5

guinea English gold coin worth 21 shillings 17.20 etc. (see note to 162.9)

guinea-pig midshipman in the East India service 255.4

gules *heraldry* red 210.8

gulfing engulfing 104.19

gulled cheated, deceived 224.37

gulph profound depth, devouring chasm 283.41

gyre-carlin *Scots* witch, hag 73.34

gyves shackles 108.11

ha' *Scots* have 35.42, 36.2

haarst *Scots* harvest 47.16

habited inhabited 49.6

hae *Scots* have 19.7 etc.

ha'en *Scots* having 47.24

hackney hired out 57.11

haggis traditional Scottish dish, made of offal, oatmeal, onion and pepper 129.3

hail-shot small shot which scatters like hail when fired 52.38

hakim (hakeem) *Arabic* physician or doctor in Muslim countries and in India 283.9, 284.26, 284.30

halberts place of punishment constructed from military spears called halberts 99.17

hald *Scots* hold 23.39

hale *Scots* uninjured 136.2

half-text size of handwriting half the size of 'text' or large hand 26.1

hank *Scots* coil or skein, hold 175.23, 200.27

hard-by close by 45.3

hard-go drinking session 26.37

harvest-moon moon which is full within a fortnight of the autumnal equinox 86.24

hasna *Scots* has not 191.8, 191.11

haud *Scots* hold 184.6

hauteur *French* haughtiness, loftiness of bearing 230.13

heartsome *Scots* cheerful 39.15

heath heather 73.1, 91.29, 93.30

heath-bird black grouse 49.19

heath-cock male of the black grouse 26.41

hebdomadal weekly, every seven days 15.19

hedge secure, compensate for 243.14

help serve, distribute food or drink 31.10

her *Gaelic English* his 49.1, 49.7

hermetically tightly, absolutely 63.5

hersell himself 134.22

het *Scots* hot 140.43

hie *Scots* high 161.8

higgler itinerant dealer 200.34

high highly-priced 132.10; noble 188.28

himsell *Scots* himself 175.18

Hindoo, Hindhu Hindu 155.32 etc.

Hindostan, Hindoostan, Hindustan Hindustan, the country of the Hindus particularly North India, but often used for the whole peninsula 155.32, 220.42, 248.13, 161.19

hobnail large-headed nail 51.3

hobnailed with the sole protected by large-headed nails 140.32

hogg *slang* shilling 213.41, 216.15

hogged with its mane cut short 131.26

hollow cry out, shout 269.25

holm *Scots* low-lying land beside a river 27.7, 27.13

home-brewed ale brewed at home, for home consumption 134.3

hoo hoo *Scots* cry used to frighten cattle or to urge them on 126.43

hookah *Urdu* Indian pipe in which tobacco and spices are smoked through water 249.25

hooly *Scots* slowly 139.40 (see note)

hooping whooping 151.10

hoot, hout *Scots* interjection implying dissent, incredulity, or impatience 36.9 etc.; for 134.13 and 184.5 see notes

horning blowing of a horn 151.10

hornpipe lively dance, usually performed by one person 188.8

hornworks projecting part of a fortification 16.24

hose stocking 125.31

hotel town house 56.30

hough-sinew hamstring, tendon at the back of the knee 112.7

houri *from Persian via French* nymph of the Muslim paradise, seductively beautiful woman 247.28, 271.42

house-leek pink-flowered herb, sempervivum 174.7

hout see hoot

howdah, howdaw *Persian and Urdu* seat to carry two or more persons, usually fitted with a railing and canopy, on the back of an elephant 279.30, 284.2

howdawed bearing a howdah 278.2

humdudgeons sulks 134.25

humour mood 45.5, 50.22, 94.24

hurdy-gurdy popular musical instrument played by turning a handle 67.9

husbandrie tillage, cultivation of the soil 23.35

hye-spye kind of hide-and-seek 178.5

ideal existing as a mental image, conceived as excellent 139.9, 199.3

ilk the same 23.12 (see note), 24.8, 193.1

ill *Scots* bad, unsatisfactory 140.16

incognito concealed identity 3.31 etc.

indenture contract of apprenticeship 194.20

Indiaman ship engaged in the trade with India, especially ship of large tonnage belonging to the East India Company 227.33, 243.17, 254.41

indifferent poor 179.25

indifferently poorly 14.18, 162.35, 172.34

indite utter, dictate, compose 147.6, 147.6, 286.14

inditer composer 24.17

involved reserved, enfolded 52.2

imp offspring, child 123.5

impassible impassive, unimpressible 267.10

impost tax 59.2

imprimatur sanction, authorisation 55.14

inclosure see enclosure

indemnified compensated 60.12

indorsation indorsement, ratification 56.1

induct conduct, lead, install 39.7, 132.20

infare *Scots* entertainment on entering a new house, especially at the reception of a bride in her new home 65.24

infer excite, bring about as a consequence 92.17, 143.4

ingle-side fire-side 127.20

intercommuned *Scots* prohibited from intercourse with others, banned 24.36 (see note)

interest influence 187.25 etc.

intestine internal, domestic 202.258

iota smallest letter of the Greek alphabet (I or i), very small quantity 75.36

jackanapes name for a tame monkey or ape, person behaving like an ape 136.29

Jacobite supporter of the Stewart claim to the British throne 7.35, 65.33, 239.41

Jacobitical favouring the Stewart claim to the throne 239.3

Jacobitism political philosophy which supported the Stewart claim in the dynastic controversies of the late 17th and 18th centuries 154.26

jade horse 30.3

jalousing *Scots* guessing, suspecting 175.4

japan wood ornamented with black and coloured lacquer 59.22

jaw *Scots* wave, surging water 171.11

jessamine jasmine, shrub with fragrant white or yellow flowers 274.15

jigger-dubber door-keeper, jailer 214.1, 214.3

jigging sporting, frolicking 210.40

jimply *Scots* scarcely 73.12

jointure-house house settled on a woman as a provision in case of widowhood 14.20 etc.

jouk *Scots* duck, evade by bending the body 171.11

kaffila (cafila) *Arabic* company of travellers, caravan 269.29

kafr (kaffir) *Arabic* infidel 275.40 (see note), 284.37

kail *Scots* cabbage, soup, meal 51.3, 140.43, 150.4 (see note)

kailyard, kale-yard cabbage patch 74.9, 192.1

kains *Scots* payment in kind, portion of the produce of a tenancy payable as rent 41.3

kale-yard see **kailyard**

keeped *Scots* kept 40.43, 41.5

keepit *Scots* kept 35.40

ken *Scots verb* know 36.10 etc.

ken *noun* knowledge 216.3

ken *vagabond's slang* house, lodging 216.14

kennel *Scots* channel, street gutter 15.1 etc.

kenning sight, view 135.16

kent *Scots* knew 49.8

key-note in music the first note of a scale; figuratively, a leading or prevailing idea 233.13

khan *Persian and Arabic* lord, prince 248.26, 275.13, 282.24; building for the accommodation of travellers 272.20 etc.

khelaut (khilat) *Urdu* dress of honour presented as a mark of distinction 278.24 (see note)

killedar (killadar) *Urdu* commandant or governor of a fort 262.42 etc.

kilt garment worn by male highlanders, skirt usually of tartan cloth reaching the knee and pleated at the back 66.8, 134.11, 136.17

kilted dressed in kilts 123.41

kind kindly 193.20

kine cattle 97.20

kingis *Scots* king's 23.25

kirk *Scots* church, the presbyterian Church of Scotland 25.15 etc.

kiven *Gaelic English* given 47.24

knitting knotting, weaving, plaiting 178.10

knowing smart, fashionable 32.14

knowingly stylishly 131.26

kyloes *Scots* highland cattle 129.41

lac (lakh) *Hindustani* one hundred thousand 199.9

lair bed, lying place 215.18

laird *Scots* lord, landowner 14.7 etc.

land *Scots* building or tenement 182.10, 185.40, 191.34, 210.9

landleddy *Scots* hostess of an inn 39.15

landlord *Scots* head of a family where one is a guest, host 152.18

landlouper *Scots* vagabond 167.25

landward *Scots* in the country, as opposed to the town 161.14

lang *Scots* long 43.18 etc.

langsyne *Scots* long ago, long since 128.31

lass *Northern English and Scots*, young girl 30.15 etc.

latchets shoe-laces, fastening 133.1

lawing *Scots* bill 39.18

lawn open spaces between woods 122.23

lazar-house house for the diseased, especially lepers 210.24

leabhar-dhu *Gaelic leabhar dubh* black book, wallet 126.38

leddy *Scots* lady 35.13 etc.

lee-side side away from the wind 35.24

legerdemain sleight of hand, juggling 51.7

leprous with diseased skin 107.15

levy body of men enrolled for military service 94.20, 202.12, 219.37

lie when writing in Latin term indicating that what follows is in the vernacular 24.32

lifted *Scots* took up, collected 41.2

ligature bond 217.15

like *Scots* probable, likely 28.10 etc.; as if about to 47.1

likely promising 205.31, 205.37, 218.17

limned painted, portrayed 39.36

linch-pin pin passed through the end of an axle-tree to keep a wheel in place 75.25

lineaments distinctive features 176.33

list choose 16.26, 191.9

lithotomical pertaining to surgery to remove a stone in the bladder 210.17

litter conveyance for a person usually enclosed with curtains and carried by bearers 280.20 etc.

llhu *Gaelic laogh* calf 130.2

lobscous sailor's dish made of meat, vegetables and ship's biscuit 211.39

lock mechanism by which the charge in a gun is exploded 80.34, 80.35

lofted *Scots* with an upper storey 49.12

longe lunge, thrust with a sword 7.13

loon *Scots* wretch, rogue, boy 133.11, 161.29, 169.1, 175.27

loophole narrow vertical opening 109.11

looten *Scots* let 35.42

lootie *Hindi* member of a band of irregular forces whose chief object in warfare was plunder, marauder 265.36

lubber sailor's term for an unseaman-like fellow, idle person 215.14

luckie *Scots* wife, old woman 41.16 etc.

lucubrations meditation, literary work showing signs of much study 150.8, 158.2, 288.13

lying-in being in childbirth 169.4

macerate waste, tear the flesh from 119.2

magisterial pertaining to a magistrate 45.13

Mahomedan, Mahometan follower of the Prophet Muhammad, Muslim 176.38 etc.

Mahomedanism Islam 277.18

mail armour composed of interlaced rings or overlapping plates of metal 279.14

main cock-fight 129.16

mains *Scots* home farm of an estate 27.43

mair *Scots* more 40.14 etc.

maister *Scots* master 19.5, 47.35, 49.5, 191.7

Mahrattas Marathas, people occupying central and south-western parts of India 262.40, 265.9, 284.21

maladroitness awkwardness, lack of skill 150.34

malison curse, malediction 120.22

mango *Portuguese from an Eastern original* fruit cultivated in India, eaten raw and cooked 246.10, 274.13, 277.17

man-service feudal obligation to work for a superior 23.24

marcats *Scots* markets 140.17

martinet disciplinarian 244.35

matchlock, match-lock musket having a matchlock, gun lock in which a match is placed to ignite the powder 269.20, 278.42, 279.13

mate assistant to some functionary on board ship 164.20, 198.27, 243.29, 255.4

matronize chaperon 61.19

maudlin tearful, sentimental 212.15

maun *Scots* must 36.10 etc.

mayhap perhaps 133.16

mechanic person in trade or industry 34.3

megrim migraine 34.20

member of Parliament 192.10

men-at-arms warriors, soldiers 145.28

menstruum *alchemy* solvent, liquid agent by which a solid substance may be dissolved 44.30

mercat *Scots* market 43.19

meridian mid-day 117.28

messenger *Scots* person who executes legal summonses 47.33 (see note) etc.

metaphysical abstract 14.37

mezzo-termini *Italian* middle terms, half measures 16.8

mhor *Gaelic mór* great 66.30 etc.

mickle *Scots* much 19.6, 41.39

mill fight with the fists 135.35

mill-horse horse used for turning or working a mill 198.23

mill water-mill 214.18

minaret *Arabic* tall, slender tower or turret connected with a Mosque, from which the muezzin calls the people to prayer 246.11, 273.22

minatory threatening, menacing 151.28

mind *Scots* remember 19.5, 19.6, 191.18

minister clergyman of the Church of Scotland 100.41 etc.

minuet slow, stately dance for two dancers 188.6

mither *Scots* mother 55.1

mizzles *Scots* measles 42.7

mohur, mohr *Persian* chief gold coin of India 222.34, 224.4, 278.23, 285.16

molakat *Hindustani* meeting, encounter 278.27 (see note)

mollach *Gaelic molach* hairy, rough-haired 86.38

monsieur *French* title of address for a man, sir 167.20, 167.21

mony *Scots* many 23.20 etc.

morning *Scots* spirits, usually whisky, drunk first thing in the morning 128.43

mortar bowl in which the ingredients of a medicine are pounded 160.19 (see note), 193.14

mort-skin *Scots* skin of a sheep or lamb that has died of natural causes 200.36

Moslem *Arabic* Muslim 176.41 etc.

Moslemah used erroneously as a plural of Muslim 155.33 (see note), 245.35, 281.30

mosses *Scots* peat-bogs, moorland allocated to tenants for cutting fuel 28.32

moullah (mullah) *Persian, Turkish and Urdu* Muslim title for one learned in theology or sacred law 246.29, 246.35, 245.40, 275.32

mountain-ash rowan tree 27.4

mountaineer highlander 145.31

mounted adjusted 201.8

muckle *Scots* much 41.9

muhme *Gaelic muime* nurse, foster-mother 127.20 etc.

muezzin *Arabic* in Muslim countries public crier who proclaims the regular hours of prayer 273.21

mulagatawny (mulligatawny) *Tamil literally* pepper water, Indian highly-spiced soup 204.38

muleteer mule-driver 69.39

mulled hot and spiced 223.7

musket hand-gun used by infantry soldiers 108.8, 110.5

musketry muskets collectively 278.4, 279.3

musnud *Urdu* seat made of cushions, used as a throne in India 280.8 etc.

Musselman (Mussulman) *Persian* Muslim 246.9, 247.33, 272.13, 272.27

muster assembly 190.15

muster-roll roll-call 8.11

mutchkin *Scots* liquid measure (3 gills; 0.2 litres) often used for spirits 160.42

mysell *Scots* myself 36.11, 123.27, 132.7, 169.35

na *Scots* no, not 35.12 etc.

nabob *from Urdu via Portuguese* (see nawaub) Muslim governor of a province 199.38

nae *Scots* no 35.25 etc.

nagara (naker) *Arabic and Persian* kettle-drum 279.2 (see note)

naig (naik) *Urdu* military officer 252.9, 254.30, 282.35

nailer *slang* marvellously good thing 135.36

nainsell *Gaelic English* own self 49.8

nane *Scots* none 39.15

natch (nautch) *Urdu and Hindi* Indian exhibition of dancing performed by professional dancing-girls 203.9

nattiest *slang* smartest 136.14

nawaub (nawab) *Urdu* title of a Muslim official acting as deputy or governor in a province of the Mughal empire 248.6 etc.

near-hand *Scots* close 25.12

needful *noun* what is necessary or essential 181.30, 227.32

needna *Scots* need not 128.35

ne'er *Scots* never 73.35, 133.10

ne'er-do-weel, neer-do-weel *Scots* good-for-nothing 43.25, 44.15, 123.26

neibour *Scots* neighbour 43.20

neophyte novice 147.18

nine-pin pin set up to be knocked down in the game of nine-pins 137.11

Nizam *Urdu and Turkish* governor, title of the rulers of Hyderabad 262.40

no *Scots* not 35.22 etc.

nonchalance apparent unconcern, indifference 256.29

nor *Scots* than 25.16

nouz *slang* intelligence, commonsense 205.38

nullah *Hindi* river or stream, watercourse 270.6, 270.32, 271.6

nuzzur (nazar) *Urdu* in India present made by an inferior to a superior 278.22 (see note)

o' *Scots* of 35.23 etc.

obeisance bow, action expressing submission and respect 10.31, 283.42

objurgation severe rebuke, chiding 111.33

och *Scots* oh 47.4 etc.

octogenarian person of eighty years old 64.27

Odd's *oath* God's 36.10

odds inequality, disparity in number 87.23 (see note), 109.10; equalising allowance given to a weaker player in a game 150.29

oe *Scots* grandchild 163.38

office *adjective* kitchen 33.21

offices kitchen quarters 57.37

officious eager to please, obliging 93.26, 177.30

officium *Latin* office 24.10

ogre man-eating monster from folklore and fairy tales, usually a hideous giant 180.22

ohellany *Gaelic* exclamation of lamentation 49.16

ohonari *Gaelic* lamentation, alas for the king or chief 49.16 (see note), 123.30

ohonochie *Gaelic och nan ochain* alas, woe of woes 76.29

oig *Gaelic òg* young 125.33 etc.

onset attack 137.34

ony *Scots* any 36.2 etc.

onybody *Scots* anybody 42.37

operative worker 288.1

or *heraldry* tincture of gold or yellow in armorial bearings 210.9

ordinary tavern 192.42

otium *Latin* ease, tranquillity 122.31

ottar (attar) *Persian* fragrant oil or essence 203.16

ou *Scots* expression of surprise or vexation 42.37

out for 132.43 see note

ouzel blackbird 227.15 (see note)

overmatched surpassed, overcome 129.13

overscutched worn out 123.34 (see note)

ower *Scots* over 43.19 etc.; too 47.13 etc.

owerloup *Scots* leap over 130.39 (see note)

owliah *Arabic* saint 246.8 (see note)

own *absolute* good, advantage 89.33

owsen *Scots* oxen 23.40

oyster-like reserved, uncommunicative, closed like an oyster in its shell 147.15

pack *Gaelic English* back 139.34

pack bundle of money 199.41

paction bargain, contract 118.24

pagoda *Portuguese from a disputed Indian original*, temple or sacred building in India and South Asia 202.15; gold coin current in south India 246.4

pairns *Gaelic English* bairns, children 132.8

palanquin *Portuguese from an Eastern original*, covered conveyance carried by bearers, litter 246.7, 271.40

pale protection, jurisdiction 164.10

pallet straw bed, poor bed 86.20 etc.

palsy disease of the nervous system causing tremors or paralysis 159.12

pander go-between in sexual affairs, pimp 34.17

panel *Scots law* prisoner, the accused 144.26

panes *Gaelic English* bones 136.2

papist Roman Catholic 101.18, 164.22, 175.28, 200.25

pargains *Gaelic English* bargains 134.21

park *Scots* enclosed piece of land, field 131.42

parole word of honour given by a freed prisoner that he will return to custody 7.28

parsonage *Scots* tithes or financial dues for the support of the parson 28.31 (see note)

parterre level space in a garden with flowerbeds 255.21

partizan member of a party of light or irregular troops, or of a volunteer force 250.25

party participant, associate 29.41

party-coloured variegated in colour 3.7, 3.18

patois *French* local version of a language, dialect 63.34, 251.16, 261.42

patronize protect, support 276.17

paughty *Scots* conceited, haughty 28.5

pavilion tent of a large and stately kind 276.42

paynim pagan 273.32

pe *Gaelic English* be 48.14, 131.40 etc.; by 131.42

peace-officer officer appointed to preserve public peace, constable 141.38, 142.1

peasts *Gaelic English* beasts 131.40, 132.7

peaten *Gaelic English* beaten 136.23

peculator embezzler 220.41

peculiar personal 225.30

ped *Gaelic English* bed 47.36

peel strip 137.30

peen *Gaelic English* been 134.14

pehaviour *Gaelic English* behaviour 135.27

pehind *Gaelic English* behind 134.16

pelongs *Gaelic English* belongs 136.7

penetralia innermost parts or recesses 59.17

pendant see note to 197.34

pendicle *Scots* small piece of ground forming part of a larger holding 49.33

pennant pennon, narrow, tapering flag especially on a ship 55.30

penny-weight measure of weight, one twentieth of an ounce 205.42

peon *Portuguese* in India, foot-soldier, messenger 271.19, 271.35

pepper-box small cylindrical pot for ground pepper 32.40

peril *verb* hazard, risk 87.26

pest *Gaelic English* best 132.7

pest-house hospital for people suffering from infectious diseases 16.27, 236.38

pestle instrument for pounding substances in a mortar 160.19 (see note)

pettah *Tamil* town or village round a fort 202.15 (see note)

petted pettish 28.6

petter *Gaelic English* better 132.7, 135.43, 136.1

petty see note to 219.1

petween *Gaelic English* between 139.35

phlegmatic calm, unexcitable, unenthusiastic 150.8

physic medicine 217.39

physic-garden, physic garden garden for the cultivation of medicinal plants 15.3, 191.37

physiognomies faces, especially when viewed as an index of mind and character 140.32

pibroch *Scots from Gaelic* genre of highland bagpipe music 114.32, 117.19, 130.8

picaresca *Spanish* adventurous and not over-honest 253.35

pick-thank *Scots* person who curries favour by discreditable means, sycophant 141.30

pickaniny small child, originally a West Indian term 218.40

pillory contrivance for the public punishment of offenders, like the stocks 13.9

pinch critical or crucial point 144.43

pit *Scots* put 39.17

plack *Gaelic English* black 136.10

plaid *Scots* length of cloth wrapped

round the person as an outer garment, in the highlands commonly made of tartan 66.7 etc.

plaided *Scots* dressed in a plaid 96.5

plashed *Scots* splashed 36.25

plaster medicinal substance spread on muslin prior to being laid on the skin 159.11

plate cup or plate of gold or silver given as a prize in a horse-race 32.8

plebeian commoner, person of low birth 190.23

pleugh *Scots* plough 23.31, 23.36, 23.39

pless *Gaelic English* bless 50.17

plood *Gaelic English* blood 136.32

plough-share blade of a plough 107.3

plover lapwing 26.41

plying employing, exerting 41.15, 160.31

po-chays *colloquial* post-chaises, carriages for hire or for use with hired horses 38.28

pocket-book note-book, wallet 126.38, 181.20, 224.4, 224.17

pody *Gaelic English* body 135.12

point *noun* short for point of the sword 136.32

point *verb* indicate, state 144.1

point-blank direct 148.27

pointer dog bred to indicate the presence of game by pointing 14.16

polish *Gaelic English* police 48.16

polypus having many feet, compound 28.36

poniard dagger 141.27, 234.28

portfolio case for keeping loose sheets of paper 173.3

portentously prodigiously 211.42

porter kind of beer originally drunk by porters 35.23, 44.9, 44.29

portico covered walk, colonnade 15.27

portion share of an estate passing by law to an heir 225.25

portmanteau bag, case 213.2

post express, with post-horses 137.1

post-boy driver, postilion 68.36

post-chaise hired travelling carriage 167.39

postern-gate, postern back door, private door 264.15, 274.7

postilion person who rides one of the horses of a post-chaise, driver

30.20 etc.

pot drinking-vessel, pewter mug for beer 135.4

pot-luck for 174.16 see note

pottercarrier *vulgar* apothecary 205.31, 205.36

pot-valiant courageous through the influence of drink 224.29

practeezing *Scots* dancing-class 187.41

prætermit omit, pass over 24.9

pragmatical forward, interfering 185.13

prains *Gaelic English* brains 135.27

pratty *Gaelic English* pretty 131.40

preccese *Scots* precise 42.15

predestinated *theology* foreordained or destined by God 37.21

predilection partiality, prepossession 73.10, 198.1, 208.4, 236.33

preferment advancement 24.3, 206.10

preferred offered, uttered, put forth 122.30, 126.29

premium reward, fee 126.14

presbyterian form of ecclesiastical organisation of the Church of Scotland, church governed by elders and presbyteries 149.27, 164.17

prescription *law* limitation of the time within which a claim can be made 201.17

presently *Scots* now, at once 162.33, 263.36

Presidency one of the divisions of the East India Company's territories in India 261.38; its seat of government 274.42

pretty *Scots* good-looking, manly, gallant, 136.38, 142.27

priming gunpowder placed in the pan of a firearm to which a match or spark was applied 269.20

primming pursing 47.21

private ordinary soldier without rank 89.41 etc.

proadswords *Gaelic English* broadswords 136.32

proem preface 11.11

professor expert or professional at a sport 129.13

proken *Gaelic English* broken 136.2

propale *Scots* talk, announce 41.39

proper own 186.37

proper *heraldry* represented in its